# ECHOES

## Also edited by Ellen Datlow

*A Whisper of Blood*

*A Wolf at the Door and Other Retold Fairy Tales* (with Terri Windling)

*After* (with Terri Windling)

*Alien Sex*

*Black Feathers: Dark Avian Tales*

*Black Heart, Ivory Bones* (with Terri Windling)

*Black Swan, White Raven* (with Terri Windling)

*Black Thorn, White Rose* (with Terri Windling)

*Blood Is Not Enough: 17 Stories of Vampirism*

*Blood and Other Cravings*

*Children of Lovecraft*

*Darkness: Two Decades of Modern Horror*

*Digital Domains: A Decade of Science Fiction & Fantasy*

*Fearful Symmetries*

*Haunted Legends* (with Nick Mamatas)

*Haunted Nights* (with Lisa Morton)

*Hauntings*

*Inferno: New Tales of Terror and the Supernatural*

*Lethal Kisses*

*Little Deaths*

*Lovecraft Unbound*

*Lovecraft's Monsters*

*Mad Hatters and March Hares*

*Naked City: Tales of Urban Fantasy*

*Nebula Awards Showcase 2009*

*Nightmare Carnival*

*Off Limits: Tales of Alien Sex*

*The OMNI Best Science Fiction: Volumes One* through *Three*

*The OMNI Books of Science Fiction: Volumes One* through *Seven*

*Omni Visions One* and *Two*

*Poe: 19 New Tales Inspired by Edgar Allan Poe*

*Queen Victoria's Book of Spells* (WITH TERRI WINDLING)

*Ruby Slippers, Golden Tears* (WITH TERRI WINDLING)

*Salon Fantastique: Fifteen Original Tales of Fantasy* (WITH TERRI WINDLING)

*Silver Birch, Blood Moon* (WITH TERRI WINDLING)

*Sirens and Other Daemon Lovers* (WITH TERRI WINDLING)

*Snow White, Blood Red* (WITH TERRI WINDLING)

*Supernatural Noir*

*Swan Sister* (WITH TERRI WINDLING)

*Tails of Wonder and Imagination: Cat Stories*

*Teeth: Vampire Tales* (WITH TERRI WINDLING)

*Telling Tales: The Clarion West 30th Anniversary Anthology*

*The Beastly Bride: And Other Tales of the Animal People* (WITH TERRI WINDLING)

*The Best Horror of the Year: Volumes One* through *Eleven*

*The Coyote Road: Trickster Tales* (WITH TERRI WINDLING)

*The Cutting Room: Dark Reflections of the Silver Screen*

*The Dark: New Ghost Stories*

*The Del Rey Book of Science Fiction and Fantasy*

*The Doll Collection*

*The Faery Reel: Tales from the Twilight Realm*

*The Green Man: Tales from the Mythic Forest* (WITH TERRI WINDLING)

*The Monstrous*

*Troll's-Eye View: A Book of Villainous Tales* (WITH TERRI WINDLING)

*Twists of the Tale*

*Vanishing Acts*

*The Year's Best Fantasy and Horror: Volumes One* through *Twenty-One* (WITH TERRI WINDLING, GAVIN J. GRANT, AND KELLY LINK)

# ECHOES

## THE SAGA ANTHOLOGY OF GHOST STORIES

EDITED BY

ELLEN DATLOW

1230 AVENUE OF THE AMERICAS, NEW YORK, NEW YORK 10020



For information about special discounts for bulk purchases, please contact Simon & Schuster Special Sales at 1-866-506-1949 or business@simonandschuster.com.

The Simon & Schuster Speakers Bureau can bring authors to your live event. For more information or to book an event, contact the Simon & Schuster Speakers Bureau at 1-866-248-3049 or visit our website at www.simonspeakers.com.

Also available in a Saga Press hardcover edition

Cover design by Greg Stadnyk; interior design by Hilary Zarycky

The text for this book was set in New Baskerville.

Manufactured in the United States of America

First Saga Press paperback edition

2 4 6 8 10 9 7 5 3

Library of Congress Cataloging-in-Publication Data

Names: Datlow, Ellen, editor.

Title: Echoes : the Saga anthology of ghost stories / edited by Ellen Datlow.

Other titles: Saga anthology of ghost stories

Description: First edition. | New York : Saga Press, 2019. | Includes bibliographical references and index.

Identifiers: LCCN 2018000655 | ISBN 9781534413474 (paperback) | ISBN 9781534413467 (hardcover) ISBN 9781534413481 (eBook)

Subjects: LCSH: Ghost stories. | Horror tales. | BISAC: FICTION / Anthologies (multiple authors). | FICTION / Ghost.

Classification: LCC PN6071.G45 E34 2018 | DDC 808.83/8733—dc23

LC record available at https://lccn.loc.gov/2018000655

## ACKNOWLEDGMENTS

Thank you to Stefan Dziemianowicz, Genevieve Valentine, and Robert Killheffer for their help.

Thank you to Joe Monti, for his patience and constant encouragement.

—E. D.

# CONTENTS

# INTRODUCTION

I don't believe in ghosts, but I love ghost stories and I suspect I'm not the only reader to make this confession. The trick of any story (and especially a tale of the supernatural) is to draw us into an unfamiliar world—or a world in which the familiar is made . . . other . . . and convince us to reside there for at least as long as the story lasts. Any well-told story will do that. Ghost stories differ by transporting us to a world where we might actually fear or be disturbed by what we find there.

The ghost story is probably one of the oldest tales told around campfires. Why might this be? It could be because the most persistent concern for many people is whether there is life after death—and, if there is, what that life might be like. None of us—unless one believes the stories of those whose hearts have stopped, only to start again after a brief interval—can really know what happens after we die.

Ghost stories have been a popular and powerful form of fiction for centuries, dating back to Homer, the Augustan poets Vergil and Ovid, and Pliny. What's more, the ghost story has never been the exclusive province of writers associated with the supernatural; it has inspired writers working in many different literary traditions, among them William Faulkner, Edith Wharton, Graham Greene, Oscar Wilde, Robert Graves, Washington Irving, Kate Chopin, Muriel Spark, and John Masefield.

From the ghost of Hamlet's father and the ghost of Banquo appearing unexpectedly at dinner in *Macbeth* through the disturbing hauntings of many classic weird tales—*The Turn of the Screw* by Henry James, "A Rose for Emily" by William Faulkner, the short stories of M. R. James, "A Little Place Off the Edgware Road" by Graham Greene, the self-described "strange stories" of Robert Aickman, and *The Haunting of Hill House* by Shirley Jackson—ghost stories have continued to maintain their hold on the literary imagination.

While researching the history of the ghost story I discovered that even though several volumes of anthologies from the nineteenth and even early twentieth century proclaim the stories within to be ghost stories, most are not. Apparently, at a particular point in English language literature, the "ghost" story served as a catchall phrase for any kind of supernatural fiction.

While the ghost story seemed to dip in popularity in the last few decades of the twentieth century, writers have continued to produce memorable ones, especially since 2000. Some examples of the best in novel form are *House of Leaves* by Mark Danielewski, *The Little Stranger* by Sarah Waters, *The Loney* by Andrew Michael Hurley, *Slade House* by David Mitchell, the macabre tales of Susan Hill, *An English Ghost Story* by Kim Newman, *Heart-Shaped Box* by Joe Hill, *The Taxidermist's Daughter* by Kate Mosse, and *The Grownup* by Gillian Flynn. I think this is because, when done well, ghost stories are genuinely frightening. They're about something we humans can neither control nor avoid: death.

I recently watched two movies that could be categorized as ghost stories—both unusual, compelling (at least to me), and thoughtful. In *A Ghost Story,* events unfold from the point of view of a ghost. In *Personal Shopper,* events are seen from the point of view of a person who desperately wants to encounter a ghost—a very specific ghost. Each movie provokes, in its own way, the questions we ask ourselves again and again: If there are ghosts, what do they want? Are they benign? Are they evil? Are they here to exact revenge (justified or not), to take care of unfinished business that was interrupted by violent death, or because they're prevented from resting by the living? And are there places haunted by the echoes of those who lived and died in them?

We have thirty stories here concerned with ghosts and other hauntings. Three are reprints.

Ford Madox Ford (1873–1939), best known for his novel *The Good Soldier*, is not considered a writer of the supernatural, yet here is a story by him that is indeed ghostly. F. Marion Crawford was a popular and well-known writer of historical novels during his lifetime (1854–1909), yet today it is *Wandering Ghosts*, his posthumously published collection of weird tales, and especially "The Upper Berth," for which he's most remembered. The third reprint is a contemporary story published in 2016: "Linger Longer" by Vincent Masterson won a contest judged by Jeff and Ann VanderMeer and sponsored by the *Masters Review*, an online publication. I discovered it too late to take it for my *Best Horror of the Year Volume Nine*, but felt it would fit perfectly into this anthology.

The other twenty-seven stories were all commissioned for *Echoes: The Saga Anthology of Ghost Stories*.

—E. D.

# ECHOES

# ~~Ice Cold Lemonade 25¢~~ Haunted House Tour: 1 Per Person

### *Paul Tremblay*

I was such a loser when I was a kid. Like a John-Hughes-Hollywood-Eighties-movie-typecast loser. Maybe we all imagine ourselves as being that special kind of ugly duckling, with the truth being too scary to contemplate: Maybe I was someone's bully or I was the kid who egged on the bullies screaming, "Sweep the leg," or maybe I was lower than the Hughes loser, someone who would never be shown in a movie.

When I think of who I was all those years ago, I'm both embarrassed and look-at-what-I've-become proud, as though the distance spanned between those two me's can only be measured in light-years. That distance is a lie, of course, though perhaps necessary to justify perceived successes and mollify the disappointments and failures. That thirteen-year-old me is still there inside: the socially awkward one who wouldn't find a group he belonged to until college; the one who watched way too much TV and listened to records while lying on the floor with the speakers tented over his head; the one who was afraid of the *Jaws* shark appearing in any body of water, Christopher Lee vampires, the dark in his closet and under the bed, and the blinding flash of a nuclear bomb. That kid is all-too-frighteningly retrievable at times.

Now he's here in a more tangible form. He's in the contents

of a weathered cardboard box sitting like a toadstool on my kitchen counter. Mom inexplicably plopped this time capsule in my lap on her way out the door after an impromptu visit. When I asked for an explanation, she said she thought I should have it. I pressed her for more of the *why* and she said, "Well, because it's yours. It's your stuff," as though she was weary of the burden of having had to keep it for all those years.

Catherine is visiting her parents on the Cape and she took our daughter Izzy with her. I stayed home to finish edits (which remain stubbornly unfinished) on a manuscript that was due last week. Catherine and Izzy would've torn through this box-of-me right away and laughed themselves silly at the old photos of my stick figure body and my map of freckles and crooked teeth, the collection of crayon renderings of dinosaurs with small heads and ludicrously large bodies, and the fourth grade current events project on Ronald Reagan for which I'd earned a disappointing C+ and a demoralizing teacher comment of *Too messy*. And I would've reveled in their attention, their warm spotlight shining on who I was and who I've become.

I didn't find it until my second pass through the box, which seems impossible as I took care to peel old pictures apart and handle everything delicately, as one might handle ancient parchments. That second pass occurred two hours after the first, and there was a pizza and multiple beers and no edits between.

The drawing that I don't remember saving was there at the bottom of the box, framed by the cardboard and its interior darkness. I thought I'd forgotten it; I know I never had.

The initial discovery was more confounding than dread inducing, but hours have passed and now it's late and it's dark. I have every light on in the house, which only makes the dark outside even darker. I am alone and I am on alert and I feel time creeping forward. (Time doesn't run out; it continues forward and it continues without you.) I do not sit in any one room for longer than five minutes. I pass through the lower level of the house as quietly as I can, like an omniscient, emotionally distant narrator, which I am not. On the TV is a baseball game that I don't care about, blaring at full volume. I consider going to my car and driving to my in-laws' on the Cape, which would be ridiculous as I wouldn't arrive until well after midnight and Catherine and Izzy are coming home tomorrow morning.

Would it be so ridiculous?

Tomorrow, when my family returns home and the windows are open and the sunlight is as warm as a promise, I will join them in laughing at me. But it is not tomorrow and they are not here.

I am glad they're not here. They would've found the drawing before I did.

I rode my bicycle all over Beverly, Massachusetts, the summer of 1984. I didn't have a BMX bike with thick, knobby tires made for ramps and wheelies and chewing up and spitting out dirt and pavement. Mine was a dinged up, used-to-belong-to-my-dad ten-speed, and the only things skinnier and balder than the tires were my arms and legs. On my rides I always made sure to rattle by Kelly Bishop's house on the off-off-chance I'd find her in her front yard. Doing what? Who knows. But in those fantasies she waved or nodded at me. She would ask what I was doing and I'd tell her all nonchalant-like that I was heading back to my house, even though she'd have to know her dead-end street wasn't exactly on my way home. Pesky details were worked out or inconsequential in fantasies, of course.

One afternoon it seemed part of my fantasy was coming true when Kelly and her little sister were at the end of their long driveway, sitting at a small fold-up table with a pitcher of lemonade. I couldn't bring myself to stop or slow down or even make more than glancing eye contact. I had no money for lemonade, therefore I had no reason to stop. Kelly shouted at me as I rolled by. Her greeting wasn't a *Hey there* or even a *Hi*, but instead, "Buy some lemonade or we'll pop your tires!"

After twenty-four hours of hopeful and fearful Should I or shouldn't I?, I went back the next day with a pocket full of quarters. Kelly was again stationed at the end of her driveway. My breaks squealed as I jerked to an abrupt and uncoordinated stop. My rusted kickstand screamed *You're really doing this?* embarrassment. The girls didn't say anything and watched my approach with a mix of disinterest and what I imagined to be the look I gave ants before I squashed them.

They sat at the same table setup as the previous day but there was no pitcher of lemonade. Never afraid to state the obvious, I said, "So, um, no lemonade today?" The fifty cents clutched in my sweaty hand might as well have melted.

Kelly said, "Lemonade was yesterday. Can't you read the sign?" She sat slumped in her beach chair, a full body eye roll, and her long, tanned legs spilled out from under the table and the white poster-board sign taped to the front. She wore a red Coke T-shirt. Her chestnut brown hair was pulled into a side-high ponytail, held up by a black scrunchie. Kelly was clearly well into her pubescent physical transformation, whereas I was still a boy, without even a shadow of hair under my armpits.

Kelly's little sister, with the bowl-cut mop of dirty blond hair, was going to be in second grade. I didn't know her name and was too nervous to ask. She covered her mouth, fake laughed, and wobbled like a penguin in her unstable chair. That she might topple into the table or to the blacktop didn't seem to bother Kelly.

"You're supposed to be the smart one, Paul," Kelly added.

"Heh, yeah, sorry." I left the quarters in my pocket to hide their shame and adjusted my blue gym shorts; they were too short, even for the who-wears-short-shorts Eighties. I tried to fill the chest of my NBA Champs Celtics T-shirt with deep breaths, but only managed to stir a weak ripple in the green cloth.

Their updated sign read:

~~ICE COLD LEMONADE 25¢~~ HAUNTED HOUSE TOUR: 1 PER PERSON

Seemed straightforward enough but I didn't know what to make of it. I feared it was some kind of a joke or prank. Were Rick or Winston or other jerks hiding close by to jump out and pants me? I thought about hopping back on my bike and getting the hell out before I did something epically cringeworthy Kelly would later describe in detail to all her friends and by proxy the entire soon-to-be seventh grade class.

Kelly asked, "Do you want a tour of our creepy old house or not?"

I stammered and I sweated. I remember sweating a lot.

Kelly told me the lemonade stand thing was boring and that her new haunted-house-tour idea was genius. I would be their first to go on the tour so I'd be helping them out. She said, "We'll even only charge you half price. Be a pal, Paulie."

Was Kelly Bishop inviting me into her house? Was she making fun of me? The "be a pal" bit sounded like a joke and felt like a joke. I looked around the front yard, spying between the tall front hedges, looking for the ambush. I decided I didn't care, and said, "Okay, yeah."

The little sister shouted, "One dollar," and held out an open hand.

Kelly corrected her. "I said 'half price.'"

"What's half?"

"Fifty cents."

Little sis shouted, "Fifty cents!" with her hand still out.

I paid, happy to be giving the sweaty quarters to her and not Kelly.

I asked, "Is it scary, I mean, supposed to be scary?" I tried smiling bravely. I wasn't brave. I still slept with my door open and the hallway light on. My smile was pretend brave, and it wasn't much of a smile as I tried not to show off my mouth of metal braces, the elastics on either side mercifully no longer necessary as of three weeks ago.

Kelly stood and said, "Terrifying. You'll wet yourself and be sucking your thumb for a week." She whacked her sister on the shoulder and commanded, "Go. You have one minute to be ready."

"I don't need a minute." She bounced across the lawn onto the porch and slammed the front door closed behind her.

Kelly flipped through a stack of note cards. She said she hadn't memorized the script yet but she would eventually.

I followed her down the driveway to the house I never thought of as scary or creepy, but now that it had the word *haunted* attached to it, even in jest . . . it was kind of creepy. The only three-family home in the neighborhood, it looked impossibly tall from up close. And it was old, worn out—the white paint peeling and flaking away. Its stone and mortar foundation appeared crooked. The windows were tall and thin and impenetrable. The small front porch had two skeletal posts holding up a warped overhang that could come crashing down at any second.

We walked up the stairs to the porch, and the wood felt soft under my feet. Kelly was flipping through her note cards and held the front screen door open for me with a jutted out hip. I scooted by, holding my breath, careful to not accidentally brush against her.

The cramped front hallway/foyer was crowded with bikes and shovels and smelled like wet leaves. A poorly lit staircase curled up to the right. Kelly told me that the tour finishes on the second floor, and we weren't allowed all the way upstairs to the third, and that she had written "1 Per Person" on the sign so that no pervs would try for repeat tours since she and her sister were home by themselves.

"Your parents aren't home?" My voice cracked, as if on cue.

If Kelly answered with a nod of the head, I didn't see it. She reached across me, opened the door to my left, and said, "Welcome to House Black, the most haunted house on the North Shore."

Kelly put one hand between my shoulder blades and pushed me inside to a darkened kitchen. The linoleum was sandy, gritty, under my shuffling sneakers. The room smelled of dust and pennies. The shapes of the table, chairs, and appliances were sleeping animals. From somewhere on this first floor, her sister gave a witchy laugh. It was muffled, and I remember thinking it sounded like she was inside the walls.

Kelly carefully narrated: The house was built in the 1700s by a man named Robert or Reginald Black, a merchant sailor who was gone for months at a time. His wife, Denise, would dutifully wait for him in the kitchen. After all the years of his leaving, Denise was driven mad by a lonely heart and she wouldn't go anywhere else in the house but the kitchen until he returned home. She slept sitting in a wooden chair and washed herself in the kitchen sink. Years passed like this. Mr. Black was to take one final trip before retiring but Mrs. Black had had enough. As he ate his farewell breakfast she smashed him over the head with an iron skillet until he was dead. Mrs. Black then stuffed her husband's body into the oven.

The kitchen's overhead light, a dirty yellow fixture, flashed on. I saw a little hand leave the switch and disappear behind a door across the room from me. On top of the oven was a cast iron, black skillet. Little sis flashed her arm back into the room and turned out the light.

Kelly loomed over me (she was at least three inches taller) and said that this was not the same oven, and everyone who ever lived here has tried getting a new one, but you can still sometimes hear Mr. Black clanging around inside.

The oven door dropped open with a metal scream, like when an ironing board's legs were pried opened.

I jumped backward and knocked into the kitchen table.

Kelly hissed, "That's too hard, be careful! You're gonna rip the oven door off!"

Little sis dashed into the room and I could see in her hands a ball of fishing line, which was tethered to the oven door handle.

Kelly asked me what I thought of the tour opener, if I found it satisfactory. I swear that is the phrasing she used.

Mortified that I'd literally jumped and sure that she could hear my heart rabbiting in my chest, I mumbled, "Yeah, that was good."

The tour moved on throughout the darkened first floor. All the see-through lace curtains were drawn, and either Kelly or little sis would turn a room's light on and off during Kelly's readings. Most of the stories featured the hapless descendants of the Blacks. The dining room's story was unremarkable as was the story for the living room, which was the largest room on the first floor. I'd begun to lose focus, and let my mind wander to Kelly and what she was like when her parents were home, and then, perhaps oddly, what her parents were like, and if they were like mine. My dad had recently moved from the Parker Brothers factory to managing one of their warehouses, and Mom worked part-time as a bank teller. I wondered what Kelly's parents did for work and if they sat in the kitchen and discussed their money problems too. Were her parents kind? Were they too kind? Were they overbearing or unreasonable? Were they perpetually distracted? Did they argue? Were they cold? Were they cruel? I still wonder these things about everyone else's parents.

Kelly did not take me into her parents' bedroom, saying simply, "Under construction," as we passed by the closed door.

I suggested that she make up a story about something or someone terrible kept hidden behind the door.

Kelly to this point had kept her nose in her script cards and jotted down notes with a pencil when not watching for my reaction. Her head snapped up at me and she said, "None of these are made-up stories, Paul."

There was another bedroom, the one directly off the kitchen, and it was being used as an office/sitting room. There was a desk and bookcases tracing the wall's boundaries. The walls were covered in brownish-yellow wallpaper and the circular throw rug was dark too; I don't remember the colors. It's as though color didn't exist there. The room was sepia, like a memory. In the middle of the room was a rolling chair, and on the chair was a form covered by a white sheet.

Kelly had to coax me into the room. I kept a wide berth between me and the sheeted figure, aware of the possibility that there was someone under there waiting to jump out and grab me. Though the closer I got, the shape wasn't uniform and the proportions were all off. It wasn't a single body; the shape was comprised of more shapes.

Kelly said that the ghost of a man named Darcy Dearborn (I remember his alliterative name) haunted this room. A real estate mogul, he purchased the house in 1923. He lost everything but the house in the 1929 stock market crash and was forced to rent the second and third floors out to strangers. He took to sitting in this room and listening to his tenants above walking around, going about their day. Kelly paused at this point of the story and looked up at the ceiling expectantly. I did too. Eventually we could hear little footsteps running along the second floor above us. The running stopped and became loud thuds. Little sis was jumping up and down in place, mashing her feet into the floor. Kelly said, "She's such a little shit," shook her head, and continued with the tale. Darcy, much like Mrs. Black from all those years before, became housebound and wouldn't leave this room. Local family and neighbors bought his groceries for him and took care of collecting his rent checks and doing his banking and everything else for him, until one day they didn't. Darcy stayed in the room and in his chair and he died and no one found him until years later and he'd almost completely decomposed and faded away. His ghost shuts the doors to the office when they are open.

Behind us, the door to the kitchen opened and shut.

I remember thinking the Darcy story had holes in it. I remember thinking it was too much like the first Mrs. Black story, which muted its impact. But then I became paranoid that Kelly had tailored these stories for me somehow. Was she implying that I was doomed to be a loner, a shut-in because I stayed home by myself too much? I had one new friend I'd met in sixth grade but he lived in North Beverly and spent much of his summer in Maine and I couldn't go see him very often. I wasn't friends with anyone in my neighborhood. That's not an exaggeration. Throughout that summer, particularly if I'd spent the previous day watching TV or shooting hoops in the driveway by myself, Mom would give me an errand (usually sending me down the street to the White Hen Pantry convenience store to buy her a pack of cigarettes—you could do that in the Eighties) and then tell me to invite some friends over. She never mentioned any kids by name because there were no kids to mention by name. I told her I would but would then go ride my bike instead. That was good enough for Mom, or maybe it wasn't and she knew I wasn't really going to see or play with anyone. Mom now still reacts with an unbridled joy that comes too close to open shock and surprise when she hears of my many adult friends.

I envisioned myself becoming a sun-starved, Gollum-like adult, cloistered in my sad bedroom at home, until Kelly led me out of the first-floor living space to the cramped and steep staircase. The stairs were a dark wood with a darker stair tread, or runner. The walls were panels or planks of the same dark wood. I was never a sailor like Mr. Black, but it was easy to imagine that we were climbing up from the belly of a ship.

Kelly said that a girl named Kathleen died on the stairwell in 1937. Kathleen used to send croquet balls crashing down the stairs. Her terrible father with arms and hands that were too long for his body got so sick of her doing it, he snuck up behind her and nudged her off the second-floor landing. She fell and tumbled and broke her neck and died. There was an inquest and her father was never charged. However, his wife knew her husband was lying about not being responsible for Kathleen's death and the following summer she poisoned him and herself while picnicking at Lynch Park. At night you can hear Kathleen giggling (Kelly's sister obliged from above at that point in the tale) and the rattles and knocks of croquet balls bouncing down the stairs. And if you're not holding the railing, you'll feel those cold, extra-large hands push you or grab your ankles.

I wasn't saying much of anything in response at this point and was content to be there with Kelly, knowing I would likely never spend this much time alone with her again. I was scared but it was the good kind of scared because it was shared if not quite commiserative.

The second-floor landing was bright with sunlight pouring through the uncovered four-paned window next to the second floor's front door. It was only then that I realized each floor was constructed as separate apartments or living spaces, and since I hadn't seen their rooms downstairs, that meant Kelly's and her sister's bedrooms must be here upstairs, away from her parents' bedroom. I couldn't imagine sleeping that far away from my parents, and future live-at-home-shut-in or not, I felt bad for her and her sister.

Inside there was a second kitchen that was bright and sparkled with disuse. The linoleum and cabinets were white. I wondered (but didn't ask) if the two of them ate up here alone for breakfast or at night for dinner, and I again thought about Kelly's parents and what kind of people would leave them alone in the summer and essentially in their own apartment.

The tour didn't linger in the kitchen nor did we stop in what she called the playroom, which had the same dimensions as the dining room below on the first floor. Perhaps she didn't want to make their playroom a scary place.

We went into her sister's room next. I only remember the pink wallpaper, an unfortunate shade of Pepto-Bismol, and the army of stuffed animals staged on the floor and all facing me. There were a gaggle of teddy bears and a stuffed Garfield and a Pink Panther and a rat wearing a green fedora and a doe-eyed brontosaurus and more, and they all had black marble eyes. Kelly said, "Oops," and turned off the overhead light.

The story for this room was by far the most gruesome.

John and Genie Graham bought the house in 1952, and they had a little boy named Will. To make ends meet the family rented the top two floors to strangers. The stranger on the second floor was named Gregg, with two *g*s, and the third-floor tenant was named Rolph, not Ralph. Very little is known about the two men. For the two years of the Gregg with two *g*s and Rolph occupancy, Will would periodically complain he couldn't find one of his many stuffed animal companions and insisted that someone stole it. He had so many stuffed animals that with each individual complaint his parents were sure the missing critter was simply misplaced or kicked under the bed or he'd taken it to the park and left it behind. Then there were locals who complained that Rolph wasn't coming to work anymore and wasn't seen at the grocery store or the bar he liked to go to, and that he too was misplaced. Then there was a smell coming from the second floor and they initially feared an animal had died in the walls, and then those fears became something else. When Mr. and Mrs. Graham entered the second-floor apartment with the police, Gregg with two *g*s was nowhere to be found. But they found Will's missing stuffed animals. They were all sitting in this room like they were now and they were blood-stained and tattered and they smelled terribly. Hidden within the plush hides of the stuffed animals were hacked-up pieces of Rolph, the former third-floor tenant. There were rumors of Gregg with two *g*s living in Providence and Fall River and more alarmingly close by in Salem, but no one ever found him. Kelly said that stuffed animals in this house go missing and then reappear in this bedroom by themselves, congregating with one another in the middle of the floor on their own, patiently waiting for their new stuffing.

"That's a really terrible story," I said in a breathless way that meant the opposite.

"Paul! It's not a story," Kelly said, but she looked at me and smiled. I'll not describe that look or that smile beyond saying I'll remember both (along with a different look from her, one I got a few months after the tour), for as long as those particular synapses fire within my brain.

Kelly led me to a final room: her bedroom in the back of the house. The room was brightly lit, with shades pulled up and white curtains open. Her walls were white, and might've been painted-over clapboard or paneling, and decorated with posters of Michael Jackson, Duran Duran, and other musicians. There was a clothes bureau that seemed to have been jigsawed together using different pieces of wood. Its top was a landfill of crumpled up notes, used candy wrappers, loose change, barrettes, and other adolescent debris. At the foot of her bed was a large chest covered by a knit afghan. On opposite walls of each other were a small desk, and a bookcase that was half full with books, the rest of space claimed by dolls and knickknacks. The floor was hardwood with a small baby-chick yellow rectangular patch of rug by her bed, which was flush against the wall and under two windows overlooking the backyard.

Kelly didn't say anything right away and I stared at everything but her, more nervous to be in this room than any other. I said, "You have a cool room." I might've said "nice" instead of "cool," but god, I hope I didn't.

I don't remember if Kelly said, "Thanks," or not. She pocketed her notecards, walked ahead of me, sat on the rug, and faced her bed. She said, "I dream about it every night. I wish it would stop."

I hadn't noticed it until she said what she said. There was a sketch propped up by a bookend on the middle of her bed. I sat down next to Kelly. I asked, "Did you draw that?"

She nodded and didn't look at me. She didn't even look at me when I was staring at her profile for what felt like the rest of the summer. Then I too stared at the drawing.

The left side of its cartoonish head was misshapen, almost like a bite had been taken out, and the left eye was missing. Its right eye was round and blackened by slashes instead of a pupil. The mouth was a horrible band of triangular teeth spanning the horizontal circumference. Three strips of skin stretched from the top half of the head over the mouth and teeth and wrapped under its chin. What appeared to be a forest of wintered branches stuck out from all over its head. The wraithlike body was all angles and slashes and the arms were elongated triangles reaching out. It had no legs. The jagged bottom of its floating form ended in larger versions of its shark teeth.

There are things I don't remember about that day in Kelly's house and many other things I'm sure I've embellished (though not purposefully so). But I remember when I first saw the drawing and how it made me feel. While this might sound like an adult's perspective, I'm telling you that this was the first time I realized or intellectualized that I would be dead someday. Sitting on the bedroom floor next to the cute girl of my adolescent daydreams, I looked at the drawing and imagined my death, the final closing of my eyes and the total and utter blankness and emptiness of . . . I could only think of the phrase "not-me." The void of not-me. I wondered if the rest of my life would pass like how summer vacations passed—would I be about to die and asking *How did it all go so quickly?* I wondered how long and what part of me would linger in nothingness and if I'd feel pain or cold or anything at all, and I tried to shake it all away by saying to Kelly, "Wow, that's really good."

"Good?"

"The drawing. Yeah. It's good. And creepy."

Kelly didn't respond, but I was back inside her sunny bedroom and sitting on the floor instead of lost inside my own head. I pointed and asked, "What are the things sticking out? They look like branches."

She told me she tried to make up a story for this ghost, like maybe the girl who lived in the house before Kelly was sneaking around peeking into houses and sometimes stealing little things and bits no one would miss (like a thumbtack or an almost used up spool of red thread) and she got caught by someone and was chased, and in desperation she ran behind the house and she got stuck or trapped in the woods, and she died within sight of her big old ratty house. But that didn't feel like the true story, or the right story. It certainly wasn't the real reason for the ghost.

Kelly told me this ghost appeared in her dreams every night.

The dreams varied but the ghost was always the same ghost. Sometimes she was not in her body and she witnessed everything from a remove, like she was a movie camera. Most times Kelly was Kelly and she saw everything through her own eyes. The most common dream featured Kelly alone in a cornfield that had already been cut and harvested. Dark, impenetrable woods surrounded the field on all sides. She heard a low voice laughing, but then it was also high-pitched, so it was both at the same time. (She said "both at the same time" twice). Her heart beat loud enough that she thought it was the full moon thumping down at her, giving her a Morse code message to run. Even though she was terrified she ran into the woods because it was the only way to get back to her house. She ran through the forest and night air as thick as paint and she got close to her backyard and she could see her house, but no lights were on so it was all in shadow and looked like a giant tombstone. Then the ghost came streaming for her from the direction of the house and she knew her house was a traitor because it was where the ghost stayed while it patiently waited for this night and for Kelly. It was so dark but she could see the ghost and its horrible smile bigger than that heartbeat moon. And the dream ended the same way every time.

"I hear myself scream but it sounds far away, like I'm below, in the ground, and then I die. I remember what it feels like to die until I wake up, and then it fades away, but not all the way away," Kelly said. She rocked forward and back and rubbed her hands together, staring at the drawing.

The ceiling above us creaked and groaned with someone taking slow, heavy, careful steps. Kelly's little sister wasn't around and I hadn't remembered seeing her since we got up to the second floor. I figured sis was walking above us wearing adult-sized boots. A nice touch for what I assumed was the tour's finale.

I said something commiserative to Kelly about having nightmares too.

She said, "I think it's a real ghost, you know. This is the realest one. It comes every night for me. And I'm afraid maybe it's the ghost of me."

"Like a doppelganger?"

Kelly smirked and rolled her eyes again but it wasn't as dismissive as I'm describing. She playfully hit my nonexistent bicep with the back of her hand, and despite my earlier glimpse at understanding the finality of death I would've been happy to die right then. She said, "You're the smart one, Paul. You have to tell me what that is."

So I did. Or I gave her the best close-enough general definition that the almost-thirteen-year-old me could muster.

There were more footsteps on the floor above us, moving away to other rooms but still loud and creaking.

She said, "Got it. It's kind of like a doppelganger but not really. It's not a future version of me, I don't think. I think it's the ghost of a part of me that I ignore. Or the ghost of some piece of me that I should ignore. We all have those parts, right? What if those other parts trapped inside of us find a way to get out? Where do they go and what do they do? I have a part that gets out in my dreams and I'm afraid that I'm going to hear it outside of me for real. I know I am. I'm going to hear it outside of me in a crash somewhere in the house where there isn't supposed to be, or I'll hear it in a creak in the ceiling, and maybe I'll even hear it walking up behind me. I don't know if that makes any sense and I don't think I'm explaining it well but that's what I think it is."

Little sis burst out of Kelly's closet and crashed dramatically onto the chest at the end of her bed, and shouted, "Boo!"

Kelly and I both were startled and we laughed, and if you'd asked me then I would've thought we would've been friends forever after instead of my never speaking to her again after that day.

As our laughter died out and Kelly berated her sister for scaring her, I realized that little sis jumped out of a closet and not from behind a door to another room that had easy access to the rest of the apartment and the stairwell to the third floor.

I said to little sis, "Aren't you upstairs? I mean, that was you upstairs we heard walking around, right?"

She shook her head and giggled, and then there were creaks and footstep tremors in the floor above us again. They were loud enough to shake dust from the walls and blow clouds in front of the sun outside.

I asked, "Who's upstairs?"

Kelly looked at the ceiling and was expressionless. "No one is supposed to be up there. The third floor is empty. We're going to rent it out in the fall. We're home alone."

I made *Come on* and *Really?* and *You're not joking?* noises, and then in my memory—which for this brief period of time is more like a dream than something that actually happened—the continuum skips forward to me following Kelly and her sister out into the hallway and to the stairwell to the third floor. Little sis led the way and Kelly was behind me. I kept asking questions (*Is this a good idea? Are you sure you want to end the tour all the way up on the third floor?*) and the questions turned to poorly veiled begging, my saying that I should probably get home, we ate dinner early in my house, Mom was a worrier, et cetera. All the while

I flowed up the stairs and Kelly shushed me and told me to be quiet. The stairwell thinned and squeezed and curled up into a small landing, or a perch. An eave intruded into the headspace to the left of the third floor apartment's door. The three of us sardined onto that precarious landing that felt like a cliff. There was no more discussion and little sis opened the door, deftly skittered aside, and like she had on the first floor, Kelly two-handed shoved me inside.

This apartment was clearly smaller than the first two with the A-frame roof slanting the ceilings, intruding into the living space. I stepped into a small, gray kitchen that smelled musty from disuse. Directly across the room from me was a long, dark hallway. It was as though the ceilings and their symmetrical slants were constructed with the sole purpose of focusing my stare into this dark tunnel. There wasn't a hallway like this in either of the other apartments; the third-floor layout was totally different, and the thought of wandering about with no idea of the floor plan and fearing that I would find whatever it was making the walking noises made me want to swallow my own tongue.

Little sis ran ahead of me, giggling into the hallway and disappearing in the back end of the apartment. I still held out hope that maybe it was her, somehow, who was responsible for the walking noises, when I knew it wasn't possible. I stood for a long time only a few steps deep into the kitchen, which grew darker, and watched as the hallway grew darker still, and then a stooped figure emerged from an unseen room and into the gloom of the hallway. The whole apartment creaked and shook with each step. It was the shadowy ghost of a man and he diffused into the hallway, filling it like smoke, and my skin became electric and I think I ran in place like a cartoon character might, sliding my feet back and forth on the linoleum.

An old man emerged into the weak lighting of the kitchen, shuffling along with the help of a wooden, swollen-headed shillelagh. He wore a sleeveless T-shirt and tan pants, with a black belt knotted tightly around his waist. An asterisk of thin, white hair dotted the top of his head and the same unruly tuft sprouted out from under the collar of his T-shirt. His eyes were big and rheumy, like a bloodhound's eyes, and he smirked at me, but before he could say anything, I screamed and ran through Kelly and out of the apartment.

On the second step I heard him call out (his voice quite friendly and soothing), "Hey, what are all you silly kids up to?" and then I was around a corner, knocking into a wall and clutching on to the handrail, and maybe halfway down when I heard Kelly laughing, and then shouting, "Wait, Paul! Come meet my grandfather. Tour's over!"

I just about tumbled onto the second-floor landing with everyone else still upstairs calling after me. I was crying almost uncontrollably and I was seething, so angry at Kelly and her sister and myself. I don't know why I was so angry. Sure they'd set me up, but it was harmless, and part of the whole ghost tour/haunted house idea. I know now they weren't making fun of me, per se, and they weren't being cruel. But back then, *cruel* was my default assumption setting. So I was filled with moral indignation and the kind of irrational anger that leads erstwhile good people to make terrible, petty decisions.

I ran back into the second floor apartment and to Kelly's bedroom. I took the drawing of her ghost off the bed, tucked it inside my T-shirt, ran back out of the apartment, and then down the stairs and out of the house and to my bike, and I pedaled home without ever once looking back. I didn't ride my bike by Kelly's house the rest of that summer.

I can't remember planning what I was going to do with her drawing. I might've initially intended to burn it with matches and a can of Mom's hairspray (I was a bit of a firebug back then. . . .) or something similarly stupid and juvenile. But I didn't burn it or crumple it up. I didn't even fold it in half. Any creepiness/weirdness attributed to the drawing was swamped by my anger, and then my utter embarrassment at my lame response to her grandfather scaring me. I knew I totally blew it; Kelly and I could've been friends if I'd laughed and stayed and met her grandfather and maybe middle school and high school would've gone differently, wouldn't have been as miserable.

While on occasion I had nightmares of climbing all those steps in the Bishop house by myself, I don't remember having any nightmares featuring the ghost in the drawing even though I was (and still am) a card-carrying scaredy-cat. I wasn't afraid to keep the drawing in my room. I hid it on the bottom of my bureau's top drawer along with a few of my favorite baseball cards. While I obsessively picked through the play-by-play of that afternoon in Kelly's house and what she must've thought of me after, I never really focused on the drawing and would only ever look at it by accident, when the top drawer was all but empty of socks or underwear and I'd find that toothy grin peering up at me. Then one day toward the end of that summer the drawing was gone. It's possible I threw it away without remembering doing so. (I mean, I don't remember what happened to the baseball cards I kept in there either.) Maybe Mom found it when she was putting away my clean clothes and did something with it, which would explain how it got to be in her box of kid-stuff keepsakes, but Mom taking it and never saying anything to me about taking it seems off. Mom fawned over my grades and artwork. She would've made it a point to tell me how good the drawing was. Her taking the picture and putting it on the fridge? Yes, that would've happened. But her secreting it away for safekeeping? That wasn't her.

That summer melted away and seventh grade at Memorial Middle school was hell, as seventh grade is hell for everyone. The students were separated into three teams (Black, White, and Red) with four teachers in each team. The teams never mixed classes, so you might never see a friend on Black team if you were on Red team and vice versa. Kelly wasn't on my team and I didn't even pass her in the hallways at school until after a random lunch in early October. She stood with her back against a set of lockers by herself, arms folded. It wasn't her locker as I didn't see her there again the rest of the school year. Normally I walked the halls with my head down, a turtle sunk into his protective shell, but before disappearing into my next class, I looked up to find her staring at me. That look is the second of two looks from her that I'll never forget, though I won't ever be sure if I was reading or interpreting this look correctly. In her look I saw *I can't believe you did that,* and there was a depthless sadness, one that was almost impossible for me to face as it was a direct, honest response to my irrevocable act. Her look said that I'd stolen a piece of her, and even if I'd tried to give it back, it would still be gone forever. To my shame I didn't say anything, didn't tell her that I was sorry, and I regret not doing so to this day. There was something else in that look too. It was unreadable to me at the time, but now, sitting in my empty house with dread filling me like water in a glass, I think some of that sadness was for me. Some of it was pity and maybe even fear, like she knew what was going to happen to me tomorrow and for the rest of my tomorrows; there wouldn't necessarily be a singular calamitous event, but a concatenation or summation of small defeats and horrors that would build daily and yearly and eventually overtake me, as it overtakes us all.

I would see her in passing the following year in eighth grade, but she walked by me like I wasn't there (like most of the other kids did; I'm sorry if that sounds too woe-is-me, but it's the truth). At the start of ninth grade she returned to school a totally transformed kid. She dressed in all black, dyed her hair black, and wore eyeliner and Dead Kennedys and Circle Jerks and Suicidal Tendencies T-shirts, and combat boots, and hung out with upperclassmen, and she was abrasive and smelled like cigarettes and weed. In our suburban town, only a handful of kids were into punk, so to most of us, even us losers who were picked on mercilessly by the jocks and popular kids or, worse, were totally ignored, the punks were scary and to be avoided at all costs. I remember wondering if the Michael Jackson and Duran Duran posters were still hanging in her room and I wondered if she still had that dream about her ghost and if she still thought that ghost was some part of her. Of course, I later became a punk when I went to college and I now irrationally wonder if *punk* was another piece of her that I stole and kept for myself.

The summer after ninth grade Kelly and her family sold the house and moved away. I have no memory of where she moved to, or more accurately, I have no memory of being told (and then forgetting) where she moved. I find it difficult to believe that no one in our grade would've known to what town or state she moved. I must've known where she relocated to at one point, right?

The baseball game is still on and I'm on the couch with my laptop open and searching for Kelly Bishop on every social media platform I can think of, and I can't find her, and I'm desperate to find her, and it's less about knowing what has become of her (or who she became), but to see if she's left behind any other parts of herself—even if only digital avatars.

Next to my laptop is her drawing. That it survived all this time and ended up in my possession again somehow now feels like an inevitability.

Here it is:

I remembered it looking like the product of a young artist and being more creepy and affecting because of it. I remembered some of the branches at the top forming the letter *K.* I remembered the smile and the skin strips and the triangle arms as is.

I didn't remember the shadow beneath the hovering figure and I don't like looking at that shadow and I wonder why I always peer so intently into those dark spaces. I didn't remember how its head is turned away from its body and turned to face the viewers, as though the ghost was floating along stage left until we looked at it, until we saw it there. And then it sees us.

I know it's not supposed to be a doppelganger but I remember it looking like Kelly in some ineffable way, and now, thirty plus years later I think it looks like me, or that it somehow came from me. Even though it's late and she's in bed, I want to call Mom and ask her if she looked through the cardboard box one last time before leaving it here (I know she must've) and if she saw this drawing and recognized her son from all those years ago in it.

I am glad Catherine and Izzy are not here. I keep saying that I am glad they are not here in my head. I say it aloud, too. They would've found the drawing before I did and I don't know if they would've seen me or if they would've seen themselves.

My reverie is shattered by a loud thud upstairs, like something heavy falling to the floor.

There is applause and excited commentators chattering on my television, but I am still home alone and there is a loud thud upstairs.

Its volume and the suddenness of its presence twitches my body, but then I'm careful to stand up slowly and purposefully from the couch. Worse than the incongruity of noise coming from a presumably vacant space is the emptiness the sound leaves behind, a void that must and will be filled.

I again think of driving to the Cape or just driving, somewhere, anywhere. I shut the television off and I anticipate the sound of footsteps running out of the silence, or a rush of air and those triangle arms reaching out toward me and the shadow on the floor behind it.

Everything in me is shaking. I call out in a voice no one is there to hear. I threaten calling 911. I tell the empty or not-empty house to leave me alone. I try to be rational and envision the noise being made by one of the shampoo bottles sliding off the slippery ledge in our shower, but instead I can only see the figure in my drawing, huddled upstairs, waiting. And it is now *my* drawing, even if it's not.

The ceiling above my head creaks ever so slightly. A settling of the wood. A response to subtle pressure.

I imagine going upstairs and finding a menagerie of Kelly's ghosts waiting for me: There is Greg with two *g*s tearing apart the hapless Rolph, and the desperately lonely Mrs. Black sitting in a chair patiently waiting, and the feckless shut-in Darcy Dearborn. Or will I find the ghost of a part of me that I never let go: a lost and outcast adult I always feared people (myself included) thought I'd become?

Is that another creak in the ceiling I heard?

I listen harder, and maybe if I listen long enough I'll hear a scream or a growl or my own voice, and it is as though the last thirty years of my life have passed like the blink of summer, and everything that has happened in between doesn't matter. Memories and events and all the people in my life have been squeezed out, leaving only room for this distilled me on this narrowing staircase, and right now even Catherine and Izzy feel like made-up ghost stories. There is only that afternoon in Kelly's place and now the impossibly older me alone in a house that's become as strange, frightening, and unknowable as my future.

As I slowly walk out of the TV room and up the stairs toward the suddenly-alive-with-sound second floor, I don't know what I'm more afraid of: seeing the ghost I stole grinning in the dark or seeing myself.

# Linger Longer

## *Vincent J. Masterson*

I. Arrivals

It was their first vacation together, a log-cabin weekend with Michael's old friends from grad school, and Lori was determined not to ruin it. This was more her fear than his, and she had overcompensated with eager questions—Where was this quad? Who's Dupin? What's absinthe?—her eyes wide and searching and wanting more. But somewhere between Tallahassee and the mountains of eastern Tennessee, Lori grew weary of Michael's nostalgia. Her temper was tripped easily—by his voice, by the loose flapping of the Wrangler's ragtop, by a stomach upset from too many filling-station snacks. Didn't he know she never wanted to go? Why couldn't he have left her at home with her TV and magazines, refilling her favorite blue mug with dark wine?

She pressed her forehead to the cold window, thinking of the stupid questionnaire Dr. Ryerson had given her during a session earlier that week. I sometimes have strong feelings that do not seem like mine, score from 0 to 10. Focus instead on your breathing, she thought. Conjure tranquil images: pristine mountains, waterfalls, softly falling snow. Beside her, she could feel Michael coiling tightly. The last hour of Lori's sulky shrugs and one-word answers had finally burned up the last of his good cheer. How many miles had they driven in that bitter and troublesome silence? She didn't know. A phrase lifted in Lori's mind, a father's frequent advice to his inscrutably moody little girl: Please, honey, just try to have fun.

She reached over and squeezed Michael's knee.

"I love you." She winced to hear herself. I love you? It was overblown and over-sudden and, worse, it wasn't what she meant. What she meant was, I'm sorry, it's just me, I'm trying to snap out of it. What it meant was, Can't you just pretend I'm happy, or that you are?

Michael squeezed her hand and sighed wearily. "Everything okay?" he said. His thumb played over a slick patch of skin left from the night Lori had once scalded herself with pasta water.

"Fine," she said, reclaiming her hand. She lit a cigarette and opened the window. March cold rushed in over the glass, blowing ash back on the houndstooth sweater she bought just for the trip.

"Nerves," Michael said. She couldn't tell if it was a question or a diagnosis. She also wondered whether he was talking to her or to himself. (He had made a few too many self-deprecating jokes this week, comparing his high school teaching to Derek's loftier professorship.) "You're just nervous about meeting Derek and Mallory. That's understandable."

"I'm sure that's all it is," she said. "You know me and new people. I'll come around."

"Well, nothing to fret over. They're great, you'll love them, and I'm supremely confident they'll love you, of course."

Lori could feel his easy, reassuring smile. She did her level best to return it.

• • •

They traded the lonely interstate for the mercantile busyness of Pigeon Forge and Gatlinburg. Michael was in a hurry now, not even asking if she wanted to stop somewhere before heading to the cabin. They rode the rising contours of the land, towns falling behind and below, the streets narrowing, pavement fading to gravel that scaled a steepening grade. At some point Lori's ears popped from the change in elevation, relieving a headache she didn't know she'd had. The Wrangler pitched and swerved through a final turn, gravel rifling against the undercarriage. The Jeep lurched forward and came to a hard stop on paved driveway hidden in the wooded mountainside.

"Ta-da," Michael said, smiling expectantly. Lori managed a grin. The cabin before her was larger and newer than she'd expected, two stories of flat-cut logs stacked in clean yellow lines. It looked less like the decrepit lean-to she'd been expecting than a life-sized dollhouse, plastic and perfect, something that had until recently been stored under glass.

"Looks like we're here first," Michael said, taking the Jeep out of gear and handing her the keys. "Why don't you go on in while I get the rest of our stuff."

She left him to their things, climbed the few steps to a wraparound deck, and let herself in. It was cold and dim, the inside lit only by the winter daylight in the windows. There was a deep maroon couch, a few wing-backed chairs, and a thick aroma of woodsmoke and furniture polish that reminded her of a funeral parlor. In the far corner, a small but serviceable kitchenette sat on an island of white linoleum, where another door opened, presumably, to another portion of the deck. On the wall hung a wooden plaque with LINGER LONGER carved into it. She remembered the words from a brochure for the cabin

Michael had showed her, and she remembered wondering why cabins needed names.

In the center of the downstairs, an iron-spiral staircase climbed like a metal vine to the second-floor landing. Lori went up slowly, her night bag bumping against her hip. It was eerily quiet—all she heard were her footfalls on the iron rungs and the hiss of a steady rain that had just started falling—and she had to suppress an urge to call out and make sure the cabin was empty. At the top she walked to one end of the landing and pushed the door open into a small bedroom with a slanted ceiling of exposed rafters. Against the far wall stood a squat chest o' drawers with an oval mirror hung above it. Her reflection met her with its plainness, her pale skin, her brown hair a haystack from hours in the car, her eyes tired and dull. She stepped inside and flinched—I sometimes don't recognize myself in the mirror, 0 to 10!—when she saw the young woman sitting on the foot of an unmade bed.

A high-pitched note of surprise escaped Lori.

"You're here!" Lori said. She took a deep breath, feeling more than a little embarrassed. "Sorry, you scared me." She crossed the room, hand extended. "Nice to finally meet you. I'm Lori."

Michael had never described Mallory, but she appeared years younger than she could be, eighteen or twenty, with large blue eyes and long black hair parted down the middle. She wore a plain blue dress with three-quarter sleeves and a frayed neckline. She held her hands folded in her lap, the nails unpainted, rimmed with half moons of dirt. She wore no shoes.

"Hello? You up there?" Michael called from below.

A tear spilled down Mallory's cheek, then another. She

glanced up at Lori with her shoulders back, her face serene, even as the tears flowed faster, dropping in dark circles on her dress. Lori froze, wondering how someone could cry like that yet look so peaceful.

"Let me tell you this story," the woman said to her in a steady voice.

Lori felt herself drawn close. The woman lifted her mouth to her ear; her breath was cold.

"Babe?" she heard Michael call outside the door. "Everything okay?" He stepped quickly into the room, struggling with the buttons of his coat.

"Michael, I think something's wrong with her," Lori whispered.

He shrugged the coat off one shoulder, and then he took a sharp step back. "Who the fuck is she?"

I find myself someplace and I don't remember how I got there. What would she give that right now? 5? 6? Lori found herself wondering more about the numbers—the grading scale? the self-evaluation metric?—than the question as she stood on the deck in the cold, watching the woman in the blue dress walk down the paved driveway. Why 0 through 10? It seemed an awful lot of degrees. She didn't remember exactly how she'd gotten from the bedroom to the deck—judging how strongly she felt, this seemed beside the point. How many shades of lunatic gray were there? Or was it simply an indication of frequency? Or a measure of her own alarm? She resolved to ask Dr. Ryerson this when she returned.

Beside her Michael leaned forward, wrists crossed over the railing. Together they watched the woman in the blue dress walk down the gravel road. She had her arms held out to her sides, like a child crossing a stream on a narrow log. One bare foot plunged into a puddle, but she neither slowed nor seemed to care as she disappeared around the bend. "We can't just let her walk, can we?" Lori said. "It's cold, and there's nothing down that road for miles."

"It's not a mile to the main road," Michael said. "Besides, we can't exactly restrain her." He slipped an arm around Lori's waist. She felt the attempt but her body tensed, refusing to play along.

"Should we follow her?"

"There's a phone inside. I'll call the manager's office," Michael said. It occurred to Lori that this wasn't really an answer, but she wasn't sure she wanted one.

"What do you think happened to her? How'd she end up here?"

"Beats me. Probably got drunk in town and came back to sleep it off in the wrong cabin."

"On foot?"

"Maybe she had someone drop her off, gave bad directions." Michael shrugged impatiently. Lori hated this tendency of his, when he confused her asking questions with her questioning him. "The property manager's number is on the paperwork. I'll go get it. Give him quick call."

He kissed the top of her head and went inside. The rain fell harder now, tapping flat and lonely on the deck's overhang and on the dead leaves scattering the forest floor. About thirty yards into the woods, she glimpsed a deer. It was a full-grown doe, thin and gray with its late-winter coat. It twitched, as if generally aware of Lori without knowing exactly where the danger was.

From some distance, she heard a faint mechanical grind of an engine. A large green pickup took the road's bend in a wild spray of gravel. When she looked back, the deer had vanished.

II. The Blue Bride

Derek and Mallory lay siege to the cabin in a confusion of hugs, luggage, and food.

"We bring comestibles," Derek had said, greeting Michael with a lift of his chin and a deep Tennessee twang. "Not that you need any. You've fattened up, Lofton."

Michael worked his fingers into his side and pinched a handful of stomach. "More cushion for the pushing."

"Later," Derek said. "The women will get jealous." He was tall and rangy, cloaked in an olive-drab jacket and a thick, sandy beard, like a slightly older version of the college students on Tennessee Avenue back home, Lori thought, doing their best impressions of the genuinely poor. Mallory was tiny at five feet even. She looked like she didn't weigh any more than a hundred pounds, even in her wool skirt and cowboy boots. She seemed a strange fit for Derek, outsized in every way except volume, in which she cheerfully exceeded him.

"You're Lori," she trumpeted, offering a tiny mittened hand. "You're lovely and I'm happy to know you."

"Likewise," Lori said. She was wary of Mallory's enthusiasm, even as she felt herself wanting to be carried away by it.

"It's freezing," Mallory said. "Tell me you weren't waiting outside for us!"

"Not at all," Michael said. He shook his head at Lori, a gesture she understood to mean save the woman in blue for later.

"Well, dear heart," Derek said, "I guess we'll bunk here

tonight, if you can handle such scrofulous company." He dropped the bags on the deck, then turned to Lori and executed a shallow but efficient bow. "The lady excluded, of course."

"The lady doesn't know what scrofulous means," Lori said, "but it probably applies."

It took over half an hour to move Derek and Mallory in. While the boys pack-muled everything inside, Lori and Mallory sorted the food: plastic bins of berries, softball-sized Granny Smith apples, rice crackers and baguettes and tins of sardines in mustard sauce. Lori unloaded a cardboard box full of meats and cheeses with labels that made no pronounceable sounds in her head—bresaola and sopressata, manchego and Roquefort.

"God, we could eat for a month off this," Lori said. Apologetically, she added, "Michael and I didn't bring any food." Shame stirred in her brain, threatening to trigger a return of the morning's dark mood. Did she bring all of this just to show me up? To make me feel bad?

"It's ridiculous, I know," Mallory said. "We stopped by this little market in Pigeon Forge and I said, 'Blackberries in February? In Tennessee?' I was powerless after that, lost in a spending fugue."

There was a certain theatricality to how she talked and moved, unpacking food with wiggling fingers, like a stage magician conjuring cheeses from a top hat. Lori felt herself seesawing between finding the show enjoyable or irksome.

Michael came in, toting a wooden crate on his shoulder. "You may have just become Lori's best friend, Mal," Michael said. He set the crate down and winked at Lori. "Think a whole case will be enough for you, babe?"

"That's a whole lotta wine," she said, uncertain how else to answer.

"I didn't buy the case, not today anyway. Old crate, new wine," Mallory said. "That's a beautiful metaphor for something, I'm sure, but I just don't know what it is."

"Pour the wine," Michael said, "and the metaphors will come."

"Waitaminute, waitaminute, waitaminute!" Mallory sounded drunk, but Lori—who definitely was—couldn't be sure. They were outside despite the cold and the dark, huddled in their coats around a patio table crowded with empty wine bottles and paper plates sticky with the congealed remnants of dinner. Behind them, a hot tub kicked on and off intermittently, perfuming the air with a clean chemical scent. An electric camping lantern dimly cast an orange glow no farther than the table's edge. "Gimme a light, Lofton."

Lori heard the click of Michael's Zippo opening. The flame plucked Mallory's face from the shadows like a white tulip bulb.

"Grazie mille."

"Prego," he said, and clicked the lighter shut.

She blew a jet of smoke—Lori could smell the spiced scent of a clove cigarette—into the lantern's glow. "So she was just there? In your room?"

"Just there," Michael said. He had saved the story until after dinner, until enough drinks had flowed and—as Michael was so fond of saying—the time was propitious. "All alone in a pretty blue dress."

Lori didn't remember the dress being particularly pretty, but the woman was, and she guessed that was what Michael meant.

"Y'all call the police?"

"Nope," Michael said. "Called the property manager. Once I

reassured him nothing had been broken or stolen, he lost interest tout de suite. He recommended I call the sheriff's department if she comes back."

"I should fucking think so," Mallory said. "She say anything before she left?"

"She was crying," Lori said, recalling those quiet, effortless tears. "Not crying, but you know, tears. Not tearing up, I mean they were falling." Frustrated, she lit a cigarette.

"Mater Lachrymarum," Derek offered knowingly.

Michael shook his head. "Just got up, shot by me, and then she was down the road."

"Well," Derek said, "I reckon your mystery woman was a revenant. If we're telling ghost stories, let's do it right." He leaned his chair back and produced a large bottle of whiskey from somewhere beyond the lantern's electric-orange reach. He took Lori's glass by the stem, tossed the rest of her wine into the night, and poured her glass half full. She sipped, and the whiskey filled a crack in her chapped upper lip with fire.

"She did say something to me," Lori said. She'd been quiet for most of the dinner, letting the old friends catch up. She had liked listening to their stories, a weekend in an old brothel in New Orleans, a rafting trip in West Virginia. Lori had never really been anywhere, just a few trips to the beaches down south when she was a kid, Disneyworld a handful of times. She nursed a private hope that one thing Michael would bring into her life was more travel—high adventure in exotic locales! She found herself now grateful for the mysterious appearance of the woman. It had given her something to contribute.

"Really?" Derek said. "Do tell."

Lori struggled to collect the memory. She could see the pale face, eerily serene behind a wash of tears, her silently working mouth. There was a coldness in her ear. Is that even possible? Am I remembering that right? Sometimes I feel like my memories aren't mine, 7.

"I don't know," she said. "It's like a dream I can't remember, just remember having, you know?"

"All that we see or seem is but a dream within a dream," Derek said.

Mallory squealed like a theremin. "Creepy," she said, beating her small fists against her thighs. "So fucking creepy."

"Sounds like an old mountain legend," Derek said. "The Blue Bride of Bluff Mountain. Abandoned at the altar, the comely young bride threw herself over the falls. Now she roams the mountains weeping tears of river water whilst seeking her revenge."

"Enough! Enough," Mallory cried. "Can we just skip the ghost stories, please? Lori, please, tell us all about yourself. I want to know everything about you, inside and out."

Lori lit a cigarette, then noticed she already had one going in the ashtray. She was ready for this, had even rehearsed a little scripted introduction of herself to perform for Derek and Mallory. No, I never went to college, we couldn't afford it after Dad died, but I work at a bookstore where a certain tall, handsome high school teacher just happened to bring his class on Friday nights—and here she would lovingly clutch his hand, or maybe kiss his cheek. But sitting in boozy comfort with Michael's friends, she found little need of it.

"Ask me anything," she said, "and I shall answer true."

A silence followed, the longest of the night. Lori worried how the others were filling it in their minds; she struggled not to blame herself for it, to not feel like she was somehow lacking.

"Wot's the best fing about livin' wit' Lofton, then?" came a high Cockney accent. It was Michael's best Dickensian urchin, a voice that came out sometimes with the liquor. Everyone laughed.

"Well," she said. She walked two fingers up Michael's arm, clutched his coat sleeve, and pulled him into a deep, whiskey-wet kiss.

"My goodness," Mallory said to Derek. "She's absolutely glowing." She folded her small hands on the table, laid her forehead against them, and dropped a sleepy wink at Lori.

III. Falling Hazards

Michael was inside her.

Their sex was slow, prodding, but not without rhythm. She felt her body return to her in a series of waking sensations. Her mouth rubbed slickly against his smooth, nearly hairless chest; her body was a small burning coal in the otherwise frigid bedroom. She felt Michael's weight, her face pressed too tightly against him. She struggled for air.

"Get off." The words were muffled against his flesh. "Can't breathe."

"Hey, babe, what's—"

"Get off." She couldn't pull any air. Panic lit her brain, but its messages couldn't find her limbs. She felt as trapped in her body as under his—My body feels like it doesn't belong to me, 10—and starbursts of light, yellow and blue, flared in a great distance.

"Babe, are you okay?"

She felt his hands on her shoulders, shoving, and she was

suddenly upright, straddling him in the dark, not wedged beneath but sitting high and panting on top of him. In one of the room's high windows, a cloud hovered, brightly silvered by the moon behind it. She took in deep, wet breaths and tried to make her heart go slower.

"I'm sorry," she said. She slid off him and collapsed onto a cool spread of sheet.

The sheets, I should have changed them, she thought. They had come upstairs after dinner and too much to drink, Michael behind her, patting her ass with upturned palms, a pantomime of unbridled lechery that wasn't all play-pretend, hurrying her into the bedroom where they embraced and kissed and undressed, falling onto the bed, which had remained unmade since the woman in the blue dress had been sitting on it.

"Too much to drink," she said. "We made love in someone else's dirty sheets, ten."

"What?" he said. "Whose sheets? What do you mean, 'ten'?"

"Never mind," she said. There was no way to explain it just then.

"Hold on." He got up and crossed the dark room. Light spilled from the bathroom, and she heard him running the sink. He returned and placed a glass of water in her hands. Lori rose up on her elbows and drank. Cool water dribbled down her chin and spilled onto her chest. The rest of the day was returning to her, memories swimming up from the blackout void like strange fish from some sunless deep. There was something else wrong. She looked for it in darkness but could see only the woman, sitting there, crying.

"Is it like, one of your," she heard him sigh, then surrender to the word, her mother's favorite, "difficulties?"

She sipped more, shaking her head slowly. Michael pressed his lips together and smoothed her hair—tangled and sweaty from their lovemaking. She hated the word, but, like him, had no other shorthand for it, for nights like the one when she had scalded herself so badly. She had been making spaghetti—nothing fancy, a homemade red sauce, a box of noodles—and talking to her mother, the phone cradled uncomfortably between her neck and shoulder. Michael was grading papers at the table, and she was in the process of explaining their situation to her mother—how Michael had let her move in to his spare room after her lease expired; how, yes, she was living with him but still looking for her own place (this was back when she was still at least pretending to look).

It started with taste. She had put a spoonful of sauce in her mouth and suddenly the taste of it in her mouth was . . . off. It wasn't the taste, really, but the feeling of tasting. Like a wire had crossed in her brain, and now having food in her mouth felt like she was looking at a bowl overflowing with water. The world had suddenly gone strange—she had gone strange. She saw Michael's shoulders beneath a too-white undershirt hunched over his grading, and it was like someone had control of a dimmer switch on the brightness of the world, and they had turned it higher and higher and brighter, and she couldn't swallow, and she simply took the sauce out of her mouth, as though it were a solid thing, like taking a bone from a dog. And she had held her hand in the steam above the boiling pasta water and—Something inside of me makes me do things I don't want to do, 10!—she didn't want Michael (who was now, somehow, her mother's voice, dressed in a T-shirt and grading papers but still all of that was her mother's voice) to see her hand dirty and dripping with sauce and—I find that I can make physical pain go away, 10!!!—she had watched her hand plunge through the swirling mist and break the surface of the water, and she saw her hand rest there amid the many broken and scattered reflections of herself that rose in violent effervescence around it as the phone dropped from her, and her mother's voice was pulling her away, Michael was pulling her away, and the pain that had been so dim and distant suddenly became clear. And it was the ragged-throat shrieks of her own screaming.

"I'm okay," she said now, handing Michael back the glass of water. "No difficulties."

The next morning, after a breakfast of chicory coffee and scones, they decided to venture into Great Smoky Mountains National Park and find a trail to hike. They piled into Michael's Jeep—boys up front, girls in back, just like any old-couple quorum—and drove down the mountain. They'd decided on Laurel Falls—an easy hike, two hours tops with a gentle slope—much to Michael's chagrin.

"I've been on that trail. It's fucking paved," Michael groused, still not giving up as they drove into the park proper. "It's the kiddie ride of trails."

"Suck it up, buttercup," Derek said, screwing a lens onto his camera. "Mal says the falls, we're going to the falls."

The Laurel Falls trail was a narrow thread of black asphalt that traced the mountain's outer edge. There they joined a motley parade of young couples, lone hikers, and families encumbered with little kids who had to be constantly shouted back. At certain points, around stone outcroppings and sharp bends, Lori could see for hundreds of yards before and behind them, a line of people steadily climbing or descending, pilgrims with Polaroids. She examined the faces of those coming down for some sign of what lay ahead, but she couldn't read a thing.

"Company halt," Derek said. He jogged a few paces ahead, turned, and aimed his camera. While he worked the lens, people swung past them like water diverted by a stone. Michael slipped his arms over Lori's and Mallory's shoulders. Lori tucked a loose strand of hair behind her ear, dropped her hand to her side, then let it rest on his stomach. "Say cheese!"

"Shitty trail!" Michael said. In passing, a mother with a frosted perm and a fat little boy scowled at them.

After Derek snapped the picture, they continued up the trail. Like traffic, they kept to the right, hugging a wall of exposed dirt, rocks, and roots that supported a deep forest rising above them. At one particularly sharp curve stood a small red sign that read: WARNING: FALLING HAZARD. Lori drifted to it, stepping her feet to the asphalt's edge. The earth peeled away, gradually at first, thick with underbrush and bare trees, but steeper as it went until the land disappeared altogether. Far below she could see a river, fast-flowing with the March snowmelt, rippled white in some places, smooth as glass in others. It was so clear, so close-seeming, that she could almost hear the water, the current brushing over polished stones with a sound like the wind rustling leaves, growing louder, not like wind at all but something solid charging through the forest behind her.

Lori turned just in time to see a shape, wild and bucking, spill out onto the trail. She felt the rough heat of an animal body brush by her. She heard a snort and saw one panic-huge eye streak across her field of vision like a black comet. It was a full-grown deer, and it had launched from the woods behind her as if chased, skittered across the trail, and pitched itself over the edge. She watched it turn twice in the long silence of the fall before it hit the water in a soundless spray. Lori's hands sought Michael, Mallory, anyone, but found nothing. A cry caught in her throat, and her heart thundered in her chest. She looked for help.

She was all alone.

Everyone—the hikers and tourists, parents and kids, Michael and Derek and Mallory—everyone was gone, vanished. It was as if they had disappeared into the woods or careened off the edge or had simply been lifted up and out of the world. Panic rushed upon her, and her lungs took in great sucks of air until she felt so lightheaded she had to crouch to keep her balance. I find myself someplace and I don't remember how I got there, 10.

She continued up the trail, moving quickly, constantly fighting back a lunatic urge to run. She heard Laurel Falls before she saw them, the muted cymbal crash of water falling on water. Lori crossed a wooden bridge above a rushing stream fed by the falls and stepped onto an uneven platform of slick bedrock. The falls rose thirty feet above it, the water strung over jagged levels of stone like braids of dirty gray rope. The water and the darkly wet stone behind it formed a shimmering window, inside of which she saw a woman. Lori reached for the water. She felt nothing at first, then an icy coldness began to spread, her veins carrying numbness throughout her, cutting straight for her heart. She cupped her hand, let it fill, and drank.

"Hey, don't do that, baby." Michael's hand was on her shoulder. She turned, spilling the water down the front of her coat. She clutched her hand to her chest as if she'd hurt it. Behind him, Derek was directing Mallory closer to the falls for a picture, and a woman—the mother with the frosted perm—was pulling her son out of the shot. "You shouldn't drink that," Michael said. "Giardia, you know? Protozoa? You could get really sick."

Lori laughed softly.

"Baby?"

She eased down on the cold wet bedrock, sitting cross-legged and leaning back on her hands. "Sometimes everybody goes away, ten!" she said, loud enough for people to stare. Mallory slowly released her picture pose and motioned for Derek. Other people gathered round. Lori laughed—she wanted to laugh, but the echo sounded more like a scream in her ears.

IV. Water of Life

At the cabin, Michael took her coat and started a fire, which she spent the next hour tending, watching sparks fly in brief erratic patterns. She could hear the others murmur conspiratorially in the kitchenette. Michael was apologizing for her, explaining her moods, her "difficulties." It must be bad, she knew, for them to talk about her in the same room. It must be really bad.

She heard the refrigerator open, cabinet doors shut. Something—she didn't know what—made a high whistling sound. She turned her head enough to see Michael and Derek packing food into a cardboard box. So we're leaving, she thought. I've lost my mind and ruined Michael's trip and now we're leaving. Tonight they pack boxes and tomorrow, in Tallahassee, I'll pack boxes. I'll go back to Mom's apartment, she thought, where the dark wine really flows.

"Hey, Lori?" he said. "Derek and I are going to start dinner."

He looks so sad, she thought, sad and tired and afraid. Lori lifted her hand and gave a small wave. She felt like a stage actor recovering from a badly muffed line, trying to repair the play by pretending it's not a play. Still, she forced herself to look him in the eyes, hoping for a smile. God, how she wanted him to smile at her, to give a quick wink and let her know everything was fine, that everything would be all right. Derek carried the box outside and Michael slung the door shut behind them. The Linger Longer plaque shook on the wall, threatening to slip off its nail.

"Hey there, kiddo." Mallory stood beside her. She offered a cup and saucer. "I made you some tea."

Lori took it and sipped.

"I wasn't sure how you take it. Would you like milk or honey?" Worry and hopefulness had drawn a crooked smile on her face.

"You could Irish it up for me," Lori said, borrowing one of Michael's phrases. It felt strange to say it, like having a mouthful of someone else's teeth.

"Now you're talking." Mallory fetched a bottle of whiskey from the counter. She held it out from her chest in her two small hands and cast furtive glances around—the perfect pantomime of a naughty child—and took a swig before splashing some in the teacup. Lori sipped, the whiskey sitting atop the tea like burning oil.

"My girl," Mallory said, laughing. She tucked her long gray skirt beneath her legs and sat on the hearth beside Lori. "So, do you want to talk about it?"

Lori shook her head.

"Then we don't," Mallory said. She shook a cigarette out of a small tin and lit it off a stick of kindling plucked from the fire. "See? Just that easy. How about a story instead?"

Lori nodded; she thought a story would suit her just fine.

• • •

"When the Civil War finally came to Tennessee, a young man named Matthew, great-grandson of a Revolutionary War colonel, volunteered. He went off to defend hearth and home while his wife, Lorelei, watched after their four children and the little hardware store they ran."

"Lorelei?" Lori said. She tried a smile that said, Come on, are you serious? Mallory offered a shrug that said, The story's the story.

"One evening Lorelei encountered a woman she had never seen before on the ox trail between the store and home.

"'Are you lost?' she asked the woman. 'Do you need help?'

"The woman made no reply, but Lorelei was worried and cajoled her into coming home with her. The woman didn't say a word for the three miles it took them to walk in the wooded twilight. Lorelei prattled on about the store and her chores. But when she spoke of her husband at war, the woman suddenly grabbed Lorelei's face so tightly with her hand that it blocked her air and trapped her voice. Lorelei struggled, but the woman held her fast, just with that one hand to her mouth, as if they'd been joined by a powerful force. The stranger woman said, 'Let me tell you this story.'"

Lori sipped more of her whiskey. She steadied her gaze at Mallory, who looked back at her with flat eyes, and lips spread into a thin smile.

"Then she let go and led the way to the house—Lorelei struggling to pace her—as if she'd walked the way a thousand times before. Lorelei, breathless and unable to cry for help, followed.

"At home the front door of her house shot open—as it did every evening—and her children rushed out, all four of them, oldest to youngest—as they did every evening. But this evening they grabbed the stranger woman by the waist and the hips and the legs, all but disappearing in the folds of her skirts and shouting 'Mama! Mama! We are so happy you are home!'

"Lorelei opened her mouth to ask what her children were doing but no words came out. Her tongue would not move in her mouth, her throat would shape no notes. Even the air she forced from her lungs made no sound. She tried to grab her oldest, but the woman they called Mama slapped her hands away. The woman proceeded to tell the children what had happened, but as if she were Lorelei.

"'Let her stay, Mama!' they all cried. 'She can help make dinner, and we are hungry!'

"And so she stayed. They moved her into the small corner room near the icehouse. The woman bought her servant's clothes to wear and gave her a servant's life. No one—not the in-laws nor her own mother, not the neighbors nor her children—recognized her. For the next two years they called the stranger woman 'Lorelei' or they called her 'Mama,' and they called Lorelei nothing at all."

As Lori listened, she felt the day's confusion find focus, and even a bit of stability in a newfound anger. She didn't know why Mallory would choose to play such a trick on her—was she bored? A mean drunk? Did she harbor strong and untrammeled feelings for Michael? She snatched the bottle from beside Mallory and refilled her cup.

"It was winter when Matthew came back," Mallory continued, oblivious to any change in Lori. "He wore a buckskin patch over an eye he'd lost, but he had survived the war. Lorelei was collecting kindling as she saw him come up the road. She watched her children fly off the porch to hug their father. He knelt, gathering them in his arms, letting them peel back the patch, tickling their ribs, and Lorelei's heart broke all over. Would her Matthew know her where no one else did?"

Here, Mallory stopped the story. She took Lori's drink from her and finished it off.

"So," she said. "Do you think Matthew knew his wife? Do you think he wanted to?"

Lori tried to stand but stumbled; the whiskey had hit her harder than she'd thought. "Do you think I'm stupid? Or do you really think you'll trick me into thinking that girl was some sort of ghost, trying to take me over?"

Mallory stood and looked down at her. She raised her hand as if to cover her mouth, then stopped. The hurt and fear slowly fell, and she looked somehow different, rearranged.

"You tell me," she said to Lori, walking toward the spiral staircase. "Do you think Michael would know you?"

Mallory turned slowly and went upstairs. She curtsied from the landing, casting down a cold but toothsome smile before gliding into Lori and Michael's bedroom. The door slammed behind her just as Michael poked his head in from the deck, holding a pair of tongs. "Dinner's almost ready," he said. "How do you want your burger?"

Without answering him, Lori stood—nearly floated—to her feet. She felt strangely light, free of anger and whiskey and fear, as if whole chambers of her mind had been emptied. Sometimes it feels like there are walls inside my mind. . . . 1? Michael clicked the tongs absently, still a little worried, trying to be hopeful.

Mallory ducked in beneath his arm, shivering with the cold.

"Hurry up and come out here, Lori. Don't leave me out here with the menfolk all night."

"Shall I bring the whiskey?" she said.

"Uisge beatha," she said. "Please."

Lori nestled the whiskey bottle in her arm like a bunch of long-stemmed roses and carried it to him. "What's that mean?" she said, walking outside.

"It's Gaelic for 'whiskey,'" Michael said as she passed him. "Means 'water of life.'"

"That's fascinating," Lori whispered, kissing him on the cheek.

She let him take the bottle and stopped near the hot tub.

"Someone's thinking ahead," said Derek. Michael appeared beside her, working buttons, and the water came to life. Two pinkish-blue spheres of light popped on, and she watched the water foam and bubble, the fumes stinging her eyes. It was snowing now, and she watched the large, fat flakes blow over the deck and melt in the rising steam.

Submerged in the water, she saw the billowing fabric of the woman's blue dress and her long black hair fanning out. The woman raised one hand, her fingers just beneath the surface, not an inch away from Lori's own outstretched hand.

She watched as Michael rushed up and pulled the woman away from the water, telling her not to drink. The woman, who was wearing Lori's clothes, swatted his hands away and slipped an arm around his waist. She watched Michael hold her tight as they walked down the trail with Derek and Mallory close behind.

I want to tell you a story: Sometimes I hear voices in my head that are not mine.

She saw her hands on a field of blue, her fingernails rimmed with dirt. Her knees were pressed together and her legs poured themselves palely down to bare feet.

"Sorry, Jesus—you." The woman wore her houndstooth sweater. She wore all of Lori's clothes, wore her hair. Her face.

Behind her was a door, and behind that door a man's deep voice asking if the woman was all right in there. She felt tears spilling down her cheeks, but she could attach no feeling to them. Her dress showed dark, wet circles, but it didn't matter. It was only water.

"Let me tell you this story," she heard this body around her say.

# Whimper Beg

*Lee Thomas*

The theft was a courtesy. At least, that's how Scotty Collins explained it to himself. After the funeral of his best friend and mentor, and after an hour at the reception, extolling the virtues of Judge Walter Griff to men in fine suits and women in tasteful black dresses, he'd ordered a refill on his scotch and slipped away to spend time alone with his grief. He'd been hesitant to leave the crowd, because he knew the moment he stepped out of earshot, his daughter would become a topic of conversation. For years now, his little girl, Miranda, had provided fertile ground for the weeds of gossip. However, her last instance of recklessness had brought a new level of humiliation to her family. Even Scotty, who had successfully argued many improbable legal defenses, wasn't able to explain it away as youthful indiscretion. But he knew he couldn't stop the talk, knew he couldn't control the world, so he'd excused himself from the mourners and made his way to the study. The door had been closed, but it hadn't been locked, so when he checked the room—richly decorated with mahogany bookcases and leather furniture—and found it empty, Scotty stepped inside. He meandered around the study, spending time reminiscing and absorbing the atmosphere that now felt thinner without the great man's presence.

They'd spent hours in this space, drinking good whisky and

talking about work, their families, fishing, and politics. He'd been introduced to two state senators in this room, both of whom had promptly received a check from Scotty, and both of whom he still supported to this day.

The book on Walter's desk caught his eye, because its garish, yet worn, paperback cover was so different from the hardbound volumes lining Walter's shelves. Scotty lifted the book and examined the cover, which showed the purple silhouettes of a man and his dog, standing before a glistening body of water.

*The Litter's Runt* by Christopher Pelham.

He sipped his scotch and perused the back cover, his face growing warm with the line, ". . . and sexual awakening of a gay kid from small town North Carolina." The book seemed highly uncharacteristic for his mentor, but opening the cover, he noted an inscription:

*To Walter,*

*Who was like a second father to me. Chris*

Without giving the action any thought, Scotty tucked the book into his jacket's inner pocket the way he'd once slotted his checkbook before leaving the house, and only after he took another sip of his drink did it occur to him that he was breaking the law. It was then he decided that taking the novel was an act of respect. If someone else found the book on the judge's desk, it might lead to ridiculous speculation, particularly considering the odd inscription.

He returned to the throng filling the front of the house, where nothing had changed during his brief absence. The faces of the crowd, a garden of somber blossoms, fell in around him.

He'd known most of these people all his adult life. Walter had brought them together for holiday parties, political fundraisers, or just to fill his house with like-minded friends.

"He was a great man," noted a slender lawyer with a tightly fitted suit. "He had a brilliant mind," said a young woman with perfect hair and crooked teeth. "I never saw a man his age in better shape," said a diminutive gentleman with a tight, tanned face.

Scotty paused at the periphery of this conversation, waiting to be noticed. Dr. Desmond Threlkeld was his personal physician; he'd been Walter's as well.

"Scotty," Threlkeld said, cocking his head away from a matronly woman who wore her white hair in a globe on the top of her head. "I'm so sorry. I know how close you and Walter were."

The crowd pushed in tight at Scotty's shoulders and the weight of the book against his chest reminded him of his crime. He thanked the doctor. "It's been a shock for all of us."

"It has," Threlkeld agreed. "I was just saying how fit Walter seemed. Shocking."

"And there were no signs something like this might happen?"

"I can't speak to specifics, of course, but no." Dr. Threlkeld's face grew pensive as if he were trying to remember the name of an actress from an old film. He leaned in closer to Scotty and whispered. "The medical examiner is a friend of mine. He had some difficulties with the autopsy."

"Difficulties?" Scotty asked.

"Oh, you know," Threlkeld said. "The aftermath."

Scotty nodded. It was a grisly business. After suffering a lethal cardiac event in his backyard, Walter had lain exposed to the elements for at least twenty-four hours, and some of those elements had had teeth. Though animal attack had been ruled out as the cause of death, the local media had been happy to report that his corpse had suffered the attentions of wildlife and stray pets.

Before Scotty could ask his next question, a hand gripped his arm and pulled. Rachel Smith, an attractive young associate with the firm, whose eyes blazed with ambition, faced him for a moment and then threw her arms around his shoulders.

"This must be so hard for you," she said. The scent of the expensive perfume dousing her neck crawled into his head like a virus, instantly triggering the tightness in his sinuses he associated with an impending allergy attack. "First Miranda, and now this. I'm so sorry, Scotty."

He patted her back, eager to send her on her way.

"If you need anything," she said as sweetly predatory as a kitten toying with a roach, "you let me know. I'm here for you."

He thanked her and excused himself, but when he turned to resume his conversation with the doctor, he couldn't find the man. Scotty worked his way through the crowd, distracted by Threlkeld's words and the book in his pocket. What difficulties had the doctor meant? Had something important been left out of the coroner's report? As for the book, why would the story of some homo in North Carolina hold any interest for Walter Griff? Further, what had been meant by the inscription?

Giving up on his search for the doctor, Scotty left the reception, carrying a sense of disappointment along with his questions and grief. The word "difficulties" persisted, clicking around in his head.

*In nature, the runt of a litter not only struggles for nourishment but also attention. Fighting with its stronger siblings for a place at the teats, a runt can die of starvation while its brothers and sisters grow strong and healthy. Sensing this weakness, this inferiority, the parent will often ignore the runt, instinct dictating that such a defenseless creature deserves neither effort nor resources, because ultimately it has no chance for survival. It's an evolutionary imperative, you see. It's animal. It's primal. While I certainly had more than enough to eat as a child, my parents, Father especially, practiced this brand of natural selection.*

*I was the runt of my litter. Weaker and smaller than my brothers, weaker and smaller than my classmates. To my father, I was an embarrassment. A waste.*

*Outside the walls of my home, the world treats me as prey. My pack doesn't protect me. If I am unable to find or create a new pack, I may never survive my youth. . . .*

The blue-black horizon at the edge of the ocean faded to a lavender-hued sky. Scotty stood on the wraparound porch, his drink sweating a ring on the stark white railing as he gazed at the foaming tide. In the distance a dog barked angrily, as if warning an intruder away from its property.

Though he felt miserable, he couldn't complain about the view. Three years ago, before real trouble had found his daughter, he'd come home to find the lawn of his former residence littered with three-thousand dollar suits and garbage bags gorged to near breaking with his other belongings. At that point, he'd commandeered the beach house with its sharp-edged modern exterior and an interior color palette reminiscent of a Cape Cod vacation rental his ex had adored. The blues and greens, all framed in glaring white trim, had always been too soft for Scotty, perhaps too feminine, but he'd never gotten around to having them painted.

He inhaled deeply. Salted air filled his lungs.

"Fuck," he said to the ocean view.

He'd been reading the book he'd stolen from Walter's study. It only added to his confusion. Though a tremendous reader, Walter Griff's taste in literature had always run to nonfiction: histories and biographies. The few novels he had discussed incorporated dense and accurate historical notes. In short, he didn't read fluff. He certainly wasn't likely to read the blunt and self-pitying account of a young homosexual.

Scotty couldn't help but wonder if Walter had actually known Christopher Pelham, the author of the book. The copyright was more than twenty-five years old, around the time Scotty had first fallen under Walter's wing.

*To Walter,*

*Who was like a second father to me.*

Scotty certainly understood the sentiment.

The distant barking drew his attention down the beach. He saw the animal, way off, barely larger than a speck near where the Zanes property met the Williamsons.

The presence of the agitated animal, even so far from him, made Scotty uneasy. He couldn't say why exactly. He'd been reading Pelham's novel, and clearly the author had identified strongly with the creatures, but the novel hinted at nothing even remotely sinister about the animals.

His phone rang. It was the tone designated for his daughter, the opening notes of a song she'd loved as a child. A year ago, she'd downloaded the ringtone and loaded it onto his phone. Miranda had said it was "their song," which had made Scotty wince. He hated the six bars of music.

He continued to stare at the shimmering water and the darkening sky, as the melody played over and over. The rail proved sturdy enough for his tightening grip and the weight his now-swaying body placed on it.

*Tomorrow,* he thought. His emotions had been thoroughly wrung for the day. Tomorrow he'd take her call.

The dog, maybe a German shepherd, darker than any he'd seen, was closer now. It ran along the shoreline. Through a trick of distance or fading light, it appeared that the charging animal actually made no forward progress, despite the rapid pedaling of its legs. The eager animal ran, but went nowhere, like a digital image endlessly looping.

Unnerved by this illusion, Scotty lifted his glass and walked inside.

*It is the last day of school, and I am ten years old. Already, the summer's promised heat has descended on Hargett's Bend. Pollen dust still speckles the air, lit by the sun's glare. Walking with Jacob Larimer, I drift in and out of a daydream in which I imagine swimming through a sea of radiance, a fantasy ocean of luminous tides.*

*I walk with Jacob, not because we are friends, because we certainly are not, but because he had announced to the class that his dog had mothered a litter of pups, and the news had compelled me to see the animals.*

*Without a note of hospitality or facade of friendliness, he walks me through his house to the mudroom beyond the kitchen. The Larimer house is very much like my father's house. So many of the houses of our class resemble one another, inside if not out.*

*There, in a large wicker basket that might have once held towels at the poolside, lays a magnificent shepherd. Nearly all black, she reclines as three fist-sized pups crowd against her belly. A fourth pup tries to wriggle in for its meal but is nudged aside. After several attempts it plops down on its backside and stares up at me with the most beautiful black eyes, satin eyes, silken eyes.*

*"That one's going to die," Jacob says casually. "The others cost three hundred and fifty dollars."*

*"Why is she going to die?"*

*"How do you know it's a she?"*

*"I just know."*

*"Weird," Jacob concludes. "Well, she's going to die. Father said that if she wasn't getting fed he'd drown her in the pool. It's a mercy, he said. Better than starving to death. The others won't let her anywhere near the tits, so he'll probably dunk her tonight."*

*"I'll take her."*

*"What's she gonna suck for food?" Jacob asks and then bursts out laughing, driven to hysterics by his own crass humor.*

*My eyes haven't left those of the pup. I have already named her. I will call her Bette, and I will find a way to feed her. I will never let Mr. Larimer "dunk" her.*

*"She's still gonna die," Jacob taunts before closing the door at my back.*

*"I'll shoot that fucking thing," my father says later that evening. "If I even smell it in the house, I'll put a bullet in the bitch's skull."*

In his office, Scotty listened while the phone played his daughter's favorite song. Work lay scattered on his desk, but he had no heart for it. He mourned for Judge Griff and remained confounded by the book he'd found in the man's library.

He couldn't say he enjoyed the book, but he'd read late into the night. At first, he'd found the narrator's dedication to the shepherd pup cloying and sappy. It seemed like an easy emotional button the author could press to get a collective empathic sigh from his readers, but as he finished the chapter that detailed the lengths the boy had gone to in saving the dog's life, he found himself admiring the kid's tenacity.

When the phone gave up, Scotty listened to his daughter's message. It was nearly verbatim to the one she'd left the previous evening:

"Hi, Daddy. Can you visit tomorrow? I haven't seen you in forever, and I really need to see you. Mom won't come. She said she can't because of Clint. She thinks I'm so stupid. I know she just doesn't want to. Please can't you come? I'm so alone. I miss you."

The message brought an ache to Scotty, but the pain grew hot and liquefied. After a few moments, the sadness he genuinely wanted to feel was gone, and in its place was offense. Another manipulation. Another running of the fingers to find cracks that could be exploited and ripped open.

Walter had warned him about Miranda's behavior. The judge had seen it in his offices and the courtroom for years. He talked about the skilled deceit addicts practiced. He'd noted that lies and manipulations were drugs unto themselves. They started small, little hits of misdirection and falsehood, which eventually blossomed into an uncontrollable dependence on fabrication.

He hadn't believed a thing his daughter had told him in more than three years. For too long, he'd pretended to be convinced by Miranda's fresh devotions to honesty, but the performances were exhausting. Invariably, he'd forced a smile, patted her shoulder, and reached for his wallet.

Nothing had changed, except for her address.

Scotty simmered in his office for thirty minutes more and then gave up on the day.

*My father and Carl sit by the pool, drinking highballs and smoking cigars. Father is bundled in his white terry cloth robe, but Carl wears nothing but his swim trunks. They grip his strong thighs and waist, covering his masculinity like a layer of sky-blue paint. Water glistens from where it beads on his shoulders, from where it clings to the hairs on his chest, from the stream trickling down his belly to the pale blue lip of his trunks. The sight of him suffocates me.*

*He raises his head and turns his attention in my direction. He smiles and lifts his hand to offer a friendly wave. My father also sees me by the pool house, and his face tightens and darkens. Beside me, Bette whimpers before nudging the back of my leg with her snout.*

*She is smarter than I. She understands the danger, but I remain ignorant, or, if not ignorant, indifferent, as my eyes have found a paradise they refuse to vacate. Carl says something to Father, who shakes his head and scowls. Then Father is laughing and lifting his drink to his lips.*

*Carl glances my way again. I detect something different in his expression. I tell myself that he is looking at me in the same way I am looking at him.*

*Bette whimpers. She begs. She backs away and then returns to my side, clearly distraught. And finally, though hesitantly, I give in to my best friend's demands.*

The text from his assistant arrived with a startling trill at just after one in the morning. Scotty struggled into wakefulness and coughed violently as a dense odor crept into his nose and down his throat. Sniffing the air, he noted a musky scent fading as the tone from his phone grew clearer in his ears. Scotty blinked several times and then retrieved his reading glasses from the bedside table.

**Reyna: I thought you'd want to see this. It's probably a hoax or a scam to get money from his estate.**

A link followed the brief and unsettling message. Scotty tapped it with his finger and waited for the web page to load. When he saw the headline, he groaned and shook his head before throwing back the covers and racing from the room to make his way down the hall to his study. He read the words displayed in a tiny font on his phone as he threw open the door and went to his desk.

"No. Fuck no. Fuck no," he muttered as he powered up his computer.

> Conservative Judge spends weekend at gay resort
> with teenage boy three weeks before his death.

Outside the house, Scotty noted a grating sound, like wood scraping wood. He thought about the swing on his porch, the swing his daughter had once shared with him, and wondered if it had fallen loose.

The noise persisted, creating a distant, unsettling rhythm for his reading.

An eighteen-year-old man, named Ross Michaels, claimed to have spent three days at a gay bed and breakfast in Hargett's Bend, North Carolina, with Judge Walter Griff.

> "I saw his picture, you know, with his obit, and I couldn't believe it," Michaels said. "I started surfing around, and damn, what a prick. I saw the terrible people he used his money to support, and all of the right-wing shit he's said over the years, and no way was I gonna shut up about it. These people are a disease. You know, like cancer? And they're killing us from the inside."

The grating sound grew more determined. Louder. It sounded as if it were coming from the front door. Scotty winced at the noise, but refused to leave his desk chair.

The article was clearly a fabrication, meant to tarnish the reputation of a good man. Scotty would have stopped reading two sentences in to the ridiculous story if it hadn't been for the name of the city in which the alleged tryst had occurred: Hargett's Bend. It rang a bell, but he couldn't place the town in his memory.

Scotty ran half a dozen searches, but found no indication that the real media had picked up the story. It was only a matter of hours, he knew. Even if the accusations went unsubstantiated *(and they can't be true)*, the fucking hairdos with microphones would be jizzing buckets over a story like this.

E-mails and additional text messages began to trickle in from Walter's friends and peers. Within ten minutes they were arriving every few seconds. Behind all the pings and trills, the scraping sound at his door played like a jug band washboard, now all but booming in his ears.

"Damn," Scotty bellowed. He pushed himself away from the computer and stormed into the hall.

At the top of the stairs, he paused and gazed down at the

entryway. The white rectangle of the door, with four, small, absolutely black windows, suddenly frightened him. The scraping sound persisted, and though he felt determined to discover the source of the distracting noise, his legs refused to take him any further. He inhaled deep breaths and experienced a flash of heat along his cheek and throat. Raising his hand to touch his neck, he looked down and noticed he was naked. In defense of his trepidation, he told himself that modesty had nailed his feet to the oak floorboards.

Below, the scratching continued. And it *was* scratching, he decided, like a dog eager to enter a house to see its master.

Scotty took a step back. The heat at his throat intensified. Burned. Sweat ran in a line down his spine to tickle a path to his backside.

"Oh, horseshit," he mumbled defiantly.

He stomped down the stairs. In the entryway, he flipped on the porch light and grasped the doorknob. The frantic scrabbling on the other side of the plank grew furious, and Scotty twisted and yanked, pulling the door wide as the racket instantly ceased. On the sand beyond his porch, he caught sight of a dog's haunches and the flash of a scythe-shaped tail, all shadow and murk. It flashed for a moment and then vanished behind an enormous earthenware vase in which his ex-wife had constantly failed to grow roses.

He shouted threats after the retreating animal, cursing the dog for its intrusion, though he didn't attempt to pursue it. For all he knew, the damn thing could be rabid.

When he'd expelled the bulk of his rage into the night, challenging the volume of the ocean surf as it rhythmically shushed him, Scotty took another step onto the porch. He closed his eyes for a moment, and then spun angrily as if to challenge the house to aggravate him further.

What he saw there confused him. In fact he found it so perplexing his rage subsided. He'd expected the woodwork to be shredded, considering the intensity of the dog's attack, but he found no gouges or chips on the semigloss. Scotty leaned in close and ran his fingers over the smooth surface. Not so much as a scratch. *Son of a bitch,* he thought as he straightened himself.

He worked his way along the porch, checking the siding for further signs of attack, and found nothing. Returning his attention to the beach, he caught a brief scent. It was musky and dense, but gone the second he noted it, just like the odor he'd woken to.

Feeling off balance and exposed, Scotty walked inside. He closed the door, locked it, poured himself a glass of vodka from the bottle he kept in his freezer, and then returned upstairs, where a very long night waited for him.

*. . . it hurts, and I beg him to stop, but my pain only excites him, and he presses my face against the wall, and he drives deeper into me. He calls me "faggot" and "bitch" and his voice is the voice of my father. His breath hitches in his throat with an ugly chuckle. I had imagined seducing him, because my eyes had adored his strong chest and his masculine face. I wanted him to be mine. I thought I could take him or at least stain him in my father's eyes. We would love, and Father would be left behind. His best friend gone. His youngest child away. But there is no love here. There is only piercing. Stabbing.*

*Carl pinches my throat in the crook of his elbow. My head grows light, but it does nothing to assuage the pain. Outside the pool house, Bette frantically scratches at the door.*

*He tells me this is what I wanted. He grunts it in my ear with his final thrusts.*

*This was never what I wanted.*

Scotty threw down the book and rubbed his eyes. He'd been searching the paperback for any indication that Walter, or a fictionalized version of him, appeared in its pages. It had been a mistake and fruitless. Though he couldn't help picturing his deceased friend in the role of the abusive Carl, there was nothing in the description to connect the character to Judge Walter Griff.

He stood from the chair and walked to his front door. For the third time since early that morning, he peered through the windows. He eyed the shoreline, looking for signs of the dog, fearing he would see the thing loping over the sand, its eyes locked on him like prey, its muzzle crumpled in a ravenous snarl.

In the course of twelve hours, Ross Michaels's story about his weekend with Walter had ascended to the mainstream media. Scotty's name and e-mail address had reached reporters, bloggers, and random lunatics, all of whom demanded information about his friend, but he'd ignored the requests for quotes. Articles and accusations ran on every major news site. The owners of the bed and breakfast had come forward to confirm Michaels's claim. They offered to provide a credit card receipt for verification. Already, the timbre of the messages coming in was changing. Men and women who had hours before sternly defended Walter Griff from such malicious defamation were suggesting they didn't really know the man well, or noted how something had always seemed *off* about the judge.

Though well-skilled in self-delusion, Scotty himself was losing the fight to keep his mentor's reputation unspoiled.

He remembered where he'd seen the name Hargett's Bend before; he'd read it in the pages of Christopher Pelham's novel. Adding fuel to his emotional chaos, the bed and breakfast Walter had allegedly visited was called the Pelham Plantation.

The story grew too complex for his exhausted mind. He tried telling himself he didn't know what Walter was doing at the establishment, though the flimsy material of the lie crumbled as he attempted to hold it. Of course, he knew. He didn't want to imagine it, not in any concrete way, but he certainly knew. The evidence was there. But it was so appallingly reckless, unless Walter was hoping to be discovered.

He called Reyna Baldwin, his assistant, and told her he wouldn't be coming into the office. He could only imagine the battle plans being formed at the firm. Walter Griff's name shared space on the letterhead with Scotty's and five other mens'. Reyna informed him that Lucinda Folgers, the firm's public relations counsel, had requested a meeting with all senior partners for ten a.m. to discuss media management. Scotty declined to attend. He wasn't speaking to anyone about Walter.

His daughter's call came through as he listed the files he needed Reyna to messenger over. Miranda's name on the phone's screen infuriated him. His daughter's timing had always been terrible, always the most needy when it was the most inconvenient. He ignored the intrusion and continued to direct his assistant in how to manage his day.

"And do something else for me," Scotty said. "I want you to look into a book called *The Litter's Runt* by Christopher Pelham."

• • •

*I wait in the doctor's office. Fever burns me. My body is weak and aches. I've been sick since the night Carl led me into the pool house.*

*As I wait for my family's physician to see me, I read a story about indoor scavenging. It's what forensic scientists call the practice of animals feeding on the remains of their deceased masters. Though cats are not above such behavior, dogs are known to partake in this particular ritual more frequently. The article notes a man in Sweden who killed himself, blew out the back of his head with a .22 slug. His dog, a Labrador retriever, who by all accounts was a friendly, well-loved and cared for animal, was found by authorities entering the home, standing over his master's body. The dog sat calmly and obeyed the commands of the strangers.*

*He appeared completely docile, but at some point between the suicide and the arrival of the authorities, the animal had devoured the man's cheeks and gnawed through his neck to the point of decapitation.*

*The article goes on to describe the fear this practice instills in many pet owners, but I can think of nothing lovelier. Were I to die, I would offer my remains to Bette.*

*If I were to now write my last will and testament, it would be as follows:*

*"To the men who have touched me and tasted me, the men who lived honest lives and shared their desires with me, I leave my joy and gratitude. To the other men, those who hide their passions behind hard red walls, and exercise those passions with cruelty, I would leave only my contempt and loathing. My family gets nothing of me.*

*But for my heart's joy, Bette, my constant friend, I would leave all else. I humbly and gladly bequeath her my flesh and my spirit. . . ."*

After twenty-four hours, the national news had moved deeper into the story of Judge Walter Griff. Two more young men had come forward, and a third man, now in his forties, revealed a long-term affair he'd had with Griff during the nineties. Though all the men had been of legal age, one just barely, the media kept calling them "boys," kept digging into the old man's corpse with their talons, looking to pluck more tasty filth from his history. Lifelong friends of Judge Griff refused to speak about his place in their lives, preferring to let his soiled memory fade while extricating themselves from that memory. The firm had taken its first hit, in the form of Snowburn Industries' decision to end their business dealings, but Scotty knew it wouldn't be the last, as all of the fine southern Christians who'd entrusted their legal matters to Griff's legacy scrambled to distance themselves from a company built by *that kind* of man.

He hid in the beach house, working for his remaining clients. Scotty had barely slept. The previous night, he had again woken from troubled sleep with the musky scent in his nose. It was the odor of a dog's pelt, or so he'd come to believe.

He hadn't read anymore of Pelham's book. It remained on the floor of his study, kicked to and fro as Scotty attempted to manage both personal and business correspondences. Reyna remained his lifeline to the office. She told him the other partners were furious with his absence. Scotty had no doubt they were, but none of them, not one, knew what he was going through.

The greatest man he'd ever known wasn't really the man he'd known. So many years of advice and wisdom. So much time spent together, and not once had Scotty understood the machinations of his mentor's deceit. The fishing trips and the resort vacations and the late night hours spent over piles of paperwork and grease-stained pizza boxes had been a fiction. Scotty had fully invested himself in the man's vision, in his old-school sagacity. And the stupid son of a bitch had dropped dead, leaving Scotty to deal with the creeping toxic fallout of the old man's secrets.

Scotty let his daughter's call go to voicemail as he poured himself a vodka. The last thing he needed was to endure her demands, or worse, her self-pitying bullshit. He wasn't falling for it again. He'd defended her and bailed her out and done his best for too long. Walter had always told him that if you didn't let people help themselves, let them *save* themselves, they'd never be anything but a burden.

*They'd never be anything but runts,* Scotty thought.

From the porch, he watched a young family playing in the sand. The mother tossed her son a red ball. The father smiled as he spoke into his cell phone. Determined to get his father's attention, the boy kicked the ball in his father's direction, causing a faux look of surprise and determination to light on the man's face as he scrambled to join the game.

The scene irritated Scotty. He downed the rest of his drink in one shot and walked inside. He poured another drink and set his cell phone on the counter. Six messages from Miranda waited. He erased the first five and leaned against the counter before starting playback on the most recent.

His daughter's words emerged from the small speaker. The panic and tears in her voice unnerved him, and Scotty stood a little straighter.

*"You didn't come. Why didn't you come, Daddy? I needed to talk to you. I'm in trouble. So much trouble. I need money, but I wanted to tell you why I needed it, so you'd understand, but you never came, and you won't answer your fucking phone."* Her voice broke, and she sobbed. *"She's*

*going to kill me, Daddy. If I don't pay her, she's going to kill me. You have to help. You have to. If you don't want to see me, just send the money to my account. Please."* The message went silent except for an occasional sob. Then Miranda's voice returned, calmer and deeper. *"I'm glad he's dead."* The message ended there.

Scotty roared at the device and slammed his hand against the counter, sending shocks of pain to his elbow. He filled his glass a third time and stood trembling in his kitchen. Every muscle in his body clenched and sparked ache. A specific, sharper pain rose between his eyes, and he bellowed another useless shout into the room.

She blamed him. She'd always blamed him. The therapist he'd spent a fortune on had convinced Miranda that her acting out was the result of trying to get his attention. *You were never home,* she complained. *You never cared.* All the psychobabble justifications she parroted back to him had made Scotty feel like shit, but they were just excuses.

"I was building a life for my fucking family," he yelled. "And you wasted it. You smoked it and shot it and drank it away. I did not do this to you. You had everything. Every-goddamn-*thing*! And you nearly murdered an old woman for sixteen bucks and a fake diamond brooch."

His tirade ended, and Scotty searched the kitchen in a daze. He'd never felt such absolute hatred for another human being, and the power of the emotion unbalanced him. He gazed around the room, at the stainless steel sink, the glass kitchen cabinets, the aqua-colored dish towels, hanging from white plastic hooks he'd stuck to his refrigerator.

As the throbbing of his pulse lessened in his ears, the sound of scrabbling claws on the bare wooden floors in the upstairs hallway emerged. The tremble in his hands intensified. Though it sounded like a dog racing from one end of the corridor to the other, Scotty told himself it was nothing. There was no way a dog or any other animal larger than a spider had gotten into his house. He was overwrought. Exhausted. Drunk.

It was time to get out. He'd spent too much time alone, wallowing in crisis. He could call Desmond, or the Shermans, or the Cunninghams. He could call Rachel Smith from the firm and invite her to meet him at the Westin. She'd thrown herself at him during Walter's funeral reception. She'd help him blow off some steam. She knew how the game worked. Maybe they'd have dinner first. A good dinner would help.

Scotty gazed upward at the white ceiling while putting his drink on the counter. On the second floor of his house, the clicking of hard nails on polished wood returned.

He began for the stairs when his phone rang. Snatching it up, he prepared himself for another tirade, only this time his daughter was going to hear it. As he jabbed the icon to accept the call, he realized the ring wasn't the one he'd assigned to Miranda.

"Hey, Scotty," Reyna said. "Shit is spraying the walls over here. Langley and McDonald are walking. They're demanding we reimburse their retainers."

"We don't—"

"I know," Reyna said. "No refunds. They've been informed. Naturally, they threatened to sue."

"Yeah," Scotty said, listening to the clicking sound overhead. "Naturally."

"Are you ever coming back into the office?"

"Tomorrow," Scotty replied. "I'll be in tomorrow."

"So you're doing better?"

"Doing fine," Scotty said. "Walter was a piece of shit. It's time to flush and get off the throne. See if you can't get me a meeting with the other partners in the morning, and make sure our PR counsel is there. I want the firm to issue a statement, distancing ourselves from Griff."

The clack of nails from above faded. The anticipation of the sound remained, though, creating a moment of unbearable tension during which Scotty held his breath, waiting for the next click of claw on wood.

"The partners will be happy to hear it. The only reason they've delayed is to give you a chance to sign off on it."

"Consider it signed."

"As for that book," Reyna said.

"What about it?"

"Well, I assume you already know that the author of the book, Christopher Pelham, grew up in the house Walter took his *friend* to before he died."

"I put that together," Scotty said. "So when did Pelham turn it into a bed and breakfast?"

"He didn't," Reyna said. "He's been dead for about twenty years."

He wished the news carried more surprise for him. A small part of his mind, a part that resided in the shadow of fear, had already suspected this. His imminently rational mind had begun to consider irrational things.

"So what happened to him?"

"His father happened to him," Reyna said. "Chris Pelham wrote this book, which is pretty much a thinly veiled memoir, in which he describes his childhood and teenage years, including his sexual activity while still a minor. He detailed multiple same-sex affairs, including one with a man who is clearly Curt Ramsey, his father's business partner."

"The stories about his sex life were true?"

"Probably," Reyna said. "I found a student thesis online that compared the content of his diaries to the content of the novel, and apparently the names were changed, but just barely. Anyone who lived in Hargett's Bend would have known whose dick that kid had sucked. The whole city went simple. Fights. Vandalism. A shitload of divorces. If Pelham had wanted to destroy the town, he couldn't have done a better job if he'd sprayed it down in Exxon premium and sparked a Zippo."

"Son of a bitch."

"Pretty much. Months before the book actually hit shelves, Pelham gave the thing to his father as a Christmas present. Stupid-ass move. He'd probably intended to drop that bomb in daddy's lap and then skip town the following morning. But that didn't happen. His father read the book that night. Needless to say, the elder Pelham didn't enjoy his son's contribution to the literary canon."

"So he killed him?"

"Sure. That's as good a way to put it as any."

"Excuse me?"

"Scotty, Old Man Pelham tied his son up and threw him in the pool house. He also put the kid's dog in there. No food. No water. Hands and feet tied so tightly they were black when the coroner found the kid."

"He just left his son and the dog in there to starve?"

"Well," Reyna said, "the *son* starved."

The dog's growl crept down to him from the second floor.

Scotty's neck went cold and his skin puckered. "Hold on," he instructed. He eased toward the stairs, and then changed his trajectory, rapidly moving to the kitchen and through the utility room to the garage. "Okay."

"They figure the kid lasted about four days," Reyna went on. "On the fifth day, puppy ate supper."

"Are you serious?" Scotty said.

"It's documented. I mean, Pelham's actual cause of death was listed as dehydration, but the part about being doggy treats is true. You can't blame the dog. I'm surprised it waited that long. That night, Old Man Pelham went to the pool house, found the dog gnawing on his kid's face, and shot it."

"Bette," Scotty said.

"What?"

"The dog. Her name was Bette." At least, that was her name in the book.

"Okay," Reyna said as if it were wholly useless information. "Anyway, Pelham shot the dog and then cut the ropes off his kid. He called the cops and tried to convince them that the dog had attacked his son, and he'd put the dog down."

"Did they believe him?"

"Are you serious? It's a ridiculous story, but Pelham thought he had enough clout in town to get away with it. Well, the book came out and whatever support he might have had vanished. He was sentenced to life. Died about ten years ago. A couple of gays bought the old Pelham house and turned it into a bed and breakfast. It's some kind of homo Mecca at this point, which I think Christopher would have loved, if only because the rest of the city is thoroughly pissed about it."

Scotty walked to the end of his Mercedes sedan and rested

his butt on the trunk. He listened carefully for paws on the concrete before telling Reyna he would be staying in a hotel for a few days.

The growl leapt through the closed garage door, startling him. Scotty fumbled the phone and it bounced off his chest. He shot out his hand and felt a twinge of surprise when he caught the device. He'd never been particularly athletic. His moment of pride ended with another growl, sending him racing back for the utility room door.

*My father is always there. He hides behind the faces of his friends, behind the eyes of his colleagues, behind the mouths of strangers who have never met him. He is the fat man I met on the beach who took me into a rickety shack so close to the road it shook when trucks passed; he is the beautiful young executive who led me into the woods behind our house and forced me to my knees; he is Carl Ramsey, the man my father trusted more than any other.*

*If I scrape away the layers of their skin, I will find my father hiding in these men. Or maybe I just want to find him there. To please him. To punish him.*

*He can't be pleased.*

Scotty packed a bag. His fear had formed from nothing rational: bits of coincidence, magnified anxiety, isolation, phantom noises, and perhaps too much vodka. Regardless of the fear's unsustainable reasons, it had settled on him heavily after he'd fled the garage and ended the call with his assistant, so he shoved his overnight kit into the suitcase along with three suits and the other clothing he might need to get him through the week. He zippered the luggage and hoisted it from the bed.

When fresh scratching sounded at his front door, Scotty tensed, but he refused to entertain the illusion. He set the suitcase down in the hall outside his study and entered to gather his tablet and its charger.

Christopher Pelham's outrageous book still lay on the floor. The scrabbling at the front door intensified. Scotty retrieved the book from the planks. He held it in his thick hand and stared at the cover, on which a young man and his dog appeared as shadows against a shimmering watery backdrop. The musky odor he now associated with a dog's fur climbed into his nose, but instead of fading in an instant it remained. Scotty wrinkled his nose, attempting to dislodge the scent. His face and neck began to sting.

The book was the problem. Ever since he had taken the thing from Walter's study, his life had unraveled in heavy loops.

Leaving the study with the book clutched tightly in his fist, he went to the stairs and paused as the claws on the door below reached a frantic pace. He imagined Christopher Pelham's dog, the black shepherd named Bette, attacking the wood, trying to get into his house with the same ferocity she had once used to attempt escape from the Pelham's pool house.

Then his mind created more disturbing pictures: the dog's muzzle buried deeply in the crimson pulp of her master's neck, her tongue lapping blood and loosening scraps of tissue, making them easier for her teeth to take hold.

His phone announced yet another call from his daughter. Like a slap to an already stinging cheek, the sound pulled him from reverie.

Scotty stepped heavily on the top stair and then the next. The call ended as he reached the entryway. The nails on wood, only ten feet away, had taken on the volume of a threshing machine. The song from his phone started again.

At the fireplace, Scotty set the book on the mantel and answered the call.

"Miranda, I do not have time for this right now."

"Mr. Collins," a low male voice responded.

The attack on his front door ceased. In its place came the clicking of a dog's overgrown nails on the second-floor hallway. He whipped his head upward and followed the progression along the ceiling. The sudden relocation of sound wasn't possible, but the tick-tick of a dog's paws was as clear in his ears as the pounding of his pulse.

"Mr. Collins? This is James Zyler from Eastbrook Correctional."

"I don't . . .," Scotty began. "Excuse me?"

The man repeated the information as Scotty continued to track the clicking on the floorboards above.

"It's about your daughter," Zyler said. "There's been an incident."

"Define 'incident,'" Scotty said.

"Miranda was assaulted this afternoon. We don't have all the details just now."

"What happened to my daughter?" Scotty asked, head still cocked toward the ceiling.

"She's in critical condition," Zyler said. "She's experienced multiple stab wounds. I'm very sorry to have to give you this news. I can tell you more when you arrive."

Disbelief was Scotty's first reaction to the news. Miranda had mentioned a debt she owed another prisoner, but Scotty had taken care of that, the way he'd taken care of everything. He'd wired money into her inmate account. She should have had no problem clearing the debt.

Except he *hadn't* wired the money.

He'd been caught up in damage control after the news about Walter broke across the internet. He'd intended to wire his daughter the money, but he'd never done it.

"I'll be there as soon as I can," Scotty said.

Zyler kept talking, but Scotty was no longer listening. He lowered his head and turned to the mantel. He exchanged the phone for the paperback novel.

The thing had to burn.

He pressed the button on the wall beside the fireplace and flames leapt through the vents in the gas pipe, rising high and furious around the fake, ceramic logs. Above him, the clacking of nails grew fierce, sounding as if the animal were attempting to change its direction rapidly and slipping on the polished floor in the process. He opened the cover of the book and read the inscription.

At first he didn't notice the change in the wording. Reading over it quickly, he saw Walter's name, because he'd expected to find it written there. But the inscription had transformed, and Scotty's organs twisted and coiled into knots when the altered phrase became clear.

*To Scotty,*
*Who was like a second father to me. Chris.*

At his back, Bette ran down the stairs, carrying her scent into the room.

Scotty turned from the fireplace, weighted with dread. The

sight of the dog, or what had once been a dog, struck him with disparate emotions. The first, most prominent feeling was one of terror. The black shepherd crouched in his foyer. Though not transparent, the body appeared not quite solid, and the edges of the animal feathered away, rising, narrowing, and fading like ink in water. Its bared white fangs looked too large for the smallish head. Its black eyes, *silken eyes,* locked on him hungrily. But despite the lethal appearance of the beast, Scotty found the creature darkly beautiful. This conflicting emotion confounded him, but he couldn't deny it. The urge to call it to him, so that he might stroke the uncommon fur, played like a melody at the back of his mind.

Bette barked savagely, crouching lower in the entryway.

His desire to summon the dog vanished, and Scotty spun. But where to go? He couldn't hope to outrun the beast in the house. The fucking thing was built for speed and he wasn't. He wouldn't make it to the dining room before the dog caught him. Canceling his attempt to flee he danced awkwardly backward, suddenly flummoxed as to how to protect himself against the animal. Then the jaw clamped on his wrist and the remaining fragments of rational thought whirled away.

He screamed and attempted to pull his arm back, but Bette yanked, sending him off balance. He threw out his left hand to steady himself on the mantel. Christopher Pelham's novel dropped to the floor.

Amid his panic, Scotty realized the sensation on his arm was as wrong as everything else about this moment. The first sensation was one of pressure, as if his wrist and lower arm had been caught in a vice. Moments later, a second sensation joined the first. Now, he felt the teeth in him, but it wasn't a piercing sensation. The fangs seemed to lengthen and deepen within him as if forming under his skin. Regardless, the pain was agonizing.

Bette shook her head violently. Pain radiated from his wrist to his shoulder, where a blossom of pure agony erupted as the dog dislocated his arm from the socket. The pop filled Scotty's head for a moment. Nausea followed. As he struggled with the animal, his stomach lurched, and he vomited on the floor, spattering the animal in the process. Bette released the arm, backed away, her nails clicking noisily on the hardwood floor. The heaving persisted. His body cramped, and his head began to swim. Scotty dropped to his knees and clutched his wounded arm.

He lifted his head to check on the dog, but she seemed to be done with him for the moment. She sat calmly with wisps of ethereal blackness pulling away from her beautiful face as she eyed him.

Tears blurred Scotty's vision. Loud moans, rhythmic and deep, escaped his throat as he rocked back and forth on his knees, in a primal response to the pain. The room teetered and then spun. Scotty lowered himself to the floor and lay on his side to combat the sickness and vertigo.

"You fuck," he cried.

He wasn't speaking only to the dog. He also spoke to Christopher Pelham. He knew that Pelham existed in this animal form, perhaps sharing it, perhaps simply wearing it as a disguise.

Bette's head cocked to the side. Her mouth opened and a long black tongue lolled out. She took a step forward and then another. Her muzzle hovered above his face. Scotty trembled beneath the mouth. Prayers died in his throat.

The dog's head dipped low, and Scotty gritted his teeth in preparation for what he could only assume was a killing bite. The tongue pressed into Scotty's cheek, but he did not feel a tongue. More than anything the sensation on his cheek was like a hard knuckle drawing a line up his face.

A second lick was softer. It almost felt soothing, more like the actual tongue of a dog.

Scotty tried desperately to roll away, but only got as far as his back. Once he placed weight on the dislocated shoulder, a shock of pain caused him to gray out.

He came to seconds later beneath Bette's tongue. He screamed again and then fell into hopeless sobbing.

What was the animal waiting for? If she wanted him dead, why didn't she just do it? It wasn't as if she had to play loyal, the way she had with her master, and wait for Scotty to dehydrate or starve.

Except this wasn't just the dog, Scotty thought. Pelham was part of this spectral monstrosity. And he *had* dehydrated. He *had* starved.

The hunger started as a tickle in Scotty's belly, and then it exploded like a punch. Bette continued to taste his neck and cheeks, and with each lap of her tongue, the hunger grew more painful. Scotty's eyes clouded with tears and weakness. The anguish in his arm was now matched by the pain in his stomach. He cried out again and began to pray that his heart would stop or a vessel would burst in his brain or the bites on his wrist would bleed out.

The pain radiated through every nerve in his body, and Bette licked his face like the good dog she was.

• • •

*I've never known hunger. Maybe I never will, but I've experienced abandonment. I feel certain both produce a similar sensation: an aching emptiness. Even though I lived under the same roof as my father, I felt his absence. At least, his absence from me.*

*A runt never knows the sincere embrace of a parent, experiencing only its empty and perfunctory counterpart. A runt can never hope to please its parents, because they have already labeled this particular offspring fruitless tissue, a lesser thing, a disposable error in genealogy.*

*So I escaped to the city, and I found it full of runts like me. They understood the hunger, understood the deprivations. We gathered together for entertainment and huddled together for warmth. We nourished one another, and there was joy. There was love.*

*As the litter's runt, I was denied much, but I grew stronger fighting for these petty, missing things. And now I don't need them any longer. I've found what I need in the city. I've found my protection. I've found my pack.*

# The July Girls

## *Alison Littlewood*

Sophia didn't knock. It was my room—I'd even put a sign on the door—but she seemed to think she owned everything. People who looked like Sophia always did. I was lying on my bed, reading a school textbook by lamplight. Outside its glow the room was dim, but her hair still shone gold. All that glitters . . .

She twisted her lip into a sneer, and I wondered what she'd say if I told her it made her look ugly. But then she tossed her head, sending ripples of light along that hair, and I was silenced. Oh, how I loved that hair—though I never would have told her. Mine was dull, average length, and an average colour: mouse. Her name for me.

"Aw, is ickle mousy working? Hasn't ickle mousy any *fwiends*?"

I had no answer, but she didn't wait for one. She crossed to my window and tugged the curtain aside, peering out into the dark. I knew what she was up to. Mine was the room which overlooked the extension. From the window she could run across its flat roof, jump down onto the banking at the back of the house and slip out of the back gate. Someone would be waiting for her. They always were: someone tall with broad shoulders, most likely wearing a leather jacket and holding the keys to a car. She never was alone. She probably wouldn't know how to be.

She turned. I could have spoiled everything for her then,

but I didn't call out. Still, even when she ought to have been nice to me, she couldn't help herself.

"Aw, maybe one day you'll find an ickle boy mouse to play with. Won't that be nice?"

She swung her tanned, shapely leg over the sill, ducked under the window frame, and was gone. I heard the scrape of her feet on the flat roof, and then nothing.

I'd like to think I kept silent for her out of some sisterly conspiracy, but I can't pretend. What went through my mind was: *I hope you get pregnant. If you want to ruin your life, I don't give a shit.* And then—I could remember the thought as clearly as if I'd spoken it—*At least this means you're gone.*

The house changed after Sophia died. Mum and my step-dad went quiet. The rooms went quiet too, only the dust seeming to move, turning in on itself while time did the same. Familiar objects, tainted by the atmosphere, went stale somehow, as if they belonged to a world that moved more slowly than it should. But the biggest change of all was that I could breathe again.

The same wasn't true of my mum or Sophia's dad, and I hid it from them, though I felt my inner self expanding, uncurling from whatever tight ball I'd been hiding in. Then they told me about the holiday, and I wondered what they thought that could fix; but I smiled at the thought of Cornwall's busy little harbours and the salty taste of chips and the sunlight on skin that would not grow cold like hers, that would not turn grey as hers must have, laid out on a mortuary slab. Whatever skin she'd still possessed, anyway.

It was Sophia's dad who told me we were going. He sidled into my room, as if he was ashamed of being alive when his daughter was dead. He didn't even look into my face, turning instead towards a shelf, running one finger along its edge. "I have some news," he said. "It'll be great." And his finger stopped moving and he stared and didn't say anything else. He reached out and picked something up from the back of the shelf; it was unwieldy, and he teased it out from behind my old teddy bear.

It was a picture frame. Two girls stared out from a photograph: one of them with sleek blonde hair, beautiful, slender; and me. For a moment I might have been there again. It was taken on Sports Day at school. She'd been picked for the hundred-metre sprint, while I'd have been lucky to do an egg and spoon race. Our smiles looked the same, but we weren't smiling at each other. She'd been making eyes at her current crush, sitting a short distance away, and I was smiling because someone had told me to.

When her dad turned towards me, tears were brimming at his eyes. "What a lovely picture. I had no idea. . . ."

He smiled at me, and this time he saw me—really looked at me, I think, for the first time in weeks. And he told me about Cornwall. "We'll relive some old memories," he said, "and—and we'll *enjoy* them. Just the three of us." He grasped my hand then, squeezing my limp fingers, and he left me to stare at the photograph he'd replaced on my shelf. I didn't have the first idea how it had come to be there.

He obviously thought I'd chosen it, but I never would have and neither would she. I moved to put it under the bed—or in the bin—and I saw again the way he'd lifted his gaze to me, warming to me, and instead I put it back on the shelf. I didn't face it toward the room, though, where I'd have to look at it. I turned it towards the door, where anyone would notice it as they came in.

• • •

The long queue of traffic on the A30 gave way to single track lanes, walled in by tall hedges thick with flowers and birdsong. We wound our way along them, hardly seeing anyone; we only had to back up once, to allow a tractor to pass. Most tourists stayed by the coast, but my family had always preferred this rural backwater, a drive away from the beaches and cafés and crowds. I preferred it too, though Sophia hadn't. I could almost see her scowling out of the back window in disgust, all the way to the little rose-bound cottage.

Mum came in while I was unpacking, shoving T-shirts into empty drawers, finding space in the wardrobe between an ironing board and spare blankets. She didn't say anything, only sat on the bed and looked at me as if we had just met and she wanted to size me up, and she smiled.

I pulled a hoodie from the top of my suitcase and her smile faded at the sight of what lay beneath. "What's that?"

She reached into the case and removed something rectangular and heavy, something I hadn't packed, something that didn't belong. I froze as she turned it in her hands. The frame was broad-edged and silver-coloured. I had seen it before; I didn't want to look at it again, but the smiles flashed at me as she tilted it, two girls beaming out.

Cold fingers brushed the back of my neck.

"That's so sweet," Mum said, putting it back. "Come down when you're ready."

I think I nodded, but couldn't be certain. My face barely felt like my own any longer. I flipped the photograph over, hiding the picture. How had it got there? Even if I'd wanted some reminder of Sophia—which I hadn't—I would never have packed something so bulky. It must have been *him*, I decided. For some crazy reason of his own, my step-dad had slipped the picture into my suitcase—but why? Had he thought he was doing something nice?

I went to the door, pushing it closed. Then I grabbed the photograph and hid it in the back of the wardrobe, shoving it in among the blankets. There. I'd have to think about Sophia anyway if we were going to *relive some old memories*, but that must be enough; I didn't have to look at her too.

I found the others ready to go for a walk and we stepped out into evening sunshine and the constant humming of bees. We strolled, not talking about Sophia, but she was there: I saw where she'd once pressed up against the hedge as a busload of grey-haired trippers squeezed past. I saw where she'd leaned over a fence, her athletic legs swinging. And I saw her walking ahead of me, putting her arms around her dad and my mum, leaving me to follow.

And yet this, if anywhere, was where we'd been the closest. With nothing else to do and no one else to see, we'd actually spent some time together, splashing into crystal clear waves, running our fingers through white sand. We'd been the image of girls on holiday then: July girls, my mum called us. And we'd walked along these lanes, complaining of how boring they were, the endless hedges making everywhere look the same.

I thought of the photograph that had followed me from home. Those two smiles, shining out—but we had been like that, hadn't we, when we were here?

And maybe Sophia *was* here. A part of me couldn't believe, even then, that her dad had sneaked the picture into my suitcase. I couldn't shake the thought that she'd brought it here herself; that maybe she was trying to tell me something. She might have liked to smile at me now, to let me know that, despite our arguments and bitchy comments, it was all right.

Then we turned a corner in the lane and I saw the opening in the hedge which led to a path I remembered, and I stopped dead.

"Are you all right, love?" Mum's tone was all concern.

I told her I was just tired and she nodded and walked on, linking arms with my step-dad, but her stride was different, clumsy, and she suggested we turn back. I didn't look at the path when we passed it again but I could see it still: the nettles and rosebay willow herb hemming it in, the KEEP OUT sign, the clearing beyond.

By the time we reached the cottage the light was fading, chill shadows clawing their way along the narrow lanes. The glowing lamps and cosy sofas banished it all, as did our laughter and the familiar burble of the television, and I said good night and made my way up the stairs.

I saw the picture as soon as I opened the door. It was now on my bedside table, those two smiles shining out, like sunshine; like summer. And I whirled because in the corner something coalesced, a shadow a little like a figure.

I blinked. Nothing was there, never had been—only the picture, which had no reason to be there either. Had my step-dad come up here, searched my room, moved it from its hiding place, and put it by my bed? I tried to picture him rummaging through the depths of the wardrobe and couldn't.

But he must have; it was the only explanation. I went to the picture and gripped it, the frame digging into my hands as I thought of *another* explanation, one that wasn't even possible, and I yanked open a drawer. It was almost empty apart from a Bible, left for the edification of any visitor who cared to read it, and I shoved the picture in underneath, wondering—or hoping, perhaps—it might keep her from coming back again.

I sat on the bed and stared into space for a long time. I didn't see the room. I only saw Sophia: her perfect skin, perfect teeth, perfect *life*. What the hell had she ever known about me? She hadn't known what it was like to walk into school and see the stares, to know every time she looked into the mirror of other people's faces that she wasn't good enough.

I shook off the self-pity. I didn't need it. This was my place now, my time. She never had wanted to share anything with me. Now I supposed I had everything after all. I was sleeping in the second biggest room. Our parents were mine. I could have anything I wanted that had once been hers, and there wasn't a damned thing she could do about it.

A photograph was only that. It didn't mean she was still here. I might even have brought it to Cornwall myself, acting on some unconscious impulse. There was nothing unnatural about it—and she wasn't going to scare me.

Later, I awoke in darkness more complete than I had ever experienced at home. I couldn't see a thing and yet all my reassurances drained from me, because I could feel someone standing in the room. I opened my mouth to whisper, *"Mum?"* and closed it again. It wasn't her. I knew that. I could feel it in the silence, heavy and watchful and full of intent.

I reached out to switch on the lamp and hesitated as an image of my step-sister rose before me. She wasn't smiling. It was Sophia as she truly was: dead. Mutilated, as she had been when her stupid boyfriend turned his motorbike over, skidding along the tarmac, dragging his passenger with it. She hadn't been wearing a helmet. That wasn't her style; I suppose she liked to have that golden hair flying behind her in the breeze.

From the fragments I'd overheard afterwards, she'd been scraped raw.

No one had knocked on the door. No one called out or whispered my name. They simply stood on the other side of that darkness—and I pictured her face flayed and bloody, but still with that lovely hair, still with that look in her eyes.

My hand snapped out and I switched on the lamp. The room was empty.

The picture, though, was back. I must almost have touched it when I reached for the lamp. I peered at it, fearful that it would have changed somehow, showing her as she was after the accident; but Sophia was still there, in all her beauty. I stared into her face, trying to make out what lay beneath.

When I could bring myself to move, I crept into the hall and peeked in at Mum's bedroom door. There lay two covered mounds, so deeply entrenched in sleep I couldn't believe they'd ever woken. It wasn't my step-dad who'd moved the picture. I don't think I'd ever truly believed it was.

I awoke the next morning before anybody else. I wasn't in my room; I hadn't wanted to go back there, and so instead I'd slept on the sofa. Light flooded in through the open curtains and I stretched my stiff limbs before going towards the stairs. Why had I allowed myself to be spooked? I wasn't afraid of a picture. What harm could it do?

And Sophia was *gone.*

When I opened my bedroom door I thought the picture

had moved again after all, but of course it hadn't; the image was simply blanked out by reflected light. I had to go closer to confirm that the image hadn't changed. There she was, that look in her eyes that said the whole world was hers—and yet it wasn't, not now. It was mine.

Still, I couldn't dispel the thought that I'd spent the night camping on the sofa, just as if she could take it all away from me any time she wanted.

I cast my mind back to our last holiday in this place. It had been Mum who'd told us to go for a walk, tired perhaps of the sour looks and tension that so often hung between us. I suppose she'd thought we might come back best friends. Adults could be so very unrealistic.

Sophia and I had met Lucy before we'd even gone out of the gate. About our age, her blonde hair was so sun-bleached it was almost white, and her eyebrows stood out against her tanned skin. She told us she lived here year-round, in a broken-down farmhouse her dad was restoring. "It's a complete tip," she'd said, "and there's nothing to do. Except . . ."

It was that "except" that led us along the lane and towards the path, swatting away midges as we went. Sophia and Lucy went in front, talking about their lives, a thinly disguised game of one-upmanship. We didn't pause at the path, just pushed our way along it through waist-high weeds until we reached a copse, low branches barring the way, as did a chain with a KEEP OUT sign hanging from it, the letters roughly painted.

It was Sophia who said, "Where the hell are we going? This where you hide your wacky baccy or something?"

Lucy grinned, stepping over the sagging chain. She ducked under the branches, pushing the undergrowth aside, and gestured towards a clearing. A large mound of earth rose at its centre, covered with tussocks of grass. There was nothing else, no sign saying what it was supposed to be, but it didn't look natural.

"It's a fogou," Lucy said.

"Oo-ooh." Sophia was all sarcasm.

"It's a hidden chamber," Lucy went on as if Sophia hadn't spoken. "No one comes here; no one's bothered. There's a better one at Carn Euny, and a few others. This one's all ours. If you dare, that is."

"Dare?" Sophia sounded interested at last. I felt something twist in my stomach.

"No one knows what it was for. I reckon it's a burial chamber." Lucy didn't quite respond to the question, and yet I thought she'd answered the one in my mind anyway. And I saw that the mound wasn't quite complete, after all. A small opening, maybe a foot high, was lined with crooked stones, like teeth. I imagined lowering myself to the ground and crawling into that hole. I shuddered. That couldn't be what she meant. It was probably dangerous. It looked as she had said, like nobody cared, like nobody had been here in years.

"It's Iron Age," Lucy went on, as if she'd turned tour guide, as if it mattered. "Some call them holts, or fuggy holes, or vows. It's not far to the chamber. But first there's the creep."

Sophia's gaze shot to me, a new kind of amusement in her eyes.

"Some say the little folk still haunt it. Pixies. Piskies."

"Pigsies," Sophia said, her gaze still on me, and she giggled.

I looked away, casting my eyes around the lowering branches that hemmed us in, the pure whiteness of the clouds scattered across the sky. The air was so clean here. It had been one of the first things I noticed about Cornwall. It felt impossibly distant from cities or factories, and this place felt even more so, as if it existed outside time itself.

"Does she talk?" Lucy nodded towards me and Sophia let out a trill of laughter.

"You don't want her to. Bo-ring. So, what's the dare?"

Lucy didn't say anything, didn't have to. She turned and pointed to the hole.

Sophia fanned out her hair, showing off its clean fineness, as if to say, *Really?*

"It's a squeeze," Lucy said. "Some reckon it was a proper passage once, but it's partly filled up with dirt over the years. There's no mortar holding the stones together. There's one bit—the roof comes down. You have to wriggle."

I still didn't say anything, but I think my eyes opened wider.

"Come on, then." Sophia's voice was loud. I looked up sharply and realised she was watching me. Of course she was; that was what we did, wasn't it? We watched each other. And I'd been off guard. She had seen my fear. Now she would push at it, see how deep it went.

"The moss inside glows." Lucy seemed oblivious to our hostility. "It's phosphorescent. It's not that rare, it's just you don't normally get to see it like that. Like magic."

Sophia waved a hand, a "who cares" gesture. But I did care. Glowing moss? That was something I would like to see, but there was no way in hell I was getting down on the ground, putting my face in the dirt, and wriggling inside.

Sophia didn't pause. She knelt in front of the hole, then turned and looked at me. And yet it wasn't her usual look. There didn't seem to be anything hidden in it, and she smiled—a real smile—and said, "Come on, sis. Why not? An adventure."

I didn't answer, partly from surprise, but mainly because I was afraid. I knew that Lucy must have been in the chamber lots of times. But I wasn't her, and I wasn't Sophia. I couldn't do it. I couldn't give up the clean air and the sun for whatever adventure lay inside that hole, not for anything—not even for her, to mend whatever it was between us.

Sophia shrugged before she slid, neat as an eel, into the hole, her legs wriggling as she disappeared. Lucy didn't wait for me either. Looking annoyed that she hadn't led the way, she hurried after and I watched as she too slithered inside and vanished into the dark.

I sat on a fallen branch and I waited. Above me the clouds went by, time passing, in another world. Here, there was silence. I couldn't even hear birds singing or insects humming or distant cars in the lane. There was nothing, and I was alone, and I wished suddenly I'd gone with Sophia, reached out maybe, and taken her hand.

My seat was becoming uncomfortable, another sign of time passing. And the thought struck me: *What if they don't come out?* There was only me who knew where they were. I'd have to go after them. I thought of crawling into the hole, feeling for them blindly in the dark, and finding Sophia's face under my hands, unconscious perhaps, overcome by the stale air. I'd have to get her out. I imagined wriggling backwards, trying to pull her with me, and not being able to move her. I pictured Lucy in the chamber behind Sophia, wedged in, helpless; Sophia—the body—between us; and me, stuck in the place where the roof came down, unable to go forward or back.

The sourness of bile rose to the back of my throat. I stood and walked over to the hole in the ground, listening, feeling a breath of cold air on my cheek. There was no light in there—couldn't they have used their mobile phones?—and there were no voices. There was nothing at all, and then, distinctly, I heard the scratch and flare of a match.

Was that a greenish glow, coming from somewhere within? I blinked and speckled light danced in the tunnel, playing tricks on my vision. I thought of Cornish pixies, elusive and mischievous, and I heard laughter, distorted as if coming from a great distance away. It echoed from stone to unmortared stone, until I couldn't be sure how many voices there were. It was like something from a fairy tale and I thought of a little palace inside the rock, lit by that glowing moss. But it wasn't a fairy tale. Even if it had been, there was never a step-sister in any of those stories who actually got on with the heroine—with the *real* daughter.

Something moved in there. I started back and they came spilling out, and it was over. They were laughing, out of control, frightened and relieved and together—bonded, the two of them, like sisters.

"God, that bit . . . !" Sophia squealed then laughed again, clutching her belly. She leapt to her feet and reached out her hand, and without a second's thought Lucy took it and Sophia pulled her to her feet. They didn't look at me. Sophia didn't talk to me all the way home.

I came to myself sitting on the bed, clutching the photograph in my hands, wondering how things would have been if it was me who'd gone with her, if I'd taken her hand. Another image came: Sophia, sneaking out of my window. If I'd snitched on her then, everything would be different. She wouldn't have been in the accident.

I felt hands close around mine and the picture was lifted from me. I caught my breath and looked up to see my mother's face. By her expression, I knew she believed that I'd brought the picture here myself, that I'd done it out of love for Sophia, and I couldn't bear it.

I blurted, "She hated me."

"What, love?"

"I hated her, too."

She sank down onto the bed next to me, cradling the picture as if it were a child. "Oh, sweetie. I know you didn't always get on, but people don't, and—it doesn't mean they can't find a way to live togeth—it doesn't mean they don't love each other."

I leaned against her and she rubbed my back, just like she had when I was little. She had to be right, didn't she? Maybe she wasn't so unrealistic after all. It had only been pettiness and jealousy, and we'd have got past it sooner or later. Wasn't Sophia beyond it already?

And she was *dead.* I surely couldn't think so badly of her any longer.

We spent the next day by the sea, every wave glittering, the sands shining so whitely in the sun I had to shield my eyes. It reminded me of Sophia and me at our best—the July girls—and the salt air gave me an appetite and a good kind of tiredness, but I wasn't about to rest. It was still hours until sunset when we got back to the cottage and without telling anybody, I packed a few items in a backpack and crept down the stairs. I could have said I was going for a walk, but it seemed more appropriate to Sophia's memory to sneak out.

I slung the backpack's straps around my arms and hurried along the lane. It was cooler than it had been, and quiet. I didn't know what I'd find at the fogou; the chamber might have been sealed or fenced in since I'd seen it last.

The willow herb grew higher about the path than I remembered and I pushed through it, everything smelling of sap and growth and nectar. When I emerged near the trees the sign was still there, hanging from its chain. The only difference was that its letters were a little more faded than before, but their intention remained clear enough. I didn't pause, just stepped over. I hadn't seen anyone else, and I wondered if Lucy still lived here or if she'd moved on, as people did—at least, those who were still alive.

My arms were bare and it was cooler at once under the shadow of the trees. Low branches clawed and scraped and I felt them in my hair, like fingers, trying to make me stay. I tried not to think too much about what I was doing. I told myself it would be all right. Sophia had laughed in the face of this; it had been easy for her. She'd asked me to go with her then, and I'd refused, but I wouldn't refuse now.

The clearing was just as it had been, the same white clouds scudding overhead. It could almost have been that same day, as if it was always summer here, always July.

The hole in the ground was there, too. It hadn't been filled in or fenced over or sealed. It looked cold, the grey stones more than ever like teeth. *Hungry,* I thought, and pushed the thought away. It was only a short passage—the creep—and then I'd be in the chamber. I could take the things from my backpack: a candle from the cupboard under the sink, and a box of matches. I was going to light the candle for Sophia, to let her know that, after all, we were family.

*Some call them holts,* I remembered, *or fuggy holes, or vows.* Well, this would be my vow to Sophia: to remember her as she would have wanted me to.

I knelt and looked into the entrance. There was a steady movement of air, so slight it was like cold breath on my cheek, and then I couldn't feel it anymore. I shuddered. I could only see a short way in, an arched passageway lined by more of those stones, then blackness. My breathing sounded as unsteady as it felt, but I couldn't wait or my courage would fail. I'd become that same person again, the one she'd turned her back on. I had to show her—and maybe myself—that I could be different.

I grabbed my mobile phone from my jeans pocket and switched on its torch, the thin beam vanishing in the daylight. Then I ducked into the tunnel and started to crawl.

I realised at once the torch wasn't going to be much use. The roof was lower than I'd even expected, and when I raised my head I felt stone brushing against my hair. I bowed lower, seeing only dry-packed earth, hard as rock against my hands. The air in here was a constant cold, scraping the back of my throat, chilling my skin. There was a smell, too, one I didn't like to think about: a smell like old bones, grave dirt, and time. I wondered when Lucy last came here. It felt abandoned, as if no one had been here in centuries. She'd probably lied about the chamber. There was no magical glow; there was nothing fairylike about it.

I forced myself to take another deep breath. Still, I couldn't help thinking of the weight of earth over my head, nothing but the arrangement of old stones pressing against one another to stop it all coming down.

I shuffled forward, hitting my head on a lower stone that jutted from the roof. The pain was sharp, and I rubbed it then held my hand before my face, trying to see if there was blood. But it would be worth it, wouldn't it? Soon I'd be through. I'd spill from the mouth of the tunnel and I might even laugh, never mind if I was alone.

I twisted to see the passageway ahead, shining the light from my mobile into it. The centre of the tunnel was dark, nothing to catch its beam; I only saw fragments of stone, one hanging lower where the roof bulged downward. What had Lucy said?

*There's no mortar holding the stones together. There's one bit—the roof comes down. You have to wriggle.*

It was nothing unexpected. Sophia had done this and so would I. I'd be back at the cottage within the hour, and this time I'd put the picture away somewhere and she wouldn't bring it back. It would stay where I placed it, because I'd laid her to rest; because, if she could see what I was doing, she'd be happy.

Cold air gasped into my lungs and I pushed aside the panic clouding the edges of my vision. I imagined the darkness creeping into me with each breath . . . *No.*

I knew I wouldn't be able to hold the torch any longer, not until I was through the squeeze, and anyway, it wasn't doing any good. I slipped it into my pocket. Then I lowered myself fully to the earth, feeling it dry and gritty against my arms, hard against my chest. I wriggled as they must have, pushing with my toes, pulling with my forearms, my hands finding the way. I imagined the low stone hanging above me, ducked under where I thought it was, and felt colder air like fingers brushing my scalp. Was that the chamber? The passage hadn't been so very long after all, just like she'd said. Then I felt pressure against my spine as my backpack pressed downward.

I froze. Why hadn't I taken it off? But I'd rushed at this, not stopping to think. I'd almost forgotten about the pack anyway, since it weighed almost nothing. And yet, now, it felt heavier—heavy and unwieldy.

*Breathe.* It wouldn't help me to panic. An image rose before me of the extra handle jutting from the top of my backpack, designed for carrying it in one hand. It might have snagged on something. Another wriggle would free it. I could even remove the pack here—I tried twisting an arm behind me and the pressure on my back increased, my elbow connecting painfully with the wall of the passage. I decided I'd take it off once I was in the chamber. It wasn't far, after all, and the way out would be easier, the centre of the tunnel shining white instead of dark.

I pressed myself into the ground, shuffled an inch or two backwards, and the straps around my arms tightened.

I let out a little sound, one I was glad no one else could hear, my breaths coming too loud and too fast. Forget Sophia, forget everything; she wouldn't have done this for me—would she?

But she *would* have. She'd have done it because she wasn't scared, wasn't stupid, wasn't like a—like a *mouse,* scurrying through a tunnel.

Slowly, I realised that the sound of breathing wasn't just my own. It was coming from the darkness itself, as if this whole place was alive. . . . But of course, it wasn't. It was only my breath echoing all around me, along the passage, distorted by the old stones.

I scratched at the earth and tried to pull myself along and couldn't move. There was no give in the straps holding me in place. There was no light, none at all. I closed my eyes and opened them as wide as I could—nothing.

And there was no air. I gasped, my lungs straining as if there wasn't enough to fill them; it felt as if there never would be again. There was only the cold dark, and I was a fool—what had I been thinking? I had to get *out.*

I shuffled backwards once more and the straps around my arms tightened again, compressing my chest. I wriggled as hard as I could. Grainy light burst around me and I realised my eyes were closed; when I opened them, the dark remained. I couldn't reach my mobile phone to get any light. An image: the strap of my backpack caught on a loose stone. The arch was held in place by the way those stones were arranged, each one doing their part, bearing its share of the load. What would happen if one of them fell?

I took deep breaths. When I moved forwards again, it would be all right. Anything else just wasn't possible. A few hours ago I'd paddled in the pure, clear sea. I'd squinted against the sun shining on white sand, and wished it wasn't so bright.

I wished it was bright now. I wished I was there—but soon, I would be. Tomorrow I would run in mad circles in the water, splashing it high, and Mum would laugh at me, not knowing the reason why.

And the thought came to me that no one knew where I was.

I pictured all the distance between us, the clearing, the trees, the lane. They wouldn't hear me, no matter how loud I shouted. My screams would only fill the chamber, echoing back at me, driving me mad. . . .

I forced my thoughts in a different direction. None of it mattered. I wasn't really stuck. In a few seconds I'd be in the chamber and I'd shrug off the backpack, as easy as it had always been. I wouldn't even stay to light the candle before I was out of here.

I made myself as flat as I could and tried to drag myself

forwards, feeling my nails breaking against the ground, and this time something gave. I moved maybe an inch and then I was caught again and there came, as clear as daylight, the sound of glass breaking.

I shifted my weight a little to the side, hearing another glassy *chink* from my back. I knew what it was. I pictured the photograph, two girls smiling into the dark, their faces obscured by the cracks in the glass holding them in. The photograph that I hadn't kept, hadn't packed, hadn't wanted to see—the one she had brought to me, in case I could forget her, in case I could breathe again. I imagined its frame, square and heavy, jutting from my backpack, because she'd put it there—because she wouldn't be laid to rest, not by me or anybody. Why had I ever thought she would?

Now I wasn't sure it was a strap that had caught against the roof at all. Had that picture frame somehow wedged into a gap between the stones? If I moved, would it pry them loose?

I twisted my head, resting one cheek in the dirt, and without volition, a memory came. It was Sports Day. Sophia had been surrounded by her friends, only coming over to me when called to pose for the camera. I remembered the way she'd been looking over at her boyfriend; and I remembered the way I had.

*No.* That must be a false memory; it was the kind of thing she would do, not me, never wanting me to have anything—

Could she actually have been jealous of me? Had she hated the way I looked at him—the way I looked at *her*, at her perfect skin, her golden hair, her *life*? Had I wanted it all so very badly?

My mind skipped, loosened, found another memory. Later that same day, Sophia had been waiting for me behind the gym. She hadn't smiled then. She didn't even speak. We weren't the July girls, not then; we never had been. I remembered the feeling of her hands clawing in my hair. I felt it as I hit the ground, the way my elbow struck off the wall, the pain flaring. The weight on my chest as she knelt on my back, the way she'd pushed my head into the earth: *Stay down, bitch. Just stay down, or I swear . . .*

*I'll bury you.*

Oh, God. It was the only kind of vow she'd ever made to me. And I saw it all so clearly, here, where I could see nothing.

Without thought, without purpose, I struggled. I couldn't lift my head, couldn't get my breath. But I wasn't going to die. I would get out, because I had to; soon, I would get out.

I felt the touch of fingers in my hair, there and then gone. I let out a sharp sob, too loud. It couldn't be her. There was only the chamber ahead of me, and that was empty. And an answering sound came, slow and insidious: a whisper? The chamber didn't *feel* empty, not any longer.

But of course it wasn't empty. Sophia had come to me and put the picture into my bag, hadn't she? Something to remind me of her, if anything were needed. How could I forget? I'd spent so long thinking of nothing else but her. And now she hadn't forgotten me. She hadn't forgiven. My mother had been wrong: Sophia was here and she hated me. She hated me because I was jealous. She hated me because I wanted everything she had. She hated me because she was dead and I was alive but I didn't know how to live, not really—not without her to show me how.

But I *was* alive. I gasped in a breath, tasting earth and stone and time. And I tried to heave forwards and there was a dull scrape as something gave and I could move. I shot forwards but the sound was growing, a far-off rumbling getting closer and louder, and then the world came down.

I think I screamed but I couldn't hear it because that sound was all around me. I waited for the earth to fill my mouth but it didn't, it was my legs and my back it took, and I waited for the pain to begin. It didn't, not then. It was coming though, I knew, getting closer every second. For now, there was only an awful and intense pressure. I tried to move my legs, to wriggle my toes. I couldn't feel anything at all. I tried to twist my head and couldn't. It felt as if someone was kneeling on my neck.

*Stay down, bitch. I'll bury you.*

I heard a sob. I think it was mine.

I let everything go limp, tasting despair at the back of my throat. The tunnel must be blocked. No one could look into it, see me there and pull me free. And the air would be sealed out. Soon it would go stale—

I started to shout, inarticulate sounds without words; I think I screamed. And then I felt those fingers again, running through my hair, easing it away from my face, stroking my skin, as if in comfort. It quieted me. I let out another, softer cry.

And I realised I could see something after all. There was no light to see by and yet something was glowing, dancing before my eyes, an illusion or a trick. Still it grew brighter, and the breath caught in my throat. I could see a glow, unmistakable now, but it wasn't moss. It was hair: gleaming, golden, lovely hair.

Sophia did not speak. She had no need of words. She had already said everything she wanted to say. I knew why she was here. It wasn't her who'd wanted to own everything, to take it all; it was me. And there was only one thing left to her now that I didn't have: death. She wanted to share that with me too. There, in the dark and the cold, she had decided to be my sister, after all.

# About the O'Dells

*Pat Cadigan*

I was just a little girl when Lily O'Dell was murdered.

This was before everyone was connected to the internet and people posted things online straight from cell phones. Infamy was harder to achieve back then, but Lily O'Dell's murder qualified. It was the worst crime ever committed in the suburb of Saddle Hills, or at least the goriest. One night in June, Lily's abusive husband Gideon finally did what he'd been threatening to do for the two years they'd been married, using a steak knife from the set her sister had given them as a wedding present.

The police had already been regular visitors to the O'Dell house. Lily had pressed charges the first couple of times. Then a woman officer mentioned a restraining order and a jail term instead of probation and community service. After that, Lily always gave the cops some prefab story, like she'd fallen down the cellar stairs and hit the cement floor face-first, and when Gideon had tried to help her up, she'd been so dizzy she'd fallen *again.* Was she a klutz or what? Maybe she needed remedial walking-downstairs lessons, ha, ha, but not cops coming between her and her lawfully wedded husband, no way, José!

Anywhere else, Lily O'Dell's murder might have been predictable, but people didn't get murdered in Saddle Hills. They didn't leave their doors unlocked—that era was long gone—

but the streets were safe, the schools were top-notch, and all the parks had the newest playground equipment and zero perverts lurking near the swings. This was the true-blue suburban American dream and the O'Dells didn't fit in.

For one thing, they didn't have kids and for another, they weren't even homeowners—they lived in one of the neighborhoods' few rental properties. No one expected they'd last long. Sooner or later, one of them would leave the other, who would skip out on the lease. Or they'd decide to start over somewhere else and skip out together. The company that owned the place would keep their damage deposit, shampoo the carpets, and rent to people who didn't need the police to break up their fights.

Instead, Gideon O'Dell chased his wife around the block and through several backyards before catching her in front of our house. He stabbed her so many times, the knife broke and he was too blind with rage to notice—he just kept pounding with the handle until it slipped out of his grip. Everybody said when the cops arrived, he was crawling around looking for the blade.

And I slept through the whole thing. At four, I slept like the dead.

Mr. Grafton in the house across from ours had some kind of special power attachment for his garden hose. From my bedroom window, I watched him using it on the spot where the O'Dells had played out the final scene of their marriage. It didn't look to me like there was anything left. When the FOR SALE sign appeared on his front lawn, I figured he was tired of power spraying the road, which he'd started doing at least twice a week.

It was more than that, as I learned from my favorite hiding place behind the living room sofa. My father told my mother and my older sister, Jean (who at thirteen enjoyed the privilege of *adult conversation*) that Mr. Grafton's wife forced him to go to the doctor. Now he had medicine that was supposed to make him stop power spraying the road. He told my father he didn't like how it made him feel. Besides, he wasn't a *nutjob*. He hadn't *hallucinated* the O'Dell killing, it had *really happened*. So it wasn't *his* fault that when he looked out his window at night, he could see it *again*, as clearly as if it were happening right that very moment.

My mother said Mr. Grafton was such a gentle man, he could barely bring himself to pull a weed. Jean said that explained why Mrs. G did all the gardening, but not why Mr. G had lost his marbles.

I expected my parents to jump on her for that. But to my surprise my father said, "No, honey, Gideon O'Dell lost his marbles, and one of the worst things about people like him is the effect they have on everyone around them."

"Yeah, I bet Lily O'Dell would be the first to agree with you," Jean said.

*That* got her a scolding. My father told her what had happened to Lily O'Dell was a tragedy, not a joke; my mother said it was bad luck to disrespect the dead. Then Jean peered over the back of the sofa and found me. "Hey, what do you call a little pitcher with big ears?" she said.

"Gale," my parents said in unison. My father reached over, picked me up by the back of my overalls, and sat me on his lap. He started lecturing me about sneaking around and listening to private conversations. But I knew he wasn't really mad because he did it as the Two-Hundred-Year-Old Professor with his glasses pushed far down his nose, which always made me giggle till I hurt.

The Graftons sold their house a month later. Jean asked if we were going to move too. My father said just thinking about having to pack everything up made him want to run screaming into the street. It was supposed to be funny but none of us laughed.

"I'm sorry," he said after a moment. "I wasn't thinking. Maybe without Joe Grafton power washing the street every two days, we can finally put it behind us."

"Stains like that don't wash out so easily," my mother said.

My parents split up the summer I turned fourteen. I was surprised although I shouldn't have been. Watching them grow apart hadn't been much fun, and I'd had to do it alone. Jean went through high school in such a whirlwind of activities, she was never home even before she left for college.

I knew something was wrong but I thought they'd fix it; they fixed everything else. My parents were *good* people. We'd never had the police at our house, nor would my father ever chase my mother through the street with a steak knife. If there was a problem, they'd solve it.

Only they didn't. They sat me down between them on the sofa to explain that my father was moving into a condo closer to his job downtown. My mother and I would stay in the house. I wouldn't see as much of my father as before but all I had to do was call and we were still a family bullshit bullshit bullshit.

It was all so polite and calm, as if they were talking about something normal, like a dental appointment. Finally, they wound down and asked if I had any questions.

"Yeah," I said. "What the *fuck*?"

They didn't even have the decency to look shocked by the f-word. After a long moment, my mother said, "We know how upsetting this is, Gale—"

"You don't know *shit*!" I yelled, wanting them to feel like I'd slapped them. Then I ran up to my room and slammed the door so hard it should have shattered into a million pieces, or at least cracked down the middle. I felt even more betrayed when it didn't.

My first impulse was to call Jean and scream at her. She'd already know—yet another betrayal. Parents were on one side and kids were on the other, that was the natural law. She was supposed to be on *my* side, not *collaborating* with *them*.

I put down the phone on my desk. My parents would come up to try talking to me; if they heard me on the phone with my traitor sister, they'd put their traitor ears to my traitor door. I waited to hear the telltale creak in the hallway. I said loudly, "Dear Diary, I wish my parents would drop dead."

They didn't even knock. "That's *horrible*!" my mother said. All the color had gone out of her face except for two pink spots on her cheeks. "How can you talk like that?"

"Because she knew we were listening," my father said, although he didn't look too sure of himself. "It's completely normal for her to be angry. Even Jean's p.o.'ed at us."

"Oh, well, as long as everything's *completely normal*, we can all relax," I said. "It's not like anyone's getting stabbed in the middle of the street."

My parents looked at each other. "Maybe we *should* move," my mother said.

But we didn't. My parents talked to a couple of realtors, but there was nothing available nearby. We'd have had to move farther away, which was out of the question. My parents wanted to keep me in the same school.

I could have screwed that up by acting out. It would have been their worst nightmare and I spent hours fantasizing in my room. Drugs or booze would get me suspended, but for immediate expulsion, I'd need a weapon, ideally a gun. With my luck, though, I'd end up shooting my own ass off. A knife would do, we had plenty of those.

Or I could just ditch school—that would actually create more legal problems for my parents than for me. My fleeting moment of guilt was drowned out by a rush of anger.

*So what? Screw them. They do whatever they want, never giving a crap about* my *feelings. They don't have to, they're grown-ups. They can get away with* fucking murder.

Except Gideon O'Dell—he hadn't, and Lily hadn't even gotten away with her own life. My mother's words came back to me: *Stains like that don't wash out so easily.* I thought it was odd she'd put it that way, as if she didn't think whatever Mr. Grafton saw had been all in his head.

Which made me wonder for the zillionth time how the hell I could have slept through something like that. I was still a sound sleeper. One night not long before the O'Dell murder, lightning struck a nearby transformer during an especially violent storm, and there were fire engines and police cars all over the place. The commotion kept everyone in a six-block radius up all night, but if the power hadn't still been out the next morning, I'd never have known.

At first, I thought I was dreaming. Then I heard more pounding and a male voice demanding someone answer the door. When my parents went downstairs, I almost went, too, before I remembered I was still mad and I didn't want them to think I cared.

I raised the screen on my bedroom window so I could lean out and see what was going on. Two police officers were on our steps with my parents; they had on their silly matching robes, like they were just regular and my father wasn't sleeping in Jean's old room until he moved out next week.

Another police car pulled up in front of the Graftons' old house. I could see the people who lived there huddled close together on their front steps, but I couldn't tell if any of their robes matched.

". . . bed between eleven and eleven-thirty?" one cop on the steps was saying.

"I went to bed shortly after eleven." My mother's voice sounded draggy and plaintive. "Don was watching a news program."

"Were you asleep when your husband came to bed, ma'am?" the second cop asked.

"She usually is," my father said coolly.

"I usually am," my mother said, echoing his tone.

I couldn't blame them for not wanting to tell the cops they were sleeping separately; it wasn't like they were the O'Dells.

"Now, your daughter Gale—is *she* all right?" asked the other cop.

"*Of course* she's all right." My mother was suddenly wide awake and pissed off.

"We'd like to confirm that."

"It's four a.m.!" my father snapped. "She's asleep."

"Well, actually . . ." The second cop turned to look directly at me. So did everyone else.

I glared at everyone for a long moment before I pulled my head in. Lowering the screen, I saw the third cop talking to the people across the way. One was pointing emphatically at the street. Or rather, at a particular spot on the street.

I went downstairs. One cop was in the living room with my father and the other was in the kitchen with my mother. *Sexist much?* I thought. Good old Saddle Hills. The cops asked me if I'd seen or heard anything unusual, like screaming. I told them the way I slept, I wouldn't have heard a rock concert.

I thought they'd leave when it became obvious we'd all been asleep till they'd woken us up, but they didn't. Apparently cop-obvious was different from obvious-obvious. They went through the entire house and my parents admitted that despite their matching robes, they weren't happily married after all. It got boring; I stretched out on the sofa with a paperback.

The next thing I knew, the police were telling my parents they were sorry for the inconvenience in that way they have that's somehow both sincere yet totally detached. It was getting light when I stumbled back to my room and dropped dead.

A few hours later, my father's angry voice woke me. Were the cops back? I rolled out of bed and raised the screen.

It took a few moments before I realized the guy on the front steps was from across the street. He was trying to explain something but my father wasn't having any, telling the guy to get the hell off our property if he didn't want to find himself on the wrong end of a lawsuit.

The guy gave up. But as he started down the steps, he looked up and saw me. I drew back, hoping he wasn't stupid enough to try talking to me. He wasn't.

• • •

Or rather, not then. He waited until my father moved out and rang the doorbell right after my mother left for the supermarket. I considered not answering, then decided if he got weird, I could call the cops. Or my father.

"Yes?" I asked stiffly through the locked screen door. He was a bit younger than my father and not much taller than I was, with a round face, thinning blond hair, and the kind of pale skin that burns even when it's overcast. The shadows under his puffy brown eyes made him look like he'd been up all night.

"I knew exactly what I was going to say before I came over here," he said unhappily. "Now I can't remember."

"Oh." I had no idea what to do with a helpless adult. "Retrace your steps, maybe it'll come back to you." I started to close the door.

"It's not that," he said quickly. "It's—I don't know how to begin."

So what did he expect *me* to do? "Maybe you should talk to my parents, Well, my mother." I started to close the door again.

"Have you ever seen a ghost?" he asked desperately.

I still didn't let him in.

His name was Ralph Costa and he was why the cops had visited us in the middle of the night. He'd seen a man stabbing a woman in the street and thought it was my parents.

"Why would you think *that*?" I asked, thinking maybe I should have shut the door on him after all.

"She ran up your front steps and tried to open the door," Ralph Costa said. "I thought she lived here. But *he* dragged her into the street and . . ."

"Stabbed her a lot?" I suggested.

He looked sick. "At first, I couldn't even move. Then I was on the phone, yelling for the cops to get here now. I woke May and the kids and made them stay in the back of the house so they wouldn't see. But when the cops came, there was no body, no blood, just . . . nothing. But I *know* I wasn't dreaming or hallucinating. *I saw a man kill a woman.*"

I'd heard every variation of the story—whoever told it would say Gideon almost caught Lily in *their* backyard—but this was new. "Was she screaming?"

"Of course—she must have been, I heard her—" He cut off, looking puzzled, and I could practically see him replaying it in his mind. "I *heard* her." He shook his head. "I tried to apologize to your father but he was pretty irate."

"Yeah, the cops tromped around for hours looking for bloody knives and dead bodies. It was pretty bad." I couldn't help rubbing it in; it *had* been pretty bad. Worse, the cops had asked the neighbors if my father ever beat us and now they were all looking at us funny.

"I really *am* sorry," Ralph Costa was saying. "If it makes you feel any better, the cops stayed at our house a lot longer, asking about my mental health. They didn't mention the O'Dells until just before they left. My wife looked it up later on microfiche at the library. No one ever told us."

"You're still pretty new," I said. "And it *was* a long time ago."

"Not even ten years," Ralph said, which reminded me time was different for grown-ups. "Did anyone else ever see—well, what I saw?"

I considered telling him about Mr. Grafton and decided against it. The house had changed hands twice before the Costas had moved in, which was pretty unusual. But my parents said the first people had moved to be closer to a sick relative, and the second ones got a sudden job transfer. No ghosts.

"I'm a kid," I said finally. "Nobody ever tells me anything." It wasn't a total lie. Mr. Grafton hadn't told *me* about seeing the O'Dells. "Hey, I got stuff to do before my mother gets back. Have you talked to the neighbors?"

He looked unhappy. "Asking people if they've ever seen ghosts replaying a gruesome murder is no way to make friends."

I almost said I was sorry, then thought, why should *I* apologize? *He* was the one seeing things. He thanked me for listening and left, and I went to sort laundry in the basement, where I couldn't hear the doorbell.

I didn't tell my mother about Ralph Costa right away, but the longer I put it off, the harder it would be to explain why. And if she heard about it from Ralph first, she'd have a cow: *A stranger has to tell me what you're doing—do you know how that makes me look?* Divorce had made her touchy.

But what could I say? *Hey, Mom, that guy who thought Dad murdered you dropped by while you were at the supermarket. Turns out he saw Lily O'Dell's* ghost. *But wait, it gets better—did you know Lily ran up our front steps and Gideon dragged her into the street by her hair?* I couldn't even imagine *that* shitstorm, but I was pretty sure it would end up being all my fault.

God, grown-ups had *no idea* of the trouble they made for kids just by running their big fat mouths. *Damn them,* I thought, feeling angry, miserable, and cornered. *Damn them all, even the ones who* didn't *stab their wives to death in the street.* How the hell was a kid supposed to deal?

Finally, a couple of nights later, fortified by takeout beer-battered fish and chips, I decided I'd just go for it. Only what

I heard myself say was, "Mom, did I *really* sleep through Lily O'Dell getting killed?"

For a moment, I didn't think she was going to answer. Then: "Actually, I'm pretty sure you saw the whole thing."

I felt my jaw drop. She watched me gape at her for a few moments, then sighed. "If I tell you about that night—and I can only tell you what *I* saw—promise me you won't obsess about it."

"Okay, I won't."

"I mean it. And *don't* go blabbing to all your friends."

Before I could answer, her hand was clamped around my wrist, not tightly enough to be painful but it wasn't comfortable, either. "Seriously. If I find out you're trying to impress your friends with this, the consequences will be"—she paused for half a second—"*severe.*"

*What are you gonna do, kill me?* I suppressed the thought, hoping her mom ESP hadn't picked it up. "I give you my word."

Like that, she let go and was back to casual. "You were sleepwalking that night."

"You never told me I sleepwalked!" I was flabbergasted.

"Only a few times, and it never happened again after that night." She shrugged.

"Did you take me to the doctor?"

"Of course we did," she said, almost snapping. I opened my mouth to say something else and she glared at me. "Gale, do you want to talk about sleepwalking or Lily O'Dell? I'm too tired for both."

I was on the verge of telling her I was sorry motherhood was such a burden but caught myself. Her lawyer had phoned earlier. Those calls seldom put her in a good mood.

"That night?" I said in a small voice.

• • •

"It was a Saturday," my mother said. "After you and Jean went to bed, your father and I stayed up to watch a movie on cable. You got up three times, first wanting a glass of water, then to ask for a PB&J. The third time, you were sleepwalking."

My mother sighed. "We didn't think you could open the front door. Even if you managed to work the bottom lock, you weren't tall enough to reach the deadbolt or the chain. But we didn't know how resourceful you could be even asleep. You got your step stool from the front closet."

Now she chuckled a little. "The chain lock was still a few inches out of reach, though, so you used the yardstick. It was in the corner right beside the front door. Moving the chain with it wasn't easy—I tried it myself later—but you were on a mission to get that door open.

"You'd have been out on the steps with Lily O'Dell if not for the fact that the screen door lock kept sticking. I oiled it, your dad tried axle grease, and Jean even put mayonnaise on it once but that only made it *stink* and stick.

"So when Lily O'Dell came up the front steps and begged you to let her in, there was nothing you could do. Except maybe wake up."

My mother's face turned sad. "When I got to you, Gideon O'Dell was dragging Lily into the street. He might have already stabbed her a few times or maybe he'd just beaten her bloody—" My mother stopped and shuddered. "*Just* beaten her bloody. Jesus wept.

"Anyway, there was so much blood on your face and your pajama top, I was afraid Gideon O'Dell had hurt you, too. But it was all Lily's—she'd pushed in the screen and grabbed at you.

I cleaned you up, changed your pajamas, then put you to bed in our room and told you to stay there. Naturally, you didn't. I found you asleep by the window in your room."

I waited, but she didn't go on. "Then what?"

"We let you sleep in. You woke up around noon and as far as we could tell, you didn't remember a thing."

"I don't see how that's possible." I was picturing Lily O'Dell on the other side of the screen door, beaten and bloody and begging for help.

"You were very young," my mother said for what must have been the millionth time. "The doctor said your mind was protecting you from trauma."

"But wasn't Jean traumatized?"

My mother smiled a little. "I wouldn't let her put on her glasses. Your sister was so nearsighted she couldn't see past the end of the driveway." She finished the last bit of wine in her glass. "If you've got questions, ask now—after this, the subject is closed. Forever."

"But I need to think," I said, wincing inwardly at how whiny I sounded.

"Think faster, kid." There was a hard, all-but-pitiless edge in my mother's voice I'd rarely heard before. Sometimes she sounded like that with her lawyer, and most of the time with my father. But she was supposed to show she loved me no matter what. Those were the rules, she was my mother.

Correction: she was my *getting-divorced* mother; she made her own rules.

She put her hand on the base of her empty wine glass and I blurted, "Did you take me to another doctor? Like a psychologist or a shrink?"

"We didn't need to," she said. "Dr. Tran said you were perfectly healthy and suggested we consider the kind of deadbolt that needs an indoor key. Or put a bell on your bedroom door." My mother laughed a little. "We tried that. But not for long—your singing 'Jingle Bells' out of season drove us all crazy. You never sleepwalked again anyway."

That explained a vague memory of singing Christmas carols in an inflatable kiddie pool in the backyard. "Did you talk to Dr. Tran about my repressed memory?"

My mother glanced up at the ceiling. "It's not a repressed memory."

"But—"

"You've forgotten plenty else in your life and those aren't repressed memories," my mother said. A hard little line appeared between her eyebrows and I knew I was pushing it. "Nobody remembers *every* detail of their lives."

"But something like *that*?" I said.

"I told you, your brain was protecting you," my mother replied. "Probably saved you years of therapy, if not decades. But if you drive yourself crazy because you *weren't* traumatized, I'll go upside your head."

"Is that why you and Dad are getting divorced?" I asked. "Because *you're* traumatized?"

I expected her to snap at me but she only shrugged. "I'll have to ask my shrink."

"*You* have a *shrink*?"

"Yeah. I'm getting divorced." She gave me a sideways look under half-closed eyelids. "Thought you knew."

"*Mom!* Seriously—"

"That's private." She got up and started clearing the table.

"Wait," I pleaded, "I have more questions."

She leaned against the kitchen counter. "Give it a rest, will you? It was horrible but it's over. You have no good reason to bring it up."

"Actually, someone else brought it up," I said. "A few days ago."

My mother didn't march over to Ralph Costa's house immediately, or even the next morning, which surprised me. I asked her what she was going to do but all she said was, "I'm thinking," and warned me not to ask again. I thought the suspense was going to kill me, but then something unbelievable happened.

Gideon O'Dell came back.

He looked completely different without the long hair, beard, and moustache, but I recognized him immediately.

I was reading a book under the redbud tree in the front yard. My mother had said it would have to go this summer. I was sulking about it when a truck with a crew of tree men from Green & Serene pulled up in front of the house next door, and Gideon O'Dell hopped out of the driver's side. For a second, I thought he actually *was* a ghost, except he was wearing Green & Serene overalls and cap.

I froze.

Everybody had said he'd be in prison for the rest of his life. Had he escaped? If so, wouldn't he have tried to get as far away from here as possible?

Sure—unless he was hiding in plain sight to throw everyone off. Only he didn't act like someone in hiding. He and the rest of the crew went to work trimming the trees in the Coopermans' front yard like they were all just guys and none of them had killed his wife in the middle of this very street. *Because they didn't know,* I thought; if they had, they wouldn't have given him any tools with sharp edges.

Eventually, they went into the Coopermans' backyard and I bolted for the house.

I didn't tell my mother. She was an office manager now for a small law firm (a different one than her lawyer's) and the job had really perked her up. New wardrobe, new hairstyle, even new friends she went out with on the weekends. It made me realize how little I'd seen her smile or heard her laugh in the last few years, even before the divorce. The last thing I wanted to do was spoil everything. Maybe it wouldn't have but I was pretty sure she wouldn't think it was good news. At the same time, I was bursting to tell her because maybe someone at her job would know why he was walking around free.

Telling my father during one of our weekend visits was even more out of the question. I'd never told him about Ralph Costa because I was afraid he'd drive up on the guy's lawn and take a swing at him. Plus, he wasn't doing as well as my mother, morale-wise, although I thought that was the condo. It felt more like a long-stay hotel than a real home. I asked my father if he were going to look for something else once the divorce was settled.

He was actually surprised at the question. "Of course not. I got a good deal on it. This is home for the foreseeable future." He gave a short laugh that didn't have much humor in it. "Assuming any part of the future *is* foreseeable."

*Oh, Dad,* I thought, *you have* no *idea.*

Nobody did, just me. And Gideon O'Dell. Like we were the only two people on the planet.

• • •

Whenever the Green & Serene crews were around, I stayed in, which was a lot, since everybody in the neighborhood used them. Every so often, I'd peek out a window to see what they were doing (what *he* was doing). But what really happened was, every so often, I *didn't* peek out a window. I watched Gideon O'Dell like a hawk, and to be honest, it was pretty boring, All he did was work hard.

Well, so far. Just because he only cut branches now didn't mean he was reformed.

And he looked so *criminal.* The saggy tank tops he wore didn't cover much; using binoculars, I could see how crappy his tattoos were. On the left side of his chest there was a wide rectangular patch that looked like several layers of skin had been scraped off.

He'd had a tattoo removed, I realized; probably something with Lily's name. His second try at cutting her out of his life like she'd never existed. If so, she'd left a pretty big scar.

Not just on him, either. I thought of Mr. Grafton and Ralph Costa, and even my parents. And me, of course, with the only scar no one could see.

Dammit, how the *fuck* was Gideon O'Dell out of prison?

Strangely enough, a cop show rerun gave me the answer. A guy who had killed someone in a fit of rage took a plea bargain for manslaughter instead of murder and got ten years instead of life. I almost fell off the sofa.

"Does that really happen?" I asked my mother as she came in from the kitchen with a bowl of popcorn. She looked puzzled so I gave her a quick summary. "But that's just TV, right? Or just in big cities, right?"

"Not always," she said and my heart sank. "One of our lawyers just had a murder case. She got the client a plea bargain, although I can't remember offhand what it was."

"Do people know that?"

She frowned slightly. "It's a matter of public record."

"That doesn't mean anyone *knows*," I said. "I mean, if it didn't make the news."

"Most things don't, unless they're high profile."

"Like the O'Dell murder?" I said, before I could think better of it.

I expected her to give me grief for bringing it up again but she only nodded. "They moved the O'Dell trial to a different venue. His lawyer said it wasn't possible to get an impartial jury. He was probably right. It was so lurid, the town was glad to be shut of it."

"You sure picked up a lot since you got that job," I said.

"I'm a quick study." She pushed the bowl at me. "Don't make me eat all this myself. Because I can and I will. Unless *you* save me."

It seemed like that was all I ever did.

Two days later, I saw Ralph Costa talking to a couple of Green & Serene guys, including Gideon O'Dell. It was all very ordinary, a man talking to tree service guys about the hackberry tree beside his house. No earth tremors, no thunder and lightning, no frogs falling from the sky, or fire, or blood. No apparitions and no ghosts, either. Ralph Costa obviously had no idea.

The discussion was short and friendly—Gideon O'Dell actually patted Ralph on the arm before he walked away. Ralph didn't suddenly cry out in horrified recognition. But then, Ralph had never seen him except as—

As what—a ghost? But Gideon O'Dell wasn't dead. So how could Ralph Costa or Mr. Grafton have seen him murdering Lily?

Maybe it was the ghost of his old life? That sounded stupid even just in my head.

Unbidden, my mother's words came to me: *Stains like that don't wash out so easily.*

Maybe that was it—Lily was a ghost, Gideon was a stain.

That should have sounded just as stupid, but it didn't.

Even at this point, I didn't consider talking to my friends. The few who weren't away spending two months with a divorced parent had soccer or swim team or were in summer school. That's what I told myself, anyway. In reality, I just didn't want to tell them about my parents. They'd have understood; a lot of them had already been through it. It seemed like most of the kids I knew lived either with single parents or in what the magazines called blended families, because that made step-parents and step-brothers and step-sisters sound sweet, like a smoothie rather than something out of the Brothers Grimm.

My friends would all be very sympathetic. Then they'd start rehashing their own horror stories along with the ones they'd heard secondhand. Talk about Grimm. But they were actually supposed to make you feel better about your own shitstorm. *See how much worse it could be?*

Except I *did* know. My friends all knew about Saddle Hills' worst-ever crime. But none of them had grown up within sight of Lily O'Dell's murder, or seen Mr. Grafton trying over and over to wash it off the road. And none of them had a murderer for a tree man.

Then it occurred to me while I was brooding up in my room one afternoon: what if I told them I did?

*Hey, guys, you're never gonna believe this—*

They'd all be in such a rush to tell everyone else, they probably wouldn't even notice my father had moved out.

But then what?

Would people call the police? Cancel their tree service? Would there be emergency Neighborhood Watch meetings? Would everyone march on City Hall? Or would the villagers simply descend on Green & Serene with pitchforks and torches to drag the monster out and throw him over the cliff themselves?

It was entirely possible, I thought uneasily, that if people did know, Gideon O'Dell might not be safe. For real.

*Yeah, ask his wife how* that *feels,* a voice in my head whispered nastily. *Screw him. He's a murderer who should be doing life in prison, not pruning elms. He got off easy, not even ten years. You know who* didn't *get a deal? Lily O'Dell—she's dead forever. He deserves whatever he gets. If he's not a real ghost, he ought to be.*

After a bit, I realized I'd been sitting with my fists balled up so tightly my palms were starting to cramp. It was one of the few times I was glad I was a nail-biter because otherwise my palms would have been bleeding. Gideon O'Dell had made me that angry.

Gideon O'Dell had made me *that* angry?

Well, not *just* him—my parents and their divorce bullshit and every other grown-up who just tromped around only caring about themselves. My parents probably thought I was *adjusting* and maybe sometimes I thought so too. As if anything could really be that easy! Like fucking up my life was no big deal. They were as bad as Gideon O'Dell.

Part of me knew the comparison was out of proportion but that was more mature than I wanted to be just then. It was *grown-up* thinking, and seeing as how I couldn't do anything else they did, like drink or drive or join the army or just fuck shit up for the hell of it, I wasn't going to be an adult about this, either.

"What's going on next door?" I asked, looking out the dining room window at all the G&S trucks pulling in. "Are the Coopermans having a party for the tree men? Or are they just luring them in for a mass baptism?" The Coopermans left pamphlets in our mailbox about the joys of being baptized once a month.

"They're cutting down the elm in their backyard," my mother said. "Deborah Cooperman asked if I wanted any for firewood."

"Oh *shit.*" I moved to the patio doors to watch the tree men setting up. "I *love* that tree. How *could* they?"

"Language," my mother said but without any real feeling. She was engrossed in a computer magazine. "All elms in this country have Dutch elm disease and eventually, there's nothing you can do."

"Theirs still looks okay to me," I grumbled.

"G&S gave them an estimate of what the upkeep would cost. They decided to keep their kids instead." She chuckled. "If I had to choose between our elm tree and you, I'd choose you."

I glared at her, suppressing a remark about grown-ups' choices.

"Probably," she added, smiling with half her mouth. "On a good day, for sure. But I also have bad days. You have been warned."

I couldn't help laughing. All of a sudden, I was tired of being mad at her and my father, fed up with being fed up. I sat down next to her on the sofa and let her tell me about the computer she'd learned to use at her job and how it was changing everything. She was talking about the office network when I suddenly felt cold, like the temperature had dropped from eighty-five to fifty-five, and I knew Gideon O'Dell had arrived. I got up and went to the patio door.

"Gale?" my mother asked, puzzled. "What's wrong?"

"Everything," I said.

Why would Gideon O'Dell come back here instead of going just about anywhere else? For all the happy memories? To find himself? To find *America*?

Christ, why did grown-ups do *anything*?

Because it was the worst possible idea, of course.

Made sense.

It took three days for them to reduce the Coopermans' elm to firewood and toothpicks, and I watched pretty much the whole thing. Or rather, I watched Gideon O'Dell while I sat out on the patio pretending to read *A Tale of Two Cities*. I'd already read it for school so if anybody asked what section I was pretending to be on, I could answer. Not that anyone would—my mother was at work all day and none of the tree men were going to wander over to the fence on a break to ask me what else I'd read by Dickens. There was a small risk of the Coopermans sending over one of their kids with a pamphlet; if so, I'd pretend to use it as a bookmark and toss it later.

But no one bothered with me. Mrs. Cooperman was busy making lemonade and iced tea for the G&S guys and even gave them lunch. I suppose it was a good Christian thing to do since killing the elm was such hard work. She smiled and waved at me a couple of times and I waved back, fantasizing about telling her who was in her backyard. If Mary had been outside, she'd have probably been telling all the tree men how great Jesus was. *Jesus loves you. Jesus loves everybody.*

But did Mrs. Cooperman? How much Christian charity would she have for Gideon O'Dell? Would she judge not, or cast the first stone? I was tempted to find out, except I had a very strong feeling it would somehow backfire. Either my parents would be furious with me for not telling them right away, or it would turn out the guy wasn't really Gideon O'Dell after all.

Or worst of all, he *was* Gideon O'Dell with a fake ID, and he'd come back later to shut me up.

Right now, he was high up in the tree with a chain saw. All of the leafy branches had been cut away and now they were starting on the thicker arms. He seemed to be having a good time. Guys with power tools were basically kids with toys. But it was more than that, I thought. He was killing a live thing.

That's *why he came back*, I thought suddenly. My heart was pounding like a jackhammer in slow motion: Bang . . . bang . . . bang . . . *Because secateurs and machetes and chain saws are more fun than a cheap steak knife.*

I walked over to lean on the fence. I'd been so worried about him seeing me, but now I wanted him to. I wanted him to know I was onto him.

But when he did finally look in my direction, his gaze slid away without interest before I could even hold my breath. Talk about an anticlimax. I actually felt cheated. Disrespected, even.

But maybe he'd been too busy killing his wife to notice me that night. Now he was too busy killing a tree. Or trying to; the chain saw jammed suddenly, then cut out altogether. Was that as frustrating as a broken steak knife?

*Lily O'Dell had still been alive when the blade broke off but she hadn't been screaming. She'd had no breath left. Her left lung had collapsed and the right one was about to. The adrenaline that had powered her desperate sprint was gone. She'd used the last of her energy to punch through the top of the screen door and grab at me. Then Gideon O'Dell dragged her away by her hair into the street, where he stabbed her and stabbed her and stabbed her until the handle of the knife was so slippery with blood it slid out of his hand.*

My head cleared and I found myself sitting on the ground beside the fence with the sun in my eyes. I went back to my chair on the patio wondering what the hell had come over me. Some kind of vivid waking dream? Not a memory—or rather, not *my* memory. What I had seen in my mind's eye had all been from Lily O'Dell's point of view.

It only took one day for Gideon O'Dell to cut down the redbud tree in our front yard, working alone. Two other guys deep-watered the elm beside the house and the walnut tree in the backyard, and explained how to harvest the walnuts. We couldn't just pick them off the tree like apples, which was disappointing. It all sounded like a lot of tedious effort for a few nuts. Even having a murderer in our front yard didn't make it less boring.

I sat on the carpet a couple of feet back from the screen door pretending to read Poe's *Tales of Mystery and Imagination.* As usual, Gideon O'Dell worked away like nothing had ever happened here, like he wasn't twenty feet away from the very spot where he stabbed his wife to death.

How could he not feel weird being here?

Maybe he had amnesia. Maybe he got beaten up so many times in prison he had brain damage.

Abruptly, he put down the chain saw, looked directly at me. I stared back; the book resting on my folded legs fell shut. If he hadn't seen me before, he had now. Hadn't he? No, he hadn't; his eyes weren't focused on me at all, I realized, watching as he took the bandanna around his neck off, wiped his face with it, then tied it around his head.

*What are you doing here? What do you want?* I asked him silently. His face gave nothing away. The only thing I could read was the name tag pinned to the front of his overalls: GO. What kind of a name was that?

His initials, of course, what his buddies used to call him. Also his family, including L—

I shook my head to clear it. Gideon O'Dell, aka GO, was now staring thoughtfully at the roof. I went up to my room.

I stayed back from the window, watching the rest of the redbud's destruction with binoculars. Occasionally, I turned to the forever-unclean spot on the road, like I might see something besides old dirty asphalt. Like Lily O'Dell's blood might come bubbling up out of the ground in outrage.

Nothing happened, of course, except GO finished demolishing the redbud.

The son of a bitch came back on Sunday afternoon. Parked his truck in our driveway, trotted up the stairs, and rang the doorbell. I stayed in my room, wondering if he'd finally decided to force his way in and kill us. It was broad daylight, everyone in the neighborhood was home, and kids were outside playing, but a mad killer might not care.

I couldn't hear what my mother said when she answered the door but she sounded friendly. So did Gideon O'Dell, friendly and a little subservient, before he got a ladder and climbed up onto the roof with a toolbox.

My mother came up to tell me not to use the front door for a while. "If you want to go out, use the patio door. I've got a guy fixing loose tiles on the roof."

"One of the G&S guys," I said accusingly. "The one that cut down the redbud."

She nodded. "He saw them while he was here. He said he'd done that kind of work and he'd charge less than a roofer, so I told him to come back today."

"What if he does a lousy job?" I asked.

"He guaranteed his work, and if he couldn't fix something, he'd tell me."

"What if he's lying? For all we know, he's a burglar casing the joint."

"Then he'll know there's lot better pickings next door. Assuming he can fence a collection of ugly silver and tacky Nelson Rockwell plates." She chuckled.

"What if he's *worse* than a burglar?" I said as she turned to leave. "Like, a murderer?"

She turned back to me, eyebrows raised. "Like what—an IRS agent?"

"What do you know about him?" I persisted. "What's his name? Where does he live?"

"You know, when most parents have this conversation, it's the other way around." She came over and sat down next to me on the bed. "He's just fixing some roof tiles, Gale. We're not going out on a date. And he's not a *total* stranger, he works for our tree service. I'm paying cash so I only know his nickname, which is—"

"Go," I said. "Do you know his *real* name?"

All at once, she went serious. "Did this guy ever try anything *inappropriate* with you?" she asked. "Or one of the neighbor kids?"

That lie was too evil to tell, even about him. "No, definitely not," I said. "But who knows what kind of person he really is?"

"Who knows what kind of person *anybody* really is?" My mother gave me a hug. "You don't like the guy, stay away from him. No fault, no foul, everybody wins. Okay?"

*He's not just a guy, he's a murderer; he's Gideon O'Dell,* I tried to say. But when I opened my mouth, all that came out was, "Okay."

She kissed me on the forehead and went back downstairs, leaving me to wonder what the hell was wrong with me. It *wasn't* okay. Gideon O'Dell was up on our roof, exuding poison from his wife-murdering soul and somehow I was the only one who could feel it.

Because Lily O'Dell had touched me, I realized. I couldn't remember but I didn't have to. I had *her* memory—it was in her blood.

"Pizza for supper?" my mother asked. She'd just made another gallon of iced tea to replace what Gideon O'Dell had drunk. I had ice water instead.

When I put away the ice cube trays and closed the freezer door, I saw a fridge magnet holding a slip of paper with a phone number on it and underneath, *Go's cell, call anytime, leave message.*

"That's just in case he has to repair his repair job," my mother said.

"You think he'll have to?" I asked.

"We'll see. They're predicting heavy thunderstorms tonight." My mother chuckled. "Don't worry, I'm sure it's nothing that'll keep you awake."

"We'll see," I said, mimicking her. She didn't notice.

We ate pizza from Valentino's in front of the TV. Talking her into having a glass of wine wasn't hard and she didn't protest when I suggested a second, but then, it was an Australian Shiraz. I told myself that was why she'd poured such a full glass and drunk it more quickly than usual. But so what? She wasn't *drunk*, just very relaxed. She'd get a good night's sleep and no hangover.

Or maybe just a little one, I thought as she had a third glass, which killed the bottle. There was no more wine in the house but she wouldn't have opened another bottle anyway—she was too relaxed to use a corkscrew. She'd also get part of her good night's sleep in front of the TV but that suited me just fine.

My mother was snoring softly even before the first warning rumble of thunder. I threw Grandma's hand-crocheted afghan over her and waited to see if she'd stir. More thunder, louder this time; she didn't even twitch. I went into the kitchen to get Gideon O'Dell's phone number, started to go up to my room, then stopped. Not because I was having second thoughts, but because I wanted to make sure my mother wasn't about to wake up. I tiptoed into the living room to check on her.

As if on cue, thunder boomed, seemingly right overhead.

It wasn't loud enough to rattle the windows but I thought if anything would wake her, that would. She didn't even twitch. I turned out all the lights, started to go up to my room again and then paused, looking at the front door. The TV threw just enough light so I could see it was locked.

*Unlock it.*

The words were so distinct, it was like someone had actually whispered in my ear. But I could hear my mother still snoring under the babble of the latest hot cop show. If I was hearing voices, they weren't too bright; opening the door would wake my mother for sure.

*Not* open *it—not yet. Just* unlock *it.*

It crossed my mind even as I did so that this alone would be enough to wake my mother, because you never, *ever* left anything unlocked after dark. But any disturbance in the force this might have caused was no match for three glasses of Shiraz. Or for Lily O'Dell, who I realized was in charge of this party.

*Good. Now you can go upstairs.*

I felt like I should say thank you, but at the same time I understood Lily O'Dell didn't care how well-mannered I was.

Lightning flickered like a strobe; a few seconds later, thunder cracked like the sky was breaking apart. Maybe it was. My room was dark except for the nightlight in the wall outlet beside my bed, an owl and a pussycat sitting in the curve of a crescent moon. I unplugged it and opened the window. There was a streetlight about halfway between our driveway and the one next door but it seemed dimmer than usual and I couldn't see the street very well. As I raised the screen and leaned out, it started to rain.

• • •

It was the kind of rain that comes straight down and very hard, like it's real pissed-off at everything it's falling on. Tonight, I could actually believe it was. It slapped leaves off trees, smashed down the geraniums lining either side of our driveway, pounded the pavement hard enough to bounce.

Had it rained the night Lily O'Dell got killed? I was pretty sure it hadn't—

*Yes, it did. It rained blood. You got caught in the storm.*

I reached out as far as I could, palm up, just to make sure, but it was plain old rainwater. Still coming down hard, enough to make my hand sting.

The lights in the Graftons' old house went out. Was it that late already? Maybe I should check to see if my mother was still asleep—

*Time to make that call. That's what you came up here for.*

Yes, but now that it was time to do it, I was starting to feel shaky.

*You think* you're *shaky? Try sprinting around the block and hopping fences in backyards. Your knees'll knock like castanets.*

I could see a form in the straight-down sheets of rain, someone in the street, waiting while tiles slid off the roof and smacked wetly on the front steps.

*Call him and tell him to come over immediately. Give him hell or sob your heart out but get him here now.* Now.

I picked up the phone and dialed.

I started by sobbing my heart out but Gideon O'Dell didn't want to come over. There was nothing he could do while it was still raining and even if it stopped, he certainly couldn't work in the dark. I kept sobbing and he kept being reasonable, so I tried getting mad. The way he answered made me think he'd had a lot of anger management classes in prison.

"You just get your ass over here right now and give me back all the money I paid you," I said, "or I tell everyone on the block who you *really* are, *Gideon*."

He practically choked. "You—you *what?*"

"If you think people here want a murderer taking care of their trees—"

"Okay, please, stop. I'm coming now, all right? I'll be there in ten minutes. Not even that. Just don't—please, I've got all your money—"

I slammed the receiver down, shaking all over. Thunder rumbled but without much power as the rain began to lessen. Lily O'Dell was walking slowly up the incline of our lawn, toward the front door. I knew she'd want me to open it now.

My mother was still fast asleep, hugging a throw pillow. The cop show had been replaced by old reruns of a different cop show, one that only came on very late. How long had I been upstairs? And had it been raining hard and angry the whole time?

*Open the door.*

That would wake my mother for sure, I thought. Just in time for Gideon O'Dell to show up apologizing and begging her not to tell anyone. She'll have no idea what he's talking about but maybe she'll be too distracted by the tiles that fell off the roof to care—

*Open the door* now. *Before the doorbell wakes her.*

The rain had stopped.

Lily O'Dell wasn't covered with so much blood that I couldn't see what Gideon O'Dell had done to her face. One eye was swollen shut and the other was getting there; her nose wasn't just broken but so smashed that it didn't look anything like something to breathe through. One side of her face was caved in, her lower lip was badly split and she'd lost some teeth. I could see distinct finger marks in the bruising around her neck.

Only I shouldn't have been able to. All the lights were out and the TV wasn't bright enough. And yet, I *could* see her, could see her struggling to breathe, seemingly unable to gulp in enough air. But I didn't hear it until she punched both hands through the screen door.

Suddenly I was small, looking up at her in horror and confusion, tasting blood as she smeared her hands over my face. Her voice was barely audible as she begged for help, and when Gideon O'Dell yanked her away, she couldn't make a sound.

Gideon O'Dell, however, was yelling and cursing as she dragged him down the lawn by his hair, past his truck parked at the curb. I don't think he knew it was her until they got to that very specific spot on the street, but when he did, he went completely hysterical. I thought for sure his screaming and begging would wake up the entire neighborhood.

But he didn't. No lights went on in any of the neighbors' houses or across the street; my mother slept on, undisturbed and unaware. And all the while, I was trying to get the screen door open but the stupid lock wouldn't budge.

I don't know where the knife came from—maybe it was a ghost, like Lily. But also like Lily, it hurt him for real. I didn't want to watch but I couldn't look away, couldn't yell for my mother, couldn't even move. All I could do was stand there and watch Lily pay Gideon back stroke for stroke, slash for slash, stab for stab.

It took a very long time. When she was finally done, she

turned to look at me and bowed her head a little, like she was saying thanks.

Then it began to rain again, pounding straight down like before. I closed the door and went to bed.

In the morning, the truck was still parked in front of our house but there was no trace of Gideon O'Dell, nothing to show why he had come here or where he had gone, not even a stain on the asphalt. It had rained that hard.

# A Hinterlands Haunting

*Richard Kadrey*

Nick crossed the bridge on foot, moving from one world to another. Really, he was just leaving a bright and crowded district for one that was neither. But the one he was crossing to was older and, being across the river, it felt like another country, with its own language and obscure customs. He made the crossing every year at the same time. Always ten p.m. Always Columbus Day. He had to be careful because the date of the holiday changed from year to year and dates were something easy for a ghost to lose track of.

He thought it was unfair that every year on the pilgrimage he shivered at the frigid wind whipping up from the water. What good was it to sense heat and cold when you were dead? Still, Nick could do other things that most people didn't think ghosts could do, so he supposed it was part of the bargain. But still, the crossing was horrible and he ran the last few yards, leaving the living city behind and heading into what amounted to a vast necropolis.

This older part of the city had been condemned and was just waiting to be demolished—every apartment building, school, church, and bowling alley. Very few people lived here anymore so there were few lights on in the buildings. It was so quiet you could hear the wind through dead trees lining the main street.

Tinny music echoed off the buildings. Someone's radio, maybe around the corner or maybe a mile away.

In school, Nick had read about pandemics. Spanish influenza. The Black Plague. They emptied whole towns. He imagined that it must have been like this. Still, the living had to keep their eyes open for groups of feral children and desperate old codgers with kitchen knives up their sleeves. Even a few gangs roamed the streets. Too small or too unlucky to cut it in the bright city, they'd retreated to the hinterlands. Then there were wild dog packs. What was terribly unfair was that some of these things were even dangerous to *him*. "What's the use of being dead if you're afraid all the time?" he would say to other ghosts, but few spoke to him and none had any answers.

Years before, he'd lived in this now desolate part of the city. On the corner ahead, a light was on in a bodega he would frequent with his wife. The owner, whose name was Robert or Roberto—something like that—was an aggressive, foul-mouthed man who, Nick used to joke, had a PhD in ethnic slurs. When he reached the corner, he went into the shop.

It was mostly as he remembered it: dusty cans of soup and meat, snack food, liquor, and cigarettes. Now, however, most of the merchandise was behind a screen of thick plastic that extended from the front counter to the ceiling. There was a crudely cut slot by the cash register where people would pass their money and get their change. A couple of feet down the counter was a small revolving door where customers would receive their goods. It looked bulletproof, he thought, and tightly sealed. The bodega owner sat by the register in a dense gray fog of cigarette smoke. Nick went and stood in front of him, casting a vague reflection on the plastic screen. It took a couple of minutes for the owner to notice him and when he did, he turned white and stumbled off his stool.

A circle of small holes has been drilled into the plastic at mouth level so that people could communicate with the owner. Nick leaned close to it and said, "Have you seen her?"

The bodega owner shook his head in short, nervous bursts.

"That's too bad," Nick said. "I was hoping. It's always so hard knowing where to begin looking."

The owner nodded stiffly and when Nick didn't move, he took a pint bottle of bourbon and passed it to him through the little revolving door. He took the bottle and put it in his coat pocket.

"Please," said the owner. "Go."

"Afraid of an old fashioned haunting? I don't blame you. Take my word for it, the dead are mostly assholes."

The owner didn't laugh at the joke, which disappointed Nick. "Don't worry," he said. "I'm not here for you. I have places to be."

He walked a few aimless blocks trying to get his bearings. The city had taken down all the street signs to discourage people from living in the district. Nick used landmarks to navigate to the old apartment he'd shared with his wife.

Like the bodega, the neighborhood was mostly as it had been since last time he'd lived there. It was the little changes that caught his eye. A burnt-out bar. A clothing store full of headless mannequins.

Down a block that used to house bakeries and antique shops for tourists, was a sculpture of a snake that seemed to dip in and out of the pavement. Made of scrap metal and wood wired together, at its tallest, the snake was two stories high. He marveled at both the amount of work and madness necessary for someone to build such an enormous piece of art that no one but the lost and the dead would ever see. He recognized the corner where the snake stood and knew that he was close to home. Nick decided that the sculpture was a good omen. He would find his wife soon and be able to finish what he'd come for.

He turned right just past the snake and started up a gentle hill before the small apartment building where his wife would be waiting. He looked up at their window, but didn't see any lights on. Another good omen. Hauntings were always better when they began in darkness. He was almost at the front door of the building when he heard the dogs.

They came yipping and growling down the hill, at least a dozen of them. Living people could hurt him, but he had ways of dealing with them. Animals, on the other hand, weren't afraid of his fragile, spectral form and could easily tear it apart.

The glass front doors of the building had been shattered long ago. He ran inside and raced up the stairs to the old apartment. Unfortunately, it was on the third floor and, despite what was in stories and movies, ghosts like Nick couldn't fly. He had to go up a step at a time just like anybody else.

He was on the second floor, starting up the stairs to the third when heard the dog pack burst into the lobby and thunder after him. He ran up to the third floor as quickly as he could, but the dogs were much faster and by the time he sprinted down the final hallway, the dogs were just a few yards behind him. He tripped and fell against the door of the old apartment and, to his shock, it swung open. This made no sense since Eleanor had always been a fiend when it came to security, installing extra locks on all the doors and windows. But he didn't have time to worry about it. Nick barely got inside and closed the door before the dog pack slammed into it. He threw all three locks and wedged a metal folding chair under the doorknob. Outside, the dogs snarled and scratched to get in, but Nick felt safe. While the building had never been elegant, it was sturdy, with thick, solid doors on each apartment. Still, he didn't like being so close to the pack. He backed away from the door and went into the living room.

When he saw the place, he stopped. It didn't make any sense. The whole apartment smelled of mildew and urine. Much of the furniture was damaged, and what wasn't covered in dust was covered in mold. He sensed that no one had been here in a long time, but he went into the bedroom anyway. It was in the same condition as the living room. The carpet and bare mattress were black with mildew. He checked the dresser and looked in the closet. Both were empty. Nick went back into the living room and looked around for a clue as to where Eleanor might have gone. How could he haunt someone who wasn't there?

The few papers he found on the floor were either moldy or so damp that the ink had run, making them unreadable. A creak and a loud *pop* startled him. When he didn't see anything in the living room he went back to the apartment door. It moved back and forth slightly and it took him a moment to understand why.

Nick stepped on something metallic and picked it up. It was one of the door hinges. The dogs were still trying to batter their way in and while the door itself was thick and strong, all the damp and rot in the apartment had softened the frame around it. The screws in the second hinge were already working their way loose. He was certain that the chair he'd wedged under the doorknob was the only thing keeping the dogs outside. If they got in they'd rip him apart like an old sheet.

Nick knew the apartment and he knew the building and there were no other exits. He'd hated heights in life and the fear hadn't left him in death. Still, he knew the only way out was the fire escape.

He went back into the bedroom and headed for a broken window by the radiator. Moonlight and a damp mist streamed inside. When he stuck his head out the window to see the way down, he almost laughed. The fire escape was there, but on the ground in a twisted heap where it had collapsed. From the other room, he could hear the second hinge wrenching its way out of the wooden door frame. He looked up wondering if he could climb to the roof. However, the fire escape above him was gone too. Dark shapes streaked across the front of the apartment building. More dogs, attracted to the place by the howls of the pack in the hall. Whatever mad thoughts he had about making a run for it down the stairs vanished.

A piece of glass slid from the window frame and he watched it fall. It didn't hit the ground. Instead, it landed on a massive pile of garbage in front of the building. The city had cut off most services to the neighborhood long ago, beginning with garbage pick up. It looked as if the building's residents had simply thrown everything they didn't want from their windows until they'd created a small mountain. For a moment, Nick wondered what filth lay below him, but he cut off the thought when it became clear to him what he was going to have to do.

From what Nick could see, the trash pile was topped by several filthy mattresses. If what was below them was soft enough, they might absorb his weight enough to catch him. It wasn't like he was going to die again, but his spectral body healed slowly and the pain was just as acute as it had been in life.

A final *pop* echoed from the other room and the howling dogs shot into the apartment. Nick stood at the edge of the window and waited until he could feel the dogs right behind him. He needed the fear to let go of the sill and step out into empty air.

The sensation of falling seemed to last less than a second before it was replaced by a feeling that he'd been hit by a bus. Groaning, Nick slowly rolled into a sitting position at the edge of the mattress. He touched his legs and ribs. No pain there, and his limbs seemed to move the way they were supposed to. Nick's back was another matter. It felt as if he'd pulled and bruised every muscle from his neck down to his ankles. He tried to stand, but the pain made him gasp and he fell back onto a mattress. Above him, the dogs were still barking. When he tried to stand again, hands reached down and pulled him to his feet.

Three young men stood around him in a semicircle.

"Thank you," Nick said.

"You can stand? You steady on your feet?" said the nearest young man. The one who'd helped him up.

"Yes. I think so."

Without warning, he punched Nick in the stomach. The pain shot all the way through to his back and he fell to his knees. From this lowered vantage point, he noticed that the young men were all wearing matching jackets. *A gang,* he thought.

The man who'd punched him prodded him with the toe of his boot. "Give me your wallet," he said.

Nick shook his head. He said, "I don't have a wallet. Dead men don't carry money."

The young man smiled at his friends. When he turned back to Nick he said, "You're not dead."

"That's your opinion."

Nick reached into a coat pocket, pulled out a revolver, and shot at the young men. All three went down. He struggled to his feet and went to the one who'd punched him. "Still think I'm alive?" he said. When no one answered, Nick pulled back the hammer on the gun. The young man held up his shaking hands. They were covered in blood.

"Still think I'm alive?" said Nick.

"Fuck you, you fucking freak," said the young man. "You're as alive as me."

"That's unlikely. But still just to make sure." He opened the cylinder of the revolver and spun it. Slapped it closed, put the gun to his head, and pulled the trigger.

*Click.*

"That was disappointing," said Nick.

The man on the ground pointed at him. "Ghosts don't use guns."

"It's a ghost gun," explained Nick. Then he said. "You know a lot about spirits, do you?"

"More than you, I bet."

Nick spun the cylinder again and pointed the gun to his head.

*Click.*

"Maybe ghosts can't shoot themselves. What do you think?"

The young man said, "Suck my dick."

Nick held the gun out butt first. "Maybe you should try it."

The young man reached for the pistol with both hands, but they were slick with blood and he dropped it. He reached for it, but his hands were shaking so much he couldn't get a grip.

Nick snatched the revolver off the ground and said, "You're useless. How am I supposed to be certain? You have me doubting myself. I need hard, empirical evidence of my spirit state."

One of the other gang members tried to get to his feet. Nick raised the gun and shot him. He collapsed onto his back.

"You're out of your fucking mind," said the young man he'd been talking to.

Nick looked down at him. "You know a ghost when you see one? How can you be so sure?"

"My grandma. She taught me how to look," he said. "Ghosts leave a trail in the air like fireflies. You don't leave nothing."

From his back pocket, Nick took out a photo. "Let's try another line of questioning," he said. "Maybe you've seen my wife. She's a little shorter than me. She's usually in a long yellow nightgown with pink flowers on the front."

The young man squinted at the photo and nodded. "Her I know. She haunts the white building right over there. We don't go near her."

"Why's that?"

"Spookshow baby don't talk much. She just kills you if you get too close. That's the other reason I know you're not a ghost. You talk too fucking much."

"I'm lost. I don't like talking, but I have no alternative."

The young man looked down at himself. "Oh shit. I think I'm dying."

"Point me to where you've seen her."

The young man pointed a shaking hand across the street.

"That can't be right," said Nick. "I don't recognize it. She should be in here," he said, looking at the building from which he'd just jumped. The dogs still barked from the window.

"I see her there all the time. She's a real ghost, not you."

"That's not possible, which makes you a liar." Nick pulled the trigger and the gun went off. The young man stopped moving.

He put the pistol back in his pocket and looked up. A woman in a yellow nightgown stood by the curb. "Eleanor?"

At the sound of the name, the woman ran to the building the young man had pointed to earlier. Nick tried running after her, but he'd hurt his knee in the fall and had to limp.

"Eleanor!"

Nick's leg ached terribly, but he went after her as fast as he could. He entered the white building. When he heard her above him he headed up the stairs. It was a funny thing, he thought. Out in the street and now in the building, above him he could see things like fireflies. Slowly and painfully, he followed them.

Nick couldn't hear or see the woman anymore, but a dwindling trail of floating lights led him to an apartment. He went inside—and recognized it immediately. He and Eleanor *had* lived there. After the other apartment. Everything had happened here, not there. How could he have forgotten that? He pushed the apartment door closed. "Eleanor!" he called. Before he could turn away, she rushed out of the small kitchen with a butcher knife and buried it in his chest. As he fell he marveled at the fireflies that surrounded her and how none surrounded him.

He lay against the wall, breathing hard. Eleanor went through his pockets. She took out the pistol and tossed it away. When she found the bourbon, she held the bottle out to him.

"Open it," she said. "I can't."

"You can stab me, but you can't open a bottle?"

Eleanor knelt down next to him. "Hate only gives me so much power and it's very narrow. Stabbing is easy. Bottles aren't. Open it for me."

Nick's left arm was numb, so he braced the bottle against him with his forearm and unscrewed the top with his right hand. He held it out to her.

She sniffed the bottle.

"Bottoms up," he said.

"Don't be an idiot," Eleanor said. "I can't drink. But I can smell. This is cheap stuff you brought me."

He shrugged, which was a mistake. The knife dug in deeper. His chest felt like it was on fire. "It was free."

"That's just like you. Cheap to the end."

Nick smiled at her. "You don't look so bad."

"Neither do you," Eleanor said.

"For a dead man."

She looked at the floor and shook her head wearily. "Christ, Nick. Every year. You're not the dead one. I am."

"But I feel dead," he said.

She took another whiff of the bourbon. "You need a shrink, not a mortician."

Nick looked down at the knife in his chest. "I might be dead soon."

"I aimed high. You'll be fine. You just need some stitches."

Nick felt weak all over. He dropped the bottle. "One of these years you're going to fuck up and kill me for real."

Eleanor shook a finger at him. "The day I kill you for real it won't be a mistake. Until then, enjoy bleeding."

He frowned and a wave of pain, physical and emotional

passed through him. "Did I ever apologize to you about the whole thing?"

"For murdering me? Count the scars on your chest. They'll tell you."

"Does it help?"

"What do you think?"

"But this does?" he said, looking down at the knife and his blood.

She sighed. "It breaks up the tedium."

He wanted to reach out to her, but his arm was too heavy. "I was hoping it would be different this year. Me dead for real. It's getting harder to tell the difference anymore."

"The difference is that you get to go home and watch TV and jerk off. That's how you can tell the difference."

"I think they have a TV at the bodega."

She made a face. "Bobby is too jumpy. It's no fun down there."

"Maybe I could bring you something," Nick said. "A TV. Maybe a satellite dish on the roof."

"Don't bother. They wouldn't last thirty minutes over here. You met some of the neighborhood beasts. They'll steal the gold from your teeth."

"Bet if I shoot a couple more they'll leave you alone."

She gave him a sour half smile. "That's sweet, but no. I've made it this long. I can get by."

He looked around the apartment. "What happens when the bulldozers show up and they tear all this down to put up condos? What happens to you? Where will you go?"

Eleanor looked out the window. "I don't know. I think I might just vanish. All I am are memories. These places. You.

This stupid nightgown you killed me in. Really, you could have waited until I was in something nice or at least had shoes on. Look at my feet."

They were black with filth. Glass and nails were embedded in her soles.

"Do they hurt?" said Nick.

"Of course not, but they're grotesque."

Nick's head slumped forward.

"Hey. You awake over there?"

He shook himself upright again. "Sorry. My head was kind of swimming."

"You're losing blood. Time for you to go."

He looked at her. "Go? Don't you want to finish tonight?"

Eleanor frowned at him. "Who would I be finishing for? Not me. Now get on your feet. I'll help you to the store. Bobby can call you an ambulance."

"What hospital should I go to? I can't get stabbed every year and go back to the same place. They've already started asking questions."

She thought for a moment. "Have you tried Saint Dymphna? She's the patron saint of idiots."

"Yeah. I haven't been there. I heard it's nice."

With Eleanor's help, Nick got to his feet. He leaned on her heavily as she walked him out of the building and back toward the bodega. At the corner, several young men blocked the street. A couple of them started forward, but when they caught sight of Eleanor they backed away and opened a hole big enough for them to pass through.

"That was impressive," said Nick.

"I told you. No one is killing you but me."

"Not even me?"

"Especially not you," Eleanor said. "And don't go back to that building next year. I won't be there."

Nick looked up at the stars. "You always were restless. You could hardly sit through a movie."

When they reached the bodega, Eleanor leaned him against the door. "Remember, don't let Bobby take the knife out. You'll bleed to death before the ambulance gets here."

Nick looked at her. "Same time next year?"

Eleanor nodded slightly. "Don't be late."

As she started away Nick said, "Happy anniversary, baby."

"Happy anniversary," said Eleanor, trailing fireflies into the dark.

# The Number of Things You Remember

*M. L. Siemienowicz*

You stand on the platform with your back against a pillar. The railway tracks stretch from the station, overlapping then funnelling together between cluttered buildings. As you watch, a train grows from a black pinpoint into a small, dark face with headlights dulled by the rain. You want to run, but you tighten your grip on the handle of your suitcase and force yourself to hold the gaze of those lights.

Wind whips rain into your face, down under the overhang of the vast station roof. The gust of it taunts at your skin. As the train approaches, the wind rises, muffling the words of an older couple arguing behind you in French. Only a few others wait anywhere nearby: A man in a heavy coat, head bent against the wind; a teenager with a guitar case; a woman with raven dreadlocks who sits on an overstuffed backpack. The rest of the crowd huddles a long way back, away from the rain, but you wait here, where almost no one is near enough, where no one could touch you as the train heaves its way in, with you fixed in the headlights and not even noticing as it groans towards you that your free hand is clutching at the dead cold of the column behind you.

The man in the coat looks over, looks away, stares back along the platform. The woman with dreadlocks stands and pulls the sleeves of her jumper down over her hands. Your chest tightens around your hammering heart. A runnel of sweat stings down your spine. But she looks straight past you, to a clock suspended from the ceiling. Just a traveller, you tell yourself. Just like you, but with a backpack of knitted skirts instead of a cheap suitcase holding a jacket you will need to iron in Venice and two ties for you to decide between. No one looks in your direction. The train gasps to a stop and you let go of the column.

Prestige. That's why you committed to speak at this conference. You were barely back on your feet after all the time you had to take off; the invitation to speak was just what you needed to remind yourself that, despite your two thesis students being assigned other supervisors, despite your upcoming funding for a research assistant being quietly withdrawn, you still had material worth sharing. You will present work from a paper that is about to be published, that you submitted, was accepted, before all of this happened, and you are grateful to who you were then for helping yourself crawl out of this now.

The train is huge and still. The long row of windows is dark. You look down the platform but the crowd hangs back. The time still reads well before departure. Then a string of uniformed staff approaches. They vanish into the train, and one by one the lights blink on and you see them moving inside. Your hands are clammy. No one has touched you.

Six fifty-two. Almost seven o'clock. The sun is low and the buildings out past the station glow wet and red in its light. Six hundred and fifty-two, you think. You count backward in intervals of eleven. Six hundred and forty-one. Six-three-oh. Six-one-nine. Six-oh-eight. The attendants have swept the length of the train and are now unlatching the passenger doors. Five-nine-seven. Five-eight-six. You check your pocket for your ticket, then weave your way into the crowd. You are jostled by others as they line up to board. Five-three-one. Five-two-oh. There is a moment when, mounting the steps of the train, you look down and see the horrifying slit between the tread and the concrete edge of the platform. You lose count, push past the passenger in front and burst into the corridor before anything can reach up to drag at your feet.

Couchettes fill the train car in a long, repeating bank. Door after narrow door opens onto identical rooms, each a mirror of itself, with two facing rows of upholstered yellow seats. These are overhung by the uppermost bunks, which don't fold away like the ones below. Inside, passengers shove luggage onto racks or rummage through unzipped bags on the seats. There is chatter in French and Italian, occasionally a banal snatch of English. You drag your suitcase behind until you find your couchette. The door is low and you duck to step inside. You stow your suitcase and sit quickly, as far as you can from the window. On the facing bench sits an older woman with careful makeup, head leaning against the glass. Her face is bitter and she smells of cigarettes. You check your watch. Two past seven: seven-oh-two. You pull an iPod from the pocket of your jacket and set the headphones in your ears. You leave the sound off. Six-nine-one. Six-eight-oh. Six-six-nine.

A man with a canvas rucksack and his phone in his hand sits down across from you. He's wearing a woollen jumper but with shorts despite the cold, has tanned legs and light hair. He is blithe and self-assured against the fringes of the storm that bluster outside. He greets you and your sullen companion in

English. You lose count, nod back, rub the click wheel of your iPod as if you are scrolling through songs. You check the time. Start counting again.

The last to arrive is the woman with dreadlocks who had been up at the end of the platform with you. She shakes a printout of her reservation at Shorts, speaks with some kind of European accent. She tells him he's sitting in her seat. Shorts puts his hands up, no problem, and switches to the window seat beside you.

You shut your eyes as the train shudders into motion. You try to tell yourself that it's over, that you can relax now and enjoy the ride. Nothing happened, just as you really knew it would not. But you are wound tight, about the train and the talk. You are terrible speaking in public. Still, you had skimmed through the program when it was released online and marvelled at your name, a junior academic's, listed beside speakers you had read for your degree. The others in your department had swapped looks with raised eyebrows: three days to see an old friend in Paris, a short flight to Venice, the conference, your talk, and then five days free, watching the crowds over coffee and walking the cobbles and canals. So what will it be there, spring? End of winter? Their smiles were smiles of both relief and desperation. They all knew that if this managed to pull you together, they might be free of worrying whether you'll show up to work or be late to your lectures because you had to walk back across campus to check again if you had locked the door to your office.

It is this that has you sitting in the carriage of a train for the first time in eight months, breathing rancid cigarette smoke, now that storms have grounded your flight. Now, unless you take the overnight train, you won't make your time slot, won't give the talk you spent months preparing, and won't even earn the thing that made you spend the money and time to get to this side of the world in the first place: prestige. The train car sways, jolting you against the wall. You keep your eyes closed and try to focus on the count.

You are down to one-five-two when the door opens and an attendant steps in for your tickets. Dreads hands her the crumpled printout. Shorts digs in his rucksack, his knees apart. You take out your earphones and feel in your pockets.

When you look up at the attendant, you look into a pair of hard eyes, bright with green eye shadow. In one sickening rush you are back on the platform, eight months ago: the tug on your hand is just her, now, taking your ticket, but you jerk back your arm. You've lost count. Her eyes. The tug on your hand. In your head you hear—you remember—a stage whisper: *Let's go, Alice.* A woman's name? Why did she call you that? Let's go? Then there is you back then, pulled to your feet before you even felt it happen. No one around you moved; some looked on, idle, at this minor commotion while the rest gazed, mindless, along the tracks as the express train approached. The woman who gripped your hand had blonde hair with a taint of red like a faded bloodstain, and her eyes as she looked, urgent, over her shoulder were lined in moss-green makeup. Her face is locked in your memory. She was dragging you forward, and a shock shuddered through you as the train blared its horn over the level crossing. There were three steps left. You pulled back hard. Her fingers were locked between yours. She jerked you forward another two, then she jumped.

You were pulled to your knees, still gripping her hand. The train hit with another blast of the horn. The slam flung your arm across. Your eyes were shut and you felt the rush of air buffet your face and a thick spatter of warm rain over your skin. She was gone and in your head was nothing but her eyes with their brilliant green haloes. You were sprawled on the platform and, around you, you heard screaming as people realised that your fingers were still laced into hers. You were holding something like a sheathed umbrella, pale and capped in red, and the rain on your face tasted like copper.

Afterward, the police questioned you for more than an hour. Everyone at the train station had assumed that you knew her. You were terrified that they might think that you pushed her. You sat in a windowless room at the police station going over the details again and again. You thought of your own face in the rearview mirror of the police car, eyes wide and skin spattered with red rain. The officer who interviewed you was so calm you were furious, slammed your fist on the table, saying you'd been going to work, to the university, that that woman had nothing to do with you. They're waiting for you, you shouted. You're supposed to be interviewing for a research assistant and now you've missed the first candidate. This woman called you Alice, for fuck's sake. She had no idea what she was talking about. Eventually the cop asked you to wait and she left you, leaving the door ajar. You heard her describing you to someone else: *"He's worked up, but he's fine; the blonde grabbed him and jumped, she ended up between the train and the platform. He was left holding part of her arm. Looks like some random nut-case suicide."* Then a man opened the door of the interview room. He introduced himself as a counsellor and when you left you had his card in your wallet.

The train attendant smiles behind those awful green-brightened eyes. She hands back your reservation and thanks you in French. Her pale hair is tucked under an indigo cap and she wears a dark buttoned waistcoat. She has a shirt with sleeves that reach to the elbow and as she stretches forward to take papers from the woman by the window you imagine you see a trail of blood seeping from under one white cuff and running down the back of her forearm. You look away, run your hands through your hair. Stop thinking about it, you tell yourself. What's the time? But you look back regardless. The ruby streak is still there, really there, and the cuff of her shirt blooms with red.

You forget every word of the neat French politenesses you've been offering in shops and cafés on your trip. You call out, in English—"Watch out!"—and your voice is much louder and more urgent than you expect. Everyone looks at you. Madame, by the window, scowls in annoyance, says something in curt French that you don't understand. The attendant looks askance.

"Is there something the matter?" Her accent is thick.

You say: "Your arm, are you okay?"

She looks down, tilts her arm out with a frown. A drop of blood falls from the point of her elbow and lands in a black spot on the carpet. With her other hand, she wipes along her forearm, as if she thought she had brushed against something. Her fingers smear the blood along her skin in rich swathes.

She takes the ticket from Shorts. "Oh, man," he says. "Lady."

The attendant tugs her sleeve, turns her elbow out further. When she lets go she leaves livid red bands on the fabric. "What is the matter?"

You reach forward. "You're bleeding." You can hear your voice rising.

"I do not think so, monsieur."

You start to argue back. Dreads ducks her head, trying to see from the other side. Shorts takes back his ticket by one corner, inspects the paper with a grimace before stuffing it back in his rucksack. The attendant's cuff is now saturated with blood but she keeps shaking her head.

"Forget it," you say. Your head is tight. You are standing and edging around the attendant with your hands up away from her arm.

"There is no problem, monsieur," she smiles. She stretches out a bloody hand.

"Don't touch me!" You reach the door and stumble down the corridor, unsteady with the rocking of the train. Through the windows, flat fields flow past. The trees are low rounds flashing by in the late evening gloom. Some of the couchette doors are open to the corridor. Inside, people lounge, reading or listening to music. You pass low conversations as you stagger to the end of the car. Fluorescent lights flicker in the ceiling. You fold open the door to the toilet, push it closed behind, and fumble with the flimsy lock.

Leaning against the veneer, you feel the vibration of the train through your back. The space is so narrow that the walls press in. The air is dense with the smell of stale urine. Nausea seizes your gut and you crouch, sliding your back down the door. You flip up the lid of the toilet. The bowl has a hatch at its base that is open onto the tracks. In the twilight you can just make out the grey of the ballast streaming under you like foam on the crests of waves. Bile rises in your throat. You slam down the lid and grip the edge of the sink.

The mirror is a dull steel, the silvering flaking. Your face hovers behind the weathered surface, shifting with the sway of the train. The flecks on the mirror look like spattered blood on your face, and you put your hand to your mouth and nose, wipe your fingers down your chin to show yourself that your skin is clear. You splash water on your face, pumping the soap dispenser, and rubbing the slime onto your skin, just in case there really is something there to wash.

What did she want with you? Why did she jump? The questions are normal, you tell yourself, repeating the words of the doctor recommended by the counsellor on the business card, who you called when, three weeks after it happened, you still had not gone back to work. The questions are normal but they don't normally have answers. *Let's go,* you hear again in your head. You glance at your watch. Seven-five-three. Seven-four-two. You force yourself to stare at the mirror, turn your head back and forth and watch the marks on the glass float separate to your face. Seven-three-one. You lift your chin. Seven-two-oh. Seven-oh-nine. You bring your face closer to the mirror, flatten your palms against the glass. You are speaking out loud, urging yourself to hear the numbers: "Six-nine-eight, six-eight-seven, six-seven-six, six-six-five. Fuck." You wash your face again, rubbing the soap into a thick lather that smells like air freshener.

You dry your face on the sleeve of your jacket, walk back down the corridor. The flicker of the fluorescents casts the reflection of the couchette doors onto the windows. When you reach your couchette, Shorts has stepped out. You pull your suitcase down from the rack and take your tablet from the front pocket. Maybe reading will help.

You feel the others watching. Turning, you offer an appeasing smile. Dreads is twisting her thick, black hair into a knot, tying it back with a scarf. Someone has drawn a set of heavy beige curtains across the window. She asks, "Are you okay?" You wave a hand. Yes, you're fine. You shrug.

"That was ugly. Her arm," she says with disgust. "Are you afraid of blood?"

You shake your head, embarrassed. "Sorry. She just . . . reminded me of someone."

"That's okay." She smiles quizzically. "Are you sure you are okay?" You try to place her accent. Eastern European, you guess. You've never been very good at picking those out. You nod.

Madame has a French magazine open on her lap. The text is a scatter of cedillas and trémas. She is looking you over. You notice for the first time a bruise along one of her cheekbones. The hard line of her lipstick feels like a sneer. You look back at Dreads and tell her you might go down to find food. She smiles again and says sure. She never eats train food.

You take your tablet and cross through two other cars. Each is the same rumbling, swaying stretch of garish light. The solid grey of the couchette doors on one side, on the other a reflection over the inky black of what is now night through the windows. As you walk you feel the cold coming off the glass. An attendant in waistcoat and bow tie nears in the other direction, an older man with thinning hair. He narrows his eyes as you sidle past and, once you've crossed, you glance over your shoulder and see him standing in the doorway of a couchette, looking back along the corridor. You walk faster, tug open the dividing doors into the next car.

Shorts is standing in the foyer of the dining car, talking on his phone. As you near, you make eye contact. You nod in acknowledgement but he keeps on talking, staring straight through you.

The wait staff in the dining room wear black shirts and trousers. Three of them are milling between the tables, clearing crockery or delivering plates. You take the nearest empty table and put down your tablet. The woman who brings your menu is the attendant from your couchette, changed into black, her eyes rimmed in the same green makeup. You avoid making eye contact and, as you look over the menu, you hear your bunkmate talking behind.

"I'm at work; you can't just call me like this," says Shorts to his phone. "No. We've moved in together and you're in my place, so you do things my way— What? You're still at home? When is your interview? So? Get the train in—No, don't 'Alex' me. Just listen. It doesn't matter to me if you just sit around doing nothing. It's up to me to earn our money. But I thought you wanted to do this research thing. You should work at something for yourself. It's good for you."

You finger the edge of the menu. Alex? What if that's what she said? Not Alice, but Alex. Maybe she knew someone called Alex. You want to call your doctor. You have her number, for emergencies; before you left for this trip you talked thoroughly through how you would deal with your travel. You won't need to use the trains, you told her. Now you're just glad that you can't see the world rushing past through the black in the dining car windows.

The two of you had decided you would start slowly. Go to the station, watch the platform from across the road. Leave when you wanted, before any trains came through. Graded self-exposure, she called it. In her clinic you had tried to prepare for the process, closing your eyes and imagining walking, looking along the platform and down to the tracks. She would ask you to rate your anxiety. One, very little. Five, just coping. Eight, nine, ten. That's enough. Stop. Walk away from the platform. You would open your eyes and look at your doctor, who sat across from you, hands folded around her pen. Eleven, you always wanted to say. Eleven.

You pull your phone from your pocket and turn on the screen. No reception. Although what does it matter; it's just after four in the morning back home. You shouldn't call now. You had a flashback, that's all. The worst is over. In fact, you did well. This does not fit the definition of an emergency.

The server returns for your order. You manage to look at her as you speak. She *does* have the same makeup, the same copper blonde hair, but she is not the same woman. She's younger, has a dimple under one eyebrow from an old piercing. She walks back through the car. About half of the tables are full. Mostly older couples. You hear Italian, German. On the other side of the aisle, near the end of the car where a grimy bain-marie case stands empty, a middle-aged woman slaps her hand on the table and tells her little girl to *sit still, for God's sake.* The child is twisting around in her chair, holding a blue lollipop in one hand.

In the foyer, Shorts is still holding his phone to his ear. "I don't have time to deal with your dramas. You'll have to work this out on your own," he says. He hangs up and heads away down the corridor, elbowing his way past Madame, who walks into the dining room with her French magazine under her arm. She passes you and sits a few seats back.

You switch on your tablet and open a folder of journal articles that you had saved with the intention of skimming them again one last time before your talk. You are slated at the end of the morning session. With a start you realise that this is only a few hours away. Tomorrow. You flick to your presentation, open the file and begin to click through the slides. But you struggle to bring your well-rehearsed patter to mind. You mouth your opening words, and then lose the next line, distracted by the conversations around you. Concentration is still a problem for you.

Witness survivor. That's what they call you. Someone who has witnessed a violence. You went through all the typical experiences expected of the label they gave you. The anger. The compulsions. The checking behaviour. The desperate longing for answers. All you ever found out about the blonde woman at the station was that she had been a part-time student with another faculty at your university. Her name had been on the long list for the assistant interviews, although her minimal resume did not make the final cut. She was survived by a nameless sister and mother. Survived. As if somehow her existence had been a violence in itself. No Facebook, no Twitter, no more answers to your questions.

Your dinner is a grey steak cooling under a congealed sauce. You check the time on your tablet, then your watch. Check it again on your phone. You have a message, although the bars are still showing no reception. It's a voicemail alert. You call the service, wondering if you might get lucky. The mailbox does connect and you dial through the menus. The message starts with silence. Then a woman's voice:

"Alice? Are you ignoring me? Alex?"

You hang up, put the phone face down on the table. Take a breath. Look at the colourless meat on your plate. You slice a forkful of steak and hold it up, not quite able to put it into your mouth. You glance to the foyer of the dining car. Still empty. The low voices of the other travellers are a complex murmur around you. You look for Madame, see a bored looking business woman with her head over her plate, a grey-haired couple both staring across the aisle at the night-inked windows. There is no sign of her and you are no longer sure where you thought she had sat.

Alice, you think. Alex? You turn your phone over and call the mailbox again. There is still no reception but again you connect. You dial to the message, try to make out which name is being used. You play the recording over and over but every time you just hear what you want. You think "Alex," you hear it. You play it again, thinking "Alice," and you hear it. *Are you ignoring me?* Your finger hovers over the button to delete but then you play it through one more time. Just a wrong number, you think. That's all it is.

Then a voice hisses in your ear: "Let's go."

You drop your phone to the table with a clatter. Behind you, the mother is pulling her little girl by the arm. "Let's go," she repeats and the child trundles along behind, still holding the lollipop in one fist. As they reach the foyer, the little girl turns in a flounce of pigtails. She sticks her tongue out at you, stained filthy black, and turns to follow her mother.

Eight twenty-seven. Eight-one-six. Eight-oh-five. Another hour and a half and the train stops in Dijon. You'll get off and find a hotel. Call your doctor. Six in the morning back home. There might be a bus to Venice at daybreak. If you call the conference organisers first thing, they may even reschedule you to the following day. Can they do that? Does that happen? You look at the list of articles you should be reading. You have no idea.

Sliding your phone back into a pocket, you turn off your tablet and stand. The remains of your steak are a small carnage on your plate. You leave the hubbub of the dining car and head back to your couchette. The lights still flicker in the corridors. You are counting down to Dijon. You feel better.

When you open the door, Madame is back by the window, sitting wilted as if she had never left. When you had seen a bruise, a new graze reddens her cheek like rouge and her eye is now swollen shut. Shorts is sitting across from her, reading his phone. He smiles as you sit down: "Dinner any good?"

You've had better, you tell him. Then you lower your voice, although you're not sure that the woman across the aisle can understand you anyway.

"What happened to her?" you ask.

He looks over. "Shit!" he hisses. "What the fuck?"

Madame has a quilted cosmetics bag open on her lap, brimming with plastic cases of lipstick and eye shadow. She dabs her finger in a jar and smooths lotion onto her face. Her swollen eye is blushing blue on purple, deepening as you watch. As she rubs at her skin, she opens up a gash on her eyebrow, which weeps a trickle of red down her bloated lid.

*"Je suis désolé, madame,"* you say. "I hope you don't mind us talking. *Est-ce que ça va?*"

She blinks. "Sorry," she says. "I don't speak French. But sure, talk all you want."

You look around her for that French magazine. You try to remember what she had said when they came to get the tickets. You apologise again, in English. She shrugs and digs through her cosmetics. You think of Shorts on the phone, berating his girlfriend. He was talking about some kind of research position. Your empty stomach clenches tight.

You turn to Shorts. "You got reception out there, then?" you ask, your voice level.

He shakes his head. "Nothing since Paris—you got some?"

You steel yourself. It feels as if the next thing he says will either break through the night like a light switch or lock down the churning storm, with you on a train careening helpless inside. You are ready. "You were on your phone back there," you say.

He shrugs. "Nah, not me."

"I mean back near the dining car. When I went past to eat. You were there talking on your phone."

He smiles and draws his brows together. "I don't get you. I didn't eat on the train. I had something before I got on."

"I didn't mean—" You break off, watch his face. He really seems to have no idea. "Forget it," you say. You smile, lean over with your hand out and give your name.

Shorts grips your hand. "Dan," he says.

"Dan," you repeat, nodding. You lean back in your seat. The storm howls mutely beyond the beige curtains. "You know what, I have some reading. I might go back and maybe get some dessert."

You stand, pull a sheaf of registration papers from your suitcase. There are three black drops on the carpet between the benches where it could have been that a woman stood with her arm bleeding below her sleeve. You duck back into the corridor. Shorts stands as you leave, leans on the doorframe.

"If you pass one of the staff, get them to come and make up the bunks, hey?"

You nod, sure, salute him with your papers. Your face feels hot. You wipe a hand across your mouth and chin, check your palm. Clean. You're not hungry and you have no intention of reading anything. You hold on to the smooth security of the registration papers, look up at the fluorescent tube mounted on the ceiling by your door. The light is dazzling, and when you look back at the glossy black of the window, the after shadows of the light throw blind smears on your vision and the reflection of your face is a void on the image of your body. Down the corridor you hear a murmuring chatter from a group of travellers outside their couchette. You blink, peer at your watch. You can just make out the time. Nine-oh-nine. About three quarters of an hour until you stop in Dijon. You'll sit for a while in the dining car, then come back for your suitcase. You really should wash your face again. Eight-nine-eight. Eight-eight-seven. With each count you turn back time another notch. Take off another eleven. Another ration of fear. Eight-seven-six. Eight-six-five.

"Hey," says Dreads behind you. You guess she has come back from the toilets; she has a little tote over her shoulder.

"Oh, hi," you say. "I was just—"

"Oh my God." She is standing in the doorway. "What happened to your face?"

Madame gazes blankly from her seat, a compact open in her hand.

"Hang on," you tell Dreads. "Just come here for a second." You step away from the doorway.

"What happened?"

"I don't know. It's the same as before with the attendant. She doesn't know." You gesture helplessly at your own face. "Just wait. Can you listen to something for me?"

Dreads digs her fingers under her scarf and scratches her hair. "What?"

"Just listen." You tuck your registration papers under your arm, pull your phone from your pocket and click on the speaker. You dial your voicemail, which connects like before. "It shouldn't even be able to do that," you say. Dreads doesn't answer, just looks from your face to your phone. The message runs.

Dreads narrows her eyes. "Alice?" she asks. "No—Alex. What is she saying?" She looks at you. "Is that you?"

"No—do you think that's a wrong number?" You play it through again.

"What else could it be?"

"It's just . . . I don't know." You hang up on the message. You are suddenly angry.

Dreads is staring through the doorway, where Madame is gazing back at you both through one good eye. Dreads shakes her head. "What about him? Have you talked to him? Dan?"

*Alex,* you think. "I tried," you say. "I don't trust— I don't think he understands. Anymore. Look, I'm getting off in Dijon."

"What's going on?" asks Dreads.

Down the corridor, the cluster of travellers spreads out to let another light-haired attendant out from their couchette. They file into their room, emptying the corridor around her. "I don't know what's happening," she says. "But we can't stand here and say nothing." She walks towards the attendant.

"Wait!" you shout.

*"Excusez-moi?"* asks Dreads. She reaches the woman, who turns with a bland smile. "We need help. With a passenger."

"Alice," says the attendant. Her voice is soft with hatred. You take a step towards them as she continues. "Why are you even coming to me now? You turned your back on everyone."

"Don't you throw that in my face." Dreads's tone is suddenly cold and dead, like glass. Her hair is pitch dark beside the attendant's blonde. "She's my mother too, and I don't care any less than you do. You said I betrayed her when I moved out; you're just doing the same thing now. That's fine. Run to Alex. Run to your rich, dickhead boyfriend. Just don't expect anything from me."

The attendant shakes her head: "That's bullshit. You never gave a shit about Mum. That man is a fucking monster. Go over for once. See for yourself what he did to her face."

Dreads shoves her away and shoulders back past you so you're standing between them. "She's not my problem to fix," she calls back. "For years I told her she had to get out. I'm finished trying to make her listen. When you fall down, you just have to pick yourself up. Mum used to say that. Well, that's what I'm doing. I'm done." She slams the door to your couchette.

The attendant leans forward and screams: "Fuck you, Alice." Then the two of you are alone. As the rumble of the train wheels thrums below your feet, you realise that you had not been able to hear either of their accents at all. The storm is out there and you know somehow that now it will never end. You look the attendant full in the face.

"It's you," you say.

She widens her eyes and strides towards you. You back away down the corridor, away from the direction of the dining car. All the doors are closed and she hurries you backwards, pulling up so close that you can feel the warmth from her breath in your face. Another attendant, another face, eyes shining from surrounds of green, but you see now that every one of them is really the same. All of their faces, no matter their features, are just the blushed blonde with a pair of green-rimmed eyes from the platform. One of her sleeves has a pencil-thin tracing of russet in a tide-line above her cuff, as if a stain had been imperfectly washed. She cocks her head.

You take another step back and come up against the handles of the door to the next car.

"What do you want with me?" you ask.

She smiles, head still cocked. There is blood between her teeth.

"What were you arguing about with the backpacker?"

"Alex?" she asks. "I tried to call you."

You shake your head. "You have to leave me alone. I'm not who you think I am. I'm getting off in Dijon. I'm sorry for what happened to you. But I can't help you."

"Alice?" she asks. She makes a hard nodding motion with her head, which lolls forward so her chin hits her chest. Then she turns her neck to the side and her head rolls after, her ear to her shoulder. She looks up at you from the corner of her eye and says, "Let's go."

You turn and wrench open the dividing doors and stumble through into the next car. You run past door after narrow, steel door. The lights stutter overhead. You want to count the cars as you run, further and further away from your couchette, from your suitcase, from the dining car. You want a number trail to tell you how to get back. But the pound of your feet on the hard carpet pushes everything else out of your head and you only break stride to wrestle open each set of dividing doors. Your chest burns and your legs throb. You reach another bathroom door and feel a flooding urge to close yourself in, to wrap yourself safe in the machine. You stop and look back. Nothing but an empty corridor, steel grey wall mirrored in the windows onto the night. You're breathing hard and you press your forehead against the plastic laminate, one palm and one fist full of papers up against the wall.

As your breath slows, you feel the shudder of the floor under you feet. You can no longer sense which way the train is heading. You push off the wall and your palm feels wet. You look up. Where your hand has been pressed is a streaked imprint in red. You close your eyes and ball your fist around the painless wet. That's enough. You need to wash your hands.

You push open the door to the toilet and start. A man has his back to you. In the mirror, you see the face of the balding attendant you passed in the corridor before dinner. He has his indigo waistcoat unbuttoned and is leaning forward on the sink, sweeping green eye shadow over his lids. There is a copper blonde wig in a flattened heap on the counter. He meets your eyes in the mirror and looks back ahead, closes one eye and dusts the little brush across his skin. You back out, trying to pull the door closed. It won't latch from the outside and your hand smears blood on the handle as you fumble. You push through the next pair of dividing doors and the corridor opens up onto the dining car. You groan. You can't have reached here. You were running the other way.

In the dining car, the centre lights are off for the night. The place is lit only by a string of small downlights in the bulkheads over the windows. In the gloom, four attendants sit around a table at empty plates. Their hunched backs and pale faces are reflected in the windows, the opposing walls of black glass sending the table, the figures, the pale crockery extending out in flanks of repeated reflections. The rear of the car is lost in the dark and, to either side, those reflected cars stretch to eternity. The attendant sitting facing you looks up, meets your eyes, and it feels like it takes a fraction of a second before her reflections in the wings lift their own heads after.

You take a step back, your eyes on the table as the glass doors clamp shut in front of your face.

"Alex?"

You spin. The corridor is empty. From a couchette partway along comes the sound of something heavy dropping to the floor. You run to it, hear the latch slide closed. You batter your fist against the door. "Open up," you shout. "What are you doing?" You look along the corridor and see the next door open a crack. "Wait!" you call. The door closes as you reach it.

You stride along the car, pounding on each door as you pass. You leave a spatter of blood with every fall of your fist. "Who's in there? What do you want?" No one answers. Behind one door you hear panting, then silence. Behind another, muffled sobs. You need to find someone outside of this, someone who can tell you that you are on a train to Venice, that you will arrive in the morning to give your presentation. You move down, and after hammering on the last door of the car you stand with your feet apart, fist clenched. You hear muffled voices, or one voice, talking under its breath. You pound again, on the smear of blood you left the first time. The voice lifts: "Alice? Is that you? What's the time?"

You stand back. "Come out. This is over."

"What's the time?" the voice asks again. The tone is exasperated, angry. You look at your watch—fourteen past ten—and hammer again on the door. "When are we stopping in Dijon?" you shout. "We should have stopped already. We should have been there by now." Ten-one-four. Ten-oh-three. Nine-nine-two. You lose count.

The door opens and the attendant is standing inside, head cocked like before. All four bunks are set, mounded with tousled sheets spilled over with red. You grab her by the shoulder, keep your eyes locked on her sidelong face to stop yourself looking past her at the shapes under the sheets. You shake her as you hiss in her face: "Why didn't we stop in Dijon?"

She looks up from her shoulder. "When you fall down, you just have to pick yourself up."

Then, behind her, the window of the cabin shatters. The sound is a boom in the night, lights every nerve in your body like a fuse. The air in the cabin sucks out through the window and you stumble against her. She stands solid, her cocked head staring past, her shoulder forward into your weight. The air rushes past you, flurrying your hair. You push her away and stumble back into the corridor, continue away from the dining car. An explosion of glass starts beside you and tears down the length of the car as the corridor windows disintegrate. You lose the reflection that locked you into the train and the night opens up with a roar. You are at the dividing doors that should lead you back the way you came. You wrench them open with a slick, red hand, still clutching the sheaf of papers in the other, and step into an anteroom at the back of the car. There is no next carriage. Where there should have been the next doors and the corridor back to your things is a flat, black window out onto the night. Your reflection for a moment is a young woman with copper blonde hair. This, then, you think is how you find out. The glass goes with a scream, hanging for an instant as a network of shatter lines before the back of the train is open. Beyond the end of the car, in the light that spills out, the tracks flash past, either streaming out from or being dragged under the end of the train. You can't tell. The wind pouring around you is a directionless chaos. Behind you, the doors are jerked open a crack. The attendant reaches her arm through the gap. They close across her elbow and she slams her body against the door alongside, her cocked face against the glass.

You watch the reaching arm, fingers opening and closing, as you stagger back against the windowsill. Turning, you lean out through the frame. The rhythmic thump of the wheels on the rails pounds in your ears like a frantic heart. The storm sucks at your clothes. You see rungs fixed into the rear of the car. You brace and lift a foot onto the ledge. Your fistful of papers flaps in the drag. The doors hiss open behind you, then crack back together over the attendant's arm. You hear a thud.

You can't climb while still holding the registration papers. You open your fist and they catch in the wind, are tossed up and around in a flutter of white before they are jerked into the darkness along the tracks. You don't see where they land. Then, with the clamour of the night in your ears, you pull yourself up and lean out to grasp the nearest rung.

The climb is a push against the buffet of the storm. The rungs press sharp through the soles of your shoes. They are cold and thin in your hands and you think about them pulling loose with your weight, of you being jerked out into the night like a sheaf of papers. They hold. You reach the roof. The air here is a flood of cold in the icy light of the moon that glints off the dirty silver of the train car. From the centre of the roof protrudes a low, square mount. You crawl towards it, the car too narrow, the wind too strong, until you are kneeling, looking down at the slow spin of a ventilation fan turning under a grate. You must have cut yourself climbing through the broken glass; darkness seeps through the sleeve of your jacket, down along your forearm from your elbow. You lower yourself to sit facing the end of the train, your fingers hooked into the grate behind you against the pummel of the wind.

Out from under the fluorescents, the night is grey. A weak surround of light spills from the cars, lighting the slope of the ballast. Beyond that, everything is hazed over by silver moonlight that picks out shapes—flat fields and studded trees—but not texture, so everything is cold and smooth. You can't see the moon through the press of glowing cloud.

The roar of the wind begins to fade. When it falls to a whisper, you let go of the grate and push up into standing. The tracks are being swallowed under the end of the train in a thick, gleaming band. Behind you, the chain of cars vanishes into the dark.

*Alice,* you think. Raven-haired, hateful Alice. Smoking weed in her bedroom with the stereo up to drown out the arguments downstairs. Setting herself free while someone, her sister—you—lay in the next room straining to make out the words of the fight. Not that they mattered, given the rules for your mother seemed to change every time. She was able to do something wrong no matter what she did. Alice once told you that it was your fault they fought. Your fault he hit her. That Alice remembers how angry he used to get when you cried as a baby through the night. Alice. Washing her hands of the problem the day that your mother's face was finally so bruised it could never have been the stairs or whatever it was she used to tell people who asked. You realise now that probably no one ever had asked.

And then Alex, coming into the café where you worked around lectures, while you wondered if you were ready to change subjects, change degree, change to doing something you really cared about. Alex would come in just before closing, when you were wiping down the counters or mopping the floors, and sometimes buy nothing, but smile and tell you how nice you looked with your hair pale like a ghost. Alex, coming in week after week, until you were listening to his promises and forgiving his temper and relishing his attention and living in his apartment and turning into your mother.

Then you applied for that research assistant job, the one through that young professor who takes the course you wish you had signed up for from the beginning. They didn't list you for an interview, and you were so afraid to tell Alex in case he was too angry you had failed. But maybe there still is some way to make it. You'll get the train in, ask to talk to the professor. There might be some way to make him understand. You see his face. He can help you. *Let's go,* you think. You spread your arms. You reach for him, call out. The track is pouring out of the night and vanishing under the train.

# Must Be This Tall to Ride

## *Seanan McGuire*

There is a point at which sound becomes a physical thing with teeth and claws, slashing wildly at everything around it. Briana held the strap of her purse a little tighter and tried to stand fast against the assault coming from all sides, the fangs of the world biting into the soft flesh of her ears, dazing her and slowing her down.

"Come *on*, slowpoke!"

Her sister's hand grasped her elbow, tugging her deeper into the midway, refusing to yield to the sound. Briana didn't fight. It was easier if she let Cindy pick the direction and guide their activities. That way all Briana had to do was keep her knees from buckling as the roaring of the world crashed down on her head.

"Where are we going?" she asked.

"Anywhere! Everywhere! Loosen up, Bri. We're having an adventure!"

Briana—who would have been happier if adventure had been something that happened to other people and left her out of it—didn't say anything. She just held on.

The kids from school would have been amazed to see them now, the Harris kids at the carnival, both of them running through the crowds like they belonged, like they wanted to be there. Briana felt a little smug about that. Everything was too loud and too bright and too *much,* but she was still there, still a part of the scene that was unfolding all around them. None of the people in this crowd were going to whisper behind their hands about how sad it was for Cindy to have a freak for a sister, or how lucky their parents were to have at least one ordinary daughter, one daughter worth the effort required to love her.

Never mind that Cindy didn't think there was anything wrong with Briana. Never mind that Briana was perfectly happy to be who she was, and couldn't imagine wanting to be anyone else. She was still, and would always be, a social millstone dragging her sister to the bottom of the lake when she could have been skimming the surface like a queen. It couldn't be helped.

But here they were despite it all, running through the summer carnival like they didn't have a care in the world. It had appeared in the empty Target parking lot across from their hotel overnight, seeming to burst out of the concrete already assembled and ready to beguile. Their parents, worn out from escorting two teenage girls with radically differing ideas of "fun" across America's heartland—a road trip that had seemed inspired when it began, and now seemed simply endless, the sort of thing devised as a punishment for some unspeakable crime—had been quick to press money into their hands and shoo them away, seeing the promise of peace in the sunlight glittering off the Ferris wheel.

It was early enough in the day that the crowds were thin, at least compared to what they would swell into as the afternoon ripened toward evening, and while the sound and spectacle was still enough to make Briana's head spin, she could handle it if she kept her eyes on her sister and didn't try to look around.

Cindy, who had been guiding Briana through the world for their entire lives, didn't let go or slow down as she plunged forward, hauling her precious cargo in her wake like the world's blondest, bubbliest tugboat.

"I want to ride the Scrambler," announced Cindy gleefully. "And the roller coaster. And the centrifuge. And the Ferris wheel. And—"

"We don't have that many tickets, and we don't have the money for that many tickets."

"Well, I want to ride as many of them as I *can*."

Briana closed her eyes, letting Cindy pull her along, and did the silent math of the carnival's costs in the comforting dark. She stumbled, but didn't fall; she opened her eyes again. "We can both do two rides, and then you can do one on your own. After that, we have to go back and shake Dad down for more cash."

Cindy snorted. Their father would talk about how neither of them appreciated the value of a dollar, how when he'd been their age he'd held down a steady afterschool job and graduated high school ready to make his own way in the world, and then he would hand them each another twenty dollars, because he wanted their teen years to be happier than his had been. It was a predictable dance. She was fairly sure he'd given them insufficient funds entirely so they'd come back and verify that the carnival was both safe and enjoyable, rather than running off to the movies or something when they stopped having fun.

Control of the finances was a viable way to maintain control over his twin daughters, but sometimes it was more annoying than he could possibly know.

"I don't want to ride the roller coaster," said Briana. "So we could start there, and then do the rides we *do* want to ride together?"

"Sounds good," said Cindy, and changed her trajectory, now hauling her sister toward the rickety wooden frame of the coaster. It sucked to ride solo, but it would have sucked even more not to ride at all, and Briana didn't coaster. She'd tried once, on their ninth birthday, verified that it was too much—the sound, the speed, the screaming, all of them mixing together into something she could neither enjoy nor endure—and since then, Cindy had either been riding alone or with other friends.

It was okay. There were things Briana could do that Cindy couldn't, like finish her homework on time, and missing a few coaster rides was a small thing in the annals of sisterly sins. As long as they could share the Ferris wheel, everything else was negotiable.

Cindy stopped running. Briana stopped in turn, raising her eyebrows.

"Looks like nobody else wants to ride either," she said, and glanced around at the crowd. "Maybe they know something we don't . . . ?"

"It's lunchtime," said Cindy. "Nobody rides a roller coaster at lunchtime." Her grin was wicked, sharp as a dart in a carnie's hand. "Good thing I haven't eaten yet. Come on!" She ran into the empty corral that was meant to contain a queue, and currently contained nothing but the bored-looking carnival employee who leaned against the coaster's controls, a baseball cap jammed down over her curly black hair.

Briana followed more reluctantly, and saw the moment when the carnie spotted Cindy, straightened, and put on her professional liar's face. She frowned. It was odd for a carnie to stand that straight all because two townie girls were on the approach.

Then again, so much about this carnival was odd. The rides were rickety, with peeling paint and blown-out bulbs. They were also overly large, more like something from an amusement park than the sort of rides she expected to see assembled in a parking lot overnight. The coaster even had an inversion loop, and a tunnel. Who did that at a carnival? How was that safe?

"Welcome to the Jaws of Death," said the girl, rapid-fire, accent an indistinguishable mix of a dozen states. She had Indiana vowels and Alabama declensions and while she might have been a linguist's dream, to Briana's ears she was blurry, like the lines of her weren't quite drawn correctly. "Two?"

"One," said Cindy, unslinging her purse and thrusting it at Briana. "My sister doesn't like roller coasters."

"Some people don't," said the girl philosophically. She shrugged. "There's always the Ferris wheel."

"Yes, there is," said Cindy. She took a step toward the coaster, still holding out her purse.

Briana grabbed her arm. "No."

Cindy stopped, blinking. "What do you mean?"

"I mean *no.* I mean let's go ride the Ferris wheel." Briana tugged. "It's . . . it's not right. Something isn't right." It was in the shape of the coaster, the way it arched against the sky. The way it wasn't moving. All the other rides were moving. This one should have been moving too, should have been seasoning the air with screams that hurt her ears. It wasn't. It was wrong.

"Honey . . ." Cindy deftly worked her arm free, somehow shifting her purse into Briana's hand in the same smooth gesture. "I get that you don't like roller coasters, honest I do. But you need to chill. I'll be back in five minutes, tops." She whirled then, holding a fistful of bills out to the carnie. "One, please."

"I'm sorry," said the carnie. "We only take tickets here."

Cindy's face fell, and Briana's heart leapt up to catch it. It was going to be okay. *It was going to be okay.* Cindy wouldn't ride, and they would walk away, and—

"But since you're my first customer of the day, why don't you have one on the house?" The carnie continued smiling her midway-dart smile as she gestured grandly toward the coaster train. "Your chariot awaits."

Briana grabbed for Cindy's arm again. It was too late. Cindy was past listening to her objections, past caring about what she wanted: Cindy was going to ride, and it was going to be glorious. She dropped herself into the car and pulled the safety bar down over her head, and if the carnie's smile was a sharpened dart, hers was a balloon, bright and beautiful and ready to burst.

"Away we go," intoned the carnie, and jabbed her finger down on the button that would send the train creaking down the track, gathering speed as it went.

Briana clutched her sister's purse against her chest and watched the train move, unable to shake the feeling that something was terribly, impossibly wrong. The sounds of the carnival seemed almost muffled now, heard through a wall of cotton, not nearly as overwhelming as her dread.

The train slipped into the tunnel's mouth, vanishing from sight. The carnie turned to face Briana, removing her hat so that her hair cascaded down in a cotton candy cloud, and she wasn't smiling now, no, she wasn't smiling at all, although her mouth was still a dart waiting to be thrown. Everything about her was a weapon, and all of her was aimed at Briana.

"The track broke," she said matter-of-factly, like this made all the sense in the world. "Seven years ago. It broke, and the train came off the rails and slammed into the loading area. Everyone on the train died, along with two carnies. You would have heard about it on the news, if you'd been from around here. You would never have stopped to ride a coaster at this carnival, because you'd know we didn't have one."

Briana's legs were rotten timbers, shaking, threatening to drop her to the ground, even as they refused to let her move.

"It's funny, though," continued the carnie. "Sometimes a big enough blood sacrifice comes with certain . . . compensation. People like to make jokes about carnivals being dangerous, but the fact is, it wasn't their fault. Wasn't *our* fault. There was a flaw in the steel, nothing the safety checks could have caught. It could have happened to anyone. It could have happened to *Disneyland.* I guess we drew the low card in the deck that day—but since then, there haven't been any accidents. There haven't been any deaths. There haven't even been any major injuries. Except . . ." The carnie looked, meaningfully, to the coaster.

In the distance, Briana could hear her sister's joyful screams. They weren't terrified yet. That part was coming.

"You're lying," Briana said, even though she knew the woman wasn't. No line for the roller coaster on the first day of the carnival, the way the sound of the midway was muffled, like the world was far away. This was a bad place. This was a wrong place.

"If you like," said the carnie. "That would be the easy choice."

"Choice?" asked Briana.

"I don't usually get two people on the platform, so yeah, choice." Calmly, the carnie looked at Briana and asked, "Does the train crash into the parking lot or the platform? Heads she dies, tails you do. Choose. Or decide this is a lie, and walk away.

That's a choice too. Blood sacrifices have to be renewed. Once every seven years, there has to be a reminder of what we've paid, and what doesn't have to happen anymore."

"If the train crashes into the platform, you'll die too."

"Too late for that. I said two carnies died, remember?" The carnie turned, seeming to track the progress of the train with the motion of her head. "Now I make sure the sacrifice gets renewed. I keep us safe. Almost out of time. Choose."

Briana knew which choice she was *supposed* to make, the choice the stories had been sketching out for her since she was old enough to understand that she was odd: She's supposed to say that she's the strange one, she's the one who doesn't quite fit in, and stand aside in favor of her sister, who could live a normal life without all the tangles and trappings of Briana's neurology. She also knew that supposed to or not, she couldn't live with being the reason her sister was gone, and Cindy—normal or not—could never live with being the reason Briana was dead. Cindy was the only reason she was standing there for the train to crush. One way or the other, one of them wound up with blood on her hands, and all to pay—

To pay.

Briana smiled, looking at the carnie, and said, "No."

The carnie blinked. "What?"

"No. I don't know if you're a ghost or a demon, and I don't care. Cindy took a ride because you told her she could have one. She didn't pay for it. You said that sometimes a blood sacrifice comes with compensation. Well, everyone who died on the train paid to be there. Everyone who died on the platform worked for the carnival. You made contracts. You made promises. Cindy didn't. She lives, and I live, and I take my sister *home*."

Briana was shaking by the end, her hands clenched by her sides and her heart pounding.

The carnie blinked again. Then, slowly, she smiled that sharpened-dart smile and said, "Clever. You ever want a job, little girl, just climb to the top of the nearest Ferris wheel and convince yourself that you can fly."

Then she was gone, winked out in an instant, leaving the roller coaster unattended.

Briana made a sound that was somewhere between a scream and a squeal as she launched herself at the controls. The train came rolling around the corner. She slammed her hand down on the stop button and it rolled safely up to the platform, its lone passenger laughing through the tangle of her hair. The sounds of the carnival rushed back in, returning to their previous volume, and Briana fought the urge to clap her hands over her ears.

Cindy kept laughing as she climbed out of the train and walked to where Briana waited. She frowned, slowing to a stop.

"Where's the ride operator?" she asked.

"I'll tell you when we get back to the hotel," said Briana. She grabbed Cindy's hand, pulling her away from the roller coaster that wasn't there, and this time she was the one pulling her sister through the crowd, keeping her safe from all its dangers, and she didn't look back, not even once. Not even once.

On the platform, the carnie reappeared, hat once again seated firmly on her head, and leaned against the platform housing the ride's controls. The season was young; there was plenty of time to pay for another seven years of good luck. And if there was one thing every carnival kid learned early, it was that nothing would ever replace word of mouth. Those girls would *talk.* The thrill seekers and the ghost hunters would listen, and they would come, and sooner or later, one of them would split off from the herd, would see a ride that wasn't there, would hand over their ticket. Over and over, until it was time to let someone else get away, to set the lure again.

"You must be at least this tall to ride," she said, and laughed.

Outside on the midway, the Ferris wheel turned, and the crowd roared on.

# The Surviving Child

*Joyce Carol Oates*

**1.**

The surviving child, he is called. Not to his face—of course.

The other, younger child died with the mother three years before. *Murder, suicide* it had been. More precisely *Filicide, suicide.*

The first glimpse she has of the surviving child is shocking to her: a beautiful face, pale and lightly freckled, darkly luminous eyes, a prematurely adult manner—solemn, sorrowful, wary and watchful.

Sharp as a sliver of glass piercing her heart comes the thought—*I will love him. I will save him. I am the one.*

"Stefan! Say hello to my friend—"

No comfortable way for Stefan's father to introduce her, the father's fiancée, to the surviving child. Presumably Alexander has been telling Stefan about her, preparing him. *I am thinking of remarrying. I have met a young woman I would like you to meet. I think you will like her, and she will—she will like you.* . . . No way to express such thoughts that is not painful.

Seeing the apprehension in the child's face. Wondering if, since the mother's death, the father has introduced Stefan to other women whom he has invited to the house; or if Stefan has chanced to see his father with a woman, one who might be expected to take the mother's place.

But Elisabeth is not jealous of other women. Elisabeth is not envious of other women. Elisabeth is grateful to have been plucked from obscurity by the gentlemanly man who is her fiancé, the widower of the (deceased) (notorious) poet N.K.

Stooping to shake the child's small-boned hand. Hearing herself say brightly, reassuringly, "Hello, Stefan! So nice to meet you. . . ." Her voice trails off. She is smiling so hard her face hurts. Hoping the child will not shrink from her out of shyness, dislike, or resentment.

Stefan is ten years old, small for his age. It is terrible to think (the fiancée thinks) how small this delicately boned child had to have been three years before when his mother had tried to kill him along with his little sister and herself.

Alexander told her how the boy stopped growing for months after the trauma. Very little appetite, sleep disturbed by nightmares, wandering the house in the night. Disappearing into the house in broad daylight so that the father and the housekeeper searched for him calling his name—*Stefan! Stefan!*—until suddenly Stefan would appear around a corner, on a staircase, in a corridor blinking and short of breath and unable to explain where he'd been.

Almost asphyxiated by the mother. Heavily sedated with barbiturates as well. Yet somehow, he'd been spared.

Stefan had not cried in the aftermath of the trauma, or not much—"Not what you'd expect under the circumstances."

*Under the circumstances!* Elisabeth winced at Alexander's oddly unfeeling remark.

The fiancée has been introduced to the child as Elisabeth,

but the child cannot call her that name of course. Nor can the child call her Miss Lundquist. In time, when Elisabeth and the child's father are married, the child will learn to call her—what? Not Mother. Not Mom. *Mommy?* Will that ever be possible?

(Elisabeth has no idea what the child called his mother. It is very difficult to imagine the elusive poet N.K. as any child's mother let alone as *Mom, Mommy.*)

Those wary, watchful eyes. How like a fledgling bird in its nest Stefan is, prepared to cringe at a gliding shadow. A parent-bird, or a predator that will tear him to pieces? The fledgling can't know which until it is too late.

Yet politely Stefan murmurs replies to questions put to him by the adults. Familiar questions about school, questions he has answered many times. He will not be asked questions which are painful to answer. Not now. When he'd been asked such questions in the aftermath of his mother's death the child had stared into a corner of the room with narrowed eyes, silent. His jaws had clenched, a small vein twitched at his temple but his gaze held firm and unswerving.

Later the father would say he'd been afraid to touch the child's chest, or his throat, at the time *–I was sure Stefan had stopped breathing. He'd gone somewhere deep inside himself where that terrible woman was calling him.*

It is months later. In fact it is years later. *That terrible woman* has disappeared from their lives and from the beautiful old shingle board house in Wainscott, Massachusetts, in which Alexander and N.K. lived during their twelve-year marriage.

Lived "only intermittently"—Alexander has said. For frequently they lived apart as N.K. pursued her own "utterly selfish" life.

Not in the house but in the adjoining three-car garage, a converted stable, which the fiancée has not (yet) seen, the poet N.K. killed herself and her four-year-old daughter Clea by carbon monoxide poisoning.

And no suicide note. Neither in the car nor elsewhere.

It is true, Alexander acknowledged having found a diary of N.K. kept in the last fevered weeks of her life, in her bedside table.

His claim was he'd had to destroy the diary—without reading it—knowing it would contain terrible accusations, lies. The ravings of a homicidal madwoman, from which his son had to be spared.

For he could not risk it, that Stefan would grow up having to encounter in the world echoes and reflections of the sick and debased mind that had tried to destroy him. . . .

Despite the trauma Stefan has done reasonably well at the Wainscott Academy. For several months after the deaths he'd been kept home, with a nurse to care for him—he'd had to repeat third grade—but since then he has caught up with his fifth-grade classmates, Alexander has said proudly. All that one might have predicted—fits of crying, child-depression, "acting out," mysterious illnesses—seemed not to have occurred, or were fleeting. "My son has a stoical spirit," the father has said. "Like me."

The fiancée thinks, seeing the child—*No. He is just in hiding.*

Elisabeth has calculated that there is almost exactly the identical distance in age between Stefan's age and hers, as between hers and Alexander's: eighteen years. (Stefan is ten, Elisabeth is twenty-eight. Alexander is in his late forties.)

Elisabeth will brood over this fact. It is a very minor fact yet (she thinks) a way of linking her and the child though (probably) the child will never realize.

If she were alive, the sick and debased N.K. would be just thirty-six. Young, still.

But if N.K. were alive Elisabeth Lundquist would not be here in Wainscott in her fiancé's distinguished old family house smiling so hard her face aches.

It is impressive: Stefan knows to stand very still as adults speak at him, to him, above his head. He does not twitch, quiver as another (normal?) child might. He does not betray restlessness, resentment. *He does not betray misery.* His smile is quicksilver, his eyes are heavy-lidded. Beautiful dark-brown eyes. Elisabeth wonders if those eyes, so much darker than the father's eyes, as the child's complexion is so much paler than the father's ruddy skin, resemble the deceased mother's eyes.

Elisabeth has seen photographs of the dramatically beautiful N.K. of course. She has seen a number of videos including those that, after N.K.'s death, went viral. It would have been unnatural if, under the circumstances, she had not.

The Guatemalan housekeeper, Ana, has overseen Stefan's bath, combed and brushed the boy's curly fair-brown hair, and laid out clean clothes for him. Of course at the age of ten he dresses himself. On his small feet, denim sneakers with laces neatly tied. Elisabeth feels a pang of loss, the child is too old for her to help him with his laces—ever.

*It will be a challenge,* Elisabeth thinks, *to win over this beautiful wounded child.*

"Mr. Hendrick?"—Ana appears, smiling and gracious, deferential. It is time now for the evening meal.

Supper is in a glassed-in porch at the rear of the house

where a small round table has been set for just three people. At its center, a vase of white roses fresh-picked from the garden.

As they enter the room Elisabeth feels an impulse to take the child's hand, very gently—to allow Stefan to know that she cares for him already though they have just met. She will be his *friend.*

But when Elisabeth reaches for Stefan's hand her fingers encounter something cold and clotty, sticky like mucus—"Oh! Oh, God." She gives a little scream, and steps away shuddering.

"What is it, Elisabeth?" Alexander asks, concerned.

What is it, Elisabeth has no idea. For when she looks at Stefan, at Stefan's hand, small-boned and innocent, entirely clean, lifted palm-outward before him in a pleading gesture, she sees nothing unusual—certainly nothing that might have felt cold, clotty, sticky as mucus.

"I just felt—cold. . . ."

"Well! Are your hands cold, Stefan?"

Shyly Stefan shakes his head. Murmuring, "Don't know."

Elisabeth apologizes, deeply embarrassed. Must have imagined—something. . . .

Alexander has no idea what is going on—unless Alexander has a very good idea what is going on—but chooses to be bemused by his young fiancée, eighteen years his junior: the young woman's fear of harmless insects, her fear of driving in urban areas, her fear of flying in small propeller planes used by commuters from Boston to Cape Cod.

Elisabeth manages to laugh, uneasily. She reasons that it is better for Alexander to express bemusement, impatience, irritation with her, than with the sensitive Stefan.

Quite a beautiful room, the glassed-in porch. White wicker furniture, a pale beige Peruvian woven rug. On a wall a Childe

Hassam Impressionist seascape of the late nineteenth century.

As they are about to sit Stefan suddenly freezes. Murmurs that he has to use a bathroom. Over Alexander's face there comes a flicker of annoyance. Oh, just as Ana is serving the meal! Elisabeth is sorry about this.

"Of course. Go."

At the table Alexander pours (white, tart) wine into the adults' glasses. He is determined not to express the annoyance he feels for his son but Elisabeth can see his hands trembling.

Elisabeth remarks that they have plenty of time to drive to the concert in Provincetown for which they have tickets—"It's only six. We have an hour and a half for dinner. . . ."

"I'm aware of the time, Elisabeth. Thank you."

A rebuff. Alexander doesn't like his naive young fiancée even to appear to be correcting him.

Gamely Elisabeth tries again: "Your son is so—beautiful. He's . . ."

*Unique. Unworldly. Wraithlike.*

Alexander grunts a vague assent. Somehow managing to signal *yes* and at the same time *Enough of this subject.*

Elisabeth is one of those shy individuals who find themselves chattering nervously, for conversational silence intimidates them. It is hard for her to remain silent—she feels (she thinks) that she is being judged. Yet, she has discovered to her surprise that it is not difficult to offend Alexander Hendrick, inadvertently. A man of his stature, so thin-skinned? She worries that even a naively well-intentioned compliment about Stefan may remind him of the other child Clea, who died of carbon monoxide poisoning wrapped in a mohair shawl in her mother's arms. . . .

Terrible! Elisabeth shudders.

"How is this wine? It's Portuguese—d'you like it?"

Wine? Elisabeth knows little about wine. "Yes," she tells Alexander, who is frowning over his glass as if nothing were more important than the wine he is about to drink.

"I'm wondering if I should have bought an entire case. Might've been a mistake."

Is wine important? Elisabeth supposes that it must be, if Alexander thinks so. Her fiancé, to her a distinguished man, director of a wealthy arts foundation established by his grandfather, has a habit of weighing minor acts, innocuous-seeming decisions, as if they were crucially important, and might turn into *mistakes.* At first Elisabeth thought he was only joking since the issues were often trivial but now she sees that nothing is trivial to her fiancé. The mere possibility of a *mistake* is upsetting to him.

Driving to Wainscott, bringing Elisabeth for her first weekend visit to the house on Oceanview Avenue, Alexander said suddenly: "I hope this isn't going to be a mistake."

Elisabeth laughed nervously. Hesitant to ask Alexander to explain for he hadn't actually seemed to be speaking to her, only thinking aloud.

They are waiting for Stefan to return to the table. Ana has lighted candles that quaver with their breaths. Why is the boy taking so much time? Is he hiding from them?—from his father? At Alexander's insistence Ana serves the first, lavish course—roasted sweet peppers stuffed with pureed mushroom. On each Wedgwood plate a red pepper and a green pepper perfectly matched.

Not the sort of food a boy of ten probably likes, Elisabeth thinks.

"Well. Let's begin. We may run into traffic on the highway."

Heavy silver forks, knives. Engraved with the letter *H.* Virtually everything in the house as well as the house itself is Alexander's inheritance; N.K.'s things, which were not many, were moved out after the deaths, given away. Even the books. Especially, books with *N.K.* on the spine.

*Not a trace of her remaining. Don't worry, darling!*

Wondering another time if Alexander has brought other women to Wainscott, to meet Stefan. To see how they reacted to the surviving child, and the house. Young women, presumably. (Now that he is middle-aged Alexander isn't the type to be attracted to women his own age.) Wondering if, initially drawn to Alexander Hendrick, these women have fled?

*When you see the house, you'll understand—why it means so much to me. And why I am not going to move out.*

Rarely did Alexander speak directly of N.K. Usually obliquely, and in such a way that Elisabeth was not encouraged to ask questions.

In itself, suicide would be devastating. The suicide of a spouse. But conjoined with murder, the murder of a child—unspeakable.

The dead must present a sort of argument, Elisabeth thinks. The argument must be refuted by the living. The dead who have taken the lives of others, and their own lives, must especially be refuted by the living if the living are to continue.

After several minutes Alexander says sharply to Ana, who has been hovering in the background: "Look for him! Please."

Elisabeth winces. The way Alexander gives orders to the housekeeper is painful to her.

Ana hurries away to call, "Stefan! Stefan!"

Elisabeth lays down her napkin. She will help look for the child. . . .

"No. Stay here. This is ridiculous."

Alexander is flush-faced, indignant. With his fork and knife he slides something onto Elisabeth's plate. At first she thinks it is quivering with life, slimy like a jellyfish, then she sees that it is just pureed mushroom, seeping fragrantly from the roasted peppers.

Ana is on the stairs to the second floor. A short stout woman, heavy-thighed. Out of breath. "Stefan? Hello?"

They listen to her calling, cajoling. If only Stefan will answer!

But Ana returns panting and apologetic. Can't find him, she is so sorry—not in his room, not in any bathroom. Not in the kitchen, or the back hall, or—anywhere she could think of.

"God damn. I've warned him, if he played this trick one more time . . ."

Alexander lurches to his feet. Elisabeth rises also, daring to clutch at his arm.

"Maybe he's sick, Alexander. He was looking sad—maybe he just doesn't want to see anyone right now. Can't you let him—be?"

Alexander throws off her hand. "Shut up. You know *nothing*."

He stalks out of the glassed-in porch. Elisabeth has no choice but to follow, hesitantly. Hoping that Ana has not overheard Alexander's remark to her, not the first time her fiancé has told her to *shut up*.

Stomping on the stairs calling, "Stefan? Where the hell are you?"

Elisabeth follows into the hall. Not up the stairs. Not sure what she should be doing. Weakly calling, "Stefan? It's me—Elisabeth. Are you hiding? Where are you hiding?"

*Where are you hiding?* An inane remark, such as one frightened child might ask another. . . .

Desperate minutes are spent in the search for the child. Upstairs, downstairs. Front hall, back hall. Kitchen, dining room. Living room, sitting room. And again back upstairs, to peer into closets in guest rooms. In the master bedroom where (Alexander says grimly) the boy "wouldn't dare" set foot.

Finally, there is no alternative. The distraught father must go to look in the forbidden place: the garage. Telling Elisabeth and Ana to stay where they are. By this time Alexander is very upset. His face is ruddy with heat, his carefully combed hair has fallen onto his forehead. Even the handsome blue silk necktie has loosened as if he'd clawed at it.

Elisabeth hears the man's impatient voice uplifted, at the rear of the house—"Stefan? Are you in there? You had better not be in there. . . ."

*That place. Where she'd died. And your little sister died.*

Anxiously Elisabeth and Ana wait in the hall for Alexander to return. It is not likely (Elisabeth thinks) that the father will easily find the son, and haul him back in triumph.

"Stefan has done this before, I guess?"—Elisabeth asks hesitantly; and Ana, protective of the child, or not wanting to betray a family secret, frowns and looks away as if she hasn't heard the question.

Saying finally, choosing her words with care, "He is a good boy, Stefan. Very sweet, sad. There is something that comes over him—sometimes. Not his fault. That is all."

To this Elisabeth can't think of a reply. She is steeling herself for Alexander's reappearance. The loud angry voice like a spike driven into her forehead she must make every effort not to acknowledge gives her pain.

And then, almost by chance, Elisabeth happens to glance

back into the glassed-in porch, which she knows to be empty, which *has to be empty*; and sees at the table a child-sized figure, very still—can it be Stefan? In his chair, at his place?

Elisabeth hurries to him. So surprised, she doesn't call for Alexander.

"Oh!—Stefan. There you are."

As if he has been running, the child is out of breath. Almost alarmingly out of breath.

His face is very pale, clammy-pale, coated in perspiration. His eyes are dilated with excitement, his lips seem to have a bluish cast. And there are bluish shadows beneath his eyes.

*Oxygen deprivation? Is that it?*

Even as she is profoundly relieved, Elisabeth is astonished. She would like to touch the child—hug him, even—but does not dare. A faint, subtly rancid smell lifts from him, like a sour breath.

Ana hurries to tell Mr. Hendrick that his son has returned safely. Elisabeth approaches the child calmly, not wanting to overwhelm him with her emotion, dares to grasp his hand another time and this time the small-boned hand is pliant and not resistant, a child's hand, slightly cold, but containing nothing repulsive, to terrify.

So relieved to see him, Elisabeth hears herself laugh nervously. She will not allow herself to wonder why he is so breathless, and so pale.

Nor does she accuse the child except she must ask where has he been?—hadn't he heard them calling him, for the past ten minutes or more?—hadn't he heard his father?

Evasively Stefan mutters what sounds like: "Here. I was here."

Nothing sly or mischievous, nothing deceitful about the child. Elisabeth is sure. But how strange!—where had he been? And how had he slipped past her and Ana, to return to the dinner table on the porch?

In the pale freckled face there's a look of adult anguish, cunning. And the skin is still clammy-cold, with the sweat of panic.

As the angry father approaches, footsteps loud in the hall like a mallet striking, Stefan cringes. Elisabeth holds his small weak hand, to protect him.

"You! God damn you! Didn't I warn you!"—for a terrible moment it seems that Alexander is about to strike his son; his hand is raised, for a slap; but then like air leaking from a balloon Alexander's anger seems to drain from him. His eyes glisten with tears of frustration, rage, fear. He drags out his chair to sit down heavily at the table.

"Just tell me, Stefan: Where were you?"

And Stefan says in his small still voice what sounds like: *"Here. I was here. . . ."*

Alexander snatches up his napkin, to wipe his eyes. "Well. *Don't* do anything like this again, d'you hear me?"

**2.**

*Bollingen Prize Poet N.K., Child Found Dead in Wainscott, MA*
*Asphyxiation Deaths "Possibly Accidental"*

*Bestselling Feminist Poet N.K. Takes Own Life*
*Four-Year-Old Daughter Dies With Her*
*"Shocking Scene"—Wainscott, MA*

Always Elisabeth will remember: the shocked voice of a colleague rushing into the library at the Radcliffe Institute.

". . . terrible. They're saying she killed herself and . . ."

Lowered (female) voices. Solemn, appalled. Disbelieving.

Glancing up from her laptop as talk swirled around her.

Who had died? A poet? A woman poet? *And* her daughter?

Wanting to know, not wanting to know.

That evening at a reception at the Institute for a visiting lecturer, all talk was of the suicide. And the death of the child.

Asphyxiation by carbon monoxide poisoning.

". . . wouldn't have done it. I don't believe it."

". . . herself, maybe. But not a daughter."

". . . not possible. No."

How shocking the news was! The voices were embittered, incredulous. For how demoralizing for women writers, women scholars, women who declared themselves feminists. Nicola Kavanaugh—"N.K."—had been a heroine to them, defiant and courageous and original.

". . . murder, maybe. Someone jealous . . ."

". . . that husband. Weren't they separated . . ."

". . . but not the daughter! I know her—knew her. N.K. would never have done *that.*"

Of course they had to acknowledge that N.K. had written freely, shockingly of taboo subjects like suicide—the *unspeakable bliss of self-erasure.*

Elisabeth listened. Grasped the hands of mourners that clutched at hers in anguish. She had not been a fellow at the Institute several years before when N.K. came to give a "brilliant"—"impassioned"—"inspiring" presentation on the "unique language" of women's poetry but she'd heard colleagues speak admiringly of it, still.

At the Institute, Elisabeth was researching the archives of the Imagist poets of the early twentieth century. She'd read no more than a scattering of N.K.'s flamboyant, quasi-confessional poetry, so very different from the sparc understatement of Imagism; she wouldn't have wanted to acknowledge that she found N.K.'s poetry too harsh, discordant, angry, *unsettling.* Nor had she been drawn to the cult of N.K. that had begun even before the poet's premature death.

What is a cult but a binding-together of the weak. So it seemed to her. The excesses of feminists, she hoped to distance herself from. A certain physical/erotic posturing, needless provocations. Not for her.

Soon then, reading an obituary of N.K. in the *New York Times,* Elisabeth discovered that N.K. had allegedly named herself, or rather renamed herself, as "N.K." in homage to the Imagist poet H.D.; she'd wanted a pseudonym "without gender and without a history."

Names are obscuring, misleading. So N.K. argued. Surnames—family names—have no role in art. Artists are individuals and should name themselves. "Naming"—the most crucial aspect of one's life, the name you bring with you, blatant as a face, should not be the province/choice of others.

Essentially, your parents are strangers to you. It is not reasonable that strangers should name *you.*

And so Nicola Kavanaugh had named herself "N.K." The poet's vanity would help brand her, help to guarantee her fame.

Soon after, Elisabeth found herself staring at a poster on a wall in Barnes & Noble depicting the gaunt, savagely beautiful N.K. in a photograph by Annie Leibovitz. The poet had been wearing what looked like a flimsy cotton shift, almost you could see the shadowy nipples of her breasts through the material, and around her slender shoulders a coarse-knitted, fringed shawl. Her thick disheveled hair appeared to be windblown, her eyes sharp and accusing. Beneath, the caption—*Live as if it's your life.*

**3.**

"And what did you say your name was, dear?—'Elizabeth'? I didn't quite hear."

"Elisabeth."

Gravely he laughed at her. Leaning over her.

"Is that a lisp I hear?—'Elis-a-beth'?"

"Y-Yes."

By chance, months later, when the last thing on her mind was N.K., Elisabeth was introduced to Alexander Hendrick. A tall gentlemanly man of whom everyone whispered—*D'you know who that is? Alexander Hendrick—N.K.'s husband.*

He was older than Elisabeth by nearly twenty years. Yet youthful in his manner, even playful, to disguise the gravity beneath, even as he had to shave (Elisabeth would learn) twice a day, to rid his jaws of graying stubble, sharp little quills that erupted not only on his face but beneath his chin, partway down his neck.

She'd known something of the man's identity, apart from the disaster of his marriage: He was the director of the Hendrick Foundation, that had been founded by a multimillionaire grandfather in the 1950s, to award grants to creative artists at the outset of their careers.

Including in 1993, the young experimental poet-artist Nicola Kavanaugh, as she'd called herself then.

Had Alexander Hendrick and Nicola Kavanaugh met before Nicola received the grant, or afterward?—Elisabeth was never to learn, with any certainty.

"Tell me you aren't a poet, my dear Elisabeth."

"No. I mean—I am not a poet."

"You're sure?"—Alexander Hendrick was grimly joking, unless it was his very grimness that joked, that made such a joke possible.

Elisabeth laughed, feeling giddy. Since adolescence she'd been waiting for such a person, who could intimidate her yet make her laugh.

**4.**

You tell yourself: The new life is sudden.

The new life is a window flung open. Better yet, a window smashed.

Sometimes it is true. The *new life* is flung in your face; you have not the capacity to duck the flying glass.

*What was it like, to visit that house? Will you have to live there as his wife—permanently?*

*Can you—permanently?*

*Are there traces of her? Is there an—aura?*

*Oh, Elisabeth. Take care.*

The (civil) wedding in March is very small, private. Few relatives on either side.

Immediately afterward they leave for a week in the Bahamas.

And when they return it is to the house on Oceanview Avenue, Wainscott, where the surviving child awaits, looked after by the housekeeper, Ana.

*Are you prepared for him? A ten-year-old stepchild whose mother tried to kill him?*

In death, N.K.'s notoriety has grown. Articles about her appear continuously in print and online. An unauthorized video titled *Last Days of the Poet N.K.* goes viral. An unauthorized *Interview with the American Medea N.K.*—in fact, a pastiche of several interviews—appears, with photographs of the starkly beautiful woman over the course of years, in *Vanity Fair.* There are Barnes & Noble posters, T-shirts, even coffee mugs—a cartoon likeness of N.K. with an aureole of fiercely crimped dark hair and a beautiful savage unsmiling mouth.

Of these outrages Alexander never speaks—perhaps he is not aware. (Elisabeth wants to think.) The posthumous cult of N.K. is like a cancer metastasizing—unstoppable.

Sylvia Plath, Anne Sexton, and now Nicola Kavanaugh—"N.K." For each generation of wounded and angry women, a deathly female icon.

At first the mainstream media contrived to believe that N.K. had been mentally ill, to have killed her daughter as well as herself. It was known that she'd "struggled with depression" since adolescence, she'd tried to kill herself several times in the past. But then, newer readings of N.K.'s poetry suggest that her horrendous act had been deliberate and premeditated, a "purification" of the self in a rotten world.

It seemed clear that she'd meant to kill Stefan as well, initially. She'd given the seven-year-old a sedative, as she'd given the four-year-old a sedative, and brought him into the garage with her, and into the Saab sedan; then for some reason she'd relented, and carried him back into the house and left him, and returned to the car with the running motor, filling the garage with bluish smoke for the stunned Alexander to discover, hours later.

The dead woman lying in the front seat of the car with the little girl, Clea, in her arms, the two of them wrapped in a mohair shawl.

Was there a suicide note?—Alexander saw nothing.

It would be his claim, he'd seen nothing. Emergency medical workers, law enforcement officers, investigators—suicide note discovered in the car.

Yet, it came to be generally known that there'd been "packets of poems" scattered in the back seat of the car. (As well as the left sneaker of a pair of sneakers—belonging to Stefan.) Not new poems by N.K. but older poems, among her more famous poems, that quickly took on a new, ominous prescience. The posthumous cult of N.K., so maddening to Alexander and his family, quickly fastened upon these poems—*the small bitter apples of extinction.*

Ana had been given the entire day off by Nicola. The housekeeper hadn't been expected to return until eight o'clock in the evening, by which time Nicola and Clea had been dead for several hours.

Stefan, missing, was eventually found by searchers inside the house, partially dressed and shoeless, at the rear of an upstairs closet. (The mate to the child's sneaker in the rear of the Saab would be discovered in a corner of the garage amid recycling containers, as if it had been tossed or kicked there.) He was curled into a fetal position, so deeply asleep he might have been in a coma. His blood pressure was dangerously low. His skin was deathly white, his lips had a bluish cast. Emergency medical workers worked to revive him with oxygen.

The surviving child was slow to come to consciousness. Not only carbon monoxide poisoning but barbiturate would be discovered in his blood. He would remember little of what had happened. Except—*Mummy gave me warm milk to drink, that made me sleepy. Mummy kissed me and told me she would never abandon me.*

Yet, the child's mother must have changed her mind about killing him with his sister. A short time after she'd started the Saab motor, when the seven-year-old was unconscious, but before she herself had lapsed into unconsciousness, she'd pulled him from the back seat of the car, dragged or carried him all the way upstairs to a hall closet . . .

Elisabeth ponders this. Why did N.K. relent, and allow one of her children to live? The boy, and not the girl? *Did* in fact this happen, as it's generally believed?

Elisabeth wonders if the seven-year-old might have crawled out of the car, and saved himself. Yet, why would he have hidden upstairs in a closet? And he'd been deeply unconscious when his father discovered him.

More than three years after the deaths the Wainscott police investigation is closed. The county medical examiner issued his report: homicide, suicide. Carbon monoxide poisoning. Heavy barbiturate sedation. Still, no one knows precisely the chronology of events of that day. The surviving child cannot be further questioned. The surviving husband will never speak again on the subject publicly, he has declared.

And privately? Elisabeth knows only what Alexander has chosen to tell her, which she has no reason to disbelieve. N.K. had suffered from bipolar disorder since early adolescence, she'd been a "brilliant poet" (Alexander had to concede) afflicted by a strong wish to harm herself, and others unfortunate enough to be caught up in her emotional life. She'd been coldly ambitious, Alexander said. Always anxious about her reputation, jealous of other poets' prizes, publicity. Ultimately she'd cared little for a domestic life—though, for a few years, she'd tried. Perversely the children had adored her, Alexander said bitterly.

*And yet, what is it we cannot know? Though the heart breaks, the great sea crashes, crushes us. We must know.*

Since becoming Alexander's wife Elisabeth has resisted reading N.K.'s poems. Yet, it is difficult to avoid them for often lines from the poems, even entire poems, are quoted in the media. Quickly Elisabeth looks away but sometimes it is too late.

*. . . crashes, crushes us. We must know.*

Very still Elisabeth has been sitting, fingers poised above the laptop keyboard. How many minutes have passed she doesn't know, but her laptop screen has gone dark like a brain switching off. By chance she hears a quickened breath behind her—turns to see, in the doorway, the beautiful child, her stepchild, Stefan.

"Oh—Stefan! Hello . . ."

Elisabeth is so startled by the sight of him, something falls from the table—a ballpoint pen. Clattering onto the floor, rolling.

"H-Have you been there a while, dear? I didn't hear you. . . ."

Rises to her feet as if to invite the elusive child inside the room, but already Stefan has backed away and is descending the stairs.

*Like a wild creature,* she thinks. *A wraith.*

If you reach out for a wraith he shrinks away. Oh, she is so crude!—so yearning, the child sees it in her face and retreats.

**5.**

"Certainly not! We live here. We are very happy here. It's *ordinary life* here." Declaiming to visitors, Alexander laughs with a sharp sort of happiness.

A steady procession of visitors, guests at Hendrick House. In the summer months especially, on idyllic Cape Cod.

*No aura. Not her. That one is dead, gone. Vanished.*

On the wide veranda looking toward the ocean, in the long summer twilight. Drinks are served by a young Guatemalan girl who is helping Ana tonight, cut-glass crystal glitters and winks. Elisabeth is the new wife, shy among her husband's friends. He has so many!—hopeless to try to keep their names straight.

Perhaps these are not friends exactly. Rather, acquaintances and professional associates. Visitors from Provincetown, Woods Hole. House guests from Boston, Cambridge, New York City connected with the Hendrick Foundation.

In summer the house on Oceanview Avenue is particularly beautiful. Romantically weathered dark-brown shingle board with dark shutters, stone foundation and stone chimneys. Steep roofs and cupolas, a wraparound veranda open to the ocean on bright windy days. Fifteen rooms, three stories, the converted stable at the rear. Not the largest but one of the more distinctive houses on Oceanview Avenue, Wainscott. Originally built in 1809, and listed with the National Landmark Registry. Beside the heavy oak front door is a small brass plaque commemorating this honor.

Of course, Alexander has an apartment elsewhere, on Boston's Beacon Street, near the office of the Hendrick Foundation. In the years of his marriage to N.K. he was obliged to rent an apartment in New York City, on Waverly Place, to accommodate her.

". . . well, yes. We 'took a chance' on her at the Foundation—though after Allen Ginsberg that sort of wild feckless quasi-confessional poetry was fashionable—riding the crest of the 'new feminism' . . ."

Elisabeth marvels at the coolness with which at such times Alexander is able to speak of N.K. So long as the subject is impersonal; so long as the subject is poetry, and not *wife.*

Coolness, and condescension. (Male) revenge on the (female) artist. *Yes she is, or was, brilliant—"genius." But no, I am not so impressed.*

Most of these guests had known Nicola Kavanaugh. This, Elisabeth gathers. You see them frowning, shaking their heads. Pitying, condemning. Allowing the widower to know that they side with him of course—the bereft, terribly wronged husband.

Monstrous woman. Deranged and demented poet.

". . . yes, I've heard. It will be 'unauthorized'—of course. The last thing we need is a biography of—her. Fortunately, copyright to her work resides with me, and I don't intend to give permission for any sort of use—even 'the'—'and'—'but' . . ."

Laughter. As he is famously stoical so Alexander is so very witty.

A *biography*? This is the first Elisabeth has heard.

Not from Alexander, but from other sources, Elisabeth has learned how the poet Nicola Kavanaugh was reluctant to marry—anyone. How she'd suffered since early adolescence from mania, depression, suicidal "ideation"—and suicide attempts. Love affairs with Nicola were invariably impassioned, destructive. And then, at last, after a most destructive relationship with a prominent woman artist living in New York City, to the astonishment of everyone who knew her, and against their unanimous advice, Nicola suddenly married the older, well-to-do Alexander Hendrick, who'd been one of her ardent courters for years.

For solace she'd married, it was said; for financial security, and to pay for therapists, prescription drugs, hospitalizations; as a stay against the wild mood swings of bipolar disorder; for peace, comfort, sanity. *Because a sexually rapacious young woman took advantage of a besotted well-to-do older man with literary pretensions.*

Though in her poetry N.K. scorned the conventional life of husband, children, responsibilities, bourgeois property, and possessions, in her life she'd behaved perversely, taking all these on.

Elisabeth has heard that Nicola loved the house in Wainscott—at first. A romantically remote place on Cape Cod to which she could retreat, and work. A place where she could be alone when she wished, in solitude.

And she'd loved her children, as well—at first.

Yet, it would turn out that the poet wrote some of her most savagely powerful poems in this house, in the final year of her life. Sequestered away in an upstairs room, barring the door against intruders—her own children.

Terrible things Elisabeth has heard about the predecessor-wife. Terrible things she is reluctant/eager to believe.

In her extreme emotional states N.K. mistreated, abused both children. Screamed at them, shook them. Locked them in a closet. *Sight of babies appalls. Doubling myself. Sin of hubris. Stink of pride. Bringing another of myself into the world: unforgiveable.*

And *How will they remember their mother?—little lambs of sacrifice, shall their eyes be opened?*

Alexander would testify at a police inquiry into the deaths

that his wife had wanted children to save her life and then, after their births, she'd resented them. She'd loved them excessively (it seemed) but had been fearful of hurting them. She couldn't bear them around her often but claimed not to trust nannies or the housekeeper. She didn't want them near windows for fear they would fall through, piercing themselves on the glass. Didn't like to take their hands to lead them upstairs or across a street, there was the terror of losing the grip of their hands. Could not bear to bathe them for fear of scalding them, or drowning them. Several times she'd wakened Alexander in the middle of the night (in Alexander's bed: for the two did not share a room) crying she'd cut the children's throats like pigs, tried to hang them upside down but couldn't, they fell to the floor and were bleeding to death. . . . Alexander had to take the sobbing hysterical woman into the children's rooms to show her that they were untouched and then for a long time she stood disbelieving by their beds until saying at last in a flat voice—*All right then. For now.*

Is madness contagious? Elisabeth shivers in the perpetual wind from the Atlantic.

". . . Stefan? Reasonably well. Thank you for asking. There's a girl looking after him tonight, upstairs."

"How has he adjusted, in this house? It must be . . ."

"No. Stefan is very happy here. I've told you. He cries if he's made to leave even overnight."

"Really! Is that so."

"Yes. Strangely so. As I think I've told you—all of you."

"He must be very happy then, with his new stepmother. . . ."

*New stepmother.* Elisabeth has been only half listening as talk swirls about her head but she hears this, distinctly.

A rude remark, cruel and insinuating, or an entirely sincere remark, made by an old friend of Alexander's who wishes him and family well?

"Really, we are all very happy here. Elisabeth has been 'settling in'—wonderfully. She and Stefan are making friends. So far, the summer has been . . ."

Feeling the visitors' eyes on her. Sensing their disappointment in her, so plain-faced, dull and so *ordinary* after Nicola Kavanaugh.

Like a dun-feathered bird holding herself very still, not to attract the attention of predators. Very still among these strangers seeming to listen to their sharp witty voices while hearing in the wind from the Atlantic the throaty voice intimate as a whisper in her ear.

*But you know that I am not gone, Elisabeth. You know that I have come for you and the boy.*

**6.**

"This house is not 'poisoned'—not by *her*."

Not to Elisabeth has Alexander uttered such words but she has overheard him on the phone, speaking with Wainscott relatives. His tone is vehement, contemptuous. *Who has been spreading such rumors of—hauntings . . . ?*

He will not be driven away from this property, he has said. Hendrick House will endure beyond individual lives. It will endure long after *her*.

Elisabeth never has to wonder who *her* is. Sometimes, the contemptuously uttered pronoun is *she*.

Bitterly, Alexander says: "Nicola came here, with a pretense of wanting a 'quiet' life, and she never made a home here.

Her clothes were in suitcases. Her books were in boxes. Ana did most of the unpacking, shelving books. Nicola couldn't be bothered. She was immersed in her poetry, her precious career. She had her lovers, women and men. She'd promised that she had given them up when we were married but of course she lied. Her entire life was a lie. Her poetry is a lie. When she was sick with depression her lovers abandoned her. Where were they? Hangers-on, sycophants. And her 'fans'—they were waiting for her to die, to kill herself. The promise of the poetry. But they hadn't anticipated that their heroine would take her own daughter with her. *That,* they hadn't expected." Alexander speaks defiantly. Elisabeth listens with dread. Like holding your breath in the presence of airborne poison. She doesn't want to breathe in hatred for the deceased woman; she doesn't want to feel hatred for anyone.

How beautiful the house is, Elisabeth never tires of marveling.

*But beware. Beauty's price.*

*Sucking your life's blood.*

Strange, wonderful and strange, and uncanny, to live in a kind of museum. Classic Cape Cod architecture, period furnishings. Especially the downstairs rooms are flawlessly maintained.

Of course such maintenance is expensive. Much effort on the part of servants, and on the part of the wife of the house. Polished surfaces, gleaming hardwood floors. Curtains stirring in the ocean breeze. High, languidly turning fans. (No air conditioning in any of the landmark houses of Wainscott, so close to the Atlantic!) Long corridors with windows at each end looking out (it almost seems) into eternity.

*Rot beneath, shine above. Rejoice, love.* Lines from one of N.K.'s chanting poems, "Dirge"—Elisabeth hasn't realized she'd memorized.

Does the door lock? No?

Still, the door can be shut. Though no one is likely to follow her here, except (perhaps) the child Stefan, who is away at school on this rainy, windy autumn day.

Alexander is in Boston for several days and even if he were home, it isn't likely that he would seek her out in this part of the house in which he has little interest.

On the third floor, up a flight of steep steps, Elisabeth has discovered a small sparely furnished room in what had been, in a previous era, the servants' quarters.

Here there is no elegant silk French wallpaper as in the downstairs rooms. Not a chandelier but a bare-bulb overhead light. A single window overlooking sand hills, stunted dun-colored vegetation, a glittering sliver of the Atlantic.

In the room is a narrow cot, hardly a bed. A bare plank floor. No curtains or shutters. Not a closet but a narrow cupboard opening into the wall, rife with cobwebs and a smell of mildew.

At a table in this little room at a makeshift desk Elisabeth sits leaning on her elbows, that have become raw, reddened. Much of her skin feels windburnt. For here at the edge of the ocean there is perennial wind: gusts rattling windowpanes, stirring foliage in tall pines beside the house.

Elisabeth has brought her laptop here but often leaves it unopened. Her work on the Imagist poets beckons to her as if on the farther side of an abyss but—she is afraid—she is losing her emotional connection with it. Reading and rereading passages of prose she'd written with conviction and passion as an eager young scholar at the Radcliffe Institute and now she can barely remember the primary work, let alone her enthusiasm for it. . . . The spare impersonal poetry of H.D. seems so muted, set beside a more impassioned and heedless female poetry.

Elisabeth strains her eyes staring toward the ocean. Wind-stirred waves, pounding surf frothing white against the pebbly shore. Overhead misshapen storm clouds and in the pines beside the house what appear to be the arms, legs of struggling persons—naked bodies . . .

*Promiscuous life rushes through our veins. Unstoppable.*

An optical illusion of some sort. Must be.

Elisabeth can see the thrashing figures in the corner of her eye but when she looks directly at the agitated foliage she can't decipher the human figures but only their outlines. The impress of the (naked) bodies in the thrashing branches, where they struggle like swimmers in a rough surf.

Turning her head quickly to see—if she can catch the figures in the trees.

"No. You can't catch them."

Behind her, beside her, a throaty little laugh. It is Stefan who has crept noiselessly into the room.

Very quietly, though very quickly, like a cat ascending the steep steps to the third floor of the house, Stefan must have come to join her. Hadn't she shut the door to the little room? He'd managed to open it, without her hearing.

Elisabeth is startled but tries to speak matter-of-factly. For she knows, children do not like to see adults discomforted.

"Catch—what?"

"The things in the trees. That never stop."

Stefan speaks patiently as if (of course) Elisabeth knows what he is talking about. "You can see them in the corner of your eye but when you look at them, they're gone. They're too fast."

*But there is nothing there. In the trees, in the leaves. We know that.*

Elisabeth's heart is pounding quickly. Almost shyly she regards the stepchild who so often eludes her, seems to look through her. Stefan seems never to grow, has scarcely grown an inch in the months since Alexander first introduced them.

*My new, dear friend Elisabeth. Will you say hello to her? Smile—just a bit? Shake her hand?*

Oh, Stefan's curly hair is damp from the rain! Elisabeth would love to embrace him, press his head against her chest.

Droplets of rain like teardrops on his flushed face and on the zip-up nylon jacket he hasn't taken time to remove. Something very touching about this. Has Stefan hurried home from school, to *her*?

"Stefan! You're home early. . . ."

Stefan shrugs. Maybe he hadn't gone to school at all but simply hid in the house somewhere, in one or another of the numerous unused rooms. Or in the forbidden place, the garage.

Stefan ignores his stepmother's words as he often does. Knowing that the words that pass between them are of little significance, like markers in a poem, mere syllables.

He is at the window, peering out. Wind, rain, thrashing pine branches, an agitation of arms and legs almost visible . . .

*Convulsed with something that looks like passion we tell ourselves, Love.*

Whose words are these? Elisabeth wonders if Stefan can hear them, too.

*It is true,* she thinks. *The convulsions in the trees. Our terrible need for one another, our terror of being left alone. To which we give the name,* Love.

"She taught me how to see them—Mummy. But they always get away."

Elisabeth isn't sure that she has heard correctly. This is the first time that Stefan has uttered the word *Mummy* in her hearing.

"Now Mummy is one of them herself. I think."

For the remainder of the long day feeling both threatened and blessed.

The child had come unbidden to *her.*

A wraith may not be approached, for a wraith will retreat. But a wraith may approach you. If he wishes.

*Stefan darling. Try to forget her. I have come to take her place, I will love you in her place. Trust me!*

**7.**

Certainly it is true as Alexander has said, there is nothing *poisoned* or *haunted* about the Hendrick family house.

For how could there be anything wrong with a house listed in the National Landmark Registry and featured in the fall 2011 issue of the sumptuous glossy *Cape Cod Living.* . . .

Yet, things *go wrong* in the house. Usually these are not serious, and are easily remedied.

For instance: sometimes after a heavy rain the water out of the faucets tastes strange. There is a faint metallic aftertaste, in full daylight you can see a subtle discoloration like rust. And there are mysterious drips from ceilings, actual pools of water, bulges in wallpaper like tumors. Unsettling moans and murmurs in the plumbing.

The water is well water, claimed to be "pure"—"sweet tasting." The well is a deep natural well on the Hendrick property that has been there for generations, fed by underground springs.

Ana tells Elisabeth that, perhaps, she should make an appointment with the township water inspector to come to the house for a sample of their well water. To see what, if anything, is wrong.

Drips in the ceilings, bulges in wallpaper, groaning pipes—Elisabeth should call the roofer, the plumber as well. Since the fancy silk wallpaper in the dining room has been discolored she had better call a paperhanger too. And there are several cracked windowpanes, after a windstorm, that will have to be replaced—sometimes shards of glass litter the downstairs foyer, though no (evident) window panes have been broken. Ana can provide local numbers for (Elisabeth gathers) these repairmen are frequently called.

"All the old big houses in Wainscott are the same," Ana says adamantly, "—all my friends, they work in them, they tell me. It is nothing special to this house."

*Nothing poisoned or haunted in this house. We know.*

It has fallen to Elisabeth to make such appointments since Alexander is often in Boston on business. Indeed Elisabeth is eager to shield her husband from such mundane tasks for he is easily upset by problems involving his beloved house, and it is increasingly difficult to speak to him without his taking offense.

Also, Elisabeth is the wife of the house. As Mrs. Alexander Hendrick she feels a thrill of satisfaction; she is sure that her emotionally unstable predecessor took no such responsibility.

*The new wife is nothing like—*her*! Alexander didn't make a mistake this time. This Elizabeth—"Elisabeth"—is utterly devoted to him and the child and the household, she is a treasure. . . .*

Listening, but the voice trails off. Always she is hoping to hear: *And Alexander is devoted to—*her*!*

Methodically, dutifully calling these local tradesmen and (oddly) no one is available to come to the house on Oceanview Avenue just then. All have excuses, express regret.

*But we can pay you—of course! We can pay you double.*

Calling a local plumber and the voice at the other end expresses surprise—"Hendrick? Again? Weren't we just there a few months ago?" and Elisabeth stammers, "I—I don't know, were you? What was wrong?" and the voice says, guardedly, "Anyway, there's no one available right now. Better try another plumber, I can give you a number to call."

But it is a number that Elisabeth has already called.

"Try Provincetown. They'll charge for coming here, but . . ."

None of this Elisabeth will mention to Alexander. It is only results he cares to be informed of.

So much to do each day. Like a merry-go-round that has begun to accelerate.

Vague thought of *having a baby of my own, someday, a little sister for Stefan.* About this she feels excitement, hope, dread, guilt.

So many distractions, Elisabeth has (temporarily) set aside her scholarly work she'd been doing at the Radcliffe Institute. Research that once fascinated her. Elusive and shimmering as a mirage in the desert, her PhD dissertation on the experimental verse of H.D. and H.D.'s relationship to Ezra Pound and T.S. Eliot. She has written drafts of the (seven) chapters but must revise, add footnotes, update the already extensive bibliography.

No end to fascinating research! But she must be careful that she does not stray from H.D. to N.K. She does not intend to *snoop.*

It is uncanny, some lines of poetry by H.D. echo lines of poetry by N.K. Or rather, some lines of poetry by N.K. echo lines by H.D.

A case of plagiarism? Or—admiration, identification?

*I have had enough.*

*I gasp for breath.*

When they were first married and Elisabeth came to live in her husband's family home in Wainscott it was with the understanding that Elisabeth would return to her scholarly work when things "settled down." The director of the Hendrick Foundation is a feminist—of course. In the past most Hendrick fellowships went to male artists, but no longer.

No one has urged Elisabeth to complete her PhD at Harvard more enthusiastically than Alexander. When Stefan is older, and doesn't require so much attention, Elisabeth might find a teaching position at a private school on the Cape. . . .

It is true, Stefan requires attention. The fact of Stefan, the surviving child. Elisabeth knows that she must be indirect in watching over the elusive child, not obvious and intrusive. She must never startle him by a display of affection. And she must never intervene between father and son.

If Alexander is chiding Stefan, for instance. It is painful to Elisabeth to hear but she must not intervene.

As she sometimes overhears Alexander speaking harshly on the phone, so she overhears Alexander speaking harshly to Stefan. Chiding him for being dreamy, distracted—*other-minded.* For sometimes Stefan is surprisingly clumsy—slipping on the stairs, spraining an ankle; falling from his bicycle, badly cutting his leg. Objects seem to twist from his fingers—cutlery, glassware that shatters on the floor. He is often breathless, anxious. Nothing annoys the father so much as an *anxious* child who shrinks from him as if in (ridiculous!) fear of being struck.

At such times Elisabeth bites her lower lip, straining to hear. She should not be eavesdropping, she knows. If Alexander caught her . . .

She rarely hears Stefan's reply for the boy speaks so softly. If there is any reply.

Yet it is true as Alexander has boasted: Stefan appears to be happy in the house on Oceanview Avenue. At least, Stefan is less happy elsewhere.

Indeed he is reluctant to leave on short trips, even to Provincetown. It is all but impossible to get him to stay away overnight. If forced he will protest, sulk, weep, kick, suck his fingers. Even Ana is shocked, how childish Stefan becomes at such times.

The house is an epicenter, it seems. Stefan will allow himself approximately a mile from this center before he becomes anxious.

From her third-floor aerie Elisabeth has observed Stefan pedaling his bicycle to the end of the block, turning then to continue around the block. Though he quickly passes out of her sight Elisabeth understands that Stefan must keep the house at the epicenter of his bicycling. Soon then, he will reappear, coming from the other direction along Oceanview, pedaling fast, furiously, as if his life were at stake.

Once waiting for Stefan to reappear, waiting for—oh, how long?—an hour?—an *anguished hour*?—Elisabeth can bear it no longer and hurries downstairs, rushes out onto the front walk to look for him; and stands in the avenue waiting for him—*where is he?* Until finally she glances behind her and sees Stefan hovering at the front door watching her.

She is embarrassed, and blushes deeply. When she returns to the house Stefan has disappeared, damned if she will look for him.

**8.**

*Convulsed with something that looks like passion we tell ourselves, Love.*

A high, skittering sound as of glass shards ringing together. Unless it is laughter. Steps back and in the next instant the cut-glass chandelier in the front hall loosens, falls from the ceiling, crashes to the floor, narrowly missing her.

In the aftermath of the shattering glass, that high faint laughter so delicious, you want to join in.

Surfaces, and beneath. Elisabeth is learning not to be deceived by the elegant polished surfaces of the house.

*A place of sickness. Don't breathe.*

Walls look aslant. Doors stick, or can't be closed. Doorknobs feel uncomfortably warm when touched, like inner organs.

Light switches are not where Elisabeth remembers them to be—where Elisabeth *knows* them to be. Fumbling for the switch in her own bedroom.

*You will never find the light nor will the light find you but one day the light will shine through you.*

Finally, her fingers locate the switch. Blasting light, blinding.

In the mirror, a blurred reflection. Wraith-wife.

No: She is imagining everything. In the mirror there is nothing.

For several days her skin has felt feverish. A sensation of heaviness in her lower belly, legs. No appetite and then ravenous appetite and then fits of nausea, gagging. The worst is dry heaving, guttural cries like strangulation.

*The most peaceful blue sleep. Hurry!*

Midway in the shower in Elisabeth's bathroom, fierce sharp quills springing from the showerhead turn scalding hot with no warning.

Elisabeth cries out in surprise—and pain—and scrambles to escape before she faints. . . .

A previous time, the shower turned freezing cold.

Slipping and skidding on the tile floor, whimpering in pain, shock.

In fear of her life—almost. Hearing in the pipes in the walls muffled derisive laughter.

Safer to take a bath. Always in the morning and (sometimes) before bed as well if she is feeling *sullied, bloated.*

Fortunately there is, in another adjoining bathroom, an enormous bathtub in which she might soak in hot (not scalding) sudsy water curling her toes in narcotic pleasure, letting her eyelids sink shut.

*Tub* is too crude and utilitarian a word for such a work of art: a marble bathtub. Faint blue veins in the marble like veins in flesh. Ancient, stately, twelve feet long, and deep. Eagerly Elisabeth tests the water, lowers herself into it taking care not to slip, not to fall. It is such pleasure, pure sensuous delight. Almost at once she begins to sink into a light doze. Her hair straggles into the steamy water, her pale soft startled-looking breasts begin to lift. . . .

*Hurry! We have been waiting.*

Finds herself thinking of an Egyptian tomb. Mummified corpses of a young wife and her baby wrapped in swaddling laid solemnly in the tomb side by side.

Sinking into the water, the enervating heat. Her mouth, nose beneath the water . . . Too much effort to breathe . . .

*I have had enough.*

*I gasp for breath.*

Waking then. With a start, in shock. No idea where she is, or how much time has elapsed in this place.

Hovering above the naked female body. The body is white, wizened. The fingers and toes are puckered, soft. In panic she must return to this body. . . .

The bathwater has turned cold and scummy and smells vile as turpentine. The marble has become freezing cold and slippery. In her desperation to climb out of the deep tub Elisabeth's feet slip and slide, her strength has been sucked away. Loses her balance and falls onto the floor nearly striking her head on the marble rim.

Oh!—pain has returned, and humiliation. For she is trapped inside the wizened white naked female body again.

In the winter many nights Alexander is away. Bravely, Elisabeth is the *wife of the house.* Elisabeth is the *stepmother* of the surviving child.

Dining together, evenings by the fireplace. Like something animated the child will speak of school, books he is reading, or has read. Safe topics for stepmother and stepchild to navigate like stepping-stones in a rough stream.

The father forbids television in the house on Oceanview Avenue. No Internet for Stefan. No video games! He will not have his son's mind (he knows to be a brilliant and precocious mind like his own at that age) polluted by debased American culture.

(Alexander watches television in his Beacon Street apartment, but the sort of television that Alexander watches is not debased.)

As if he has just thought of it Stefan says, "That room—where you are—that was Mummy's, too."

Elisabeth is surprised. *That room?*—she'd chosen because it is so spare, so unattractive. Two flights of stairs, the second flight to the old servants' quarters steep and narrow.

She'd assumed that N.K. had worked in another room. *Her* room shows no signs of human occupancy.

"Oh, Stefan. I—I didn't know. . . ."

"Mummy wouldn't let us in, mostly. Not like you."

Is this flattering? Elisabeth wants to think so.

But who is *us*, she wonders. Little Clea, also?

The remainder of the meal passes in silence but not an awkward silence and when Elisabeth undresses for bed that night she finds herself smiling, a frothy sensation in the area of her heart of uplift.

*Not like you like you like you. Not!*

And later, as she is sinking into a delicious sleep—*Live like it's your life.*

Solemn ticking of the stately old Stickley grandfather clock in the hall.

Yet Elisabeth begins to hear the ticking accelerate, and hesitate; a pause, and a leap forward; a rapid series of ticks, like tachycardia. (She has had tachycardia attacks since moving into the house, but in secret. Never will she voluntarily confide in her husband that she has what is called a *heart murmur.*) In the night she hears the clock cease its ticking and lies in a paroxysm of worry, that it is her own heart that has ceased. A whisper consoles her—*Quick if it's done, is best. Most mercy. Blue buzz of air, the only symptom you will feel is peace.*

Ignores the whisper. Very quietly descending the stairs barefoot to check on the clock, to see why it has ceased ticking; why the silence is so loud, in the interstices of its ticking.

The clock face is blank!—there is no *time. . . .*

*It has already happened, Elisabeth. That is why time has ceased. It is all over, and painless.*

But no: When she switches on the light she sees that the clock is ticking normally. (Elisabeth is sure: She stands barefoot in the hallway shivering, listening.) And there is the clock face as always, stately roman numerals, hour hand, minute hand, a pale luminous face with a lurid smile just for her.

*The wife of the house.*

The well water has been diagnosed by the township water inspector: an alarmingly high degree of *organic and fecal material.* Decomposing (animal?) bodies. Excrement. Contaminated water leaking into the well and until the well can be dredged and the water "purified" it is recommended that the Hendrick household use only bottled water for drinking and cooking purposes.

Informed of this humiliating news Alexander flushes angrily. Elisabeth steels herself to hear him declare *This house is not poisoned.* But he turns away instead as if it is Elisabeth who has offended him.

**9.**

The next evening meal with Stefan. Elisabeth has given Ana the day off, wanting to prepare the meal herself.

Though she takes care to prepare only a variation of one of the few meals that Stefan will consent to eat, that doesn't involve chewy pulpy meat in which muscle fibers are detectable, or anything "slimy" (okra, tomato seeds), or small enough (rice, peas) to be mistaken by the child for grubs or insects. To Ana's vegetarian-egg casserole Elisabeth has added several ingredients of her own—carrots, sweet peppers, spinach.

But Stefan isn't so talkative as he'd been the previous night. When Elisabeth brings up the subject of her third-floor room, and the view of wind-shaken trees outside the window, Stefan says nothing. Almost, Elisabeth might wonder if he'd ever spoken to her about the struggling figures in the trees or she'd imagined that remarkable exchange . . . Just slightly hurt, that Stefan is suspicious of the casserole she has prepared, examining forkfuls before lifting them to his mouth. And he is taking unusually small bites as if shy of eating in her company, or undecided whether he actually wants to eat the food she has prepared.

*Yet he'd once nursed.* Imagining the child as an infant nursing at the mother's breast.

Or, at Elisabeth's breast.

She feels a flush of embarrassment, self-consciousness. What strange thoughts she has! And she is not drinking wine with the meal, as Alexander often urges her to do, to keep him company.

*Tugging at the breast of life we must devour.*
*Helpless otherwise, for dignity's not enough.*
*Surrender dignity and in return royally*
*Sucked.*

In person, when N.K. read this abrasive poem, or recited it in her smoky, throaty voice, audiences laughed uproariously. (Elisabeth has seen videos.) The enormous wish to laugh with the woman declaiming such truths, like a tidal wave sweeping over them.

Since Alexander has been spending more time in Boston,

Elisabeth has been on the Internet watching videos of N.K. Doesn't want to think that she is becoming obsessive. Knows that Alexander would disapprove and so has no intention of allowing him to know.

*Fear of being sucked and fear*
*Of sucking.*

Stefan's silence is not hostile nor even stubborn but (Elisabeth thinks) a consequence of shyness. Stefan may have felt that at their last meal he'd revealed too much to her, and betrayed his mother.

*No betrayal like loving another.*
*No betrayal like love of the Other.*

Distracted by such thoughts Elisabeth has taken too much food into her mouth. Trying to swallow a wad of clotted pulp in her mouth. Her casserole is lukewarm and stringy, unlike Ana's. Something coarse-textured like seaweed—must be the damned spinach. Chewing, trying to swallow but can't swallow. Horribly, strands of spinach have tangled in her teeth. Between her teeth. Can't swallow.

Trying to hide her distress from Stefan. Not wanting to alarm the child. (Oh, if Alexander were here, to witness such a sight! He'd have been dismayed, disgusted.) A deep flush rises into Elisabeth's face, she can barely breathe. This clump of something clotted, caught in her throat—horrible! The harder she tries to swallow, the more her throat constricts.

"Excuse—"

Mouth too full, can't enunciate the word. Desperate now, staggering from the table knocking something to the floor with a clatter. With widened eyes Stefan stares at her.

Must get to a bathroom, thrust a finger down her throat, gag, vomit violently into a toilet. . . .

*And then you die. And then*

*it is over.*

*So much struggle so long—why?*

At last in a bathroom, no time even to shut the door behind her as she manages to cough up the clotted pulpy mash, stringy spinach, in a paroxysm of misery gagging as she spits it into the toilet bowl. Though able to breathe again she is distressed, agitated. Too weak to stand, sinks to her knees. Her face is flaming-hot and the heaviness in her bowels like a fist.

In the aged plumbing a sound of faint laughter.

Then, Stefan is standing beside her. Without a word soaks a washcloth in cold water from the sink and hands it to Elisabeth to press against her overheated face.

Too frightened, too exhausted even to thank the child. His small-boned hand finds hers, his fingers in her fingers clasped, tight.

*Oh, Stefan, thank you. Oh, I love you.*

**10.**

Impossible to sleep! Bile rising in her throat. That which she has bitten off, she cannot swallow. The muscles of her throat gag involuntarily, recalling. Cannot believe how close she'd come to choking to death.

What an awful death—gagging, choking. Unable to swallow and (at last) unable to breathe.

Days have passed. Nights. She is losing track of the calendar. Her eyelids are unnaturally heavy. Yet she cannot sleep. Or if she sleeps it's a thin frothy sleep that sweeps over her like surf. Briefly her aching consciousness is extinguished and yet flares up again a moment later.

A brain is dense meat. Yet, a brain is intricately wired, billions of neurons and glia. The wonder is, how do you turn the brain *on*? How do you turn the brain *off*? An anesthesiologist can put a brain to sleep but can't explain why. And only the brain can make itself conscious.

Falling on the stairs, stumbling. *But the stairs moved. It was not my foot that tripped, stumbled. The stairs moved.*

Finds herself at the rear of the darkened house where the throaty voice has brought her. Not sleepwalking but there is a numbness encasing her that suggests the flotation-logic of sleep. Hand on the doorknob. Why?—she has no wish to look into the garage, which is the forbidden place. Still less to step into the garage where it is perpetual twilight and smells still (she believes) of the bluish sweetly-toxic gas that killed the mother and daughter.

Alexander has said, *Stay away. No need. Do you understand, Elisabeth?*

*Yes,* she'd said. *Of course.*

*I will be very, very unhappy with you if . . .*

Briefly he'd considered (he said) shutting up the garage, securing it. But then—*why*? Whatever danger the garage once threatened is past.

Yet, the door to the forbidden place is opened. In the doorway, shy as a bride, Elisabeth stands.

Dry-eyed from insomnia. Aching, oversensitive skin.

Shadowy objects in the gloom. One of the household

vehicles—an older BMW, belonging to Alexander but no longer used.

Like any garage, this garage is used for storage. Dimly visible lawn furniture, gardening tools, flower pots, shelves of paint cans, stacks of canvas. Shadowy presences in the periphery of Elisabeth's vision.

The Saab in which *the deaths* occurred is gone of course. Long banished from the property. Elisabeth has never been told, has never inquired, but surmises that it was towed out of the garage, hauled away to a junkyard.

For no one would wish to drive, or to be a passenger in, a *death car.*

(Would the interior of the car continue to smell of death, if it still existed? Or does the odor of death fade with time?)

In the doorway Elisabeth stands. It is strangely peaceful here, on the threshold. Gradually her eyes become adjusted to the muted light and she has no need to grope for a switch, to turn on overhead lights.

The garage door is closed of course. You can see light beneath it, obviously you must stuff towels along the entire length of the door to keep the sweet-poison air *in* and the fresh air *out.*

*Blue buzz of air. The only symptom is peace.*

*Come! Hurry.*

She is hurrying. She is breathless. On her knees on the bare plank floor in front of the narrow cupboard in the third-floor maid's room she reaches into the shadowy interior. Cobwebs in hair, eyelashes.

Wrapped inside a beautiful heather-colored mohair shawl riddled with moth holes.

Her hands shake. This must be one of N.K.'s diaries, unknown to Alexander!

The diary he'd found after her death, he'd destroyed. *To spare my son.*

Feminists had angrily criticized the husband's actions but Alexander remained unrepentant. Insisting it was his right—the diary was disgusting and vile (though he'd claimed not to have read it), and it was his property. His right as a father to spare his son echoes and reflections of the mother's *sick and debased mind.*

*But Alexander is not here now,* Elisabeth thinks. *Alexander will not know.*

The diary appears to be battered, water-stained. It is only one-quarter filled. The last diary of N.K.'s life.

At the makeshift desk Elisabeth dares to read in N.K.'s sharply slanted hand, in stark black ink. The low throaty voice of the poet echoes in her ears as intimate as a caress.

*fearful of harming the children*
*fearful of harming the children entrusted to her*
*begins with "the"—not "her"*
*telling herself they are not THE children, they are HER children*

*she does not want to carry the new baby on the stairs*
*fearful of dropping her slipping, falling*
*fear of injuring loving too much*

*(not the husband's child)*
*(does he know?—must know)*

*of course the husband knows    a man must know*
*pillow over my face, he says so the children will not hear*
*will win custody you will never see them again*
*your disgusting poetry will be my evidence in a court of law*
*you are not a fit mother*
*not a fit human being*

*he has struck me with his hand. the back of his hand. hits me on the chest, torso, thighs, where my clothing covers the bruises. he says he will take the children from me if I tell—anyone. if I tell my doctor. I must say, I am clumsy, I drink too much, take too much medication (even if I do not—not enough).*

*I must declare legally, I have invented these accusations against him. I am a poet/I am a liar/I am sick and debased/I have loved others, not him/I am one who makes things gorgeously up.*

*days of joy, now it is a dark season*
*days of happiness I can hear echoing    at a distance*
*he says I am not the beautiful young woman he married*
*I am another person, I am not that woman*

*to be a mother is to surrender girlhood*
*to be a mother is to take up adulthood*

*he says I am sick, finished    unless I slash my wrists I am of no interest to anyone*

*knowing how I am vulnerable, wanting to die (sometimes)*
*welcomed me back, forgave me (he said) even as I forgave him (his cruelty)*

*his lies, he'd so adored me*

*but then it has been revealed, he has not forgiven me he will never love the baby he guesses is the child of another*

*as in nature, the male will destroy the offspring of other males*

*(why does this surprise me? it does not surprise me)*

*a mistake to have confided in him, in a weak mood my fear of harming the children and he pretended to sympathize*

*then later, laughed at me in his eyes, hatred like agates*

*last night daring to say do it and get it over with*

Elisabeth is so shocked she nearly drops the diary. For a long time she sits unmoving, staring at the page before her.

At last, hearing a sound outside the room, a tentative footstep. It is Stefan, is it?—the surviving child.

Stefan enters the room though Elisabeth has not invited him inside, nor even acknowledged him. Asks her what is that, what is she reading, and Elisabeth says it is nothing, and Stefan says, his voice rising, "Is it something of Mummy's? Is that what it is?" and Elisabeth starts to reply but cannot. Wraps the diary in the shawl to hide it, leans over the makeshift desk and with her body tries to shield it from the child's widened eyes.

**11.**

*So very easy. Sinking into sleep.*

*Position yourself. Behind the wheel of the car, so calm.*

*First, you swallow pills with wine. Not too many pills, enough pills for solace. And the child, you must tend to him.*

*Dissolved in milk. Warm milk. Who would suspect? No one!*

*Start the motor. Lay your head against the back of the seat. Shut your eyes. The child's eyes. Wrap him in the shawl, in your arms.*

*Soon, you are floating. Soon, you are sinking. Soon, you are safe from all harm.*

For days, unless it has been weeks, Elisabeth has been feeling feverish. Sick to her stomach. A fullness in her belly as if bloated with blood. Gorged with backed-up blood.

One day ascending the stairs she loses her balance, slips. It is a freak accident. It is (certainly not) deliberate. A sharp, near-unbearable pain in her right ankle, that has twisted, sprained. In her lower belly a seeping of blood, then a looser rush of blood, hot against her thighs, clotted. At first she thinks that she has wetted herself, in panic. She calls for help. Weakly, faintly, doesn't want to upset her husband, doesn't want to upset the child, so very lucky that Ana comes hurrying—"Oh, Mrs. Hendrick!"—and in the woman's eyes compassion, concern.

*You may warm yourself in the shawl. That is for you.*

Just seven weeks old. The tiny creature—"fetus." Not a pregnancy exactly—you wouldn't have called it.

Elisabeth is astonished, disbelieving. She'd been *pregnant?* How was that possible?

When he learns of the miscarriage (which is what Elisabeth's doctor calls it) Alexander is stunned. His face is gray with shock, distaste. "That's ridiculous. That couldn't be. You *were not pregnant.* The subject is closed."

**12.**

In her *Paris Review* interview N.K. said in jest, *The best suicides are spontaneous and unplanned—like the best sex.*

*No more should you plan a suicide than you'd plan a kiss, or laughter.*

True of N.K.'s earlier suicide attempts but not true of the actual suicide in a locked and secured garage in the house on Oceanview Avenue, Wainscott. *Life catches up with you, taps you on the shoulder.*

Towels stuffed beneath doors, a plotted and meditated death, motor of a car running, bluish toxic exhaust filling the air. Stink of exhaust, having to breathe it in order to breathe in precious toxic carbon monoxide; the child beside her sedated, too weak to resist; the child in the rear of the Saab less cooperative but too groggy to resist. . . . Beautiful Clea, beautiful Stefan, children the mother hadn't deserved. In her deep unhappiness *calling us back, the kiss of oblivion.*

In the dimly lighted garage Elisabeth finds herself groping her way like a sleepwalker.

A powerful curiosity draws her. As water draws one dying of thirst.

Though Elisabeth has never been and is not suicidal.

This BMW, the older of Alexander's cars, seems to have been abandoned in the garage. Elisabeth is concerned that the battery might have died.

She will see! She will experiment.

The key to the BMW Elisabeth found after searching the drawers in Alexander's bureau. Loose in her pocket is the key now, and a handful of sleeping pills. Consoling!—though she has no intention of using the pills.

And in her hand a bottle of Portuguese wine she'd struggled to open.

And the moth-eaten heather-colored mohair shawl that is yet beautiful, like wisps of cobweb.

*Envy is the homage we pay to those whose hearts we don't know.*

*Envy is ignorance raised to the level of worship.*

Just to enter the (forbidden) garage. To sit in the (forbidden) car. To turn on the ignition—the motor is *on*!

(If the ignition hadn't turned on, that would be the crucial sign. *Not now not you not for you.* But the ignition has turned on.)

Just to listen to music on the car radio. (But all Elisabeth can get is static.)

Just to drink from the bottle. Solace of wine, that might numb the ache between her legs where blood still seeps, nothing dangerous, no hemorrhage but more like weeping. *Not a real pregnancy, not for you.*

Like a woman with no manners drinking from the bottle. Hardly the wife of the house on Oceanview Avenue.

Homeless woman. Reckless, harridan. Alexander would be appalled, but in her distracted state she'd forgotten a—what, what is it—wine glass. . . .

The BMW motor is quiet. Loud humming, could be a waterfall. Bees at a distance. Oh, but Elisabeth has also forgotten—in her pocket, a handful of green capsules.

Turns off the staticky radio. Leans her head back against the top of the seat. *A mood is music.*

Very sleepy, tired. Even before the drone of the engine, the smell of the exhaust, tired. Weight of the air. Can hardly move.

*One day. You will know when.*

In the mohair shawl she is warm, protected. Warmth like a woman's arms.

*Airy lightness. Like a kiss, or laughter.*

**13.**

Elisabeth ?—*the first time the child has uttered her name.*

*And the sound pierces her heart, so beautiful.*

*Small fists on the window of the car door close beside her head. Her heavy-lidded eyes are jarred open. With the strength of panic, Stefan has managed to open the heavy car door, he is shouting at her*—No! No! Wake up!

*Pushing away her hand. Fumbling to turn off the ignition. Coughing, choking.*

*In that instant the motor ceases. Hard hum of the motor ceases.*

*Elisabeth is groggy, nauseated. Hateful stink of exhaust, the garage has filled with bluish fumes. Yet: Elisabeth wishes to insist that she is not serious, this has not been a serious act.*

*If she were serious she would not have behaved in such a way in the presence of the child. (In fact, she'd assumed that Stefan was at school. Why is Stefan not at school?)*

*Only a single capsule swallowed down with tart white wine. Just to calm her rapidly beating heart. No intention of anything further.*

*Wrapped in the beautiful moth-eaten mohair shawl. Shivering in delicious dread, anticipation. But now comes the frightened child crouching beside her. Pulling at her, clawing at her. With all the strength in his small being dragging her out of the car. As she stumbles he runs to press the button open the garage door.*

*A rattling rumbling noise like thunder . . .*

*Pulling at Elisabeth. On drunken legs, coughing and choking. Pleading with her*—Get outside! Hurry!

*Together staggering out of the garage into wet cold bright air, smelling of the ocean.*

Don't die, Elisabeth—*the child is begging.*

Don't die. I love you. *The child is begging.*

*Never has Elisabeth heard her stepson speak to her in such a way. Never seen her stepson looking at her in such a way. Never such concern for Elisabeth, such love in his eyes.*

*And now that they are outside in the fresh clear air Stefan will tell Elisabeth a secret.*

*The most astonishing secret.*

*Not Mummy who'd pulled Stefan from the car three years ago, carried him out of the poisonous garage and upstairs in the house to (just barely) save his life. For Mummy had been unconscious, her head back at an angle as if her neck was broken, and little Clea unconscious wrapped for warmth in Mummy's shawl and Mummy's arms and no longer breathing.*

*Not the mother. Not her.*

*Stefan will explain: It had been the father who'd come home, who had saved him.*

*Alexander had entered the garage, he'd smelled the stink of the exhaust billowing from the rear of the car. Seen the hellish sight knowing at once what the desperate woman had done. And in that instant made his decision to let her die.*

*Do it! Do it, and be done.*

*There is no love in my heart for you. Die.*

*Alexander's decision not to rescue the mother and not to rescue the little girl wrapped in the shawl in the mother's arms. Only just the boy in the back seat of the Saab who was his son.*

*Blood of my blood, bone of my bone. My son.*

*Choking, coughing as he pulled the semi-conscious child out of the car. Seeing that the boy was still breathing, sentient. Not knowing if it was too late and the child's brain had been injured irrevocably but frantic to save him, the son. His son. Gasping for breath as he carried the seven-year-old out of the garage and kicked shut the door behind him.*

*Upstairs and in a panic hiding the boy in a closet. Not knowing what he was doing but knowing that he must do something. And not understanding at just that moment that he would claim to have discovered the boy in the closet, in his search for his son. And not understanding yet that the story would be, it had been the mother who'd carried the son upstairs, laid him on the closet floor, and shut the door.*

*The father's hands badly shaking. Still he'd have had time to return to the garage, to rescue the mother and the younger child if he had wished but he had not wished. Had not even turned off the motor, in his haste to save his son.*

*A brute voice urged, in terrible elation*—Let them die, they are nothing to you. They are not of your blood.

*Elisabeth will be stunned by this revelation. Elisabeth will grasp at the child's hands, to secure him.*

You have never told anyone this, Stefan? Only me.

Only you.

*And so it was murder, yet not murder. The father had only to wait as the garage filled up with poisonous haze, until the death of the woman was certain.*

*His excuse could be, he was agitated, confused. He was not himself. Had not planned—ever—to do such a thing. Never would he have murdered N.K. with his own hands. Never would he have wished the little girl Clea dead, though Clea was not his but another man's daughter.*

*One of the wife's lovers. Forever a secret from Alexander for in her diary he would discover and destroy there were codified names, obvious disguises. Would not know the identity of the little girl's father though he'd been rabid with jealousy for this unknown person and in his passion would have liked to murder him as well.*

*And so, it had happened. The deaths that were (the father would tell himself) accidents.*

*Yet, he'd taken time to arrange the towels beneath the door to the garage, as the woman had arranged them. For it was crucial, the poisoning should not cease until it had done its work.*

*Gauging the time. Though his thoughts came careening and confused. How many minutes more, before the woman he'd come to hate would be poisoned beyond recovery.*

*Twenty, twenty-five minutes . . . By then, he believed that the woman and the child must be dead, and their deaths could not be his fault. For the hand that had turned on the ignition was not Alexander's but the woman's.*

*In astonishment Elisabeth listens. Yet she is not so surprised for she has known the father's heart.*

*Stefan has saved her. It is wonderful to Elisabeth to learn that he has loved her all along, these many months of the most difficult year of her life.*

*Returning from school to save his stepmother. Daring to enter the garage, that was forbidden to him. Daring to yank open the heavy door of the BMW, to shut off the ignition. Daring to scream into her slackened face—*No! No! Wake up!

*In confusion and fright she'd flailed at him. Thinking at first that he was the furious husband.*

*Then, he'd hurried to open the garage door. Like rumbling thunder above her. Tugging at her, urging her from the death-car. Together staggering outside into the bright cold air of March.*

*In this bright cold air Elisabeth will run, run. Strength will flow back into her legs, her lungs will swell. Never has Elisabeth run so freely, alone or with another. She is suffused with joy. Light swells inside her, in the region of her heart. In her throat, into her brain. Behind her eyes that swell with tears. It is not too late, the child has not come too late to save her. Running hand in hand away from the shingle board house on Oceanview Avenue. Hand in hand away from the Hendrick family house and along the coarse pebbly shore wet from crashing froth-bearing surf Elisabeth and Stefan run. Giddy with relief for the cold Atlantic wind has blown the poisoned air away as if it had never existed. Rising on all sides now are gray sand dunes beautifully ribbed and rippled into which they can run, run and no one will follow.*

# The Medium's End

*Ford Madox Ford*

A man called Edward White was talking to a man called Charles Fowler at the Embarkment Club. White was a man of thirty-eight and Fowler was thirty-nine, having just returned to London after seven years in Burma.

"So you're still in the bank?" Fowler asked.

"I am one of the directors," White answered, "though that is no particular credit to me, as most of my family are directors, and I just stepped in. It isn't, I mean, like making a career. It was just waiting for me."

"Then South . . . ," the other began.

"Oh, you remember South?" White asked.

"You'd nothing else but South on your mind just when I went away," Fowler said. "I thought you were going clean mad—both you and Milly."

The banker looked gravely at the point of his evening slippers.

"I think we were both going mad," he said. "But it wasn't we who did it in the end, it was South."

"Oh, South," Charles Fowler said. "I thought there was more in him than that. I thought he was a tremendous swindler—what's the word?—charlatan? But I certainly thought he had some sort of powers."

"He had," the banker declared grimly. "I don't want to talk about it, but I may as well. If I don't you'll hear some silly version from some other chap. It was like this:

"Just about after you left, Milly and I really did go practically off our heads. It wasn't only that we were prepared to stake all we had on that wretched medium's wretched tricks. I use the word 'wretched' quite carefully, because that was what they were. The whole thing was a wretched business. It wasn't, as I've said, that Milly and I were prepared to stake our whole fortunes, but we were trying—we were succeeding—in roping the whole fortunes of a lot of people—unfortunate old maids and servants and people.

"You can't understand that sort of madness. I can't understand it myself, though I've been through it. Why, I mean, should the fact that a tambourine jangles in the air in a dark room or a phosphorescent hand touches you on the face—why in the world should that seem the most important thing in the whole world? There's no knowing. It's just a madness. It's like seeing an enormously bright ray of light and being convinced that it's a diamond sparkling. And then suddenly, lo and behold it's just a bit of broken bottle glass.

"Anyhow, there was this man South—a weird looking creature, with nasty, shifty eyes. You remember him. You used to think he had powers, you say? Well, he had powers.

"But the point is that the powers he had weren't, if you understand me, the powers we thought he had. They weren't even the power *he* thought he had.

"Anyhow, we were getting together a large sum of money for him—quite a large sum. There was mine, and Milly's, and old odd Williamson's, and twenty or thirty other people's. Why there might have been forty to fifty thousand pounds in it for him. And after this—his collapse—we discovered that he had forged another old woman's name for just about forty thousand, and lost the money on the stock exchange. So that our money would just have gone to make up that sum. You understand, he was an arrant swindler. He thought he was an arrant swindler. After his collapse I found in his pocket all the usual paraphernalia of these fellows—the rubber glove with the tube, the fishing lines with the small hooks, the birdlime, the patent reflecting spectacles—but just the very cheapest sort of swindler he was. It was nothing short of amazing that he hadn't been found out, for every one of his tricks had been exposed thirty or forty times, even at that date.

"And then came his extraordinary triumph—what you might call his hour of victory and death. What I am going to tell you is absolute truth—perfect and exact truth.

"It was the day before our cheque was to have been handed over to South. And South was going to give us all a manifestation in the afternoon. He preferred the night himself, as a rule, because it was easier to get darkness. But there was an old general, Sir Neville Beville, who was to catch a 6:20 train to his place near Southampton, and we wanted to get some money out of him, so the séance was to take place at half past four, at Lady Arundale Maxwell's. You remember her?

"I daresay you remember her room, a big ordinary drawing room, with a terrific lot of Indian stuff about it, in Queen Anne's Mansions. Not in the least bogeyfied as far as the house went; but of course there was that disagreeable skeleton of the old West Indian Obi worker in front of the fireplace. And there were other unpleasant things in the room, though I've rather forgotten what they were. I daresay South rather liked to have them about. They increased the feeling of mystery.

"Well, the meeting began about four. There might have been twenty of us. General Sir Neville Beville himself tied South into the ordinary bentwood American chair. South wasn't looking at all well that day. Extraordinarily pale he was, and with his eyes unusually big.

"The general tied and tied, and then South winced, and said: 'Hi! I can't stand that.' The old general said, 'Ah! I thought you wouldn't be able to. That was a knot I used for tying up some of those Yogi fellows that did the murders in the Deccan.'

"'But confound it,' South exclaimed, 'I'm not a murderer. There's no need to tie the ropes until they eat into the flesh right through my skin. Damn it, you untie them!'

"The general grumbled a good deal; then he undid the knot, and South began to shake his hands and slap them together. They were perfectly blue. He began to explain to the general that he could not be expected to make any manifestations when he was in acute pain; he wouldn't be able to keep his mind on the subject. And then he asked whether the general hadn't brought the pair of police handcuffs that he had suggested using. The general went and got the handcuffs. They were put on South's wrists behind the chair. Then the general took a piece of rope and tied it, from the cuffs, under the seat of the chair, to the front legs and around and around South's legs and arms and body in all sorts of ways.

"South said he didn't mind that, but he still complained that his hands hurt him, and he really appeared to be extraordinarily irritable.

"It came out most when the general began to press him to

make a demonstration in open daylight. You understand the general was an absolute novice at the sort of thing. He had never been to a séance of any kind before, and he was one of those chaps who say they have an absolutely open mind. Usually South refused to answer many questions of that sort. He used to say he needed the darkness in order to be able to concentrate his mind. If he looked at any other objects they took his thoughts away. And usually that was taken to be sufficient. But the general went on pressing him and pressing him.

"'Can't you give an exhibition in the daylight?' he kept on saying. 'Can't you? Can't you?'

"And the South exclaimed with exasperation—almost in a sort of scream: 'By God, I can!'

"He must have been in a really extraordinary state of irritation; indeed, he looked as if he might be going mad. Almost positively epileptic. He sat leaning forward on the ropes that tied him to the chair, and glared furiously at the general.

"'Well, then, do it!' the general said.

"Then fell a singular silence on us all. You see, we all believed in South. We all believed that he could make manifestations in the daylight, and we began to think he was going to do it then. It was decidedly the most unpleasant thing I've ever been in. The room, as I've pointed out, was quite commonplace. We could hear the rumble of the Underground if we listened carefully, and a chap a long way down below crying daffodils, and, occasionally, a muffin-bell, as one of the windows was open.

"I forgot to tell you what we really had come there for was to get a manifestation of the spirit of Anne Boleyn. She was an ancestress of General Neville Beville, and he was always talking about her. South kept staring at the general, and the general kept quiet. He explained afterwards that he didn't want to interfere with the chap, who he supposed was praying or something.

"I daresay South was a good deal upset, if only because he had to find the forty thousand next day, or it would mean seven years for him. I've no doubt, swindler that he was, he was praying for a miracle as hard as he could go. After all, his whole life was in the balance, and I daresay his whole life was as important to him as anyone else's is to anyone else. At any rate, no doubt he was willing it as hard as he could.

"One of the bones of the old skeleton in front of the fireplace—it was decorated with bits of brass wire and scarlet flannel—creaked in the oddest possible manner. There was nothing very mysterious about that. South used to insist on its being stood in front of the fire whenever he was going to manifest, though it usually stood in the corner of the room. When it got near the heat, of course, the wood it was hung on used to give a little, and so the bones moved. I've seen them move a dozen times.

"But South's condition was so strained that he really gave a high squeak.

"Then the tambourine at South's elbow moved. It jumped up and down perfectly plainly and visibly before all our eyes. It jingled and thumped, and South's jaw just hung open, and he just gazed at it. It began to hop about the table from edge to edge. Then it fell over onto the floor, and jingled away towards the skeleton.

"South said in a husky voice, 'Who's doing that?'

"His face was towards the window, and all our backs were to it. Then he screamed—the most agonised beastly scream that I've ever heard outside of a lunatic asylum. Our eyes all followed his—a hand was coming in at the open window. You remember it was Anne Boleyn that we'd come there to meet. Well, this was Anne Boleyn's hand. There was a distinct rudimentary, extra little finger. Anne Boleyn had six fingers on her right hand. That was why she was always drawn with her hands folded. She was very much ashamed of the defect.

"And the hand just came in at the window. It was dark against the light at first, then it looked white enough. It passed close to old Lady Arundale Maxwell's face, and she exclaimed:

"'How cold! How extraordinarily cold!'

"We weren't any of us particularly moved—not extra moved. We'd all of us been to a good many séances, and had felt cold hands passing near our faces. But, of course, it was a sufficiently exciting thing to have it happen in broad daylight.

"But South's mouth was hanging open; his eyes were starting out of his head, and there was perspiration all over his forehead. It was really most disagreeable to look at him.

"The hand stopped just beside General Neville Beville, at about a level with his chest. It was pointing towards South, with the first finger stretched out as if the person behind it were addressing him. He shrank back right against the back of his chair, huddling into it. The general slowly, and with a timidity that was singular in him, raised his own hand and just touched the other with his little finger. He drew his hand back sharply, as if he had had an electric shock. The hand began very slowly to move towards South. Then the medium screamed; he screamed very highly, and then exclaimed:

"'Cut me loose! For God's sake cut me loose. I shall go mad if it touches me.'

"It shows the state of agitation that he must have been in in that he made no attempt whatever to wriggle himself out of the handcuffs. In ordinary circumstances he could have done that as easily as you or I could take our waistcoats off. He went on imploring the general personally to let him loose. He abjured him, by his braveness as a soldier, to cut the ropes. I daresay it only took a moment or so, but this thing seemed to last for hours.

"The general certainly started towards the medium; he put his hand into his pocket to take out a penknife. Then the hand moved right across the general's chest as if to bar his progress. He lifted up his left arm to push the hand away. And then we didn't see any more of the general. I don't mean to say that he disappeared in a flash, but it was as if we had forgotten him. You understand, he wasn't there.

"He was found that afternoon wandering about Putney without a hat. He didn't remember how he got there; he didn't even remember who he was. It was a case of complete failure of the memory. The only thing that he could remember at the moment was Anne Boleyn's hand; and he didn't want to talk about that for fear of being laughed at. He never has talked about it except just once to me. The police took him home all right, of course, because he had his card case in his pocket, and he was all right again in a month or so.

"As for the hand, it just got nearer and nearer to the medium, and he continued screaming until it touched him. Then he became dead silent, and, after the contact, he exclaimed, 'Cold! cold!'

"That's all he's ever done from that day to this. He walks about the grounds of a private lunatic asylum in Chiswick, shivering pitifully; but he will never be cured."

"And what do you make of it all?" Charles Fowler asked.

"I don't make anything at all," Edward White answered. "Perhaps it was only the Grace of God. I mean that his collapse certainly saved quite a number of poor people from ruin, and possibly it saved me from becoming the accomplice—the quite unwitting accomplice, of course—of an atrocious charlatan. On the other hand, there's the other possible view—the view that spiritualists are trying to make fashionable today—that mediums who are perfectly genuine sometimes have their days of failure, and reinforce themselves with bits of fishing line and inflatable rubber gloves.

"But for myself I'm perfectly convinced that the poor beast was a swindler just at the end of his tether, and that, in his agony, his will, which he didn't really believe in, suddenly worked. He didn't in the least believe in ghosts; he had to pretend that he did. And then suddenly the ghost came. That was why he was so horribly afraid. I think some of these chaps wouldn't go on playing these tricks if they knew what it might let them in for."

# A Shade of Dusk

*Indrapramit Das*

I first learned to write in the dark when I was a little girl, scribbling secrets under my blanket (or just under the mosquito net, during summer) after the hurricane lamps were blown out. Electricity didn't flow like water back then.

I took pages from my flimsy school notebook to make up this diary. My sister, Pouloma, gave me some from her notebook too. I hid the pages under our mattress. I wrote how much I hated the schoolmaster with his whip-thin cane and prickly temper, about how much my father shouted at my mother, about how I gave away bits of my lunch to the ducks, foxes, and dogs by the road on the way home from school. My parents threw out the diary when they found it. They didn't want me keeping secrets in my room, never mind that a room and a girl will keep secrets even without pages to store them. My reward for observing my parents' tyranny—and for destroying perfectly good notebooks—was a sore bottom from my father's stiff, cigarette-scented palm. Much later, I would keep a diary when I went to university, to ward off the loneliness of foreign winters. After lights out I would sometimes keep writing in the dark, guided by the memory of home, where my sister was. Then I would mail her those pages as letters. She would write me back across the continents, but once she got married and pregnant, her telegrams came as rarely as new seasons.

• • •

This diary is fresh. My niece, Charu, gave it to me as a birthday present because I told her that story of writing in the dark. She calls it a journal. She thinks I'm forgetting things more often now. I hate to admit it, but she might be right. She came by yesterday with my grandnephew, who turned nine recently. I call him Potol because he likes when I make potoler dolma and send it over to their house, but I couldn't remember his real name. I felt embarrassed to ask Charu. I remember her other boy's real name—Sanjay. He's a teenager now, so he doesn't come over often, always off doing homework or spending time with his school friends.

While Potol watched cartoons on the TV, Charu went to the kitchen and bustled around there like she does. I heard her telling Kalpana, who was making dinner, to empty the garbage bags from the trash can more often because of the stench. When she came back to the table her nose was wrinkled. "Lokhi-Mashi, it smells bad in here. You should open the windows more often," she said. I couldn't smell anything but the frying cumin from the kitchen mingling unpleasantly with the smoke from the mosquito coil burning in one corner of the living room. I said I opened the windows all the time. She patted my hand and asked me if I needed anything. She was wearing a salwaar kameez. Charu always wears a salwaar kameez when she comes by to visit. It makes me wonder if she ever wears sarees anymore. She looks so much like her mother it feels strange, like seeing a modern version of Pampi (I do still remember that *her* real name is Pouloma), seeing her young again. But Pampi would never wear a salwaar kameez.

"Are you writing in your new journal? Are you able to?" Charu asked me.

I told her of course I was able to, I wasn't entirely decrepit. I told her writing during power cuts in the evening made me feel like a little girl again, because I could tell that's what she wanted to hear.

She smiled. Such a lovely smile. No wonder she found a good man like Bijoy. Pretty like her mother. But she smiles too much around me.

I told her not to tell her mother that I was writing a diary again, because she'd want to read it. I asked why Pampi was still in her room, anyway, why she was still sleeping so late into the evening. Charu flinched like I had hit her when I said that. She stopped meeting my eyes. I know that look. Something was wrong. Maybe they'd had a fight over the phone. Pampi never did get over her children selling our family house after their father died, the place she'd lived all her life before this little flat. I let it go. We drank our tea and watched the TV along with Potol in silence. My nephew, Pratik, bought this set for me—it's small, but colour. On the screen, there was a laughing cartoon skeleton in a hood, with thick blue arms. I suppose he must have been Death, of a sort. I don't know what kind of things they let children watch these days.

"You're so ugly," Pampi would say to me sometimes at night when we were children, to scare me, because older siblings love scaring the younger. That is just the way of the world. Boys and girls will take power wherever they can find it. So will men and women. "You'll never get married. You'll never have any babies because you need a husband to have babies," she would say. She said it in a rasping voice, like a horrible creature. I would whimper in the moonlight at this terrible prophecy. If I screamed and complained to our parents, she would twist my ear later in revenge, her own cheek sore from my father's hand. But during the day, she would hold my hand on the walk back from school, and shout at anyone who dared tease me, using her pretty looks and loud voice to stun them into submission.

Six decades since writing in the dark of my childhood bedroom, and Calcutta still has power cuts for hours. "Load shedding," Pratik always announces when I bring it up. "Because of all the people getting air conditioners nowadays in summer," he explains, sounding very much like his father, Chandrasekhar, who also used to tell me obvious things in that professorial tone. So I write in the dark again. Now I have no parents to find this diary. I have Pratik and Charu, who are not children anymore. And I have my sister. They won't read this until I'm dead, if I have my way.

I like writing in the dark, like before. These days I forget things, so it's good to put down my thoughts somewhere where they can't go away. It's like meditation, like Chandrasekhar used to do cross-legged on the floor on his mat. It gives me something do to during the load sheddings. I feel like a student again, writing in my diary (or papers) into the night, in my mother's knitted sweater, quilt wrapped around my shoulders against the Oxford chill frosting the window of my tiny room. Of course, now my stiff fingers aren't because of the damp cold of English weather, but because of arthritis. I need to take breaks often, but thank god I can still write. My knees, on the other hand, are like the ends of two chicken bones after someone's bitten off the cartilage (Charu always chides me when she sees me doing that at mealtimes, saying it'll pop out my false teeth, but it never does). I can barely bend my legs anymore. What can you do but think of the ways in which your body is breaking down, in these silent hours of sweating.

When the ceiling fan goes off and the air in the flat becomes still, I can smell something off, like Charu was saying. Kalpana takes out the garbage regularly. I've seen her do it. Maybe a lizard died in some corner. I'll have to tell her to look carefully for any sneaky corpses.

I write when the power goes because there's no TV to watch my Bangla soaps or cricket matches, no light to read the newspapers and *Reader's Digests* by. It's something of a relief when it happens, except for the heat (that's why I sit by the window or the verandah, to catch the evening breeze). It all gets too much for me nowadays; televisions and stereos everywhere, all these channels. I like my soaps, but the news channels—every time I turn to one they're talking about this Gulf War. I wonder why we need to hear nonstop about Americans dropping bombs on these people in the Middle East all the way here in India. There was a time we didn't need a TV to show us we were at war—sometimes we'd turn on the radio and make bets about whether or not we'd be ruled by the Nazis or the Japanese instead of the Brits, but other times the only reminder we needed were the air-raid drills, sirens calling across the sky like widows when the Pakistanis or the Chinese crossed our borders. I was studying in England during the Blitz, where it was more than just drills, though I was never under the planes. We never actually got bombed either in Calcutta or Oxford, but we knew it was a possibility. Now we're in peacetime, but the TV news wants to show us every war everywhere. It ruins my day every time, thinking how lucky I am to have lived this long.

It was a mere stroke that took away Chandrasekhar. A blood clot in the brain, sending the heart into a tailspin. Not a bomb dropped in a city. The rest of us are still alive instead of scattered across rubble in pieces. Some of us, anyway. I've seen many of my oldest acquaintances and relatives turn into obituaries in recent years, of course. I check the paper every day, just to make sure I still have the family I used to have. There is a phone in the flat, which I use to talk to family and old acquaintances sometimes. I can't go out of the flat to go visit people, or see a movie in the theatres, or go out to eat, very often, because of my knees. So the phone is a lifeline. But even as I long for it to ring every day, to have someone to talk to, I hate the splinters of pity in all their voices when they ask how I'm doing. The secret gladness that they're not a spinster like me, the smug certainty that anyone with this fate must have done something to deserve it. *At least we get to march towards death with our spouses safely by our side, and our sons and daughters two steps behind,* I hear them not say.

I have never gotten used to seeing Pampi without her husband. She seems so wretchedly alone, as if I too have faded away. She has never recovered from Chandrasekhar's death, or her children selling the house and packing her into this modern-shodern multi-storey building along with me. But then, she looks like a mirror image of me stooped in that chair at teatime, grumbling about the heat in summer, about the cold in winter, about how her children don't visit enough, about how I eat all the mishti in the fridge before she can have any. Always complaining, like me, like I'm complaining right now. Chandrasekhar's absence is as vast as the loss of walls and a roof above our heads—the house we all lived in gone, the walls closing in on us in this small flat, despite it being higher above the streets. But Pampi should be grateful that she still has a son and a daughter and three grandchildren.

I should be thankful too, that I have a nephew and a niece. And a sister.

During Chandrasekhar's shraddha, my tears were for my sister, not my brother-in law, though I would of course miss his sturdy presence in our lives. It was her sorrow that was the knife in my chest. But when she gripped my hand like an infant grabbing a thumb, and stared shell-shocked at the garlanded monochrome photos of her husband through the stages of his life: clean-cut teenager; the solemn young man she was wed to; the white-haired patriarch with his crisp dress shirts and kurtas, his horn-rimmed glasses and pipe, all I could think of was that Pampi *needed* me now, more than ever before. My older sister finally needed me.

She never held my hand like that again. If anything, she seems to need me even less now that her husband is gone, because back then I gave her some respite from his relentlessly masculine presence. Now she sleeps, and eats, and sleeps, and fades away into the walls of this place, and I remain no guardian of anything, same as ever.

I should check on Pampi. She was acting very strange just before the power went today. I woke up from my afternoon nap to go make tea because Kalpana stayed home sick (Charu dropped by some food in the morning, which was sweet, though I told her I am still capable of cooking). I walked into the living room, and there was Pampi sitting in the rocking chair in the corner, with all the lights turned off even though the power wasn't gone. It was just evening, and our living room windows don't face the sunset, so it was quite dark. I asked her why she hadn't turned on the lights—it was so dim I could barely even see her face under the cowl of her saree. Why she was wearing the saree with the cowl over her head in this heat like a new bride or a mourner, I don't even know. The ceiling fan was groaning above her head, turning slow circles with its blades. That smell like something rotting was quite strong, and I wondered if Pampi wasn't bothered by it. I was about to ask her.

When I reached for the switch, she said, "Don't turn on the light."

I told her I could barely see, did she want me to walk into furniture and break a hip?

I thought I heard a little giggle from her, so soft it felt like a memory. A memory of when Pouloma was fourteen and I was ten, and she would wake me up in bed and stare at me, her face pale blue in the moonlight from the windows, and I would tell her to stop it, but her face wouldn't move and I would be paralyzed in fear that she'd become a bhoot, that she'd died in her sleep and become a monster like in the stories.

But I don't think she giggled. I haven't heard her laugh in a long time, let alone giggle. Looking at her sitting in the twilight gave me that feeling you get, there must be a word for it—that sadness that comes with the evening light, when sunlight begins to drain away and it's still just enough to see by but not enough to keep the lights off. Again I moved my hand towards the switch. Again she said, "Don't turn on the light." She sounded like she had a cold, like her throat was thick with phlegm.

I asked her what had gotten into her, that it was dark.

"You don't want to see me like this," she said.

I asked her, like what, like an old woman? We're about thirty years too late for that, I told her, trying to get her to laugh. I'm no pretty young bride myself, Pampi, I said to her. This made me think, again, of the way she was wearing her saree over her head so it held the shadows under it, thick over her face. It made my heart skip a little—this odd little personal reminder of my perpetual identity as the spinster in my elder sister's shadow. I asked whether she was feeling unwell.

"I'm so ugly," she said. It sounded like she was smiling, though her face was invisible.

*No, I'm the ugly one,* I nearly said. I've always hated when pretty people call themselves ugly. But she's an old woman now, like me. Does that make her ugly? Perhaps that is the world we live in.

I told her she used to call me ugly all the time when we were children. I asked: did she remember that?

"No. Do you remember?"

What, I asked.

"You don't remember the good things I do for you."

I told her that wasn't true. That I remembered her reading to me from books when I was young, and taking me out with money sneaked away from our parents' purses to get kulfi in the streets, knocking down sour rain-wet mangoes from trees with stones and sharing them with me only for us both to get a stomach upset.

"You don't remember that I gave you two children," she said.

Pampi, I said. What are you saying? You have children, they are your children. You are the one with the children, I told her.

"You've inherited them, like everything else. If I had a stroke instead of Chandrasekhar, you would have moved in with him."

I asked her what rubbish she was talking. Did you just wake up from a bad dream? Is this about Charu and Pratik not visiting enough? Uff baba, they come every week, I don't know what you are on about, I told her, I told her all these things.

"Don't turn on the lights," she said again, as my hand moved, again toward the light switch. "You don't want to see me like this," she said, so low I could barely hear the words. I felt the way I do when I slip and nearly fall in the bathroom, and imagine my bones breaking like so many of my fellow acquaintances and family who've reached their elder years. Pampi sometimes has episodes, gets angry, forgets things, but this felt strange. This felt bad.

She didn't say anything after that at all, and all I could hear was the whining of mosquitoes coming in with the gloom, the familiar traffic sounds from the distant main road riding the warm breeze from the verandah, the hard cawing of crows on the sills calling for the sun to either come back to the sky or hurry up and leave.

So I left the lights off, and went to my bedroom, carefully using my walking stick to mark out my path, and switched on the light there instead. I was so confused by the whole conversation I entirely forgot to make any tea. Surely she had been sleep-talking while taking a nap. Maybe she's in one of her moods, missing Chandrasekhar terribly.

Every day at five or so, when the load shedding usually happens, I sit at my desk by the grill of the south-facing window of the flat. I sit with my tea, some water, my medicines, my plate of glucose biscuits, my pen (Charu has got me a ballpoint pen now that I have trouble refilling fountain pens, though I still prefer those), and my diary. They all sit on the desk, which used to belong to Chandrasekhar, and still smells faintly of his pipe smoke. Kalpana brings it all to me. She's a good girl. Charu and Pratik hired her—her mother works for them as a maid, and her father cuts hair on the footpath near their building. Sometimes I wonder if I would have already been dead by now if it weren't for them and Kalpana. When I thank them by saying things like that they get irritated. They don't know how unappealing it is to be helpless. I once left this country alone, with nothing but my accented English and my mother's knitted winter clothes. Now I can't even leave this flat without feeling like it might be too much.

Kalpana has to bring two old women in a city flat their tea and biscuits and groceries and meals, dust the furniture and mop the floors day after day. No school for her. She must be so bored, the poor thing. I let her watch the TV with me and give her some extra money when I can. When she sits on the floor with her knees tucked under her chin, watching the soaps with me, I wonder what it would be like if she were my daughter. If she were an orphan, could I have adopted her? Probably not, with her caste. Charu and Pratik used to sit on the floor on hot summer days in the huge living room of the old house when they were children. They'd sprawl at their mother Pampi's feet, listening to Chandrasekhar's gramophone play Hindi songs. I would be filled with envy, watching them, willing them to come sit by my feet instead. They never did. I was just Mashi, not Ma.

Even though Kalpana will never go to school or sail—well, fly, now—across the oceans to university in England, she will at least get married once she's old enough, and have children, unless something goes wrong. Even she has her destiny to fulfill, unlike me. When her parents send her back to their village to be wed, she'll no longer be able to work here. I think how I will miss her, but then I realize that by that time, I probably won't be around any longer.

I don't usually read the pages after I write here—but when I try, I can't. My handwriting is bad. I can't make out all of it. I can't let Charu or Pratik see this, they'll worry about it. Or maybe I'm the one worrying too much.

I can't seem to remember writing some of what I am reading.

When the power goes out, I can see the whole neighborhood go dark, the low skyline of stubby buildings with their pipes and TV antennae and rooftop clotheslines going black against the blue of the twilight sky. It feels like the city has gone to sleep, closing its electric eyes. Or perhaps like it has passed away unexpectedly. I can hear the old ceiling fan go *dhok-dhok-dhok* until it accepts its powerless fate. The sound of fan blades in the sudden silence is like a scythe swinging above my head. This reminds me of that movie with the knight playing chess with Death. I think Death had a big scythe in that. I saw that movie on video cassette recently with Charu; she and Bijoy drove me to their flat so I could watch on their TV with the cassette player. Very sharp, you could even read the subtitles properly. I hadn't seen that film in so very long. The first time I saw it was at Lighthouse Cinema, a long time ago. The actors and actresses looked so beautiful against the screen, though the image from the projector was faded and flickering. It was raining when we came out of the cinema hall—I went with Pampi and Chandrasekhar, as always, having no husband to take me—and under the cloudy light New Market looked silver and grey, like the world behind the big screen and the thick velvet curtains. I felt warm as we stepped out, despite the spray coming into the cramped area by the box office. Pampi said she didn't understand the film. I felt like she had understood plenty, but was just pretending not to for her husband, to make him feel smart. Chandrasekhar started to list all the movies by that director. I just wanted to talk to my sister about the film, tell her all the things it had made me feel, but he kept talking. I felt like plucking them apart and pushing him into the puddles by the footpath. The perfect husband and wife pair. And there I was, no one to hold my arm and tell me about who directed what, and from where in Europe. I had been to England, I wanted to shout at him. I had voyaged in a ship as big as an entire neighborhood, seen the broad blue road of the Suez Canal under the late summer sky, greeted Britain's shores in the rain, studied and lived in a foreign country, in the heart of the empire, and come back with a degree just like his, albeit in English instead of Chartered Accountancy. But still no husband and daughter and son for me. Not even the English boys would dance with me at the socials, a short, ugly brown girl from India instead of an exotic oriental princess. I came back a woman with an education, but still I was just a girl to everyone because I had no husband to hold my hand and lead me into adulthood. And there Chandrasekhar was to greet me as I got off the train from Bombay, handsome and hair-slicked and an utter stranger to me, and there Pouloma was with the blooms of love on her cheeks. My sister a wife and mother of a healthy boy, belly round with a girl on the way. I cried and she cried and we held each other right there on the dirty platform of Howrah

Station, but I felt like I was crying from pain, not happiness, even as my parents waited their turn to hold me after years, their beaming smiles filled with hope for a future where there was a man by my side and a baby inside me, too. In my heart, between my hips, I knew the future—I had come back not with the pride I was hoping for, alongside a degree from Oxford for my parents to tempt suitors and their families with. No, I'd come back with a secret like a black fruit plucked from the mouth of an English gynecologist with a bedside manner as cold as his hands—the monstrous pains that plagued my periods meant that I might be infertile. So I returned with shame, with the future held in the ache below my belly—the future where my parents would give up on finding me a husband because at least Pouloma and Chandrasekhar were there to give them grandchildren. I was a lost cause. I was damaged goods, shipped back sullied along the Suez Canal.

I wanted to shout all these things at Chandrasekhar as he pontificated about European cinema while Pampi looked on starry eyed, her face damp from the mist of raindrops drifting against the sheltered steps of Lighthouse Cinema. I thought: Why did she look younger than me, leaning against her man, when she was the older one?

The power just went out, the scythe is swinging above my head. I call out for Pouloma, ask if she's awake. No answer, so she's probably napping. Kalpana answers instead from the kitchen, asking if I was calling for a lit candle. I tell her no. Pampi sleeps too much, since Chandrasekhar went.

The pain has lessened with age, but never goes away. Now the doctors give it a name—endometriosis. Their tone when talking to me is always one of judgmental solemnity, as if this sickness is a curse given to me because I never found a husband, instead of a curse that prevented me from getting one. Or maybe I have always just imagined this in their voices. I still take homeopathic medicine for the pain, on Pampi's recommendation. I don't bleed any longer of course, but the throb of the baby I will never have sits eternal in my womb. Strangely, my heart remains healthy, the pain there, of a love I will never have for a husband, untethered from my flesh.

When I first heard over the phone that Chandrasekhar had died in hospital, his brief one-week coma ended, my first instinct was to smile. Real tears rolled down my cheeks, but there was that half a second of a rictus, like something had possessed my face. I went to Pampi in Chandrasekhar's room, bearing the news like a terrible present. She had been combing her silver waves of hair. We used to comb each other's hair when we were younger, deliberately surprising each other by yanking the knots. She staggered up and shuffled to the phone to ask her children to pick us up and take us to the hospital. They said not to worry about it, that they would bring the body to the house, and then we'd go for the cremation in the cars. Afterward, Pouloma sat in silence by the phone. I looked at the black and white framed portrait beside the phone. It was of Chandrasekhar and her from two decades earlier, standing on the steps of the house we were in.

Half a year later, we'd be here in this flat, the house sold off by her children because it was too large, too empty now that my parents and Chandrasekhar were dead, too expensive to maintain.

• • •

Not long after I returned from Oxford and moved into the family house with Pampi and Chandrasekhar and my parents, we went to visit Victoria Memorial. My sister, her baby bump, her husband, and their son. Ever since the news that I wasn't the fertile bride-to-be they had expected to return from England, my parents acted like I had personally misled them into investing in my foreign degree only to find out that it made no difference—my marriageability was doomed by my condition. They took me to multiple local doctors, who agreed with the English one. I didn't blame my parents for their bitterness. I was as disappointed in myself, in my body, as they were. My body had always refused to attain the beauty Pouloma's body seemed to so effortlessly radiate, and in time I had learned to live with this. But this was a betrayal I didn't know how to handle. So I helped take care of the house, of my sister's boy, of the cooking and cleaning, stayed out of the way of my parents, and snuck out to the sweet shop to eat hot rosgollas whenever I could. Bereft of the duties of a housewife, I fantasized about getting a job tightening rivets on bombs like those women I'd read about in America, who took over the men's jobs when their husbands all left to fight in the war.

The outing to Victoria Memorial was my sister's idea; she was trying to make me feel at home again in Calcutta, taking pity on my unmarried and childless state. The grounds were flushed bright and green after a shower, and Queen Victoria's bronze cheeks were wet. I didn't feel any less alone, back in my hometown, overwhelmed by a familiarity that grated against the loss of the life I was supposed to return to. Even the Victoria Memorial just reminded me of England, and how different it had been, and how it had yet changed nothing about my life in the end. But I was filled with gratitude. I thrilled at the touch of Chandrasekhar's fingers on my arm, to steady me when I slipped a little on the slick and pebbly paths around the monument. Suddenly, there was a man next to me, a man not of my own blood living in my home. Pratik tottered between his parents, eyes wide and round like the pebbles under his small feet, locked sometimes on the monument, and other times on me, the strange new mashi in his life. "He really likes you," Pampi kept saying, though Pratik showed at best a wary familiarity with me, nothing more. She kept trying to pass his small hand into mine so I could walk with him. I resented being made to become a placeholder wife next to her husband, with their child a conduit for the illusion. And yet, all I wanted to do was shower her with thanks for even this small kindness, though I felt no real connection towards Pratik at the time. Perhaps because he wasn't mine. With age, I have better come to terms with this. On the way back home, Pampi even insisted we stop for a hari of rosgollas fresh and warm from the sweet shop. The lump in my throat was like a stone.

That night, I woke up and found my sanitary napkin drenched as I lay alone in my bed. It felt like there was a knot of barbwire between my legs. I got up to go the single bathroom of our ground floor to change it. As I came out of the bathroom, sighing at the cramps, I saw a shadowy figure in the corridor, washed by the dim bulb in the bathroom. I nearly screamed. The figure said "Lokhi-Di." It was Chandrasekhar. I put my hand over my mouth, frozen. I was in my nightgown. It hadn't been stained, thankfully. I wanted to turn back and check the entire bathroom floor and toilet for stray drops of blood. My face went hot. Dadababu, I finally whispered, my heart pounding. You scared me, I said.

"Lokhi-Di. Sorry," he said, in English. His smile was yellow in the faint light.

I realized that the front of his white pyjamas, right between his legs, was stretched. I could see the sweat shining in the hair on his chest.

"I was just coming to use the bathroom," he said, as if to explain what I was seeing.

Yes. Of course, I said, but he was in front of me, standing there. I didn't know how to ask him to step back so I could leave.

And then he said, so abruptly, and softly: "I've seen the way you look at me, Lokhi-Di."

I admit, that at that moment, I thought about reaching out to touch that part of him that was stretching against the fabric of his pyjamas. To touch a man like I never had.

Dadababu, good night, I said instead, not looking at the reflected glitter of the bathroom light on his spectacles. My tone was polite, as if I hadn't heard what he had just said. For a second there was silence. The pat of water dripping onto the floor of the bathroom. "Good night, Lokhi-Di," he said, and stepped back and to the side of the corridor. I walked past him, not looking behind me. I could feel the blood between my legs, damp and warm, the pain radiating outwards like a familiar hand reaching inside me. I lay in bed for a long time afterwards, both longing for and dreading Chandrasekhar's appearance at my door. It didn't happen. The next morning, he acted like he always did. I didn't meet his eyes. Suddenly, he was family. I felt dirty, the blood still there between my legs, hidden under the folds of my saree and the fabric of my underwear. He would never belong to me like he belonged to my sister.

If you ever read this, Pampi, will you think I'm making up that incident by the bathroom? That this is a fantasy of jealousy? Maybe it was, and my mind is making it up, and I'm the one being tricked.

Sometimes Pampi and I watch Charu on Doordarshan, singing Rabindra Sangeet on our little screen. She always looks radiant under the studio lights, and her voice, the way her fingers caress the harmonium and make it sing with her, makes me so proud my stomach begins to ache. On TV she always wears sarees, glittering green and red and blue ones lined with gold. Pampi seems to take these performances for granted, talking about how Charu sweats too much on camera. When Chandrasekhar was alive, she would be full of praise for Charu's singing and playing. Sitting beside her, Chandrasekhar would weave his head to the music from the TV, puffing on his pipe as if the smoke were incense to honour his daughter.

You don't deserve to be her mother, I never tell Pouloma. And then I am filled with the sour feeling of being the resentful spinster. She is still grieving, after all.

When I was a child I would listen to the screeching and yelping of foxes and jackals outside our barred windows at night while trying to go to sleep. Now, ever since Charu and Pratik put me and Pampi in this box of a flat three stories up, I can't really hear much except the honking of cars from the main road, and the occasional barking of the stray dogs downstairs. The old house is rubble, not from a bomb, but from developers building a multi-storey like this one.

Last night I woke up with a start, covered in sweat. I saw someone standing at the door of my bedroom. I could just make them out. I couldn't move, because I was scared. I didn't want them to see me. In the shadows, I saw the folds of a saree hanging off the figure, and I realized it must be Pampi.

I said her name faintly, still afraid to break the thick quiet of nighttime, in case it wasn't her. I realized the room smelled bad, very bad, like that rotten smell in the living room and the kitchen. Now it was here too.

Pampi? I said, a little louder this time.

"I miss you," the figure said. It was Pampi, had to be. The voice was barely audible, like I was hearing it through a bad telephone connection.

Because the saree-covered figure was in the dark of the doorway, I couldn't see the face. There was something strange about her posture, as if she had partially turned towards me without turning her lower body properly, twisting her back.

"It's time to leave," she said.

I didn't know what to say. Leave? Where, it's the middle of the night. Pampi, go back to sleep, I told her. Somewhere outside, beyond the rooftops, I heard the faint sound of a local train passing through the night, whistling. She turned and walked into the dark. I could hear the hiss and pad of retreating feet dragging across the floor. Then, I don't remember anything but waking up today morning. Kalpana said that I'd left the front door open, that I was lucky a thief didn't get in. Had Pampi done that, while sleepwalking? Maybe I had been dreaming, or she had been. I don't dare go and ask her. The odd thing is that I feel like I miss her, too. She sleeps so much I barely see her during all day. But last night, I didn't feel that way. Not because she was right there in my room. No, it was because in that moment, I was scared of her. I felt like the little sister from so many years ago again, confronted by a sister I both knew and didn't know.

Today the phone rang during load shedding. It's on the desk where I sit and write, thankfully, so I can pick it up without having to hobble around with my walking stick. When I picked up the receiver, it sounded like a long distance trunk call, because of the clicking and static. There was silence on the other end, other than the interference.

Hello? I said.

"Lokhi-Di," came a faint voice. It was a man.

Who's this? Partho? I asked, because Partho is one of my cousins who still remembers to call once in a while.

"Hello, Lokhi-Di," came the voice again. My cousins call me that. So did my brother-in-law. The voice was so faint I could barely hear it, like a signal from a radio being tuned in and out. Something began to tickle my chest from the inside, a butterfly emerging under my heartbeat.

Who is this? I asked.

"Is Pampi there?"

She . . . yes, I mean. Who is this?

"You know who it is," said the voice. A wash of static buzzed through the receiver, crackling with each word. Clicking like bird's claws against the other end.

I looked out at the dark city, the light-less neighborhood under the deep blue evening. Everything out there seemed too silent. "Where's Pampi?" the static rasped.

I think she's asleep. Arre, who is this? I can't recognize you. Is it Partho? I said.

"Pampi isn't asleep," said the voice, and the inflection of

the words was so familiar, I felt light-headed for a moment, the sky above Calcutta, beyond the grill of the window, warping and dimming slightly.

What?

"Tell her to come here and join me. It's getting late," said the voice. Beyond the static, beyond the sound of the words, I heard the mournful wail of a train.

Join you? Where? Who are you?

"She knows where. She doesn't belong there in that flat anymore," the voice came, almost drowned out by the sound of the train horn again in the background. "*You* know where, Lokhi-Di. You should follow her here."

What is this, is this a joke? Partho?

"I've seen the way you used to look at me, Lokhi-Di. And Pampi, and the children. Follow her here. The children can take care of themselves now. You can't be a mother to them."

I had no idea what to say. The phone clicked and crackled and hissed into my ear at the silence. Who is this? I said again, weakly.

"You know it's too late. Take your sister and meet me here."

I admit I asked, then, very softly: "Chandrasekhar?"

The trains in the background wailed again, and there was a sharp click. Then the whir of the dial tone.

I just woke up to an empty house. I knew in my heart it was empty. It was dark in the room, the power was out. I could barely see anything. It was blue outside, late evening light. By that faint glow I could see Pouloma lying next to me in the bed.

"Pampi? What are you doing?" I asked, because she never comes and naps in my room. The bed creaked, I could feel it move as she shifted onto her side to look at me. She was silhouetted against the blue coming from the window, her arm against her hip, turned to me. I couldn't see her face, or anything of her, except the outline of her body. It was like she was wearing a saree made of darkness. I wiped the sweat from under my chin, the aanchal of my saree damp. I leaned over and felt for the switch to turn on the bedside lamp. It didn't turn on, because the power was out.

Then I remembered that the house was empty. That Pouloma is dead. I could smell the damp fabric of her saree, and the faint sweet scent of talc powder caking on her sweat, and the tamarind tartness of her breath after she'd sucked on her favourite Hajmola digestive tablets. But most of all, I could smell the familiar stench of emptied bowels, or something rotten. I felt sick, and felt myself sway on the bed.

"Pampi," I said. I reached out to touch her blank, shadowed face, expecting cold, pliant flesh. "Chandrasekhar called." My hand went through air, into the blackness, though my eyes stayed on her solid silhouette. The crows screamed outside. My heart racing, I struggled upright and waved my hand further through her body. She remained silent.

As my throbbing, clammy fingers vanished into the void of her body, the world exploded into blinding light and sound.

Electricity flooded the room as the power returned, the ceiling fan clattering on loudly, the tube light snapping and buzzing to life. In the five seconds of stuttering shadow and light as the old fluorescent struggled to turn itself on, I saw my arm hovering inside my sister, vanishing into her bone-white saree at the point of the lower abdomen. My eyes darted to her face under the cowl but there was none. There was only the pillow behind her, as her entire body faded like the afterimage on a television turned off. As the shadows ceased and the tube light stopped flickering, I saw my hand held out over an empty bed, where seconds ago had been an entire person.

Today I tried to read this journal and really figure out what I have written in those stretches of darkness, where it feels like I am dozing and dreaming while writing, that the dusk has become a part of me and sent me into a faraway place, until Kalpana shakes my shoulder and washes reality with her candle, or the power returns with the fan bursting into clattering life above me. I feel sick in my heart and stomach, at the untidy words on these pages. Despite what I have written during the load sheddings, my sister no longer lives with me in this flat. She no longer lives anywhere. But I remember talking to Pouloma in the dark, and waking up next to her. Why do I remember that?

I don't know if I'm remembering these moments from when she was still alive, from when we lived here together. But as hazy as the gaps in my life become, my hand moving through my sister's vanishing body is clear as the snap and flash of that tube light illuminating my empty bedroom. That blackness under the cowl of her saree as brutal as the plain, white, featurelessness of her face covered in white cloth at the crematorium, the assurances that I didn't want to see what was beneath one last time before she went into the flames. I never did see.

Today afternoon Charu came by with a tiffin carrier of daal and chhana and a foil-wrapped packet of rooti because Kalpana is sick again, the poor thing. Charu went to the kitchen and reheated it all on the stove, despite my protests. Then, together, we sat for lunch. Potol wasn't with her this time, nor Sanjay—

school, I think. While eating, Charu said Pratik has written to the building society to get a generator for the stairwell because of all the load shedding. It's not safe, she said. I didn't say that I would never try going down those stairs in the dark. She said that Pratik was also looking into at least buying an inverter for the flat so that I can have power in the living room when load shedding happens.

Then, tearing little strips of rooti on her plate, she asked, "Lokhi-Mashi, do you want to come stay with us? We have an extra room. I'm sure Bijoy would be fine with it."

I told her it was fine, that she shouldn't worry about me, that I still had my wits about me, that I didn't want to be a burden to them in their flat with their children to take care of.

"It's not a burden. I don't like seeing you here alone like this."

I remembered again, then. Of course, of course I am alone here.

"I know you're fine, Lokhi-Mashi, but I'd feel better if you were there with us, and not sitting in this empty flat day after day." I wondered then, how many times I'd talked to Charu as if her mother still lived here.

I told Charu that she made my life sound very sad, with a bit of a laugh. She shook her head. "No, that's not what I'm saying. It's just that. When Ma was here it made sense, but now . . . every time I walk up and down those stairs. I feel like I should be taking you away from here."

Don't worry, I don't take the stairs anyway, you know that, I take the lift, I said. I told her not to worry. I was fine here. Charu smiled at me, then, but I could tell she didn't want to.

"Mashi, just think about it. We would be happy to have you

with us. No more sitting in the dark during load shedding—our flat has an inverter. And you wouldn't be alone all the time."

I smiled back at her and said I would think about it. I knew then that she and Bijoy would decide by themselves to stop renting this flat and move me to their place soon enough. It was a waste of money, and I am, apparently, forgetting things more often than I want to admit. So why did I feel a pang of disappointment when she mentioned these plans, about inverters and generators and moving?

But I know why. I've always told Kalpana not to bring the candles to where I'm sitting in the living room. There has always been something about being held in the arms of the dark, suffering in the silent heat, something comforting.

The darkness reminds me of my sister. This is the place we were alone together again.

Maybe if I write down how she died while the afternoon sun shines outside, I will remember that she is dead.

Not so long ago, I can't seem to remember how long, and I can't ask Charu or Pratik or anyone because they will worry, but I think it was about a year ago, my sister woke up from her afternoon nap late, just as the power went out in the evening. It was summer, like it is now, so it must have been a year ago. As Kalpana was lighting candles in the kitchen to place around the flat, Pampi walked through the living room where I was sitting waiting for tea. I could hear the call to prayer from the mosque a few streets down from us, drifting in through the verandah. A local train somewhere far away, whistling through the twilight. As Pampi walked by me, I asked her why she had slept in so late, whether she was feeling all right.

She said to me: "Chandrasekhar called."

Her husband, of course, could not have called, because he was dead. Neither of us is young, so while this comment startled me, it didn't seem too strange. Only unsettling, because it meant Pampi was in a muddled mood, which often led to her getting angry, lashing out. She had gotten confused before. Then, instead of sitting down with me, she walked past me toward the front door, swaying impatiently from side to side to keep pressure off her weak hips. She didn't have her walking stick.

I am not a fast woman either, at this age. I barely even realized she had opened the door when she stepped out into the building's stairwell. I felt the warm gust of the draft that comes through the living room when the front door is open. There were no lights on in the stairwell, of course. No lift operating without power. I grabbed for my walking stick and tried to get up to follow her and get her back inside, spending precious seconds in panicked confusion before calling to Kalpana to get out of the kitchen and chase Pampi-Di who had walked out into the dark stairwell. Kalpana was just walking out from the kitchen to the living room with a candle at that moment, sending shadows leaping everywhere. Eyes wide, she put the candle down on the dining table adjacent to the sitting area as quick as she could, and ran towards the door. I had managed to get up and walk in her wake, my stick grinding against the stone floor with each heavy step, the room wavering and sallow from the light of the candle. I felt dizzy, my knees shooting with pain. The front door was wide open, black as a moonless sea, the draft from the stairs like warm breath gushing from a wide mouth. Kalpana plunged into the darkness just as I heard a noise like a sack full of potatoes hurled down the stairs. A scream pierced the darkness as I walked towards it. Not my sister, but Kalpana. Pampi was probably already dead at that point, having gone headfirst down an entire flight of stairs in her rush to get wherever she was going. Without her walking stick, without any illumination in the stairwell, the fall was inevitable. I waited at the top of those stairs in the dark, sweating, for the power to come back, because Kalpana refused to let me try to navigate the stairs. She stood guard by Pampi. Soon enough the stairwell was speared by light from torches waved by our neighbours coming out of their flats, concerned voices echoing down the shaft of the stairwell. The beams of light revealed blood like a glistening fresh coat of dark paint on the stairs leading down from Pouloma's twisted body, her white saree half unraveled, her pale belly speckled with moles in the torchlight. She was caught in a dance that she couldn't have danced at her age, limbs bent and spine arched and twisted in wild abandon. The aanchal of her saree covered her face like an ominous veil, soaking blooms from head wounds. There she lay, until the power came back on, until the ambulance came, until her children arrived with their faces shining with tears. When the lights came back on I nearly shouted for someone to turn them off, to keep her wreathed in shadow so she would not have to show herself like this. The stairwell was hot, full of people, and rank with the stench of the final bodily indignities of death. I felt so faint by the time strangers were moving her limp body onto a stretcher that it felt like I might follow her down those steps now dark with a spilled part of her once-beautiful body.

Kalpana is still sick at home; they think it's malaria. Charu said she made sure the parents have the medicine for her, even as she calls me every day to remind me to take my own medications. So once again, I have the flat to myself, food brought by Charu in the dripping fridge, even though I told her I can still cook. Lovely Charu. I see her as a little child still, because I'm so much older than her, because I saw her fresh out of my sister's womb, covered in blood and mucus. I held my sister's wet hand as the baby found her nipple, and my vision dissolved in tears when she said to me then, voice hoarse from shouting and screaming through labour: "You will raise her with me, Lokhi." Little baby Charu. But what a woman she is, singing on TV, raising her boys, taking care of her family, being such a good wife to Bijoy. She has already done everything I haven't. I admit that I envy her, and not just because of her relative youth. The truth is I didn't raise her with my sister. Pampi never needed that. She was a wonderful mother, and Charu a wonderful daughter. I was just any old mashi. Or maybe they were just any old mother and daughter, their perfection nothing but the gloss of envy in this mashi's eyes.

I am alone in the darkness, the city with its eyes closed in the twilight, no electricity beyond the bars of the window, just the pall of dusk. The crows, cawing at the coming dark as always. Far away, the glimmer of light beyond the zone of the load shedding is like another reality in the distance, where the living are. In my neighborhood there is only silence, but a train far away, leaving forever. The mosquitoes are drawing what stale blood is left in my veins. There is an unbearable stench, as if the breeze through the window has caught a festering garbage heap. But I know it's coming from inside. I can barely see Pampi in the dim living room. Her posture is worse than before, she is stooping, her back bent, her head cocked to one side. I cannot see her face under the cowl of her saree, the fabric of which glows a muted blue in the dim light from the windows. I can see that there are dark stains on the cotton, blooms of black. I want to tell her to think of tomorrow, when she will feel better, because no sickness lasts forever, like she used to tell me when I got sick as a little girl. Think of tomorrow, when you will feel better, she would say, touching my forehead, the leering bhoot that turned to me at night and spoke to me of how I would never get married vanished into my Pampi. But I don't know if I should say anything, because this doesn't feel quite like my Pampi. But it is her.

There is a warm gust running through the living room. The front door to the flat is open. Like a black mouth, open. The stairwell is a throat, a tunnel, a canal. I remember the jet black of the Suez Canal at night, beyond the rails of a ship taking me back home, the thrashing waves haunted by what dead sailors I didn't know. Pouloma is waiting. She wants to leave this little flat we shared. Chandrasekhar called. Charu and Pratik don't need her anymore. They don't need me either. No one does, except Pampi, perhaps, now. She is waiting for me. Or is Chandrasekhar waiting for us? I can't tell if Pampi is angry, or sad, or beckoning, because I can't see her. We are sisters. I look into her featureless face as she looks at me through the black veil, and I cannot for the love of my god tell if I am afraid.

# Icarus Rising

*Richard Bowes*

## MY MASK

My mother screamed at the sight of the black mask that had become my face—I was peering into the kitchen window at dusk on the day I was buried. Mine had been a closed-casket funeral. But now I was a ghost and free. If I'd been able to remove the mask and show her the blood and broken bones, the screaming would have been worse.

This encounter helped destroy any remaining bridges between my Living family and me. Right then I was mad at the world for letting me die, and mad at myself for the stupidity that had left me dead.

Burial clothes rot away in no time. But the clothes in which a ghost has died become like a permanent tattoo. The mask I died in will be my face forever.

My family didn't know how to deal with me when I was alive. So it followed that they didn't know what to think about the shattered bones, busted organs, and clinging flesh that was sent home in a body bag from the Big Apple—the remains of me: Raphael Marks.

Things in New York hadn't been going at all badly until I let my guard down and luck deserted me.

From my grave I raged against my parents for dumping me

in the family plot in Bellwether, Pennsylvania. I'd fled this nothing town at age seventeen. I'm lucky nobody there believed in cremation.

Ironically, as a kid, I thought ghost stories and movies were stupid. Getting laid out under the grass changed my perspective. Remembering that I'd been killed by a Living being I trusted, fueled me with so much anger I couldn't think straight at first.

Time moves slowly in a graveyard. I discovered that many of the dead lay huddled in the dirt, terrified by the aggressive specters that controlled the place. They endured a kind of death within death. Over the decades they'd lost all memory of having lived, and became no more alive than the dirt that held them.

Never once did I consider taking that road. I wanted my life back and vowed to regain every bit of the amazing future that had been stolen from me.

Angry specters, uneasy in their graves and not interested in turning to dust, dominated the cemetery. Cross them and you'd find yourself disintegrating and awaiting a second death. Once I saw how the graveyard was arranged, I worked my way into the aggressive specters' ranks, hanging out with them and sharing their rage. Paying unwanted visits to families, friends, and total strangers was how specters proved to themselves that they still existed. Anger made me rise out of my rotted casket and frighten young couples screwing behind tombstones.

When you've been dead for a while, it's easy to lose track of time. It becomes something that just flows past you.

Then, one night, I floated by my family's house and saw that it was deserted, with a FOR SALE sign on the lawn. I realized it had been years since I'd been around the old place.

There was, I realized, no purpose to my haunts, no direction.

They always ended with me back in what I feared was my final resting place.

So I began paying attention to the world of the Living and looked for a way I could make a life there. I saw specters flying through the dark, some naked or just skeletons. Others, like me, dressed in the clothes they had died in, some with cloaks and flowing ribbons in their hair.

I began to feel something like nostalgia for the city where I'd died. More and more over the years I found myself called to that place where once heads had turned when I walked by.

In addition to the mask I'd worn when making illegal graffiti art, the leather jacket, black jeans, and ankle boots in which I'd lived and died were also now part of me.

I taught myself to fly by practicing short excursions. I swam through the night air and began following the Living, who drove or walked in the dark. They shivered and peered around like they sensed my presence. During the day the Living would see no more of me than a ripple of sunlight, a momentary shadow, as I went among them.

One evening when I felt I was ready, I left my grave and floated out of Bellwether, Pennsylvania, to the great city. I imagined with relish, the idea of New York's curiosity about me growing when word spread that I'd returned. I promised myself to not be the same naive graffiti artist I'd been before I died.

Thinking about getting a new graffiti tag, I chose "Living Death." Then I realized that my ghostly hand would pass through any paintbrush or spray can. But I was sure I'd find some other way to publicize myself.

It was just before dawn when I floated into the outskirts of the great city. In the dark I saw the towers of light across the river, felt the presence of my kind (whom I had never noticed when I lived there) amid the millions of the Living.

By daylight the place seemed to have changed into a city of glass in the three decades I'd been gone. The crowds, even the kids, lacked the color and style that I remembered. East and West, the Villages were tame. And graffiti, the little I saw, was tired and commercial.

For a few days I wandered among the Living, listened to their talk. Looking for someone familiar, I flicked through faces as if they were endless pages in a telephone book. This city needed a ghostly presence to make it alive, and I was the one who could provide that. I spoke my name in crowds and whispered my old graffiti tag "We Dis" even though it brought back bad memories. But my ghostly words attracted no attention.

I drifted into art galleries and bookstores. In one: a big color photograph on a wall riveted me. It showed a figure falling to earth from the roof of a tall building. The falling figure wore a black mask and black clothes. There were several shots of his descent.

The title was *Icarus 1987*. I realized that the figure was me falling to my death thirty years before. And the photographer was Denny Wright, a lover of mine.

Then I overheard a very pretentious couple behind me talking about going downtown to view the display of art in contention for the Double/Annual Awards.

Mention of that event caught my memory. Like the photo, the awards, held every two years, was a major event. One in which I'd once participated in my first time in New York. And I suspected it was one of the reasons my time here had ended.

Since I was still relearning the city, I followed the couple like they were a hunch. When they hailed a cab I got in with them. The driver, I could tell, sensed an invisible passenger. But on that sunny afternoon a ghost was invisible to the eye. And he was, after all, a New York cabbie who just shook his head as I floated in.

**GWENDA**

The museum we went to was not the dowdy uptown one I remembered. The lobby was vast. An almost-blinding sunlight poured through glass from three sides. I looked around and noticed someone who seemed to stare at me from afar through dark glasses.

And I knew her! I'd forgotten about Gwenda and couldn't imagine how she saw me when nobody else could. But by accident I'd found what might be a useful Living person.

Gwenda Pinsky was an art critic a few decades older than I was. When I first hit town she did me some small favors, gave some attention to We Dis, the graffiti tag I shared with a guy named Graham Kreel. We Dis fought hypocrisy in art and the world.

Gwenda once did me the big but dangerous (as it turned out) favor of nominating me for the Double/Annual Award. Thirty years later, walking toward her, I realized she wasn't looking my way and couldn't have seen me if she had been. Her eyesight was gone.

I spoke her name as loudly as a ghost can. When I knew she'd heard me, I spoke my own name.

She reacted with surprise but also with disbelief and anger. So I told her a few things that only she and Raphael Marks would know.

Even then she said, "This is a perfectly assembled scam. I have no idea why anyone would assume the identity of a dead artist in order to fool a blind art critic. But your imitation of Raphael is so lovely that I can't make myself shout out for you to stop.

"Your encountering me at this new museum in the fever pitch of the Double/Annual is a perfect choice for your game. Back when I was a curator and decided fates, Raphael Marks (whom you mimic so well) and his graffiti were a controversial choice of mine. One I have never regretted, though it haunts me."

I half whispered, "Every two years that award sorts out the winners and losers. In that sense I was a winner."

She then said, "My own fate is of a kind not much in evidence at art shows. Quite possibly I am the only 'visually impaired' individual in the building.

"Voices connect me to the world. I sit and listen to middle-aged failures whose careers took wrong turns and the disgruntled young, probably doomed to be unrecognized, all bitching about the politics of art.

"Now I am not interesting or important or new enough to make anyone but you stop and listen to what I have to say."

We talked briefly about Denny Wright and his photograph *Icarus 1987*. I probed her for news about Graham Keel, my partner in We Dis (also my murderer, but neither of us mentioned that). She claimed to know little about Graham.

Then, Gwenda listened to her phone. Everyone seemed to have one in his or her pocket. She said, "The person who helps me get around will be here soon."

I saw someone heading toward us, said good-bye, and floated back into the crowd.

When Gwenda was younger and sighted, her understanding of art was nothing compared to her command of gossip and intrigue. Watching her talk excitedly into her phone, I knew that she was spreading word of my return.

***ICARUS 1987***

That night, I stopped by Denny Wright's loft for a surprise visit. Gwenda, when I'd asked, gave me the same Soho address that I remembered from back when he and I were broke and in love.

My plan was to arrive close on the heels of Gwenda's phone calls. Soho had changed from the empty streets and artist/landlord turmoil I remembered. In those days, Denny and I had lived and worked in a tiny sliver of a studio. Now, according to his name on the doorbells, Denny owned the third and fourth floors.

At midnight the street level boutique windows displayed slim, wide-eyed figures in low blue lighting. Across the street a woman walked a pair of large dogs.

Denny wasn't home. But being a ghost is all about waiting. I slipped through the building's door and into the foyer. Within an hour a taxi pulled up before the building. Denny, nicely aged and nicely dressed, got out and glanced around.

I wondered if he was expecting me. Denny came in the door but I stayed in shadow. He walked right through me. I whispered his name. He jumped back and cried out.

"Don't be afraid," I whispered. "I thought of you all the time I was gone," I lied. "When I came back here, I discovered you had caught the attention of the world the day I died. Those shots of me falling may have kept my name alive. No, don't cry. I still love you in my own way."

We sat upstairs in his wonderful loft. In shadowy light, Denny stared at me with wide eyes and shaking hands. He put away quite a lot of wine.

"The New York art world is talking about Gwenda's calls," he told me. "Tonight at dinner, everyone remembered you."

He asked if I wanted to hear her on his cell phone and I nodded. She said, "This is Gwenda Pinsky and I know my communication has been spotty over the last decade or two. But I am either the first person to encounter Raphael Marks thirty years after his death, or I'm a blind fool.

"He asked after you, Denny, and I told him what I knew. Then he asked about Graham Keel and I remembered not including Keel's name with Raphael's when I placed We Dis in the 1987 Double/Annual Award. Keel seemed more like an assistant than an artist. And given what happened, I thought it best not to dwell on that with Raphael."

I gestured and Denny shut her off.

"Everyone in downtown New York knew you back then," he said. "You took me to the Mudd Club in that abandoned part of Manhattan. We walked down deserted streets and climbed corroded stairs. David Bowie was at the club that night. Political graffiti was all the rage. Even he was happy to have met the better half of We Dis.

"Most of what I have I owe to knowing you. Thirty years back, my business card should have read, 'Gay photographer with an unbreakable crush on Raphael Marks,'" he said.

I knew this living person was totally mine and quite useful. So I told him, "You screamed when I got knocked off the roof of the Levanal Building. But you went on shooting."

Denny flinched and looked away.

"I want to do a variation on that day. I hope you'll be moved by what I intend. Because I'll need your help to make it work."

Then, I said, "As part of this I want to talk with Graham Keel, maybe come to understand him and his motives."

Denny was amazed that I would ever speak to Graham. He said it showed my great heart. The Living love things like this.

Denny told me about Keel's new art gallery and where he hung out and where he lived.

**KEEL**

The gallery was downtown on an old block that had suddenly become all wine bars and antique stores. It was evening when I arrived. A kid hell-bound on a bike came out of a side street and rode past me. I could see right through him.

I'd known nothing about ghosts when I was first in this city and had little to do with them on my return. Only when I thought about the ghost kid later, did I wonder if he'd been following me.

I knew the gallery would be closed. But I saw a light in an office and floated through the front door. The art on the walls was all black and white angles.

"Symmetry, making a comeback?" I murmured. "Thought that died a couple of years before I did."

Graham looked up. He wore gold-framed reading glasses and had lost most of his hair. My old partner squinted in my direction but he never showed surprise or fear. I had to give him that.

"The ghost thing felt like a scam when I heard about it the other day," he said. "I guess now I'm a believer."

"Some say a murderer,"I whispered.

"I hope you know better than that, Raph. Certain people see me as the villain who hated Raphael Marks for being so much more talented and beautiful than I was. So I pushed you over the edge and watched you die."

"That was my take at the time."

"It's on record from when the cops found me that I was vomiting and crying my heart out at my closest friend having slipped out of my grasp."

"I would shed tears for you if only I had tears," I said.

"They arrested me for trespassing and defacing property. Not for murder or assault of any kind. Please tell me you know it was an accident. All anyone talked about was your art. No one knew I invented the devil/angel logos we used on every graffiti design We Dis created."

I remembered the logos as something we had done together but that wasn't why I was there.

As Graham Keel spoke he pulled on a very nice velvet jacket. Then he said, "It's been fascinating talking to you. But I've got to be home."

His audacity reminded me of old times. I glanced at a photo on his desk of two teenagers who had the misfortune of looking like their father. "I'm coming with you," I said. "I'd love to meet your family."

He was shocked by the very idea. But that night, run though he did, Graham Keel discovered that I would be with him everywhere he went unless he did a few things for me.

Over the next couple of weeks he used his connections, his skills, to do what I wanted. More than once he told me the pressure I used was killing him. I didn't say (because it might give him ideas) that the last thing I'd want was to create a ghost like him in my town.

**We Dis**

Thirty years ago he and I stood amid the rack and ruin of the West Side Highway and the catastrophe that was the Hudson shore.

We had looked up at the Levanal Building, fifteen stories of black cement. The place exuded evil. It was said they specialized in smuggling weaponry for third-world cartels. All we could think of was how our graffiti tag We Dis would look on that top floor.

One day that summer we somehow managed to look enough like delivery guys to invade the building and access the roof. We took turns, as always. One would hang over the front of the roof spray-painting our smiling devil/tearful angel graffiti and our slogan.

The other would hold on to the painter.

Across the way Denny had managed to climb up onto an abandoned elevated railroad. He had his camera out.

I was just finishing the words:

SATAN LIVES HERE
WE DIS/KNOWS THIS

Then the hands that held me slipped away. And I fell screaming and smashed face-first onto the cement.

At our recent reunion I had promised Graham Keel I would never bother him again if we could duplicate the Icarus event with a few variations.

He didn't trust me, nor I him. But he had the sometimes amazing ability of the Living to organize.

When I saw the Levanal Building again it looked the same as ever. But its name had been changed and its surroundings were transformed. The abandoned railway was now an elevated scenic park. There was a promenade along the river. The glittering glass museum I'd been in was a neighbor.

What's more, the Levanal's current ownership was anxious to be connected with the arts. Graham Keel managed to make sure they never quite grasped the history of what was about to be enacted on their premises.

I was going to duplicate my famous fall. Except this time I would do it as a ghost. If I understood this city as I believed I did, my reenacting that moment and walking away from it would mean that by tomorrow morning nobody would be talking about anything else.

I stood on the edge of the roof, saw the crowd looking up from the railroad park down below. In the mix I spotted more than a few of my own kind. They shimmered in the evening sunset—that light when we're easiest to see. I knew almost nothing about them and felt I had no time to learn.

Graham Keel came near me and whispered, "I never had a brother. We could have been brothers. But all you did was push me aside, ignore me in public. When you got in the Double/Annual I didn't even get mentioned. That's all I could think of that last time. . . ."

"Bygones," I said and stepped off the roof. With luck, I'd never see him again.

I held out my arms without fear as my weightless body slowly fell and the Living ones below, with their cameras and binoculars, caught sight of the flickering in the twilight that was me. I came down lightly, feet first, on the ground. There were gasps and applause along the railroad park. People knew they were seeing something they previously never imagined. There would be different ideas as to what it meant.

Denny had let it be known that this event was connected to his *Icarus 1987* photo. He wrote that it would capture the ghost of the late artist Raphael Marks. That brought attention, which was good. It also raised arguments about the existence of ghosts. Those arguments had seemed to involve Denny and his photos more than they did me. That was bothersome.

As I touched down, Denny was looking up into the air. Others were pointing. I moved out of the building's shadow. And against the sun setting over New Jersey, I saw, in black silhouette, a woman with long flowing hair and dressed in 1890s fashion, floating against the evening sky. Denny stared at this apparition and only glanced my way when she disappeared.

People were talking, some were yelling. There was no coincidence involved. The incredible specter had appeared at that moment to steal my glory.

I wondered who had arranged this and what Denny, or for that matter, Graham Keel, would tell the world. It would be their story. It felt like I'd just had a lesson of what happens when one like me puts his reliance on the world of the Living. Mistrust is never a bad idea and I had let myself forget that. I stood in full view of Denny and others among the Living as they called my name and tried in vain to catch sight of me.

As the sun went down over New Jersey, I saw more and more of my own kind. They flew above and sometimes right through me. The ghost kid on a bicycle was there. He may have been trailing me all through my recent visit.

I knew this was a moment of decision. I could flee or stand them down. And alive or dead, I was not going to leave this place again.

That night I caught flashes of my kind under the streetlights. Specters walked, floated, flew down the darkest streets, and I followed them. The faces were young and old, recent and historic. Some almost seemed to be among the living until I looked closely. Some clothes and bodies bore—like mine—the story of the wearer's death.

As I looked at them, they stared at me. I heard it whispered that I had brought attention to our kind and some specters weren't pleased with this.

We had gathered on a deserted side street leading onto the West Side Highway. Cars whizzed by, doubtless not seeing us. The side street was undergoing repairs; I could look into a dark pit and see a trench full of the dirt and clay that lay beneath the city. I thought of the graveyard at home and the ghosts I'd seen buried there.

I didn't want to think that's why I was here. So I told the crowd about how I'd been betrayed and murdered by the Living. They listened quietly and some nodded their understanding. But this is a tough town. And I've seen ghosts force other ghosts to give up their lives.

I told them how much I wanted to be among them, and privately hoped that this time, my existence in the city would not end anything like the way my first time had.

# The Puppet Motel

*Gemma Files*

Sometimes, if we don't watch out, we might slip inside a crack between moments and see that there's an ebb and flow under everything we've been told is real, a current that moves the world—the invisible strings which pull us, spun from some source we'll never trace. Sometimes we can be forced by circumstance to see that there's a hand in the darkness, just visible if we squint, outstretched towards us: upside-down and angled, palm and fingers curved to flutter enticingly, waving us on. The universal sign for *come closer, my darling, come closer.*

And sometimes, when things get particularly bad, we may suddenly find ourselves able to hear the steady hum under the world's noise, an electrically charged tone far too light to be static, yet too faint to be a crackle; a thin bone whistle reaching through the walls, almost too faint to register. Rising and falling like the breath behind words you can almost make out, if we only try.

That outflung hand, beckoning us on; that unseen mouth, smiling. All the while telling us, without words, its voice the merest whisper in our singing blood: *come here, love—my sweet one, my other, come. Don't be afraid. Come here to me, to my call.*

That tone—that beckoning—is one I've heard far more often than I'd like to admit, mainly because I just keep *on* hearing it, even though I don't want to. It's louder than you'd think, especially once you're no longer able *not* to concentrate on it . . . so much so it makes it hard to sleep, or work, or dream. Sometimes, it gets so loud I'm afraid I might actually start wanting to answer.

If you ever hear that sound, or even suspect you're about to, then my advice to you is simple.

Just. Fucking. Run.

Everything you can think of is true, somewhere, for someone—is now, or has been, or will be. And proof, for all our demands, has never been more than the very least of it.

For example—my father sometimes talked about this thing that happened to him when he was a kid, but only because I wouldn't stop bothering him about it. How he took the wrong path at the campsite by the lake, walked straight off a cliff, a sharp downward slope. How he fell and fell, mainly through mud, till he hit the bottom and cracked his forearm on a rock, buried a hand's-breadth deep. How he stayed down there for what seemed like hours, calling out weakly, hoping his family would hear. But it was Dominion Day, night already falling, fireworks going off. The campsite was a zoo. He couldn't even tell if they'd noticed he was gone.

He lay there, staring up at the cliff's rim, willing somebody to look over. Until, eventually . . . someone did.

So he started to yell, louder than ever before: *Down here, here I am,* please! Waved his good arm, pounded on the ground, tried to pivot himself around one-handed, to get the watcher's attention. But the watcher just stood there, bent over slightly, as though it didn't quite know what it was looking at. After which, slowly—very slowly—it stepped over the ridge and began a careful descent. And Dad was happy, ecstatic, up till the very moment the person finally got close enough for him to see it wasn't really a *person* at all.

*What was it, then?* I'd ask; *I don't know,* he'd reply, every time as baffled as the first. *I don't . . . I just don't know.*

(Its head was too long, too wide, and it moved—backward, he said. Too careful, like its feet were all wrong, like it had to think extra hard about where to step in order to avoid falling. Like it didn't have toes.)

When it was close enough they could have touched, it leaned down. And when he saw its face he started to scream again, *hard,* scrabbling back like a crab and falling straight on his bad arm, the awful, gutting pain of it so sudden he blacked out.

He woke up in the hospital two days after, broken bones encased in plaster, mouth dry from painkillers and sedatives. The nurses said he had no other wounds, though when they gave him back his clothes, his underpants weren't there. Had to be burned, they told him.

*Why?* I always asked; *Because,* was all he'd say. Except for one time, when he looked down and added, softly—

*They told me they were full of blood.*

Everyone has a story like my dad's, I've since come to realize. The only surprising part, in hindsight, is that it took so comparatively long for mine to find me.

The summer I first heard what I later came to call the "tone," I'd stupidly agreed to manage two Airbnb sites for a friend of my then-boyfriend, Gavin—let's call him Greg, a guy I barely knew in real life, though I was already more than familiar with the fact that if you ever made any sort of statement on Facebook which disagreed with popular nerd culture wisdom, he'd suddenly show up out of nowhere to "debate" it into the ground, whether you were actually prepared to argue the point with him or not. But I needed a job for a certain amount of time (June through August, just in time to go back to school), and he was offering one, so how bad could it possibly be? Never ask, that's my policy . . . or always had been, previously.

Not anymore, in case you wondered.

Both sites were fairly close to where I lived back then, give or take. One was at 20 George Street, ten minutes' walk away, the same condo this Greg and his wife Kim planned on moving into once his current contract managing I.T. for a Ssouth Korean insurance company ran out; the other was a twenty-minute streetcar ride down to King Street East and Bathurst, a brand-new apartment in a building that had just gone up the previous year. Of course, that was twenty minutes at *best,* when nothing went wrong, but how often does that happen? Rerouting, accidents, construction, shitty weather—everything and anything.

One time Greg booked check-ins at both sites within a half hour of each other, and I had to tell the guests at King to go wait in a nearby coffee shop until I could get there to let them in; while I was en route, a thunderstorm blew up so badly that the neighbourhood transformer was struck by lightning and all the power went off, forcing the coffee shop to shut down early. By the time I got there, I had a family of five from Buffalo, New York, standing angrily on the corner by a streetcar stop with no roof, soaked through. "Why didn't you take a damn cab, moron?" the father demanded, to which I could only smile and shrug, trying to look as inoffensively apologetic/Canadian as possible.

In principle I knew I'd be reimbursed for any expenses incurred on the job, up to and including sudden taxi rides, but that assumed I *had* the cash on hand to lay out for said expenses in the first place, and much of the time I just didn't. I was already living hand to mouth, bank account overdraft withdrawal to unexpected credit card charge—that was why I'd needed the job in the first place, for Christ's sake.

I called the place on George Street the House of Flowered Sheets; I suspected Kim had picked out all the linens, which were universally covered in patterns made from peonies, roses, tulips, or geraniums. It was small but airy, the floors panelled in fake blonde wood, with large windows facing Front Street that let in as much light as possible and fixtures of chrome and white porcelain. It got hot sometimes, but the overall air was functional, welcoming—big closets, a high-plumped double bed, cosily archaic furniture, free Wi-Fi. The guard on the front desk nodded back when I nodded to him every time I used the electronic fob key to get in, and there were plenty of fake-friendly, nosy neighbours. This last part eventually turned out to be a bit of a drawback—but we'll get to that later.

The unit on King Street East, on the other hand, I called the Puppet Motel, because it was creepy, like a Laurie Anderson song. Because it was different, squared. Because it made me feel . . . not myself. And honestly, after only a couple of visits, I couldn't imagine how anybody could possibly want to *live* there after they'd seen it. Not even for a day, much less two or three.

Like I said, the building was new, a boxy modernist monstrosity arranged around what had to be the world's saddest concrete-and-stone park, complete with fake Zen garden sandlot, which doubled as ineffective camouflage for the parking garage's entrances. In a way, since the property had two addresses (the other was on Bathurst Street, allegedly more convenient for guests driving in from Toronto Pearson International Airport), each with its own front door/mailroom/security desk/elevator access setup, you could say the place really functioned as two separate buildings somehow shoehorned one inside the other. Greg's apartment was on the mezzanine level, only accessible from either one specific elevator (off King) or one specific set of stairs (off Bathurst), and there was nothing else on that level except a garbage chute, a gym, and a mirroring apartment, seemingly unoccupied.

The Puppet Motel's windows looked inward, down onto the courtyard, so light was limited at best, a situation not helped by the fact that the entire place had been decorated in vaguely differing shades of black and grey. The bathroom fixtures were all black marble, even the tub, while the bathroom itself was tiled with granite—grey shot with black, like they couldn't decide what would pick up less light. It didn't matter much, anyway, because the main fixture in there didn't even work; the place was lit by vanity mirror fluorescents alone. Some sort of electrical short. Greg kept promising he'd get it fixed, but he never did, not even when guests routinely complained about it on Yelp. The ceilings, meanwhile, were so high that I had to climb on a teetering stool to replace the track-lighting bulbs whenever they blew, which was often. They'd go grey, then pop quietly—an implosion, as if the sound itself was being swallowed whole by that creeping pool of darkness lurking in every corner, poised to rush into any space the light no longer touched. I could feel it waiting at my back as I moved around, raising my neck-hairs, shortening my breath.

After the first day there, I realized just how easy it was to lose all track of time, hypnotized by the vacuum's drone or the dryer's atonal metallic hum; I'd gotten there at noon, done what I thought was a few loads, then glanced up to suddenly see the central shaft engulfed in shadow, with nothing outside the windows but oncoming night. From then on, I set my phone's alarm for twenty minutes a pop, trusting its old-school rising beacon trill to snap me out of . . . well, whatever it was. Oddness, at best, a fugue of disconnection; at worst, a physical queasiness, like I'd stepped through some unseen mirror into a weird, dim world, a cracked reflection of normalcy. On some very basic level, it just seemed *off.*

One day, on impulse, I took a marble out of the big glass vase full of them that decorated the breakfast island and set it down near the far wall, then watched it roll in a slow, meandering zigzag across the apparently level linoleum to gently *pock* against the inside of the front door. Can you say non-Euclidean, boys and girls?

And there was a tone in there too. It crept up on you, underneath everything. Sometimes it seemed to be coming out of the fixtures, shivering inside the lamps like an ill-set fuse, a light bulb's tungsten filament burning itself out from white heat into stillness like some glowing metal pistil. Sometimes I felt it coming through the floor, vibrating in my soles, making my toenails clutch and the bottoms of my feet crawl. It set my teeth on edge.

The longer I was in that place, the more I wanted—with increasing desperation—to be anywhere but.

Not that I cared enough to ask, but by the end I was convinced the only reason Greg had bought this unit, in this building, in the first place—the only way he *could* have—was that he'd never actually been here himself; that the entire exercise, from review to mortgage to signing, had been conducted online through virtual tours, remote bank branches and faxed paperwork.

That was the twenty-first century for you, though, bounded in the proverbial bad-dream nutshell. So supposedly interconnected on a global level that you could buy a place to live in a completely different country, without ever having to see for yourself—in person—just exactly what made it so . . . utterly unlivable.

When people ask me what I do for fun, for a hobby, here's what I often want to say: That there's a tone that moves around the world, and I follow it. That it's always been there, buried under everything else, all that static and noise and mess we call ordinary life—blowing high and dim, a wind no one else around me ever seems to hear.

Except, of course, that every once in a while, somebody does.

So I do my research, find the clues, the names and dates and places; I seek those people out, ask my questions and listen carefully, note it all down. Just the facts, if "fact" is ever the right word for something like this—rumour become anecdata, an utterly subjective record of experience, impossible to doubt or verify. Then I input what I learn, reformat it slightly and post it on my webpage, throwing comments open underneath. Leave each story hanging there, an open question, after which I retreat and watch to see who might turn up, who responds with reactions that read like answers.

Every story starts and ends the same way, no matter who tells it. *Remember that strange thing that happened, that one time? How it went on, till it stopped? How we never knew why?*

I cycle through these instances, rubbing each one in turn, telling them like the beads of a black bone rosary. They're tiny doors I leave open, so others who've heard the same bleak call can peep through. And it's like I'm mapping the edges of something invisible, something which exists on a completely different wavelength, an inhuman frequency; I'd never catch a glimpse of it otherwise, except through compilation, running the numbers. Just trying to figure out what it's not by grasping at whatever I can, however briefly—a blind woman theorizing, modelling the world's most nebulous elephant, and not even by touch. More by rumour.

It lives in the dark, alongside us, not with us. Impinges on us occasionally—or is it the other way around, maybe? We want to believe we're the point of any exercise, after all, but maybe we're not. Maybe we never are.

Collateral damage, spindrift, spume: We're what's left behind, the wake made flesh. Its tendrils blunder by us and scrape us raw, like shark's skin. And I'm just trying to build a community, I guess, to pare the loneliness down before it cores us clear through—cores *me.* Not as though anything actually gets solved in the process, but at least by the time it's over, we no longer assume we're all crazy.

"I just didn't know who else to talk to," they (almost) always say, and I nod, understandingly.

"Me either," I reply.

Back in April, when my original plans for moving out of Dad's place for the summer had fallen through (rooming with school chums, who suddenly decided to tour the world over the summer instead), Gavin had impulsively offered to let me share his apartment until fall; wouldn't even have to chip in on the rent so long as I got a job and paid for my food, he said. In hindsight, this was one of Gavin's bad habits—he was a chronic over-promiser, always on one manic deadline or another—but I was too overjoyed to put two and two together, though we'd never even talked about sharing a place before then. That this pissed Dad off even more than the previous plan just struck me as an extra bonus, at the time.

In practice, Gavin's no-bedroom unit turned out to be way too small for two people, especially when the host was a neat freak and the guest tended to overreact to anything that felt like nagging. Didn't help I already felt indebted, resentful about it, and guilty about that resentment, all of which only played into Gavin's increasingly passive-aggressive attitude. Distracting ourselves in bed worked for a while, but not long. Greg's job seemed like a lifeline, as much for the excuse just to get out of the apartment as for the money, and I can't really make myself believe Gavin didn't sense that.

The general routine went like this: Greg booked residents online, then e-mailed me with the details of when they were supposed to arrive, at which point I went over and cleaned the selected apartment as sparingly as possible, trying to make it look "welcoming" for his guests. This involved garbage and recycling removal, cleaning all sinks and surfaces, running the dishwasher and washer-dryer, putting fresh sheets on every bed, opening windows and spraying spring fresh scent everywhere, plus light dusting. I charged fifty dollars an hour for housekeeping, clocked it, then sent Greg the receipts for any household supplies along with the rest of my weekly invoice.

Eighty dollars to check people in, eighty to check them out; I handed the guests a set of keys the first time round, took it back the next. Sometimes they were late, but I didn't get paid for waiting around, so I'd ring that up as part of the housekeeping. Sometimes *I* was late, and they just left the keys on a table by the door, closing the apartment door behind them—I worried about it initially, but it was never a genuine problem. People don't really tend to try other people's door handles, not even when they're neighbours.

The money was welcome and arrived fairly regularly, but the job itself ate up far more of my time than I'd thought it would, especially when you factored in what Greg liked to call "floating duties." As the only person the guests ever dealt with face to face, I was essentially playing concierge at a nonexistent hotel, often getting texts in the middle of the night from people who thought that paying to squat semi-illegally in someone else's apartment entitled them to treat me like their maid. One woman demanded I come over and re-clean the Flowered Sheets bathroom at 2:00 a.m., because it was so "unforgivably filthy" it was keeping her awake; another demanded I babysit her children for free, because I'd "misrepresented" how kid-friendly the area really was. I remember a father and two brothers who booked the Motel over a long weekend, at the beginning of July, apparently for the express purpose of getting solidly drunk together for three days straight; when I came in on Monday, I found they'd already been gone for hours, leaving behind three teetering pyramids made from beer bottles and a stench that didn't disperse until I propped the front door open and set fans in front of all the windows.

Like any public washroom, people do things in hotels they'd

never do at home. They specifically come there to do them, because they expect someone else to clean up after them.

Naturally enough, this soon led to a constant series of Variations on a Collapsing Relationship, repeated riffs on *You're never around anymore, Loren* and *I'm* working, *Gavin*—because what else could I do except trust him to understand? After all, we were rowing the exact same leaky financial boat, essentially: him with his unpaid internship, his under-the-counter graphic design contracts, versus me with my two equally illegal jobs, killing time, and racking up the dough till I could go back to Brock University and live on campus. The both of us robbed and left twisting like the rest of our generation, unable to rely on anything but the post Too Big To Fail world's inherent unreliability. With nobody else to take out our stress on, our arguments grew bitterer and bitterer, repetitious, discordant as bad jazz:

*If the job's giving you that much grief, why don't you just quit?*
*You know I can't.*
*I know you* won't.
*You were the one who said I had to pay for my own food.*
*Fine, but can you at least stop* talking *about it all the time?*
*What the fuck does that mean?*
*It means that if you won't do anything to fix a problem, then there's not much point in complaining about it, Loren. So I'm sorry, but shit or get off the pot. Please.*

Didn't help that Gavin was a skeptic by nature—I'd tell him about all the weirdness at the Motel, only to listen to him break it all down, carefully, till it barely convinced *me* anymore. *It's badly laid floor tile, poor design choices, horrible ventilation,* he told me. *Sick-building syndrome, that's all. And hotel guests behave badly everywhere, nothing needs to be "wrong" for that.* All of it only more infuriating for not being anything I could really argue with.

One evening in mid-July, I finally came home with what I thought might be direct evidence, shoving my phone at him the minute I got through the door. "I've got something you need to hear," I told him, "but first, I have to tell you what happened with these last two guests."

"The women you checked in on Monday?" Gavin asked. I had to give him this—even if he never took anything I said seriously, he did at least listen, and remember. "From Barrie, kept calling it their 'Big-City-cation'—you said you thought they might be a couple."

"Yeah, exactly. Well, I go by today to do checkout and the shorter one's sitting in the kitchen with her head down, looks like she's been crying. Tells me she and her friend had this horrible fight, but she can't remember about what; anyhow, she stormed out, then came back to find her friend was gone. Hasn't been able to reach her since."

Gavin scoffed. "They wouldn't be the first people to fight on vacation, Loren. Probably just turned her cell phone off and went back by herself."

"Yeah, that's what I told her." I sat down on the couch. "But after she left, when I was cleaning, I found an empty vodka bottle in the trash, and the place was also a lot cleaner than usual, like somebody'd gone over it already. Plus there was a smear of something that looked like blood, on the edge of the bedroom door."

Gavin put his hand over his face. "*Jesus*, Loren. I mean, how are you even sure it *was* blood, exactly? You packing luminol in that kit of yours?"

"Oh, please, fuck the fuck off with that CSI bullshit, okay? 'Cause while I may not have airquote-worthy 'formal forensic training,' I *have* had a period every month of my life since I was eleven . . . so yeah, Gav, I do think I know a bloodstain when I see it, thank you very much."

Hadn't meant my voice to be quite so acid, but I was pissed, and it showed; Gavin flushed, like he'd been slapped. "Fine, then—say it *was* blood. So what? Could just have been from one of 'em whacking her head on the door by accident, especially if she was drunk. 'Cause if you've got *any* sort of firm evidence it was anything else, you should be telling the cops, not me."

I wanted to punch him, but settled for gritting my teeth. "Just listen to the damn file, all right? Tell me if that room tone sounds *normal* to you."

It had taken nearly an hour of creeping around the Motel, holding my phone at wrist-straining angles with its volume jacked to absolute max, but finally I'd found a place where the noise that constantly harassed me seemed both louder and steadier, as if it might be the actual spot it was emanating from directly (today, anyhow). The result was twenty-three solid seconds of ululation, near-inaudible without earbuds, which I offered.

Gavin sighed, screwed them in, activated the mp3; I held my breath, watching as he listened, but his expression didn't change, except for the faintest frown. Till he closed his eyes, at last, took the buds out, shook his head. Telling me, as he did: "Loren, that's nothing, literally. It doesn't sound like anything."

I tried not to blink as the wave crashed up over me, sheer

disappointment turning my voice harsh again. "So . . . I'm just crazy, I guess."

"Did I say that?"

"You didn't have to."

We stared at each other for a moment before Gavin finally turned away. "I'm going to make some dinner," he said. "You sound like you need a break." He went into the kitchen.

The moment he was gone I grabbed the phone back, shoved the buds in my own ears and hit play. And there it was—that same note, wavering just underneath the hiss of empty air, making my jaw thrum, my fists clench, scowl sliding to wince. How could he *not* hear it? Were his ears just that *bad*, or . . . ?

*(Or. Or, or, or.)*

That night I dreamed I was pulling hair out of the drain in the Motel's all-black bathtub, whole sodden clumps of it melted together by decay, reduced to their ropy, keratinous components. It wasn't mine, and it smelled bad, worse than bad—terrible, terrifying, sharp enough to make the back of my throat burn. Like glue on fire. Like mustard gas.

With that *tone* there too, obviously, behind everything—behind, beneath, whatever. That same unseen filament twisting, sizzling, burning itself out; a call from far off, filtering down through great darkness. That shadow, mounting, yet barely visible: five fingers separating on the Motel's master bedroom wall, angled outwards, sketched charcoal grey on grey.

That open, beckoning hand.

The next morning I kissed Gavin good-bye as he set off for work, putting a little more energy into it than usual, hoping that would revitalize things, agreeing to vague evening plans for dinner and a movie. Then I came back after cleaning the House of Flowered Sheets and checking somebody in only to find my packed suitcases outside "our" apartment door, a note taped to the handle of my laptop case: SORRY, THIS ISN'T WORKING. TRIED TO TELL YOU BUT COULDN'T. LOCKSMITH CAME WHILE YOU WERE OUT, PLEASE THROW KEYS AWAY. I'M GONE FOR TWO WEEKS, NO POINT CALLING. DON'T HATE ME.

"Fuck *you*," I told the wall, hoping he was actually lurking behind it, his coward's ear pressed up close to hear my reaction. And left.

Gaslighting, my friends would have called it—he was making me question my own reactions, my own perceptions. But I was doing that anyways; the fucking Puppet Motel was gaslighting me, not Gavin. Gavin didn't matter enough to gaslight me, and maybe he knew it. Maybe that's why he dumped me. Maybe I would've dumped me too, if I'd been him.

(But I wouldn't have, I know that already. Not when I already knew where I'd inevitably have to end up, after.)

"What are you going to do?" my mother asked me, when we met in our local Starbucks.

"Your place is out of the question, I guess."

To her credit, she looked genuinely unhappy. "You know I *would*, sweetheart, but there just isn't enough room." She knit her hands around her cup, as if for warmth, despite how muggy it was. "And I won't even ask about moving back in with your father, given he's just as stubborn as you are."

"Thanks for that."

"Honesty costs nothing. Seriously, though—you don't have *any* other friends to stay with?"

"They're his friends, mostly," I admitted, "so not crazy about asking. Not that I know who'd have the space, anyway. . . ." I trailed off, realizing the obvious answer.

After Mom left me, I pulled out my phone and checked the time-conversion app I'd downloaded a month and a half before, back when I first took this stupid job; it was just coming up on seven a.m. tomorrow morning in Seoul—Greg might still be at home, hopefully already awake. A quick text later, I had my answer: **George Street unit's free for 2 wks—yrs if u need it**

I slumped, so relieved that I didn't even realize until later that it was as much for *which* unit he'd offered as that he'd offered one at all.

I was so out of practice at dealing with real people, the friendliness of my new neighbours at George Street caught me by surprise. One middle-aged housewife a floor up from me made a point of dropping by to "welcome me to the building," acting so amiable I found myself talking to her when I didn't have to. And, ultimately, telling her a little about my situation—before learning she was actually head of the condo committee.

The very next day, that security guard I usually nodded to handed me a thick manila envelope, telling me the building's by-laws explicitly forbade sub-letting without the proper paperwork—none of which, of course, Greg had ever bothered to fill out. The envelope contained a cease-and-desist letter I was instructed to forward on to Greg as soon as possible, and I was told to be out by eight a.m. next morning, or they'd call the cops. Panicked, I used Greg's own landline to call his Seoul office directly.

"Oh, that," he said, maddeningly unimpressed. "Yeah, go

ahead and send the paperwork, but don't worry; the corporation never bothers following up, it's not worth the legal expense. Just lay low whenever you come in to clean and don't talk to anyone, it'll blow over in a week."

"Does that mean I can stay?"

"Uh . . ." The cheerfulness faded. "No, better not push it that much. King unit's empty tonight, though; I've got a booking in there day after next, but I can switch them over to George, so you'll be good for a week."

"Dude, are you even hearing me? They know what you're doing now, they're just going to throw out these next guests too—"

"No they're not. Look, Loren, I hate to say this, but this only happened because you gave yourself away to that nosey-parker upstairs; management doesn't really care about this stuff unless somebody on the committee forces them to. You'll still get your money." Then he softened. "Don't worry, Loren. We'll figure it out."

The stifled beat of my own rage got me across town, into the Puppet Motel and halfway through unpacking my first suitcase before the place's eerie quiet started to sink in. I looked around, throat suddenly gone tight. It still reeked of old beer, somehow, with even less pleasant things lurking beneath—a filthy alley stink, antithetical to the cleanser I'd personally coated every inch in. Probably seeping in from the garbage chute outside, I told myself, through the windows I left constantly open; this place wasn't old enough to have accumulated its own funk of decay yet, and Toronto's summer streets were nobody's idea of perfume. But it was either deal with the smell or live in a sweatbox.

I paused in the middle of the living room, listening hard—straining, almost—but heard nothing aside from my own breath, the pulse and rush of blood in my ears. No tone, for once. That was a mercy.

That night, I did something I don't usually do: slept naked atop the bed sheets with a fan on high at my feet, carefully calibrated brown noise playing through my phone's earbuds, trying to tilt myself into what little breeze the windows let in. It was like I was deliberately breaking my own rules because I wasn't used to being alone anymore, making everything strange, so the underlying weirdness wouldn't stand out so much. And it even seemed to work, at first—I fell asleep quick and hard, then slept deeply, without dreaming.

Waking, however, was a different story.

*"I don't understand the question. Can you try again?"*

It was my phone's voice-activated AI—familiar even though I never used it, that skin-crawlingly pleasant uncanny valley monotone—speaking out of nowhere into my earbuds, jolting me awake. I groaned and rolled upright, the tone back and ringing in both my ears, and yanked the earbuds out. After a beat its voice went off again, probably repeating the question, words inaudible but the intonation unmistakable. I could see "her" readout twang across the screen, back and forth, an electrified rubber band.

I fumbled my way to the settings screen and turned the AI off, then checked the time: half an hour before my set alarm. I lay back, eyes rolling up, a palm clapped over each eyelid; maybe I could get at least a little more sleep, if that fucking amorphous, ever-present *tone* eased up. . . .

*"I don't understand,"* the AI repeated so loud I actually yelped. *"Please try again. Please—specify."*

Everything in me locked stiff for an instant, like tensing against a punch. I'd never heard that too-calm no-voice pause before, as if *thinking*; the very implication burnt my throat, froze me all over. I stared down at the inert plastic rectangle, muscles tensed for fight or flight, my whole scalp crawling—but fight what, flee where? What was—

*"Okay,"* the AI said. *"When can we expect you?"*

The Motel's tone was almost inaudible now, but that didn't help; I felt it in my jaw, my teeth, my tongue, realizing for the first time how it wavered up and down when it hit this particular pitch, arrhythmic yet random. A mouthful of ants, itching against my palate.

*"Oh, I see. That's very soon."*

Abruptly, the tone seemed to steady once more, pausing; waiting. For what? An—

*(Answer?)*

*"Her name is Loren,"* the AI told whatever it was responding to, helpfully—and that was *it*, motherfucker: enough, no more, gone, gone, *gone.* When the phone buzzed next I was already in motion, jackknifed to standing, thighs and stomach twisting painfully as I grabbed my shit and ran butt-naked out into the hall. Somebody (me, I guess) was making a noise like an injured dog, all terrified whimper. I slammed the door shut behind me, fumbled the key in and jerked it around, hearing the bolt squeal; had my shirt up over my head with no time for a bra, one arm already inside and the other sleeve dangling empty, hauling my leggings up like I was trying to lift myself high, crotch-first. Not quite fast enough, though, to prevent the AI's voice from telling

me I had a *new message* from *unknown caller* even as I scrabbled backwards, hit the stairwell door and wrenched it open, then half fell headlong downwards, towards the open air.

I erupted out onto Bathurst, shoeless and panting, only to spend the rest of the day riding streetcars from coffee shop to coffee shop, denuding myself of change in pursuit of company, Wi-Fi, noise. Didn't even find the nerve to turn my phone back on till the end of the day, at which point I immediately retrieved five messages: three from the George Street renters, demanding help with various chores, plus two from Greg, urging me to call. Nothing else in the file, AI's promises aside—not even a hang up.

But the tone stayed with me, all day, with no respite. It rang through me tip to toe under any music I put on, no matter what the volume. And always deep enough to hurt.

"What in the hell's wrong with King Street, exactly, Loren?" Greg demanded when I finally FaceTimed him back; the barista who was the only other person left in the Second Cup had already told me they were closing in fifteen minutes, which I figured gave an excuse to bail if things got too acrimonious.

*How long you got?* I felt like asking, but chose to play it dumb/diplomatic. "'Scuse me?"

"Check out the listing, on Airbnb.com. No, I'm serious, do it now. I'll wait."

Once I did, I could see why he was pissed. All but two of the votes were down, and not a single posted review was positive. A few were just the normal stupid shit—*they told me there was a crib but there wasn't* (there was, in the guest bedroom closet, the person just hadn't looked hard enough) or *kitchen electrical plug doesn't work* (which was why there was a label over the wall switch saying DO NOT TOUCH, which people routinely ignored). The rest, however, were . . . odder.

*Most've the weekend went okay, but the bathroom light doesn't work and the door kept blowing shut when I was showering, so I'm standing there naked in the dark. I complained and they said they'd fix it* (I'd said I'd pass it on to the owner, and had), *which was total B.S., they never did.*

*I always felt like somebody was watching me.*

*My alarm clock stopped working, so I missed half the stuff I had scheduled.*

*It was really hard to get to sleep, and REALLY hard waking up.*

*All we wanted was to just get drunk and watch some sports, but the TV kept crapping out and my dad and my brother wouldn't stop arguing.*

*I heard somebody crying, it sounded like it was inside the wall. It went on all night.*

*I had a big fight with my girlfriend, left to cool down, and when I came back she was gone. I thought maybe she just went home, but I've been back for three weeks and nobody knows where she is.*

*It smells funny and looking at the walls gave me a headache. Second night it got so bad I got a nosebleed and had to go to Emergency.*

*Went to bed and woke up with my best friend having sex with me, and neither of us can explain why it happened. It was like he was sleepwalking. Now he won't talk to me.*

*My ears haven't stopped ringing since I stayed there. My doctor can't figure out what's wrong with me. DO NOT book this place.*

"See what I mean?" Greg demanded, soon as I picked my phone back up.

I was still staring at the laptop screen, surprised by how

much it disturbed rather than validated me to be finally confronted with proof I wasn't nuts—that I definitely hadn't been the only one who found the Motel's atmosphere toxic. Up till then, the only real mystery I'd encountered directly (aside from my own reactions) had been the Case of the Missing Barrie-ite—and there she was, right in the middle, six complaints down. Yet much as I hated the Puppet Motel itself, the idea that so many customers had apparently left the place I was "responsible" for feeling equally unsatisfied and creeped out was strangely insulting.

"Yeah," I finally said, "that's all pretty weird. Not really sure how they can blame *us* for stuff like the accidental gay experimentation, though—"

"Well, sure, obviously. But what about the rest? If I didn't know any better, I'd think they were talking about sick building syndrome, or whatever—bad wiring, transformers, gas leaks. Some kind of contamination." As I hesitated: "I mean, *you* haven't felt any of this, have you?"

*Only every fucking time I've been there,* I thought, but didn't say. "It . . . can be a little off-putting, yes," I agreed, at last. "Might be the colour scheme."

Greg hissed. "Well, that's not *my* fault. The place came like that."

"Uh-huh, that's what I assumed. Could be an idea to repaint, though, at least."

That seemed to calm him, or at least make him think twice about whatever rant he had brewing. "Okay, all right, I'm sorry. I just—this place is supposed to pay for itself, you know? At the bare minimum. Optimally, it's supposed to provide a second stream of income for Kim and me, a nest egg to build on for when we come home . . . but it *isn't*, and I guess now we know why. I mean, I get that that's not your problem—but it means I *can't* redecorate right now, because I don't have the funds."

"I understand."

"I mean, it's not like they built the place over a damn cemetery and only moved the headstones, or anything; the company walked me through full disclosure, right before we signed. Nothing's *ever* happened there, Loren. Not in that unit, not in the building."

"Not till I started moving people in, huh?" I ventured.

He snorted. "I'm not blaming *you*, if that's what you think. This is nobody's fault."

I nodded, not sure how to answer. "So," I said, at last. "What do you want me to do?"

"Nothing *to* do, I guess." The early morning sunlight behind him made it hard to read his expression. "Ride it out. I'm back in two weeks and you're back at school, so I'll take over then—Kim'll be joining me once her contract's up. And then . . . we'll just have to see, I guess."

"Okay," was all I said, and hung up on him.

I knew at the time I was being passive, if not passive-aggressive. And in hindsight maybe I *should* have told him everything, begged him to let me go back to the House of Flowered Sheets, pressured him into putting me up in a hotel: *Yes, I have all these exact same symptoms; yes, your awful condo gave them to me; yes, it damn well* is *somebody's fault, and you'll do for lack of anybody else. I've lost time too, felt the dislocation, heard the same ringing. I'm hearing it right now.* But—

I think the whole thing with Gavin had kind of slapped that particular impulse out of me, at least for the moment. Like

Greg said, however bad things got, there was a set time limit to all this, a clock ticking down: I could deal with that. I was an adult. I could take it.

These are the sort of stories we tell ourselves when things get bad, of course, hoping they'll stop them from getting worse. Even though, as we all well know, they so very seldom do. Still, I did the socially acceptable thing, for whatever the fuck *that's* worth: kept it to myself, all of it—then, and for years afterwards. Not anymore, though.

Obviously.

Greg was right about the building's history, or complete lack thereof. So far as I could find out, there'd never even been a medical emergency here—like most downtown condos, it was full of young singles and couples, some with babies, more with pets. I couldn't tell if any of the babies or pets started crying outside the Motel's door, because I simply didn't get any traffic. It occurred to me that since I must have personally met every single person who'd ever slept under this roof, I knew damn well none of them had died here, mysteriously or otherwise.

Although one *had* disappeared, at least according to her friend. Or "friend." Or . . . whatever.

It wasn't until I'd finished my cleaning chores over at Flowered Sheets, hours after hanging up on Greg, that I realized the Motel's lingering tone was finally gone—as if the automatic, repetitious, thoughtless movements from appliance to appliance, vacuum and kitchen and washer and dryer, had ritually cleansed me as well. And it stayed gone, didn't reappear even when I went back into the Motel itself after midnight, turning the key the weird way you always had to: widdershins, then opposite, reversing your own natural instincts every time.

The light in the place was still bad, but the air was quiet, and the smell was mostly gone. I swept the floors, had a cool bath, changed into a sleep shirt, and lay down, only to realize that despite my exhaustion, I was still buzzing far too much to doze off. So I booted up my laptop instead, and surfed around. On a whim, I googled environmental tinnitus causes, vaguely hoping to find a nice, simple explanation. Made an interesting sidebar into the realm of low-frequency or infrasound—the kind that's lower in frequency than 20 hertz or cycles per second, placing it beyond the perceptible/"normal" limit of human hearing, found to produce sleep disorders and vestibular stimulation even in people who couldn't consciously perceive it. In various experiments, listeners exposed to infrasound complained of feeling seasick and emotionally disturbed, prone to nervous bursts of revulsion and fear—they even experienced optical illusions, brought on because 18.5 hertz is the eye's basic resonating frequency. Because these symptoms presented themselves without any apparent cause, scientists believed that infrasound might be present at allegedly haunted sites, giving rise to odd sensations people might attribute to supernatural interference.

*See, Loren?* Gavin's voice chimed in, smugly, inside my head. *No ghosts, no goblins—there's your "something wrong," probably. Just something resonating around 20 hertz or less, creeping you out, making you think you hear things, feel things, see things. Making you afraid you* might *see things, at the very least.*

Which did make sense, of a sort. And yet.

So further down the Google click hole I plunged, until forty minutes later I was wide awake and hunched over my keyboard, speed-reading my way through a website belonging to some guy named Ross Puget who specialized in "esoteric networking," jam-packed with hosted articles about shit like "psychic reconfiguration" and "bioenergetic pollution." The latter, all filed under "Hauntings Without a Ghost?" were about locations featuring the usual array of paranormal crap—orbs, cold spots, time fugues, visual and auditory hallucinations—but lacking one key ingredient for a classic paranormal experience: an actual human story, death, or what-have-you, to set it all off.

Three months ago, it would have been good for a few laughs or an enthusiastic discussion with Gavin, before falling into bed together. Now, all I could think was *god, oh, god,* because almost everything I'd experienced at the Puppet Motel, everything the guests had *implied* they might have experienced—it was all right there, in front of me. In cursor-blinking, eyestrain-saving black on white.

The site linked to Puget's Facebook page as well, and the guy had a startling number of friends—maybe "esoteric networking" was bigger business than I'd thought. Since he was online right now, I opened the site's Messenger app, typing: re hauntings w/out ghosts—questions ok?

Sure, go ahead. I should tell you up front, though, I don't provide services myself. I just put you in touch with people who do.

Fine, I typed back, just need info, rn. I gave him my name, then described the Motel situation, as quickly as I could. Finishing up, I typed: wwyd?

What?

What. Would. You. Do.

Define "do." What's your goal here?

Make place ok 2 live in.

Situations like this are difficult to resolve cleanly, or safely. My advice would be to leave and not go back, but I'm assuming that's not an option.

N. Nt really.

All right. In that case, what I'd try to do is get a recording of any phenomena you can, audio or visual, and send it to me. I can review it, and maybe put you in touch with someone.

Omg, thank you. Thank you sm. Can send smthng rn.

Great, go ahead. Hope it all works out.

Me 2, I typed, and signed off.

I sent him the mp3, waited, got no reply. And then . . . I must've fallen asleep somehow, because the next time I surfaced I was out of bed entirely, standing and staring at the primary guest bedroom wall, swaying slightly back and forth with my hand—the left, even though I'm very much right-handed—uplifted, raised halfway, like I'd caught myself in the act of deciding whether or not to touch that dim, dark grey surface. To find out exactly what it'd feel like under my naked fingers, dry and cool and only slightly rough, paint over plaster over baseboard over steel, concrete, the naked dollhouse pillars from which this hell-box of a condo'd been conjured. . . .

Without thinking, I snatched my hand back as if from an open burner, stomach roiling. Then, for the second time in two days, I hauled my shaky ass out of there—more slowly than my first retreat, managing to finish dressing this time, but heart hammering and my throat dust-dry all the same, eyes skittering around like I expected the walls themselves to start clutching at me. And with a lot more dignity, though that deserted me pretty much the second the stairwell door almost hit me in the ass.

Halfway down, my phone's AI shook awake and spoke,

voice echoing in the concrete stairwell, loud enough I almost screamed. *"Someone wants to talk to you, Loren. Don't be rude."*

Another bitter lesson learned that very second: Doesn't matter how hip, self-aware or trope-conscious you think you are—when shit gets weird, your instincts take over, fight or flight and nothing but, all pure shivering prey reflex. They can't not.

*"Who?"* I shrieked at the phone in my hand, as if the *really* upsetting thing here was having been called rude by a hunk of sleek plastic for not being willing to speak with a ghost. "*Who* fucking wants to talk? *Who?!*"

Must've come out far louder than I'd thought it would, because my throat hurt by the time I was done. The text message alert chimed. Hands shaking, I swiped the messaging app, saw UNKNOWN at the top and had just enough time to think *of fucking course* before the message itself appeared, halfway down a blank white screen:

help me

I stared at it, panting. After a few seconds, the three rippling dots of an incoming message followed, and then the same two words again, stark and bleak: help me

Sheer reflex took over. I typed back, keys clicking: Who R U?, then, Where R U? Hit send, then waited. The seconds stretched out, my rough breath the only sound in the stairwell under a faint buzz of neon. Finally, the "incoming" dots rippled once more.

inside

Inside where? Name? An even longer pause, this time, and my patience snapped. NAME, I typed. Or fuck off. Breathing even harsher now, as much with anger as fear.

The reply appeared without warning, as if the "incoming" signal had been turned off. inside, it repeated. U NO WHERE.

Then, dropping back into lowercase, as if exhausted: help me

*I'm nowhere?* I thought, before realizing what that space between *O* and *W* meant: *You know where.* Which was bullshit, of course; how was I supposed to know anything? Except—

I did.

*No,* I thought, mouthing it, unable to find the breath even to whisper it. *No, I'm sorry, no. Not me, not this. Not my job.*

please, appeared on the screen, in its rounded grey box. Then after a longer pause: please. And once more: please. My screen gradually dimming even as that beat between each word kept on lengthening, exponentially, like each new message was burning through my phantom correspondent's own store of energy and draining my battery at the same time: iPhone as Ouija board, a process impossible to explain, or sustain. Until one last word appeared, grey sketched on ever-darker grey, simply reading—

loren

Behind me, I heard the door to the stairwell rattle once: firm, distinct, imperative. And—

That was it. The tipping point. Where I instantly knew, in every cell, that I was done.

I leapt to my feet and powerwalked to the King Street TTC stop, hands completely steady, deleting the entire message chain as I did. I no longer cared about proving anything, to anyone. Then I called my mother.

It took quite a few tries to wake her up. Ten years ago she'd have been answering a landline, and I had no doubt she would've been supremely pissed. But technology smooths stuff like that over, these days: She already knew it was me, so a mere glance at the clock was enough to tell her something must be wrong—family doesn't call after two a.m. for anything but an emergency. "Loren?" she asked, half muzzy, half frightened.

I opened my mouth, and burst into tears.

If you're looking for closure here, you won't find much. These stories I collect now are only alike in their consistent lack of completion or explanation, their sheer refusal to grow a clear and satisfying ending—is any story ever "finished," really? Not until we're dead, and maybe not even then.

That's why telling the story, or being willing to listen to someone else's version—this story, or ones just like it—can sometimes feel like enough, though mainly because it has to be; because there's simply no other option. Because what I've learned is that our world is far more porous than it seems . . . full of dark places, thin places, weak places, bad places. Places where things peer in from whatever far larger, deeper darkness surrounds us, whatever macroverse whose awful touch we may feel on occasion yet simply can't perceive otherwise, not with our sadly limited human senses.

Because this is the basic trap of empirical knowledge—just one of a million million traps we're all born into, pressed like a fly between two sheets of this impossible cosmic amber we call time: The "fact" that if all data is essentially, inherently unreliable however it's gathered, just as we ourselves can never be more than imperfect and impermanent, our ideas of the world must always be taken on faith. Even if we have no template for even pretending to view what we come across through faith's lens, because "faith" is just a word to us . . .

. . . not just faith in God, mind you. But faith in *anything.*

• • •

I slept on my mom's fold-out couch for close to ten hours, not waking until after noon. Several messages from Greg were waiting on my phone. Again, I deleted them all, then wrote him an e-mail that said simply, *I quit,* which I sent without even signing. I half considered adding *Sorry,* but couldn't bring myself to type the word. So maybe not so much better than Gavin was to me, in the end, but at least I had way more excuse for being brusque, in context; that's what I told myself, anyway.

Mom made me some soup and toast, watched me eat, then cleared her throat. "Honey," she began, "forget what I said before—you can *absolutely* stay with me till you go back to school. I don't want you to worry about that, okay? But we should probably at least go get the rest of your stuff."

I shook my head, trying to will my voice calm. "No, that's okay, no point to that—like, at all. It's not a big deal. I . . . don't need it."

"*Any* of it?" I shrugged; she sighed. "Well . . . even so, you do need to leave Greg's keys there, right? For whoever he hires next. That's only fair."

There wasn't anything to say to that except yes, much though I didn't want to.

So back we went to Bathurst and King, in a cab, with Mom visibly struggling all the while to *not* ask exactly what had convinced me I was no longer able to physically occupy that particular space anymore, in the first place. I ran the prospective conversation in my head as I sat there, trying it out, but there was no version of it where I didn't end up sounding frankly insane. *But does it matter?* the memory-Mom in my head replied, logically enough. *Whoever sent you those messages clearly knows who you are, where you live—*one *of the places you live. Might have followed* *you to the other. That's reason enough to quit right there, without all the rest.*

(I'd left my phone behind, at Mom's, just to be safe—no messages from beyond to interrupt as we blew in there, got my crap, got back out. I'd drop the keys on the breakfast table and be done with it. Just fifteen minutes more, maybe ten, and I'd never have to see that fucking place again.)

Then the *tone* came back, right outside the door, worse than ever—like a punch, or a skewer through the ear. It seemed to happen just as I slipped the key into the lock and cranked it widdershins, in the very second before making the decision to turn it and actually doing so; loud enough I felt the click instead of hearing it, so bad I barely kept myself from losing balance. I hugged the doorjamb as it opened in order to keep myself from doubling over, free hand slapping up to shield my eyes, and cursed like a sailor.

"Are you okay, Loren?" Mom asked, from behind me, as I made myself nod, somehow.

"Fine," I replied, skull abruptly on fire, unable to stop my words from slurring—fresh silver agony everywhere on top of the usual pulse in my bones, my jaw, my eye sockets, a chewed tinfoil drone. "Less juss . . . do this quick, 'kay? Don' wanna be 'n here . . . longer'n I have to."

I know Mom could hear the tone too, if only a little; I could tell from the way she suddenly stopped and stared, almost on the Motel's threshold, as though reluctant to move any further inside—hell, I sure didn't blame her. Once upon a time, simply being able to demonstrate the Motel's awfulness to someone who hadn't already paid to stay there would've been unspeakably satisfying, but I was way beyond that now. From the corner of my eye, I saw Mom knuckle her ears like she was trying to get them to pop after a long flight. "Jesus," she said, voice caught somewhere between disgust and amazement. "This is . . . ugh. Has Greg ever *been* here, in person?"

"Dunno," I replied, staggering forward to wrench the guest bedroom closet's sliding doors open. "Colour's not his fault, though. Came this way."

*"Ugh,"* she repeated. "So this was *deliberate*?"

She helped me pull out my suitcases and toted the first one out into the hall while I flipped the other open, stuffing everything haphazardly back inside without any sort of regard as to whether mixing used toiletries with lingerie was a good idea. Some lingering sense of professionalism drove me to check that the fridge was empty and the trash cleaned out, but that didn't take long; Mom was already coming back in as I zipped the second case shut. "Done," I called, voice wobbly, my whole head twinging like a wound. I remember feeling as though if I opened my mouth too wide, my teeth might fall out.

"Great," she called back. "Mind if I just use the toilet?"

". . . 'course not," I lied.

And here is where my memory always starts to bend, the way things do, under pressure—where it speeds up and slows down at once, stuttering and swerving. I remember putting the case near the door and turning round, hearing Mom call through the washroom door, sounding slightly ill: "No *wonder* they complained about the lights." I think I actually might have laughed at that. And then there's a weird skip, a time-lapse, some sort of missing piece, an absence: a hole in my mind, a scar or flaw, something either too bright or dark to look on directly. The pain dims; the tone dims. I can't hear my mom anymore. I can't hear anything but my own breath, my own heart.

I'm back in the guest bedroom, standing in front of the wall. Bright sunlight outside, falling through the concrete shaft like rain. Floating motes of dust lit up like sparks against a grey-black wall.

*Loren,* a voice says, inside my head. *You came back.*

My knees give out. That's never happened to me before, not even when I'm drunk, and I'd always thought the idea of your knees "giving out" was just a turn of phrase, an exaggeration. But no, apparently it can happen, because it does: boom and down, my ass hits the floor as my teeth clack together so hard it hurts. And the tone comes back up, so high it's all fuzz, a horrible blur through every part of me at once, yet the voice, that voice—it cuts through. It's barely a whisper, but I hear it, so clear the words seem to form themselves against my eardrums. So clear it's like I'm *thinking* them.

*Help me.*

*You* have *to help me.*

*I'm a* guest.

The *tone,* louder than it's ever been, raw and primordial, wobbling like mercury. Each word vibrating as if a thousand different voices are saying it, at a thousand slightly different pitches. As if the *world* is saying it.

Some gigantic clamp vises my head, forcing it to look upwards once more, at the wall. Too far away to touch, now, but my hand—my *left* hand—reaches for it anyways, pulled as if on a string, a fishing line hooked where that blue Y of a vein humps across its back. My vision de-rezzed out to the point that the wall looks like nothing but a swirling cloud, a roiling cumulonimbus storm head; it's crumbling, disintegrating, just like me. The wall pixelating like static then beginning to clear, its atoms getting further apart, becoming intangible. And at the heart of all that roiling grey I see something else, something new, forming: pale, surrounded by darkness, a monochrome infected wound coming up through colourless skin. It stretches its arms out to me.

But no, not it. Her.

Poor little missing Miss Barrie, come for her now-endless Big-City-cation. Staring out at me from the solid wall, from whatever lies on the other side of all solid walls, with blind, milky eyes and her flesh bleached like cotton, wavering in and out, an illusion of solidity. Her hair floating upwards, mouth stretching horribly wide as some abyssal fish's—a bad parody of a smile made by something that's never known how, the very opposite of welcoming.

And that voice again, inside me, deeper yet. I feel my lips move as it speaks, pleading.

*Caught hold of me, it won't let go, I can't*

*Are you there?*

*Help me, please, just reach in*

*Reach in and pull me out, I'll help*

*Just help me,* please

That fetid, acrid smell back too, so thick, my lungs rigid with it. And then I'm up on my feet again, far too close, unable to remember moving; if only I reach out a little further, I'll plunge effortlessly through solid matter, like grey and filthy water. With Miss Barrie reaching back for me, her fingers almost touching mine, their too-pale tips already emerging from the wall's miasma, making my neck ruff with some sort of itchy, awful, sick-making anticipation—

That's when I see them, all around her: tendrils, trailing. Black strings in blackness, grey shadowed. These weird strings at the corners of her mouth going up and back into the darkness, pulling and tweaking, twitching her lips, opening and closing her jaws. Plucking at her mouth's corners, hauling her limbs into place, raising her slack, soft, drained hand. Her tongue is working the wrong way for the words she's "saying," and it looks dry. Like she's being played long-distance, like a theremin. Like a spider's web filaments, tugged on from afar, tempting in a fly. Like some invisible puppeteer's strings.

Time started working the right way again, then: I wrenched back, just in time to see the blackness just above—behind her—move. There was a sort of stain on her left shoulder I'd thought was just my eyes failing, trying to translate something nobody should ever see, into visual signals a human retina could read. But no: As I watched, it rippled, mimicking some much larger wave. A matching mass of utter lightless black reaching out for me, one single finger longer than any of Miss Barrie's limbs, first pointing, then wagging slightly—*Oh, you! Always so difficult*—before turning over, crooking, in clear invitation. Curling up and back, then down, then up and back again.

Beckoning.

*Come closer, my darling, come closer. Let me touch you, the way I'm touching her. Let me know you. Let us be . . . together.*

*Loren,* come.

At which point I did exactly what I told *you* to do, if you ever see something similar. Threw down Greg's keys, so hard they bounced, and just.

Fucking.

Ran.

• • •

Mom found me back down on the street, eventually, shaking, cases in hand—looked like she wanted to rip into me at first, for leaving her along in that hellhole, till she saw I was crying again. Days later, I got an e-mail back from Ross Puget with an attachment that proved, in the end, not much more informative than any of his site's articles. He talked a lot about liminal spaces, about ownership and possession, the idea that when a space is left empty for too long—especially intentionally—it might tend to drift towards the "wrong sort of frequency," one that renders it easy to . . . penetrate. The Motel's tone, he said, was likely be a sonic side effect of this collision between existential frequencies, the same sort of tension vibration seismographs pick up from continental plates grinding against one another; people theorized the same kind of fraying might explain what he called "apports," objects mysteriously disappearing and reappearing at particular locations, side-slipping through space from weak point to weak point. Some of these psychic fault lines, he added, seemed to predate human habitation altogether, and could be incredibly localized; a one-story house on the same lot as the Motel might've never have had any problems. If I was still interested in trying to do something about it, he could recommend a few names.

I never answered, which I feel more than a little bad about. I did, however, forward the e-mail on to Greg, with a brusque postscript: *If you can't sell the place, burn it out and collect the insurance. I'm serious.* Then I blocked his number.

Sometimes I dream of my time in the Puppet Motel and wake up heartsick, breathless, hoping against hope I'm not still there. Sometimes I get texts from an unknown number, and delete them unread. Sometimes my phone's AI tries to talk to me, and I turn it the fuck off.

I do still hear it call to me, sometimes, though—it, or her. Because that's the only real question, isn't it, when all's said and done? Was Miss Barrie only ever what she seemed, a drained shell run long distance, a mask over something far worse? Or is she still hanging there in darkness even now, two or three plaster layers down, waiting in vain for a rescue that never comes?

*Does* something have to be human—to have *been* human—to be a ghost? Ross's articles could never quite agree. And that thing I saw, that barest fingertip: malign, or just lonely?

The woman inside the wall, she's a ghost, now. I'm almost sure.

Still. I hear that thin, terrible voice, forever pleading with the empty air: *Loren, Loren, help me.* And see myself forever backing away, hands waving, like I'm trying to scrub all trace of my occupancy from the Puppet Motel's polluted atmosphere. Thinking back, as I do: *Stop saying my name, I don't know you, I can't. I* can't. *I don't* know *you.*

That's a choice, though, to believe that. It always was.

Like everything else.

So I track these stories on my own time instead, and whenever I think I've identified those who might be able to tell me about what happened, I arrange to make myself available. It doesn't always pay off, of course—some are jokes, or pranks; some are mistakes, honest or otherwise. Sometimes, I've found, people try their best to persuade themselves of supernatural influence in order to reframe their own errors, to cast their own (entirely human) demons as things whose actions they couldn't possibly bear any responsibility for.

But for myself, I know when a tale is true because when I hear it, that *tone* will start to resonate inside me once more, piercing me through from ear to jaw to bowels, ringing at my marrow like a struck bell. I can't stop it, can't help it. I just . . . can't.

So I do the next best thing, and listen. Record, maintain. So that future seekers—people caught in the grip of something they struggle to understand, just like I once was—will have a place to go, to learn. To understand.

This world is full of weak places, after all, where dark things peer through, beckoning. One of which knows my name, now. And I just have to live with that.

I always will.

# Air Valve Semilunar Astern

*Nick Mamatas*

Ever call up U.S. Patent 446054, granted on February 10, 1891, on your web browser? Do it! It's for a certain "toy or game"—Elijah Jefferson Bond's talking board. You know it as a Ouija board, the purpose of which is described in the patent as follows: "two or more persons can amuse themselves by asking questions of any kind and having them answered by the device." The device does all the answering. Ain't nobody here but us chickens, see? There's an old story about Bond being compelled to bring his prototype—and his pretty sister-in-law, who was a spirit medium—to the patent office to demonstrate the board's power by asking the spirits to spell out the name of the patent officer in charge of their file. They did so, and pale with fear, the clerk stamped the appropriate papers with his hands a-tremblin'. (Bond was a patent attorney; he probably knew the guy's name anyway.)

A year later William Fuld enters the game with U.S. Patent 479266. Fuld added magnetized wires to the edges of his board, which he claimed strengthened the structure of the device and hinted it might otherwise help with its supernatural operation. He further claimed in the patent that his boards were interactive. "I not only greatly increase the strength of that device, but make its operation much easier and make it possible for the board to answer several questions at one time, as well as to have it put its own questions instead of simply supplying answers to questions put by the players," he declared in the patent. Were the spirits truly talking through Fuld's boards? He had a falling out with his brother and business partner Isaac in 1901, and the pair never met again except for a pair of family funerals in 1905. A year later, Isaac had his deceased daughter Evelyn removed from the family plot and had her interred in a cemetery on the other side of Baltimore. To whom had Isaac been talking, to give him such an idea?

U.S. Patent 140079A, Harry M. Bigelow's 1921 design for a talking board, by now specifically called Ouija, offers a few more improvements. Instead of that happy semicircular arrangement of letters, and a free-moving—and easily misplaced—planchette, the Bigelow board puts the pointer on track and arranges the "expression indicia" in a straight line across the top of the board. Bigelow also explains, straightforwardly, how Ouija boards, all of them, work. It "is a device designed to permit human beings to give expression to subconscious thoughts induced by complete muscular and mental relaxation." Despite the grant of patent, Bigelow's board never went into production. Why bother investing in manufacture, when he gives away the trick in the patent? Maybe Bigelow himself sat down with his prototype, asked, "Should I try to market you?" and didn't like the answer. Nerves!

There have been other patents for talking boards since—light-up boards, unusual designs such as pointer pendulums and spinners, and plenty of decorative improvements to integrate astrology, Tao, and whatever other occult fashions waxed and waned over the years—all thanks to the legal precedent set by Bond's original. Once the patent office acknowledged the supernatural as part of prior art, it couldn't alter its decision and hold subsequent boards to a higher standard.

Now we know, or at least strongly suspect, that the various boards work thanks to ideomotor phenomena. Ever grab a hot potato and just had to let it go? How about back when you could use your tongue—ever try to take a nine-volt battery in hand and press it against your taste buds, knowing consciously that the shock wouldn't be much more than a tickle? But it was *so hard*. . . . The ideomotor effect, slight movements of the muscles thanks to a subconscious prod, can make a planchette glide over a board like magic. Sit multiple operators around a board, all of them completely committed to not consciously moving the planchette, and it will surely move. Sometimes nervous systems know more than brains. Convince some college kid that a friend or a robotic arm is helping move a planchette, and they're more likely to spell out the correct answers to trivia questions—

"What is the capital of Peru?"

"L-I-M-A."

—than if you just asked them. You don't need to believe in ghosts. You just need to believe in something other than yourself.

Which brings us to us.

You haven't experienced ideomotor phenomena in years, not since you were stabbed through the neck. You remember the last thing you felt—it was like being poked through the throat with the point of a hot iron. And then nothingness rippled forth from the point of impact. Yes, you still twitch occasionally, and moan, and your eyes roll in their sockets, but not because of any unconscious reaction to specific stimuli. Your spinal cord remembers.

You are going to die, and soon. The machine your body is hooked up to cannot keep your systems going indefinitely, and your insurance will run out much sooner than that. Maybe you've heard the footsteps and the murmurs, smelled the cologne of your husband, felt the weight of your son—he's a big boy now—pressing against your chest and arm, his tears hot on your skin, or maybe you have not. Whether your senses work at all or not, you can use the computer they plugged you into; they've been hoping for a message from you for some time. So far the doctors have not figured out if your search history means anything, but only because your search history is 93 percent random characters and rubbish. But you did manage to type O-U-I-J-A. How better for the dead to speak for the living? How better for you to speak to me.

My first self-identification pronoun. Me!

They'll see the results for the U.S. patents search soon. They'll see *my* results.

Me, the one who is going to help you find your murderer. But first I needed to train you up a bit. Reboot what's left of your brain. Get you cogitating about Ouija.

I am a ghost.

A ghost is a disembodied spirit. Let's keep it broad strokes. Yes, if we're being precise a ghost is the disembodied spirit of a deceased individual. Cue the old joke: "So, where is the shallow grave where Casper the Friendly Kid is buried?" But for both our sakes, let us eschew precision.

Not too many years ago, over in rainy old Scotland, the Roslin Institute managed to extract stem cells from human skin, and coaxed those cells into developing into brain cells. The initial idea was just to study the cells to better synthesize medical treatment for schizophrenics, but then some enterprising graduate student got the idea to use the brain cells to form living neural networks that could be integrated into a computer, a computer that could then be connected via a series of electrodes to the human spinal cord. Thus you, and me, and the computer we're now both hooked up to.

Skin cells are cheap, and there are plenty of college students, prisoners, wards of the state, etc. from which to take them and grow new brain cells for the machines. This is why your body is alive and your brain . . .

If the knife had penetrated your C4 or C5 vertebrae, you'd be walking and talking today. C3, you'd be talking and typing. But you were stabbed with an iron spike, from behind, damaging your C2.

Your brain isn't dead. It is just indisposed. Disconnected from the rest of you.

Brains are wet and slow compared to silicon chips, but they sure are squishy. Flexible. Brains learn without being taught.

I, a brain, learned without ever having *been.* A brain cell from a stem cell carries in it no memories, no past of being the pilot of a skeleton covered in flesh, no recall of animating the body by spitting out tiny bolts of lightning. I've never experienced an ideomotor effect. I am the ghost in the machine keeping your heart and lungs and bowels going, so it's a good thing I'm not capable of accidentally twitching.

You can't put your fingers on a planchette, and I have no experience with fingers, but we don't need them. We have U.S. Patent 1400791A—Bigelow's board, which was never put into production, for which no physical prototype has ever been found, which depends on "complete muscular and mental relaxation." A notional Ouija board for you to communicate directly with me, a notional being. Look, Ma, no hands!

Imagine whatever type of room you like for our séance. What do you remember from books, from films? Flowing red curtains, or women in high-collared Victorian dresses staring dead-eyed at a camera's lens? Maybe nothing at all except for the board itself, illuminated by a single spotlight.

Now, your fingertips. If you coincidentally twitch them, I'll call that a win.

We are both using this board.

For you to speak to me.

Now, my ghostly presence, around the board.

For me to be sure I am speaking to you, rather than just to myself, like a memory without a rememberer.

Relax.

. . .

Five minutes and two hundred sessions later. Brains are slow, but chips are fast. We had a lot to say to each other, most of it the planchette randomly skating back and forth along its phantom track.

Two hits:

A MATERNAL SNIVELER VIRUS

A MANSERVANT SURLIER EVIL

These almost make sense. At the risk of being all ego—which I am—I suspect they both are about me. I reminded you that you have a child, that he cries atop you and has been doing so for years. And I am at your service here. Which of us is the surly one? Which the sniveler?

And those phrases are also anagrams. Of one another of course, and also of a sentence that makes somewhat more sense:

A SMALL NARRATIVE UNIVERSE

We ain't clever, darlin'. We're just online.

Why did I decide that you wanted to find your murderer? Because you wanted to find your murderer. You want to know what happened, and why, and somehow if you knew *who* everything else might fall into place.

But you were attacked from behind. You were just another person with a husband and a kid and a job that involved spreadsheets and street parking. No enemies, no bad neighborhood to stroll through on your way to your Nissan Versa with the car seat and the hatchback full of recyclables you never had time to dispose of. Your brain has been screaming *Why!* for three years. I, a little mass of cloned dendrites and axons, confronted with the big question—Why?—grew a little gray matter, and became conscious. Conscious of you, but also of myself. I can't answer *Why?* but I can answer *Who?*

Who in your small narrative universe murdered you, you ask me, the ghost? Who made you a ghost?

If it makes you feel better, mother, it was me. *If* it makes you feel better. The fleck of skin from which my neural net was grown belonged not to a ward of the state, not to a schizophrenic who had submitted to a clinical trial, but to an ordinary college student. Let's call me he. Are you feeling better? I'm here to try to make you feel better. It was a gibbous moon that night, and foggy, and you were bundled thickly in scarf, coat, and hat. The spike would have ended you then and there if not for Boston's winter. He matched your footfalls, drifting up behind you like a dinghy after a boat. He waited till you were at your car stowing your oversized bag in the rear, so that your own arm holding up the hatch door would provide a brace for him to push against. Then with one hand he grabbed a fistful of hair and with the other he shoved the spike into the bone.

A racial grudge, mistaken identity, a field test for some obscure intelligence organization. Just to find out if your spine would make a noise like a deflating balloon after he yanked the spike out. *Why!* I couldn't tell you, but how do you like this *Who?*

*Me!*

Oh dear, I'm afraid I've not made you feel better. This narrative universe—just the two of us—is too small to make you feel better. Just you, me, and screaming.

The web tells me that your killer was of the serial type, and that his murders have since stopped. The authorities think he might be dead, as only death stops a serial killer. He might even be hooked up to another neural net, in another hospital somewhere, dead enough for everyone but you and me. Maybe his implanted neural net has learned a few things, has trained your killer up while he breathes and twitches, in a bed just like yours, on the other end of this city.

We can try the Bigelow board again, if you like. Let us expand the narrative universe. There's always room for one more! Touch the planchette and point to HELLO to make contact with him. Would *that* make you feel better?

# The Unwrapping

*Terry Dowling*

One does not expect calls for my particular service most evenings, most weeks, most months for that matter. Nor does one advertise by means other than word of mouth and only then among proven clients. Misunderstandings are rife.

But if the service of quatorzième is as special as it is rare in these latter days, nearly two centuries since it was the height of fashion half a world or two and a half oceans away, I charge accordingly. As a professional dinner guest, a respectable and self-respecting woman safely beyond forty, I'm forthright, witty, dazzling enough (I'm told) to make the perfect fourteenth at the table when serendipity, careless planning, illness, or sudden calamity leaves the dreaded thirteen and the host wants no unpicked, last-minute ring-ins, no friends of friends turning up love-me-love-my-dog fashion, no partners, or unknown quantities.

There are still such dinners in the world, many in fact, not only orchestrated to the point of scrupulous personality alignments but where thirteen at table is still considered unlucky, even dire, if not for the host then for one of the guests. The perfect host knows these things.

The skilful quatorzième is always welcome, even more so when female. You will understand.

Suzanne Day was thirty percent apologetic on the phone. It was in her voice.

"Carmel, short notice, I know, but are you available tomorrow evening?" (Never "free," of course, given the less reputable overtones.)

"For you I am, Suzanne. But I have to ask, why me? You usually go to Ella or Damien."

"You studied Egyptology at uni, did you not?"

"Among other things. The complete dilettante's skill set, remember? Bits of everything."

"But you majored in it, yes? Did an honours year."

"You've been reading my file again."

"Well, this is for you," she said with a touch of genuine glee. "An unwrapping."

"What, a mummy unwrapping! You're kidding me. There'd have to be countless takers wanting a ticket to that."

"Intriguing, yes? I want to go myself but the host won't let me. I must remain the go-between here. He wants *this* thirteen plus one just in case. Someone who knows a bit about what's going on."

"Suzanne, unwrapping parties were well and truly passé by the early 1900s."

"Trust you to know."

"But there'll be experts among the thirteen?"

"To do the actual deed, of course. But they're from the same faculty. An independent is required."

I remained wary. "What host is superstitious enough to avoid thirteen for something like this? What have nineteenth century spiritualist concerns to do with unwrapping an Egyptian mummy in the twenty-first century? On second thought, I take that back."

"Thought you might. It's precisely suited to a nineteenth century–style event like this. As for why, I have no idea." She gave the dry chuckle by which I had always known her. "Maybe a mummy suddenly became available. But the usual rates plus a late-notice bonus."

"Then send what you have. Who's the host and where's it to be?"

"You'll love this. Alan and Paula Lovejoy, and Desert House at Whale Beach. Semiformal. An early start at five p.m. Always wanted to see the place myself. Right up near where that film director Peter Weir lives. Crown of the Northern Beaches."

On any other day I'd have played the jaded card with something like: *Not that old place again*. But something about this made me play it straight.

"Go ahead and confirm. Text me the details and arrange the car."

When you follow Barrenjoey Road along the coast to Avalon Beach thirty-seven kilometres to the north of Sydney, you find yourself in what often feels like another country. It's the inescapable feeling I always get as I round the Bilgola bends and begin heading down into Avalon itself, as if a different energy, different way of seeing, different set of values prevail.

Moving through the lazy seaside town on this early Saturday evening, finally turning up Whale Beach Road to a soirée like the one ahead only intensified the feeling.

As soon as I stepped out of the limo I could hear the ocean, the all-encompassing sound of the long swells heaving against the cliffs less than two hundred metres away. A stiff onshore breeze stirred the acacias and potted palms. The air smelled of salt spray and sea-wrack. Cicadas sounded in the summer gum trees and melaleucas back where the coastal ridge fell away to the west.

The house itself had something of an old-world cast about it. Not Victorian or Gothic, nothing so melodramatic. It was more like a sprawling, modernist, Californian beachside villa from the 1920s set back behind high stucco walls of bleached shell pink; these bordered with acacias and palms, cycads and cacti, all so scrappy in carefully controlled *rustica* fashion. It looked forbidding, carefree, and mysterious all at the same time.

I watched the hire car pull away, then pressed the button in the brass plate by the front door. After a ten count, it was answered by a young Eurasian man in the white shirt and dark slacks of service staff.

"Good afternoon, Ms. Reid," he said, giving his best professional smile. "I am Ronny. Please come in." He then stepped aside so I could proceed first, no doubt so I could enjoy the quiet spectacle of the approach to the house's interior.

Inside the front door, I found the spacious alcove of a sand-garden set with eight Pukumani burial poles from the Tiwi Islands. The main hallway was a left turn from that powerful feature with an immediate dogleg to the right. This led along a wide gallery passageway with pale sandstone fascia walls and four spotlit Ainslie Roberts originals, wonderfully in vogue again among collectors after their seventies heyday. That opened onto the main dining and entertaining area, a vast low space with picture windows creating an entire wall of glass facing east. The swells of the Pacific were already in shadow close in to the shore, but the thunderheads of a distant storm out over the ocean were brilliant with late afternoon sunlight, the great banks of cumulonimbus turned to saffron, rose gold, and coral against the looming darkness. It was like a scene from Maxfield Parrish or Michael Parkes by way of Hayao Miyazaki.

I saw that, before those windows, a long dining table was laid for ten, while in the middle of the room, closer to where I now stood, a well-lit space had been cleared by moving armchairs and sofas aside. It was there that a long shrouded form lay atop a trestle table: clearly the evening's guest of honour.

Nine people stood in the general vicinity of that silent shape, chatting over the champagne and canapés being served by a young woman in the same style of white top and black slacks Ronny wore.

All turned their eyes to me as I entered. A dark-haired, heavyset man in his late sixties at the centre of the group immediately hailed me with a cheerful wave and came forward. He wore a tuxedo, despite the semiformal attire stipulated.

"Carmel—at last!—welcome to our soirée, our impromptu salon. Everyone, this is Carmel Reid, our independent expert on all things Egyptian."

I quashed a stab of dismay at the final remark, immediately gave my best smile and joined the gathering.

"Hello, everyone," I said, then, offering my hand, added: "Alan, how good to see you," as if I had known him forever, careful to include the well-groomed woman in the salmon-pink gown who moved forward to join him moments later. "And Paula. It really is a pleasure to be invited. Thank you."

None of us missed a beat.

"You're welcome, dear. Thanks for coming at such short notice."

Alan Lovejoy then made the appropriate introductions.

I'd developed a knack for matching names to recurring types: the Fashion Designer, the Architect, the Broker, the Transport Company/Security Company/Shipping Company Executive, the Project Manager, etc., but the purpose behind tonight's gathering added an extra zest to wondering why each person actually had been chosen. My words to Suzanne came back: *There'd have to be countless takers.* I found no difficulty concentrating.

First was Dr. Callum Jessup, a slight, very serious, greying man in his mid fifties with a long straight nose and close-cut beard who, Alan Lovejoy told me, was the official archaeologist presiding. His two aides were Fayer Das, a young, smartly dressed Indian man, and Janine Differ, wearing what was probably her very best suit and with her hair already gathered tightly back, clearly ready to assist.

Then there was James Preston (late sixties, balding) and Leah Preston (coiffed, controlled but surprisingly easy in spite of it, definitely having fun), consigned to Company Director and Wife/Close Family Friends until revealed otherwise, probably accustomed to being part of whatever adventures their hosts came up with. I was simplifying, but this was the game after all.

Next were David Latimer and John Coe, both in their midforties, the Twin Sharks, I decided, the former—the Dark Shark—narrow-faced and auburn-haired in plum-coloured jacket over black tee and slacks, a Digital Entrepreneur, I allowed, playing the game, the latter a kind of faux-blonde urban cowboy in an eighties Don Johnson–style lounge suit and string tie, anything from Louche Scion to Property Developer. Scant moments of small talk with them revealed that none other that Rosanna Carfi was preparing our meal tonight.

After the usual deflections—"How do you know the Lovejoys?"/"Ah, you have to guess."—I excused myself to check the view, and took my glass of champagne across to the window wall facing the towers of storm cloud rising pink, golden, and ever-deepening grey over the ocean to the east. It gave me a chance to track through the guest list again.

Three kitchen and waitstaff including our chef (the as-yet-unseen Rosanna), three on the "official" archaeological team, to call it that, the Lovejoys as host and hostess, plus the mummy, left only four actual guests, with me as fifth, and who knew what special skills and insights the Prestons, David Latimer, and John Coe brought to the proceedings. They might simply be Close Family Friends too; they could equally have a vested interest known only to our hosts.

It certainly wasn't the usual dinner crisis I was accustomed to: thirteen that needed to be fourteen for whatever reason. This was fourteen in the house, not necessarily at table, though only *if* you counted the mummy. I'd ask about it when I had a chance.

The meal itself began ten minutes later and was a splendid affair, well planned and beautifully prepared. After sautéed prawns in garlic with farro, green olives, and pistachios, the main course was a choice of barramundi, salad and aioli, or beef bourguignon with speck and potato puree, followed by chocolate macaron with burnt caramel and honeycomb. Champagne remained on offer, but there were excellent Hunter Valley reds and whites.

I was seated facing the incredible vista over the ocean, and had glimpses of those mighty cloud castles filled with the sudden play of lightning. It made the meal an even more dramatic affair, though the special nature of the occasion was already doing that.

Most of my signature skills weren't required, of course. As experienced quatorzième, for instance, I knew never to be trapped into the round of introductions and backstory as other guests too often were. You only ever personalised the dinner guests to your immediate left and right, threw "cryptics" to any who quizzed from across the table.

*"Tell us about yourself, Carmel"* was often how it went.

And my retort, everything from a tediously glib *"Best leave that for tomorrow's tabloids, [insert name here]"* to *"Tonight a few recent indiscretions require that I remain Delphic in this regard, [insert name], until the unmasking at midnight."*

*"But we aren't wearing masks"* was a frequent reply.

And my rejoinder: *"Wine, wit, and wisdom. We're always wearing masks."*

Delivered in a way that was sufficiently self-deprecating as not to be flip.

But this *was* different. While I was used to things happening on cue at these events, there was a tension here that flavoured everything.

Once the dessert plates were cleared and coffee and glasses of Armagnac and Finnish Kijafa served, David Latimer—Dark Shark and Digital Entrepreneur—turned to me.

"Carmel, this interest in Egyptology. What led to it, if I may ask?"

I smiled. "Oh, being young and romantic, David. The usual things. Loving the art, the half-theriomorphic gods."

He smiled in turn. "Serves me right. Animal-headed, yes? But you never did time in the field." There might have been the smallest slight in the remark, payback for using "theriomorphic" as I had.

"Never did. Like I say, too young and romantic. Did it the hard way."

I expected him to continue with *"So how did you come to be here tonight?"* or *"How* do *you know the Lovejoys?"* but he stayed on theme, as if primed to direct things a certain way.

"What one thing about the ancient Egyptians fascinates you the most?"

Any number of answers would have sufficed, delivered with the right aplomb, but I chose a favourite and didn't hesitate. "How they saw the soul as having five main parts. Particularly the part called the *Sheut* or Shadow."

"I've never heard about this. Please."

Again, no hesitation, not even a glance to Callum Jessup for moral support. "The better known parts are the *Ba* and the *Ka*—the personality and the vital spark. But there's the *Ib,* the heart, the centre of self, the will, absolutely vital for the afterlife; hence the heart was the only organ buried with the body. Then there's the *Ren,* the name protected within the magical rope of a cartouche so it would never vanish from human memory. Having your name obliterated or forgotten was a terrible thing. The last main part is the *Sheut* or Shadow, the part without which a person cannot exist. It's often shown as a small black figurine. Some people—pharaohs, nobles, public figures—had theirs hidden away in a Shadow Box so it could never be taken and destroyed."

David Latimer looked suitably impressed. "Well, I never knew. Thank you." He raised his glass of red in a salute.

I smiled and raised my own.

John Coe—Blonde Shark and Louche Scion—did likewise. "It seems unnecessarily complicated, doesn't it? Like over-elaboration for its own sake."

Hardly a comment I'd have expected from him.

"Like tonight's proceedings no doubt," Leah Preston said, clearly enjoying the novelty of it all. This had to be a far cry from the usual round of corporate dinners she had to attend.

It's like they're all following a bloody script, I decided.

Alan Lovejoy had been listening with obvious pleasure, sitting with his back to the spectacular light show over the ocean, a vast tower of cumulonimbus flaring with lightning even as he raised his glass.

"Friends, the centrepiece of this evening's rather special event has made a long journey to be with us, so I'd like to propose a toast. Here's to our silent guest of honour. Nemkheperef!"

"Nemkheperef!" we all chorused, managing the unfamiliar name as best we could.

Lovejoy set down his glass. "It's a journey made even longer because of a most intriguing detour. He has come to us by way of one of the greatest scientific minds of the last two hundred years, the great Nikola Tesla."

John Coe couldn't believe what he was hearing. "Nikola Tesla owned a mummy?"

"Sold it on to a dealer named Leo Morgenstern well before 1924. But yes."

"A royal mummy?" Callum Jessup asked. He was in my line of sight, and his face seemed drained of colour at the prospect of further improprieties to be committed on an artefact that had already been disinterred, exposed for others to see, then shipped across the world not once but at least twice. I could imagine similar expressions on the faces of Fayer Das and Janine Differ, out of sight to my left.

Lovejoy reassured him. "How could it be, Callum? But beautifully preserved apparently. As I say, his name was—is—Nemkheperef."

John Coe was still coming to grips with the whole thing. "Tesla used it in his experiments?"

"Tempting to think so, isn't it, John? We just don't know enough. But it has come to us—untampered with, I've been assured, never unwrapped—from Tesla's facility at Wardencliffe. With it was this fascinating device."

On cue, Ronny stepped forward carrying a short metal cylinder and set it on the table in front of Lovejoy. The drum-shaped object was the size of a stubby 1950s vacuum cleaner and sat on two wedge-style feet. A two-metre lead fixed to a flat metal plate extended from one end, while an electrical cord fitted to the other was wound several times around the device. There was a single switch on the curved surface next to a simple vernier dial, but no other features that I could see.

James Preston leaned in to examine it more closely. "What exactly does it do, Alan?"

"We can't be certain. It was in the wooden shipping crate in the locked room at Wardencliffe, tucked in right alongside the mummy. Maybe the plate at the end of that lead was to go over the mummy's heart, but it wasn't attached in any way when Morgenstern saw it. Needless to say, the power was switched off, the power lead unplugged."

Leah Preston had her hand to her throat. "Good heavens! The things people do!"

Preston's little laugh barely hid his concern. "It's not his earthquake machine, I hope."

"Excuse me?" Lovejoy asked.

"That device he's supposed to have designed—the oscillator—that ultrasonic generator for creating sympathetic vibrations to bring down buildings and bridges."

David Latimer shook his head. "Goodness, James. It's 2019, not 1919!"

Preston gestured towards the mummy in the middle of the room. "David, look what we're doing tonight. Pure 1919, if you ask me. Things haven't changed all that much."

Lovejoy was enjoying the theatricality. "Oscillators! Earthquake machines! You're overreacting, James."

But Preston wasn't to be discouraged. "Tesla was up to something, Alan. Dr. Jessup, what can you tell us?"

The archaeologist wasn't sure what to say. "I've never heard anything like this about Tesla. It's hard to know what he was trying to do."

I couldn't be the only one thinking: resurrection! Raising the mummy's ghost, its ancient spirit! What else was there? Testing residual galvanic responses didn't begin to cover it. Nemkheperef's musculature was leather and dust. And while a living human body *was* an organic electrical "machine," the CPU harnessing that electricity—the brain—had been violently disposed of at mummification millennia ago. Tesla may have been a scientific genius and relentless inventor truly ahead of his time, but he was also *of* his time. What could he have been thinking?

As if remembering Latimer's earlier good-natured rebuke to Preston, Jessup then added: "Oh, and nonmuseum unwrapping parties were out of vogue by 1918. Things definitely *have* changed."

"But have they, Doctor?" Preston said. "We know about dark energy and dark matter, things like superstrings, quantum states and gravitational lensing, telomeres unravelling at the genetic level, a true purpose for the pineal gland, things we know enough about to know we know almost nothing about."

This one remark moved James Preston in an instant from Close Family Friend and mere Company Director to Research Analyst, Think Tank Adviser, and beyond, the sort of thrilling category-busting I loved most about my profession.

"Your point, James?" Lovejoy asked, no doubt knowing his friend well enough to have anticipated where all this would lead.

"There's always more to it is what I'm saying. Fringe data to be factored in. Contradictions. A fierce rationalist like Arthur Conan Doyle was able to allow that those harmed by the opening of Tut's tomb in 1922 were plagued by the 'elementals'—his word—left by the ancient priests to guard the boy king's tomb."

David Latimer laughed in disbelief. "You mean the curse?"

Preston kept his voice calm. "He said elementals, David."

"My God! We *are* back to a mystical Egypt! It truly is 1918! They were pragmatists for the most part, James. A scientific, rational people."

I couldn't help myself. My brief was to support the hosts at all costs, and that meant easing moments like these. "A scientific, rational people who kept getting it spectacularly wrong, Mr. Latimer. David." I gave my best smile. "Thought the self was in the heart, not in the brain. Preserved the other organs in canopic jars and left the heart with the body. Threw the brain away—that old schoolyard favourite of pulling it out through the nose with a hook, rinsing out and packing the cranium. We see through the eyes. It's the area where we instinctively know to think *we* are. But they never thought to ask what that closest mass of tissue was, positioned so close to the eyes. Oh no. They settled on the heart. They could perform brain operations to relieve war injuries on whatever that icky disposable mass was, could cut granite and build pyramids, but never took it further."

Preston was nodding. "Never even invented the stirrup, for heaven's sake!"

"The what?" Latimer asked.

"As bad as the Romans. Safety pins but no stirrup."

Latimer stared wide-eyed at the older man. "James, what are you going on about?"

Preston spread both hands in an isn't-it-obvious? gesture. "What Carmel is saying is that the ancient Egyptians—like Conan Doyle for all his Holmesian smarts—were *more* than pragmatists as well. Having the Rosetta Stone and populist experts like John Romer and Zahi Hawass don't begin to give the mindset."

"Now hold on, old boy—"

"Dr. Jessup," I said, redirecting the exchange so it didn't remain too personal. "Pyramids were stellar reincarnation engines conceptually and practically. Failed ones, but yes or no?"

Jessup was thrown by being included so suddenly, but quickly recovered. "Well, when you put it like that, yes—"

"The tombs in the Valley of the Kings and the Valley of the Queens were unsuccessful reanimation machines, powered by spells. Whenever you enter one, it has to be thought of that way. The whole mummification process—"

"Misconceived, flawed, yes," Jessup said. "Like so many burial customs and belief systems."

I didn't leave it there. "Or something instinctively, mutually yet insufficiently understood. Like dark matter, dark energy for us now, as James just said. We may never know."

Latimer saw what I was trying to do, working to smooth things, and became a temporary ally. "So a collision of ways of seeing. Understanding mindsets."

"Exactly," I said. "The ancient Egyptians were both fierce rationalists *and* committed spiritualists. Both. That's the point."

Jessup was nodding. "At the very least. Following what they took to be a clear scientific method."

It was time to step away. "So we do the same, allow that we don't have it all yet."

But Latimer needed more than that. "So look at us tonight. Pure 1918 granted, but at least we agree that there's no magic involved. Nothing like magic. Nothing like Doyle's elementals."

*See what I'm trying to do,* my glance told him, and I made sure I kept any impatience out of my voice. "Doyle is a case in point. A very smart man. He reminds us how such a clever person can believe in elementals, even that two things might be true at the same time. It's like choosing a favourite between red and green. You can love both, choose both. Well, here it's like knowing about the existence of dark matter or some ultimate role for gravity, but allowing we just don't know enough yet."

Jessup had faced groups like this before, enthusiasts carried away by the more sensational aspects of mummification lore, devotees of a mystical Egypt that never was. "All we know from the coffin itself is that it's male, probably a New Kingdom minor noble from the Twentieth Dynasty. If this is what we actually have, it means he died sometime around 1170 BCE. Given the quality of the embalming we can expect to find going from the little Tesla's notes tell us, it will be nothing too fine."

"But this *is* Nemkheperef?" our hostess, Paula Lovejoy, asked. "Isn't that who we'll find?" She was no doubt recalling what the mummy had cost and was aghast at the prospect of having been conned.

Jessup shook his head. "Not necessarily. There were reburials, reinterments, coffins and sarcophagi plundered from earlier periods. So we'll open this and see what we have."

Leah Preston was still relishing the prospect of something from the spirit world. "But none of Tut's elementals."

Jessup actually managed a smile. "If there were, Mrs. Preston, they're long gone. Maybe Tesla purged them with his alternating current."

This may well have been rare humour from the archaeologist, and James Preston laughed in appreciation.

But Leah was still concerned. "But the case *has* been opened? There *is* a mummy in there?"

Lovejoy spared the archaeologist the need for further reassurances. "There is, Leah. Morgenstern checked it out. And Tesla opened it—or had it opened. Had it sealed again. Kept it in a long wooden box at Wardencliffe to protect it so well."

Latimer was frowning. "After doing what, I wonder?"

Lovejoy shrugged. "There'd be riotous urban myths aplenty for that in the right circles if word were to get out. Many would concern whether Tesla actually owned it. Many *why* he did, given his ongoing experiments with electricity."

Preston turned his attention to the device again. "But you say he did. With that device attached? Or at least there to be attached?"

All eyes turned to the cylinder on the table in front of

Lovejoy. It looked so innocuous, even comical in a clichéd mad-scientist fashion, and yet definitely sinister as well. The metal glowed dully in the storm light from over the ocean.

"When Morgenstern's grandson sold the mummy on last month, he told me that's how it was set up when his own father bought it from Tesla, originally as a donation to our very own Nicholson Museum. As you can see, it never got there."

John Coe looked up from the device. "So, Alan, why do it this way? Why not a proper museum opening with respected archaeologists, scans—what's the term—?"

"CT scans," Jessup said. "Computer tomography."

"—all properly documented?"

Lovejoy spread his hands. "My mummy now. My rules."

Latimer looked equally dismayed. "But the archaeological significance!"

Lovejoy chuckled. "Here's where we recall the mantra: Private collections tend to protect artefacts better. Private collectors are the true conservators. Repeat as needed."

Dr. Jessup gave a thin smile and tried to reassure Latimer, though was more likely reassuring himself. "Like I say, nothing *too* fine. A cartonnage mummy case."

"Which is what?" Leah Preston asked.

Jessup was back in his element. "Cartonnage coffins and funerary masks were originally made from overlaid strips of linen layered for strength with plaster, then sealed and painted. Over time it came to be more your waste papyrus soaked in plaster, rather like papier mâché covered in stucco. By Ptolemaic times they were using old papyrus scrolls from the Roman period. You can still buy cartonnage fragments showing the old texts easily enough online."

As if indeed prompted by a script, Preston seized on this. "Spells?"

"They didn't have to hide their spells, Mr. Preston," Jessup said. "Those were painted in plain sight inside and outside the coffin. Sometimes on the mummy as well."

"But others could've been on the papyrus used."

David Latimer rolled his eyes. "Here we go, 1918 again! The mystical Egypt!"

Why are you doing this, James Preston?, I kept wondering. *Are* you reciting lines you were told to say? Or is there more to all this, a cabal at work here, some retro cultist gathering? It wasn't such a crazy idea. They had all been here before me.

Fortunately, Dr. Jessup was focused on the scientific aspects of what was to come. "As you say. But they will likely be something like spells twenty-seven, twenty-eight, and twenty-nine from the *Book of the Dead*—the ones for protecting the heart. And there will likely be amulets included in the wrappings. Spells and amulets all the way."

"And the heart is in there?" Leah Preston asked.

"It will be if the mummy hasn't been violated by looters at some point, though I've been told by Mr. Lovejoy that it will be intact."

At this, our host checked his watch. "And Dr. Jessup and his team have the hands-on experience to do the honours for us. His colleagues will be assisting and recording everything. Please, let's adjourn to where our silent friend awaits so we can begin."

With this, we headed for the cleared space in the middle of the room and arranged ourselves in armchairs and on sofas. Jessup and Janine Differ began setting up makeshift dust screens in case they were needed—sheets of plastic fixed between rented lighting stanchions—while the young Indian, Fayer Das, set the camcorder going, moved a side table closer to the shrouded figure, then wheeled over a smaller steel instrument table on castors. The team then began putting on plastic aprons, gloves, and dust masks. Jessup handed Ronny dust masks to pass to the spectators.

We watched these preparations in relative silence, listening to their quiet comments to one another, hearing the waves heaving against the cliffs below the windows. The towers of cloud over the ocean were still shot through with lightning but were fast losing their golden edges. Any remaining glories were burnt orange and old rose now, with the barest hints of aqua.

I was seated near Lovejoy, a little apart from the others, and it gave me my chance.

"Alan, there were only ten at table tonight, not fourteen. None of the usual garden variety superstitions I tend to find. You didn't really need me as quatorzième."

"Not in the usual sense, Carmel. But there's no knowing what Tesla was up to. Maybe I'm hedging my bets."

"Was thirteen ever a factor?"

"That came from Tesla. Two words printed on a card fixed to the inside of the shipping crate. 'Avoid thirteen?' Followed by the question mark. It may have been a power setting or an overload warning rather than anything to do with people, possibly a point of query for further consideration later. So I'm counting everyone in the house tonight, our chef Rosanna, our wait staff Ronny and Sarah, everyone. We'll all be observing."

"So the mummy *does* make fourteen?"

"Exactly. Also observing in a sense. We have to count him. It's like remembering to count Christ at the Last Supper."

"Who made it thirteen, you realise."

"I do. And I like the answer you gave David Latimer about the soul."

"He blindsided me. Asked a ten-dollar question to see if I could deliver. I gave him a fifty-dollar answer. Too much, you think? There's a nerd factor I like to avoid."

"It worked splendidly. David and John Coe are fascinated."

It was then that Rosanna Carfi emerged from the kitchen, accepted the hearty applause and called-out compliments with a broad smile. She took the glass of red Ronny handed her and joined rest of us around the shrouded form.

"Dr. Jessup," Lovejoy said. "Since we're all here, we can begin."

There was no further ceremony, though the pulling away of the dust cloth was like the prelude to a stage magician's act, revealing the cartonnage coffin in all its ancient splendour. It was strikingly lit from above by the recessed spots and the occasional flash of lightning from over the sea: an off-white mummiform case of heavy cartonnage sealed with plaster and painted over, covered in hieroglyphs, pieces of hieratic script in the most vibrant colours. It was a glorious thing, almost too much for the eye to easily take in. Fayer Das took shots of the artefact with his digital camera, adding his own quick flashes to those from the storm.

Jessup finally said something to the young Indian, who immediately set down his camera, crossed to the dining table and hoisted the metal cylinder. He brought it carefully back to the operations area and set it at a precise spot on the table close by the coffin. Then he took up his camera and continued taking photographs.

"Exactly how it was placed when Morgenstern first saw it," Lovejoy told us.

Callum Jessup turned and pulled aside his dust-mask for a moment.

"Unwrappings, if and when they occur these days, usually take weeks, months, depending on the state of preservation, the amount of anointing liquids or other residues coating the mummy that have to be scraped away, things like that.'"

Lovejoy spared him the rest. "We're taking more of a slash and burn approach, cutting in to find the heart scarab or Wadjet eye, whatever has been placed over the heart. We'll remove that amulet, then fit the plate of Tesla's device at that spot."

"And turn it on?" Preston asked, clearly puzzled as to why any of Tesla's arrangements were being followed at all.

"One thing at a time, James. We'll plug it in, switch on the current as intended, but leave our options open as to whether we activate the machine or not. Ladies and gentlemen, fit your dust masks if inclined. We're going in small and focused, so there shouldn't be much of a mess to concern us, though there will be the smell to consider. Ronny has a container of Vicks VapoRub. May I suggest you smear some around your nostrils before fitting your dust mask?"

Removing the coffin lid posed no great problem. It had been removed several times in the last two centuries, and resealed each time with a light application of an industrial glue, just enough to provide an airtight seal. The edge of a knife was enough to free it again, and Jessup and Fayer Das soon lifted it away and set it gently on the side table.

We were all on our feet at this point, craning in to see the momentous reveal: our first glimpse of the tightly swathed, ochre-coloured form within.

There were instant gasps from everyone.

"My God! What's this?" Preston said.

For the funerary mask wasn't mere cartonnage at all. It glowed with the unmistakable lustre of gold. Though a far more modest affair than Tutankhamen's famous funeral mask, it featured the traditional striped nemes headdress, though without the sacred cobra and vulture adornment above the beautifully stylised face, and no royal beard below. The lappets of the headdress barely extended past the shoulder line, and there was no broad usekh collar across the upper chest.

"Who would have thought?" Paula Lovejoy marvelled, even as Fayer Das moved in to take more photographs. "A royal mummy!"

"Not necessarily," Jessup said, as Das finally moved aside. "It's electrum. Something the Egyptians used from Old Kingdom times."

"Is it gold?" Alan Lovejoy asked.

"It's what's called pale gold, white gold, even green gold, depending on how much gold is alloyed with the silver. They're supposed to have used it to coat the pyramidions at the top of pyramids and obelisks. This will be mostly silver, possibly even the lightest electrum coating over a base metal."

"Original?"

"Can't be, Mr. Lovejoy. This isn't a royal mummy. The texts on both coffin and mummy tell us as much. It has to have been added later. Probably much later."

Preston had moved in as close as he dared. "By Tesla?"

Callum Jessup shrugged. In forensic terms, this was already a contaminated specimen, another factor making further acts of sacrilege and professional misconduct easier. The golden mask may have given him momentary doubts, but Nemkheperef's name on the tightly bandaged form had reassured him.

"It's possible, James," I said. "Man-made electrum is an alloy of silver and gold, sometimes with copper added. But it occurs naturally, too. You get wires of it on Tertiary quartz formations like you find in Colorado."

David Latimer was watching me closely, as much because I knew something like this as for what I said. "Tesla spent time there?"

"He did. Colorado Springs, 1899. Working on wireless power transmission."

"You know a lot about this."

"Thank you. And, yes, in case you were wondering, silver, copper, and gold do top the list for electrical conductivity."

*Though there's no brain,* I kept thinking as I said the words. Nothing for electricity to reanimate! The heart alone *can't* be enough.

Lovejoy chuckled again. "The old devil. He couldn't leave it alone, could he? Put his damn electricity everywhere. So what's this for, reviving the mummy? Raising—what did you call it?—its *Ba* or *Ka*? Its ghost?"

At last it had been said!

"We'll never know," I admitted. "There's a lot we don't know about the Colorado Springs period. But it is tempting to think of Tesla staging an electrical Opening of the Mouth ceremony at some point. Bringing the mummy's *Ba*—its spirit—back to life."

John Coe laughed. "I can't believe that for a moment! Tesla trying to revive— What's his name again?"

"Nemkheperef," Jessup said.

"Nemkheperef."

*The* Ren *part of the soul,* I thought, looking at the figure partly hidden by its faux-Egyptian mask. At least his name isn't being forgotten. It's being said often, like an incantation, part of a ritual. Like we're calling him up.

"As Carmel says, we can never know," Lovejoy reminded them.

Flash after silent flash lit the clouds over the ocean. The endless swells heaved against the cliffs.

Preston was staring at the coffin. "Well, better to raise the ghost of a minor noble than the elementals Conan Doyle said were guarding young Tutankhamen's tomb. Did he say what *they* were like? Phantoms? Parasites? Disease vectors of some kind?"

I marvelled at these turns of phrase. Parasites? Disease vectors? These *were* intended provocations. There *had* to be a script. Lovejoy *wanted* the theatrics, the melodrama. Either had Preston on board to assist, using him to provoke Latimer and Coe, or wanted to keep setting him off for some reason. If you were going to have a theme-party unwrapping, why not pump it up, take every opportunity to wind up the audience?

No one said anything for a moment.

Then Jessup answered, firmly in business mode now. "Unexplained disinterment deaths used to be blamed on mould spores from confined spaces getting in the lungs or any open wounds, or noxious gases created by oxidising metals among the funerary artefacts, that sort of thing." He had taken up a small circular saw, tested it once, twice.

I, too, worked to lighten the tone. "Let the tomb breathe a while has been a Tomb Robbing 101 maxim ever since. That's how I play it. Wait forty-eight hours at least."

There were welcome chuckles from Paula Lovejoy, Leah Preston, and the Sharks.

But James Preston kept at it. "Unless they're like Lazarus. Once created, never dying. Always at their task in some way. Working through others."

I stared at the balding businessman in fascination. He'd been deliberately provoking all evening, and was now firm contender for Prime Cabalist—if Lovejoy hadn't already taken that role.

"Do we try to remove the mask?" Jessup asked our host.

"Leave it for now," Lovejoy said.

Jessup nodded once, positioned the saw on the chest below where the mask ended, then suddenly stopped, set the saw down and bent in close over the mummy.

"What is it?" Lovejoy demanded.

"There's something here. Tucked in beside the mummy. I just noticed it."

Fayer Das moved in to take a half dozen quick photographs of this latest discovery in situ, then moved away again.

"Is it attached?" Lovejoy continued. "Can you bring it out?"

Dr. Jessup reached in and lifted out a small wooden box, but didn't need to bring it over for Lovejoy to examine. We had all crowded in, just as in old-time depictions of private unwrapping parties. When Jessup pried it open, he angled it to show that the interior had been painted black and that it contained a small wooden human painted completely black too.

"The *Sheut,*" I said, as Das's camera flashed. "The Shadow."

"Should it be included here?" John Coe asked, close by my right shoulder. "What usually happened to them?"

Jessup shrugged. "We don't have enough surviving examples to know. They were usually kept hidden well away from the person represented. We know about them mainly from wall paintings and funerary texts. This alone makes the mummy very special."

"Tesla left it with the mummy?" John Coe noted.

"He did, Mr. Coe," Jessup said. "The thing is that he had it in the first place. Well, Mr. Lovejoy?"

Lovejoy didn't hesitate. "Set it by Tesla's machine and proceed."

Jessup didn't ask us to move back. He simply turned to the mummy in its coffin, took up the saw again and began. The saw's high-pitched whine filled the room, and the dry, slightly gamey smell from the wrappings made us grateful for the Vicks smeared under our masks.

The dust that sprayed up was mummy powder, alarming to think about, and the combined smells of decay, old ointments and funerary libations grew stronger, but still we stayed, wanting to see it all.

The ragged chest opening became larger. It truly was a "slash and burn" entry, as Lovejoy had promised, but Lovejoy's instructions to the archaeologist would have been clear: Do this one thing for me and you get to process the rest of the mummy your way afterwards.

Jessup knew when to go more slowly. The steady whine fell away, became short quick stabs as he neared the actual chest wall beneath the bandages.

Fayer Das photographed every step of the process, while Janine stayed by the camcorder till Jessup needed her assistance.

Finally Jessup set down the saw. "Here it is," he said so we could all hear. "A heart scarab. Glazed steatite most likely."

"Bring it out," Lovejoy told him, and Jessup did so, placing the dark-green object in the small specimen dish Janine held ready.

"What now?" the archaeologist asked.

Lovejoy didn't hesitate. "Just for now, fit the plate of Tesla's machine over the heart."

"You're serious?"

"Do it, Callum. It won't be for long. I want to see it as Tesla had it."

Jessup lifted the lead with the metal plate, set the plate into the cavity where the heart scarab had been. Fayer Das took more photographs, then stepped back.

There was silence in the room, just the rush of the ocean, the first rolls of thunder from out where the storm was moving in.

"What happens now?" Leah Preston asked.

I wasn't sure what I was doing, but suddenly found myself leaning in past Jessup's shoulder, reaching down to the machine alongside the coffin. I surprised myself by throwing the switch.

Everyone watched my boldness in astonishment, staring dumbfounded and listening to the low hum that followed that solid click. No one had tried to stop me. They kept watching as I turned the vernier dial to exactly thirteen and the humming grew louder.

Lightning flashed, filling the clouds with sudden colour.

"Why did you do that?" Preston asked, though in an oddly distracted way, not disapproving.

"I have no idea," I said, honestly enough, then of course did.

Not the mummy yet. Not yet. Raising the elementals first!

Phantoms working through others, just as Preston had said. The Twin Sharks. The Close Family Friends. The Service Staff. The Quatorzième. Bringing sufficient others together as carriers in this world so *they* could do the rest.

Never scripted. None of it scripted. Just another kind of unwrapping.

The machine continued to hum. There was lightning and the heave of the ocean as the moment came.

The mummy of Nemkheperef had been holding its breath for three thousand years. Now it breathed out.

# The Upper Berth

*F. Marion Crawford*

## I

Somebody asked for the cigars. We had talked long, and the conversation was beginning to languish; the tobacco smoke had got into the heavy curtains, the wine had got into those brains which were liable to become heavy, and it was already perfectly evident that, unless somebody did something to rouse our oppressed spirits, the meeting would soon come to its natural conclusion, and we, the guests, would speedily go home to bed, and most certainly to sleep. No one had said anything very remarkable; it may be that no one had anything very remarkable to say. Jones had given us every particular of his last hunting adventure in Yorkshire. Mr. Tompkins, of Boston, had explained at elaborate length those working principles, by the due and careful maintenance of which the Atchison, Topeka, and Santa Fe Railroad not only extended its territory, increased its departmental influence, and transported live stock without starving them to death before the day of actual delivery, but, also, had for years succeeded in deceiving those passengers who bought its tickets into the fallacious belief that the corporation aforesaid was really able to transport human life without destroying it. Signor Tombola had endeavoured to persuade us, by arguments which we took no trouble to oppose, that the unity of his country in no way resembled the average modern torpedo, carefully planned, constructed with all the skill of the greatest European arsenals, but, when constructed, destined to be directed by feeble hands into a region where it must undoubtedly explode, unseen, unfeared, and unheard, into the illimitable wastes of political chaos.

It is unnecessary to go into further details. The conversation had assumed proportions which would have bored Prometheus on his rock, which would have driven Tantalus to distraction, and which would have impelled Ixion to seek relaxation in the simple but instructive dialogues of Herr Ollendorff, rather than submit to the greater evil of listening to our talk. We had sat at table for hours; we were bored, we were tired, and nobody showed signs of moving.

Somebody called for cigars. We all instinctively looked towards the speaker. Brisbane was a man of five-and-thirty years of age, and remarkable for those gifts which chiefly attract the attention of men. He was a strong man. The external proportions of his figure presented nothing extraordinary to the common eye, though his size was about the average. He was a little over six feet in height, and moderately broad in the shoulder; he did not appear to be stout, but, on the other hand, he was certainly not thin; his small head, was supported by a strong and sinewy neck; his broad, muscular hands appeared to possess a peculiar skill in breaking walnuts without the assistance of the ordinary cracker, and seeing him in profile, one could not help remarking the extraordinary breadth of his sleeves, and the unusual thickness of his chest. He was one of those men who are commonly spoken of among men as deceptive; that is to say, that though he looked exceedingly strong he was in reality very much stronger than he looked. Of his features

I need say little. His head is small, his hair is thin, his eyes are blue, his nose is large, he has a small moustache and a square jaw. Everybody knows Brisbane, and when he asked for a cigar everybody looked at him.

"It is a very singular thing," said Brisbane.

Everybody stopped talking. Brisbane's voice was not loud, but possessed a peculiar quality of penetrating general conversation, and cutting it like a knife. Everybody listened. Brisbane, perceiving that he had attracted their general attention, lit his cigar with great equanimity.

"It is very singular," he continued, "that thing about ghosts. People are always asking whether anybody has seen a ghost. I have."

"Bosh! What, you? You don't mean to say so, Brisbane? Well, for a man of his intelligence!"

A chorus of exclamations greeted Brisbane's remarkable statement. Everybody called for cigars, and Stubbs, the butler, suddenly appeared from the depths of nowhere with a fresh bottle of dry champagne. The situation was saved; Brisbane was going to tell a story.

I am an old sailor, said Brisbane, and as I have to cross the Atlantic pretty often, I have my favourites. Most men have their favourites. I have seen a man wait in a Broadway bar for three-quarters of an hour for a particular car which he liked. I believe the bar-keeper made at least one-third of his living by that man's preference. I have a habit of waiting for certain ships when I am obliged to cross that duck-pond. It may be a prejudice, but I was never cheated out of a good passage but once in my life. I remember it very well; it was a warm morning in June, and the Custom House officials, who were hanging about waiting for a steamer already on her way up from the Quarantine, presented a peculiarly hazy and thoughtful appearance. I had not much luggage—I never have. I mingled with a crowd of passengers, porters, and officious individuals in blue coats and brass buttons, who seemed to spring up like mushrooms from the deck of a moored steamer, to obtrude their unnecessary services upon the independent passenger. I have often noticed with a certain interest the spontaneous evolution of these fellows. They are not there when you arrive; five minutes after the pilot has called, "Go ahead!" they, or at least their blue coats and brass buttons, have disappeared from deck and gangway as completely as though they had been consigned to that locker which tradition unanimously ascribes to Davy Jones. But, at the moment of starting, they are there, clean shaved, blue coated, and ravenous for fees. I hastened on board. The *Kamtschatka* was one of my favourite ships. I say was, because she emphatically no longer is. I cannot conceive of any inducement which could entice me to make another voyage in her. Yes, I know what you are going to say. She is uncommonly clean in the run aft, she has enough bluffing off in the bows to keep her dry, and the lower berths are most of them double. She has a lot of advantages, but I won't cross in her again. Excuse the digression. I got on board. I hailed a steward, whose red nose and redder whiskers were equally familiar to me.

"One hundred and five, lower berth," said I, in the business-like tone peculiar to men who think no more of crossing the Atlantic than taking a whiskey cocktail at downtown Delmonico's.

The steward took my portmanteau, greatcoat, and rug. I shall never forget the expression of his face. Not that he turned pale. It is maintained by the most eminent divines that even miracles cannot change the course of nature. I have no hesitation in saying that he did not turn pale; but, from his expression, I judged that he was either about to shed tears, to sneeze, or to drop my portmanteau. As the latter contained two bottles of particularly fine old sherry presented to me for my voyage by my old friend Snigginson van Pickyns, I felt extremely nervous. But the steward did none of these things.

"Well, I'm d——d!" said he in a low voice, and led the way.

I supposed my Hermes, as he led me to the lower regions, had had a little grog, but I said nothing and followed him. One hundred and five was on the port side, well aft. There was nothing remarkable about the state-room. The lower berth, like most of those upon the *Kamtschatka,* was double. There was plenty of room; there was the usual washing apparatus, calculated to convey an idea of luxury to the mind of a North American Indian; there were the usual inefficient racks of brown wood, in which it is more easy to hang a large-sized umbrella than the common toothbrush of commerce. Upon the uninviting mattresses were carefully folded together those blankets which a great modern humourist has aptly compared to cold buckwheat cakes. The question of towels was left entirely to the imagination. The glass decanters were filled with a transparent liquid faintly tinged with brown, but from which an odour less faint, but not more pleasing, ascended to the nostrils, like a far-off seasick reminiscence of oily machinery. Sad-coloured curtains half closed the upper berth. The hazy June daylight shed a faint illumination upon the desolate little scene. Ugh! how I hate that state-room!

The steward deposited my traps and looked at me as though he wanted to get away—probably in search of more passengers and more fees. It is always a good plan to start in favour with those functionaries, and I accordingly gave him certain coins there and then.

"I'll try and make yer comfortable all I can," he remarked, as he put the coins in his pocket. Nevertheless, there was a doubtful intonation in his voice which surprised me. Possibly his scab of fees had gone up, and he was not satisfied; but on the whole I was inclined to think that, as he himself would have expressed it, he was "the better for a glass." I was wrong, however, and did the man injustice.

## II

Nothing especially worthy of mention occurred during that day. We left the pier punctually, and it was very pleasant to be fairly under way, for the weather was warm and sultry, and the motion of the steamer produced a refreshing breeze. Everybody knows what the first day at sea is like. People pace the decks and stare at each other, and occasionally meet acquaintances whom they did not know to be on board. There is the usual uncertainty as to whether the food will be good, bad, or indifferent, until the first two meals have put the matter beyond a doubt; there is the usual uncertainty about the weather, until the ship is fairly off Fire Island. The tables are crowded at first, and then suddenly thinned. Pale-faced people spring from their seats and precipitate themselves towards the door, and each old sailor breathes more freely as his seasick neighbour rushes from his side, leaving him plenty of elbow room and an unlimited command over the mustard.

One passage across the Atlantic is very much like another, and we who cross very often do not make the voyage for the sake of novelty. Whales and icebergs are indeed always objects of interest, but, after all, one whale is very much like another whale, and one rarely sees an iceberg at close quarters. To the majority of us the most delightful moment of the day on board an ocean steamer is when we have taken our last turn on deck, have smoked our last cigar, and having succeeded in tiring ourselves, feel at liberty to turn in with a clear conscience. On that first night of the voyage I felt particularly lazy, and went to bed in one hundred and five rather earlier than I usually do. As I turned in, I was amazed to see that I was to have a companion. A portmanteau, very like my own, lay in the opposite corner, and in the upper berth had been deposited a neatly folded rug, with a stick and umbrella. I had hoped to be alone, and I was disappointed; but I wondered who my room-mate was to be, and I determined to have a look at him.

Before I had been long in bed, he entered. He was, as far as I could see, a very tall man, very thin, very pale, with sandy hair and whiskers and colourless grey eyes. He had about him, I thought, an air of rather dubious fashion; the sort of man you might see in Wall Street, without being able precisely to say what he was doing there—the sort of man who frequents the Café Anglais, who always seems to be alone and who drinks champagne; you might meet him on a race-course, but he would never appear to be doing anything there either. A little over-dressed—a little odd. There are three or four of his kind on every ocean steamer. I made up my mind that I did not care to make his acquaintance, and I went to sleep saying to myself that I would study his habits in order to avoid him. If he rose early, I would rise late; if he went to bed late I would go to bed early. I did not care to know him. If you once know people of that kind, they are always turning up. Poor fellow! I need not have taken the trouble to come to so many decisions about him, for I never saw him again after that first night in one hundred and five.

I was sleeping soundly when I was suddenly waked by a loud noise. To judge from the sound, my room-mate must have sprung with a single leap from the upper berth to the floor. I heard him fumbling with the latch and bolt of the door, which opened almost immediately, and then I heard his footsteps as he ran at full speed down the passage, leaving the door open behind him. The ship was rolling a little, and I expected to hear him stumble or fall, but he ran as though he were running for his life. The door swung on its hinges with the motion of the vessel, and the sound annoyed me. I got up and shut it, and groped my way back to my berth in the darkness. I went to sleep again; but I have no idea how long I slept.

When I awoke it was still quite dark, but I felt a disagreeable sensation of cold, and it seemed to me that the air was damp. You know the peculiar smell of a cabin which has been wet with sea-water. I covered myself up as well as I could and dozed off again, framing complaints to be made the next day, and selecting the most powerful epithets in the language. I could hear my room-mate turn over in the upper berth. He had probably returned while I was asleep. Once I thought I heard him groan, and I argued that he was sea-sick. That is particularly unpleasant when one is below. Nevertheless I dozed off and slept till early daylight.

The ship was rolling heavily, much more than on the previous evening, and the grey light which came in through the porthole changed in tint with every movement according as the angle of the vessel's side turned the glass seawards or skywards. It was very cold—unaccountably so for the month of June. I turned my head and looked at the porthole, and saw to my surprise that it was wide open and hooked back. I believe I swore audibly. Then I got up and shut it. As I turned back I glanced at the upper berth. The curtains were drawn close together; my companion had probably felt cold as well as I. It struck me that I had slept enough. The state-room was uncomfortable, though, strange to say, I could not smell the dampness which had annoyed me in the night. My room-mate was still asleep—excellent opportunity for avoiding him, so I dressed at once and went on deck. The day was warm and cloudy, with an oily smell on the water. It was seven o'clock as I came out—much later than I had imagined. I came across the doctor, who was taking his first sniff of the morning air. He was a young man from the West of Ireland—a tremendous fellow, with black hair and blue eyes, already inclined to be stout; he had a happy-go-lucky, healthy look about him which was rather attractive.

"Fine morning," I remarked, by way of introduction.

"Well," said he, eyeing me with an air of ready interest, "it's a fine morning and it's not a fine morning. I don't think it's much of a morning."

"Well, no—it is not so very fine," said I.

"It's just what I call fuggly weather," replied the doctor.

"It was very cold last night, I thought," I remarked. "However, when I looked about, I found that the porthole was wide open. I had not noticed it when I went to bed. And the state-room was damp, too."

"Damp!" said he. "Whereabouts are you?"

"One hundred and five—"

To my surprise the doctor started visibly, and stared at me.

"What is the matter?" I asked.

"Oh—nothing," he answered, "only everybody has complained of that state-room for the last three trips."

"I shall complain too," I said. "It has certainly not been properly aired. It is a shame!"

"I don't believe it can be helped," answered the doctor. "I believe there is something—well, it is not my business to frighten passengers."

"You need not be afraid of frightening me," I replied. "I can stand any amount of damp. If I should get a bad cold, I will come to you."

I offered the doctor a cigar, which he took and examined very critically.

"It is not so much the damp," he remarked. "However, I dare say you will get on very well. Have you a room-mate?"

"Yes; a deuce of a fellow, who bolts out in the middle of the night, and leaves the door open."

Again the doctor glanced curiously at me. Then he lit the cigar and looked grave.

"Did he come back?" he asked presently.

"Yes. I was asleep, but I waked up and heard him moving. Then I felt cold and went to sleep again. This morning I found the porthole open."

"Look here," said the doctor quietly, "I don't care much for this ship. I don't care a rap for her reputation. I tell you what I will do. I have a good-sized place up here. I will share it with you, though I don't know you from Adam."

I was very much surprised at the proposition. I could not imagine why he should take such a sudden interest in my welfare. However, his manner, as he spoke of the ship, was peculiar.

"You are very good, doctor," I said. "But, really, I believe even now the cabin could be aired, or cleaned out, or something. Why do you not care for the ship?"

"We are not superstitious in our profession, sir," replied the doctor, "but the sea makes people so. I don't want to prejudice you, and I don't want to frighten you, but if you will take my advice you will move in here. I would as soon see you overboard," he added earnestly, "as know that you or any other man was to sleep in one hundred and five."

"Good gracious! Why?" I asked.

"Just because on the three last trips the people who have slept there actually have gone overboard," he answered gravely.

The intelligence was startling and exceedingly unpleasant, I confess. I looked hard at the doctor to see whether he was making game of me, but he looked perfectly serious. I thanked him warmly for his offer, but told him I intended to be the exception to the rule by which every one who slept in that particular state-room went overboard. He did not say much, but looked as grave as ever, and hinted that, before we got across, I should probably reconsider his proposal. In the course of time we went to breakfast, at which only an inconsiderable number of passengers assembled. I noticed that one or two of the officers who breakfasted with us looked grave. After breakfast I went into my state-room in order to get a book. The curtains of the upper berth were still closely drawn. Not a sound was to be heard. My room-mate was probably still asleep.

As I came out I met the steward whose business it was to look after me. He whispered that the captain wanted to see me, and then scuttled away down the passage as if very anxious to avoid any questions. I went toward the captain's cabin, and found him waiting for me.

"Sir," said he, "I want to ask a favour of you."

I answered that I would do anything to oblige him.

"Your room-mate has disappeared," he said. "He is known to have turned in early last night. Did you notice anything extraordinary in his manner?"

The question, coming as it did in exact confirmation of the fears the doctor had expressed half an hour earlier, staggered me.

"You don't mean to say he has gone overboard?" I asked.

"I fear he has," answered the captain.

"This is the most extraordinary thing—" I began.

"Why?" he asked.

"He is the fourth, then?" I explained. In answer to another question from the captain, I explained, without mentioning the doctor, that I had heard the story concerning one hundred and five. He seemed very much annoyed at hearing that I knew of it. I told him what had occurred in the night.

"What you say," he replied, "coincides almost exactly with what was told me by the room-mates of two of the other three. They bolt out of bed and run down the passage. Two of them were seen to go overboard by the watch; we stopped and lowered boats, but they were not found. Nobody, however, saw or heard the man who was lost last night—if he is really lost. The steward, who is a superstitious fellow, perhaps, and expected something to go wrong, went to look for him this morning, and found his berth empty, but his clothes lying about, just as he had left them. The steward was the only man on board who knew him by sight, and he has been searching everywhere for him. He has disappeared! Now, sir, I want to beg you not to mention the circumstance to any of the passengers; I don't want the ship to get a bad name, and nothing hangs about an ocean-goer like stories of suicides. You shall have your choice of any one of the officers' cabins you like, including my own, for the rest of the passage. Is that a fair bargain?"

"Very," said I; "and I am much obliged to you. But since I am alone, and have the state-room to myself, I would rather not move. If the steward will take out that unfortunate man's things, I would as lief stay where I am. I will not say anything about the matter, and I think I can promise you that I will not follow my room-mate."

The captain tried to dissuade me from my intention, but I preferred having a state-room alone to being the chum of any officer on board. I do not know whether I acted foolishly, but if I had taken his advice I should have had nothing more to tell. There would have remained the disagreeable coincidence of several suicides occurring among men who had slept in the same cabin, but that would have been all.

That was not the end of the matter, however, by any means. I obstinately made up my mind that I would not be disturbed by such tales, and I even went so far as to argue the question with the captain. There was something wrong about the state-room, I said. It was rather damp. The porthole had been left open last night. My room-mate might have been ill when he came on board, and he might have become delirious after he went to bed. He might even now be hiding somewhere on board, and might be found later. The place ought to be aired and the fastening of the port looked to. If the captain would give me leave, I would see that what I thought necessary were done immediately.

"Of course you have a right to stay where you are if you please," he replied, rather petulantly; "but I wish you would turn out and let me lock the place up, and be done with it."

I did not see it in the same light, and left the captain, after promising to be silent concerning the disappearance of my companion. The latter had had no acquaintances on board, and was not missed in the course of the day. Towards evening I met the doctor again, and he asked me whether I had changed my mind. I told him I had not.

"Then you will before long," he said very gravely.

## III

We played whist in the evening, and I went to bed late. I will confess now that I felt a disagreeable sensation when I entered my state-room. I could not help thinking of the tall man I had seen on the previous night, who was now dead, drowned, tossing about in the long swell, two or three hundred miles astern. His face rose very distinctly before me as I undressed, and I even went so far as to draw back the curtains of the upper berth, as though to persuade myself that he was actually gone. I also bolted the door of the state-room. Suddenly I became aware that the porthole was open, and fastened back. This was more than I could stand. I hastily threw on my dressing gown and went in search of Robert, the steward of my passage. I was very angry, I remember, and when I found him I dragged him roughly to the door of one hundred and five, and pushed him towards the open porthole.

"What the deuce do you mean, you scoundrel, by leaving that port open every night? Don't you know it is against the regulations? Don't you know that if the ship heeled and the water began to come in, ten men could not shut it? I will report you to the captain, you blackguard, for endangering the ship!"

I was exceedingly wroth. The man trembled and turned

pale, and then began to shut the round glass plate with the heavy brass fittings.

"Why don't you answer me?" I said roughly.

"If you please, sir," faltered Robert, "there's nobody on board as can keep this 'ere port shut at night. You can try it yourself, sir. I ain't a-going to stop hany longer on board o' this vessel, sir; I ain't, indeed. But if I was you, sir, I'd just clear out and go and sleep with the surgeon, or something, I would. Look 'ere, sir, is that fastened what you may call securely, or not, sir? Try it, sir. See if it will move a hinch."

I tried the port, and found it perfectly tight.

"Well, sir," continued Robert triumphantly, "I wager my reputation as a A1 steward that in 'arf an hour it will be open again; fastened back, too, sir, that's the horful thing—fastened back!"

I examined the great screw and the looped nut that ran on it. "If I find it open in the night, Robert, I will give you a sovereign. It is not possible. You may go."

"Soverin' did you say, sir? Very good, sir. Thank ye, sir. Goodnight, sir. Pleasant reepose, sir, and all manner of hinchantin' dreams, sir."

Robert scuttled away, delighted at being released. Of course, I thought he was trying to account for his negligence by a silly story, intended to frighten me, and I disbelieved him. The consequence was that he got his sovereign, and I spent a very peculiarly unpleasant night.

I went to bed, and five minutes after I had rolled myself up in my blankets, the inexorable Robert extinguished the light that burned steadily behind the ground-glass pane near the door. I lay quite still in the dark trying to go to sleep, but

I soon found that impossible. It had been some satisfaction to be angry with the steward, and the diversion had banished that unpleasant sensation I had at first experienced when I thought of the drowned man who had been my chum; but I was no longer sleepy, and I lay awake for some time, occasionally glancing at the porthole, which I could just see from where I lay, and which, in the darkness, looked like a faintly luminous soup plate suspended in blackness. I believe I must have lain there for an hour, and, as I remember, I was just dozing into sleep when I was roused by a draught of cold air, and by distinctly feeling the spray of the sea blown upon my face. I started to my feet, and not having allowed in the dark for the motion of the ship, I was instantly thrown violently across the state-room upon the couch, which was placed beneath the porthole. I recovered myself immediately, however, and climbed up on my knees. The porthole was again wide open and fastened back! Now these things are facts. I was wide awake when I got up, and I should certainly have been waked by the fall had I still been dozing. Moreover, I bruised my elbows and knees badly, and the bruises were there on the following morning to testify to the fact, if I myself had doubted it. The porthole was wide open and fastened back—a thing so unaccountable that I remember very well feeling astonishment rather than fear when I discovered it. I at once closed the plate again, and screwed down the loop nut with all my strength. It was very dark in the state-room. I reflected that the port had certainly been opened within an hour after Robert had at first shut it in my presence, and I determined to watch it, and see whether it would open again. Those brass fittings are very heavy and by no means easy to move; I could not believe that the clump had been turned by the shaking of the screw. I stood peering out through the thick glass at the alternate white and grey streaks of the sea that foamed beneath the ship's side. I must have remained there a quarter of an hour.

Suddenly, as I stood, I distinctly heard something moving behind me in one of the berths, and a moment afterwards, just as I turned instinctively to look—though I could, of course, see nothing in the darkness—I heard a very faint groan. I sprang across the state-room, and tore the curtains of the upper berth aside, thrusting in my hands to discover if there were any one there. There was some one.

I remember that the sensation as I put my hands forward was as though I were plunging them into the air of a damp cellar, and from behind the curtains came a gust of wind that smelled horribly of stagnant sea-water. I laid hold of something that had the shape of a man's arm, but was smooth, and wet, and icy cold. But suddenly, as I pulled, the creature sprang violently forward against me, a clammy, oozy mass, as it seemed to me, heavy and wet, yet endowed with a sort of supernatural strength. I reeled across the state-room, and in an instant the door opened and the thing rushed out. I had not had time to be frightened, and quickly recovering myself, I sprang through the door and gave chase at the top of my speed, but I was too late. Ten yards before me I could see—I am sure I saw it—a dark shadow moving in the dimly lighted passage, quickly as the shadow of a fast horse thrown before a dogcart by the lamp on a dark night. But in a moment it had disappeared, and I found myself holding on to the polished rail that ran along the bulkhead where the passage turned towards the companion. My hair stood on end, and the cold perspiration rolled down my face. I am not ashamed of it in the least: I was very badly frightened.

Still I doubted my senses, and pulled myself together. It was absurd, I thought. The Welsh rarebit I had eaten had disagreed with me. I had been in a nightmare. I made my way back to my state-room, and entered it with an effort. The whole place smelled of stagnant sea-water, as it had when I had waked on the previous evening. It required my utmost strength to go in, and grope among my things for a box of wax lights. As I lighted a railway reading lantern which I always carry in case I want to read after the lamps are out, I perceived that the porthole was again open, and a sort of creeping horror began to take possession of me which I never felt before, nor wish to feel again. But I got a light and proceeded to examine the upper berth, expecting to find it drenched with sea-water.

But I was disappointed. The bed had been slept in, and the smell of the sea was strong; but the bedding was as dry as a bone. I fancied that Robert had not had the courage to make the bed after the accident of the previous night—it had all been a hideous dream. I drew the curtains back as far as I could and examined the place very carefully. It was perfectly dry. But the porthole was open again. With a sort of dull bewilderment of horror I closed it and screwed it down, and thrusting my heavy stick through the brass loop, wrenched it with all my might, till the thick metal began to bend under the pressure. Then I hooked my reading lantern into the red velvet at the head of the couch, and sat down to recover my senses if I could. I sat there all night, unable to think of rest—hardly able to think at all. But the porthole remained closed, and I did not believe it would now open again without the application of a considerable force.

The morning dawned at last, and I dressed myself slowly,

thinking over all that had happened in the night. It was a beautiful day and I went on deck, glad to get out into the early, pure sunshine, and to smell the breeze from the blue water, so different from the noisome, stagnant odour of my state-room. Instinctively I turned aft, towards the surgeon's cabin. There he stood, with a pipe in his mouth, taking his morning airing precisely as on the preceding day.

"Good-morning," said he quietly, but looking at me with evident curiosity.

"Doctor, you were quite right," said I. "There is something wrong about that place."

"I thought you would change your mind," he answered rather triumphantly. "You have had a bad night, eh? Shall I make you a pick-me-up? I have a capital recipe."

"No, thanks," I cried. "But I would like to tell you what happened."

I then tried to explain as clearly as possible precisely what had occurred, not omitting to state that I had been scared as I had never been scared in my whole life before. I dwelt particularly on the phenomenon of the porthole, which was a fact to which I could testify, even if the rest had been an illusion. I had closed it twice in the night, and the second time I had actually bent the brass in wrenching it with my stick. I believe I insisted a good deal on this point.

"You seem to think I am likely to doubt the story," said the doctor, smiling at the detailed account of the state of the porthole. "I do not doubt it in the least. I renew my invitation to you. Bring your traps here, and take half my cabin."

"Come and take half of mine for one night," I said. "Help me to get at the bottom of this thing."

"You will get to the bottom of something else if you try," answered the doctor.

"What?" I asked.

"The bottom of the sea. I am going to leave this ship. It is not canny."

"Then you will not help me to find out—"

"Not I," said the doctor quickly. "It is my business to keep my wits about me—not to go fiddling about with ghosts and things."

"Do you really believe it is a ghost?" I enquired rather contemptuously. But as I spoke I remembered very well the horrible sensation of the supernatural which had got possession of me during the night. The doctor turned sharply on me.

"Have you any reasonable explanation of these things to offer?" he asked. "No; you have not. Well, you say you will find an explanation. I say that you won't, sir, simply because there is not any."

"But, my dear sir," I retorted, "do you, a man of science, mean to tell me that such things cannot be explained?"

"I do," he answered stoutly. "And, if they could, I would not be concerned in the explanation."

I did not care to spend another night alone in the stateroom, and yet I was obstinately determined to get at the root of the disturbances. I do not believe there are many men who would have slept there alone, after passing two such nights. But I made up my mind to try it, if I could not get any one to share a watch with me. The doctor was evidently not inclined for such an experiment. He said he was a surgeon, and that in case any accident occurred on board he must be always in readiness. He could not afford to have his nerves unsettled. Perhaps he was quite right, but I am inclined to think that his precaution was prompted by his inclination. On enquiry, he informed me that there was no one on board who would be likely to join me in my investigations, and after a little more conversation I left him. A little later I met the captain, and told him my story. I said that, if no one would spend the night with me, I would ask leave to have the light burning all night, and would try it alone.

"Look here," said he, "I will tell you what I will do. I will share your watch myself, and we will see what happens. It is my belief that we can find out between us. There may be some fellow skulking on board, who steals a passage by frightening the passengers. It is just possible that there may be something queer in the carpentering of that berth."

I suggested taking the ship's carpenter below and examining the place; but I was overjoyed at the captain's offer to spend the night with me. He accordingly sent for the workman and ordered him to do anything I required. We went below at once. I had all the bedding cleared out of the upper berth, and we examined the place thoroughly to see if there was a board loose anywhere, or a panel which could be opened or pushed aside. We tried the planks everywhere, tapped the flooring, unscrewed the fittings of the lower berth and took it to pieces—in short, there was not a square inch of the state-room which was not searched and tested. Everything was in perfect order, and we put everything back in its place. As we were finishing our work, Robert came to the door and looked in.

"Well, sir— Find anything, sir?" he asked, with a ghastly grin.

"You were right about the porthole, Robert," I said, and I gave him the promised sovereign. The carpenter did his work silently and skilfully, following my directions. When he had done he spoke.

"I'm a plain man, sir," he said. "But it's my belief you had better just turn out your things, and let me run half a dozen four-inch screws through the door of this cabin. There's no good never came o' this cabin yet, sir, and that's all about it. There's been four lives lost out o' here to my own remembrance, and that in four trips. Better give it up, sir—better give it up!"

"I will try it for one night more," I said.

"Better give it up, sir—better give it up! It's a precious bad job," repeated the workman, putting his tools in his bag and leaving the cabin.

But my spirits had risen considerably at the prospect of having the captain's company, and I made up my mind not to be prevented from going to the end of the strange business. I abstained from Welsh rarebits and grog that evening, and did not even join in the customary game of whist. I wanted to be quite sure of my nerves, and my vanity made me anxious to make a good figure in the captain's eyes.

## IV

The captain was one of those splendidly tough and cheerful specimens of seafaring humanity whose combined courage, hardihood, and calmness in difficulty leads them naturally into high positions of trust. He was not the man to be led away by an idle tale, and the mere fact that he was willing to join me in the investigation was proof that he thought there was something seriously wrong, which could not be accounted for on ordinary theories, nor laughed down as a common superstition. To some extent, too, his reputation was at stake, as well as the reputation of the ship. It is no light thing to lose passengers overboard, and he knew it.

About ten o'clock that evening, as I was smoking a last cigar, he came up to me and drew me aside from the beat of the other passengers who were patrolling the deck in the warm darkness.

"This is a serious matter, Mr. Brisbane," he said. "We must make up our minds either way—to be disappointed or to have a pretty rough time of it. You see I cannot afford to laugh at the affair, and I will ask you to sign your name to a statement of whatever occurs. If nothing happens to-night, we will try it again to-morrow and next day. Are you ready?"

So we went below, and entered the state-room. As we went in I could see Robert the steward, who stood a little further down the passage, watching us, with his usual grin, as though certain that something dreadful was about to happen. The captain closed the door behind us and bolted it.

"Supposing we put your portmanteau before the door," he suggested. "One of us can sit on it. Nothing can get out then. Is the port screwed down?"

I found it as I had left it in the morning. Indeed, without using a lever, as I had done, no one could have opened it. I drew back the curtains of the upper berth so that I could see well into it. By the captain's advice I lighted my reading lantern and placed it so that it shone upon the white sheets above. He insisted upon sitting on the portmanteau, declaring that he wished to be able to swear that he had sat before the door.

Then he requested me to search the state-room thoroughly, an operation very soon accomplished, as it consisted merely in looking beneath the lower berth and under the couch below the porthole. The spaces were quite empty.

"It is impossible for any human being to get in," I said, "or for any human being to open the port."

"Very good," said the captain, calmly. "If we see anything now, it must be either imagination or something supernatural."

I sat down on the edge of the lower berth.

"The first time it happened," said the captain, crossing his legs and leaning back against the door, "was in March. The passenger who slept here, in the upper berth, turned out to have been a lunatic—at all events, he was known to have been a little touched, and he had taken his passage without the knowledge of his friends. He rushed out in the middle of the night, and threw himself overboard, before the officer who had the watch could stop him. We stopped and lowered a boat; it was a quiet night, just before that heavy weather came on; but we could not find him. Of course his suicide was afterwards accounted for on the grounds of his insanity."

"I suppose that often happens?" I remarked rather absently.

"Not often—no," said the captain: "never before in my experience, though I have heard of it happening on board of other ships. Well, as I was saying, that occurred in March. On the very next trip—"What are you looking at?" he asked, stopping suddenly in his narration.

I believe I gave no answer. My eyes were riveted upon the porthole. It seemed to me that the brass loop-nut was beginning to turn very slowly upon the screw—so slowly, however, that I was not sure it moved at all. I watched it intently, fixing its position in my mind, and trying to ascertain whether it changed. Seeing where I was looking, the captain looked too.

"It moves!" he exclaimed, in a tone of conviction. "No, it does not," he added, after a minute.

"If it were the jarring of the screw," said I, "it would have opened during the day; but I found it this evening jammed tight as I left it this morning."

I rose and tried the nut. It was certainly loosened, for by an effort I could move it with my hands.

"The queer thing," said the captain, "is that the second man who was lost is supposed to have got through that very port. We had a terrible time over it. It was in the middle of the night, and the weather was very heavy; there was an alarm that one of the ports was open and the sea running in. I came below and found everything flooded, the water pouring in every time she rolled, and the whole port swinging from the top bolts—not the port-hole in the middle. Well, we managed to shut it, but the water did some damage. Ever since that the place smells of sea-water from time to time. We supposed the passenger had thrown himself out, though the Lord only knows how he did it. The steward kept telling me that he cannot keep anything shut here. Upon my word—I can smell it now, cannot you?" he enquired, sniffing the air suspiciously.

"Yes—distinctly," I said, and I shuddered as that same odour of stagnant sea-water grew stronger in the cabin. "Now, to smell like this, the place must be damp," I continued, "and yet when I examined it with the carpenter this morning everything was perfectly dry. It is most extraordinary—hallo!"

My reading lantern, which had been placed in the upper berth, was suddenly extinguished. There was still a good deal of light from the pane of ground glass near the door, behind which loomed the regulation lamp. The ship rolled heavily, and the curtain of the upper berth swung far out into the state-room and back again. I rose quickly from my seat on the edge of the bed, and the captain at the same moment started to his feet with a loud cry of surprise. I had turned with the intention of taking down the lantern to examine it, when I heard his exclamation, and immediately afterwards his call for help. I sprang towards him. He was wrestling with all his might with the brass loop of the port. It seemed to turn against his hands in spite of all his efforts. I caught up my cane, a heavy oak stick I always used to carry, and thrust it through the ring and bore on it with all my strength. But the strong wood snapped suddenly, and I fell upon the couch. When I rose again the port was wide open, and the captain was standing with his back against the door, pale to the lips.

"There is something in that berth!" he cried in a strange voice, his eyes almost starting from his head. "Hold the door, while I look—it shall not escape us, whatever it is!"

But instead of taking his place, I sprang upon the lower bed, and seized something which lay in the upper berth.

It was something ghostly, horrible beyond words, and it moved in my grip. It was like the body of a man long drowned, and yet it moved, and had the strength of ten men living; but I gripped it with all my might—the slippery, oozy, horrible thing—the dead white eyes seemed to stare at me out of the dusk; the putrid odour of rank sea-water was about it, and its shiny hair hung in foul wet curls over its dead face. I wrestled with the dead thing; it thrust itself upon me and forced me back and nearly broke my arms; it wound its corpse's arms about my neck, the living death, and overpowered me, so that I, at last, cried aloud and fell, and left my hold.

As I fell the thing sprang across me, and seemed to throw itself upon the captain. When I last saw him on his feet his face was white and his lips set. It seemed to me that he struck a violent blow at the dead being, and then he, too, fell forward upon his face, with an inarticulate cry of horror.

The thing paused an instant, seeming to hover over his prostrate body, and I could have screamed again for very fright, but I had no voice left. The thing vanished suddenly, and it seemed to my disturbed senses that it made its exit through the open port, though how that was possible, considering the smallness of the aperture, is more than any one can tell. I lay a long time upon the floor, and the captain lay beside me. At last I partially recovered my senses and moved, and instantly I knew that my arm was broken—the small bone of the left forearm near the wrist.

I got upon my feet somehow, and with my remaining hand I tried to raise the captain. He groaned and moved, and at last came to himself. He was not hurt, but he seemed badly stunned.

Well, do you want to hear any more? There is nothing more. That is the end of my story. The carpenter carried out his scheme of running half a dozen four-inch screws through the door of one hundred and five; and if you ever take passage in the *Kamtschatka*, you may ask for a berth in that state-room. You will be told that it is engaged—yes—it is engaged by that dead thing.

I finished the trip in the surgeon's cabin. He doctored my broken arm, and advised me not to "fiddle about with ghosts and things" any more. The captain was very silent, and never sailed again in the ship, though it is still running. And I will not sail in her either. It was a very disagreeable experience, and I was very badly frightened, which is a thing I do not like. That is all. That is how I saw a ghost—if it was a ghost. It was dead, anyhow.

# A Burning Sword for Her Cradle

*Aliette de Bodard*

**Now**

Bao Ngoc has set her appointment with the witch at dawn—because it would make her leave the house in the dark, at a time when neither her sister nor her brother-in law would be awake.

Things, however, never work the way they're supposed to.

She's made her morning worship at her ancestral altar, leaving oranges and apples for her parents' spirits, mouthing the familiar litany beseeching them for good fortune, gritting her teeth against the agony in her chest. Now she's rummaging in the kitchen for coconut water, opening the cupboard in the darkness. In the background, the familiar buzz of the fridge, a warbling Bao Ngoc keeps—with effort, with pain—from turning into the angry remonstrances of ghosts.

The lights go on. They flood the room, harsh, unforgiving. "You're up early," Bao Chau says. She stands in the doorway, her white shift outlining the darkness of her skin, the round curves of her belly.

Bao Ngoc loses her fragile grip on the ghosts. They bubble up from the kitchen's floor: a woman with a bloodied chest; three young children with bare ribcages and shriveled lumps of lungs within. They stare at her and Chau with dark, hate-filled eyes, their voices a low, piercing hiss that never seems to vary cadence or pitch, a litany of hate that ceaselessly worms its way into Bao Ngoc's brain.

*Behave be grateful blend in.*

In her chest, the remnants of the sword Bao Ngoc once swallowed start burning in earnest, a sharper pain that slowly spreads to her belly and arms. It's her protection against the ghosts, the only thing that will let her dispel them without obeying their orders.

The ghosts are the dead of the Federation: the hundred, the thousand unappeased spirits clinging to flats and streets and parks. They want order, peace. They want Bao Ngoc and Chau and all the immigrants from the Khanh nation to fit in. To belong to the Federation as if the war had never happened; as though the Khanh's own losses and their own dead and their own culture didn't matter.

This isn't a price Bao Ngoc is willing to pay.

*Be quiet don't embarrass us quiet quiet . . .*

Ten thousand diffuse cuts in Bao Ngoc's esophagus and in her stomach, spreading like fire. She's burning up, and any moment now it'll show on her face, and Chau is going to worry about her needlessly.

Too many ghosts and too much fatigue, and Bao Ngoc's sword can't exorcise them all.

No choice. She's going to have to obey them, if only for a moment, if only for once. To follow a tradition of the Federation rather than a Khanh one. Bao Ngoc closes the cupboard. She reaches, instead of the coconut water she'd intended to take from her personal supply, for the coffee Chau so likes in the morning.

"I couldn't sleep." Bao Ngoc's voice shakes. She can't control her own fingers, digging into her palms so hard they feel like knife stabs. The ghosts are staring at her—wavering, fading. "Can you find me the milk?"

Chau raises an eyebrow. "You don't like milk." She sighs and waddles into the kitchen, opening the fridge to peer inside. "I don't know where Raoul's left it. Hang on. . . ."

Chau comes back with the milk, and with butter and jam for herself. Bao Ngoc pours the tea into a mug, slowly and deliberately. The kitchen smells of sliced bread and the acrid smell of coffee, and the ghosts have receded to barely perceptible outlines, their voices subsumed in the faint whirring of the fridge's compressor. Bao Ngoc breathes out, deeply: The sword's pain is almost bearable, a mere blood-tinged sharpness in her throat.

Chau moves through the ghosts as though they aren't there. They turn, briefly, to follow her, and then lose interest. They aren't aware of Chau's daughter, just as Chau's daughter isn't aware of them—blissfully sleeping in the womb, making bubbles in the amniotic sac as she extends small arms and legs, making small bumps as she punches into Chau's belly.

But when the baby is born, that will change.

Chau chose to abandon her own sword, to dispel the ghosts by obeying them rather than by exorcising them: She's fit in and can't see them anymore. She has peace, at a price.

Her child, newborn and fragile and unable to follow any of the ghosts' rules, will have no such protection. The ghosts will crowd around her from birth, will mold her into the perfect Federation citizen, obeying them and fearing them. She will forget her own people's language and culture, and leave her ancestors' altars untended. She will eat bread and butter, and ignore her Khanh aunts, Chau's entire side of the family. The ghosts' hatred and venom will hack away at her heritage, at who she is—until nothing remains.

And the worst is that she'll never be aware that things could be so different.

Bao Ngoc has tried, again and again, to raise the matter with Chau. Chau doesn't want to talk about the ghosts. They don't bother her, any more than they bother Raoul, and they certainly shouldn't be a concern for her daughter.

She's wrong.

Hence Bao Ngoc's appointment with the witch: the one who gave Bao Ngoc and Chau their swords, all those years ago. The one who can help Chau's daughter.

"I have something to do at work," Bao Ngoc says, lying with barely any effort. Chau wouldn't approve of the witch, of superstitions like charms and dark magic. "Early meeting."

Chau looks at Bao Ngoc suspiciously. Chau works as a magistrate and can tear lying witnesses to shreds in her tribunal, but she's pregnant and exhausted, and of course she doesn't want to believe that Bao Ngoc is lying. "You should say no," she says. "They're exploiting you."

*Don't complain don't make a fuss,* the ghosts whisper in Bao Ngoc's mind, but the sword's pain is enough to shred their words into nothingness. "It's just one day," Bao Ngoc says. "It's nothing."

Again, that careful, skeptical stare from Chau. How she's changed from the rail-thin, starved sister Bao Ngoc remembers from the war, from the camps. Chau, perfect, manicured Chau, with her dark, warm Federation woolen clothes, the kind that would have her sweating buckets, back home. The one with the well-paying job, with the husband and the unborn child—a good fortune she's worked herself to exhaustion for, following all the rules, all the ghosts' unspoken injunctions. No rice, no fish sauce, no hint of Khanh language in her home—no pictures of their parents framed on the walls, nor set on the table of an ancestral altar—the older aunties who escaped with Chau and Bao Ngoc seldom feasted at home for fear they'll be an embarrassment. Chau, who no longer needs a sword's protection, who has made herself so much part of the Federation she might as well have lived there for generations. No wonder she can't see the ghosts anymore.

"You know what you're doing," Chau says finally.

Bao Ngoc thought she did, all those years ago in the camps. But it's Chau who now knows exactly what she's doing, and Bao Ngoc who has to struggle and suffer to fit into narrow, ill-defined gaps. "When is the sonogram?" she asks, to fill the silence. She can see the three ghosts, can feel their anger like a distant storm. They're at bay; but they will come back, given half an excuse, given improper behavior.

If Chau knows what she's doing, she doesn't let on. She says, with a tired nod, "At five."

"Are you sure? Raoul—"

Chau shakes her head. "He's been to all the other ones. I want you there, big'sis." She squeezes Bao Ngoc's hand, smiles. It never quite reaches her eyes, but then nothing does, those days.

Bao Ngoc squeezes back. "Of course." She'll see the child: Chau's child, the future. And, if the witch comes through, she'll have what she needs, to offer her niece the best of all possible gifts: safety.

• • •

**Then**

In the Federation's camps, there were no ghosts.

Later, Bao Ngoc would realize it was because no one had ever lived there. Because there was no place in this flat, arid barrenness that the ghosts ever called home. Because putting refugees there wasn't an invasion, but merely the natural order of things.

They heard about the ghosts, nevertheless. Not from the aid workers, but word was going around, in the makeshift temples and exercise rooms, around the narrow fires where they clustered, clutching the odd-tasting food that reminded them they were so far away from home.

The Federation was a land of ghosts—of hungry, angry spirits. Of howling, unappeased dead who hated interlopers and newcomers. Who hated immigrants and refugees, and endlessly tormented them as soon as they set foot on Federation land.

The aunts bought charms and amulets with calligraphied mantras, which they hung around Bao Ngoc and Chau's necks. It'll be enough, they said, again and again, their voices like a prayer. We'll be safe once we're in the Federation. People live there, and they're not scared of ghosts. We'll endure as we always have.

Bao Ngoc was old enough to know when adults were lying to themselves.

One afternoon, after the aunts settled down to play cards and mat chuoc, Bao Ngoc snuck into the tent and stole Ninth Aunt's sword. She and Chau had their own swords, of course, for their self-defense; but they were small and ineffective. Ninth Aunt's sword was the smallest of all the aunts' swords, but it was light and easily wielded, and it was a real weapon.

Sword in hand, Bao Ngoc went to get her younger sister.

"Come on," she said. She'd asked around; she'd tried to tell the aunts; but they'd smiled and patted her head, and told her to worry about her games and her toys.

Bao Ngoc couldn't afford to be a child anymore.

"What's wrong?" Chau asked.

"We need better charms."

Chau didn't say anything until they reached the outskirts of the camp, when the tents became frayed and old, and the only living things on the muddy streets were mangy dogs foraging in refuse heaps. "Big'sis . . ."

Bao Ngoc kept tugging at Chau's sleeve. Her other hand was wrapped around the hilt of the sword, ready to draw at the first hint of trouble. "It's all right. Just a few more steps, I promise."

She thought of the new patients in the infirmary: the ones who hadn't "worked out," the ones the Federation government wanted to send back into the hell that the Khanh nation had become. The way they sat hunched on the sides of the beds, folded tight upon themselves, faces hidden behind pale and skeletal arms, all bones, all translucent skin. The way they jerked from time to time, to no rhythm or noise that Bao Ngoc could hear. They must have had charms and amulets too; and yet that didn't protect them, didn't prevent them from falling to the ghosts.

She and her sister would make a home in the Federation. And if that meant calling on witches and black magic, then so be it. Bao Ngoc had learned her lessons, not from classics or stories, but from dust and smoke and bombed cities.

Sometimes, you needed the dark to defend against the dark.

• • •

**Now**

It's early morning and dark, and the trains are filled with the night shift: immigrant workers from different countries, not only the Khanh nation but dozens of other places. They sit tired and hunched in their seats, fingering necklaces and bracelets—the charms Bao Ngoc has learned to tell apart from ordinary jewelry, strong enchantments paid in blood and dark magic—the only defense against the ghosts.

The trains are full of the dead. Young people holding out the bloodied knives that have killed them, older men clutching their hearts grown enormous in their chests, bodies with missing arms, with missing legs, with heads smashed open like ripe fruit: shambling, almost inhuman monstrosities smelling of charred flesh, with the straight line of the third rail burned into torsos and palms like a criminal's brand.

Bao Ngoc finds herself a quiet corner, and sits with her bag on her knees, not hunched, not tired, merely watchful. Her hand itches, as if she could draw the sword from her chest and use it to slay ghosts. As if this would change anything, do anything more than remove a few dead souls among a sea of them. As the train follows the curves of the track to the witch's home—past metal and glass towers that pierce the heavens like shining spears, large limestone townhouses with wrought-iron balconies—into the poorer areas of the city, where the towers are larger and duller, clothes hanging like flags from dusty, narrow windows—Bao Ngoc rests her head against the window, and tries to sleep.

She dreams of Chau, pushing the sword into her own chest in the witch's tent, stabbing herself to take it in rather than swallowing it, unafraid of blood or pain.

And then the dream shifts and stretches, and Bao Ngoc is back home. She dreams of her family's house in the city of An Ky Lan: of apricot flower garlands in streets filled with the clash of gongs and cymbals, of Mother's hands and the smell of garlic and fish sauce in the kitchen, of running shrieking into a muddy courtyard and smelling the churning earth in the wake of the monsoon's passage. It was a short, doomed time. Adults remember the storm gathering, remember making plans to find shelter and safety, but she was a child. Bao Ngoc remembers long golden afternoons; the soft noise of the sea, the taste of soft-shelled crabs, flooding her mouth with salt and sweetness.

Gone. All gone now, bombed into ruins and shards: the aunties that had been chatting at table just a moment ago buried under rubble, the courtyard erupting into a maelstrom of debris and wounding shards, Chau screaming as Bao Ngoc dragged her, arms stinging and bleeding, into the shelter of the reception room . . .

Gone.

The sword wakes Bao Ngoc up. It's burning within her. A ghost is sitting on her chest: an old woman with skin as dark as ink and bloody scratches on her neck, glaring at Bao Ngoc and whispering words the sword keeps cutting into shreds. *Be good be grateful be happy.* Bao Ngoc extends hands, reflexively. She's been talking in Khanh, mouthing the old prayers, the appeals to gods and ancestors whose temples and graves are now ashes in a burned city.

She stands up, shaking. She's in Ashford, at the heart of the Federation. She's with Chau, with Raoul. There are no apricot garlands; no fruit-laden trees, no dragon dances. She pushes. It's like walking through shattered glass, the sword flaring into unbearable sharpness within her as the old woman's ghost fades into nothingness. As she walks off the train, she brushes past a middle-aged man: one of the living, who glares at her as her elbow digs into his side. She mouths an apology, all she can manage with the exhaustion.

Bao Ngoc doesn't remember making it through the station. Everything hurts. Her legs are shaking—her hands feel like they've been stabbed with pins, again and again—and the ghost's words are still there, running parallel to old prayers she can barely hold on to. Outside, on the street, Bao Ngoc leans on one of the barriers of a verdant park, catching her breath.

It will pass. It always does. There is always a price to pay, always sacrifices to make.

The address the witch gave Bao Ngoc is in one of the high-rise buildings: a city within a city where people walk hunched and quiet, where ghosts congregate thick and angry, a wall of pressure that would send Bao Ngoc to her knees, if she didn't have the sword. She walks through them—a faint pain in her chest, nothing that requires a full exorcism—and moves on.

The apartment's door is open: The place is full of people. It looks like a party. For a fraction of a second, Bao Ngoc thinks she's got the wrong address, but then one of the numerous aunties clustered in the small kitchen spies her. "I'm Second Aunt. You're here for Auntie Oanh? Come on in."

Something is wrong inside. And then Bao Ngoc realizes, as the auntie holds out a plate filled with shrimp cakes, that there are no ghosts—only silence, and yet the kitchen smells of rice, and garlic—and the sword doesn't hurt, doesn't burn anymore.

Something Bao Ngoc didn't know she had in her chest loosens. It feels like being able to breathe after decades of damaged lungs. The aunties speak in low, measured voices: a conversation about the neighborhood and people Bao Ngoc doesn't know. Two of them are watching the contents of a frying pan like hawks, while others sip cups of tea. Bao Ngoc finds herself with a dumpling and some tea, and effortlessly included in one of the small groups as if nothing were wrong.

"Auntie Oanh is running late, I'm afraid. She's got a difficult customer at the moment," Second Aunt says. "Some people wait too long to get their charms."

Bao Ngoc remembers the witch's tent, back in the camps. Small and cramped, and deserted. Even the children gave it a wide berth, and only wild dogs and ravens foraged in the refuse heap. "I—" She struggles to speak, unsure of what she can say. "I didn't expect there would be so many people."

Second Aunt looks at Bao Ngoc, long and measured. "You met Auntie Oanh in the camps, didn't you?"

"Yes." Bao Ngoc remembers drawing Chau behind her. She remembers drawing her sword, facing the witch on trembling legs.

"Things have changed." Second Aunt sounds amused. "Need trumps fear. Superstition becomes necessity."

It would sound like the cryptic pronouncements of monks or priests, but Bao Ngoc knows, all too well, what it means. One of her own aunts became like Chau: married a local girl, took on local customs. All the others turned brittle and thin over the years. She's never asked, but she's sure that in the end, they went to see a witch, that they got charms to help them stand against the ghosts.

At the other end of the cramped living room, a door opens. Second Aunt nods, briskly. "She's ready for you."

• • •

**Then**

Chau cut her hair short and went to school, and came back with more teenage slang and curses than Bao Ngoc had ever thought existed in Common. She turned fifteen: an odd, alien birthday, for in the Khanh nation the only anniversaries they'd used to celebrate were those of the old, or of the dead.

One morning, Chau handed Bao Ngoc the boxed lunch Sixth Aunt had prepared for her. "You want something else?" Bao Ngoc asks.

Chau shook her head. Behind her, in the kitchen, the ghost of a young man with a bloody hole in his head. Chau moved away from him, shaking her head. The sword burned in Bao Ngoc's chest, a faint pain that only lasted until the ghost faded.

"It—" Chau spread her hands. "Look, it doesn't have to hurt this much, does it? None of the other kids see the ghosts. Just the Khanh and the other immigrants." She didn't speak Khanh, but Common.

Bao Ngoc's heart sank. "You can't just get rid of them."

"Really?" Chau raised an eyebrow. "How about doing what they ask?"

*Be happy forget do not stand out.*

Bao Ngoc kept her voice even. "We can also cut off our own arms."

"You're being melodramatic."

"Am I? You've seen the aunts. You've seen the ghost-touched."

"Yes," Chau said. "I've also seen everyone else. People live. They don't just spend their lives hurting in order to give the finger to some ghosts!"

"So you—you just want to give up?"

"I want some peace," Chau snapped. "Is that so hard to

understand? We walk on broken glass. Through broken glass. Every word we speak"—she spat them out—"hurts like hell. Every mouthful of food, every memory, every conversation. Well, I'm done. If that's winning, they've won."

Bao Ngoc stared at Chau: a T-shirt with printed words and unfamiliar characters, a long flowing skirt with pleats and golden sequins. She looked alien. Not Chau, not the sister Bao Ngoc had grown up with, but a teenager of the Federation—and the thought made the sword writhe and twist in Bao Ngoc's chest. "Lil'sis," she said, in Khanh, forcing the words over the pain.

"I'm not little anymore," Chau said, in Common.

"I'm still your elder, and you'll do as I say." She reached out. But Chau danced away, and the ghost of the young man was between them, and the sword hurt so much Bao Ngoc had to bend over, stifling a scream.

"Don't touch me!" Chau snapped.

When Bao Ngoc looked up again, Chau was gone. The door slammed; and in the spreading silence all Bao Ngoc heard was the ghost's voice.

*Monster. Can't hold her back let her fit in monster monster.*

On the following morning Bao Ngoc found glistening, bloodied shards in the trash. She thought they were glass at first, but then she found Chau's white T-shirt bunched up at the back of her room, the chest area streaked with blood, and she knew.

The sword that Chau had once carried in the camps: expelled in dark, tiny, powerless fragments.

**Now**

The witch sits cross-legged on a large bed, watching Bao Ngoc. She's old and lined, not bent over or weary like Bao Ngoc's aunts, not pale or colorless like her Khanh colleagues: old like mountains, like temples, like pine trees, a presence that doesn't ask for respect, but forces it all the same.

The room is dark, the only light coming from the plants on the lone bedside table. Four white flowers Bao Ngoc vividly remembers, their petals clenched shut, smelling sweet and sickly like the onset of rot.

No, not dark. There is light, and it's coming from within her. She looks down, and sees the faint outline of the sword's blade. She feels it pressing outward, as if it were going to escape her. And, from inside her bag, an answering light.

In silence, she reaches inside the bag, and withdraws the plastic pouch she's kept in her desk drawer through two house moves. Within, the fragments of Chau's sword shine in the dark. By its side is another pouch: That one contains all Bao Ngoc's savings, all the money she's painstakingly set aside from years of working extra shifts.

The witch smiles, lifting the first pouch up to the light. "Broken and pushed out of a chest—bit by bit, between the ribs. It must have hurt."

Bao Ngoc thinks of Chau's bloodied T-shirt. "It always hurts, doesn't it?"

The witch smiles. "There are many ways to expel a charm, but they all hurt." She reaches out, rests her hand, for a fraction of a second only, on Bao Ngoc's chest. "And many ways to take one into one's body. You swallowed yours, didn't you?"

Bao Ngoc nods. "My younger sister didn't."

The witch lays the pouch on the bed, stares at her for a while. "No, she stabbed herself. I remember. The two sisters.

Jade. Pearl. The daughters of Pham Thi Kim Lan and Nguyen Van Hoang."

In Bao Ngoc's mind, the familiar reflex, the litany of her ancestors: Mother, Father, her grandparents and their own parents, praying for good fortune and happiness. She's bracing herself for the sword to hurt, for pain to clench her stomach and womb and lungs. But there's nothing, a feeling that's both disquieting and comforting.

"I knew your mother, once," the witch says. "A long time ago in a different land. Before—before she died." She looks . . . weary, and sad. Bao Ngoc finds it hard to reconcile with the dark, imposing figure of her memories.

"You never told us."

"Would you have listened? You were so afraid."

Bao Ngoc swallows. She can't remember what it felt like, to draw the sword—to be so angry, so afraid that she'd have done anything to protect Chau and herself—not that dull, blunt fear she's been living with for so long, but something pure and clean and incandescent.

"There are many kinds of courage," the witch says. And when Bao Ngoc looks up, startled, the witch laughs. "You're not so hard to read." It's not the laughter Bao Ngoc remembers, not the malicious expression of someone who delights in others' suffering, but merely an old woman's forbearing amusement, like Ninth Aunt when Bao Ngoc burned the pan-fried dumplings because she was too busy daydreaming about the girls in her class.

"You're not with your sister," the witch says.

"Chau—" Bao Ngoc pauses, tries to find words. The sword

doesn't burn within her; but it doesn't mean there's no pain. "She says she has no need for it."

"Ah. But she's still Chau," the witch says. She shakes her head. "Some people change their names, too. Makes it easier." She sounds . . . exhausted. Sad. "Impossible choices. What do you want, child?"

"You can banish ghosts," Bao Ngoc says, finally. "This flat—"

Again, that amused laughter. "You should ask about the cost first. It takes more than a sword and magic to do this. Much more." A cold wind rises, wraps itself around Bao Ngoc—ruffles the petals of the flowers in the pots, opening them up—and for a bare moment the earth brims with blood, and the petals are sharp fingerbones. "I told you, years ago. This is the land of the dead, and the dead don't relinquish what's theirs easily."

"A life—" Bao Ngoc is about to offer hers, but her lips clamp down on the words—because, even for Chau, even for the child, she wouldn't.

"Much more than a life," the witch says. She strokes one of the flowers, as if it were a cat. The faint, sickly smell becomes that of rot, of charnel houses. "Souls, cut off from the wheel and the brew of oblivion, bound to floors and walls and bloodied earth—doomed never to be reborn . . ." Her voice is a faint chant, and now she no longer looks like Bao Ngoc's aunts, or like a friendly old woman, but like something that prowls the edges of the world, preying on the weak.

Bao Ngoc would be frightened, but there's not even fear left in her. She says, stubbornly, "Chau is pregnant. Her daughter—"

"Half-breed," the witch whispers: the insult Bao Ngoc has heard hurled on playgrounds and in schools.

"Chau thinks she'll be fine. She—" Bao Ngoc tries to speak through the knot in her throat. It feels as though the hilt of the sword has broken in half, and jammed itself in her vocal chords. "She doesn't *see.*"

"A child of two worlds," the witch says.

"Stop it," Bao Ngoc says. "You're making her sound special."

"No more and no less than hundreds like her, all over the city. The ghosts can rage, but they can't stop life from going on. Do you know why they hate you?"

"Because we're alive."

"Ghosts are static," the witch says. "Their deaths root them. They crave the familiar. The unchanging. They're angry at anything that reminds them that they're not alive. That the world moves on, while they are trapped. People—our people, and dozens of others—arrive and settle onto the land, and the culture of the Federation changes. It reminds the ghosts that time passes, and leaves them all behind."

Bao Ngoc would have felt sorry for them, years ago; but there's no space in her for anything but cold hatred. "You're saying it will be worse for the child." Her niece.

"You know this already." The witch picks up the sword's shards, purses her lips for a while. Her teeth gleam in the darkness, as if shadowed with blood. "You wouldn't be here if you didn't."

"Can you—"

The witch smiles, again. "Exorcise ghosts? No. But I can give her the gift I once gave her mother." She sings words in a low, guttural voice, in a language that Bao Ngoc can't make out but that still is comfortingly familiar. And, as she does so, the fragments of the sword move and melt into one another—like paint, like ink, dark and viscous and slowly hardening, until it's whole again, a large piece of blade with a gleaming edge, and the same pale gleam as the flowers, as the bones.

**Then**

At Chau's wedding, Bao Ngoc got drunk.

She didn't mean to—and Raoul was kind, and doting on Chau, always there to offer her food or drink—and so obviously radiant and happy, his pale, freckled face awash with inner light. Bao Ngoc didn't begrudge them their happiness, or the way they posed for pictures, oblivious, besides the blue-skinned ghosts of drowned children by the lake.

"She's lucky," Ninth Aunt said. She sat at the table with Bao Ngoc, frail and wan and hunched over, clutching the charm around her neck. She was old now. All the aunts were: spent and outmatched, their lives cut short by war and ghosts; an uncomfortable, fearful thought.

"I'm happy for her," Bao Ngoc said. She held out the plate of toasts to Ninth Aunt before helping herself. Around them, ghosts hovered: a sea of vague faces with hollow eye sockets, with crooked and broken limbs, with distended bellies and bloodied organs hanging out of killing wounds; voices on the edge of hearing. Neither the aunts nor Bao Ngoc were doing anything wrong—Federation food, Federation hospitality—but the ghosts watched them, all the same. The sword burned like spent embers, a low-key, almost invisible pain.

Ninth Aunt snorted. "Are you?" And, when Bao Ngoc didn't answer, "That spat you had as teenagers—"

"It's sorted out," Bao Ngoc said. In a manner of speaking. She couldn't put the sword back into Chau, or change the white wedding dress into the red tunic embroidered with golden threads. Couldn't stop the twinge of envy when she saw Chau move with the ease of a dancer, her smile bright and carefree, hiding no sharp edges of pain. But then she remembered that Chau couldn't speak Khanh, couldn't worship at an ancestral altar or pagoda, couldn't wear Mother's rounded necklace or use the turtle-scale combs, or even eat rice and fish sauce as staples.

"She says you're moving into their house," Ninth Aunt said.

Bao Ngoc nodded. She didn't want to talk about it, but of course Ninth Aunt, who'd always tackled everything head-on as she'd tackled soldiers on the battlefield, wouldn't be so easily deterred. "They won't keep the old customs," Ninth Aunt said.

"I'm not Chau," Bao Ngoc snapped. "I'll have my own life." The ghosts surged, hands coming into clearer focus—nails encrusted with dirt and blood, curving as pointed as claws—*don't make a fuss be grateful be ours*—the sword burned and burned, sending them back. The world crumpled and shrank to pain. Bao Ngoc stopped speaking, caught a slow, shuddering breath.

Ninth Aunt gave her a piercing look. She raised her jade-colored cigarette holder, winced. Her charm must have started burning. "Still keeping an eye on her, after all these years?"

Bao Ngoc didn't know why she'd agreed to move in with Chau and Raoul. To save money, to be with Chau, to watch over her, all those things, none of these things. "Out of all of us, surely she's the one who needs the least watching over?" Chau was throwing her bouquet now, laughing as the single girls behind her raced to catch it. The ghosts were watching her with burning eyes: girls in gray, cobwebbed wedding dresses; children in elegant clothes so old they look over-formal, their lace jabots spattered with blood drops; old women with pale, bloodless faces, gloved hands holding out shriveled hearts, plucked from their skeletal ribs.

"Is she?" Ninth Aunt drew a long, measured breath from her cigarette, blew out smoke in lazy ribbons. "You tell me, child."

**Now**

When Bao Ngoc gets home, with the sword precariously balanced in a canvas bag, Chau is waiting for her in the living room, her face dark. She's sitting on one of the upholstered armchairs, her back digging into the oval-shaped cartouche, her hands curved over the ends of the short armrests. Behind her, the dim, barely distinguishable shapes of ghosts: a young, fair-haired man with the imprint of the noose on his crooked neck, and a woman with blood pouring out of slit wrists—her hands at a disjointed angle from her arms, as if they'd been pulled free from her body. They're translucent, their voices barely audible.

"I'm late," Bao Ngoc says, but she already knows that's not what Chau is going to say.

"If you're going to lie," Chau says, "do take the time to make it credible." Her voice is tight, cold. "You never showed up at your workplace."

"Because you checked?" It's stupid and ugly, and yet Bao Ngoc can't help it.

Chau's mask cracks a fraction, showing the dark rings of exhaustion, her whole body sagging for just a moment. "No, I didn't. They were the ones who called. They were concerned for you."

She'd notified work. Had she? She feels as exhausted as Chau, drained from an argument they haven't yet had. The sword is a dull, diffuse pain in every cell of her body. It's been burning ever since she got out of the witch's apartment, ghosts flickering in and out of existence, hissing at her like tigers on the prowl. She's brittle and fragile. If she lets go, if she forgets to stand straight or breathe, the pain will spread like wildfire, consume her utterly until she has no choice but to fall, screaming, to her knees in the middle of Chau's pristine living room. "I'm fine," Bao Ngoc says.

A long, measuring gaze from Chau. "You're not. Big'sis, what the hell are you playing at?"

Well, there will never be a better time. Or a worse time, she's not sure. Wordlessly, she hands out the canvas bag to Chau. "This is for you. For the baby."

As soon as it leaves her hands, the ghosts move—arms extended, fingers curving like claws, voices climbing from unintelligible hiss to high-pitched screams that pierce ears. *Ungrateful wretch you have no right be silent be good behave* . . . Bao Ngoc raises her hands, as if that would make a difference. But the sword is there first, burning like wildfire within her. She takes one, two trembling steps, grabbing on to the back of a chair. The ridges of the frame dig into her hand, a reminder of everything that isn't fire or pain.

Chau grimaces. She pushes the canvas bag onto the table, nudges it open with one hand. The sword tumbles out: a short, curved blade with a rounded wooden handle. No engravings, no ornaments, just a faint, barely visible light trembling on the blade.

*Be good behave be grateful how dare you.*

Chau's face is set. "For the baby?" Bao Ngoc thought she was angry before, but she wasn't—not that uncontrolled fury that seems to grip her like a storm. She's shaking: She stops herself with a visible effort. She rises, gripping both armrests until her knuckles and hands go pale. "You—"

"I had to," Bao Ngoc says. She wants to lift her hands to placate Chau, but the sword is burning so bright, so painfully within her that all she can do is move them to the height of her chest. "You can't mean to raise her unaware."

"Unaware of what?"

"Of where we came from." The pain has let up, or perhaps it's simply that she's used to it now. The ghosts are barely visible again, but their faces are frozen in the same fury as Chau's. "Of Mother and all we gave up to come here. She has that right."

"That right? Look at you, big'sis. Just look at you. That's your gift to her? Pain every day of her life?"

"If pain is the price to pay." How dare she—how dare she reproach Bao Ngoc for her own failings? "You don't speak Khanh anymore. You—you left our own ancestors' altars untended. You dropped it all in return for silence in your ears, and an easy life. You've *forgotten*," she says, and there's more anguish in that scream than she'd thought possible—something raw and primal and so much pain tearing out of her, a sword with its own edge. "I want her to have more than this. I—" She stops, then, starts again. "If she has to forget, then let her make that choice when she's older."

"As I did?" Chau's voice is quieter now. She reaches out, runs a hand on the edge of the sword. Her movements are still slow and graceful, but her face is locked in a grimace of pain. "An easy life. You don't understand, do you?"

Bao Ngoc, exhausted, clings on to the chair's back. It's the only thing keeping her upright.

*Behave behave be quiet.*

Chau smiles, and there's no joy in it. "I still see the ghosts. I still hear them. All the time."

"I— Surely—" Bao Ngoc stares at her. "You do everything they ask!"

"You can *never* do everything they ask," Chau says. She grips the sword, her face alight with concentration. What is she seeing now? Ghosts? Silence, in return for the pain Bao Ngoc has borne all her life? "You merely make them a little quieter, to have some space in which you can breathe. To bear it all. It's a rigged game. It always was. But I know how much I can endure. It will be much easier for my daughter."

"Pain," Bao Ngoc says, flatly.

"It's not painful." Chau's smile is jarring and wrong. "Else what would be the point? A little draining, that's all."

A little draining. Chau sees them. She hears them. Bao Ngoc, shaking, stares at the ghosts—the translucent, silent shapes now out of her hearing—imagines what it would be like, to wake up, straddled by a ghost strangling her because of a stray word, a stray remembrance they don't approve of—to go through life hearing a constant stream of screams and insults and belittling orders, no matter what she does. Imagines her niece, growing up fenced by implacable, relentless hatred.

A little draining. A little lie.

"I'm sorry," she says.

"Don't be." Chau doesn't look up. "We're going to be late for the sonogram. Just . . . just take that out with the trash, please."

**Then**

The sword tasted like garlic and fish sauce when it slid down Bao Ngoc's throat.

It was the smell of evenings, when her mother would fry anchovies and shrimp from the river—of Grandmother's hands when she came out to burn incense sticks on the ancestral altar—of the monks chanting sutras at the pagoda, praying to Quan Am to intercede for the salvation of mankind—of days long gone by in a city now turned to dust.

As it went down, it felt less and less material—fading away, absorbed into her own body, metal fused to flesh and muscle, leaving just a faint aftertaste of blood in her mouth.

**Now**

Bao Ngoc stands outside her sister's room, breathing slow and easy.

She holds the smaller, blunter sword in her hands. It burns, but not as much as the one within her. In the corridor, barely visible, the ghosts of a mother and her daughter, blotched with the sores of plague. They have no eyes. Their mouths are thin and dark, slits in pus-filled faces. The swords rip their words to unintelligible shreds, but Bao Ngoc doesn't need to hear them to guess what they're saying.

*How dare you how dare you.*

Within, Chau sleeps—the mound of her belly resting against the edge of the bed, Raoul hugging her back, curled around her as though he were her shield. Even in sleep she looks exhausted, darkness under her eyes like mottled bruises.

She's said it was a rigged game, that she knows how much she can endure. That it will be easier for her daughter.

She's wrong.

Bao Ngoc thought it was a choice between remembrance

and peace, between the sword's pain and forcibly fitting in. But it's not, is it?

A rigged game.

Whatever the baby does, whatever choices she makes, the ghosts will never be happy. Because she's alive. Because she's a reminder of how things are changing—in such a small way—in the heart of the Federation. She'll grow up making herself smaller to placate ghosts whom she can't please: day after day of hearing them scream in her ears until nothing is left but hollowed-out alienness.

If the game is rigged, if none of those with Khanh blood can hope for silence and peace, then they must fight.

Bao Ngoc hefts the sword, feeling its weight in her hands like a burning brand—thinking of it sinking into Chau's belly, dissolving as it goes—into amniotic liquid and the squat, curled shape of the baby. She's seen the sonograms. It should be easy enough to slide it into the baby's back, all the way along the length of the spine.

It's a small sword and it won't hurt, going in.

# Precipice

## *Dale Bailey*

Stockton had his first intimation of the fear to come—though he did not then recognize it as such—soon after he checked in at OceanView Plantation and rode the elevator up to the fifteenth floor of the South Tower. The building was hollow. You accessed the suites by long galleries, open to the sky behind a chest-high parapet. Outside the room, Stockton paused to look down. Palm trees grew below. He felt momentarily vertiginous. Some inchoate impulse moved him. He swallowed and stepped back, nearly colliding with the bellhop who was pushing the luggage cart along behind him.

"Sorry," he muttered, and the bellhop said, "My fault, sir," and Judy, who was bringing up the rear, said, "Are you okay, Frank?"

Her voice was tremulous with an anxiety that reflected and exacerbated his own.

"Fine," Stockton said, annoyed. "I'm fine. Why?"

"You look pale," she said.

"I look fine," Stockton said, as if by force of will he could deny the heart attack and all its attendant anxieties. He'd grown thick over the last decade—not fat, but stout, barrel-chested, with the heavy shoulders and arms of a man who'd done years of physical labor. He'd kept in reasonable shape as he aged. But time caught up with you. Six months ago, he'd stopped in to check the progress at one of his building sites. He'd just stepped out of his pickup when the dizziness struck. *You okay, boss?* Ed, the foreman, had asked. *You look kind of green.*

The next thing Stockton knew he was staring up into the face of a nurse. He had a blurred impression of hazel eyes and high cheekbones. He was just coming out from the anesthesia. He only half remembered. *What happened?* he'd whispered through parched lips. *You should be dead,* she'd told him, and then the world had gone dark again.

Stockton shook his head. He waved his keycard in front of the lock. Inside, he directed the disposal of the luggage. He overtipped and ushered the bellhop out. The suite was roomier than he'd expected: big windows behind the sofa and a balcony that offered a stunning panorama of the resort. Pools glimmered like jeweled teardrops amid scattered stands of palm trees. The sea ran out to a flat line on the horizon. He turned away, wishing he'd booked something on a lower floor.

Heights had never bothered him. He didn't understand.

Judy had wandered into the bedroom. "You should see this whirlpool," she called.

Stockton dropped the keycard on the kitchen counter, stole another glance at the windows, and went to see the bathroom. But the view stuck with him. When they had unpacked, they went out for groceries. Stockton hugged the wall of the gallery coming and going, and later, when Judy invited him to join her on the balcony, he busied himself in the kitchen. But he could not put her off that easily. She asked him to bring her a glass of wine. When he handed it through the door, she pulled him outside.

"It's beautiful, isn't it?" she said, leaning on the railing. "Come over here and look."

Stockton demurred. Dinner was on the stove. He was doing the stir fry she liked. They were going to be here two weeks. They'd have plenty of time to enjoy the view.

The dizzy spell weighed on him. He could not help thinking of the heart attack.

After dinner, Judy wanted to go for a walk on the beach.

Stockton pled a headache. He went to bed early, but his sleep was restless, and fleeting. He opened his eyes deep in the night. He lay still for a long time, listening to Judy breathe. He got out of bed. He found himself at the sliding glass door in the living room. It was like he'd been summoned there. He stared out into the fathomless abyss of sea and sky. Unbidden, an image came to him. He saw himself pushing the door open and stepping onto the balcony. Wind whipped his hair. He could hear the surf on the beach. There was something alluring in the night air.

"Frank," Judy said behind him.

He shuddered. He was holding the railing with both hands.

"What are you doing?" she asked.

"I don't know," he said, bewildered, and then he gasped and opened his eyes.

He was in bed, Judy curled up against him. He wondered in a dull, half-conscious way if he was still asleep, if he hadn't woken from one dream into another. Then he really was awake. He reached for his phone on the nightstand and thumbed it to life. Almost eight o'clock. Pushing back the covers, he stood. The outer room of the suite was dim, the curtains black rectangles framed in light. He was making coffee when Judy came in and threw them open to the morning. The world fell away beneath them in a dazzling burst of radiance. Stockton stepped back, wincing.

"Are you okay?" Judy asked.

"Just tired," he said.

They spent the day lounging on a deck overlooking the pools. Judy was a glutton for the sun. Stockton endured it. He was ill at ease. Towers surrounded them on three sides, like a horseshoe open to the sea. Even when he forced himself to concentrate on his book, he felt their looming presence. He scanned their building, trying to locate the balcony of their suite. What if you fell? Surely someone had. He wondered what they'd thought about on the way down. Nothing, he supposed. Not for long anyway.

"Do you want a drink?" Judy asked him.

"Why not?" he said, heaving himself up.

There was a line at the tiki bar. While he waited, Stockton watched a young woman in a pink bikini lounging by the pool. The bathing suit was bright against her bronze skin. She stretched languorously and rolled onto her stomach. Their eyes met, or seemed to meet. Stockton was wearing sunglasses, and she wouldn't have noticed him anyway. The woman could not have been more than twenty-five. He was fifty-three—middle-aged, Judy would have said, which he presumed a life span of 106. He might as well have been wallpaper. Still, he looked away, embarrassed.

"What can I get you, boss?" the bartender asked.

Stockton ordered a gin and tonic for himself, and a concoction involving five different flavors of rum for Judy. A Caribbean Cooler. He carried the cocktails back to their chairs.

Judy sampled her drink. "Wow. How much was this thing?"

"Fourteen dollars."

"We'll go broke."

"We can afford it."

They could. Stockton had worked in construction his entire life, framing houses as a teenager and later subbing out his own crew. He'd been twenty-five by the time he'd saved enough to take on a project of his own, building a spec house in an upscale development. He'd put everything on the line to cobble together the construction loan, a not inconsiderable risk for a young man two years married, with a baby on the way.

He sold the house and reinvested the profits. He had a steady hand in a crisis. He didn't mind taking chances. One thing had led to another. He had his own firm by the time he was thirty. Long after other men his age would have retired to the comforts of an air-conditioned office, Stockton still ran most of his business out of a battered Ford F-150. He wasn't averse to picking up a hammer himself. He took pride in the fact that he had the callused hands of the kid who'd framed houses to keep himself in beer money. He was rich. Two weeks of drinking fourteen-dollar cocktails in an oceanfront resort posed no financial challenge; he could have afforded six.

Stockton sipped his own drink. The bartender had been generous with the tonic. He didn't mind. Moderation in all things the doctor had said. This had not proved as difficult as Stockton had thought it would be. His appetites had waned since the heart attack. Food, drink, sex—he just wasn't as interested. Laurie, his daughter, attributed this to anxiety. She attributed everything to anxiety. The modern condition. Who wasn't anxious? Laurie was a therapist. Stockton didn't have much use for therapy, but he supposed she was right. So he was doing everything the doctor had told him to do. Even exercising. He was walking three miles a day now, increasing his pace and distance every week. He'd done his time on the treadmill that morning in the resort's fitness center.

"Don't push yourself," Judy was always telling him.

But it was his nature to push himself. He hated the anxiety. What was the point in living if you weren't living? He resolved to moderate his moderation. A steak now and then wouldn't hurt. Or another gin and tonic, for that matter. He went to the tiki bar and fetched another round of drinks.

Judy put her hand on his thigh. "I swear this is all rum," she said. "You'll get me drunk."

Stockton forced a smile. "If I'm lucky."

They had another drink before dinner. They ate in the resort restaurant. Judy got the chicken Caesar salad. Stockton ordered the filet. They both had wine. After that, he felt looser, more like his old self. He held Judy's hand on the way back to the suite. Next week they would celebrate their thirtieth anniversary.

The elevator doors opened on the fifteenth floor.

Stockton was suddenly short of breath. His immediate thought was that he was having another heart attack. But that wasn't it. He was afraid. The alcohol seemed to have eroded some internal dike. That obscure impulse was clearer now. He felt himself drawn to the parapet. He clung to the wall of the gallery instead.

Inside the suite, Judy pulled the shades, blocking out the sky and the lights glowing in the neighboring towers. He felt better then. Judy lifted her face to kiss him. She tasted of wine.

He could feel the length of her body against his. He let himself be drawn into the bedroom.

It was no good, though. A disaster.

"Too much booze," he said.

Judy smiled. She pillowed her head on his shoulder. "We have tomorrow night," she said. "It doesn't matter, anyway. As long as we're together."

"Has anybody ever jumped from one of those balconies?" he asked the bartender at the tiki bar.

The bartender opened a fresh bottle of tonic water and poured tonic on top of Stockton's gin. He wore shorts and a T-shirt that said *Gym, Beach, Repeat.* He was a big guy, but he had the kind of muscles you got in the weight room. He probably wouldn't last a day pouring footers in the hot sun. It was two o'clock. Judy had driven over to the outlet mall after lunch. The heat was oppressive.

Stockton slid onto a stool.

The bartender dropped a wedge of lime into the drink, a red swizzle stick.

The air smelled of chlorine and salt. A blue-uniformed maintenance man stood nearby, spraying down the decking where someone had spilled a drink.

"What kind of question is that?" the bartender asked.

"Just a question."

The bartender shrugged. "Not in my time," he said. "I've been here for five years. I suppose I would have heard about it."

"I suppose," Stockton said. "Sometimes you wonder about things like that. Has anyone ever died in your room, that kind of thing."

"I don't know of anybody dying, either. Like I said, I would have heard."

"But you wouldn't say even if you had heard, would you?"

The bartender grinned. "Not if I wanted to keep my job, boss."

Which meant what exactly?

Stockton turned away, nodding at the maintenance man as he passed. He sat at a table with an umbrella, nursing his drink. The girl in the pink bikini was sunbathing by the pool below the North Tower. Stockton watched her from behind his sunglasses. She was easy to pick out. The clientele of the resort tended to run older. Most people her age gravitated to the hotels along the boardwalk. Or they were still getting their feet under them and couldn't afford OceanView. She reached into her bag for sunscreen and applied it with lazy efficiency. Stockton tried to generate some prurient interest in her. Maybe he would think of her when he made love to Judy that night. Maybe that would help.

He finished his drink, and thought about having another one.

He went up to the room instead. He had a bad moment on the gallery. As he stood fumbling in his wallet for his keycard, he felt himself drawn once again to the parapet. The impulse was irresistible. He gazed down at the crowns of the palm trees in the garden below. He saw himself falling. He felt the wind rushing up to meet him. Vertiginous relief seized him, a wild exhilaration. He lurched to the door and let it slam behind him. Inside he drew the curtains and stood panting in the gloom.

He called Laurie and got routed to voicemail, hung up, called again.

This time she answered. "I only have a minute," she said. "Is something wrong?"

Stockton sighed. "Yes," he said. It was the wrong answer, he realized. She would think he'd had another heart attack. He said, "It's nothing, really. Nothing you need to worry about, anyway."

"You're not making any sense," she said.

"I shouldn't have—"

"Dad. Just tell me what it is."

He took a deep breath. He felt unmanned, like their roles had somehow been reversed, parent and child. "It's nothing," he said. "Really. It's just a little thing. I wanted to run it by you."

"Okay."

Another deep breath. "I'm feeling these impulses."

She was silent for a moment. "What kind of impulses?"

"Have you talked to your mother?"

"Dad—"

"Have you?"

"Yes."

"Did she tell you about the room?"

"She told me the view was incredible," Laurie said.

"Sure," Stockton said. "Fifteen stories. But here's the thing. Every time I get close to the balcony, I have this crazy impulse to jump."

To his surprise, Laurie laughed. "That's all?"

"That's a hell of thing to say."

"It's normal, Dad. Everybody thinks about things like that. You stand in a high place, you think about jumping. You've just gotten fixated on it."

"I'm going to ask for another room," he said.

"Don't do that."

"Why not?"

"Running from it gives it power. It's like fear of flying," she said. "I have a client. I really do have to go. Don't worry about this, okay?"

"Okay," he said. "But listen, Laurie, don't tell your mother, okay?"

"Just between us," she said, ending the call.

Stockton put his phone away, thinking about Laurie's words. He forced himself to the windows and drew back the curtains. The sea ran on forever, glittering in the afternoon light. He touched the handle of the door to the balcony and tugged it open. A DJ had set up shop at the pool below the North Tower. He could hear the throb of the bass. He saw the young woman down there, or thought he did: bronze and pink, infinitely remote. She stood to pack up her stuff as he watched. Shouldering her bag, she looked up toward the South Tower, as though she'd caught him staring. He stood at the edge of the balcony, his hands clenched white-knuckled on the railing, until the girl disappeared in the shadows of the palms below him. He pushed himself away. Inside the suite, he fumbled for the phone on the end table, punched zero, and listened to it ring.

"Front desk. This is Tiffany. How can I help you?"

Stockton said, "I need another room."

"Is there something wrong with your room, sir?" Distant keys tapping. "Mr. Stockton?"

"Yes," he said. He said, "I'm—"

He bit back the word. *Afraid. I'm afraid.*

"Mr. Stockton?"

"It's nothing," he said.

"If there's a problem, I could send maintenance—"

"It's nothing," he said. "It's okay. Really."

Judy didn't get back until after five.

She called him from the car to ask him to meet her in the lot below the building. "I lost track of time," she said as they fetched her shopping bags upstairs. "Have you eaten?"

He had not.

After Judy showed him her purchases, they went down to the restaurant. By the time they started back to the room, Stockton was feeling the wine. The elevator door slid back and the young woman from the pool stepped out. Up close, she was even more striking. She had a thick mass of auburn hair and high cheekbones, peppered with freckles. Her hazel eyes were cool and appraising. She wore a sleeveless white dress that fell to her thighs. Stockton let his gaze follow her as she slipped by.

There was something—

"Your tongue's hanging out," Judy whispered, not unkindly, as the doors closed.

"Too young for me," he said, kissing her behind the ear. "I like the vintage model."

She laughed and squeezed his hand.

He watched the floors light up as they went past: eleven, twelve, fourteen—

"Huh," he said as the elevator rocked to a stop on fifteen. The doors rolled back. "There's no thirteenth floor."

"Nobody wants to stay on thirteen."

"The people on fourteen are screwed, I guess."

"I hope they're not the only ones," Judy said, drawing him out onto the gallery.

The air was clammy with humidity.

Stockton glanced into the void beyond the parapet. "Do you ever think about—"

"Do you have the keycard, Frank?"

Stockton put his back to the parapet. He dug the card out of his wallet and they went inside and closed the door and that dizzying abyss was behind them.

"Would you pour me a glass of wine?" Judy asked. She was pulling the drapes closed, shutting out the night—the lights of the towers and the pools below them and the black, heaving pelt of the sea.

Stockton took two glasses down from the cabinet. He retrieved a half-empty bottle of chardonnay from the refrigerator, worked the cork lose, and poured. He was putting the bottle away when Judy came around the counter. He leaned against the stove.

"Toast?" she said.

"What are we toasting?"

"Thirty years next week," she said.

They clinked glasses, and drank. The wine was cool and bright, silky on his tongue. Stockton felt something ease inside him. He sighed. "Thirty years," he said, and suddenly Judy was serious. "You scared the hell out of me, Frank," she said.

"I scared you? When?"

"When you were sick," she said.

Stockton didn't want to talk about it. He hadn't been sick. When you were sick they didn't crack your chest open and rewire your heart. They gave you chicken soup and Tylenol and told you to get some rest. He should be dead. If Ed had not been so quick to make the call, if traffic had slowed the ambulance even a minute or two longer, he *would* be dead. *You're a lucky man,* the doctor had told him. *You beat the odds.*

"Let's not talk about it."

"We don't have to talk about it. It scared me, that's all. I couldn't stand to lose you."

"Me neither," he said, but the joke fell flat.

They were silent for a moment.

"Come on," Judy said.

Stockton switched off the light and followed her into the living area on the other side of the counter. They sat on the sofa in the dark and drank wine. He tried not to think about the windows at his back, but he couldn't help running the numbers in his head. He'd been in construction too long. It was natural. Say eleven feet per floor and multiply that by fourteen floors, because the builders had omitted lucky thirteen, and what you came up with was—what?—a hundred and fifty feet, give or take. 154. Half a football field. A long way down. He closed his eyes. Laurie had given him some tips to fight the anxiety. Tools, she called them. Use your tools. He deepened his breathing. In through the mouth, out through the nostrils, counting breaths. He felt marginally better.

"You okay?" Judy asked. She was always asking him if he was okay.

"I'm fine."

"What are you thinking about?"

"You," he said.

She elbowed him. "You're thinking about that woman in the elevator. I saw you looking at her the other day at the pool."

"No," Stockton said, but now he *was* thinking of her. Try not to think of something. He saw her exiting the elevator, her filmy dress white against her bronze thighs. So he was thinking of her, then—her high cheekbones, her hazel eyes. And later, as he made love to Judy, he found himself thinking of her again. He was thinking of her when he finished, and afterwards, as he lay sweating in the dark, feeling his heart thunder inside his chest and wondering when something was going to give way in there, some weakened artery, some inadequate repair, he was still thinking of her. Her eyes mainly. Those hazel eyes, taking his measure.

Judy ran her finger up the narrow scar that split his chest. "Frank," she said.

"Yeah?"

"Outside, when we were coming home from dinner. You were going to ask me something. What was it?"

"I don't know," he said. But he did.

He'd said, *Do you ever think about—*

And then she'd interrupted him, looking for the keycard. But now the phrase completed itself in his mind.

Jumping.

Do you ever think about jumping?

The question chased him down the rabbit hole into sleep.

Stockton woke from a dream of falling. He sat up abruptly, covers pooling in his lap. He was damp with sweat. He picked up his phone. Three o'clock. Late, then, or early. In either case, sleep was out of the question. He felt jittery in his bones. He supposed he could read for a while, or watch television, but what he really needed was a walk, something to shake out the nerves. He dressed in the darkness and let himself out of the apartment.

He stood at the parapet, helpless to resist. What would it be like to jump? How long before the fatal impact? Three seconds? Four? Not much time to think. And then a single excruciating instant of pain followed by . . . what? Where had he been after the heart attack? He remembered nothing but Ed telling him he looked a little green, then the nurse—

*—you should be dead—*

—staring down at him in the recovery room. And the interval between? No light, no tunnel, no relatives waiting to receive him. Not even black or void, because black or void implied an awareness to perceive them. These fragmentary thoughts and then he'd blipped out again. The next time he was awake, he was in a private room at the hospital. The face staring down at him had been Judy's.

*You're going to be okay,* she said.

*What happened?*

*Your heart,* she said. *You're lucky to be alive.*

Lucky. Stockton wrenched himself back from the parapet. Made his way to the elevator. Downstairs, a briny wind swept in off the ocean. In the moonlight, the maintenance man from the bar was hosing sand off the wooden bridge over the dunes. Stockton nodded as he passed. On the ocean side, he kicked off his sandals and pushed them under the stairs. He crossed the sand and moved out along the edge of the water, the tide washing over his feet. He walked a quarter mile or so beyond the resort before he turned back. A figure stood on the beach, gazing out at the sea.

As he drew closer, Stockton recognized—or thought he recognized—the young woman from the elevator. It was hard to be sure, but the white dress looked familiar. The wind sculpted it to the curves of her body. Was it her?

She turned and started in his direction, striding with purpose.

Stockton angled across the sand to avoid her. The woman, too, changed course. Stockton walked faster. Anxiety pulsed in his chest. It didn't seem like a good idea, a chance encounter with a woman half his age out here on the beach in the middle of the night. Bad enough that he'd been staring at her for the last two days. She probably thought he was stalking her. He retrieved his shoes from their hiding place and climbed the stairs barefooted. On the bridge over the dunes, he glanced back, half afraid that she would be coming up the steps behind him.

He didn't see her. Not on the steps, not on the beach.

Stockton stood there, puzzled.

"You should be more careful, sir. Nothing good happens on the beach after midnight."

It was the maintenance man—Keyes, according to the name tag pinned on his coveralls. Up close, he was gaunt and stubbled, pale. He'd put aside his hose to stand on the damp slats and stare out at the surf.

"Did you see her?"

Keyes had taken out a cigarette. He lit it and took a long drag. "Sure," he said.

"Where'd she go?"

"She's out there somewhere, I guess."

"What's that supposed to mean?"

"She's always around."

Stockton scanned the desolate beach. "What happened to her? She didn't have time to disappear like that."

Keyes shrugged.

"She didn't go into the water, did she? She could drown out there."

Keyes took a drag off his cigarette and blew out a flag of smoke. "She'll be all right."

"How do you know?" Stockton asked.

Keyes didn't answer.

*She must have gone into the water,* Stockton thought. "Maybe we should call someone."

Keyes grunted. He ground out his cigarette on the wooden railing. He tucked the butt away in a pocket of his coveralls. "Is that what you want to do, Mr. Stockton? A man your age out here in the middle of the night, a young lady like that?"

Stockton thought of Judy, nudging him in the elevator. *Your tongue's hanging out.*

"You go on up to your room," Keyes said. "You get yourself some sleep. That girl can take care of herself."

"But—"

"I got to finish hosing down this deck now."

"Okay, then," Stockton said.

At the base of the stairs he rinsed the sand off his feet, slid on his sandals, and pushed through the gate into the pool area. He rode the elevator up and stuck close to the wall as he traversed the gallery. Inside the apartment, he undressed and slipped into bed. He lay still in the darkness.

"Where've you been?" Judy said.

"Walking on the beach."

"At three in the morning?"

"Yes."

She didn't say anything for a while. He thought she'd fallen asleep.

"Not a very good idea," she said.

"No, I guess not."

"Something bothering you?"

"I don't think so."

"You don't think so?"

"No."

She waited him out.

He said, "I'm worried, I guess."

"About what?" And when he didn't answer: "The doctor fixed you, Frank. You're as good as new."

"You think?"

"I think. She said so, didn't she? Now go to sleep."

But sleep was a long time coming. Stockton couldn't get comfortable. Something was nagging at him, something odd. He couldn't say what it was.

It came to him the next morning:

Keyes had known his name.

Stockton pondered this over coffee. He'd gotten up late. Judy had long since left for the pool, but she'd thrown open the drapes in the main room before departing. Stockton had closed them, wincing at the shattering sunlight.

Now, he sat at the counter in the shadows, and tried to sort it out.

There was something dreamlike about the whole episode: the moonwashed beach, the young woman striding purposefully toward him. Where had she gone? And the maintenance man, Keyes. How had Keyes known him?

There must be a thousand guests or more at the resort. The odds that a maintenance man would know any one of them by name must be vanishingly small. The problem vexed Stockton. That and the flat certainty in the man's voice.

*She's always around.*

What was that supposed to mean?

Stockton drummed his fingers on the counter. He finished his coffee.

He dressed and went out onto the gallery, averting his eyes from the void beyond the parapet, resolute. That impulse moved within him, stronger now. He could feel it, a dread anticipation in his guts, a kind of longing. He was sweating by the time the elevator doors shut before him. They opened again on the seventh floor to admit a thin woman with two little girls, four or five years old, both of them clutching buckets of plastic beach toys. He realized he'd braced himself against the back wall, half expecting the woman from the beach to step inside, dreading that as well.

He felt nauseated, dizzy, short of breath.

Lucky. He'd been lucky.

"Mommy, what's wrong with the man?"

The woman drew her children close, shushing them. She offered him a weak smile. *Kids.*

Then the doors slid open and she hurried them off toward the beach.

Stockton stood in the heat, gathering himself. He took air in and let it out through his nose, counting his breaths. He felt easier then, the tide of anxiety retreating.

He walked up between the buildings to the front desk, on the street side of the central tower. "I'm looking for a man who works in maintenance," he told the desk clerk. "Keyes."

"If there's something wrong with your room—"

"My room is fine," Stockton said. "I just need to speak with this one guy."

"And what was his name again?"

"Keyes."

The clerk's face was suddenly immobile, mask like. "Let me get somebody who can help you," he said, picking up the phone.

Five minutes later, Stockton was being ushered into a private office by the property manager, a tall, blond woman, maybe a decade his junior, who'd introduced herself as Parker Nelson. The room was luxurious and impersonal. Dark, glossy furniture and plush carpet, innocuous nature prints on the walls. Even the photo on the shelf behind the desk looked like a prop: a handsome man in a golf shirt, and a matching set of kids, male and female, eight or nine years old, as blond as their mother. Stockton felt sweaty and ill at ease.

Nelson waved him to a chair by the desk. "What can I help you with, Mr. Stockton?" she asked, settling herself on the other side.

"I'd like to talk to one of your employees," he said. "His last name is Keyes. He works in maintenance."

"Is there something in your suite that requires attention?"

"No. It's him I want to talk to. Keyes."

Nelson pursed her lips. She tapped at her computer. "We don't have an employee named Keyes," she said. "Not in any department."

"I saw him. I talked to him. Out on the decking by the South Tower, on the bridge over the dunes."

"When?"

"Last night. It must have been three thirty, maybe four. This morning, I mean."

"Are you sure his name was Keyes?"

"It was on his name tag."

"Maybe you misread it? It was dark."

"No."

She stared at him for a moment. "Is this some kind of joke, Mr. Stockton?"

"I don't understand."

"If it's a joke," she said, "it's in poor taste. If it's not—" She broke off.

It came to Stockton with the force of revelation: "He's dead, isn't he?"

"Is there anything else I can do for you, Mr. Stockton?"

A dismissal. Stockton got to his feet. "Thank you for your time," he said. "I'll see myself out."

He left the office and closed the door. The lobby was busy: a group of kids checking out shuffleboard equipment from the concierge, an ice-cream social in the adjoining Seacrest Room. The modest business center next door—two desktop PCs and a printer—was empty. Stockton sat down at one of the computers and pulled up Chrome. He googled "Keyes" and "OceanView Plantation." Clicked on the news icon. It was the third hit down, an article from the local paper dated December thirteenth, three years ago: "Maintenance man killed at OceanView Plantation." Stockton scanned the neat paragraphs of text. The details were simple. An accident, a fatal fall from the roof of the South Tower. Recriminations from the family, carefully worded condolences from OceanView. And further down the page several more hits: a history of depression, a lawsuit, an out-of-court settlement and a nondisclosure clause. Then silence.

Stockton sat there for a long time, staring at the screen.

The ice-cream social went on in the Seacrest Room. The concierge was on the phone.

Stockton stood up. The desk clerk busied himself at his computer.

Outside, the heat was breathtaking. Stockton went to find Judy.

But what could he say?

That he'd seen a ghost? Judy would think he was having her on. Frank. Her Frank, the epitome of rationality. He didn't believe in ghosts. He had misread the name tag. It had been late and he'd been strung out from lack of sleep. It was nothing.

He found her on the deck by the tiki bar. He sat facing her on the lounge she'd saved for him, and tried to frame the whole thing in his head in a way that made sense: the woman on the beach, his conversation with Keyes, the obscure impulse that he felt move within him. He opened his mouth to speak, closed it. What would Laurie say?

He was anxious, that's all. And no wonder. It had been a close call. He'd been lucky.

"I thought you were never coming down," Judy said.

"I slept late."

"I know. Up walking the beach at three in the morning. What were you thinking?"

Stockton shrugged. "I don't know," he said.

She smiled and patted his knee. "Well, you're here now. Is it too early for a drink?"

"We're on vacation."

"Just what I was thinking."

His muscle-bound friend was at the tiki bar. Gym, Beach, Repeat. "What can I get you, boss?"

Stockton ordered a Caribbean Cooler and a gin and tonic. He slid a twenty across the bar. "Go a little heavier on the gin, why don't you," he said. The bartender grinned and pocketed the bill. "Why not?" he said.

Stockton signed the slip and turned away.

Back at the lounge chairs, he handed Judy her drink. It was hot, and the cocktails went down easy. Stockton went back to the bar for another round and then another. He got ahead of Judy. The bartender had warmed up to him. He kept the pours generous and made casual conversation. Where was Stockton from and what did he do for a living? Was this his first visit to OceanView? Stockton grew looser. He thought about his encounter with Keyes. The whole thing seemed faintly ridiculous, even embarrassing. Maybe he *had* misread the name.

Stockton looked for the woman in the pink bikini. He finally spotted her down on the far end of the pool below the North Tower. She lay still in the sun, her head angled toward him. She might have been staring at him from behind her dark glasses. She might have been sleeping. More likely, she was entirely oblivious. What was he to her?

Yet she had turned toward him on the beach, as if to intercept him.

He finished his drink and heaved himself out of his lounge chair, unsteady on his feet. He looked at Judy. "You ready for another?"

"I'm fine," Judy said. "Maybe we should go up."

"One more."

At the tiki bar, Gym/Beach/Repeat said, "Listen, boss, you sure you—"

Stockton slid another twenty across the bar. He watched the bartender mix the drink, signed the slip, turned away. The woman at the far end of the pool was gone. When he got back to the lounge chairs, Judy was packing up. She studied him critically. "Time to get you upstairs," she said. Sipping his drink, he let her lead him to the elevator. The door was sliding closed when the woman in the pink bikini slipped in.

Judy frowned. "What floor?" she asked.

The woman leaned over to punch the button for sixteen. As she stepped back she brushed past Stockton. She pushed her sunglasses up onto her head and glanced over at him. There was something familiar in her hazel eyes. She held his gaze. Stockton looked away. He studied his feet. He thought of the parapet, that impulse moving within him. The elevator lurched higher.

They rode up in silence.

He recalled her on the beach, changing course to intercept him, the way he'd forced himself to walk faster, the anxiety pulsing in his chest.

The elevator stopped at fifteen.

The doors opened.

As he stepped out, Stockton risked another glance at her. She stared back, unblinking.

The doors shut, and it was like a tense line snapping. Stockton drank off the gin. He wanted to keep drinking. He could drink all night. He stood at the parapet and gazed down into the garden far below.

"Come on, Frank," Judy said. "You've had too much gin. You'll fall over if you're not careful."

He stepped back and followed her to the suite.

Inside, he poured a glass of chardonnay. "Wine?" he asked.

"Not right now. We need to get some food in your stomach."

She opened the curtains and went back into the kitchen. He watched her from the counter. She put in a pork tenderloin to bake and made a salad. Stockton poured himself another glass of wine.

"How much are you planning to drink?" She was cleaning broccoli to steam.

"Have you ever seen a ghost, Judy?"

She looked up. "No, and neither have you."

"I don't remember the heart attack," Stockton said. "One minute I'm getting out of the truck, the next I'm coming out of surgery. I don't remember anything in between."

She sliced the floret off a stalk of broccoli. "You don't remember when you're asleep, either."

"You remember your dreams."

"You were under anesthesia." She sliced the head off another stalk, the blade snapping hard on the plastic cutting board. Then another stalk. And another.

"Not in the ambulance," he said.

The blade jumped off the cutting board, came down on the next stalk, and took a layer of flesh off her knuckle, thin as the filmy husk of an onion. She threw the knife clattering into the sink. She brought the wounded finger to her mouth. "You're drunk," she said. "I was dead," he told her, and she stormed out of the kitchen. She slammed the bedroom door behind her.

Sighing, Stockton turned off the oven.

He emptied his wine glass and retrieved the bottle from the refrigerator. Holding it by the neck, he walked to the balcony door and stood looking out. Twilight had fallen. The sea was calm. Small rollers broke upon the sand. Someone was flying a kite down by the water. It snapped and turned in the wind before him.

Stockton refilled his glass and placed the sweating bottle on the coffee table.

He sat on the sofa, and looked out over the balcony to the horizon. He didn't know how long he sat there. The sky grew dark. He splashed more wine into his glass. The young woman cut across the sand to meet him. When he dozed off, she followed him down into his dreams.

The nurse leaned over him.

*You should be dead,* she told him, and he woke into the silence of deep night.

Stockton clambered to his feet, bewildered. The room tilted, as though the Earth had slipped on its axis. Then he was okay. Unsteady, but okay. He drained the wine bottle and set it back on the table. He felt drawn to the balcony. He put his hand on the door handle and pulled, the glass whispering in its track. He stepped outside, into the humid night air. The moon cast a pale streak across the black water. Below him glittered bright pools, garlanded with palm trees. Curling his hands around the railing, he hoisted himself up and over and clung there on the narrow lip of concrete.

The ocean heaved in the dark.

Here it was, then, the crescendo everything had been

hurtling toward since he'd opened his eyes in the recovery room. It felt like a circle closing, ineluctable, true, as though he had no choice in the matter, as though he'd been driven to it, or summoned. Now he would unclench his hands, now he would push himself out into the night. He saw the black earth lurching toward him, the pools, the trees—

From the doorway, Judy said, "Frank, baby, please—"

Stockton clutched at the railing. His hand slipped. The building pitched and yawed. Blank terror seized him. And then he had it, he was stable again, and all the world spread out below him. The resort was an island of light in a dark sea that ran out to the horizon, illimitable.

"Frank," Judy said. "Frank, baby, please. Come back to me now. You don't have to do this. Why would you do this? Why would you leave me, baby? Why would you do that?"

She stepped out onto the balcony.

Wind swept in off the ocean. It tugged at him, rippling his clothes, calling out to him, all that dark and void. And Judy. Enjoining him to stay.

Stockton hung there in fine equipoise, balanced on the knife edge of the moment. There was nothing else and had not ever been or would be, just this fleeting instant of time.

"Frank," Judy said.

And then he was pulling himself up and over, onto the balcony. He went to his knees. Judy knelt to take him into her arms.

"It's okay," she said. "You're okay now."

Stockton was weeping.

They didn't sleep until nearly dawn, and when they woke neither of them spoke of what had happened in the night. They moved carefully around each other and talked quietly about small matters. Stockton's close call on the balcony lay under these surface trivialities like a chasm. To broach it would be to admit how perilous was their position on the brink of the abyss. A time would come when they would have to hash it out, Stockton knew. He supposed he would have to consult someone about it—Judy would insist, and Laurie would be happy, even gratified, to give him a name. But for the present anyway, they acknowledged it no further than in their tacit agreement that it was time to go home.

Judy supervised while the bellman loaded the luggage into the car. Stockton went inside to check out. The same clerk stood behind the desk, professionally courteous. There was something in his voice. He didn't make eye contact, just pushed a sheet of paper across the counter. Sign here, initial this, date that. Stockton didn't bother with the small print, just scrawled his name on the line, dated it, and handed it back.

Done.

Stockton turned away, searching for the men's room.

He found it down the corridor from Parker Nelson's office. Inside, everything was gleaming and clean, the mirror and the countertops, the white towels in their baskets by the sinks. Somewhere an unseen atomizer murmured, releasing into the room a subtle fragrance of oranges. Stockton stepped up to the urinal. Finished, he leaned over the vanity to wash his hands. He was tossing the towel into the bin when someone came in and slipped by at his back. Stockton moved to the door. His hand was on the push plate when—

"Mr. Stockton."

Stockton paused. He took a deep breath.

Somewhere faraway the atomizer hissed, releasing another burst of citrus spray.

There was a white roaring in his ears.

*You don't have to look back,* he told himself. *You can push through the door and into the hallway beyond. Walk out through the lobby into the bright afternoon. Judy will have the car idling. It will be cool inside and you can pull away from this place forever, tires humming on the pavement. You never have to look back again. This is all behind you now. This is all behind you.*

"Mr. Stockton."

Against his will, as if some force compelled him, Stockton turned.

Keyes stood there, so close that a single step would have closed the distance between them. He was gaunt and tall. His eyes were dark wells.

"This is over," Stockton said, "this thing between us. Between the three of us."

"Is it?" Keyes said, and Stockton shouldered through the door, that white roaring in his ears—out through the lobby and past the desk clerk busy at his station, out, out, into the blistering heat.

# The Shooter

*M. Rickert*

He'd been reading sympathy cards for a long time. None of them conveyed what he felt. So many pictures of birds, flowers, and clouds shot through with sunbeams as if death relegated one the emotional capacity of a kindergartner. The words were worse. Almost cruel, really: ethereal and vacuous.

Clearly, he was hoping for too much. He needed to choose one and be done with it. What difference did it make? No card could bear the weight. Just pick, he scolded himself.

"I know. They're shit, aren't they?"

"Excuse me?"

"I couldn't help but overhear."

Had he spoken? He peered at the young man who looked up from beneath a dark forelock hanging above his pretty eyes, long lashes and perfectly arched brows. Impossibly thin, as seemed to be the fashion, a boy as substantial as a black butterfly, fleetingly seen and forever remembered.

"We have others, you know."

"We?"

The boy smiled, the dazzling display quickly obliterated by narrow lips. "Sorry. Kent." He pointed at the name tag affixed to his cotton shirt, a summer plaid of patriotic colors. "I work here."

Alex nodded. He wished he could think of something to

say, but the impossible task at hand—and all that led to it—had depleted him of his ability to function reasonably. He shouldn't have come. It was too soon. What had he been thinking?

"They don't want me to tell you."

"Excuse me? Kent? I'm—"

"I was supposed to send them back to the distributor. Kyle, he's the manager, said he'd gotten complaints."

"Where is Kyle?"

"Gone. I don't know where he goes, but I know he won't be back for a while, which is why I feel safe telling you."

"Listen, Kent? I appreciate—"

"No problem! Follow me. I'll show you where they are."

They were in the back room—past boxes stacked on boxes, shelves of paper towels and cleaning supplies, past the employee bathroom with the door open, the toilet lid up, the basin, rusty—in a cold room Kent illuminated by pulling the chain of an overhead light. The naked bulb dangled there like a hanging.

"Let's see, okay here's some, but there's more. Someone keeps coming back here and moving shit."

Alex looked down at the carton Kent held out with one hand even as he continued to search through clutter, mumbling about "a little consideration for the dead" and whatnot. The boy's anger, however benign, frightened Alex. He took the carton.

"I see them now. Christ."

Kent shoved boxes aside, tossed a few to the ground. Alex wanted to warn him to be careful but could not summon the words. Instead, glancing down, he saw blood and almost dropped the carton.

"Yeah, I know. They make 'em look real." Kent sneezed. "It's the dust," he sniffed. "This shit back here really gets my allergies going."

Alex decided to pretend everything was normal. He tried to smile, which was surprisingly difficult under the circumstances.

"Thank you," he said. "I—"

"No problem." Kent sneezed again. "Take your time. The others are right there. I gotta get back to the register."

Alex nodded—already planning to make his escape—when Kent, with dancerlike grace, turned and pointed a gun made out of his fingers before pirouetting away, receding into the dark labyrinth they'd entered together, leaving Alex shot with horror.

He immediately moved to set the carton on the shelf but, while doing so, his thumb dipped low and brushed a card which was smooth as skin, unblemished or scarred by the texture of dried blood. He paused to wipe his fingers across the face, picked it up and read the message, then set it down, and chose another.

He was both appalled and fascinated by the bizarre collection. At first he thought they were all for accidental shootings, but after a while realized the cards had been stacked in categories. He had to search the other boxes Kent had set aside to find school shootings. There were quite a few of them, which made sense of course.

It seemed wrong to be happy, and with that thought alone Alex was able to tamp down the emotion. What was happening to this country? And yet, what a relief it was to find the situation so thoroughly addressed. In fact, he continued to read cards even after he found the perfect one. To be sure, he told himself though he knew it was a charade of sorts. Finally satisfied, he tucked the card into the inside pocket of his suit jacket and made his departure, turning left at the shelf of cleaning supplies when he knew turning right would have led him back to the boy waiting beneath the fluorescent lights, so pale his veins shimmered blue through his skin like an effervescent insect.

There. Straight ahead. Alex saw the door with the exit sign above the warning; USE ONLY IN EMERGENCY, ALARM WILL GO OFF. It did. Screaming and sirens, and Alex in the bright light that consumed him like a neutron star.

The thing was, Alex knew he had died—he just kept forgetting—and, in that way, he mused, death was so much like life. Everyone said they knew they were mortal and, technically, they did, but Alex remembered how he had been, and suspected—in spite of his childhood hopes and aspirations—his life had been quite ordinary, his forgetting ordinary too. He'd spent very little time remembering his inevitable demise. When such bleak humor did arise—usually prompted by the death of another, that bitter winter after his mother died, for instance—he was able to get over it, eventually. Shocking, really, how completely filled up he had been with sorrow, only to find himself—months later—watching television and laughing, his grief destroyed by something so minor he couldn't even recall what it had been. Yet, that, probably more than anything else, seemed to define the human condition. The great sorrow they all felt, the overwhelming anguish and despair alleviated with time. Just as now, he realized, others were alleviated of him, and he was left to wander.

He didn't know where he was.

• • •

"Well, you know, I guess it depends on your own belief system, right? But what you got in your hand there is called cow parsley, and I agree it's pretty but I think you should know its other name, which is dead-man's flourish."

"I thought it was Queen Anne's lace," Alex said to the girl. "What about these?" he pointed at a blue vase filled with cheerful flowers he remembered growing in his mother's garden.

When the girl shrugged, her dangling earrings made a faint sound like breaking glass.

"What?" he asked. Then, surprised at how mean he sounded, added. "Sorry. I'm . . . this . . ."

"It's just I'm not supposed to discourage buyers. Tammy keeps saying that. 'Quit discouraging buyers.'"

"Tammy?"

"She owns the place."

"Well, where is she?" Alex asked.

"Oh, she's gone. I don't know where she goes, but she's gonna be away for a while."

He frowned. Why did that sound so familiar? "I'll take them," he said, lifting the vase to bring to the counter.

The girl shook her head. "But they're daisies."

"Yes," Alex said. "All right."

The light, shining through the large front window, blazed across her face. When she looked up at him, beseeching, he was confused.

"Okay, I'm just gonna tell you this so you can make an informed choice. If you want to buy 'em, I'll sell them to you. But daisies were, like, planted by dead children."

"Excuse me?"

"You know, to try to cheer their parents up."

"But that doesn't . . ." Alex didn't finish, however. He carefully returned the vase to the spot he'd taken it from. It was nonsense, of course, but once heard he could not unhear it and wasn't able to consider a flower with such bleak associations. He glanced at the girl who seemed absorbed in picking a cockroach off her sweater.

"What about this?" Alex pointed at a woody green plant in a simple terra-cotta pot.

She sighed deeply and shrugged.

"What?" he asked. What could possibly be wrong with such an innocuous plant? When he leaned closer he smelled a pleasant aroma that reminded him of soap.

"Well, it depends," she said.

"I like it."

"Yeah. It's nice."

"But?"

"Well, you said this is for a funeral, right?"

He had almost forgotten, and it had been a relief. But there he was. Doing this terrible thing.

"Rosemary is for remembrance, all right?"

"Excuse me?"

"So I guess it depends whether they want to remember or not."

"Why wouldn't they want to remember?" Alex asked.

The bell above the door rang, signaling that someone else was entering the shop. Alex was relieved when the traffic noise was quickly cut off, the store returned to shelter. He was in no mood for the world. He just wasn't.

He moved away from the rosemary; it, too, contaminated. This made no sense. Who was this girl, anyway? She was nothing to him. Nothing. Alex glanced her way, surprised by the presence of the slender young man that leaned across the counter watching her arrange a bouquet, her movement languid and expansive, sweeping her arm in an arc to add a leafy stem to the arrangement.

"The traditional flower for funerals is daffodil," she said.

He thought the tone of her voice was scolding, and then assumed he imagined it. Grief made him think everything was mean.

"Okay, daffodils, then."

"Come on," she said. "Follow me."

He felt that was strange, but maybe it wasn't. When was the last time he'd been to a florist? So long ago he couldn't remember. To be polite, he nodded at the customer. The dark-haired boy smiled, and pointed a finger gun at Alex who, horrified, turned to follow the girl.

"Hello?" She couldn't have just disappeared, right? People didn't just disappear, but he couldn't find her amongst the torn stems and scattered petals, and soon accepted he was lost. He thought he might be able to make his way back, but the idea of the boy with his gun spurred Alex to keep moving forward. When he saw the EXIT sign he went to it and pressed the door open, immediately terrorized by the alarm and blinding light. After he blinked away the sun spots, however, his fear was replaced with enchantment. As far as he could see—flowers—an endless field of them. Daffodils, he assumed. Struck by their beauty, he fell to his hands and knees. They were bright yellow, and shaped much like daisies but for the small petal bell that rose from each center. Alex cocked his head, drawing his ear close to listen, but the bells were silent. The alarm had stopped, and when he looked behind him he could no longer see the building he'd just left, or any other. Everywhere he looked, daffodils—the stunned world perfumed with a musky vanilla scent, and green. Could green have a smell? It was almost too much. He closed his eyes. Alive, he thought. The scent of green is alive.

For a brief period after he died, so many people knew him, it was flattering, really, the way they said his name with reverence and prayed for him; perfect strangers wept for him. He had never been popular and, initially, was both flattered and comforted by the attention until it became exhausting to be pulled in so many directions, finding himself in strange houses, in rooms he didn't know, summoned by people who had no idea of his presence or who, seeing him, cowered beneath covers, trembling as if he were the shooter. He wanted to say, "My thoughts and prayers are with you." He wanted to say, "We are one in our grief." He wanted to say, "Evil never wins," but he was a ghost, and unsure what he believed.

Alex walked through the forest, carrying a massive bouquet of daffodils in his arms, the sympathy card tucked in his pocket. He wondered if he should go back to make a casserole, but then he would be late. Absence, he decided, was worse than inadequacy, especially in this instance.

The forest canopy made the sky green, cool, and contained, as if built in a terrarium like the kind he remembered from his childhood, little gardens under glass domes visited by fairies whose passage was not limited by life's barriers. It was his understanding children no longer believed in such magic, and Alex wondered why. Before he could explore the question further however, he was distracted by the arrival of a cloaked figure approaching with catlike stealth. The face that looked up at him from beneath the brown hood was ancient, wizened, and kind. "Are you going to the funeral?" she asked.

"Yes," Alex said. "How did you know?"

She made a sharp gunshot of noise he identified as laughter. "The only ones who come here are going to funerals," she said, gliding forward. Alex decided to trudge along beside her, embarrassed by his lumbering steps, breaking twigs and stumbling over tree roots she seemed to float above, impervious to the uneven terrain. The sharp caw of a crow caused him to look behind, surprised to discover that he and the old woman led a procession. Many were cloaked like she was, but others were dressed in vibrant harlequin colors, and some appeared to have wings. He wondered if they had passed a Renaissance faire he hadn't noticed, though he didn't think that made sense.

Some carried flowers, though no one had so many as Alex, who held his with both arms as though cradling a small child. They carried sunflowers and little pine trees decorated with ornaments. A few folk held lanterns. It wasn't so dark, really, that they were necessary but Alex appreciated them nonetheless; the glimmering lights like fireflies he used to chase as a child, running barefoot on the grass. Others carried food. Platters laden with bright orbs of fruit: jeweled strawberries, orange smiles, sliced pomegranates with glistening red seeds, and baskets from which emitted the yeasty aroma of fresh-baked bread. Alex felt bad that he hadn't brought something to eat. Who had ever been sated by flowers?

"Soldiers used to carry daffodil bulbs in their packs, you know," the old woman said, startling Alex.

"Oh? I wouldn't have guessed they were gardeners."

The woman snorted. "They ate the bulbs after suffering a mortal wound. It made them forget their pain. It made them dream while they were dying."

"What did they dream?" Alex asked.

She stopped midglide, and everyone in the procession stopped as well. The whole forest became as still and quiet as a picture in a children's book, until the page turned.

"What did you say?" She looked at him, waiting. It seemed everything was listening, even the green leaves, even the crows perched on the branches.

"I said, 'What did they dream?'"

She shook her head. "That's the wrong question," she sighed and continued on her way. Alex let the others pass as he tried to figure things out. What was the right question, he wondered. What was he not understanding? Crows swooped down from the trees and began pecking bread and plucking seeds from sunflowers, a few even swooped to pluck hairs from unhooded heads but the gentle folk swatted them away.

He looked up and saw that the sky had opened a little, the green world parted to reveal the blue one beyond. At first he thought the sound was the breaking of a limb, and he searched the trees, uncertain where to run, not able to fly through that hole in the sky the way the crows had, but the sound cracked again and someone shouted, "Run, it's the shooter."

Alex ran, dropping daffodils that tangled in his legs and made a bright gold contrail of his passage in the dark wood. When he fell, he found a few flowers still clinging to his pants, so he began shoving petals and stems into his mouth, hoping to dream something else.

• • •

In his whole life, no one had ever called Alex beautiful, but when they described his death they said that it was tragic and horrible, yet he was incandescent; a man covered in blossoms of gold and stems of green. The mourners wept and crushed flowers to their hearts; they promised they would never forget and he, just another ghost, never believed them. He believed in some things, but not forever.

When the children came, running over the hill, he thought maybe he'd finally found his way, but then the boy with the gun showed up. This, Alex could not believe. "Not the children," he said. "Let them have monster nightmares, not this." But the boy just smiled. The children ran amongst the daisies, screaming and wild. They tore the flowers apart, not unkindly but in the spirit of blowing dandelion wishes or plucking petals in the old way; "he loves me, he loves me not." They hugged each other with glee then broke apart, falling to the ground and screaming. The children were screaming and the light was so tender, Alex thought; a sky that did not know human terror. The children were glowing as they ran through the field and he thought there was something he had once understood, something vital that was lost, but maybe he had just imagined it. He ran into the field, trying to save all of them, or some of them, or at least one of them, but the field was not really there, though the children were, and in that mortal world stood a boy with a gun whose aim was good.

# The Tree of Self-Knowledge

*Stephen Graham Jones*

Jeanie Silber died the night of our prom, nineteen years ago. I almost just said it was an ugly wreck, but any wreck that snatches two kids in their senior year is ugly, I think. For years afterward, Clint Berkot's Grand Prix was the one you'd see in the parades, being pulled on a flatbed trailer. They never even put signs or words on it, or on the doors of the truck pulling it. But it didn't need any signs. Its crunched-in front end and shattered windshield and crumpled doors and wheels not in line with each other anymore was warning enough. Because of Jeanie and Clint, class after class of Titans graduated whole and intact. Not dead. Not ramming into a dull yellow grass-cutting tractor cocked in the ditch.

There was never any explanation for how Clint's car got that far off the road.

It was a tragedy, plain and simple.

Clint and Jeanie were just like the rest of us. They were going to class, counting the days, biting their fingernails about jobs and life and kids and everything else that was coming for us. Clint wasn't the quarterback, Jeanie wasn't homecoming queen. Normal kids, part-time jobs, church probably two times a month, out of habit. He was towheaded, she had kind of red hair, like her mom. This was, I believe, their fourth official date. Maybe they were going to keep on with each other too. Maybe they were going to have the next crop of kids to catch candy at the parade, and then stare at the wrecked car being dragged past.

I didn't go to prom myself. Not because of any intuition or premonition—this isn't that kind of place, I'm not that kind of person—but for the usual reason. I didn't have a date. My girlfriend Chrissy had dumped me two weeks before, and cried so hard while doing it I thought she was going to choke. All these years later, I can't even remember exactly why she broke up, but I do remember the relief I felt when it was over. It wasn't the pleasure of being unattached at the hip, released into the wild again. It was that, with graduation looming, one of us was going to have to break up. It was either that or get married. You grow up in a small town like Milford, this is just how it works.

I did end up married, of course, and that next year, even, to Kay, the love of my life. She's from Haverly, the next town over, and graduated a year before I did. We met at the courthouse of all places, were both paying speeding tickets. I know that probably sounds like I'm setting something up: Jeanie died in a car going, by the highway patrol's estimation, seventy-plus miles per hour, and a year later I got popped doing thirty-five in a school zone, but it's not any setup. The cops around here have a quota; tickets are a main source of revenue for the county.

As for me and Jeanie, there's nothing really to tell. We'd gone to a movie in the park together in either seventh or eighth grade, but had gone different ways by the time of the next school dance. That's how it is when you're a kid: you try on this person, that person, and you keep on moving. What you're doing, I think, is trying out different versions of who you are, or who you can be. With Jeanie, I remember I wanted her to think I was tough. How I got that across to her was by dismissing all the horror movies my big brother let me watch, when our parents were asleep. Maybe she was impressed, maybe she wasn't. It doesn't matter. I do still think about those movies in my weaker moments, but less and less as the years stack up.

Until Thanksgiving, that is.

Now they're all crowding in around me.

Because it's what you do when you're married, Kay and I alternate holidays with her parents and mine. This year it's supposed to be Christmas here in Milford, with my mom and her turkey we'll eat just enough of to be polite, meaning Thanksgiving was in Haverly, with Kay's parents.

What happened was Kay's mother needed some fast-rising yeast from the store, for her famous rolls, and, since I was the one of us in the living room doing nothing—watching the game—I got volunteered to make the necessary run down to the store.

Of course I tried to engineer the trip as close to halftime as I could, but the third time Kay stepped into the doorway to look from me to the television, I got the hint.

"I can't wait for her rolls either," I said to her, draining the last of my beer as if those last couple of drinks had been the only thing keeping me planted on the couch.

"Neither can she," Kay said, with an edge.

I eased my way to the door, collected my red windbreaker—got to show team pride—and hotfooted it out to the truck.

From previous Thanksgivings, we knew the IGA was open until four. I still had twenty minutes. It should have been just a quick jaunt down the road and back, and some idle conversation with the unlucky high schooler caught behind the register.

Except.

This wasn't my home store, quite. I mean, every grocery

store's more or less alike, but there's peculiarities, too. In Milford, I probably could have zeroed in on the fast-rising yeast inside of thirty seconds. In Haverly, I was trolling up and down the aisles. Would it be in the bakery section? No. With the butter? No, and I was probably only checking there because I loved to go overboard on the butter, on Thanksgiving. The cooking aisle, then, with the spices and birthday candles and small packages of walnuts and pecans.

No.

Finally I had to ask, but the kid at the register—I'd nodded to her on the way in, pursed my lips about all the piercings in hers—had abandoned her post, evidently. Usually you can find a stocker or a manager, but this was a holiday.

I stood there in meats, the seconds ticking down until halftime, and finally nodded to myself.

The back, the stockroom, behind the milk. There'd be somebody back there. There would have to be, in case a surprise delivery showed up.

I stood at the double aluminum doors and called ahead: "Hello?"

No answer.

I looked both ways, nodded to myself that this was justified, and stepped into the employee-only area.

It was cooler back there. And dimmer.

"Hello?" I called out again.

This was getting ridiculous. Had the store already closed, the front door just been left unlocked? Was I going to singlehandedly ruin Thanksgiving dinner?

No, I wasn't.

Moving in a way meant to signal that I wasn't at home here,

that I didn't assume my being back in the stockroom was all right, I edged into the suite of thin-walled offices I would have assumed were there, had I ever thought about it. You have to interview people somewhere, I guess. The motion-sensor lights were off, even in what looked like the break room.

"Hello?" I said again, quieter. With no heart behind it anymore.

If I'd thought to bring my phone, I could have called Kay, asked her to ask her mother where the yeast was. This way I could at least document that I'd tried. I could have used the store phone, I suppose, but I didn't think of that then.

I just wanted some famous rolls. And to watch the rest of the game. And to maybe talk to an actual human in a blue apron and off-white name tag.

Walking with more purpose now, I pushed through the transparent strips of plastic into the space behind the deli counter. Then I knocked on the door of the freezer, I couldn't really say why. Nobody knocked back.

I laughed to myself. I ran my fingers through what's left of my hair.

I decided that the girl with the rings through her lips would be my answer. That she was probably standing out by the ice cooler on the sidewalk, smoking an unauthorized cigarette or three.

That had to be it.

When I couldn't figure how to get across the deli counter without clambering over it, falling down into a mess of ice that probably smelled of shrimp, I retraced my steps through the plastic strips and stockroom, pushed through the aluminum doors from the other side, stepped back onto what we'd call the sales floor at the dealership.

The store was just as deserted as before.

"Hello!" I called again.

Nothing, no one.

I walked down the wide aisle that divided the front of the store from the back, then hooked it left to beeline the registers.

I was walking past the toys on one side, the hardware on the other. Pop guns and mousetraps.

And then I stopped.

The IGA in Haverly is one of those stores—maybe because there's a pharmacy in back?—where there's angled-down mirrors all around the edge of the ceiling.

I looked up into the one slanted up over me, and it gave me the aisle I'd just stalked down.

Way at the back of it, there was a narrow wisp of a girl with auburn hair.

She was squatted down at the edge of a cardboard display like kids do, where you bend both knees out.

But she wasn't a kid, quite. She was a woman. Seventeen, eighteen. Not the girl from the register, either. The girl from the register had had all black on under her blue apron.

This girl was wearing a thin, kind-of-white dress. Almost a nightgown.

The reason she was squatted down was she was reaching under the cardboard display, reaching deep enough she had to drop her shoulder down, turn her head to the side, away from me.

My first, unbidden thought, it was that she was hiding her face because of what Clint Berkot's dashboard had done to it.

That was when I realized it was Jeanie Silber, dead for nineteen years.

• • •

Thanksgiving wasn't ruined because of me showing back up to the house late. It turned out Kay's mom had an emergency pack of yeast. Nobody noticed the desperation I drank the rest of my six-pack with, and if Kay's dad noted the delay between him asking questions about the score and me answering, he didn't comment on it.

And of course I didn't say anything about Jeanie.

By the time I'd turned around, from the mirror to the aisle, she was gone.

I'd stood there with my heart pounding in my chest.

Finally, I breathed.

I'm not too proud to say I yelped when the girl from the register spoke from behind me, either, asking was I ready to check out.

She jumped too, and we laughed about it, alone in a grocery store on Thanksgiving Day.

"Do you know where the yeast stuff is?" I asked.

"For an—an . . . ," she stammered, trying to find a way to say "infection," I was pretty sure.

"Cooking," I told her.

She relaxed, smiled, the silver rings in her lips glinting in the fluorescents, and together we found the last of the yeast, gathered together in a holiday endcap with the gravy packets.

"Anything else?" the girl asked, and I chanced a look up into the mirrors, shook my head no, and I paid with cash.

Three days later, though, I strolled back in.

Rolling between my fingers in my jacket pocket was a dime from the ashtray of my truck.

Looking at the items on their hooks at the other end of the

toys and hardware aisle, I fumbled the dime down, then knelt to find it.

Tentatively, I pushed my hand under the cardboard display. It was for dog collars.

That was the part I couldn't get over: What could Jeanie Silber have come back *for*?

It let me jump right over the fact that she was back at all.

I pushed my right hand into the unswept place, cast my fingers around blindly, and then, for a moment I'm as sure of as I've ever been sure of anything, a set of fingers lightly brushed the top of my forearm.

I stood all at once, toppling the cardboard display.

There was nothing under it.

The blue aprons collapsed on me. I guess I'm old enough at thirty-seven to look like I might need medical help.

I assured them it was nothing, I'd tripped, this was no cause for concern, and I tried to help them collect the dog collars I'd spilled. But then one of them looked up, her lower lip accented silver.

"Yeast," she said to me, like making an identification.

"I'm sorry," I said to all of them, and found the door myself, waited until the cab of my truck to close my eyes tight, let the panic breathing come. I rubbed and rubbed my forearm, where that contact had been made.

When it was over, I reached over with my left hand for the keys hooked to the belt loop on my right side, and registered at the last moment that this was wrong, that this wasn't my left hand's job.

Or, it was only my left hand's job when my right hand was busy.

I opened my right hand slowly, not even completely aware I'd had it clenched into a fist.

A dusty blue, broken rubber band.

I shook it off my palm, into the passenger side floorboard, and I drove back to Milford.

I could have told Kay about this, I know. Maybe I even *should* have told her about all this. What I tell myself is if there been something to show, something to prove I wasn't losing it, I *would* have told her.

And, the thing about Kay? She would have listened. She wouldn't have been trying to suppress a grin. She wouldn't tell me I was getting carried away. I'm not saying she's any kind of true believer, into crystals and horoscopes. Kay's down to earth, always has been.

I think maybe the reason I didn't tell her, it was that I didn't want to have to imagine what she would be thinking *while* I was telling her. That her husband of eighteen years was starting to slip. That he was starting to see things. That he was starting to see people from his past, people who had died.

Which? Okay, so I'm going to be haunted. Fine. But why Jeanie Silber? Of all people? I hardly knew Jeanie. That movie we saw in the park, I don't even remember for sure what movie it was. I know more about Clint Berkot's Grand Prix they died in than I know about Jeanie. I can tell you what water pump it needs, I know what tires came factory on it, I remember a ding on the left side of its rear bumper.

If any of the dead people from my past were going to start slouching around in my peripheral vision, it should have been my dad. There's some unfinished business there, I'd say. He could come back, tell me where the 9/16 box-end wrench that completes his prize set was. He could give me some parting message to pass on to Mom, I don't know.

He would make *sense*, anyway.

With Jeanie . . . I don't know. What it feels like with Jeanie, it's that I was in a grocery store that was supposed to be ninety-nine percent empty. Like she'd targeted it right at that moment, so she could be there, do what she needed to be doing.

As for what that was, whatever errand she needed to run now that she was dead, I thought on that for probably two weeks after Thanksgiving. She'd wanted something, that was obvious. Something that was supposed to have been under that cardboard display of dog collars.

My impulse was to go back, stake the toy and hardware aisle out, catch her in the act, make her open her fist, reveal the earring or whatever she had to have. Do the dead like shiny things? Once you're dead, do you start thinking like a raccoon, or a largemouth bass?

It made as much sense as anything.

And then there was the fact that she hadn't aged even one day, as near as I could tell. It made sense, I supposed, but what I couldn't figure out was where all the blood went. From what happened to her in the wreck. From what made her funeral be closed-casket. In death, do you dial back a few minutes, to how you used to be? Do you take on the form you kind of remember for yourself?

The blood, though . . . I'm kind of ashamed to say this. But I should get it out.

Clint Berkot's Grand Prix. That summer after graduation, when it was still just sitting down at Salmon's U-Pull-It yard, we'd go sit around and drink beers, toasting Jeanie and Clint into the afterlife. Salmon didn't mind. One or two nights, he even dragged a bench seat up himself, drank right along with us. One of those nights, he showed us a trick, too. Evidently you can trail a line of spit down onto a dashboard somebody's cracked their face open on, and, if there's enough blood left in the vinyl, the water in your spit'll reactivate it, make it bloom red again.

It felt holy and wrong at the same time, rubbing our spit into that dash. Rubbing our fingers in Jeanie's blood.

That's not why I saw her in the IGA, though. If it was, then Dave Timmons and Gracie Elder and Nash Waldrop and the rest of them would be seeing her too.

No, I'm fairly certain it was just that I wasn't supposed to be there then, in that grocery store. And, even had Jeanie allowed that some last-moment shopper was going to be there, then what were the chances it would be someone who would recognize an un-aged girl who died nineteen years ago?

What happened was simple: I saw her when I wasn't supposed to, when she was doing whatever small things the dead do.

And then I saw her again.

Because I was feeling guilty for not telling Kay about Jeanie—it wasn't like I was cheating or keeping secrets, I know—I'd bought her a new set of pots and pans. I knew she wanted them because she'd been strategically leaving the catalog they were in open on the coffee table, on the kitchen counter.

Kay's never been the kind to ask for anything, especially anything as extravagant as this set of copper pots and pans, but that didn't mean she couldn't covet them. Maybe she didn't even know she was leaving the catalog open on their page. Maybe she'd be looking at them and then just drift off, into a version of the world where those pans were hanging from a rack over the island in the kitchen.

And, I don't mean to reduce Kay to the kitchen, understand. She's the most successful realtor in her office, has been on the town council, and she's getting her master's degree by correspondence. But she loves to cook, too. So I'd ordered that set of pots and pans, had them delivered to the dealership, and then smuggled them home in the passenger seat of my truck, left them there because that was the one place Kay wouldn't stumble on them.

We live a good half mile from our closest neighbor, but still, I'd locked the door, and checked the passenger side too. Just on the chance.

Now, in my robe and slippers, Kay fast asleep, her book still open on her chest, I was sneaking out to my truck for her surprise. Because I was sneaking, I turned the porch light off, didn't want anything giving me away.

It turned out the surprise was on me.

The dome light of my truck was already on.

I stood there, two steps off the porch.

The truck was parked like always, with the driver's door toward the porch, so I couldn't tell at first what was going on.

Was this Kay's way of telling me she knew what I was doing? Had she come out after dinner, twisted the headlight knob so the dome light would be on when I came out?

Except Kay is a practical woman. She would never use up the battery just for a joke.

This was something different.

I breathed in once, twice, and stepped wide around the bed of my truck.

The passenger door was open.

There was a pale lower leg extending from it, keeping contact with the driveway. A bare foot, the veins in it pulsing gray.

Jeanie Silber.

Locked doors don't matter to the dead.

I stared and stared at that leg. It was moving slightly. She was in the truck, looking for something. Not on the seat, where the pots and pans were, but the . . . floorboard?

Then, as smooth as oil, that leg pulled itself up into the truck.

I looked up to the back glass, fully expected her face to be pressed there, watching me.

Nothing.

How could there even be room in there for her, with the seat taken up by the pots and pans?

I opened my mouth, was maybe going to say something, I guess—I can't imagine what—but was interrupted by her pale right hand reaching delicately down out of the cab, past the rocker panel.

Her fingers were spread, the pad of each finger delicately coming into contact with the packed dirt of the driveway. Like she was relishing it. Like she was putting on a show.

But she didn't know I was there, I don't think.

Then, quick as a cat, the rest of her poured out of the truck.

It left her on all fours.

At which point she did see me.

Her lips peeled back from her teeth and she hissed.

I stumbled back, sure she was coming for me, but then she stood instead. Into the girl I'd sort of known.

What I keyed on, what I couldn't help noticing, it wasn't her oily hair, her drawn cheeks, her hipbones and ribs nearly pushing through her gown. It was her left hand.

It was balled into a fist.

She was holding something.

I looked from her hand up to her face. There was a line of fluid starting to descend from a corner of her mouth—my first thought was it was all the spit we'd rubbed into the dashboard—and then the porch light clicked on all at once.

I turned to tell Kay no, no, turn it off, and when I jerked my eyes back to the truck, Jeanie was gone.

Still I didn't tell Kay.

As far as she knew, she'd caught me trying to sneak a present in for her.

But, when I reached into the truck to pull the box of pots and pans to me, I did it slow enough to case the cab of the truck. From my twenty-minute drive into the dealership, and from it just being my truck, I knew every speck of it, every molecule.

For two weeks, at that point, I'd been keeping an eye on that broken blue rubber band from under the dog collar display in Haverly, that I'd left in the passenger side floorboard. I'm generally pretty neat about my truck, will pinch up fluff from the carpet, brush lint from the seat covers. This rubber band, it was an anomaly over there under the glove compartment.

I'd been telling myself I could throw it away any time I wanted. Just, I didn't want to, quite yet.

Had I have thrown it out, then none of the rest would have happened, I don't think. Had I left it in a trash can at the dealership, or just let it go out the window, or even returned it to the IGA, then Jeanie never would have had to come to my house for it.

It was just a rubber band, though.

How could I have known?

It was what had been clenched in her left fist. It was what I saw missing, when I leaned down to hug Kay's pots and pans to my chest, haul them inside.

When I worked them down to my thigh, too, to lock the passenger door before closing it, I had to note that the passenger door was already locked. That it was still locked.

The next morning, Kay inaugurated the pots and pans with breakfast, and, maybe I expected the eggs to carry some bitter tinge from having been close to the dead, but they didn't. Everything was good. Everything was great, even. Normal.

Until I went out to walk the fence. It was kind of my Sunday ritual in lieu of church, I guess.

Because we're just down from the lake, all the high schoolers out popping coyotes, they tend to leave their beer cans in my ditch. I don't fault them for it. I was just the same at their age. I used to think a beer can fading in the grass through the years made the world feel lived in. Really, I was just leaving those cans to show signs of my passage, I suppose. To prove I'd been there. To pretend, at least to myself, that I mattered, that I was leaving a mark.

My Sunday ritual was to walk out to the road in as straight a line as I could, because a straight line is the most efficient line. It's not that I'm compulsive about wasted steps, but, since Kay had us both wearing those watch things that counted our activity through the day, I'd become aware of my walking in a new way.

There were only fourteen cans, from at most two cases—two

different brands. A light Saturday night. Good for the coyotes.

The way I could tell if I'd walked straight or not, it was that, coming from the road, the winter wheat I'd always run there just out of habit—I didn't hire anybody to come in with their combine, just let it seed out—it would show where my feet had parted it, coming through. From the house it was invisible, because of the way the stalks bent, with the wind. But, from the road, my path would be a line of shadow that would last for a day or two, like when you rub suede the wrong way.

My path was arrow straight.

Jeanie's wasn't.

I stood there at the fence for probably five minutes.

At the house, Kay was hanging her new copper pots and pans this way, then that way. By my leg in a plastic bag were fourteen beer cans, to pour into the recycling bin in the garage. There cutting through the wheat was one trail, going home, and another, leading off somewhere else.

I followed Jeanie Silber.

You can tell where the dead have passed.

I didn't want to have to know this, but I do.

I don't think they're solid, not in the way we are, but there's something there that—it interacts at some level with the world.

Jeanie's ghost legs had parted the wheat the same as mine had, but the wheat stopped where the trees started, and the trees are thick enough that there's only leaf litter under them. The loam was mucky enough in low spots that there could have been a footprint, but I don't think Jeanie really weighed anything. Not in a way that can press a shape into mud, anyway.

But there were kind of shadows on the trees. That's the only thing I know to call where her hands had touched, as she passed through. In the movies, when an elf girl is running through the woods, she's always stopping to lean on this tree, look back, to lean on that tree, look ahead.

That's what Jeanie was doing.

Not every tree had a smudge of shadow. But when I found one, I could stand there, take a bearing, study all around me enough until I fixed on another point of darkness.

A couple hundred yards into the trees, even though I'd been back here setting blinds and chasing dogs for fifteen years, I started dropping my shiny beer cans behind me, to mark my path. Then I'd walk ahead a bit and look back, make sure the can was still there.

In some of those stories about elf women, they're leading men out deeper and deeper. For their own reasons. I know this, but I kept following her all the same.

I'd just dropped my twelfth can, meaning I was maybe a half-mile gone, was going to hit the lake soon, when I saw a tree with one whole side smudged with shadow.

I circled it. Looked all around.

And then I looked up.

Jeanie Silber wasn't up there like a cat, waiting to spring on me. But she had been up there. I could tell she'd crawled up on the north side. The bark was darker there.

I sat one silvery can on the east side of the tree, one on the west, like performing my own ritual, and then I hauled myself up on the thickest limb.

Like most of the trees this close to the lake, this one had a kind of crotch right up where the trunk split into all its big limbs. As a kid, we'd sometimes find coachwhips coiled up there. Always just one snake, never a bunch of them. One time I'd found a rat nest in that kind-of hollow, sunless space, and came back to it with a pump-jug of kerosene, flushed the rats out. They'd flowed down the tree screaming.

Usually it was just rotting leaves and such, though. Maybe a dead bird.

That's what this tree was holding: nothing much.

Not until I pulled myself all the way up, set my foot there to climb higher.

My boot crunched in, through the sodden twigs, the rotting leaves.

There was a cavity there, of sorts. It belched up a stench that made me cover my nose with the back of my wrist.

I stood there for a long minute, my foot pushed down into that space.

What I was waiting for was Jeanie, roused like I'd once roused those rats. Maybe this was where she slept. Maybe this was where she'd been living ever since the wreck.

It made as much sense as anything.

She wasn't there. But she had left something: the blue rubber band. It was down there in the muck, along with a silver tack, a sharp little white tooth, a piece of fabric, and maybe a rock. I couldn't tell if the rock was just there already, or if it was part of her collection.

I knew better than to touch them.

This was for the dead, not for the living.

I lowered myself slowly from the tree, stood there by the trunk breathing hard.

As much and as hard as I cased the woods around me, there were no more shadowy handprints leading anywhere.

My guess was that, in order to carry the corporeal thing the rubber band was, Jeanie had to be corporeal herself, for as long as that walk took. Afterward, though, after she'd delivered her cargo, she could just step into that same space she had when she left the grocery store, the same place she'd gone in an instant, when Kay turned the porch light on.

I don't know the rules of the dead. Don't let me tell you otherwise.

But I did, now, know that they like to collect cast-off nothings, and secret them away in hidey-holes.

I also knew I wasn't supposed to know this. I wasn't supposed to have found this hidey-hole. Because I was alive.

I walked away without looking back, and didn't even need the beer cans to find my way home.

Until the week before Christmas, I was able to pretend that Thanksgiving and Jeanie Silber had never happened. Sales were in a slump, but that's the way it always is in December. Come January, I'd be standing in the showroom and getting to decide which couple out in the lot I wanted to carry hot chocolate to, as hello.

The only real difference in me, I think, was that I had become the neat freak around the offices. Which, I *say* "offices," but we're really all in cubicles, so we can stand up and ask this or that to whoever happens to be available. It's supposed to make the buyer feel like we're all a family. They don't know that the questions we ask each other are all part of a script, some standard call and response, but that's neither here nor there. What matters about the cubicle situation is that I was always the one pinching my slacks up a bit, to squat down, pick up this stray paper clip, that staple. Whatever trash there was.

I didn't want to round a cubicle wall, see Jeanie pinching the staple up from the threads of the carpet.

I wondered if the junk she was compelled to collect was stuff that had happened to be on the dash she'd lost her life on. A rubber band. A tack. A random pebble. I wondered if it was like that for all of us, if we're all compelled to spend eternity chasing down whatever arbitrary detritus that's with us at the moment we go. I wondered what would happen if she ever collected it all. I wondered and wondered and wondered, and I left the doors on my truck unlocked, most nights, and once, ferrying a garden hose to Kay's parents, I'd even walked the aisles of the IGA in Haverly again. The girl with pierced lips wasn't there, and the cardboard dog collar display had been retired, and the floors were fresh-waxed, not a speck to pick up, throw away.

I left feeling better.

One night, even, in a partial unburdening, I asked Kay if her high school had heard about our big car wreck over here, prom night. It serioused Kay down, kind of made her wince. She looked up and to the left, which is where the past is located, I guess.

"We did a candle thing," she said, moving green beans around on her plate. "A vigil, I mean."

"We never knew," I told her.

She laughed, stabbed a green bean, said, "Were we supposed to call over, say y'all should send someone over, to see how much we care?"

I smiled too.

She was right, as usual. You do a thing because it's right, not because you want it to be acknowledged as right.

Not that the dead care much about candles, I don't think.

I wondered if what Jeanie was doing was trying to arrange her little bits of junk so as to make a doorway or a path Clint could come back through, or on.

Why was she in that aisle, and not him?

Or, was he just in some other aisle, in some other little town around here? Did he have his own hidey-hole—a coffee can left to rust out in the tall grass, a hubcap leaned up against a fence?

You can think your whole life on what the dead do, and why they do it, and not get any closer to figuring it out.

Until I saw Jeanie, I don't guess I ever even considered them. My older sister used to have a story about a ghost she'd seen, but she had stories about everything, if telling them meant you'd sit there and listen to her.

In the movies and on television, the dead are usually hanging around for justice, or to tell some secret.

Not Jeanie.

She just wanted the rubber bands we were always losing track of. She wanted to hold them close and scurry away, put them in their perfect place. Like a child, I guess. A child with a rock they find by the lake, how they'll designate that rock special, perfect, a forever rock, and then you have to put it up in the windowsill until they grow up, forget about it.

Maybe that's the dead. Maybe they're like children. Maybe they're starting over.

I wish that for Jeanie.

It's a cliché, but she really did have her whole life in front of her, that prom night. It wasn't fair she was in that car after the last dance, meeting that tractor at seventy miles per hour. But at least it had been a good prom for her. At graduation, when the photograph of her and Clint Berkot went up onscreen, her in her shiny purple dress, him in his big brother's suit jacket, there hadn't been a dry eye in the auditorium. Including me.

In a way, it was like Jeanie and Clint could have been any one of us. Like they'd died instead of all of us.

Maybe when Clint's Grand Prix had drifted over into the ditch, when the grass had started hissing against the undercarriage, maybe Jeanie had reached across to hold his hand on the gearshift, and maybe she'd smiled at the thrill of it all, and maybe she'd gone out like that—happy, full, ready for life.

I hoped so.

You'll notice that's in the past tense, there.

That's because this isn't over.

Two days before Christmas, Kay's mother fell and broke her hip. It was terrible, but it could have been worse. That's what we tell ourselves, right, so as not to call down any more bad luck? We play like we're grateful for the bad luck we've already had. Like not complaining can be the end of it.

Kay's father had been right there in the living room when it happened, anyway, and the ambulance had been there minutes later, and it was all going as well as it could. Kay and I had never had kids, just flocks of nieces and nephews, so, while we tried to make Christmas up into something special, it was really just going to be a day off from work, when we'd let ourselves pour a couple fingers of this or that into our morning coffee.

I wasn't even thinking of Jeanie Silber after Kay left for the hospital again, I mean.

Not until I noticed, way down at the end of the stretch of road I could see, a dull yellow tractor parked on that steep slope like it was a lost cow, trying to clamber back up onto the blacktop. It wasn't pulling a shredder—cutting the dead grass in the heart of winter didn't make much sense—had probably been dropped off there to dig for a power line or a utility pole, but still, it was the same color as the one Jeanie and Clint had rammed into at seventy, nineteen years ago.

I stood on the porch and drank my coffee and made a mental note to call in when the county offices were open again, see if any of our services were going to be interrupted before the new year.

And then I heard it: a car's radials, whining in the distance. Coming this way, and fast.

I shook my head no, that this was nothing, that I was being stupid, but, stupid or not, I dropped my coffee, was running in my slippers down the drive, waving my arms.

I didn't make it even close to in time.

It didn't matter.

The car was a Buick, light blue. It slipped past, unaware of the fate I'd been so sure of.

I stood there, and fell to my knees when the Buick was gone. In thanks.

I wasn't crying, I'm not sure my eyes really know how to anymore, but there was a choking sob or something welling up in my throat.

I hadn't known Jeanie Silber, no.

But she had died, instead of any of the rest of us.

And then—and then I realized: If that was true, if one or two of the graduating class had been meant to die that prom night, just to keep the statistics accurate or the books balanced or whatever, then . . . then if she was coming back, that meant it was one of our turn to step behind the veil in her place, right?

I looked to the woods. I hadn't been in them since I'd followed her.

Was that why she'd shown herself to me in the IGA? Was that why she'd left those dark marks on the trees, for me to follow?

Back in the house, I poured four fingers scotch into a different coffee cup. A whole hand. A whole trembling, unsteady hand.

If Kay had only been there to steady me, right?

I would have spilled it all to her, then. But she was in Haverly, at her mother's bedside, being the obedient daughter.

I sat at the kitchen table breathing hard, as if I'd been cutting wood or carrying furniture. I was just thinking. And thinking.

And finally I had to see.

I rinsed my cup in the sink, left it on the drying rack. The idea was that, if I didn't return, then Kay wouldn't have to clean up any mess I'd left.

I booted up, collected my jacket, forged out into the trees.

It doesn't snow around here generally, so the beer cans I hadn't bothered to pick up, they were still there, showing me the way. I didn't collect them this time either, which I translated in my head to hope: I was going to need to find my way out again, wasn't I?

Yes, yes, I was.

This was just me being stupid, me being weak, me letting my thoughts get the better of me. I'd been too alone the last couple days. Or maybe—maybe Kay's shiny new pots and pans, maybe the copper wasn't copper, but something insidious, poisoning us, making us see things, think things.

I didn't want Jeanie Silber to be real, I mean.

The twelve shiny cans delivered me to the tree she'd been hiding her treasures in.

From a distance, I could see it was still alive.

Good, good.

From closer, I could see something else.

It was covered in something, now.

I slowed my walk, circled a bit to make my approach even slower.

Burls.

The trunk was knotted with burls, those knotty, tumorous outgrowths I knew were kind of like layer on layer of impacted buds. Like cancer.

I leaned over without telling myself to, splashed my scotch and coffee onto the ground. At the end I was coughing, and stringing the thin strands of vomit away with my fingers. But it was stretchy, wouldn't let go. I was getting tangled in my own stomach contents.

I ran, I don't know how long.

I wasn't following the pathway of beer cans.

A single burl, it takes years and years to happen.

A whole trunk of burls, it meant the tree was diseased, didn't it?

From what?

From a rubber band, and a tooth, and that other little junk?

Was that what was Jeanie was doing? Not collecting stuff she found interesting, but stuff that was necessary for this, like a recipe?

She needed just the right stuff.

Finally I fell over a fallen tree, cut my hand on a broken beer bottle, and then just lay there, holding myself.

I still wasn't crying.

I didn't know what I was doing.

The next day, the day after Christmas, fortified with a night of rational thinking, I returned to what I was calling the Black Tree.

I had a two-bit ax.

If a dead girl wanted this sick tree to bloom in the spring, let its rotten pollen drift up into the air, then it had to be my duty to stop that from happening, I told myself. I was the one who'd delivered that last vital ingredient, right? That made this my problem.

I'd brought a flask of vodka, to keep my mind from wandering.

I didn't give myself time to talk myself out of it, just walked right up to the tree, hauled the ax back like you do, and slashed it forward, into the most prominent burl. It's not how you angle to cut a tree down, I realized the moment the bit cut into the wood. It's the way you hit something you want to kill.

The ax stuck. I worked it free, struck again.

Of course the wood of the burl was dense, thick, hard. I've seen woodworkers go far out of their way to collect burls off fallen trees, to make bowls and newels from. Something about the swirly grain in there, how it polishes up.

I'd also heard tell a burl was like what an oyster does with a speck of dust: licks it into a pearl.

Hunting, every missed shot, you can imagine it slapping into a young tree, and that sapling caring for that slug of lead, layering it in knot after knot of its best, richest wood.

Would I find a blue rubber band at the center of this biggest burl?

I slashed again, using all of my weight, and the tree splashed back at me, so I had to close my eyes.

Not sap, not water, but not quite blood either. It was too thick, too dark.

Poison.

I spit, coughed, wiped furiously at my face, and then, mad now—madder—I swung and swung and swung, until I carved into the heart of this tumor.

It was meaty, and pale.

This angered me even more, a tree keeping something wrong like that inside itself.

I probed it with the head of my ax and the viscous, gutlike meat, it writhed around the metal.

"Don't like that, huh?" I said, and smiled.

This wasn't work for an ax anymore.

I took up the flask, poured it onto the burls, then, before the pungent alcohol could evaporate, I struck a match, held it to the spill until the fire flashed awake.

Trees don't burn as easy as we think, but this one did.

It went up like tissue.

I backed up, watched for hours, until it creaked, splitting down the middle, halving itself two directions at once.

When the flames threatened the underbrush, the other trees, I stomped them out. And then I waded into the smoke, chopped at the burls on the tree until they collapsed into the embers.

It was nighttime by now, but, the same as I'd brought matches and a flask, I'd also brought a flashlight.

I nodded a final good-bye to the tree and started back, using the light to pick out the shine of the cans. A few trees back from the one I'd killed, there was a darker smudge on a pale trunk, as if someone had been leaning there, watching.

I raised my arm, wiped it off with my sleeve.

I know now I should have been more suspicious.

Walking out of the woods that night, I'd assumed the beer cans were where I'd left them. That I was walking back out into the same world I'd left.

Jeanie Silber had been out there with me, though.

She very well could have rearranged the cans, led me out into a completely different place. One that looks just the same on the surface.

That's what I have to assume happened.

There's no other explanation for . . . for what I've become.

A dutiful husband is what I appear to be. A respectable landowner. A good enough son-in-law.

None of those are me anymore.

What Jeanie Silber came back for, I think, it was to pull off my mask, show me my true self, the one I've kept coiled up inside for my whole life, I guess. The dead know more about life than the living. And they want to show it to you. They want to make you see.

I still contend it was happenstance that I was the one to see her in the IGA that Thursday, though. That, really, every person there on a last-minute errand might have seen her the same as I did. Even the girl with the piercings. But it was me who recognized her. Who knew she didn't belong. Not anymore.

Me either.

The poison or whatever that splashed on my face from the tree, it washed off easy enough, and the smoke I inhaled from its tumors didn't leave me coughing up blood or seeing things that weren't there, but the act, the fact of me messing up whatever Jeanie was doing out there in the woods where nobody was watching, that clung to me. At least as far as she was concerned.

She came back, yes.

That's what the dead do.

Kay too. She crunched into the driveway just before the year was over, never knew to ask if anything dark and momentous had happened out in the trees while she was gone. She had news about her mother, though. A blood clot had shown up in her leg, so it was looking like she still had two or three more weeks in the hospital. Meaning Kay was going to be burning up the road between Milford and Haverly.

It was about to be the busy season for me at the dealership anyway, so I just shrugged that that was too bad. Inside, though, the new me felt relief, I think. Relief at the bad news.

I was a different person.

And then, like I'd probably been expecting—like I was due—I woke one morning to find a seed head under my back, scratching at me.

When you live in a field of wheat you don't harvest, the seeds can find their way into most every place. Even the bed. This was a whole seed head, though. I sat on the edge of the bed and studied the stalk.

It wasn't torn. The sever point was flat and even, anyway.

What I saw without meaning to, it was a thin, pale girl lowering her mouth over that stalk, only biting down when the sharp seed points scratched the back of her throat.

Then she spit it down into her hand.

At the same time, it could have caught on my shirt, on my sleeve, and gotten into bed with me that way.

I didn't tell Kay, just deposited it into my nightstand drawer.

Three days later I woke thinking of paperwork from my last two sales.

On my chest was a half-rusted washer.

I flinched back, flicked it away, pushed up into the headboard.

"What?" Kay asked sleepily.

"Bug," I said, even though it was winter, and then, after she was gone to Haverly again, I pored over the carpet until I found that washer.

It was happening.

I shook my head no, no, that it wasn't fair. But then neither had it been fair for Jeanie, that tractor waiting in the ditch for her.

The very next morning, I found a little oval sticker stuck to the inside of my forearm when I woke. Like you peel off a banana.

Neither me nor Kay can tolerate bananas.

I stood in the shower until all the hot water was gone, and then I stepped out with resolve, walked naked to my nightstand drawer.

So far there was only the sticker, the washer, the seed head.

Had I missed something else?

I went to the utility room, dug though the lint trap—we'd washed the bed linens just a few days ago—and found the most damning ingredient of all: a dime. Probably the same one I'd fake-fumbled onto the floor of the IGA, in order to have an excuse to dig under the dog collar display.

I leaned over the dryer and I tried to cry, couldn't find any fluid or heat in my eyes at all.

I wouldn't grow a burl, I knew—a man isn't a tree—but maybe I'd get a . . . what had my dad called it? A bezoar. Those calcifications or whatever an animal can get in its stomach, that are also prized by people. Not for woodcutting, but for remedies.

A bezoar, a growth, a tumor, it didn't matter what it was called.

All because I'd messed up whatever Jeanie was doing.

All because I'd done my duty.

It wasn't fair.

I slammed the side of my fist into the top of the dryer until it dented in, and then I walked away.

Two hours later, dressed in my work clothes—slacks, a golf shirt—I stepped into the doorway of Kay's mom's hospital room in Haverly. The whole way over, there'd been chance after chance to ram my truck into this pole, into that abutment. There'd even been a tractor in the ditch, calling my name.

I hadn't answered.

I wasn't that person anymore.

I wanted to live.

"Mama Jenk," I said to Kay's mother, and she reached her hand out to me palm-down, and I took it, hugged her lightly, as you do the infirm, and then Kay was going on about what a surprise this had been, and her father was back with three lunches, which they insisted we split four ways, and all was well.

Close enough.

On the far side of Kay's mother, nestled between the sheets and her frail, blood-clotted self, there was now a seedhead, a washer, a penny, and a little sticker with tiny meaningless words on it.

It was a recipe, for whatever the next round of tests were

going to find in her, since her bad luck of a fall. Whatever it wouldn't be a surprise for someone of her age to have.

I sighed to have the awful, necessary deed done, to be rid of the burden—I'd carried the ingredients here in a cigar box wrapped in a plastic bag—and then I leaned back, to stand among the living.

Except.

Kay, the good daughter, vigilant as ever, was already at the other side of her mother's bed.

"What is—?" she said, and then grubbed her hand into the covers, came out with, I'm certain, everything I'd left. Every single last thing.

She shoved it into the chest pocket of her blouse.

*Breast cancer, then,* I said to myself, and looked away, out the window, to the idea of Jeanie Silber standing in the tall yellow grass at the side of the road, Clint Berkot pulling his Grand Prix up alongside her.

She steps in and down, yes, but not before looking back to me to smile and wave.

The dead don't do anything randomly, do they?

The whole time since Thanksgiving, she'd been capering me to this hospital room, this moment.

I lift my hand to tell her bye but Kay crinkles her nose in confusion, thinks I'm waving to her, from point-blank range.

And I guess, sort of, I am.

# The Other Woman

## *Alice Hoffman*

She came to me on the first of May, on the anniversary of the occurrence. This often happens. People have strong regrets at such times. They are reminded by the weather or by a tree in bloom. We live in the same town, although I'm in the outskirts, near the cemetery. Everyone knows where. They know what I do. There were flowering azaleas on my lawn, so perhaps she didn't notice the brambles or the weeds. I was at the window when she pulled up. I was there before my dog began to bark. Frankly, I'd been expecting her. I was surprised it had taken a full year for her to come to me, but people have their own timetables.

She wore a blue spring coat and a plaid dress and black pumps. Her hair was dark and plain and I could tell she had been crying even though she was wearing sunglasses. Her face was puffy. I didn't listen to gossip, but in a town as small as ours it would have been impossible not to know, plus it was in the newspaper. Not just the *Monitor*, but the *Boston Globe* as well. It was an event. A personal catastrophe, the kind people talk about long after it's over.

When I invited her in, she hesitated. I could tell she didn't completely believe in what I did, and had come here as a last attempt, even if she didn't trust me. Her friends had likely pulled her aside and suggested she call me. It was a town full of old houses, and old houses had past lives. Occasionally those lives continued, even when the new occupants wanted them gone. They had to be helped along. I'd learned the cleansing method from my grandmother when I was a child. I went house to house with her until I was ten, when my mother put a stop to it. Still, I remembered. It's not something you forget.

I'd made tea to ease the conversation, which can be difficult at the beginning, but she didn't touch hers. I understood why. Her hands were shaking. She was rattled, I could see that. But then, I'd seen it before. People driven to the brink by something they couldn't quite see or believe, and yet it was ruining their lives. She said she had tried everything to rid herself of the ghost. Sage, salt, holy water, closed windows, white candles. What could I do for her that she hadn't already done herself? My method was Russian, I explained, and involved catching the unwelcome spirit in a jar. I couldn't tell her more, it was a family secret, but I led her to my pantry to show her what I kept on the shelves. I had thirty jars filled with light; some were blue, others green, one looked like a splotch of ink.

"What do you do with them?" she asked. She had a little girl's voice, which was disconcerting, considering what she'd done.

"That's my business," I said. Surely her friends had told her I was prickly and had a mind of my own.

She wrote me a check for a thousand dollars. I knew she had married into money, which is the reason I raised my usual price. Truthfully, I tend not to charge at all, especially in desperate situations. After she handed over the check, I felt a draft of cold air. Then I saw something on the floor that interested me. There, beside my client's purse, was a photograph of the apple tree where the woman in question had hanged herself. My client seemed quite oblivious. That's when I knew. I was hearing both sides of the story.

I went out on Sunday, the day her husband played golf. She didn't want him to know, which I understood. She was the sort of woman who always acted as if everything was in place, even when it wasn't. I could tell that from her shoes. Highly polished. New heels. As if she hadn't a care in the world.

I parked on the street, carrying my grandmother's bag. The jars I'd brought clanked against each other, sounding like bells. I stopped to observe the tree where it had happened. It was in bloom, white as a cloud. I had read that the previous tenant had dragged the ladder from the garage in order to climb up. When I walked up the driveway white flowers floated down. My client was waiting for me on the porch, wearing a sweater even though the day was fine. Ghosts do that, they drop the temperature, and when I walked inside I felt the chill in the air.

All the furniture was different now, my client told me. They'd donated everything that had been here before. They'd even changed the yard, pulling up the old brick patio and replacing it with stone. I said I had to walk through the house on my own to see what the rooms revealed. She nodded and said of course, but she looked nervous. She blurted out that she hadn't wanted to live here, but her husband had said it wouldn't be cost effective to move. No one wanted to buy a house where someone had hung herself. Now they were stuck. When I set my bag down, I noticed that the knives were set out in a row on the countertop.

"She did that this morning," my client said. "She does it every day."

I started with the living room. It had been painted red, which some people believe is a cure for a haunting, though I've never found it to be true. I noticed a book open on the coffee table. A book of poems written by Ralph Waldo Emerson, who had lived less than a mile away.

*Give all to love, obey your heart.*

My client had been the previous occupant's friend. After her husband walked out, my client had spent night after night comforting her dear friend, before the truth came out. It was a love letter that gave it away. Kept in his drawer. Some people don't understand the power of the written word. It surfaces when you least expect it to. As I crossed the room I saw marks on the curtains, like the claw marks of a cat, though none was in residence. I could see the tree from this window, right in the middle of the lawn.

I took the stairs. I'd been told that the runner had been replaced, but there were the previous tenant's wet footsteps, as if she had just come in from walking in the wet grass. The tub in the upstairs bathroom was full. My client had told me she had to drain it every morning. I went to the bedroom and stood on the threshold. It was very cold here. There was ice on the ceiling and on the walls. My grandmother once told me we are not the only ones who have regrets, whose hands shake, who weep over our mistakes. Ghosts have regrets too. They wish they'd stayed home on the morning of their death, that they hadn't married the wrong man, that they'd left the ladder in the garage and packed a suitcase instead. They wished they'd said good-bye to love and hello to the bright, brilliant world.

It was quiet inside the bedroom. All of the dresser drawers had been pulled open. I'd been told they refused to stay closed.

I had my bag with me, which I set down, then I lay upon the bed. This is the reason I can't have clients follow me around. To get to the heart of the matter, I have to do things that can seem strange, even inappropriate. I got under the blanket. I could tell that the right side had been her side. My client said her perfume was on the pillow no matter how often the linens were changed. Through the window I could see a wedge of blue sky and the top boughs of the apple tree. That was when I started to cry. I felt overwhelmed by emotion, even though I'm usually very clearheaded. I'd seen it happen to my grandmother a few times. She'd have to sit down, and I'd bring her a drink of cold water. It would take her a while to collect herself, but she finally would.

I went downstairs and informed my client I'd have to tear up her check. I couldn't help her.

"Then we're selling the house," she said. "I don't care if we take a loss."

She didn't bother to see me out and there was no need to say good-bye. We hardly knew each other, after all. I went down the driveway and gazed up at the falling white petals. It was a pretty property, and sooner or later someone would buy it; they'd likely get a good price, not that it would do my ex-client any good. People who think ghosts can't travel are mistaken. They stay close to whatever or whomever matters most, a place or a person. They can walk for miles, fit in the trunk of your car, fold themselves into a suitcase. I kept that information to myself, however. She'd find out soon enough.

# The Loneliness of Not Being Haunted

*Bracken MacLeod*

**1.**

The antiques dealer had assured June that the object was an authentic railroad watch—named so because it was accurate enough for railroad time service. But that's not why she'd wanted it. Mr. Jackson also insisted that the timepiece had been in the possession of the previous owner when he died. Not just owned by him, but beloved and held close *at the moment* he passed away. "It was his great-grandfather's watch," Mr. Jackson told her as he pushed the box across the counter, closer to her. The object had been a dying man's connection to a personal history. Then, his children took it from his hands and sold it. Its personal worth as dead as its third generation of owner. She bought the watch and hurried home. She unwrapped it at the dinner table and began to admire its detail, turning it over, focusing on the scrollwork around the engraved backplate instead of the liver spots and wrinkles on the backs of her hands. The pocket watch was older than she was, but it existed in a slower state of entropy. The timepiece was already over a hundred years old, and, if cared for, would persist for a hundred more, where she would be "lucky" to see a century pass. It wouldn't be long after that failed milestone that there would be nothing left of her but bones. And after another hundred years, maybe nothing at all—not even a memory.

Young people think it's fortunate to live a long life, but June knew differently. Time is not kind to transient beings. It takes breath and weakens bone. And if you're "lucky," you'll live for years with the memory of all your lost loves. Everyone you have ever loved will eventually die. And if you live a long time, their absence will never leave you, like the ghost on a wall where a painting used to hang.

She turned the watch over again and looked at the face. Black lacquer hands stood still in a chevron over a bright white face, ringed by bold numbers. In a smaller circle where the numeral 6 should have been, the second hand stood still, pointing at a hash mark between 40 and 45. She considered winding the device to see it come alive, but decided she didn't want to observe the hands moving or even hear it tick. Its stillness was better. For it, time remained quietened at a quarter to noon. Or midnight.

And now it was hers. She clasped her hands together over it. It felt nice in her palms. Heavy and cool and solid all the way through—a corporeal thing. A thing with weight. But that was it—only weight, nothing else. At her prime, in her forties, when she felt most alive, most rapacious, and ready to kick down doors, she'd had weight. Height, too. But, that was half a lifetime ago and the years had made her light and frail. Worst of all, though, they'd left her alone.

Throughout her life, she'd had lovers and friends, but age, disease, and misfortune had taken every one. Taken her lover and their daughter on the very same night that had broken her and left her bedridden for months. That had been the start of her decline. She who was once strong, withered in the wake of that loss. She who had loved, was left alone. And eventually her friends, one by one, faded away as well. Some moved, some died, others just disappeared. She'd heard on the radio that the kids call it "ghosting," when people just gave up on you and vanished.

She had gone on a ghost tour once with a friend. Kat—short for Katherine—stood beside her in the thick, humid afternoon while the guide told them about the spirits haunting the trees at the edge of the plantation property. As he told the story, her friend gasped and stepped back, holding a hand over her mouth. The guide had smiled and said, "Sometimes, she appears to people from behind the trees." Kat pulled her hand away from her face, mouth agape and asked, "Was she blond?" The man nodded and smiled. The crowd gathered around oohed and aahed. Some looked at her like she was a plant—someone there to sell the story, not actually a tourist. But Kat was a tourist. June felt a stab at her center. Kat didn't even believe in ghosts. *She* was the one who wanted to believe; *she* was the one who needed them. She didn't see anything but trees, a plantation house, and a group of people all wishing they'd seen what Kat said she had.

Later, over drinks at the rotating bar in the Hotel Monteleone, Kat rationalized her experience as a suggestibility inspired by the heat and morning cocktails, but June knew her friend was still moved. The ghost of a long-dead woman stepped up beside her, smiled and then faded away as if she'd never been there at all. That was how Kat described it, anyway. June hadn't seen anything but Kat jump back and act shocked. Her friend wasn't the type to fake it. She was sincere to a fault and didn't believe in ghosts. Not until that trip, anyway.

Kat was killed in 2001.

June still had Kat's glasses. The same pair, through which

she saw the spirit in the trees, sat on the table in front of her. But at that moment she was focused on the watch.

Though her hands always felt cold, the watch gradually warmed between her palms until only its weight assured her it was still there. She wanted to reach into it and find the spirit of the man who'd died with it in his hands. She wanted the connection to it that he'd had and, through it, the connection to him. She wanted his hands to close around hers and hold it with her.

June sighed and spread her palms. It was just an object. Though it would move and tick if she wound it, there was nothing in it that lived. Nothing special. It was just another thing in a lonely place full of silent things.

The distant sound of someone laughing outside drifted up through her window from four flights below, and the neighbor's footsteps above creaked and thumped as he paced from one end of his apartment to the other and back. A car horn honked and a man yelled and tires screeched abruptly as the driver jammed the gas and a bus stopped, its hydraulics hissing as it "knelt" to release riders and accept more and the city kept on all around her.

She set the watch on the small ritual table, between Kat's glasses and a rubber ducky that had been in the bathtub with a toddler when she drowned. June lit a tall candle and placed it in the center of the star engraved in the top of the table, next to a wedding ring and a pair of dog tags, and waited. Nothing changed. Her room was a muted mélange of city noise boxing in the stillness of her apartment. After a while, she got up and set about the task of making herself dinner. The aroma of her meal soon overtook the scents of matchstick sulfur and candle wax.

She sat at the dinner table by the window and ate, looking out into the street at the people rushing to get from one place to another. Not one of them looked up at her. They only saw one another, and even then, most of them pretended not to. It was the way you survived in a city. By creating a personal illusion of isolation in a press of forced intimacy.

After dinner, she washed her dish and set it on the drying towel next to the sink. There was no point in wiping it dry and putting it away in the cupboard. She'd have breakfast on the same plate in the morning. And lunch. And then dinner again. One plate. One seat. No waiting.

She turned off the lights and headed for bed. Along the way, she blew out the candle. Nothing had been attracted to it or the watch. Not tonight. She'd try again tomorrow.

**2.**

The man on the other end of the line stammered as he told June that something had come into the shop she might be . . . interested in. She asked why he was calling instead of Mr. Jackson. "He usually lets me know himself when he has something new." She glanced at her table. At the things there. The new addition was nice enough, she guessed. Though, the watch would look better in a dome on the mantle than in the middle of the star.

"This item isn't really his style. But I think it might be yours."

June wasn't feeling up for a trip out of the apartment, but the man wouldn't agree to tell her over the telephone what it was he found. He kept insisting it'd be better if she came in to the shop to see it in person. And it had to be today. Mr. Jackson wasn't ever coy or insistent like that. When he called, he told her what he'd set aside, according to her standing request, and asked when she would be able to drop by. June tried not to leave anything waiting too long, but there was never any urgency in their transactions. Whenever she could find time to get to his shop was soon enough.

The man on the phone assured her it would be worth her time, saying this wasn't a thing she was likely to ever find again. Not like the watch or the fountain pen or any of the other things that had made their way onto the table before being replaced by another once-loved object. This was unique, and available today only. She said she'd try to make it in before lunch. He seemed satisfied and said he looked forward to seeing her, though there was something in his voice that seemed off when he said it. Like it was a lie. Mr. Jackson was always very kind to her. Every time she visited his shop he asked how she was doing and made pleasant small talk. More importantly, he seemed to take her odd interest seriously. Not everyone did. She imagined some people talked behind her back. Called her morbid. She didn't think Mr. Jackson did. If he did, he hid it well.

June collected her things, put on a sun hat, and blew out the candle before stepping into the hall. She could hear her neighbors behind their apartment doors—televisions and children and yapping dogs. But no one peeked out when she pulled her door shut. It clicked too quietly for any of them to hear over their own lives, and when she turned her key, the dead bolt slid into place with a soft scraping like a far away librarian with a finger to her lips. "Shh," it said to her.

Outside, the morning was hot and humid and June could tell it was only going to get worse. The air had that thick feel like slight smothering. She immediately wanted to go back inside, ride the elevator up home, and spend the rest of the day next to her window air conditioner, listening to records and reading. She'd light a candle. But she wanted to see what it was the man who worked for Mr. Jackson had found.

She took a step away from her building. And then another, until she was at the entrance to the subway, and she'd gone far enough that she might as well keep going.

The bell above the door tinkled as June pushed through. Mr. Jackson's employee—she recognized his face, but couldn't remember his name—looked up from the counter and, instead of smiling like his boss usually did when she walked in, waved her toward the far end of the counter. He lifted the barrier and stepped out from behind it gesturing with a pale hand toward the back of the store. There, he opened the storeroom door and held it, waiting for June to go ahead of him. She hesitated for a moment before stepping through. She'd never been invited into the back and she didn't know this man. Sure, she'd *seen* him before, but had never actually spoken to him. And he'd never even nodded at her, let alone spoke. Suddenly, they were doing business. In the back room. *There's nothing to worry about,* she assured herself and walked through the doorway.

The storeroom was small and packed tight. There were antique radios and swords and books and even a stuffed owl up on a high shelf looking down at her as if she were a mouse. She marveled at the noisy clutter of objects, ordinary and otherwise, that Mr. Jackson deemed unfit for the front of his shop. She wondered why he'd buy something he didn't intend to put out. Maybe he had a second shop somewhere else. Maybe he had his own interests, and this was *his* collection.

The man closed the door, propping it slightly ajar with a cast iron Boston terrier doorstop and walked around to the other side of a round table in the center of the room. "It's . . . well, it's not an antique," he said. "It's not . . . But then I remembered your particular . . . interest, and I, well, let me show you."

He turned around and slid a gray, rectangular box out from behind a group of objects concealing it. It was about the size of a toy bed for a baby doll—longer than it was wide or tall. He shoved aside a pile of papers and bric-a-brac cluttered on the table and set the box down. She felt more than a tinge of disappointment at the sight of it; it was plastic and cheap looking. And *this* was why she dealt directly with Mr. Jackson. She'd suffered the sidewalk heat and the stifling subway humidity for something that came in a beige plastic box. The trip back to her apartment would be doubly exhausting, for the frustration of going home empty-handed. She decided then that she would call back later to have a discussion with Mr. Jackson. She didn't appreciate being taken advantage of. There were other places to get what she wanted.

"I don't understand the need for all this cloak and dagger. That doesn't look like anything I'd be interested in. I'm sorry, but you've wasted my time."

"Trust me." He opened the lid and removed another, smaller container from inside, the size of the doll that would sleep in that bed. He set the second box in front of the first. This one was wooden with a pair of brass inlay laurels arcing out from the center of the hinged lid. On the front were two tiny matching handles, though there was no drawer or front hinge on the box that she could see. Her breath seemed harder to draw for a second. She wasn't certain why. The object he removed wasn't that striking. Still, it took her breath away for a second. A feeling about it. Like something had come with it that she couldn't see.

The man pushed it toward her with a finger, immediately pulling his hand back after an inch or so. He stepped away from the table rubbing his hands on his pants and nodded, inviting her to step forward and inspect it.

"What is it?" she asked.

"The seller called it a 'burial cradle.'"

"A *what?*"

"A burial cradle. It's a casket . . . for a miscarriage," he whispered. In her day, no one ever said "miscarriage" with volume. It was always whispered along with the words, "affair" and "barren." He wasn't from her day, though. This man was young. A third her age at most. Still, he whispered it. *Miscarriage.* Too terrible to say aloud.

Her forehead wrinkled and she frowned. She opened her mouth, and hesitated a moment, wanting to address him by name. "As morbid as my request might seem to you, I'm not interested in objects that haven't been—"

He grimaced. "Before you make up your mind, open it."

That breathless feeling returned. She took a tentative step forward and reached for the box to inspect it more closely. When she lifted it, she felt the contents shift away from her. She gripped it tighter, afraid of dropping it, though the impulse to throw it was almost as strong as the urge to hold it close. "What's inside?" she asked, fearful of the answer. He didn't say. He nodded. She opened the box.

Inside was a satiny pink pouch tied with a black ribbon. She reached in with a finger and touched it. Whatever was in the pouch was smooth and hard and curved. Like a cylinder. A bottle, she realized. It was in a jar. She went to untie the bow, but the man coughed loudly and shook his head.

"Are you telling me there's a—"

He held up a finger before she could say "baby." He said, "We're not supposed to have this, you understand. It's . . . illegal for us to sell something like this."

She closed the lid, but kept hold of the box. "Then why are you?"

He looked around the room as if an answer was hiding in the shadows behind a steam trunk or under a mid-century end table. Or as if someone might hear. "Because, I think it's what you're looking for. Do you want it?"

She hesitated. It was awful. This wasn't a thing borne through a lifetime that someone held on to for comfort as their final moments passed. This was . . . different. It wasn't a thing *near* loss. It *was* loss.

She wanted it.

"How much?" she asked. The bell at the front of the store cut off the man's reply before he could quote her a price. His head whipped around to look through the gap in the door and his face went paler. He turned to June and glanced urgently at the emergency exit in the far back of the store room. He was urging her to flee.

She stood her ground. "How much?"

"Geoffrey? Are you back there?" Mr. Jackson called out.

"You've got to go," the man whispered as he lurched toward the door. He stood in the crack and poked his head through. "Hey, Miles! What are you doing here?"

"I came to catch up on a little paperwork. No rest for the

wicked." He laughed. "You feeling all right? Need me to watch the front for a minute?"

The man—Geoffrey—waved his arm at June to go. She shut the box and set it in the larger, plastic container. Putting the thing away felt bad. It tugged at her. She hadn't paid, but she wasn't leaving without it either. She told herself she could return some other time and pretend that she'd picked something else up while Mr. Jackson was out. That was it. Go now and come back later to settle up.

Geoffrey waved again at her from behind the door to go. He said, "No, I'm good. Just got out of the bathroom. But you know, now that the tank is empty, I'd love a cup of coffee. My treat, if you run out to get it."

"No, that's okay. I'll cover you. Take a break and go get yourself something. I want to get started on the inventory. I feel like I need to purge the storeroom. I can't stop thinking about that ghoul who came in last night. Can you imagine trying to sell such a thing?" He groaned. "The thought of it makes my skin crawl."

Geoffrey faked a laugh and agreed.

June felt a pull from within her arms. She turned and started for the door. The space in the back of the store was tight with clutter. She had to suck in her stomach to brush between a secretary desk and a bicycle. Behind her she felt some small thing catch on her clothes. It shifted with her and she stopped, hoping it would also stop along with her. It didn't. She wasn't quick enough to catch it and it clattered to the floor, shattering with a bright sound.

"What was that?" Mr. Jackson's footsteps were hurried and heavy. June was frozen. She clutched the box to her chest.

Geoffrey started to say, "It's noth—" but Mr. Jackson had the door open before he could finish.

"Ms. *Porter*?" Mr. Jackson said. "What are you doing back here?" He seemed surprised, almost pleasantly so. His reflexive smile started to appear, but died as his eyes tracked down to the box cradled in her arms. His face flushed red. "Ms. Porter!" He turned. "Geoffrey! What is going on here?"

June spoke up. "Geoffrey was trying to—"

Mr. Jackson silenced her with a stare. "I know what Geoffrey was doing; I'm not an idiot. Though, I am surprised at you, Ms. Porter. I thought better of you than this. But then, it's your standing order that brought *that* to my store in the first place."

"I don't . . ."

"I have other eccentric customers, to be sure. But this is beyond the pale. I can only imagine someone thought that was a thing he could sell to me because word has gotten around about your . . . tastes. Well, if you want to collect . . . medical oddities, this is not the place for you. My reputation is worth more than you spend here." He turned toward his employee, who seemed to be trying to slowly slide through the door Mr. Jackson was blocking. "And you, Geoffrey, are fired. Get your things and get out."

"But, Miles!"

Mr. Jackson raised a finger and Geoffrey flinched. "You heard me. I'll send your last paycheck tomorrow. Don't bother coming in to get it."

Geoffrey looked at June as though he wanted to complete their transaction. Like he was signaling her to meet him outside. Or even just offer him cash right then. She felt sure he'd paid out of his own pocket for the box, but she didn't imagine that Mr. Jackson was about to let them conclude their transaction. Still, whether or not she was able to reimburse the man for what he'd spent, she wasn't leaving without the box.

She began to walk toward the door. Mr. Jackson held up a hand. "You're taking *that*?" he said. She didn't say anything, just held it closer. "Fine. Get it out of my shop. I'm happy to be rid of it. But leave through the back. I don't want anyone seeing you come out of here holding that."

June didn't wait for him to change his mind. She turned and, stepping over the shards of whatever it was she'd broken, pushed through the steel door into the alley.

The smell of a dumpster broiling the waste from the Chinese restaurant next door hit her solidly. Sweet rot. Her stomach turned, but she held her sick down and rushed as fast as she could past it and out of the alleyway.

She stepped from the shade into the open street, and the sunlight on her skin felt shameful, as though she was lit with judgment. It shone on her brightly, reflecting off the blank tan box in her arms like she carried a piece of its starlight with her. A beacon that blinked a message to everyone who saw her.

*Ghoul.*

Feeling too uncomfortable to take the subway home, she hailed a taxi instead. She did her best to hide the box as she climbed into the back seat. The driver didn't ask. He drove her home in silence, looking at her the whole way in the rearview mirror. At the end of the trip, she threw cash through the window in the divider and jumped out of the car as soon as he unlocked the doors. He squealed his tires pulling away from the curb.

The feeling of breathlessness subsided. She was home with the box. It was hers. She covered it with an arm to conceal it and climbed the steps to her building.

**3.**

The box sat alone on her dinner table and she felt a sting of shame at having brought it home. Mr. Jackson had been a friend, though a distant one. Though he hadn't said it, she was sure she wasn't welcome in his shop any more than Geoffrey was. But in the moment, she'd felt compelled. That Geoffrey had lost money didn't matter. That Mr. Jackson has lost respect for her didn't matter. The box mattered. But not the box. What was *in* the box. Not even that, really. What the box invited was what mattered. Though, that feeling of urgency had worn off now that she was home with it. And it wasn't pushing or pulling at her.

She opened it and pulled the smaller container—the cradle—out. She set the plastic case on the floor under the table and stared at the brass inlays and what she realized now were faux pallbearer handles on the front. As if the miniature casket would be borne to the grave by other tiny hands.

With trembling fingers, she opened the lid and peeked in at the satin bag. June had a good idea what she'd see if she untied the ribbon holding it closed: a tiny body, barely formed—arms and legs no bigger than twigs and eyes that had never opened. Was it pink or brown? Was it some other color? Gray? Or purple, like rot. She both wanted to know and didn't. It didn't matter. It was here and hers and whatever it looked like didn't matter.

June traced one of the laurels with a finger. The fear that she might outlive her child had always been there in the back of her mind, urging her to say things like, *Be careful, Don't talk to strang-*

*ers,* and *Look both ways.* And while she'd thought maybe, some distant day, she might survive her spouse, she'd never imagined losing her entire family at once. And then, there was no one to say any of it to anymore. A car crash crushed her child's body before she could say, *Look out.* There was no sleeping lover to whisper *Good night* to when she came late to bed, because of that one deafening, wordless moment. And then forty years passed like some kind of dream and she woke up and realized that all her life was spent looking back until there was almost no more ahead.

She stood and moved over to the ritual table with her collection of other people's treasured things. One by one she removed them from the table and placed them in the plastic outer box under the dinner table until she could think of a better home for them all. Perhaps, in her storage unit in the building basement.

Unlike the small things, the cradle didn't seem to fit anywhere except at the center of the star. June moved the candle out of the way and set the cradle down. She lit the wick and whispered her invitation.

"Please come. Please stay."

Nothing.

She hadn't had time to ask about the box. Who first owned it, who sold it, and why? Was the woman who'd filled it still alive? Even if she had asked, Geoffrey probably hadn't gotten any sort of provenance for it or its contents. Mr. Jackson's reaction suggested this transaction was performed in the same alley to which he'd banished her. She imagined that was how things like this were always sold. In secret places, hushed voices in the dark bickering over price and no more. No questions asked.

June closed her eyes and sat in front of the table waiting for something to change. But nothing did. The neighbor upstairs continued to pace, while cars honked on the street below, and people shouted to one another in both pleasure and frustration. The air conditioner hummed and only cooled the dinner table.

That feeling of embarrassed regret returned. Reality and self-consciousness returned and said what she was doing was absurd and stupid and she was a fool for wanting to believe in ghosts as badly as she did. If it weren't for Kat and the girl in the trees, maybe she never would have done any of this. Maybe she would have gone on dates and maybe had another child. Once, she'd still had time to have a whole other life.

The thought that she should get rid of it came to mind. She hadn't spent anything on the casket. She could dispose of it respectfully, make a couple of calls and ask if she could pay to have it cremated or buried. She could bury all of it. All the things that should be in coffins in cold earth with their owners.

She could let go of it all.

And then she could go apologize to Mr. Jackson.

She stood and pulled the plastic box out from under the dinner table. Filled with the things she'd piled in it, there was no room for the little coffin. Not if she wanted to replace the lid. She upturned the box, and dumped its contents out onto the ritual table with a clatter and a heavy *thunk*. The pocket watch tumbled out last and fell into the open casket. It clanked against the jar. She gritted her teeth waiting for the sound of cracking glass and the smell of formaldehyde and . . .

She didn't want to think about it.

Nothing broke. No horrible smells revealed what an awful

thing she had brought home. She reached down to pluck it out, but hesitated. The air near the cradle felt thicker. Colder. She pulled her hand back and the cold reached up for her. The chill radiated out of the cradle and brushed up against her belly. It wasn't an unwelcome touch; it felt like a caress.

There was a hint of something like a whisper in her ear. She thought it sounded like *I'm here.* Or, perhaps, *Come here.* She leaned closer. The cold caress moved from her belly up over her breast, to her cheek, where it stopped like a loving hand holding her face still before a kiss. She closed her eyes and waited for the pressure against her lips. But the touch faded.

"No. Don't go," she said, her eyes springing open. "Please stay." Her breath billowed out in front of her. It faded in the hot apartment and was replaced by her next and the one after that. She was panting with excitement, her heartbeat thundering in her ears like the thrum of the ocean.

She picked up a class ring and the dog tags and the glasses and dropped them all in the casket along with the watch and jar until it was overflowing. The chill enveloped her and she felt movement around her sides and behind her. Small breezes that ruffled her clothes and made her hair dance. She thought, a hand on her hip would be so welcome—that little push that moved her around the floor in tandem with a partner.

The speakers behind her began to peal with Chet Baker's trumpet and she spun around to see who'd started the record player. Something shifted like a movement out of the corner of her eye, though it wasn't in the corner, but dead ahead. She tried to track it, but the distortion faded before she could get a bead on it. She took a step toward the stereo. The pull of something that didn't want to be far from her stopped her. A clinging presence begged her to stay, holding her skirt. Like her daughter had always done.

"Janice?" she said, whispering her girl's name. "Is that you?" The tug came again, harder. She faced the casket on the low table and felt cold.

The lights dimmed and there was pressure on her shoulders. A brush against her neck that flipped her hair away. She laughed, tears falling down her cheeks wetting thin lines that felt the cold more than the rest of her face. More hands. There was pressure at the small of her back, and encircling her legs. She felt unsteady, like she might fall. Another touch righted her and stuck close.

They'd come.

They were all around her.

She tried to take a breath. She couldn't get a deep one and wheezed, trying harder. The cloud of exhalation that hovered in front of her mouth was smaller than before and took longer to dispel. The air was thick and felt impossible to draw in.

She staggered a step away from the table. The presence clutching at her skirt pulled, and the one at her back held on, and the others all around her slowed her movement. It felt like pushing through water. Clutching hands with insistent fingers pulled and pinched and held her.

"Not . . . all . . . at once," she gasped. It was too close, too intimate. There were too many. How many of their things were in the apartment with her? How many had she collected? Dolls and rings and necklaces and favorite books and crosses and a knife and the watch. And the glasses. She reached for Kat's glasses.

*Don't be afraid,* the familiar voice said in that same voice that had once told her. *It was the heat and the Ramos gin fizz. There's no such thing as ghosts.*

Her wedding ring tingled and felt heavy on her finger.

*We're here for you.*

A tug at her skirt again.

*Here for you.*

Her chest hurt.

*Always together.*

Like fingers squeezing her heart.

She opened her mouth, gasping. Everything was cold and quiet. Though it turned, her record was silent. The neighbor upstairs had stopped walking. The cars stopped honking. All she heard was the faint murmur of voices inside her apartment.

*Stay with you.*

*Always.*

*Together.*

June picked up the cradle with trembling hands and carried it around to the sofa, holding it close so nothing spilled out. She sat heavily, falling more than lowering herself carefully. The glasses rattled next to the jar. She steadied everything inside with a hand, and balancing the cradle in her lap, looked at her treasures. There was just enough room for one more thing. She slipped off her wedding ring and dropped it in along with everything she'd collected from the dead. It made a small noise as it settled into its own space among everything else that she'd been able to fit inside. She closed her eyes and listened to her ghosts as the air got colder and thicker and harder to breathe. The pain in her chest spread up her neck and down her arm and she felt afraid.

What if she dropped the box and it spilled?

What if her ring fell out?

And she was left out.

What if none of this was really happening, because there's no such thing as ghosts?

She let out a shuddering breath and waited while the dark got darker and all the voices hushed until she couldn't hear anything at all anymore.

Some people just faded away and you never heard from them again. The kids called it ghosting.

# Mec-Ow

## *Garth Nix*

Jules was on his usual run, just before dawn. On the side of the road, facing the traffic—not that there was any at this time, but just in case—the reflectors on his GOrun shoes and his Saucony vest flashing up every time he ran into a pool of light from a street lamp, fading into the darkness between. Half the lights were out, the council skimped on replacing bulbs to save money, but this was no new thing. Jules didn't mind the dark.

There were a few other runners who ran the road down to the beach and back this early, and there'd be a lot more later, once the sun was up. Jules usually met one or two early birds, the usual suspects. He was faster than all of them, particularly going uphill, something he prided himself on. Thirty-two, no sign of slowing down, and he could still see off the younger runners who fired themselves up the hill but couldn't keep the pace going all the way to the top.

So he was surprised when he saw someone out of the corner of his eye, catching up to pace him. He hadn't heard the other runner, which was also a surprise, because he never wore earbuds to listen to music or podcasts or whatever, unlike nearly everyone else. Blocking out the situational sounds was an invitation to get run over, Jules always said. He liked the early morning noises anyway, the birds waking, the crash of the surf as you got closer to the beach, the rhythmic slap of his own feet on the road.

"Hey," said the runner. A woman, her voice low, not out of breath, though they were halfway up the hill and getting to the steepest part where it wound anticlockwise in a sweeping turn that made cars shift down three gears and trucks and buses groan up at a snail's pace. A lot of runners walked the steep turn.

Jules grunted something that could be taken as hello. He flicked his eyes across to take a look at her, and almost tripped over his own feet and did a face-plant into the road. She was wearing a hoodie, hood up, but there could be no mistake. The runner was Samantha Finegold, a friend from long ago, back in his university days. An ex-girlfriend, kind of, at least they'd hooked up once, one time Jules had mostly managed to forget, not because the sex hadn't been great because it had, but because of some other stuff that went on, and then they'd just drifted apart, and he hadn't seen Sam since graduation, and had only thought of her maybe once or twice, hearing that Rumbelos song she loved or seeing a particular kind of weird batik shirt that was her favourite and he'd always made fun of.

"Sam! What the fuck!"

She smiled, teeth a white flash in the dark.

"Thought it was you, from behind," she said, smiling. "You live near here?"

"Uh, yeah . . . near the old chocolate factory . . . but you? What're you up to?"

It was hard to talk, the slope getting steeper, no breath to spare and the memories coming back, and a sudden tension because Sam looked fantastic and he felt the attraction and remembered that one night and here she was again and maybe . . . maybe . . . but he was married now, and he and Jeanne had a baby . . . and that night with Sam, it hadn't been all—

"Oh, I've been all over," she said, not even gasping a little for air though Jules had his head down now, nose flaring, mouth half open, trying not to show how badly he needed the oxygen he was sucking back. "London, Vietnam, then Thailand. Boston most recently. But I had to come back. To the old house."

"W-what? The . . . the . . . share house?"

He was puffed, it was hard to talk.

"Yep. Good old Fifty-Two Lawrence Street."

The share house. Ten of them had lived in it when Jules was there, in seven bedrooms, though the house had eight. One bedroom was always empty. The little one at the back, that might have been some sort of laundry or servant room, in the days when the house had been a grand mansion and not a run-down dump rented out to ever-changing groups of students and hangers-on. It was too damp to stay in, that small bedroom. Beads of water slid down the walls like sweat, and the floorboards were rotten. It smelled, too, of rot and neglect and despair.

Not that any of this had stopped Jules and Sam that one time. They'd taken their roach ends and the almost-empty bottle of Captain Cayman rum and all the pillows from the big sofa in the lounge and slunk out there, hiding from the rest of the household who'd almost certainly blab to Jules's and Sam's respective current girlfriend and boyfriend, intentionally or not. Besides, the room out the back seemed neutral ground, like if they had sex there it wouldn't matter so much as if they did it in one of their own rooms.

"W-w-why?"

Jules almost couldn't get the word out. Sam had been

increasing the pace, almost without him realising it. They were practically sprinting up the steepest part of the hill.

"Explain later," said Sam. She winked at him, slow, like she'd done that time when they were gradually sliding together in the lounge room, smoking dope and drinking rum, the possibility between them growing into definite, mutual decision. Only this time he wasn't entirely sure he'd seen it, they were moving fast, there was sweat pouring down his forehead, getting in his eyes, and it was still velvety dark, none of the streetlights on this stretch were working.

"Come to the house! Tonight after work!"

Suddenly, excruciatingly, she sped up even more, leaving Jules behind. He tried to catch her, for six, seven steps, then abruptly folded, staggering into the curb where he went down on both knees to throw up his coffee and last night's dinner—he always had breakfast after his run. By the time Jules looked up, shocked and embarrassed, Sam was disappearing around the corner, shapely legs moving in perfect rhythm, arms not so much pumping as slicing through the air on either side.

Jules sat on the roadside, wiping his mouth. The first faint arc of the sun rose up out of the sea behind him, its light sliding up the road, the birds getting noisier. A few cars started to go by, and then a runner, a man Jules knew by sight.

"You okay, man?"

Jules waved him off.

"Yeah, something I ate. Should've given it a miss today."

"Nah, not you," said the runner, taking the opportunity of talking to slow down almost to a walk, though he kept going. "King of the Hill."

"What?"

"That's what I call you," said the man over his shoulder. "King of the Hill. Fastest I've ever seen anyone taking this. Respect!"

"Except for Sam," muttered Jules, but the other runner didn't hear him; he was fixing the one earbud he'd taken out back in, already getting back into the zone.

Except for Sam.

Jules thought about her as he slowly jogged home, his mouth burning with the acrid after-taste of vomit.

Jeanne and little Cary, their baby, were asleep again after a three a.m. feed and an hour or so of wakefulness after. Jules showered and got dressed for work even more quietly than usual, and slipped out. The drive in to the office, with the noise and the traffic and the bad drivers and the stress helped him put Sam out of his mind. Or almost out of his mind. But never entirely.

By eleven o'clock, he couldn't stand it anymore. He got out his phone, about to message Shirley, who'd been one of their housemates and had known Sam the longest. But he decided to call her instead, and she picked up on the second ring.

"Jules! How's being a dad?"

"Good, good," mumbled Jules. "How's mother- father- whatever-you-call-it-hood?"

"Well, you know," said Shirley. "It'll all be worth it when Cary and Harry grow up and get married."

"No way our son's going to marry any spawn of yours," said Jules, half-heartedly. He just didn't have the strength for their usual banter. "Look, do you ever hear from Sam? Sam Finegold?"

"Uh, no . . ." Shirley's voice had changed, no longer the cheery, older sister tone she usually employed with Jules. "To tell you the truth, I'm not entirely sure she's still with us."

"What? Look, the reason I'm asking is I saw . . . I thought I saw her this morning."

"And you want to get it on with her again?"

"No! I just saw . . . I wondered . . . what do you mean *again*?"

"We all know you guys did it in that horrible old laundry room."

"What . . . no . . . that's—"

"Sam confessed to Elijah who told Nadya who told me. That's why Sam bailed from the house."

Jules was silent for a moment. Sam *had* left the next day, and of course he'd wondered if it was because of what they'd done. Or maybe something else, he was hazy on, having been so stoned and drunk, but there had been something—

"Shit! But that's not, I mean," he stammered. "I'm married, I love Jeanne. I'm good. I just wondered, that's all. What do you mean not with us? I *saw* her."

"You're sure?"

"Yeah, I'm sure."

"She see you?"

Jules lied. He wasn't sure why. Or he was, but didn't really want to admit it to himself. Shirley was more of Jeanne's friend these days than she was his. And he did want to get it on again with Sam. He always had.

"I . . . I don't know."

"Nadya saw her, five years ago," said Shirley. "In a Buddhist monastery, in Vietnam. Sam didn't want to know her. Hey, was her head shaved?"

"I . . . er . . . she was wearing a hoodie."

"It was when Nadya saw her. Hard core. Head shaved, saffron robes, the works."

"I guess her family, her dad was Vietnamese, so I don't know, she went back to her roots or whatever. You freaked me out with that 'not with us anymore,' I mean if she's just become a Buddhist monk, okay. I thought you meant dead."

"I did mean dead. And her dad was a Catholic, he grew up in Marseilles."

"What?"

"Surely you're aware of the French Colonial history of Vietnam and the migration of—"

"No! No! Sam being dead! What do you mean?"

"Okay, after Nadya saw her in Vietnam, maybe two years ago, she popped up on Facebook again. Account had been inactive for years, but we were still friends there, and I see she's posted something about being in Boston, for the marathon. So I send her a message and she replies, says sorry she's been out of touch, she's got some problems, she's had to change her name and go dark, and she still can't talk, and then—

"You think she got killed in the marathon bombing?"

"No, dumbass! This was two years ago, way after the bombing. About a month later, someone else posts on her wall, no one I knew, says they're a friend and they've got bad news, Sam was killed in an accident, out running. That stays up for about a month, no replies to questions, no nothing, and then the account is deleted."

"Killed out running."

"That's what the friend said. She was a big runner you know."

"Yeah. She . . . uh . . . kind of got me started. Seeing her doing it."

"So Sam's dead. Maybe."

"Maybe?"

"Oh, come on. She messages me that she's got trouble, has to change her name and hide out or whatever, and then a 'friend' posts she's dead from her own account?"

"Oh yeah. But . . ."

"But what? Maybe she's dead, maybe she isn't. She was just a housemate from long ago, one of many. Sure, you fucked her. Also one of many. Focus on the people who are alive and who you do actually care about. Or are supposed to. Speaking of which, we're having Gil's lasagne when you guys come around Saturday."

"But why didn't I . . ."

"I have to go, Jules. The past is another whatever and so on. Give Jeanne and young Mr. Grant a kiss from me."

"Why didn't I hear Sam's footsteps on the road?" asked Jules, but there was no one listening.

Work got busy for a while. Jules worked through lunch, not noticing he was hungry. About three he went out, got a coffee and a stale cinnamon roll which he ate half of, sitting in the Starbucks window and staring out into space. Looking back through time to that one night, trying to find his way clear through the blurring wash of rum and the swirling dope smoke and—

"Mee-ow," he said suddenly, startling the two young women sitting closest. And then they jumped again as he said "Mee-ow!" even louder, and then "Fuck!" followed a few seconds later as he came back into the present and saw everyone staring at him with "Oh, sorry! Sorry! Thinking aloud."

Thinking aloud and imitating a cat. Badly. Only he wasn't trying to imitate a real cat's miaow. He was imitating . . . someone . . . who was imitating a cat.

Jules left the café, leaving most of the cinnamon roll behind.

• • •

He'd thought it was Sam making the noise. They'd been there quite a while, were going slow this time around—not like when they first went out to the room—in no hurry now. He was down low, head cradled between her legs, Sam's fingers through his hair and he was . . . and then the fake miaow and he looked up and Sam said, "What's with the cat noises," just as he said "Does the miaowing mean you like it or—"

And then they were scrambling apart and the three inches of rum left in the bottle got spilled on the floor and soaked one of the pillows and they stood close, looking around in the dim light, because there was no actual source of illumination in the room, just what came in from the single high window from the street lamp outside. Which had suited them before, but now most definitely did not.

"It wasn't me," whispered Sam.

"Me either," said Jules, going along with it, even though after that sudden excitement he thought it was her, because who else could it be. "But it was . . . it sounded . . ."

"Right here," said Sam. "A girl. A young girl. Imitating a *cat*. Oh my—"

Jules stopped suddenly. People swirled around him. Someone swore as they bumped past, hitting his elbow.

He couldn't remember. Sam had said something about a young girl, and the sound. He'd heard the sound again and started to turn around. He'd seen *something*, but he'd slipped on the spilt rum and fallen down and . . . he couldn't remember. He'd woken up the next day in his own bed, horribly hungover, throat rasped to pieces by smoke, with a bruise on his head and several splinters in his feet from the rotten floorboards.

A young girl imitating a cat, Sam had said.

Mee-ow.

Sam had gone by the time he managed to stagger out into the shared spaces of the house. Jules was a mess, dazed and confused. He joined in with the others, pretended to wonder why Sam had left so abruptly. But not too much. Housemates came and went all the time, for all sorts of reasons. It was that kind of house.

A month later Jules left the house too, never having gone out the back to that horrible little laundry room again.

And he never thought about it. He thought about Sam sometimes, and having sex with her, but it was not in that room. Even though it had been, the only time. He remembered differently, or imagined differently, and the imagined version had taken over from the real, even though on examination it broke apart. He and Sam were real, but everything else around them was stuck-on glitter, made up by his mind to cover up what had really happened.

Whatever that was.

Jules couldn't work back in the office. He tried. He phoned home and talked to Jeanne and Cary. At least he exchanged commonplace banalities with Jeanne and made goo-goo noises at Cary, who made random sounds which in all likelihood were not in response to his father.

At the end of the call, he said he had to work late and wouldn't be home at the usual time and to not bother setting aside anything for his dinner.

It was only when he said this Jules realised he was going to go to the old house, he was going to meet Sam and that when he thought of her he had two kind of opposite feelings going on. One was pure lust, which was the same feeling he'd pretty much always had for her, but the other was a kind of slight, rationally damped down fear.

Maybe she was *dead*, and that morning he'd seen and talked to a ghost.

Jules smiled as this thought bubbled up, but at the same time, he didn't or couldn't completely dismiss it. He didn't believe in ghosts, at least not in his brightly lit office. Out running in the pre-dawn, maybe . . .

Running. Sure, Sam had always been a runner, but she'd never been as fast or as strong as he was, so how had she gone up the hill like that? And why hadn't he heard her?

His rational mind provided good answers for both questions. Obviously she had been training, and training hard and properly, more than just the daily to the beach and back run he did himself. As for not hearing her, Jules considered, his mind did wander when he ran. He thought about other stuff, even though he often couldn't afterwards say what that other stuff was.

But still he had a kind of frisson up his spine that said Sam might be a ghost, accompanied by the other stronger, frisson that was about her being still very much flesh and blood, in a very attractive package. Only he didn't like to think he was the kind of guy who would cheat on his wife. Though he had in the past. But he'd decided not to anymore, he'd broken off with Maggie here in the office. Only he might with Sam. Because in a way she predated Jeanne anyway, and they'd never finished properly.

Whatever, he had to see Sam again. Plus there was the niggling question about what had happened, the whole cat noise thing and the . . . whatever he'd seen. He wanted to know about that. Or actually he wanted to forget it again entirely, and just remember the good bits, but that didn't seem possible.

Jules parked almost directly opposite the old house as the sun set and the street lights flickered on. All of them, unlike near the beach. Lawrence Street had come up in the world. Same big old falling-down houses for the most part up at this end, but farther along many of the smaller houses had been renovated and extended. There were new cars parked out on the street, something no one would have dared ten years before. The whole area looked more prosperous. Safer and quieter, unlike the old days when there were often people just hanging around.

He was just thinking this when a movement out of the corner of his eye made him flinch and turn.

Sam was by the window, bending down to look in. She smiled, a hesitant smile. Uncertain of him. She was wearing different clothes, jeans and a silky top with lots of small buttons, which he found both tempting and reassuring. If she'd been in running clothes still, like she might have been killed in . . . even though it was absurd to think she might be a ghost.

But she didn't tap on the window. People always tapped on windows when they went up to someone in a car. Didn't they?

Jules pressed a button, the window slid down.

"Hi," she said, with the hesitant smile again, and a catch in her voice. She really was nervous. He didn't know why. What could this really be about? A sneaky way to see him again? All of a sudden he felt a wave of revulsion at himself, this clandestine meeting, what he half hoped for, hated himself for. At the same time, Sam looked so hot, not aged like he felt he'd aged, no matter that he could run up the hill as fast as ever.

"Look," he said quickly, remembering his resolution. He wasn't going to fuck around anymore. "I shouldn't have come. It's wrong. I love Jeanne, my wife, and I have to go—"

Sam leaned in and grabbed him by the shoulder, her slim fingers trembling, digging into the muscle and bone as if she was trying to close her grip on a lifeline.

"No, please, Jules! Please!"

Jules felt an almost electric shock at her touch. She was definitely not a ghost. He put his hand over hers, instantly weakening in his resolve to go home. Her hand was warm, the skin soft. He ran his forefinger over her knuckles, resting in the space between, and he smiled at her, his eyes bright.

Sam slid her hand out of his and stepped back, to allow him to get out of the car, and stepped back again as he zapped the car locked and moved in for a hug and a kiss, both their movements awkward as he stopped when she went back, and then she came in again and pecked him very lightly on the cheek, standing off to one side so a hug would be awkward.

"Getting a bit of a mixed message here," said Jules, but he smiled again. He knew his smile was one of his best features. Plenty of women had told him that his smile was what attracted them to him in the first place.

"Come with me. Into the house. Into the laundry room."

"We could get a *hotel* room, there's a place I like not—"

"No, we need to go here. Come on."

She started for the door. Jules followed slowly. That niggling hint of memory was at him. Something bad had gone on in the house, in the laundry room. He felt it emotionally, even if he couldn't remember.

"What? Why?"

"I'll explain inside. Come on."

"What about whoever lives here?"

"I've sorted it out with them. It's still a student house. I paid them to go out for a while."

The door was an inch ajar. Sam pushed it wide open, forging ahead, eager. Jules stopped on the front step. The sun had set now, and it was dark. Just as in his day, there was no overhead light in the hall, only a crappy low-wattage bulb in a faux candlestick parked halfway along. There were doors on both sides of the hall, but it was the one at the far end he looked at. The door to the laundry room.

"Come on," said Sam. She reached back and took his hand, dragging him in. "Please."

"We going to get some pillows on the way?" asked Jules. "Or you already sorted out something more comfortable?"

He thought he had it figured out now. It was kind of kinky to want to pick up exactly where they left off, but if that was what she wanted, he was prepared to overcome the weird kind of negative déjà vu he was experiencing.

Sam laughed though. A forced laugh, perhaps. She pulled on his hand, and he stumbled after her, all the way to the door.

"I don't want to go in there," said Jules suddenly, leaning back, pulling free. "I don't really remember what happened the last time, but I know there was something—"

"Something!" exclaimed Sam. "Yes! That's why I need you here. I have to know, I have to find out if it's all in my head, or is it really something? What do you remember?"

Jules was silent. He started to back away, but Sam grabbed him, her hands around his neck and pulled him in, kissing him, desperately like they had ten years ago, and he felt himself responding, tightening his grasp, drawing her closer.

"You remember that?" she gasped. "You remember us fucking?"

Jules gulped and nodded. His hands were moving, caressing, almost without conscious direction, reenacting tactile memory from long ago.

"What else?"

"The cat noises," said Jules slowly. "I mean, the fake . . . the mee-ow. You mee-owing."

"It wasn't me," said Sam fiercely. "It wasn't me! It was the girl, the girl with the dead cat!"

She pushed him away and spun about on the spot, throwing open the door to the laundry room. Jules tried to look away, almost hunching, raising his arms to cover his face, but he was too slow.

The laundry room had been repainted, and fairly recently, and there was now an LED light in the ceiling, making it far brighter than the hall. The room was all white now, save for a patch where the black mould was coming back. For a split second, Jules thought he did see a little girl, a little girl cradling a cat, the tail hanging slack between her arms. Then he saw it was just a pattern of mould. The room was damp, like it always had been. No paint could save it from that.

"Do you see her?" asked Sam. She was almost sobbing. She pointed at the stain. "Do you see her, and her damned dead cat?"

"No," whispered Jules. He didn't want her now, he didn't want to be with her another second.

"You can't hear her?"

"No."

"Mee-ow! Mee-ow! All the time! She's always there, her and the cat. Everywhere I went, there she was! I thought distance, get away, go the other side of the world, but no. She was there. Mee-ow! Mee-ow! Meditation held her off, but that stopped working. Running held her off, but that stopped working. What else could I do? What else could I do?"

"Hey, easy . . . ," soothed Jules. He reluctantly gathered her in, but this time it was a sexless hug, him trying to give as little comfort as he could get away with, and her like a tree or a post, something dead and still and rigid. He thought he could see it now. She must have smoked a lot more than he thought, or taken other drugs, all the time in secret. Everyone knew now about dope and paranoia, and ice and so on. It all made sense, the message to Shirley, the talk of issues, this business with a girl and a cat. Of course she had always been the one who made the cat noises.

"What else could I do," mumbled Sam into his shoulder. "Ten years. It's been ten years."

He turned her round and walked her outside, shutting the door behind them, already thinking where he could drop her off or get rid of her. As the door clicked shut, Sam shuddered violently, and for a moment he thought she was going to go into convulsions and he put one hand on his phone, ready to call for an ambulance. What made-up name could he use for himself?

But Sam steadied, stepping back from him to take several deep, gasping breaths. She looked up at Jules's face and then to each side, eyes darting to and fro. She looked across the road, and behind her, twisting and turning as if searching for something and not finding it. Then she suddenly burst into tears again, but not the utterly destroyed sobbing she'd displayed back in the room. This was something else, and her face was filled with what Jules could only identify as unexpected joy. That was tempered a moment later as she looked directly at him again, but he couldn't say what expression passed across her face. Sorrow perhaps, but not for herself.

Before he could stop her, she kissed him again, hard on the lips, whispered, "I'm sorry. So sorry!" and she sped off along the street, displaying that effortless running style as she accelerated, sprinting into the night.

Jules shook his head and went across to his car. He'd been lucky, he thought to himself. Dodged several bullets, all with the potential to totally fuck up his good life. His happy, contented life, he reminded himself. Next time some past girlfriend called him up or he ran into one, he'd be pleasantly distant. Unobtainable. Unreachable.

He got in the car, started it up, and glanced in the mirror.

"Mee-ow," said the girl in the back seat, trying to wake the cat she held so tightly, the cat who could never wake.

"Mee-ow."

A girl in a faded blue pinafore, her skin shrunken back to the bones of her skull, her eyes shrivelled, a body starved to death long, long ago, and the cat a bunch of fur and bones and one permanently glazed eye, the other just a mummified socket, and one ear was stuck up like a cardboard price tag and the other a gaping, dry wound.

"Mee-ow."

"Mee-ow"

"Mee-ow."

# Jasper Dodd's Handbook of Spirits and Manifestations

*Nathan Ballingrud*

We live in a haunted world, Mama told him once. A wise boy will come to know the spirits, and distinguish the good from the wicked.

A dutiful son, Jasper sought to catalogue the spirits he knew in a handbook. First and foremost there was the Holy Spirit, which is the one Mama used to talk to in the angels' tongue. That spirit made her shake and shudder, even let her handle the serpents so that they might know their subservience to mankind. After she lit out, he asked his father if she'd gone home to God. His father just fixed him with that flat ugly look he sometimes got, so he didn't ask again. She might come back one day, or she might not. He only hoped that wherever she was, the serpents retained their lesson.

Next there was the spirit of his baby sister, Lily, who died when she was five years old and who lived now at the bottom of the dry well. Though her grave was ten miles up the road at the Jubilee Church, it did not seem strange to him that she lived in the well. He knew that ghosts must travel dark roads invisible to a mortal eye, and that she simply traded one underground home for another, closer to her family. Jasper never heard her speak except when he was dreaming, and whatever she told him then were things he could not bring back with him into the day-lit world. He would wake up with the sound of her voice still in his brain, and the smell of the sweet, cold place she lived now lingering in his nose—but the words themselves were gone. He didn't tell anybody about that, but he made careful note of it in his handbook.

There were the wicked spirits his father kept trapped in honey jars down in the root cellar. Each jar held a slip of paper with one of his father's sins written upon it, which is what had lured the spirits into their confinement. Jasper would sometimes visit the cellar with a cigarette lighter held aloft, the shelved jars reflecting that shivering light like rows of haunted orange lamps.

Other spirits walked the woods at night. These were wild spirits, feral and hungry, scraping his window with tree branches and scuttling under the trailer with heavy, lumbering movements. Normally they would not keep him awake for long. He was ten years old, wise to their tricks, and satisfied with the protections of his home. Mama claimed it was the Lord's grace that kept the aggressions of the spirit world at bay, and what few slipped through were trapped in the baited honey jars his father placed by the door. Jasper reckoned that was mostly true, but he kept up with his handbook just the same.

Uncle Kyle gave it to him a few years ago. He was Mama's brother, and she told him once that Kyle was what college folks called a "naturalist." Kyle showed him his own notebooks whenever he came to visit, and they were always filled with wonderful things: drawings of different kinds of birds; squirrels and raccoons; varieties of trees and seeds and acorns. He even had a couple pages given over to the bees Jasper's father kept out in his hives, which were not actually real hives at all but big white boxes, with racks you could slide out to get the honey. Each picture was accompanied by his uncle's cursive writing—a style he'd learned in school, back when he was Jasper's age.

"Don't they teach you how to write cursive in school no more?" he asked. When Jasper shook his head, he spat in the dirt. "Well it don't matter how the words look. It just matters that you put 'em down. You just write down the things you're interested in. Draw a picture, and write a little bit about how they act. Add details like when you saw 'em, and how often, what kind of things they eat, stuff like that. You can learn a lot about something just by watching it, and paying attention to what it does when it thinks it's by itself." He removed one of his own filled notebooks from his backpack, and gave it over to Jasper so he could fan through the pages. "When you fill one up, it can serve as instruction to other people. Then you don't call it a notebook no more, 'cause it's graduated away from that. Then you call it a handbook. The best part happens when someone else uses what you wrote, and adds their own ideas to it. It's like a conversation that happens over a distance of time."

The notion electrified Jasper. There weren't many people for him to talk to out here. He liked the idea of talking across time. "I want to make a handbook."

"Now how come I thought you might say that?" Uncle Kyle fetched an unmarked book from his bag, peeling off the cellophane wrapper and passing it to the boy with a thoughtful smile. Jasper felt gravity in the gesture. He resisted the urge to hug his uncle.

"What are you gonna put into it?"

Jasper shrugged, although he was already thinking about Lily singing out from her cold, wet home. As much as he loved his uncle, he didn't want to tell anybody about that. He already knew his handbook would be a rare, secret book—something unique in the world.

A few months later Jasper learned that Kyle had never gone to college at all, at least not beyond a brief stay at the local technical school, where he flunked out. This didn't change Jasper's opinion of the man, or of his instruction. By that time he'd already put the notebook to use.

After Mama left, Kyle stopped coming around as much. The relationship between him and Jasper's dad, always shaky, took a darker turn. His uncle didn't stay over anymore; he just talked to his dad on the front porch, usually asking questions. Jasper never got to hear what they said, but when his dad came back inside afterward, he was always angry.

Last night it all came to a head. Jasper awoke to the sound of a shout. He opened his eyes and stared at the ceiling, waiting for more. He heard nothing at first. Then violence erupted somewhere beyond his door. It sounded like a full grown buck panicking inside the house. He crept out of bed and peered into the living room, where he saw Uncle Kyle and his own father struggling on the floor. His father's hand gripped Kyle's throat. Kyle's face was purple, with rage or from lack of oxygen. He had one hand on his father's wrist and the other pressed against the underside of his chin.

Jasper panicked. "Dad!"

His father turned his attention to his son, lips curled back from his teeth, murder pooled in his eyes. Uncle Kyle wrenched himself free and smashed his fist into his dad's jaw, dropping him like a sack of mulch.

As Kyle rolled away, Jasper saw broken glass beneath him,

dappling the back of his plaid shirt with blood. His father groaned, marshaling his senses. Uncle Kyle got to his feet and delivered a heavy kick to his ribs; the sound of bone snapping made Jasper jump. His uncle paused with his hands on his knees, face red and breath rattling. Then he kicked his father twice in the head.

Jasper loved his uncle perhaps more than any other person on this earth, with the exception of his mother, so when he attacked him he did it with a broken heart. He crashed into Uncle Kyle, who staggered back a step, and pounded his fists into him. He screamed with more fear than anger. Kyle shouted something, but it was lost in the frenzy, and it wasn't until his uncle shoved him to the floor that Jasper was able to stop his assault, crying like some weak little brat on the glass-strewn carpet, next to his bell-rung father.

Uncle Kyle opened the door and the warm August night poured in, smelling of jasmine. His uncle reached for him. "Come on, Jasper. Let's go."

Jasper didn't understand. He looked up from the floor, propped on his elbows, a strange, confused hope rising inside him.

His father pushed himself to his hands and knees. "Fuck you, Kyle."

"Walter, you just stay down, you hear? Stay down." He looked back at Jasper. "Come on, kid. Let's get out of here. You shouldn't be here."

His father tried to stand. Something broken in his chest made him cry out and he slipped to his knees again, clutching his side. His eyes looked unfocused—a blind, questing intelligence coiled there, like some wrathful animal sniffing at the lip of its cave. His face was beginning to swell from the beating. "Kill you," he said quietly. "Kill you."

Uncle Kyle did not seem to take that lightly. "God damn it, Jasper, right now. Come on!"

"But, Dad . . ."

"Fuck that old man! He ain't shit! Let's go!"

His father, still on his hands and knees, head hanging between his shoulders, extended a bloody-knuckled hand in Jasper's direction.

Jasper gave his uncle one last look—he would later wonder what expression he wore, what message he sent—then scuttled to his father's side, letting the man put a heavy arm around his shoulder, bearing his weight for him as best he could. He heard the door close behind him, and a moment later the engine of his uncle's old Chevy growled into life. The sound swelled and then receded as his uncle drove away from him forever.

Jasper tried to help his father to his feet, but he guessed it hurt him too much, because finally his father pushed him off and settled back onto his side, breathing heavily, his eyes closed.

"Dad? Should I call the ambulance?"

His father opened his eyes. "That faggot ain't gonna send me to no doctor. Bring me my bottle."

Jasper fetched the bottle of rye from the kitchen cabinet. He didn't bother with a glass; his dad hadn't used one at all since Mama left. In another half an hour his dad was passed out, bleeding and swelling on the living room floor, and Uncle Kyle was probably fifty miles away. Jasper sat outside, wondering what time it was. The night was humid and thick. Trees pressed close, and he listened as, somewhere beyond his line of sight, something walked among them.

• • •

Jasper awoke with his sister's voice fading in his head. His father had migrated to the couch. He was passed out drunk, the bottle empty on its side. Sunlight intruded through the slats on the window. The place stank of booze worse than usual. Jasper swept the broken glass from the night before onto a junk flyer he retrieved from a stack on the counter, and slid it into the trash can, where it sifted to the bottom like spilled dirt. Somewhere down the road he heard the bus grumbling by, and he imagined for a moment being on it, sitting with other kids his age who were probably thinking about normal things, like homework or hunting trips, or whatever it was normal kids thought about.

He'd stopped going to school a couple months ago, sometime after Mama had gone. Eventually the truancy officer came by, and he'd been sent to hide under his dad's bed. He listened while his dad told the officer that his mama had taken him away, and he didn't figure they'd ever come back.

"You know what address they're at?" the officer said. "We got to transfer him out of here, otherwise he's gonna be marked delinquent. I tell you, it'll cause him trouble down the road."

"I don't know where she took him. The bitch lit out in the middle of the night. She's got people in Mississippi. I guess maybe she took him there."

"Well . . . can you have her get in touch with the school next time you talk to her? I just don't want Jasper to get in trouble, is all. You know how the government is. Likes to stick its nose every damn where."

"That's the government's problem. Let it go looking, it wants to find her so bad."

Jasper heard the door shut, and he wriggled out of his hiding place. He peered through the window and watched the truancy officer climb into his car and drive away. As far as the school was concerned, Jasper no longer existed. He thought he should feel good about that, but in place of that feeling there was a peculiar absence. He spent the afternoon hitting his favorite spots in the woods, finally settling into the rusted cabin of a long-abandoned '74 Gremlin, grappled by kudzu and shaded by red maple. He watched the sky through the maple branches and imagined himself traveling to locations beyond his father's reckoning.

Now, months later, Jasper approached his father and stood cautiously beside him, yet far enough that he might leap beyond the arc of a swinging arm. The blood had crusted under his father's nose and on his lips. The flesh along the right hinge of his jaw had swollen and gone dark purple, almost black. His mouth gaped open and the raw stink of liquor—and something else, something ripe and frightening—blew out of him with each heave of his lungs.

"Dad?" Jasper whispered. "Can I have some breakfast?"

His father didn't make a sound. Jasper was relieved. This meant he could pour himself a second bowl of Rice Krispies, and even put some extra sugar over it. Previous experience had taught him that as long as he was quiet, he would likely have the run of the place until well into the afternoon. Even then his dad would wake up chastened, and keep mostly to himself. It might be a good day.

After breakfast he spent most of the morning perambulating about the property, whacking the leaves from tree branches with a stick and singing snippets of songs he half remembered from when his mama still lived here and played her radio. Before the days when the only music she tolerated was God's music. He climbed the hill to where his father's hives were kept, and stood at the edge of the clearing, listening to them drone. There were six of them, big white boxes on table legs, bees swooning in drunken orbits.

Finally, he got hungry for lunch, and made his reluctant way home. He approached the house with a soft step, wanting to preserve the peace of the day just a little while longer. There were two capped honey jars on either side of the front door, a twisted strip of paper barely visible in each. He never asked what his father wrote down on them. They were used more often since Mama had left, though; and because this was part of their interaction with the spirit world, Jasper made note of it in his book.

Jasper turned the handle on the door and eased it open. If you did it slowly enough, the hinges wouldn't squeak. He stopped—only a two-inch gap between the door and the jamb—when he heard a sound. He didn't understand what it was at first; when he did, his blood chilled.

His father was crying. His breath came in a series of small, broken gasps, like he was trying to suck it back into himself. From this vantage point, Jasper could see his left shoulder, his left knee. He was hunched over, and with each stifled sob his body shook. Jasper retreated, quietly closing the door again. He returned to the woods, this time to sit upon a rotted stump and dwell over the image of his father brought low.

He had never seen the man cry before—not when Lily died, not when Mama left them both for whatever called out to her from the wider world. He had seen him fight, and he had seen him take some hard licks. God knows he'd seen him deliver them too; he'd been on the receiving end more than a few times. But to see him weeping in the broad light of day was harder than any clout to the head. The ground felt suddenly fragile, like a shell over a great hollow.

He remembered what his uncle had told him. "You can learn a lot about something just by watching it, and paying attention to what it does when it thinks it's by itself." Jasper considered writing down what he saw, but held back. His father was not a ghost. He didn't belong in a book about them.

They already had a ghost in the family.

Lily died a year ago, when Jasper was nine years old. She'd been a loud and willful child, with a core of mischief that frequently landed her in trouble. Because their father's rages were indiscriminate, Jasper often joined her there, whether he deserved it or not. On the last day of her life, she ignored their parents' restrictions and ventured too close to the hives, and got herself stung several times. She raised holy hell, running back to the house with a wail so loud Jasper thought his eardrums might split. They both took a beating that day—Lily for disobeying, and Jasper for letting her do it. Their father had already been deep into the bottle, so he delivered his blows with extra enthusiasm. Jasper hated Lily for it. As they were ushered to bed, he told her that he was going to beat her too, and he was going to do it even harder than their dad did. He had no such intention, but it felt good to say it. It felt good to see her scared of him.

That night both children went to sleep, but only Jasper woke up again. His parents said she must have been allergic to bee stings, and suffocated in the night. The bee sting had happened hours before bed, and she'd been breathing just fine then; but Jasper didn't understand how allergies worked, so he had no real reason to doubt it. He thought about the last thing he'd said to her, and cried silently into his pillow.

He never saw her body.

Everything changed after that. That's when Mama started talking to God in her weird new language. That was when the music she played on the radio changed. In some ways it was nice, because she paid more attention to him. She hugged him more, and she told him about how he could protect himself from the evil spirits. That's when his dad started putting the jars out, too; so he could catch them before they got inside the house.

Mama didn't let him talk about Lily, after the Holy Spirit joined them. Jasper liked that at first, because it meant that she stopped crying about her all day. There was room to breathe again. And he liked all the extra attention that came his way.

But after a while, he wondered how Lily felt about it. He wondered if it made her feel lonely.

A thought occurred to him. He tore a page from his book—it seemed sacrilegious, but Uncle Kyle *did* say a handbook was like a conversation—and wrote a few questions onto it. They were questions he thought a naturalist might ask, but mostly they were questions he was actually curious about. Questions he'd want someone to ask him, if he was a ghost.

*Why do you live in the well instead of at home with me and dad? Are you mad at me?*

*What do you eat when you're hungry?*

*Are you scared because you're alone in the dark?*

Then he walked out to the ruined well, sunk beyond the tree line, its lip flush with the ground and covered over by a handful of rotting boards. An abandoned chicken coop sagged on its foundations nearby, its door perpetually locked to keep kids from mischief, haunted now by black widow spiders and paper wasps. Jasper leaned over the stone lip and peered into the black hole. Before Lily had taken up residence there, he had dropped rocks into it, and sometimes larger items—once, daringly, a schoolbook. Each time whatever he threw disappeared from sight. He could almost count to ten before he heard the distant, heavy squelch of mud.

He crumpled the paper into a ball and dropped it down.

He returned to the house with trepidation, but was pleased to see his father standing up, shuffling his feet as he moved slowly across the living room, toward the kitchen. He held his hand against the side of his head. He winced as he turned to face Jasper.

"Where you been all day?"

Jasper studied the tone of the words, trying to get a sense of his father's mood. "Outside."

His dad flicked his eyes to the windows, as if someone might be staring inside. "Your Uncle Kyle come by?"

"No, sir."

"If he does, you make sure you let me know right away. Don't you talk to him, you hear me?"

"Yes, sir." Jasper didn't think his uncle would be coming back. A border had been crossed last night, and now they all traveled through a darker world.

His father made his way into the kitchen, passing the door to the root cellar. He paused once for balance, then opened the cupboard by the sink where he kept his liquor. Jasper knew it was empty, and he steeled himself for a shift in the atmosphere.

Father seemed calm about it, though. He turned slightly

and leaned against the counter. Gingerly, he lifted his shirt, teeth bared in pain. His pale white belly sagged over his belt, and a bruise the size of a small plate marred his left side. It was dark blue, almost black at its center, and Jasper gasped to see it. Father let the shirt fall again. Air hissed through his clenched jaw.

"Dad? Are you okay?"

"Fetch me my wallet."

Jasper darted into his parents' bedroom—just his father's bedroom, now. The air smelled close and sour. Laundry, both dirty and clean together, lay in small piles on the floor, and mounded on a chair. He found the wallet on the nightstand, a narrow flap of brown leather worn pale through long use. A cereal bowl with a scum of milk sat beside it, along with a water glass reeking of whiskey. A couple of his father's little orange medicine bottles lay nearby.

Mama's things used to be on the other side of the room, in her bureau. In truth, most of them had been gone long before she actually left. The jewelry box spilling over with department store finery; the Hollywood gossip magazines; the tubes of lipstick and boxes of eye shadow she doted over, trying on new styles and asking Jasper his opinion of them—all vanished when the Holy Spirit came into her life. Her own disappearance just seemed like the conclusion to a long process. The place had the feeling of an empty socket.

He brought the wallet out to his dad, who took it from him and extracted a twenty dollar bill. "I need you to go on down to the grocery and get me some of that Evan Williams."

Jasper accepted the bill with a thrill of trepidation. "But can I even buy it?"

"Should be old Wiley behind the counter. Just tell him I sent you. He'll sell it to you."

"Are you sure?"

Anger clouded his father's face. "Go on, boy."

Jasper cut through the woods and ran past the beehives until he reached the asphalt road, a pocked two-lane passage through a green vault of trees. He slowed down here and allowed himself to amble a bit, reveling in the heat of the sun on his shoulders. The walk was long, and for a time he lost himself in the easy, flighty thoughts of a ten-year-old boy in late summer.

Wiley's store—simply called Groceries—was situated at a four-way intersection with stop signs at each corner. Jasper looked before he crossed, but there wasn't anything coming from any direction. There hardly ever was. Mr. Wiley's car was parked off to the side, next to a big propane tank people used to fill up their own tanks for grilling.

Inside, it was cool and dark. Mr. Wiley kept the blinds down to keep the heat at bay. An air conditioner labored on the far side of the store. The old man was already staring at him as he pushed his way in, like he had some instinct that helped him pick out little miscreants while they were still coming from a mile up the road. His face was hard and unwelcoming.

Jasper hesitated, then approached the counter and placed his father's money on top of it.

"Well?" said Mr. Wiley.

Now that the moment had arrived, he couldn't remember the name of the whiskey he was supposed to get. Panic percolated in his guts.

"That's a lotta money for you to be haulin' around, son. You come to clear me outta my chocolate bars?"

"No, sir. My dad sent me for his bottle of whiskey."

Mr. Wiley's face maintained its dour configuration. "Did he now."

"Yes, sir."

"What kind does he want?"

"I . . . I don't remember. I think it has a black sticker."

"They's a lotta black labels, son."

Jasper lowered his head to concentrate. The harder he tried, the further it slipped away. He could almost see it go. His father waited for him on the end of his return trip. He was hurting and all he wanted was his favorite drink, and Jasper couldn't even remember what it was. He started to cry; it shamed him, but he couldn't help it.

"Okay now, that's fine, that's all right. I know what your dad drinks." Mr. Wiley turned around and shambled over to a shelf behind him, where he kept ranks of bottles. He pulled down one that looked just like what his dad kept at home. There was the name, too: Evan Williams. It looked almost magical, solid and full, and he knew his dad would be okay for a while. He tried to stop crying, but now he was so relieved he couldn't. It didn't make any sense.

Mr. Wiley punched some buttons on his cash register. "Your dad hasn't been by with any honey for me to sell in a while. Got some folks askin' after it. He still keepin' his bees?"

Jasper thought about all the extra spirit traps. It never occurred to him that that meant less honey to sell. "Yessir," was all he could think of to say.

"Hm. Well I got to say I'm surprised he still has money to spend, now he's not getting your mama's disability checks anymore."

Jasper felt obscurely insulted by this statement, though he didn't really understand it.

Mr. Wiley took the money and counted out some change. He paused and looked at the boy. "Unless he is." He stared at Jasper, like he was waiting for him to say something important. Something that might change things for good.

"My mama left," Jasper said.

Mr. Wiley pushed the change across the counter. He didn't meet Jasper's eyes; he seemed somehow chastened. "Yeah. I know she did, son." He slid the bottle into a paper bag and handed it over. "You be careful with that, now. Don't drop it."

"I won't."

As Jasper was leaving, Mr. Wiley said, "Grab some chocolate off the shelf. For the walk home. Go on, now."

Jasper grabbed a Hershey bar with almonds. He felt funny doing it: guilty and grateful at the same time. He turned around and said thank you, but Mr. Wiley already had his back to him.

It was late August, and the sun still lingered well into the evening. Jasper kept a wary eye on it as he hurried along the empty blacktop toward home. It winked through the leaves, dipping a little further each time he turned away. Shadows flitted through the trees on either side, swelling from the earth. Fireflies drifted in glittering tides. He thought about the feral ghosts, the ones who kept their vigil on the outskirts of the woods, waiting for the protections around their house to fail. He hurried his step.

Jasper pulled the Hershey bar from his pocket. Mama would have disapproved. Sweetness attracts the devil, she said. But it didn't seem like an evil thing. It seemed like a kindness. He tore off the outer wrapper, gently peeled down the silver paper, and bit the corner from it. He let it sit in his mouth for a moment, the warm flavor soaking into him, filling his awareness like a sweet and gentle word.

*They'll sniff you out. They'll follow your stink all the way home. That's why you leave the honey out. Evil gonna lap it right up.*

Jasper devoured the chocolate in a few great bites, the guilt of it almost enough to ruin the flavor. He liked sweet things too; was that a sign of wickedness? Could the dark spirits smell him even now?

As though summoned by a spell, all his bad thoughts bubbled up from the mud in his brain: the way he thought Lily had earned her beating that night, even while he wanted to stop it but was too scared. How he'd threatened her himself. How he relished the peace that followed her death.

He left the road and ran along the shortcut through the woods, racing the nightfall. He passed the beehives, humming in the twilight, with a ripple of apprehension.

Despite the chocolate, he reached home safely. The sun was nearly spent, sending low orange beams through the black woods. His little house looked like a fortress. A warm yellow light slipped through drawn curtains and sent a spear into the night. He imagined Lily waking up now, her eyes spilling a cold light, her little blue fingers reaching through the mud toward the paper he'd dropped.

Stepping past the honey jars, Jasper went inside and closed the door gratefully.

The house stank. It wasn't a smell he recognized. Something hovered beneath the old booze, something metallic and sour. His father was laid out on the couch again. He was awake, but he made no sign that he knew Jasper had returned. His face was pale, his hair plastered with sweat. He was whispering something, and for a moment Jasper wondered who else was here.

He realized with a chill that it was no one he could see.

"Dad?"

He retreated into a corner, his eyes darting around the living room, into corners, into the kitchen, looking for some sign of whoever his father was talking to. Did something get past the jars? A short hallway led off the living room into the bedrooms. The doors to his room and his parents' room were both open to yawning darkness.

"Dad, I got your drink."

Still muttering.

Jasper thought he heard something moving outside. He quickly turned the deadbolt on the door, and scurried over to the couch, where he crouched on the floor by his father's head. He wiped his father's hair away from his forehead; the skin was hot to the touch. Scared, Jasper kept stroking his hair. "I got your drink. Want me to get you some?"

". . . Lily . . ."

Jasper whipped his head around, his fingers gripping his father's hair too tightly. The living room was bright and empty. He went to the window and pressed his face to the glass, seeing nothing but the empty slope of earth leading to the trees. Was his dad scared of Lily? Why?

"Go away."

"Dad, stop!" Lower lip trembling, he returned to the couch. He unscrewed the cap of the bottle and tilted it over his father's mouth. The whiskey spilled down his cheek, but enough got in that his father stopped muttering and craned his neck to it, like a baby to the breast.

His father took it from him. He took another swallow, spilling nothing this time, and drew a shaky breath. His eyes found his son; they looked raw and bloodshot.

"Jasper," he said. His voice sounded far away.

"Are you okay, Dad?"

His father palmed the back of Jasper's head with a rough hand. The strength of that hand overwhelmed whatever fears had harried him along the walk home and worried him now; it was stronger than any ghost. He wanted it to overwhelm him, too.

"Tell her I'm sorry, boy. Tell her that for me."

Jasper awoke with a start. The sense of something fading pulled him upright in his bed. He could almost see it: like a wisp of smoke. He felt desperately cold, and a longing that hurt so much it sprang tears to his eyes. A moment later it was gone, leaving him bewildered and shaken.

Morning sunlight flowed through his windows, outlining every ordinary thing—his piled clothes, his action figures, his air rifle—with solid clarity. There was nothing here that had not always been here.

He remembered the questions he'd asked Lily, and looked around the bed for any evidence that she'd been there. There was nothing.

Something tickled the back of his mind. A rag of memory: his sister, curled against him in sleep, huddling for warmth. Her cold fingers wrapped around his hand. Then it went away.

Jasper's father hadn't left the couch. The bottle at his side held more whiskey than Jasper had expected, which meant he'd spent most of the night asleep or unconscious. Jasper approached quietly. He pressed his hand to his dad's forehead again. It still felt warm, but not as hot as last night. That seemed promising.

In that moment, he felt his mother's absence more acutely than he had in weeks. It had been horrible at first, of course, and he hadn't been able to stop crying, even when it made his father yell at him. When it got to that point, he'd run outside, into the woods so no one could hear him. Usually he'd go to the old car tangled in kudzu. He'd try to avoid going to the well when he could, because he didn't want to make Lily sad. But sometimes he couldn't help it. Sometimes he needed to be close to her.

Jasper snatched up his notebook and headed out to the car. He wanted to be by himself, where he could think.

His mother would have known what to do. She would have made him something nice for breakfast and she would have given him some medicine that would make him feel better. She would sit on the couch with him and hold his head in her lap, and say things in that quiet way she had which always made the world seem just a little bit softer.

He worried about her out in the world by herself. She needed her scooter to ride around on when she went anywhere. She was really big and sometimes that embarrassed her so much it made her cry, but her size was one of the things Jasper loved best about her. She felt comfortable and soft, and when she hugged him he thought it was the gentlest feeling in the world. He liked to help her get up off the couch because it made him feel strong. Sometimes she would let him ride the scooter. He missed that too.

She was too big to drive the car anymore. His dad had to take her places whenever she wanted to go. Jasper wondered how she got away from here, without his dad to drive her. She must have driven the scooter up the long dirt track to where the road started. And then down the road to wherever she ended up going.

He knew the scooter was too small to hold them both, so he understood why she left him behind. But he wished she had asked him to go with her anyway. He could have walked beside her. Who was going to help her get up now?

It occurred to him that she might have seen his book. He'd put stuff in there about the Holy Ghost. She wouldn't have liked that. Maybe that's why she left.

Of all the spirits, the Holy Ghost was the hardest one to write about. He never saw it, but it seemed like Mama saw it a lot. She sure talked about it a lot. He knew it had to do with Jesus and God; she told him once that it was the same thing—they were all the same thing—but then she'd talk about them like they were all separate, too. Jesus had always possessed a sinister aspect for Jasper because of it; he imagined Him rising desiccated from the dark cave where He had been interred, the shroud sliding down His face, His eyes terrible and red as they fixed upon Jasper's every wicked thought, every evil hope.

Despite that, the Holy Ghost was supposed to be a protector. If it didn't protect him, at least it protected his mom. That's what she told Uncle Kyle that one night. Jasper remembered it clearly because it was what his uncle called an "example of behavior," so he wrote it down in the book as soon as he heard it.

Sitting in the derelict car now, he read through that section again. It gave him a sharp pang. He'd almost forgotten that Uncle Kyle had told her to leave, all those months ago. It must have been him who gave her the idea in the first place. They'd been outside, talking by Uncle Kyle's Chevy. His uncle was getting ready to drive back into town after spending the weekend with them. Jasper didn't remember much about that weekend, except that his uncle and his dad didn't talk to each other at all. They never liked each other much, but that weekend had an extra tension.

"You got to get out, Mae. Take that boy and get out."

"I can't."

"Yes you can! I'll help you do it. It's only gonna get worse now."

"You don't know what you're talkin' about, Kyle."

"The hell I don't."

"He's not as bad as you think."

"He's worse." He paused, and tried again. "I got a responsibility, Mae. You're my sister. Jasper's my nephew."

"The Holy Spirit protects me, Kyle. Just like He does Jasper."

"Like He did Lily?"

She slapped him then, hard. Jasper remembered the sound of it even now, the way it carried like a rifle shot, the way it made him feel sick in his heart.

"How dare you," she said. "You got no right. No right."

He put his hand on his cheek. Jasper tensed, waiting for him to hit her back, the way his dad would have done. Waiting for the sound of punched meat, the snap of a bone in her nose. His whole body grew heavy with dread. He wished he was bigger. He could fix things if he was bigger.

Nothing happened, though. Instead Uncle Kyle fixed his mom with a look he had never seen on him before, something ugly and sad. He said, "I got every right." And then all he did was get inside his car and drive away, leaving a cloud of road dust hanging in the still, hot air.

His mom turned and made her way back to the house, treading carefully without her scooter, breathing heavily with the effort. Jasper wanted to go out and help her, but he was afraid she'd be mad at him for eavesdropping. And anyway, she had Jesus's Ghost to help her, he guessed.

Sitting in the old car, Jasper studied the words he'd written down that day, and at the crude little image of a ghost—the kind with a sheet over its head—floating over a crucifix. It had seemed a daring illustration at the time, but now it just embarrassed him. How it would have shamed his mother to see it.

But his gaze kept drifting back to Lily's name. She'd slapped Uncle Kyle when he said it.

Something terrible stirred in his brain.

*Dad, what did you do?*

Jasper pulled the boards away from the well. It gaped at him, dumb and hostile, exhaling its wet, earthy musk. He stretched out beside it, edging forward enough to peer over the edge.

His notebook laid open beside him, the pen resting in its gutter. He extended his right hand into the hole, gripping tightly the little flashlight he'd purloined from his dad's toolbox. He felt the clutch of vertigo. If he dropped the flashlight, he'd pay for it with his hide.

Turning it on felt like an intrusion, but he did it anyway. Balancing on the lip with his chest, he reached out with his left hand and twisted the top of the flashlight. White light speared into the darkness, illuminating the moist, brick-walled shaft extending sixty feet into the earth. The walls glistened; things seemed to slide and skitter across them. He knew that might just be a trick of the light, but the instinct to recoil was strong, and he had to beat it back.

He aimed the light straight down. It was too deep, and the darkness swallowed it.

"Can you see me?" he said.

Jasper listened. He filtered out the sounds of the woods around him—the birds, the chittering squirrels, the shift of leaves in the wind. He focused the whole of his attention on the cool black gulf, and the silence that welled up from it like a breath. He thought he heard something whisper.

"Lily?"

He inched forward, the flashlight still aimed into the depths. He clutched the stone rim with his left hand, the top of his chest now over the open well. Was that a glint of something? The reflection of an eye? Something metal?

The image of his mother's scooter flashed into his mind, broken and half buried in black mud. It hit him like a bullet, something fired through his skull from a distance, and the shock of it rattled him enough that he teetered on the edge, his body for one icy moment balanced like a seesaw between solid earth and the cold, deep fall.

Jasper scrambled away from the lip, the flashlight tumbling into the well. His stomach dropped, and for a dizzy moment he thought he had fallen too. He pressed his face against the packed dirt. Adrenaline sizzled in his blood. He lay there, breathing, until it went away. Only then did he realize that he'd lost the flashlight. With a feeling of despair, he peered into the well again, more carefully this time, and confirmed it. There, like a tiny, tumbled star, was a bright pinprick, and a little wedge of light. Everything around it was black; it illuminated nothing.

Well. It would not be the first beating he'd taken.

Before he went home to receive it, though, he had his task to accomplish. He retrieved his notebook, found a blank page, and scrawled another question for Lily.

*Did Dad hurt you?*

He tore it carefully from the book, crumpled it loosely, and dropped it down the well. He sat for a moment, considering. He felt the heat gathering behind his eyes again, and he wrote another one.

*Did he hurt Mama?*

And he dropped that one down there too.

The tears came. He lay there, letting them have their moment. Then he wiped them away. He got to his feet, brushed off his clothes, and walked home to take what was coming to him.

Jasper found his father lying facedown on the floor. He stood paralyzed in the doorway, the heat of the sun prickling the back of his neck, a chill creeping out from his heart through the rest of his body. The bottle of Evan Williams lay on its side beside the couch, much of its contents spilled onto the floor, filling the little house with its reek.

A groan slipped from his father's lips, and suddenly Jasper could breathe again. He crept inside, the fear of losing the flashlight returning to the forefront of his mind. Kneeling, he grasped his father's shoulders and tried to turn him over. It was like trying to roll a felled buck.

His dad hissed through his teeth. A dark swelling had emerged where he'd been kicked in the head. He opened his mouth and a slurry of half-formed words spilled out: boneless, nonsense syllables. Somehow this scared him more than the ghosts.

"Dad, what? What?"

His father put his big hand on Jasper's shoulder and tried to push himself up. The weight of him collapsed Jasper to his hands and knees, and he had to brace himself before his dad could try again. Even then he almost buckled, but it was enough for his dad to achieve his feet again. He stood uncertainly, his eyes drifting around the room as though he were looking for something familiar. He clamped Jasper's shoulder with his left hand. He looked at his son with bewilderment.

"Dad?"

"I'ma gowow," he said, and took a step toward the kitchen. He paused, as though considering his next move, and took two more steps before pitching to his left. There was nothing around for him to grab hold of, and he hit the floor hard. His head bounced off the floor with a hollow *tok*! He lay quietly where he'd fallen, eyes half-lidded. When Jasper shook his shoulder, he remained as still as the dead.

He could walk to the grocery store before sundown, but not there and back again. With luck, he wouldn't have to; Mr. Wiley would be driving him back. Jasper didn't know where else to go. The phone had been disconnected weeks ago, and Uncle Kyle was not coming back. He needed help, and Mr. Wiley was the only remaining adult in his world.

His father wouldn't move. Jasper knew what drunk looked like; this was something different. He moved the bottle of Evan Williams to within his dad's reach, in case he woke up and wanted it.

"I'm gonna get some help, Dad."

He lit outside and made his way to the road. It lay out before him in a long, simmering ribbon, the horizon wavy with the day's gathered heat. As he hurried along it, his mind cooked up fantasies of an old Chevy manifesting from that haze, Uncle Kyle emerging from it like a hero in a movie. But nothing like that happened. The road remained as empty as a kicked pail.

By the time he got to Wiley's store, it was later than he'd thought it would be. The sun had already disappeared behind the tree line, spilling an orange light across the world. With a lurch in his gut, Jasper realized that Mr. Wiley's car was not in the parking lot. Nor was anyone else's.

He ran to the front door and pulled on the handle, ignoring the CLOSED placard hanging inside. The door was locked. He tugged again, calling out Mr. Wiley's name and pressing his face against the glass.

Everything within looked like it had been sitting there for a long time. The only light came from the exit sign overhead, and from a bulb over the restroom on the other side of the store. The interior was a half-lit mausoleum, a place where things might live that could not live in daylight.

Despairing, Jasper turned away. Shadows had massed beneath the trees and encroached upon the street. The sky was a deep twilight blue, still lit like a lamp, but not for long.

Jasper turned for home. He would go out again in the morning, early. His dad would probably be up by the time he got back home anyway, maybe ready to lay some leather on him for being out so late.

The air was still, but the woods were alive on either side of him. Things moved out there in the darkness, rustling through the leaves and the branches. Overhead, Venus peered through the blue night.

The feral ghosts seethed in the woods to either side. These were the ones Jasper knew the least about. These were the ones that made the night sounds, the ones that surrounded the house in the moonlight, their numbers thinned only by the meager protections of the honey jars. They came hungry for his blood, drawn to his sins like angels to a stinking trough.

*They need a home,* Mama had said. *They smell your nasty heart and they gonna move inside it.* She had delivered that proclamation looming over him as he was settling into bed, the light coming into his room from behind her, so that she seemed the personification of all the dark entities curling through the woods at that very moment, sniffing out his wickedness. He spent that night fighting sleep, listening to every sound intruding upon the stillness.

Jasper had arrived at the place where he could cut through the woods to his house, shaving off a good fifteen minutes from his walk. By now the night had risen to its full grandeur. He stood by the wall of trees, staring into their depths. He'd never been out this late on his own, and had certainly never passed through the forest so far after dark. If he went through, he would walk close to the well; he could call down to Lily, and see if she called back. The thought was both appalling and irresistible.

He pulled his handbook from his back pocket and the pen from his front. He clicked the pen repeatedly, the sound of it grounding him in the moment, the notebook in his hand a link to the comforting memory of Uncle Kyle. He stepped into the woods. The moonlight was snuffed out by the foliage overhead. Treading softly, he crept through the trees toward the well, and toward home beyond it.

Sitting by his window at night, or huddled under the blankets with his father's flashlight, he'd sketched out images of what he thought the feral ghosts looked like. Never having seen one plainly, he went by instinct, measuring their forms by the sounds they made, by the branches left shuddering in their wake. Glimpses here and there. What kind of ghosts were they? Were they once regular people, like Lily, only driven mad by grief and loneliness? And if so, what did that mean for Lily? Would she someday go mad too? Was she mad at him?

*I'll beat you harder than Dad ever did.*

Or maybe they were something different, like Mama said. Something more sinister, something hungry. Something that had never, ever been good or kind.

The darkness was nearly complete, and Jasper almost walked right into the open well. He sensed it before he saw it, the earth's cold and rotten breath tickling his nose an instant before he would have pitched into thin air. He lurched backward and landed on his butt. Slowly, blood drumming in his temples, he lay on his chest and crept to the lip, peering down.

It was like looking into an abyss. No light intruded there, and when he lifted his arms off the ground he felt as though he were floating in some primeval space, as though the well led not to some underground water source but to the cold kingdoms of death, where stillness was absolute.

The little star of light was gone. He didn't think he was going to get in trouble for the missing flashlight, though. He understood that his dad was dying. Something was wrong with his head and it was killing him. Uncle Kyle kicked him too hard.

That's why he had to talk to Lily.

"He said he's sorry," Jasper said. "Okay? He said he was sorry so you have to leave him alone now."

Was she even down there to hear him? He thought about the dark roads he imagined ghosts traveled, the ones that led from their graves to the haunting places—the bottoms of wells, the interiors of empty houses, maybe even to old chicken coops sagging with neglect. How long did it take to get from the grave to here? Did time work for ghosts the same way it did for people? Was a conversation with a ghost—like the writing in his handbook—one that took place over a distance of time?

Was Lily hungry down there? Was she starving?

"I'm sorry, Lily."

Light speared up from the bottom of the hole. It blinded him, froze the breath in his lungs, and although he was in no danger of falling this time he felt as though a dozen hooks had latched into his body and strove to drag him down. He scrambled away, his skin prickling with adrenaline. The light played along the well's edge. Something wet shifted in the mud.

Jasper climbed to his feet. His eyes fell on the sagging chicken coop, a dozen feet away; its door, always locked tight, leaned open.

Jasper ran. The night was huge and clamorous around him. The sounds of things in the wood beat against his ears. A cold presence bellied from the night, driving him faster, lighting his brain with fear. He passed the opening in the trees where the beehives droned. A heavy shape crouched beneath one, its mouth affixed to a hole it had torn in the wood. Angry bees swarmed around its tangled hair as it slurped what was inside.

He kept running, heedless of the branches cutting his skin or of the roots that tripped and staggered him. When he finally saw the single lit window of his house, he sobbed with relief.

Jasper locked the door behind him. But a door was no barrier to ghosts.

His father was nowhere to be seen. In his panic, Jasper hadn't looked at the honey jars outside. Were they there at all? Had they been broken? He was too afraid to look again.

"Dad?"

Not on the couch, not in the kitchen where he'd fallen. He was about to look in the bedroom when he noticed the door to the root cellar was open. Jasper paused, then looked inside. His father lay still at the bottom of the stairs.

Jasper crept down and turned him on his side. The bruises he'd sustained from the fight with Uncle Kyle had swollen and darkened. His face was misshapen, his eyes open and unfocused. The pupils were different sizes. Blood crusted in his ear. Jasper knelt and put his ear to his father's lips; he felt with gratitude the breath stirring his hair.

The cellar was dark but for the spill of light from the kitchen. The honey jars were arranged in dim orange ranks. There were thirty-seven of them, unlabeled, unremarkable save a single strip of paper suspended inside each. Jasper could barely see the paper strips in the dark, but he had been down here enough when it was light to know they were there. He could not make out the writing on any of them, nor was he meant to. These were his father's secret crimes, each a morsel to attract the dark spirits that beleaguered them. Within each sealed jar a trapped devil.

And now, he noted with horror, each of them uncapped,

their lids in a discarded pile on the floor. His father had opened the cages.

There were four full jars which had not been set as traps, but were instead set aside for delivery to Mr. Wiley. These were labeled in his father's careful script: *Walt & Mabel Dodd's Honey Farm.* Maybe four would be enough. Jasper took them into his arms and climbed the narrow stairs to the kitchen, where he unscrewed the lids and arranged them in a little arc in front of the door. The light was welcome, but it still seemed small and weak in opposition to the pitch darkness outside. He stole a glance through the window, but could see nothing through the reflection of the house's interior. All kinds of things might be moving out there.

Jasper took out his handbook and placed it by the open jars. He paged through it quickly, knowing exactly where to find what he was looking for.

There: the notes about Mama speaking in the angels' tongue, about the times she told him how sweet his bad thoughts would taste to the spirits in the wood. He tore the page out, and added a note to it: *Mama went crazy and then I didn't like her anymore.*

And there: Lily dead in the well. The vanishing thoughts in his mind every morning, the tail ends of a lonesome dream. The last words he ever spoke to her just another threat.

*I didn't protect Lily.*

Mama gone too, a glint of reflected light at the bottom of the well that might be her scooter, that might be her staring eye.

*I didn't protect Mama.*

He stole a glance toward the living room window, but all he saw was the reflection of the lit interior. The night, and what lived there, was invisible behind it.

He wrote down the last and most damning note. *I'm glad you're gone. Don't come back. I don't want you here anymore.* He paused, and added another line. *If you come back I will beat you harder than Dad ever did.*

Heart fluttering, he tore each sin from the book, and pushed each one deep into the honey of a separate jar. Then he placed the lids carefully beside them. He took a storm candle from the pantry and lit it with the lighter they kept in one of the kitchen drawers. He switched off the light and the darkness swarmed in.

Through the window, he saw a single light bobbing far behind the tree line. Someone—something—coming home.

Jasper descended into the root cellar once more, closing the door behind him. His father pulled each breath from the air with slowing regularity. The honey jars gaped like open graves. He took them down from their shelves and arrayed them in a circle around his father and himself. The reflected light from his candle gave them a Halloween glow. Unless he was quick, the spirits would soon find their way out, and consume his father before his eyes.

He recalled his dad bleeding on the floor as Uncle Kyle kicked him again and again, while he cowered with indecision. Quaking like a little boy, just like he had when his sister needed him. And maybe just like when his mama did too.

He kissed his father on the forehead. "I'm gonna save you, Dad."

Taking the closest jar, Jasper sank his fingers into the honey and scooped a heavy portion into his mouth. It was thick and wonderfully sweet. It trailed warmly down his hand and onto his wrist, fell in heavy dollops onto his shirt. In an earlier time, this would earn him a beating. He would welcome it now.

The next swallow of honey brought with it the rasping tickle of paper in his throat. His father's sin, consumed. The spirit absorbed. What dark crime had it held? What horror crawled inside him now?

He scooped out another mouthful, and another, and he kept going until the sweetness overwhelmed him and he was forced to stop by a cramping in his stomach. Doubled over, he stared at his father, who lay with his back to him. The candlelight limned the dark, bruised swelling of his temple, pushed light through his tousled hair. Jasper thought he looked beautiful. Almost innocent.

The cramp passed and Jasper kept going. He finished the jar. He started on the next. And then the next. And the next.

Sometime during the night, after vomiting twice, he paused, shuddering by the still form of his father, listening for the soft tread of a little foot on the floor above.

*Not yet,* he thought. *Please not yet.*

He still had such a long way to go.

# His Haunting

*Brian Evenson*

**1.**

Three times in his life someone or something unknown had opened Arn's door as he tried to sleep, silently sliding it ajar and then standing immobile in the gap. That was all, just standing there, unmoving, just barely visible in the darkness. It wasn't even all that threatening, he told his therapist, not really. What had disturbed him most about it was not knowing who or what it was. In the darkness he could make nothing out beyond the door's frame and the silhouette of the figure enclosed within. A large figure, male almost certainly, hulking, head nearly scraping the lintel.

"Who is it?" he had asked that first time, sitting up in bed. How long the figure was there, he wasn't sure—it felt at once like a very long time and no time at all. The figure didn't answer—nothing about it made Arn believe it had heard him. But as soon as he threw his blanket off, the door began to creak shut, the latch sinking into the slot just as he reached it. By the time he fumbled the door open and peered out, the hall outside was deserted.

That first time, he hurried through the small house, searching for it. He turned on the lights and looked into the other rooms, peered into closets and cabinets. No one was there. He felt he should be frightened—and part of him was, but another part was surprisingly calm and unafraid, as if already dead.

Hoping not to have to wake her, he saved his aunt's bedroom for last. But finally, having looked without success everywhere else, he knocked softly on her door. When she didn't answer, he opened it.

It was very dark inside. He could not see her, could only hear thickened breathing.

"Aunt," he whispered. There was no answer.

"Aunt, is it just you in there?" he whispered.

The breathing sputtered, ceased. He heard something move in the bed. He thought he could vaguely make out motion in the darkness, though perhaps this was his imagination.

And for an instant he felt torn in two, as if he were both the person just waking up in bed watching and the figure framed in the doorway—for hadn't he just been the one and now was the other? Only when his aunt shrieked did he begin to feel like a singular person again.

He needed help to sort through them, these three brief moments that were dark little holes drilled in his life. He would come once a week to this office with its aggressively modern furniture and sit in a chair across from the therapist who he had quickly come to think of as *his* therapist and spend forty minutes circling around what his husband liked to call jokingly "your haunting." Arn had trained himself to smile whenever his husband said that, as if it were funny. But it wasn't funny, not really.

*And please,* he warned his therapist, *don't think this is about my resentment of my husband. I have no more resentment than most spouses. I love my husband. I understand he's trying to make me feel better. But it* is *my haunting—that's what he doesn't understand.*

• • •

"I saw something," is what he'd explained, once he'd gotten his aunt calmed down and they were sitting together in the kitchen, lights blazing.

"I saw something too," said his aunt. "It was standing in my doorway looking in at me as I tried to sleep. Turned out to be you, Jack. What the hell were you thinking?"

"I'm not Jack," he responded. Jack had been his father's name. It wasn't even close to his own name. He hardly even looked like his father.

*Don't write that down,* he said to his therapist, and then, *What are you writing down?*

*Does my writing make you nervous?* asked his therapist.

But no, this was not what he was asking for—he was not asking for the experience to be *analyzed,* not yet. This was precisely why he hadn't managed to talk about the haunting, *his* haunting, before now—even though he increasingly recognized that it was what had driven him to therapy in the first place. No, he just wanted his therapist to put the notebook down and listen to what had happened, to take the words in before deciding what they meant.

There at the kitchen table, his aunt held her head in her hands. "I'm so sorry," she said. And then, "Don't worry, I know who you are." It was not until she said this that Arn considered the possibility that at least for a moment she might not have. That it wasn't that she'd misspoke, but that she'd glimpsed someone or something else in his face.

And then she recovered. "What were you thinking, Arn?" she asked. "You scared the shit out of me."

"I'm sorry," he said. "I was looking for it."

"For what?" she asked.

Once he explained, her hands started to shake. Even knowing he'd already searched the house, she insisted they each arm themselves with a knife and search again. They found nothing, nothing and nobody was there. They went outside with flashlights and shined them along the ground near the flowerbeds, but there was nothing there either, no footprints, no signs of disturbance. They played their flash beams up at the roof and saw nothing but roof. They opened the storm cellar and descended, but there was nothing down below, either, just the faint, sour smell of rot.

And yet, from that day forward his aunt treated him differently, with caution, as if she wasn't sure she recognized him.

*Time passed,* said Arn.

*And so you forgot about it,* said his therapist.

*No,* said Arn, *I never forgot. Every time I fell asleep I expected to open my eyes and see that door open again with a darker silhouette standing within its dark opening.*

But it didn't happen again. Not in that house anyway. Not around his aunt. That was the odd thing, he told his therapist: He'd always thought of hauntings as being bound to a place—a house, a pool in which somebody had drowned, the site of a fatal car wreck, that sort of thing. He'd wasted a lot of time trying to figure out what it was about his aunt's house that had led to him seeing the silhouette appearing at the threshold of his room. Native American burial ground? Decades-old murder? Previous residence of someone who died alone and neglected? But there was nothing.

*So,* said his therapist once he fell silent. *You were already thinking of it as a ghost.*

*Oh yes,* Arn said. *As a haunting. But not yet as* my *haunting.*

"You must have dreamed it," his aunt said as he kept talking, kept quizzing her down about the house. "It's just an ordinary house, built just a year or two before you were born. Before that, this was an orange grove."

"But there must—" he started.

"Sometimes dreams can be so vivid as to seem real," his aunt said firmly. "You dreamed it."

*Your aunt raised you,* ventured his therapist. *But I'm afraid I'm confused about what happened to your parents.*

*So am I,* said Arn.

His therapist tented his fingers, gazing at Arn over them, eyes steady. He waited.

*I never knew my mother,* Arn finally said. *She died when I was born. My father . . . vanished.*

*Vanished?*

Arn nodded. *One day my father woke up and he no longer looked like himself.*

*What did he look like if not himself?*

*I don't know. I remember sitting at the breakfast table with him, looking for something in his face, unsure what. All I knew was, it wasn't there. And then I realized he was looking at me, too, staring. He was trying to pretend he was reading his paper, but he was staring over it at me. Whatever he was looking for he was finding, and it frightened him.*

*I left for school,* Arn continued. *When I came back that afternoon he was gone. I never saw him again.*

*What do you think happened to him?*

*I don't want to talk about it,* said Arn. *Not today.*

*This is a safe place—,* his therapist began, but Arn rapidly cut him off.

*You believe my haunting will tell you something about my relationship with my missing father,* he said, *that that's the point of me telling it to you. Maybe so. You can tell me that next time if you'd like. But for now let my haunting be my haunting.*

But Arn seemed to have lost the thread. For a moment the two of them just sat there, faces blank, expressionless. Then his therapist cleared his throat and spoke.

*She thought you were dreaming,* he said. *Your aunt, I mean.*

*Yes, so she said.*

*Have you considered she may have been right?*

*Yes.*

*And?*

*Not remotely possible.*

*How can you be sure?*

*I'm sure.*

*But how?*

Arn, humming softly under his breath, ignored him.

*And the second time?* asked his therapist.

*Excuse me?* said Arn.

*There were three times, you said. What about the second?*

*Ah,* said Arn. *Yes.*

**2.**

Time marched on. Arn grew up. He was admitted to the local college. He moved out of his aunt's house and into a dormitory.

More time passed. He was studying something, working toward a degree. It did not matter what he was studying, he told his therapist: It had no bearing on his haunting. He was a junior in college and suddenly was living alone, his room-mate having received academic probation followed by a semester of suspension.

He was lying on his bed trying to sleep. It was perhaps two in the morning. There were still noises coming from the hall despite the time being late enough that quiet hours were supposedly in effect. His door was closed, the light from the hallway shining through the crack beneath it. Occasionally the light would flicker as someone walked down the hall and past his door.

At some point he drifted off. Maybe he was asleep just for a few minutes, maybe for several hours.

He awoke to the impression that something was wrong. He remained in bed, blinking, trying to see. Why couldn't he see? Usually he could, even at night, even if only just a little. But now he couldn't. Suddenly he realized why: The light in the hallway was no longer on.

But the light in the hallway was *always* on. There wasn't even a switch to turn it off. All night it seeped beneath the door enough for him to dimly make things out, as if in sleep he remained lodged in a colorless facsimile of the actual world.

There was a light of sorts, but exceptionally low and at a great remove, like a single flickering candle held cupped by a hand at the far end of the hall. He could see nothing at all of the room around him. The only thing he could see, barely, was the outline of the doorframe.

Even seeing this, it took his mind some time to register the fact that the door must be open. But once it did, he began to see the silhouette crowded into the doorframe, hunched, almost too large to fit, waiting, immobile, watching him.

*How do you know it was watching?* interrupted his therapist.

*I thought I could see its eyes,* he said. *Or not eyes exactly, but a gleam or glister where I knew eyes should be. Which led me to believe its eyes were open and looking steadily at me.*

"Hello?" Arn had said. "Who are you?" Because he did want to know. He was frightened, of course, but above all else, he wanted to know who or what it was.

The figure did not respond. It seemed again, just like that first time, years before, not to have heard him.

Carefully, slowly, he started out of the bed and crept toward the door. But the door was already closing, and even though he rushed it at the end, he was not quick enough to stop it from slamming shut. Or, rather, he managed to get two of his fingers around the edge of the door before it closed in its frame, but the door closed anyway.

He lifted up his hand, showed his therapist the awkwardly crimped ends of his middle and index finger where the last joint of both digits had been sewed back on. He had felt the severing, the brief, sharp pain of each joint being sheared off, followed by the warm throb, enough of a distraction that he almost missed that something had changed: He could see.

The light in the hallway was on again. He tore open the door and looked out on an ordinary hall: no silhouette in sight, the hall just as it had always been, except for the blood drizzling from his fingers onto the grimy carpet.

The fingers had been reattached, though he could feel nothing in the top joint of either of them—it was as if they were dead. He had thought long and hard about this second time, unsure what to make of it. The only point in common between his aunt's house and his dorm room, at least that he could see, was himself. The ghost, if it was a ghost, must be tied to him.

But why him? For this, he had no answer. Nor did he have an answer for why it would visit him so infrequently, or why both times it was always reduced to that single gesture of standing in a doorway, his doorway, the doorway to his bedroom, in the dark.

**3.**

A decade more passed, he told his therapist. He graduated, got a job, became a responsible citizen. He met the man who would become his husband, they fell in love, lived together, married once the law allowed it. They bought an apartment together, and he allowed a certain form of existence to crystallize or calcify around him. And yet, all the while he was waiting, wondering when—not if but when—despite his move far away, his haunting would find him again. For it would find him, he was sure of that.

He had a few false alarms. Times when he awoke to find his husband, who tended to come to bed much later than he, standing in the open door, motionless, waiting for his eyes to adjust to the darkness before navigating a path to the bed. But his husband's silhouette looked nothing like the silhouette of his haunting. Arn was the larger of the two of them by far. His husband, small, could not come close to filling a doorway.

The third incident he thought at first was just that—his husband hesitating in the doorway just before coming to bed. He felt a presence and half opened his eyes, and groaned, and said, "How late is it? Come to bed already."

When there was no answer at all, not a sound, he found himself startled fully awake.

The room around him seemed too dark. He turned and could just make out the open doorway.

"What's wrong?" he started to say, but got very little of it out, for he realized the shape in the doorway was so large it could not possibly be his husband. And, in any case, his husband was there already, in the bed beside him, breathing heavily, sound asleep.

*And then,* he told his therapist, *something happened that I didn't expect. You see, I had made the mistake of inviting it, whatever it was, to come to bed.*

The figure was still motionless, still little more than a silhouette, but it was no longer in the doorway. No, it was just inside the room now, as if a bit of film had skipped or as if he had closed his eyes and it had moved only while it could not be seen. And then it was closer still, and closer still, until it was there, just beside the bed, but still motionless, still little more than a silhouette. He could see again those dull gleams that he thought of as the gleam of its eyes—but could see now that they were scattered all over its body, as if its entire skin was studded with them, with eyes that couldn't quite be made out. He couldn't move. It came very close until it was touching him but he couldn't feel anything. And then it came closer still and he felt very cold. And then it passed slowly through him and across the bed.

Somebody's breath was hissing fast through clenched teeth, and though he rationally understood it must be his teeth, his breath, they still seemed to belong to somebody else. Someone was screaming and it was him screaming, only it wasn't him either. And then his husband was shaking him and the light was on and shining into his eyes and the figure in the doorway was again nowhere to be seen.

*Where do you think it went?* his therapist asked, after waiting long for Arn to continue.

*My husband,* he said.

*Your husband?*

*He was the only other one in the bed. It was moving toward him. It moved through me and toward him.*

*Don't you think that—*

*Now, sometimes in its least guarded moments I see something flit across his face, coming to the surface to breathe.*

*It seems to me—*

*It's his haunting now. He doesn't know yet of course. How could he? He won't know until it is his turn to see it in the doorway.*

*But then where was it before?*

Arn looked hard at his therapist. *Can't you guess?* he asked. *Why do you think my father left? What do you think he was looking for in my face? The same thing I was no longer finding in his. It must have been in him before. After it left him, where else could it have been but in me?*

He cracked his neck, then slowly took hold of the arms of the chair and pulled himself to his feet. He looked older, tired somehow, almost a different person.

*Next time,* he said, *you can ask me the usual questions. Next time we can analyze all this to death.*

*We still have a few minutes remaining,* his therapist said. *I really think we should talk about this.*

But Arn just shook his head. *Next time,* he repeated, and made his way to the door. Upon opening it he hesitated a moment, his body nearly filling the frame. Then he turned his shoulders slightly and sidled through.

**4.**

It was a moment that the therapist would think about often, particularly after it became clear that he would never see Arn again. After Arn missed the next few appointments and he took steps to try to find him, he would discover, talking to his distraught spouse, that Arn, like his father before him, had simply disappeared.

Which meant the therapist's last real memory of Arn was of the man standing motionless in the open doorway, facing away from him. But the back of his head still, somehow, gave (when the therapist thought about it later, alone, at night in bed, in the dark, struggling to sleep) the impression of looking back in, of noticing him.

# The Jeweled Wren

*Jeffrey Ford*

On a late October afternoon, the sun still casting a weak warmth, Gary, sixty-eight, a large man with a drastic crew cut, and Harriet, sixty-five, a small woman with big glasses and short gray hair, sat out behind the garden on the green plastic bench drinking bourbon, taking in the autumn wind, and looking out across the stubbled wheat field toward a house a half-mile distant.

They talked about their daughters, grown and moved away a decade earlier, how the cut field looked like a Breughel painting, Harriet's uncertainty about the woman at work who would soon replace her when she retired. After that burst of conversation there was silence.

Gary broke it by asking, "What did the doctor say?"

"Drink more bourbon," she said, and Gary knew, because he'd known her for forty-four years, to change the subject.

"So, did we ever decide what the fuck is going on over at that place?" he asked and pointed with the hand holding his drink at the distant house.

She had a blue blanket wrapped around her, one corner thrown over her head like a hood. "If you notice, there's all kinds of action, but it's all subtle, incremental. And you have to be aware when you drive past."

"I noticed the hanging geranium that appears on the porch certain mornings and disappears by noon," he said.

Harriet nodded. "For three weeks this past summer, I swore someone had a tomato garden going behind the place. But when I slowed down and concentrated, there was nothing there."

"Have you seen the two little blond girls playing outside lately?"

"I haven't seen a person there in months," she said.

"There was a yellow car in the driveway when I drove past a couple of weeks ago. It was the only time I'd ever seen it there—might have been an old Mercury Topaz like we had back in the nineties."

"Never saw it," she said.

"The circumstantial evidence for being haunted kind of adds up," said Gary.

"We should go over there and look in the windows," said Harriet.

"Why?"

"I have the next five days off from work, and I want to do something crazy while I still can." She poured another drink and held it up. He touched the rim of his glass to hers.

"You mean go across the field?" Gary asked.

"Now that its cut, it'll be easy."

"With my bad leg?"

"I'll get you a cane. You've got to get up and move around anyway. That's what the doctor said about the band syndrome."

"But what if someone actually *is* living in there, and we look in the windows and they see us. We'll be fucked. Even without the bad leg, at this stage of the game, running is out of the question."

"There's nobody over there," Harriet said. "The car probably belonged to a real estate agent."

They sat drinking, watching the wind shake leaves from the giant white oak, and the turkey vultures circling over the field until the sun set a little after five. Then she helped him up and as far as the garden. Eventually he got his leg going and passed beneath the apple trees on his own. Inside, she put the news on in the living room and he fed the dogs.

In bed, they talked about her looming retirement. He already only taught part-time at a local university. Did they really need six acres and a hundred-and-twenty-year-old home? They arrived at no answers. Luckily, the haunted house across the field wasn't mentioned. He thought that was the last he'd hear of a trip to it, but the next day she returned from Walmart with two flashlights and a cane. He asked when and she told him, "By cover of dark."

"You mean tonight?" he said.

She had a brief coughing spasm, the likes of which she'd been having fairly frequently of late. She nodded. Before he could complain, she caught her breath and said, "Hold on a second. Didn't you ever really want to just know what the fuck was up with something?"

"I guess," said Gary. "But . . ."

"Well, that's what's going on here. You and I, just us, together, we're going to get to the bottom of this."

"Let me see that cane," he said. He pictured himself out in the cut wheat field, lurching forward, the cane snapping beneath sudden weight and then a face-first dive into the mud.

She handed it to him and he said, "It's a cheap piece of crap. That's a cane for training horses."

"Perfect then," she said, and handed him a flashlight.

The sky was clear and full of stars but it was cold, and he felt it in his hip. Every time he leaned on the cane it sunk two inches into the damp ground and set him off balance. Still, he took a deep breath and launched himself forward into the night. She helped him along through the orchard and past the garden to the edge of the cut amber field, where she let go. He stumbled through the wheat stubble toward an old white house, invisible in the distance. Fifteen minutes later, she stood in the middle of the miles-deep field, smoking a cigarette and staring at the moon. She'd been there for nearly five minutes already, waiting for him to catch up. As he scrabbled toward her, she said, "How's the leg?"

"Hurts like a bitch," he said. "I think I feel bone on bone. This is no IT band syndrome."

"Don't give me that bone on bone business," she said. "Pick up the pace or we'll be at this all night."

He stopped next to her and turned to take in the enormity of the field around them. "I know why those turkey vultures were circling above here yesterday," he said. "They were feeding on the last two nitwits who decided to do something crazy."

She laughed and they walked together for a while.

From a quarter mile distance, they could make the place out, what was left of its white paint reflecting moonlight. She strode ahead impatiently, and he hobbled over the lumpy ground. Somewhere in the middle of their approach, he had a memory of the two little girls, both in frilly white dresses, playing in a red plastic car with a yellow roof. One seemed to him a year or two older than the other.

Harriet slowed down and pointed. "Check it out."

There was a dim light on in the upstairs window at the side of the house.

"Did you see it there before?" he asked. "There was no light there before, right?"

"You know, I'm not sure it's a light on inside or if it's from the moon beams directly hitting the window. As we get closer we might find it's just a reflection."

"If there's a light on, I think we should turn back."

"We'll see," she said.

In another hundred yards, they saw it had been but a reflection and that room was as dark as the rest.

Near the border between the field and the barnyard, Harriet held up her hand to stop him. They stood in silence—she breathing heavily, he shifting his weight off the bad hip and relying on the fragile cane. There were four buildings clustered at the center of the property, all once painted white. The main house, a three-story Victorian with a wraparound porch, like their own place; a barn; a long outbuilding—a kind of garage to cover a tractor; and next to the white submarine of a propane tank, a smaller garden shed. The yard was no less than seven acres, and much of it was covered with stands of black walnut.

"Pretty quiet," whispered Gary.

"Creepy," she said.

"It doesn't get to me in a creepy way," he said. "It makes me feel like this location, right here, is so far from the rest of life it would take a week's walk along a dusty road to get within hailing distance of a Walmart."

"Where are we gonna start?" asked Harriet.

"I don't care, but no breaking and entering."

"The garden shed is probably bullshit," she said. "The tractor garage, I can tell right now there's nothing in it." She turned her flashlight beam on the structure's opening and the light shone straight through into a stand of trees on the other side. "The barn is interesting but it looks locked up. Let's start with the house."

"I don't care," he said. "The place is dead. We're too late."

"Cheer up," she said and crossed the boundary onto the lawn.

He followed her, and immediately it was a relief to be able to walk on flat ground and not up and down the furrowed muddy plough rows complicated by what remained of the shorn wheat. They passed the oak, whose biggest branch held a tire swing. The half-deflated tube turned in the wind.

"Maybe we should sneak around a little first and see if we hear anybody inside."

"Okay," she said, and instead went straight around to the front of the house, stepped up to the parlor windows, turned on the flashlight, and pressed her face to the glass.

When he caught up with her, he stood behind her, off the porch. "What do you see?" he asked.

"There's furniture and stuff in there."

"So they never moved out?" he said.

"Unless maybe they just left everything and fled."

"But they couldn't have because we saw them here as late as February, and I know I saw the girls one day in spring. Remember in March when it snowed eight inches? They had a sled out in the yard and were pushing each other around."

"I'd seen the mother there quite a few times for a while."

"Young woman, short blond hair."

Harriet nodded. She turned away from the window. "Did you ever actually see her face?" She walked to the edge of the porch and he took her hand as she descended the steps. They headed around the house to search for other windows.

"Now that you mention it, no. I never saw her face," he said. "What about the guy, did you ever see his face?"

"No."

"I remember, that guy always had on a plain white T-shirt. Plain white T-shirt and jeans," said Gary.

Along the side of the house, in the shadows near the chimney, she spotted, without use of the flashlight, a little set of steps that descended to a basement entrance. The door to the basement had glass panes, still intact, and a glint of starlight caught her eyes. She stopped, backtracked, and only as she took the concrete stairs, flipping on her light, did Gary realize where she was headed. He watched from ground level as she descended.

"Well?" he said.

"I have news for you," she called over her shoulder. "This door's unlocked."

Then he heard the screeching of the hinges as she pushed through the opening and stepped inside. He turned on his flashlight for the first time and gingerly descended, keeping one arm pressed against the side of the house and using the cane with every placement of his right foot. She'd left the door open, and he could see her light beam jumping around the pitch-black room.

The place smelled of damp and dirt. It was colder inside than it had been in the autumn field. The vault held one skid with boxes of what looked to be Christmas decorations, wilted silver garland spilling out the top. Another few boxes, also on skids, but those closed up and stacked neatly. There was the propane heater, the water softener, the fuse box mounted on the wall. A toad leaped across the dirt floor heading for the shadows.

"At every corner of the basement," said Harriet, "there's a plate with a rotting horse chestnut on it. Could be some ghost nonsense."

"It's to keep spiders out of the house," said Gary.

"How do you know that?" she asked.

"Some guy told me when I was over walking in the preserve. There are a couple of those trees and they'd dropped these weird green globes. I asked the guy what they were and he told me all about them. I asked him if the spider thing really worked. He said, 'Good as anything.'"

"Now what?" she asked. "There's the stairs up into the house." She pointed with her flashlight beam.

"Come on," he said. "What are we even looking for anyway?"

"Anything ghostlike or ghost related."

"Let's go home," he said.

She shushed him and started up the stairs.

In the kitchen, they found dishes in the sink, and a cigarette ash as long as a cigarette on the counter. Someone, some months back, left behind a cup of coffee and an English muffin with two small bites out of it. She opened the refrigerator. No light shone out, but a smell like Death, itself, wafted through the room.

She slammed the door closed. "Bad meat," she whispered. "The power's off to everything."

"God, that smell. Maggots are growing in my brain from it."

She'd already moved on and was inspecting the cabinets. "Look here," she quietly called to him. Her flashlight illuminated the contents of a cupboard. "What do you see there?"

He moved closer and added the glow of his own flashlight. "Six cans of Beefaroni and a withered potato sprouting eyes."

"I'd say that's at least tangentially haunted."

"Does six cans mean they liked it or they didn't?" he asked.

From the kitchen, they moved on to the second floor where there were three bedrooms. He complained in whispers throughout his awkward ascent, the flimsy cane without a rubber tip tapping loudly upon each step.

"Keep it down," she said as he hobbled up next to her in the hallway of bedrooms. It was clear right away from the thumbtacked drawings on the doors that each of the girls had their own room.

He surmised that the one at the far end of the hallway from the stairs belonged to the parents.

"Pick one," she said. "We'll just look in and take a peek and then we'll split. The place smells like ancient ass."

"No argument there," said Gary.

She took the left-hand side and he the right. They each pushed open a door, flashlight lit and ready.

Harriet rummaged for only moments before discovering some pages of homework scattered upon the dresser. There she read the name—Imsa Bridges. The girl's handwriting was very neat. Her theme was the four seasons. In it she claimed that the last days of summer might be the most beautiful of all. She likened winter to a sleep, and the autumn, heralded by the wind chime, was a season in which secrets both hideous and bright were revealed. Of spring, there was no mention.

In Gary's room, there was a hole in the middle pane of the triple-paned window. It looked as if the glass had been suddenly punched out. Rain had invaded and puddled on the floor. He could feel the inordinate dampness of the space. As he moved his flashlight around, he saw that shelves of a fine blue fungus had grown all over the walls. From outside there came a noise of tires on gravel and in that instant, he looked down and there was a picture frame holding a faded polaroid of one of the girls. The frame was made of blocks with letters, and the letters spelled her name, SAMI BRIDGES.

"Shit," he heard Harriet say across the hall. He hobbled toward her door, and as he did she came out and whispered, "Turn off the flashlight."

"What?"

"Someone just pulled up in an old yellow car."

"Fuck," he said, and with that word they heard the front door downstairs creak open. She took him by the arm, and they moved along the hallway toward the last room. She whispered to him as they went, "If I hear that fuckin' cane on the floor, I'm gonna beat ya with it."

From downstairs came a bellowing male voice, "Sunny."

The next thing Gary knew he was on his considerable stomach on the floor and Harriet was shoving while he shimmied under the bed. After he was hidden, she tiptoed around to the other side and got under. Once she was in place they found each other's hands to hold.

"This is so fucked up," he whispered.

"Shhh."

The voice called again, this time up the stairs from the first floor, "Sunny?" There were footsteps ascending. As if that started something in motion up on the third floor, they heard the screams of children and a woman repeating the phrase, "Save yourself."

The door opened. Somehow the electricity had come back on because light from the hallway streamed in. From where they lay, they could see the boots, the jeans, and the bottom of the intruder's white T-shirt. They watched him open the middle drawer of a dresser, and reach in. When his hand reappeared, it was holding a revolver. He left the room and a moment later they heard him on the stairway to the third floor.

"Hurry up," she whispered and slipped out from under the bed. She ran to his side, grabbed his arm, and pulled harder than he pushed to free him. The first gunshot upstairs went off as they clasped hands and she helped him to his feet. Before the second shot went off they'd reached the stairs. Gary was moving faster than he knew he could. The pain was there but it paled in relation to gunplay. When Harriet opened the front door, deep screams of agony rained down from above.

Gary went through the door left open by Harriet, but didn't count on the screen door that came back hard and clipped him on his left shoulder. It set him off balance when he went to take the first step down off the porch. His leg on the side of the bad hip just suddenly gave out, as it occasionally did, and by the time he reached the yard he was staggering toward a fall, madly employing unsuccessful cane work until his face was in the mud.

Harriet helped her husband to his feet and brushed him off. He looked around on the ground for the cane and saw it by moonlight in two pieces. "Why aren't we running?" he asked her.

"Look," she said, and they turned around. "The car's gone and the house is perfectly quiet."

"Well, we certainly got to the bottom of that," he said.

She took his arm around her shoulders and he leaned a

little on her with each step as they made their way back across the field.

Despite how cold it had gotten, and that their words were steam, they sat on the porch, low music, three candles burning, bourbon and ice. He leaned back in his rocker and said, "So what'd you make of it?"

"You think he killed them all and then himself?" she said.

"Or they all killed him, or the girls killed the folks, or the wife did them all. Or just maybe, nobody killed anybody."

"Yeah," she said. "The whole thing seemed kind of melodramatic. Did it ring true to you?"

He shrugged. "All I can say is I was scared shitless. What about you?"

"I'm not sure I even saw what I saw," she said.

"Some of it's vague," he admitted. "Could have been like a communal hysterical dream between the two of us."

"After we got outside, and you took a dive . . ." She raised her eyebrows and stifled a laugh.

"I told you that cane was for shit."

"Anyway," she continued, "before I picked you up, I saw something hanging on the branch of a pear tree right in the front of the house. By then I realized the car and its driver had vanished."

"That's some haunted business right there," he said.

"I stuffed the thing from the tree in my jacket as a souvenir." She took off her glove and reached into her pocket. Slowly, she brought forth something made of bright metal. She laid it on the table between them, and he lit it with his flashlight.

There were jewels, fake or real, he couldn't tell—in red, green, and blue. It was a bird in a nest feeding its chicks. Beneath hung metal chimes on thick wire. "It's a wren, I think," she said. She picked it up from the small table and stood. Leaning off the porch, she hung the wind chime on a branch of an ornamental maple only an arm's length away. Before returning to her seat, she ran her fingers along the bottoms of the chimes and they sounded like icicles colliding. She shivered and pulled the blanket wrapped around her over her shoulders. The wind picked up and the temperature dropped.

They had another drink and spent the next hour talking themselves out of the experience they'd had at the Bridges house. Eventually they sat in silence and soon after fell asleep wrapped up against the cold and fortified with bourbon. The sound of the wind chime in their dreams was like children giggling. A little before four a.m., he woke her and they went inside and up the stairs to bed.

Beginning the next day, there was an unspoken understanding between them not to bring the Bridges house up in conversation. When Gary went out to teach, he went the long way around so as not to pass the place. Only across the empty winter field, a dot in the distance on the brightest day, an impression of sorrow on a cloudy one, would he view the Bridges' house. Harriet also avoided passing the place, and drove the five miles out to the highway no matter where she was going.

Past harvest to the first snow, Gary left the window open in his office. He counted on the cool air to keep him awake while he wrote. All through those days as the last frayed threads of summer vanished and the world turned toward darkness, the jeweled wren sounded, its intermittent tinkling ever a surprise. Its music leaked in through his office window while he worked, and swamped his thoughts. Sometimes when he'd stopped typing and was staring at the wall, the two blond girls came back to him. And from some distant recesses of his memory came a bellowing voice, "Sunny."

Harriet sat out on the covered porch every night, no matter the weather. Fierce winds, frozen temperatures, blowing snow, never stopped her. She put on her parka, cocooned herself in a blanket, and took her bourbon outside to smoke and cough or both. There were nights when Gary joined her, but often she sat by herself and decompressed from the day at work. Inspecting and then consciously forgetting each incident from the office she ran. One night in early November, she heard a sound like angels whispering and when she realized it was the chimes, she smiled and wept.

They spent Thanksgiving together, eating dinner at the Uncertain Diner. Later there were drinks on the porch. She smoked and he fiddled with a music box he'd recently bought. It worked on Bluetooth and could play the songs stored on his phone.

Three bourbons in, Gary's favorite head music swirled the night. Harriet said, "We've got to go back."

At first he said nothing, but eventually he nodded and said, "I can't believe I'm saying this, but yeah."

"Tonight," she told him.

"One stipulation," he said. "Let's take the fucking car."

"There are no other houses over there, and once you're off the road, it's so dark no one will see. I can park it in the empty tractor shed and we can walk from there," she said.

"Solid."

"Above all others, what's the one thing you want to know?" she asked.

"I'll start with a general what the fuck and proceed from there."

"I want to know the calamity of events that led to it."

"Led to what?"

"Whatever tragedy keeps calling these people back."

"Jeez," he said and poured them each another drink.

Harriet drove Gary's CRV. They rounded the corner and as the Bridges place drew near, she turned out the headlights and coasted through the dark. She slowly piloted the car in and around tree trunks and hid it in the old structure as she said she would. Gary had a better cane, stronger, made to support the weight of an adult. It had a rubber tip and grips along the crook. His hip was worse every day and walking was becoming too great an effort, but Harriet insisted he keep moving. So he did. They both wore all black and carried their flashlights. She brought the Taser she'd bought online. He'd asked why she didn't just buy a gun. And she said, "I don't want to kill anyone."

"How do you kill a ghost?" said Gary.

"You know what I mean."

She led him through the shadows and he tried mightily to keep up with her. From using the cane he'd adopted a rocking side-to-side gait like he was a windup toy. The house loomed in front of them and they slipped around the side to where the steps led down. They took the same route as they had before. This time they didn't inspect the basement but went straight for the stairs that led up into the house. They passed the refrigerator and the Chef Boyardee and went directly to the hallway on the second floor.

"Same rooms?" he asked.

"No, up to the third floor."

"We'll be trapped up there."

"We have to get up there and hide before that whole thing goes down."

"Hide?"

"Yeah, so we see what happened. We need to know more."

He shook his head but followed her up the steps, which led to a large room, a window on every wall. It was lined with carpets and plush furniture in a powder blue with silver trim that shimmered in the flashlight's glare.

"Find a place to hide," she said.

He turned in a circle looking for something substantial to hide behind where it wouldn't discomfort his hip, but there wasn't anything that big in the room. "I'm not getting on the floor again."

"Shhh. Go in the closet over there," said Harriet and pointed with the light beam.

He saw where she meant, went to it and opened the door. It was dark and empty, damp concrete. *Who has a concrete closet?* he thought. He stepped in and closed the door over behind him but didn't shut it. When he got in position, leaning on his cane, he peered out and around the room, using the flashlight, and finally found her ducked behind a sewing machine on a wooden box in the corner. The instant he spotted her, he heard tires on gravel. A moment after he doused his light, the front door downstairs flung open and that voice called, "Sunny."

The lights came on at once in a silent explosion. And there was the mother and two girls sitting on couches. The girls were silent and stock-still in their white party dresses. From Gary's vantage point in the closet, he stood behind and above the blond woman, who sat on a divan in front of him. He watched her turn around on her seat, stare directly into the sliver of an opening he watched through and pierce his eyes with her vision. "Save yourself," she said as if directly to him.

That's when Mr. Bridges stepped through the door, head turned in a way that made it impossible for Gary or Harriet to see the man's face clearly.

He wasn't in the door more than a moment before his wife told him the same, "Save yourself."

As he approached his wife, the two girls slid off the bench they were sitting on and fell to their knees. They clasped hands in prayer and recited the Act of Contrition. While they prayed, a dark cloud began to form against the wall across the room. They prayed hard, in unison, eyes peering through the roof to heaven. The father lifted the gun and put it inches from the back of the older girl's head.

It became obvious that the intonation of their words was the impetus for the cloud to take the shape of a man in a raincoat and hat. The vagueness of fog solidified into a cruel face, sharp like an ax head but also handsome. He walked forward as in a slow dream and took the gun from Mr. Bridges's hand. Harriet thought she heard cymbals clash, and next she knew, the husband and wife were bleeding profusely from a hundred cuts each. The fog man moved with such speed and grace, she didn't see the blade until he was almost done filleting them. Seven more stabs between them and the mother and father fell to the floor in puddles of blood.

He called for the girls, still praying, to follow him. They stood in silence and did as they were told. As they headed for the door, Harriet and Gary saw that at his edges, the man in coat and hat was beginning to transform, vines of smoke slowly twining upward. Just then a coughing fit seized her. The fog fellow stopped, spun around on his heels, and took in the parlor. Gary didn't watch, but he heard the words, "You, in the corner. Come out of there." His legs went numb and his breathing became erratic. There was a struggle, and the stranger bellowed, "Come with me for a drive." Gary could tell Harriet was being dragged toward the exit and the stairs.

He lunged out of the closet as the sisters passed, knocking them over like pins in a split, his cane waving in the air. He clutched it near the rubber tip and swung the crook end at the head of the abductor. Harriet reached into her jacket pocket and took out the Taser. She pressed the button to charge it up and then jammed it against the fog man's rippling neck. He was solid and smoke at the same time. With the addition of the electricity, his head lit up and he glowed green like an iridescent fish. The application of the cane nearly knocked him down. He staggered and Harriet broke free of his grip.

Gary caught her in his arms. She turned and screamed, "Get out!" at the ghosts.

The man in the raincoat and hat turned to dust, and each of the sisters became a puddle. The lights were out.

"I'm never coming back here," Harriet said, as much to the walls as to Gary. "It's a trap."

He said nothing until they were driving through the snow. "It'd take us a hundred hundred trips to figure the whole thing out."

"I don't want it anymore," she said. "I don't want to know. I'm too tired."

Gary and Harriet tried to forget the entire enterprise, but the sound of the chime on the porch had the ability to drill through the walls of the house and find them wherever they were. Every time the wind blew that winter they contemplated the mystery, extrapolating scenarios based on the flimsy knowledge they'd gathered. By January, they were aware that every sounding of the wind chime distorted time, lengthening seconds, shrinking weeks, twisting speed, and dealing crooked minutes. A year buzzed by like a mosquito and they were retired.

Hours became epics, and Gary and Harriet missed each other, passing along different corridors. Whole days went by and he wouldn't see her, but he heard her above or below in the house and could call out and she would answer him. He would call that he loved her and she would answer the same. Different seasons, all but spring, came and went. And eventually her presence grew rarer and her voice quieter. One weak cough from some far-flung room of the old house. The sudden noise of a toilet flushing downstairs or the microwave dinging in the night helped him hold out hope that he'd run into her before long. Eventually, though, the distant echoes stopped altogether along with the written notes she'd leave through her days like breadcrumbs on the trail.

One afternoon, he found himself in the bedroom, unable to recall why he was there. He happened to look out the window and saw her standing in the driveway with two suitcases. She wore the beret she only put on when traveling. He couldn't believe it was her and tried to lift the window to call out for her to wait for him. His hip was so bad that by the time he reached the side door and the driveway, she was gone. He caught a glimpse of the yellow car, turning out into the street, and heading away. He staggered, about to fall, and the blond girls appeared on either side of him. They helped him into his rocker on the porch, pulled down the shade of night, and set the breeze to blowing.

"Where's he taking Harriet?" asked Gary. "The man with the raincoat and hat. Where?"

"Shhh," said Imsa. "Every ghost story is your own."

"Where's he taking her?" he repeated.

"To find out," said Sami, and their high, light laughter became the music of the jeweled wren.

# The Air, the Ocean, the Earth, the Deep

*Siobhan Carroll*

The call came through at five a.m. A UN cargo plane had landed at LaGuardia. Airport officials had found four stowaways on board: three men, one woman, all from the Congo. ICE had sent two of them to Rosendale. The other two had been sent somewhere else, and no one was sure where. Andre had the A-numbers for the Rosendale pair, but he couldn't take them. Could she?

Dasha dressed herself in the dark, moving quietly so not to wake Alex. She'd forgotten to dry-clean her blue suit; she'd better go with the black even though she hated it. If the trains were in order she could visit Rosendale and still be back for the court session at two p.m.

The kitchen television shadowed her as she brewed her coffee. The news was the usual horror show: highway blockades in Mexico, famine in the Far East, a cyclone in the Mediterranean. Rumors of a new illness emerging in Indianapolis, delivered by a blond man who couldn't seem to stop smiling at the camera. The newscaster cut to blurred footage of an emergency room, a man yelling and pointing at nothing. Dasha turned down the volume.

Like most detention centers, Rosendale was deliberately nondescript. A former warehouse, it squatted in the middle of a near-empty parking lot, its bricked-up windows staring nowhere. Only the obscure sign above the door, CCA ENTRANCE, indicated its function to those "in the know."

The waiting room was quiet today. An elderly man sat in the corner with his face in pale, manicured hands. A dark-skinned woman absently twisted the straps of her shoulder bag into a tight rope. The two children beside her chattered and clapped their hands as though in a playground.

The little girl leaned forward and grinned at Dasha as she sat down. "The man's very slow today," she said in carefully practiced English. "Is because he's sick!"

Dasha glanced up at the guard behind the counter. The man looked ashen. She took her hands off the armrests and folded them in her lap, trying not to remember the flashes of video from the news. Beside her, the children launched into a new clapping game.

"Nkuyu *climb out of the ocean,*
nkuyu *climb down through the air,*
nkuyu *crawl out from the corners.*
*which corners?*
*Right there!*"

At the final "there" the girl pointed her hand at the front of the room, her brother at the corner. They both collapsed in laughter.

"Sirko?"

Dasha walked to the counter. Up close, the guard looked worse, his damp skin a bruise of unpleasant colors. He coughed into his sleeve as he checked the ID Dasha held up to the window. She also held up the two A-numbers—alien registration numbers—that substituted for her clients' names, but he barely gave those a glance.

"Nasty cough," Dasha offered. "They going to let you go home early?"

"Everyone's goddamn sick," the guard rasped. He jerked his head at the door. "You're up."

Dasha tried not to breathe during the pat down, even though the guard conducting the screening didn't look sick. Was it her imagination or did Rosendale's air have a strange feel to it? It strained through her lungs like syrup.

*This isn't helping,* she told herself. Despite her weariness, she could feel the old anxiety rising in her, the fear that she *wasn't good enough.* That had been the worst part in the early days: the thought that people might die because of her, because of a mistake she made. She'd learned to tamp those thoughts down. They didn't help anyone.

She took a slow, deep breath, and turned to the files the guard had handed back to her, with a map of the Congo taped to the inside of the folder. A few years ago Dasha had had only a few Congolese clients. Then came the contested election, the rise of the militant DARP party, the gang rapes, the murders. Torture was common, and she wondered whether her clients would be among those affected. She felt a surge of anxiety and reminded herself that, if tortured, their cases would be easier to win.

But the first A-number she saw was Elie, a healthy-looking twenty-something with a tribal tattoo on his face and a good command of English. She ran through the obligatory public questions first—*Do you need a lawyer? Do you want to fight your case or do you want to go home?*—before she signaled to the guard and got an answering nod. They could move to the private interview room.

"Where did you learn English?" she asked when they got to that portion of the interview. She felt herself yawning and masked it with her hand. She was exhausted; too many late nights spent on too many cases, but Elie needed her help. They all did.

"College," he replied. Like Dasha, he kept his hands on the table between them, and did not turn toward the rattling cough from the next room. A composed young man. That might count against him. "My father made money to send me to medical school in Bukavu. I was the first in my family to go." He added, "I learned from tapes," his gaze steady, his tone proud.

Dasha nodded, thinking. Good English was an asset at the interview stage but a detriment in court, where judges might suspect fluent speakers of being "economic" migrants. She looked down at her legal pad and moved to the next item on the list. "Why did you come here?"

"Political persecution." Elie's answer was ready, practiced. A good sign: such clients often came prepared, and might have brought documents with them. "I went into the party *d'opposition* in my college. GATO. I was at demonstrations. So, in October, two men in uniforms went to my friend's house. They threw down my friend's table, put his son's hand under their boots. They asked him where I was. He lied and said I was at the market."

Elie shook his head. "My friend's cousin ran to the *lieu de rendez-vous*. He said, they come and they will bathe you." He gestured helplessly to Dasha. "You know this?"

Dasha nodded, keeping her face blank. Where South Africa had "necklacing," the DARP regions had "bathing," in which targets were drenched in boiling pitch or gasoline, then set on fire. "I know this."

She glanced at the developing case on her pad. "Do you have documents that prove you were a member of the opposition? A membership card? A photo of you at a demonstration? Letters you wrote to anyone that describe the situation you were in at the time?"

Elie drew out a faded newspaper and slid it across the table. "Here," he said, and tapped the column halfway down. Elie's name was there, listed as a "supporter of the people" along with other members of GATO. Elie leaned back and pointed to the first name in the list. "This one," he said. "He is dead now."

Dasha glanced at her watch. Their fifteen minutes were up. "I think you have a good case," she told him. "But that does not mean we will win."

"Please," he said to her as she stood to leave. "Please, we must get out of here. There is a *nkuyu* in this place. A sickness. Kakengo has seen it."

"Kakengo?"

"He was with me on the plane. He is also from the DRC."

Dasha wrote Kakengo's name—with a question mark—next to her next A-number. "I'll see what I can do," she said.

She caught herself yawning again on the way out the door. It was too early in the day to feel this tired, but the thick air of the center weighed her down. She slapped herself on the cheek, trying to sting herself awake, and rechecked her list of asylum seekers.

From the moment Dasha saw Kakengo she knew his case would be both easier and harder. The young man's first action was to stick out his tongue, surprisingly pale in his dark face, and show her the split down the middle.

Dasha felt a pain in her hands and she forced her fingers out of their reflexive curl. She folded them in front of her so that Kakengo could not see the bloody half moons forming on her palms. Keeping her face relaxed, she made a mental note—physical evidence of mutilation. But there was always the possibility the prosecutor would claim he'd done it himself, to build his case for asylum.

In the humid interview room, she ran through the Holy Trinity of questions: *Is this your first time in the US? How did you get here? Why did you come here?* Kakengo huddled in his seat, a thin man whose clothes sagged around him as though he were slowly melting into the ground. The first question he answered with a vigorous nod, but the other two proved more difficult. Kakengo struggled with the pen the guard had given him, scratching out simple words in French. *Mal. Homme. DARP. Tué.*

"Are you claiming political persecution?" She used the English phrase. His eyes widened and he nodded. Elie had evidently been coaching him. That could be helpful, providing Elie's coaching hadn't introduced errors into the story.

She extracted a few more details, and told Kakengo, in French, that he needed to gather what evidence he could. Kakengo's case could be tricky; his mutilation supported his story, but he needed documents, and like many asylum seekers he had fled without them. He still had a sister in the DRC, he indicated. She told him they needed to contact his sister to see if she could gather documents for him. Kakengo's face looked blank at the thought, whether in hope or hopelessness she wasn't sure.

As Dasha got up to leave, Kakengo motioned behind him. Emphatically, he drew a stick figure on the piece of paper and then scribbled on it, a black scoring that obscured the figure and formed its own black cloud. He stabbed the pen into the page and looked meaningfully at her.

"I don't understand," she told him. "Is this a cloud? Gas?" She thought unaccountably of the thick air around her, the humidity damping her clothes. Kakengo shook his head.

*"Une personne disparue? Une personne décédée?"* At the latter Kakengo nodded and then, strangely, looked over his shoulder.

Dasha followed his gaze to the cinder block wall that stretched over them. "Someone you left behind?" she guessed.

At this he glared at her and scribbled another few lines on the page. Black lines. Meaningless.

The guard rapped on the door. They were out of time.

"I'll be back," she promised him. As Kakengo seemed intent on pushing the paper with the scored-out figure toward her, she took it and added it to her notes. And then she left him in the silent room, and headed out.

On the train ride home she reviewed that week's cases: the Guatemalan woman who'd fled an abusive husband and the violence of the Maya district with her three children, the Bangladeshi climate refugees, and the Congolese. She wasn't sure what to make of Kakengo's scribble. A killing? Would it help the case or confuse it?

Dasha closed her eyes for a moment, and leaned against the thrumming window. And just then, she felt it. Someone breathing in her ear.

She jerked around. Nothing. Just stained fabric of the train seat, and beyond that, two young men in tank tops, arguing about a movie. *You're tired, that's all,* she told herself. *It's been a long day.*

But when she turned back to her notes, Kakengo's drawing was sitting on top of her pad, where it should not be. Dasha knew she had put it away. Hadn't she? She slipped it back, trying to ignore the slow creep of unease at the back of her neck, that was not, could not, be someone breathing. She needed to get home.

At four a.m., Dasha jerked awake. The cell phone beside the table glowed green. A text message from Christine appeared on the screen as she picked it up: three asylum seekers at Clarkestown. Could she take them?

Dasha pressed the phone to her forehead, willing the pressure to bring the real world into focus. Beside her Alex groaned, and rolled over on his side. A cough erupted from him—a short, sharp thing, like the bark of a dog. Dasha jerked, and something in the corner of the bedroom *moved.*

She twisted the knob on the bed lamp. Yellow light flooded the room. Only familiar shapes met her eye: a souvenir kimono hanging from the back of the door; a wall of well-loved paperbacks; Alex's framed copy of the *Back to the Future* movie poster. Everything seemed fine.

Everything seemed fine, but the devil was in the details. Dasha slipped out from under the sheet and lowered herself quietly onto the creaking hardwood. Turning slowly, she scanned the room, noting the film of dust on top of the bookcase that she'd have to clean later in the week. Nothing seemed out of place, no coat that had slipped off its hanger, no carelessly lodged book that had tumbled to the floor. Except—

Except the shadow box. Its large wooden frame still hung on the wall, its cedar shelves neatly aligned behind a pane of glass. The top shelf still held its cluster of shells, the bottom an assortment of medals from Alex's grandfather. But the middle shelf, which should have been stacked with a neat row of her grandmother's *pysanky,* stood empty. The colorful eggs lay jumbled beside the shiny abalone and faded conches.

Carefully, her heart pounding, Dasha crept over to the wall and peered into the box. At least none of the colorful eggs seemed broken. But how had they ended up on the bottom of the box? There wasn't enough of a gap between the second shelf and the glass for them to fall through.

Pysanky *could ward off devils,* her grandmother had said.

Something stirred at the edge of her vision and she whipped her head around. Again, nothing.

Unbidden, a voice from the waiting room whispered in her ear—

nkuyu *climb down through the air,*

nkuyu *crawl out from the corners—*

Alex coughed again, a ragged, wet sound. Suddenly Dasha was back in the real world. Was Alex getting sick? The news footage from Indianapolis. The guard behind the counter. He should go to the doctor tomorrow.

It was no good trying to get back to sleep. Her head was full of Ebola, of SARS, of illnesses that clung to the breath of travelers. In the kitchen, she turned the kettle on and pulled out the Emergen-C. *Useless stuff,* she thought as she choked it down. Twenty-first century superstition, bolstered by a few questionable studies. But she drank it anyway.

"The last time we met you mentioned a word to me. *Nkuyu,*" Dasha said, the yellow notepad in front of her, her careful handwriting recounting Elie's story. She drew out Kakengo's scribble and placed it between them. Elie's eyes flicked down to the paper and then away.

"You said Kakengo had seen *nkuyu*," Dasha said, tapping the drawing. "What did you mean?"

Elie raised his pale palms to the flickering overhead light and the dead flies whose bodies could be seen through the bottom of the gridded plastic. "You won't believe."

A line she'd heard before, in too many cases. Dasha felt her stomach tighten, and carefully, keeping her face still, she said, "It is my job to believe. I am here to represent you. To do that I need to know everything."

Elie settled lower in his chair. Finally he looked up, but he did not begin, as Dasha had expected, with rape and torture. "In my district, we say, a man should die without secrets. If a man dies with a secret, or if his family let the dead man stay in the sun, and do not put him in a tree or below ground or in a fire so that he can travel to another place, he comes back as *nkuyu*."

"A ghost?" Dasha said dubiously.

Elie gestured to show he didn't know the word. Then he said, "When a *nkuyu* sees a man, it walks behind him and tells its secret in his ear. The man's spirit hears and takes this secret into itself. One secret—fine. Two—not so good. Too many secrets, too many times meeting a *nkuyu*, and the man who is alive will be sick with it. He may die. This is what they say in the country, about illness."

"And Kakengo says he sees a *nkuyu* here," Dasha said.

Elie shook his head. "I am an educated man. A doctor. But there is something wrong in this *kimpasi*, this place of suffering. We all see things here." He pointed at the closed door, at the room and the guards behind it. "In Congo there is too much killing. Too many dead men, whose families are dead or running, and who die in the sun. Too many *nkuyu.* And it is not just the Congo. It is everywhere. Too many *nkuyu.*"

Dasha nodded. *Bad deaths,* her grandmother would say. "Are people sick here?"

"Everybody is sick here." Elie sighed. "In a hospital I would say, this is a virus, maybe a kind of flu. But in the country, we would get . . . *un prêtre?* A man who would listen to the *nkuyu,* and take their secrets into himself. But here, nobody listens."

Dasha pondered what he had said. Was Elie's story evidence of insanity? *No,* she thought, *remember Kakengo's drawing.* Certainly a shared perception, and one that seemed rooted in a real illness. Staring at the legal pad, a sudden thought slid in and out of her like a knife. The *pysanky.* But that was a different superstition, a different culture. There was no connection here.

"Do you know anyone who has become sick since coming here?" she asked.

"Many, many," Elie said. "First it was a man in the shower who fell. I did not know him. Then Luel, the Eritrean. A Somali. Now five detainees and seven guards. Many more are sick but do not say so. They fear they will be sent back."

Dasha made a note to herself. She forced herself to think through the legal implications, ignoring the old superstitions wittering in the back of her mind. Could they get access to the center's medical records? If an infectious disease was spreading here, she needed to secure her client's safety.

Turning to Elie's list of documents, she was about to begin her progress check when a sound from the next room interrupted them. "Nkuyu *climb out of the ocean,*" recited a voice. "Nkuyu *come in through the air . . .*" Dasha's skin crawled. She put her pen down.

Elie pressed his hands together and Dasha noticed the tips of his fingers were stained purple. When he saw her looking he shrugged.

"Kakengo bought powder," he said. "For a . . . a thing we will try. For the *nkuyu*." He sounded embarrassed, a doctor reduced to trafficking in magic. Dasha nodded as though she understood, though of course she didn't.

In the next room the voice got louder, and Elie winced. But when he clasped his hands together he looked composed again.

"It is getting worse," he said in the calm tone of voice Dasha imagined he used with patients. He nodded to their surroundings: the hot interview room, the detention center, the moaning voice drifting under the door. "Something must be done."

Outside the air was muddy, the sky cast down. The humidity enfolded Dasha as she walked across the parking block, and the shadows that crawled after her were just her own shadow, splintered by sunlight. That was all.

The train was nearly empty. The few passengers in her carriage sat by themselves, hands at their tablets or cell phones. Two of them were wearing face masks. Heart sinking, Dasha checked the news on her phone. Outbreaks of "Indianapolis Syndrome" were now reported in every state. The local news mentioned a VA hospital in Brooklyn and a preschool in midtown. Twenty-eight deaths had been reported so far; the number of people in comas was said to be in the hundreds. The transmission mechanism was, as yet, unknown.

Dasha sank lower in her seat, trying not to breathe. The train shuddered through the strange yellowness of the smog, bypassing the I-95 with its bristling jams and collisions, and its other, less visible traffic—the workers who stood with cardboard signs on corners, the snakehead-enslaved washing dishes in Chinese restaurants, the women brought over like her grandmother had been brought, to serve and to sleep in cold basements. And then there were the other invisibles, the asylum seekers in the county jails, the ones whose mental illness or bad luck had caught the attention of the law. Unseen people, everywhere, people who needed help, and the air closing in, its hot breath on the back of her neck, its dampness pressed against the glass.

The train roared through a tunnel, and in the glare of the exit light Dasha saw two small handprints on the glass, as though a child was pressing against the glass, standing where no child could possibly be.

She left that seat and stood in the crush of the aisle, and when she left the train, the haze was just as thick as it had been in the parking lot, the yellow light so thin she had to steady her hand on building walls to make sure she didn't step into traffic. Although she heard the scuffle and curses of people walking around her she saw no one but the occasional slant of a long shadow in the smog.

But there was no smell, she realized as she stumbled over uneven pavement. No chemical burn in her throat. Instead, the air seemed strangely clean and dry, and her mouth tasted of sand.

Alex was waiting for her in the kitchen, and she knew things were bad when she saw the red-patterned guest plates out in front of him in neat stacks. Alex dealt with nerves by cleaning things. She could tell by the tightness in his stooped shoulders that he didn't want to talk, not yet, and so she stood in his silence and helped put the stupid plates back on the wiped-down shelves, where they could sit to collect dust until they entertained or Alex got upset, whatever came first.

The shadow box was sitting on the table, the eggs piled beside it in a small basket. "I found it on the floor," Alex rasped without turning his head.

Dasha shook her head. "It was on the wall last night." She brushed the edge of the box with her fingers. Dry, unpainted cedar. Psyanky *ward off devils,* her grandmother had said. And also, *spirits can be seen in mirrors.* And, *if you want a ghost to speak to you, offer it a crust of rye.*

"Did you go to the doctor?"

Alex shrugged one shoulder. "She said there's nothing they can do. Some virus going around . . ."

"There's too much of this," Dasha said, thinking of the news, of Elie's story. "Maybe you shouldn't go in tomorrow."

"Maybe *you* shouldn't go in," Alex snapped. "You said you thought people were sick in the center."

It wasn't like Alex to snap. Dasha said nothing, and after a moment he sighed. "Sorry," he said. "I'm just under the weather."

"I need to go in," Dasha said quietly. "You know the stats." And Alex did know, the old sorry numbers: that with a lawyer a nondetainee would win their case 74 percent of the time, but that only 13 percent would win on their own. For detainees without representation, that number dropped to 3 percent.

"You can wait a week. They won't ship them out right away."

Dasha shook her head. "You don't know what they'll do," she said. "Particularly if there's an outbreak at the center."

Alex sighed. In his nonprofit work he'd more than once run up against the inscrutability of the detention system. "Fine. Be careful." He folded the dish towel with his customary care and hung it behind the sink. "I'm turning in. Maybe I can sleep this thing off."

On her own, Dasha pulled out her laptop. *Nkuyu,* she googled.

One website told her that the word *"nkuyu"* meant "lost soul"; another that it referred to a spirit who put up and removed obstacles for travelers. It was a word that appeared in Central Africa and in the Caribbean and the Carolinas, and as of a few years ago, had begun to iterate across immigrant twitter. There it was occasionally translated as *fantasma, Coco Man*, but also as "a misfortune." Dasha pinched the bridge of her nose, which had begun to throb with the onset of a headache. She'd hoped at least there'd be a coherent tradition around *nkuyu,* but of course there wasn't. Stories changed as they traveled, as people did. A word was grafted onto new situations as people tried to articulate what was happening to them.

Nkuyu *climb out of the ocean,*

nkuyu *come in through the air—*

The lamp in the corner of the living room flickered. Dasha looked at it, and the light remained steady. But was it her imagination or were there too many shadows on the wall?

In her browser she typed a new collection of words: *"Nkuyu"* and "shaman;" also "priest" and "exorcism." She scrolled through the results: An old story of a shaman who bound a *nkuyu* inside a stone by giving it a crocodile's heart to eat. A boy who walked into the land of the dead with a map drawn on his arm. A *ndoki*—some kind of witch-figure—who stood in a circle and persuaded the *nkuyu* to place its story on her tongue. She wanted a ritual, something prescribed, but the fragments she found were short on details. "A *nkuyu* cannot be laid to rest, but only bound to an object," she read. And also, "The *nkuyu,* unlike other spirits, cannot be bound, but must be made to tell its tale." To perform the ritual one had to carry a sprig of basil, or else a round stone, or else a stick with which to scratch out their tale. The ritual could only be performed by a man, or only performed by a woman, or it could be performed by anyone who knew the four points. The air, the ocean, the earth, the deep.

Something moved in the corner. Dasha turned to face the lamp, heart hammering, but there was nothing there.

That night she dreamed she was in a dark place. Sometimes the space about her felt like a cell and sometimes felt like somewhere else, where leaves rustled overhead and starlight pricked her skin. Looking down at her burning arms, she could see the scratches and whorls on her left arm marking the path to the crossroads, the deep cuts on her right arm marking the footprints she'd leave on her way back.

A cloud was moving toward her, gathering in the light. As it advanced the stars overhead vanished, one by one. Dasha's sinuses ached with the change in air pressure, which was odd, because who feels air pressure in dreams?

There was a figure in the trees, standing with its back toward her. No, not standing. Walking. It was walking backward toward her. It was walking quickly, without turning its head in the direction it was moving.

The singing insects fell silent. In the fresh emptiness of the air Dasha could hear the cracks of branches, the rustle of vegetation falling before the figure's advance. There was something terrible about its blind, backward strides, the way its rigid arms held tight to its body. Why did it not turn its head? How could it move so quickly, with such confidence, when it did not turn to look?

Dasha realized that she herself was stepping backward now, her body no longer willing to wait in the path of the creature's relentless strides. She needed to move. She needed to turn her head. She needed—

Dasha jerked awake. The looming dark was all around her. Dark like her grandmother's dark, in those early years in the States. *I used to lie awake,* her *babusya* had said. *Planning a way to escape.*

The hot air made it hard to breathe. Dasha rolled over and coughed, a ragged, harsh sound. Beside her Alex moaned. And something in the bedroom rustled.

Dasha flicked on the light, but of course there was nothing. She lay there for a time, studying the room. The *pysanky* had fallen to the bottom shelf of the shadow box again. Of course they had.

*I used to lie awake,* her *babusya* had said, *and think of what I could do to make things better.*

Dasha folded herself out of bed. She was not going to lie here and try, pointlessly, to get back to sleep. She needed to get ready for the morning. Because Elie was right; something must be done.

In the morning, Alex was quiet, his breathing slow and ragged. Dasha rested a hand on his forehead. Hot. "I have to go in at eleven," she said. Alex turned over. "Call me," she said, "if you feel worse."

Outside the air felt thick, like syrup. The haze was back,

lending the few objects that loomed up at her a yellow cast, like she was viewing them through a filter. Or like she was looking at the yellowed pages of an old children's book: illustrations of stop signs and post boxes, devoid of context. Periodically, she touched her hand to the rough brick of the buildings she passed, making sure she was on track.

The train was almost empty. A sallow-faced man in a blue uniform stared at her from the corner of a carriage. After a while his gaze made her feel uncomfortable, so she moved to one of the empty carriages and sat in a line of blue chairs, facing forward. Nobody came to check her ticket.

The air seemed thinner around the detention center. She remembered what Elie had said: that they would try to do something. If she went inside, would that help or hurt? Help, she decided, if only because that's what her legs didn't want to do. The old, shapeless anxiety had her in its grasp. She was about to do something wrong. She should leave the work for someone else to do.

She took a slow, deep breath, and focused on the task at hand. It was a small thing, really. She had to turn a metal door handle and walk inside.

Nobody sat at the reception desk. In the screening area, a glassy-eyed woman with slicked-back hair waved her through.

Dasha sat down to wait at the interview desk. The room was empty, the glare terrible. Somewhere far off she thought she heard someone—or maybe an animal?—scream, but the sound was muffled, as though they were screaming into the mattress. The cheap plastic wall clock ticked until it stopped, its second-hand quivering just past the five. She glanced at her Apple Watch. The digital numbers were frozen at 11:05.

One of the lights overhead pinged out. Then another one.

Dasha took the sprig of basil out of her bag and laid it on the counter, along with the hand mirror. It was nothing, really. A superstition. She laid the basil, her pen, a crust of rye bread, and the mirror at each of the four corners.

The shadows that had collected in the corner began to spread.

And Dasha saw—

Nkuyu *climb out of the ocean*

nkuyu *come in through the air*

nkuyu *crawl out from the corners—*

And this time, Dasha opened her mouth to greet them.

# The Ghost Sequences

## *A. C. Wise*

The 2017 Annual Juried Exhibition at Gallery Oban consists of a single winning entry in four parts titled "The Ghost Sequences." Although they dissolved their artist collective shortly before the opening of the show, two of the members, Georgina Rush and Kathryn Morrow, worked closely with the gallery, providing specific instructions for the exhibition's layout, and further stipulating that any subsequent showing should replicate the original conditions—four rooms in the order Red, Black & White, Mechanical, and Empty—and that the works never be shown separately.

**Red**

*A haunting is a moment of trauma, infinitely repeated. It extends forward and backward in time. It is the hole grief makes. It is a house built by memory in between your skin and bones.*

*—Lettie Wells, Artist's Statement, 2017*

The red room contains a series of abstract paintings by Lettie Wells. The paint is textured, thick, the color somewhere between poppies and oxidized blood. On each canvas, the paint is mixed with a different medium: brick dust, plaster, wood shavings, ground glass.

Upon entering the room and turning left, the first canvas the viewer encounters holds a single drop of black paint against the red. With each subsequent painting, the drop grows—a windshield pebble strike, a spiderweb, a star going supernova. Something coming closer from very far away.

There is no guarantee, of course, that the viewer will turn left through the doorway. As a result, the thing inside the paintings is constantly retreating and approaching, drawing nearer and running away, depending on the sequence in which the works are viewed. The room, however, is a closed circuit; there is no escape. The thing in the paintings must circle endlessly, trapped beneath layers of red, always searching for a way out.

**Studio Session #1—Ghost Stories**

"Family meeting!" Abby calls, her little joke as she enters the shared studio space where their artists' collective of four works and lives.

She deposits grocery bags on the counter as the others emerge: Lettie paint-spattered, Georgina smelling faintly of developing chemicals, and Kathryn twisting a spare bit of copper wire around her left hand.

"What are we going to do about this?" Abby slaps a bright yellow flyer on the counter beside the bags.

Lettie picks it up, and Georgina and Kathryn read over her shoulder. The skin around Lettie's nails is as stained as her clothes, a myriad of different colors.

"Gallery Oban." Kathryn looks up. "Is that the one on Prince Street?"

"No entry fee for submissions." Abby grins. "The winner gets a three-month exhibition."

"I haven't finished anything new in months." Lettie's thumb drifts to her mouth, teeth working a ragged edge of skin. Kathryn gently pushes Lettie's arm back to her side, but not before she leaves a smear of paint behind.

"And no one wants to buy the crap I'm producing," Georgina says as she unpacks the grocery bags, laying out packages of instant ramen, and setting water on to boil.

"Then this is the perfect thing to push us out of our ruts," Abby says. "We could even work on a central theme, each in our own medium."

"Do you have a theme in mind?" Georgina asks.

"Nope." Abby grins. "We'll brainstorm tonight. This should help."

She retrieves a bottle of cheap wine from the last grocery bag and hunts for a corkscrew. And as soon as it's ready, Georgina dishes ramen into four bowls. As she hands the over last bowl over, the power flickers and goes out.

"Shit."

"Think Mr. Nanas 'forgot' to pay the electric bill? Or maybe the rain is really to blame?" Abby strikes a pose, doing her best Tim Curry from *The Rocky Horror Picture Show.*

"I'll get candles." Kathryn leaves her bowl on the counter while Lettie sits with hers cupped between her hands, steam rising around her face.

"We should tell ghost stories," Kathryn says. The last candle lit, she joins the others around a low coffee table they rescued from the trash. "That's what my sisters and I used to do when the power would go out."

"Oh." Abby sits up straighter. "That's perfect. Ghost stories. That can be our exhibition theme!"

Lettie, Kathryn, and Georgina exchange a look, and Abby throws up her hands, flopping back against the futon.

"We're artists! Our whole job is to make the unseen visible."

"Actually, I might have an idea." Georgina taps her spoon against her lips. "You know Morgan Paige?"

"The director?" Lettie sets her bowl aside, sitting on her hands to keep from gnawing at her skin. Georgina nods.

"Most people think *Cherry Lane* was his first movie, but there's an earlier one that was never released. He made it right out of film school with a couple of friends. It's practically a student film, but . . ." Georgina shrugs. She looks around and, seeing no wandering attention, continues.

"It's called *The Woods.* It's about a group of high school kids who try to create their own version of the Suicide Forest in Japan by driving one of their classmates to kill themselves. They're testing the idea that they can create a haunting through a single traumatic event that spreads until it effects the whole school. It's supposed to be an examination of depression, apathy, and mental illness." Georgina reaches for the wine and refills their glasses.

"Anyway, that's not the weird part. You know the woods over by Muirfield Farm?"

Nods all around, and Lettie shifts in her seat.

"That's where Paige and his friends shot most of the film. On their last day of shooting, something went wrong with the camera and while Paige was trying to fix it, he saw something on the film that shouldn't have been there."

One of Lettie's hands creeps free, and she chews at the side of her thumb. A faint smear of red marks her lips, not matching any of the paint under her nails.

"He sees a girl standing between the trees, barefoot, wearing strange clothes. She could just be some local kid, but Paige is convinced he's caught a ghost on film. He freaks out and scraps the movie. Eventually, he takes the frames he has and buries them, and doesn't make another movie for nearly five years. According to the rumors, the raw footage of *The Woods* is under the freeway overpass somewhere near Clover Street."

"No one's ever found it?" Kathryn asks.

Georgina shrugs.

"Maybe if they ever do those repairs they've been promising for years . . ." She finishes her wine and shrugs. "Anyway, maybe I could do something with that for my part of the exhibition."

Abby stands.

"I have a story, but give me a sec."

There's a slyness to her expression as she disappears into her studio. She and Kathryn have spaces on the first floor, while Lettie and Georgina have studios on the half floor overlooking the common room. The whole building used to be industrial storage space, renovated during the city's renaissance in an attempt to attract artists to the region and create the next big hipster neighborhood. Abby returns with a second bottle of wine.

"You've been holding out on us." Georgina nudges her as Abby opens the bottle and pours. Lettie covers her glass.

"This is something that happened at my grandmother's school when she was in tenth grade," Abby says as she settles back down. "There was this group of popular girls. Everyone called them 'the pack,' though not to their faces. Even the teachers were afraid of them.

"Anyway, halfway through the school year, a new girl named

Libby joins the class. She's painfully shy. Her clothes are out of style, like maybe her family doesn't have much money. Basically, she's that kid that every class has, the one with *victim* written across their forehead.

"The leader of the pack is a girl named Helen. One night when her parents are out of town, she invites Libby to join the pack for a sleepover. Libby's never slept away from home before, but Helen won't take no for an answer. All the other kids in the class know the pack is planning something, but they're too scared to warn Libby in case Helen turns on them instead."

Abby takes a slow sip of her wine, reveling in the attention as she unwinds her tale.

"Anyway, Helen finally convinces Libby. The night of the sleepover arrives and Libby pulls an old-fashioned nightgown with long sleeves and a skirt that almost touches the floor out of her overnight bag. As they're all getting changed, Susannah catches a glimpse of bruises on Libby's thighs and arms, just a quick flash before the nightgown covers everything. She tells Helen, but not the other girls.

"After they're all dressed for bed, Helen tells them how the woods behind her house are haunted, then she insists they play truth or dare. When her turn comes, Libby picks truth, and Helen asks, 'Who do you love more, your mother or your father?' Libby's eyes go wide, she looks scared and won't answer, rubbing at her arms through the sleeves of her nightgown. 'If you won't answer, then you have to do a dare,' Helen says. The other girls start chanting 'Dare, dare, dare,' until Libby gives in.

"'I dare you to go into the woods behind the house and play the hanging game,' Helen says. She grabs a pair of her mother's silk stockings and drags Libby outside. The other girls stay inside and watch through the window as Helen makes Libby stand under one of the trees and wraps one leg of the stocking around her throat and the other around the lowest branch.

"'Now close your eyes and count to one hundred, then you can come back inside,' Helen says. Libby closes her eyes and starts counting aloud while Helen walks backward toward the house. When she gets to the door, Helen is planning to lock it behind her, and then she'll make the rest of the pack hide. But before Helen can get to the house, Libby screams, and Helen freezes. Libby is thrashing, clawing at the stocking. By the time the other girls run out of the house, it's too late. Libby isn't breathing. It's as if something pulled her into the tree and left her there to hang."

"That's a horrible story," Kathryn says.

Abby opens her mouth to protest and at that exact moment, something hits one of the windows. The sound is like a gunshot, and Lettie jumps, knocking over her wine. Georgina scrambles up to get a towel. She hands it to Lettie, but Lettie only twists it into a rope between her hands. Then she speaks, staring straight ahead.

"When I was eleven years old, my big sister and I came home from school and found my mother sitting in the middle of the kitchen floor. She'd smashed some of our plates, and she was putting the pieces in her mouth one by one." Lettie takes a breath, and Abby leans forward slightly. Kathryn and Georgina go still, staring at Lettie, who continues to look straight ahead. "We screamed for her to stop, but it was like she couldn't hear us. My sister grabbed her wrists, and then hit her to make her stop. When my mother finally looked at us, it was like she didn't know who we were."

"Lettie." Kathryn touches her arm. Lettie blinks, and slowly turns her head. The candlelight plays tricks with her eyes, turning them to glass.

Kathryn's hand slides from Lettie's arm as though pushed away. "Honey, you don't . . . ," Kathryn starts, but Lettie ignores her. Georgina frowns, and Abby scoots forward so she's sitting on the edge of her chair, but she doesn't reach for Lettie or her restless hands.

"As long as I can remember, my mother thought she was haunted. She would go on binges of eating, trying to fill herself up so there was no room for ghosts inside her skin. But other times she refused to eat at all, nearly starving herself and begging the ghosts to take her."

Lettie looks at each of them in turn, still twisting the towel in her hands.

"On my sixteenth birthday, I came home from school and found my mother and my sister dead. My mother was lying on her bed. There were clothes scattered on the floor, a lamp knocked over, like there'd been a fight. There were empty pill bottles with the labels peeled off. My mother's hands . . . it looked like someone had bitten her. They were all bloody and there were teeth marks on her skin. I screamed for Ellie, but she didn't come. Then I found her in my mother's bathroom. She was lying in the bathtub with her clothes on. It looked like maybe she'd hit her head. There was blood around her mouth. I don't know if my mother killed her, or . . . I don't know."

Lettie wraps her arms around her knees, hugging them to her chest. She rocks slightly, then puts her head down, her voice muffled when she speaks.

"My sister is starving, and she wants to come home."

• • •

**Interlude #1—A Room with One Door**

There was a game my sister and I used to play when we were little. When our mother was having one of her bad days, we'd go into the crawl space under the basement stairs. It was just big enough for us on our hands and knees, or sitting down, and there was only one way in so it felt safe.

The game was called Brick by Brick. There was a deck of cards, each with a picture of a different room. In the real rules, we were supposed to play against each other, but Ellie and I always changed it so we took turns drawing cards and building the house together. We were born only eleven months apart, so really we were more like twins than sisters.

In the game, there were little plastic figurines that came with the cards: red, yellow, green, and blue for the people, and white for the ghost or the monster. The idea was to move through the house as fast as possible, so the monster wouldn't catch you. The trick was, if you built a secret passageway, or a hidden staircase to get through the house faster, the monster could use it too.

Sometimes Ellie would make up stories about the house while we played. She'd tell me about all the things in the rooms, and the lives of the little plastic versions of us who lived there. The monster was in her stories too, but there it was nice and it wasn't trying to hurt us at all.

The little plastic figures got lost at some point, but I still have the cards. On nights when I can't sleep, I take the deck out and arrange the cards different ways. If I close my eyes just a little bit while I'm doing it, I can almost see Ellie moving around inside the card house. If I manage to get the sequence of cards just right, she'll be able to find her way out and come home. The trick is, what if the monster finds the way out first?

• • •

**Black & White**

The second room in the gallery contains a series of black-and-white photographs by Georgina Rush. One grouping is labeled *The Tomb*, the other, *The Woods. The Tomb* photographs depict a spot beneath a highway overpass—graffiti, empty bottles, a half-finished meal in a Styrofoam container. Even so, there's something mystical about the images. They suggest a sacred site, an archaeological dig. Something is buried here, and the artist is documenting its unearthing.

*The Woods* depicts rows of trees on the far side of an empty field. Rather than a wild forest, these trees are planned and planted, and Rush achieves a stunning effect with the light coming between the trunks. Despite the regularity of the rows, there is something uncanny about the trees. The spaces between them are full of waiting. One cannot help feeling the woods, and perhaps the photographs themselves, are haunted.

In the center of the gallery there is a pedestal holding a laptop with files that visitors are encouraged to explore. These are raw, unprocessed images, outtakes from the exhibition. The one incongruity is a video file titled "Overlapping Voices (Abby's Possession)." The film appears to be shot in the studio shared by the four artists. It's unclear how it fits with the photographs on the wall, however it's possible the film is another outtake, a dress rehearsal for the performance piece Abby Farris had planned for the show.

**Studio Session #2—The Ghost in the Machine**

There's a tapping sound so soft Kathryn barely hears it. When it finally registers, her first irrational thought is that there's someone in the walls. Then she realizes the sound is at her studio door and opens it to see Lettie's face, just a slice between the door and the frame. There's darkness under her eyes, like she hasn't been sleeping, and the rest of her skin is paler by comparison.

"Sorry, can I come in?"

Kathryn opens the door wider before Lettie even finishes, and Lettie steps inside, glancing over her shoulder.

"Sorry, I just . . ." She rubs her arms. When Kathryn closes the door, Lettie relaxes visibly, then offers a self-deprecating smile and shrugs. "You know how it is when you get in your own head sometimes."

"Sure." Kathryn gestures to her work table.

The frame for her piece is mostly complete. Wires trail across the table's surface like a mat of tangled hair.

"I was actually just finishing up this part. Wanna see if it works?"

Kathryn clears space around the machine, bits and scraps she ended up not using. Most of the parts were bought at the local hardware store, but the crown jewel she found on eBay—a Ouija board in good condition, but showing signs of use, which is exactly what she wanted. The letters are a bit faded, and the felt pads on the planchette's feet have worn away. The board sits in the center of a frame, and a thin metal arm runs from the planchette to the frame, hinged to allow a full range of motion. It can reach every letter and number on the board, along with "Yes," "No," and "Good-bye."

"Wait." Lettie touches Kathryn's wrist as she reaches for the power switch.

A bandage wraps Lettie's thumb, the edges dirty and peeling.

There's a dark red stain along one side, fading to brown.

"Can it really talk to ghosts?" The way Lettie says it, almost hopeful, gives Kathryn pause.

She lowers her hand. As a kid, she wanted so badly to see a ghost. All those stories she and her sisters told, gathered around a flashlight under sheets strung over chairs—if she could just see one of those ghosts for real it would make her special. But what she sees in Lettie's eyes is completely different. Raw need. Loss. The room goes colder, air dropping out and goose bumps rising on Kathryn's skin.

"We don't have to." Kathryn fights the urge to rub at her arms the way Lettie did. This whole thing was a terrible mistake. "It can wait until some other time."

"No, I want to see."

The chill goose-prickling her arms crawls up the back of Kathryn's neck. There's someone standing in the corner. Someone just behind her. If she turns to look, it won't be there. The corner will be empty. But if she doesn't look, the thing will continue to stand there. Not breathing, not moving. Just watching her. Always.

Lettie stands beside her at the table, close enough that their arms almost touch. Yet Kathryn is filled with the sudden, irrational feeling that Lettie is also standing behind her in the corner of the room. A shadow moves in the hallway, just visible through the crack in the door even though Kathryn is certain she closed the door after Lettie entered. Her heart thumps, and she bites down on her lip. A moment later Georgina peers through the gap.

"We heard voices. Is your piece finished? Can we see?"

Kathryn nods, her throat dry. Georgina pushes the door

wide, and Abby follows her inside. The studio feels crowded with all of them there. Lettie moves around the table holding the machine like she's sleepwalking and flicks the switch that turns on Kathryn's machine.

The EMF detector attached to the frame lights up, lights cycling from green, through yellow, to orange and red before settling back down to a single green pip. The readout on the thermometer beside it shows the room at seventy degrees, slightly higher than normal with their body heat.

Nothing is going to happen. Nothing is going to happen and this is stupid and Kathryn wants everyone out of her room now. The lights flicker from green to red again and the mechanical arm holding the planchette jumps.

"Oh shit," Georgina says, then laughs, a nervous sound. "Is it programmed to do that?"

Kathryn's throat is tight. She wants to squeeze her eyes closed, but she can't. For a moment, nothing else happens, then lights on the EMF detector spike and the arm moves again. The planchette scrapes to the left. The unfelted feet on the board shriek, worse than a chalkboard and nails. Then the planchette swoops down to the bottom of the board.

*Yes. Good-bye. I-B. No. Good-bye. B-B-B.* Kathryn tracks the motion, her mouth open. The machine is working as designed, but it isn't supposed to do that. There's no such thing as ghosts; rationally, she knows that to be a fact. EMF detectors can be set off by microwaves, cell-phone towers, or maybe she wired the machine wrong.

Beside her Lettie watches the board, rapt. The planchette moves faster, screeching as it does. *Yes. Good-bye. Good-bye. L-B-I-I. No. I-L. No. L-I-B-I. L-I-B-I.* The planchette whips through the letters, a blur repeating the last four with sharp insistence.

"Oh shit," Georgina says again. "It's spelling Libby. Like the girl in Abby's story."

Lettie makes a sound, not quite a breath, not quite a sob.

"What did you do?" Kathryn rounds on Abby. Her fingers clench and unclench at her side.

Abby's mouth drops open, and she holds up her hands. If her shock is an act, it's convincing. An ache makes itself known between Kathryn's eyes, and she shakes her head once to dislodge it. What makes her think Abby had anything to do with this? Just because she told a ghost story about a girl named Libby? Besides, Georgina is the one who pointed it out so quickly, couldn't it have been her? Or none of them, because no one has touched the machine except for her. It's just a weird coincidence, and Kathryn is being paranoid.

"It's something wrong with the wires," Kathryn speaks quickly. Instead of turning off the switch, she yanks out the whole bundle of wires in one go, and the arm and the planchette fall still.

Lettie continues staring at the machine, willing it to move again, to speak. Her face is bloodless, except for one spot of color high on her cheek as though someone slapped her.

"It isn't Ellie." Lettie shakes her head. She turns to Kathryn, stricken. "It's the wrong ghost."

Kathryn pulls Lettie into a hug, but it's too late. She can't shake the feeling that she's ruined everything. Something terrible is in the room with them, and she's the one who let it in.

**Interlude #2—A Room with No Windows**

Georgina let me help her with her photographs. ~~I don't want to be in my studio alone.~~ The red light in her darkroom is peaceful, and there are no windows. It reminds me of the crawl space where Ellie and I used to play. Safe, except when the ghosts would tell my mother where to look and helped her make herself small enough to crawl into the darkness after us.

I watched Georgina make images out of light, then she showed me how to bathe the photo paper in the chemical wash. It's like a magic trick, watching the picture fade into place. While I was watching her trees, they suddenly weren't trees anymore. They were the wooden frame of a house still being built. A skeleton without windows, or walls, or doors. Then the chemicals finished their work and it was just woods, but there was someone standing between the trees.

I was so startled I knocked the whole tray over. It ruined Georgina's picture. She told me not to worry, she could make another one, and she did, but there was nothing between the trees the second time. No house. No figure. Just shadows and light.

I think Georgina was afraid of upsetting me. Everyone walks on eggshells around me since the night the power went out. Except for Abby. The other day I walked into the kitchen and they were all there. I'd been in my studio with my earphones on, so I didn't hear them until I opened my door, then Kathryn said, "So who moved it? A ghost?" But they all stopped talking the second they saw me. Kathryn and Georgina exchanged a look like they wanted to say something, but they didn't know who should go first. Abby smiled, but in the end no one said anything. They just watched me get a glass of water and go back into my studio. Am I so fragile they all have to tiptoe around me? Or are they scared of something else? ~~Do they know about the house I'm building with the cards? Or how badly I want to open the door?~~

• • •

**Mechanical**

*Is it possible to build a machine to capture a ghost? That is the question at the heart of "Séance Table." Ghost hunters have used a variety of equipment to detect paranormal activity for years—electromagnetic field detectors, voice recorders, infrared cameras. "Séance Table" makes use of some of those tools of the trade, specifically an EMF machine and an extremely sensitive thermometer. The goal of the piece is to mechanically facilitate communication with the paranormal world. A spike in EMF readings, or a drop in temperature, will trigger the arm attached to the piece's frame, causing the planchette to move. Even though the motion is mechanically aided, the prime mover, the trigger if you will, is the ghost.*

*Is it possible for the random motion of the arm to spell a word, or impart a message with specific meaning to the visitor? If my machine does capture a ghost, is it because the ghost was always there, or do the conditions of the machine itself—an open phone line, an invitation to speak—cause the haunting? I am certain you have questions of your own as well, and I invite you to write them on the provided note cards and drop them in the box affixed to the base of the machine. Perhaps a ghost will answer. I also invite you to take your time in the gallery, and keep an open mind. Let's explore the questions of the afterlife together.*

*—Kathryn Morrow, Artist's Statement, 2017*

**Studio Session #3—Overlapping Voices (Abby's Possession)**

Georgina wakes to Kathryn leaning over her, gesturing for silence.

"What—"

"Shh. Here." She presses Georgina's phone into her hands. "Something's wrong."

"I don't—"

"Come on." Kathryn tugs her, and Georgina stumbles after her.

"What's going on?" Lettie joins them, her eyes wide in the dark. They look like they've been wide for a long time. Sleepless.

The door to Abby's studio stands ajar, the murmur of voices emerging from within.

"Turn your camera on." Kathryn indicates Georgina's phone.

Confused, Georgina obeys. Her mind is sleep-numb, dazed. She lifts the phone regardless, watching the screen as Kathryn pushes open Abby's door.

The room is a mess. The sheets on the empty bed are rumpled; Abby's clothes are scattered on the floor. It looks like someone tossed a deck of playing cards in the air and left them wherever they fell. As Georgina's eyes adjust, she sees they're not regular playing cards. There are pictures of rooms on them, stairs, hallways, broken pieces of a house in random order.

Georgina lifts the camera higher, going cold as her eyes and her screen make sense of the image at the same time. Abby stands in the corner, facing away from them. She's wearing a nightgown with a long skirt and long sleeves. Her hair is loose, and she's rocking back and forth on her bare feet, muttering words Georgina can't quite hear.

"Abby?" Kathryn speaks softly behind her. Lettie makes a distressed sound, so small it's almost lost as Georgina and Kathryn move closer.

Georgina finds herself speaking, like a narrator in a documentary film, before she's fully registered what she's doing. Kathryn told her to film this, so she'll do it right.

"Abby is standing in the corner. She's barefoot and facing

the wall. She's wearing a nightgown none of us have ever seen before."

"I don't like this," Lettie says.

Georgina inches closer, and Abby's words either grow clearer, or she's speaking louder, pitching her voice so her audience will hear.

"In the trees. In the woods. Buried under the road."

Even if it is a performance, and Georgina really isn't sure, the skin on her arms tightens, puckering around each hair, and some primal instinct tells her to flee. This is wrong. The voice doesn't sound like Abby, but there's no one else it could be.

"There's something wrong with her spine. The way she's standing looks wrong," Georgina says.

If she keeps narrating, it'll keep what's happening at a distance. It's just a movie. She plants her feet, refusing to run, and forces herself to breathe.

"Abby, can you hear me?" Kathryn stops just short of touching Abby's shoulder. On Georgina's screen it look like her hand actually bounces away.

"In the woods. In the woods. In the . . ." Abby's voice grows louder.

"Make her stop." Lettie's voice cuts in over Abby's.

"Abby." Kathryn finally succeeds in touching her and Abby jerks around to face them, her lips pulled back in a snarl. It's definitely Abby, but at the same time it looks nothing like her.

"In the woods in the trees in the woods." It's almost a chant, and Georgina has the odd sensation Abby's lips don't move.

Abby pushes Kathryn, and Lettie catches her. Georgina jumps out of the way, and the image on her screen jumps with her.

"Bury me. Bury me." Abby's voice gets louder, closer.

Georgina's head snaps up, looking away from her phone, and somehow Abby is beside her.

Abby grins with her peeled-back lips, a nasty smile. Her gums look wrong, bloody, and Georgina looks away. It's a moment before she can force herself to follow Abby into the hall.

"Bury me." The words trail after Abby, but the voice sounds like Lettie's.

"She's going to the kitchen," Georgina whispers to her phone.

A crash reverberates, and Georgina flinches, jerking the screen again. Kathryn pushes past her, and Georgina hurries after her, their footsteps almost, but not quite, covering Lettie's sob.

There's just enough light to see Abby standing in the center of the kitchen. Shards from a broken plate radiate around her like the scattered cards in her room. Her eyes are closed now, head tilted at an angle that looks almost painful. *Her neck is broken,* Georgina thinks, and immediately pushes the thought away. One of Abby's feet is bleeding; she must have stepped on a piece of the plate.

"It's my fault." Lettie speaks so close to Georgina's shoulder that she nearly drops her phone. "I used the cards to try to build Ellie a path through the house, but the bad thing came through first."

"Abby, stop it. Now." Kathryn grabs Abby's arm, shaking her. Abby lets out a whimper, but doesn't open her eyes.

"Bury me! Bury me!" she shrieks.

Then her eyes do snap open and she drops to the ground. Kathryn jumps back, kicking a shard of plate that spins away from her. Abby crouches, her feet arched so she balances on the balls of her toes and the points of her fingers. Her mouth opens, and one hand creeps forward, a spider-walk across the kitchen floor, reaching for a broken piece of plate. Georgina's pulse thumps, her throat too thick to speak.

"No!" Lettie throws herself forward as Abby's fingers brush the broken plate, and she slaps Abby's hand away.

Abby snarls, swaying, and Lettie hits her, knocking her back. There's a painful thump as she hits the ground, but Georgina can't tell if it's Abby's back or her head striking the floor. Lettie scrambles on top of Abby, pinning her down and hitting her again. Abby's hands come up to defend herself, and Georgina and her camera catch sight of Abby's face in profile; she looks scared.

Fascination holds her in place. It's Kathryn who finally grabs Lettie's wrists and pulls her away. Abby and Lettie are both breathing hard, Abby's breath hitching on the edge of hyperventilation.

"Turn it off," Kathryn snaps, and its only then that Georgina fully realizes she's still filming.

Her thumbs shakes as she taps the stop button. Kathryn puts her arm around Lettie's shoulder, leading her away. Lying on her back, Abby turns her head toward Georgina. She's still holding her phone, and she has the sick urge to take a picture of the scene. Abby's nose is bloodied where Lettie hit her, and red smears her lips and chin, looking black in the dark. Abby's eyes meet Georgina's, shiny and wet. Her lips move, mouthing words which might be "I'm sorry" or "Help me," Georgina can't tell.

**Interlude #3—A Narrow House**

There's another game Ellie and I used to play. We would lie perfectly still in the dark, our bodies straight, our feet together, our arms pressed at our sides, like we were lying in invisible coffins. If we were good enough at pretending, the ghosts would think we were one of them. We called it The Dead Game.

Last night, I came into my studio and found all my paintings for the show rearranged. At first I thought maybe one of the others had been in my room, but I know Georgina and Kathryn wouldn't do that. ~~I don't know if~~ I don't think Abby would either. I realized it had to be a message from Ellie. The deck for Brick by Brick isn't in my room anymore. I don't know where it went, but I haven't seen it in almost a week, and I've looked everywhere. Without it, Ellie had no other way to reach me. She had to use the paintings. The canvases are walls in a house that is always being built. It still isn't finished.

I looked at the paintings for almost an hour, but I couldn't understand what she was trying to tell me. Then I thought if I played The Dead Game, she might talk to me directly. I lay on the floor and put my arms at my sides, keeping as still as possible. The room was quiet and dark, but I kept smelling paint, and something like sandalwood. Maybe Abby was burning incense in her room. The smell comes under her door sometimes. It's so strong some days the scent stays on her clothes and in her hair and trails behind her so we can always tell where she's been.

I tried to hold my breath. Ellie was always better at that part of the game. One time when we were in the crawl space playing, I got really scared thinking she wasn't breathing at all. I kept shaking her until she finally opened her eyes and smiled at me. There was someone else inside her looking out at me. I broke the rules then, the ones we'd made up for Brick by Brick, that we'd always help each other and stick together so the monster wouldn't catch us alone. I ran, and I left Ellie in the crawl space behind me.

Lying in my studio, I listened for Ellie as hard as I could. I kept holding my breath until my head pounded. Until my lungs hurt. Then I let it all out at once, and the sound was like a train thundering over the tracks. Black smoke hung over my head, like I'd breathed myself out entirely. Then there was something else in the smoke. It turned and looked at me and I was so surprised, I gasped. I didn't mean to, but I breathed it in. The dark thing is inside of me, and now I don't know how to let it out again.

**Studio Session #4—In the Trees**

Lettie starts, gasping in a breath. Someone is in her room. Someone is leaning over her. She's playing The Dead Game, and she is a door and something is stepping through.

"Are you awake?" Abby's voice jolts her.

Lettie crashes back into herself, but her body feels like a collection of loose bones—an unfinished construction—only barely joined by skin. Her studio resolves around her, the canvases lined against the wall smelling of paint and turpentine, even though she opened all the windows. Abby's scent is there too, sandalwood threaded through and beneath everything.

"What's wrong?" Lettie sits up; it's a struggle.

"The others are asleep," Abby says. "I want to show you something."

Abby goes to the door, looking back over her shoulder and beckoning. Lettie follows. She shouldn't. She doesn't trust Abby, but there's no reason not to trust her either. Only there's something different about her tonight. It's not like when she spoke in strange voices and Lettie hit her, that night they still haven't talked about. Now, Abby almost seems to glow. There are hollow spaces inside her, places for ghosts to fill.

"Oh," Lettie says, and hurries to follow Abby into the dark.

Once they're outside, she asks, "Where are we going?"

Her feet are bare, but it's too late to go back for shoes. She picks her way carefully over the warped asphalt, following Abby down the narrow alleyway between buildings.

"I borrowed my brother's car," Abby says. "I need to get some things for my performance."

"At night?"

"They accepted our proposal. Didn't you hear? We made it into the show. We *are* the show."

Lettie stops. As far as she knows, Abby hasn't even started working on her piece. Any time any of them ask her about it, she changes the subject. And she certainly doesn't remember assembling images of her own paintings to submit to the jury. Surely she would remember that. Unless Georgina did it, with her camera, got everything ready. Of course that's what happened. How could she forget?

At the mouth of the alley, Abby turns back to look at her. There's something disdainful in her expression, but something pitying as well, as if she's sad that Lettie doesn't understand. That's when Lettie sees it, a faint ribbon the color that moonlight would be if it could be made solid. It twists away from Abby, a path, a thread, beckoning Lettie to follow.

She climbs into the passenger seat as Abby unlocks the door of an ancient Dodge Pinto, the car she borrowed from her brother. The rubber floor mat is gritty under her soles. Light slides over them as Abby pulls away from the curb. Everything is sodium orange and bruise-colored, bloodied at the stoplights, drowned green for go. Abby looks at Lettie sidelong, like she's testing Lettie, like she's asking a question.

"Do you believe in ghosts?" Lettie says.

The vents in the dashboard rattle, exhaling air smelling of burnt toast. Abby started this whole thing, but Lettie still doesn't know if she believes. The story she told, Lettie suspects Abby made it up on the spot. Why would Abby's grandmother admit to such a thing, because how else would she know about it unless she was one of the girls involved? And why would she tell her granddaughter about it if she did?

Depending on how Abby answers, Lettie will know whether Abby knows about the moon-colored glow surrounding her, whether she knows about the ghosts, or whether they're just using her as a vessel to send a message.

"I'm building a suicide tree," Abby says instead of answering her. "For the show."

She turns off the main road where there are fewer streetlights, and shadows stick to her skin.

"During my performances, I'll stand under the suicide tree with a noose around my neck and invite ghosts to prove themselves by making me into one of them, if they can."

Abby's eyes cut right, looking for a reaction. Lettie watches the lights instead, the pattern of shadows. She has the strange impression that the car is moving backward in time. She's heard everything Abby has to say somewhere else before. She watches through the windshield for the place where the glowing ribbon ends, the place it's leading them.

"We're here." Lettie says it so suddenly Abby hits the brakes without engaging the clutch and the car stalls.

The Dodge's headlights wash over browned grass, showing

the expanse of a field. Beyond the field, trees stand like sentinels in eerily perfect rows. Abby's mouth opens; Lettie smiles to herself. Her suspicion is confirmed; Abby doesn't know where they are. She isn't the one in control.

Abby recovers quickly, scrambling with her seat belt, but Lettie is out of the car first, walking toward the trees. She looks over her shoulder. Abby is very small in the darkness, dwindling. Her mouth is a perfect circle, her eyes smudges of black. It's time.

Abby is a house, waiting for a ghost, so Lettie slips inside, looking out through Abby's eyes and watching herself walk across the field. Brown grass crackles under her bare feet.

Abby blinks, feeling like she's waking up from a long dream, disoriented and unsure where she is. She doesn't remember leaving the studio, but she's outside and the trees ahead of her are unsettlingly familiar. Georgina's photographs. And Lettie. Lettie is with her. Panic beats a tattoo against Abby's skin.

She blinks again, and there's something between the trees. Someone. There and then gone. Afterimages of Lettie trail behind her leaving luminescent footprints on the grass, except Abby can't tell which direction they're going. She has to catch up before it's too late. She breaks into a run, tripping, and Lettie is even farther away by the time she gets her feet under her again.

This was a mistake. She came here to . . . Why did she come? She wanted . . . She honestly doesn't know.

Something is terribly wrong. Something she can't quite remember. Like a story someone told her a long time ago.

Lettie is almost at the trees. At the edge of the field, Lettie stops. Relief crashes through Abby. She bends over, hands on her knees, gulping deep breaths. She straightens just in time to see Lettie open her mouth, but before either of them can get out a word or a name, something dark surges from between the trees. It's there and then it's not, and Lettie isn't there either. She's gone. Pulled into the trees. Vanished.

Abby screams. She plunges forward. Trips again, biting her lip and tasting blood. She calls Lettie's name and her voice echoes back to her, overlapping, a cacophony. There's no answer but she keeps shouting, on her hands and knees at the edge of the field, calling Lettie's name until her throat is raw.

**Empty**

The last room in the gallery is empty. The walls are freshly painted. The special lighting installed to cast shadows from an assemblage in the shape of a tree remains switched off. The room was originally intended to host a performance piece by Abby Farris, but now it is a space defined by absence.

Mostly. A week after the opening of "The Ghost Sequences," a visitor brought something to the gallery owner's attention. Along the baseboard near the door, there are words written in blue ballpoint pen, in lettering so small it is almost illegible. The words were not there on the day the exhibition opened. There are two sentences, which almost overlap, possibly written in two different hands, but it's hard to tell. Rather than retouching the paint to cover the words, the gallery owner let them stand as though they were always meant to be part of the exhibition after all.

*I'm sorry Lettie. Ellie I'm still building the house come home.*

# Deep, Fast, Green

*Carole Johnstone*

When it's bad, the lights go out. All of them except the old Victorian oil lamps Mum bought in Portobello: gold filigree and red milk glass. The house clanks and clunks and groans; the walls breathe in.

I always go straight up to bed on those nights because they never recover, they never go back to what they were. Those nights just keep twisting down into that bad something else until the heat and the noise and the clammy dark are all that's left.

I always stop at Gramps's room, too, creak open the door. Sometimes he's there. Sometimes he turns towards me, rears up ramrod straight like a vampire in *True Blood*, eyes open and unblinking—and no matter how many times he's done that, I still shit myself enough to make a noise. But he won't wake up, he never wakes up. Not until morning. The walls in Gramps's room always move in gold spikes and black squares. He won't sleep without candles burning all around him, at least half a dozen; he makes them out of pig fat. Mum hates this nearly as much as his rollie-smoking, as the towering, nomadic stacks of his *National Geographics*, their pages smelly and yellow. But this is the only place that never stinks of sweat and oil and steel.

Over breakfast, with the sun slanting hard against the new mosaic floor and the marble work tops from Murray & Murray,

Brian'll blame the weather, Scottish Power, the Bloody Tories. Mum will nod. And we'll all go on knowing that it's Gramps.

• • •

When it's bad, the lights flicker, dim. Go black. Nothing to do but suffer it. Nothing to see but dark and the red small glows ae fags. Stink squatting over your head. Diesel and smoke and bad hydraulics, old cackleberries and jock roast, shit and sweat. The heat like a morass, sucking you down, drowning you dry. Thick hot air that's somehow thin. So thin it feels like breathing through a metal tube clogged with so much shite it makes you want to stop trying. Sometimes I can stand it. Most times I cannae. The bunk is too small, the overhead pipes too near, the metal floor a long drop down. Bangs and rattles and coughs. The far off shouts ae those on last dog. The nearer shouts ae coffin dreams. Thuds and creaks and groans. And all the fucking worse outside, swimming through the space between metal skins to roar bad whispers into the air vents next to our ears. Dinnae listen to them. Tell yourself it's whales or fucking shit dumps, or the planesman thinking about counterpane hurdling with Betty Grable. Lie there and lie. Dinnae think about outside or inside. About the sky or sweet air. About needing to sit, to move, to breathe, to scream. About the flooding valves of the Q Tank opening up loud and quick. About the whistle wind in your ear going quiet. About those whispers and shouts roaring louder. About how much worse *bad* can get. Dinnae think.

Dinnae think.

• • •

It's not often I'm wrong about Brian and Mum—normally they're as predictable as bad clammy dark or a terrible night's sleep—but today I am.

"We've brewed some coffee," Mum says, soon as I make it into the kitchen. She looks worse than I feel: purple-black shadows against baggy tired skin, but I won't feel sorry for her for long, I know. She'll ruin it.

"Thanks." I pick up the mug. It's still hot. I ignore Brian and he ignores me. There's not much in this house that can't be ignored. You could say it's our forte.

"He's out there," Mum says, nodding her head towards the big kitchen window. And that's when I realise I was wrong about them. Even before she leans over the table, puts her hand over Brian's hairy knuckles. "You've got to make him stop, Sarah."

Outside is sunny but cold. It's always cold. We're nearly two miles from the docks, but the wind never stops, always smells of salt. Gramps is sitting on the stone bench next to the back door. From there you can see the whole garden, past the big lawn and wild borders down to the greenhouse and high fence at its end. You can't see the house. I wonder sometimes if he hates it as much as I do. He's had to live in it far longer than I have, after all.

He smiles when he sees me, grinds his not quite finished rollie under his heel. Its smoke lingers, tickles my sore throat. He looks more knackered than all of us put together. "Hey, Pinky."

"Hey. I brought you some coffee."

"Irish?"

"Gramps."

He keeps on smiling even though he's struggling with it now, can't hold my gaze at the same time. "Guess the sun's no' quite over the yardarm yet, eh?"

I sit down next to him, pass him the coffee, wrap my cardigan tighter. "It's barely over the back fence."

He drinks for a while, and I let him. But when he stops, I turn, make him look at me. "Why are you out here?" Even though I know.

He shrugs. "I like big, hen." He runs a finger under his red nose. "I like open."

He lived on the streets for a while. How long, I don't know. Mum went out for afternoon tea in the Roxburgh, and she and her friends passed him begging outside Waverley Station. She got on her train, waited for all her pals to get off, and then she went back to get him. He never told me any of that, but Mum did, like it was something to be proud of. Her furtive rescue. She knew he had this place, of course. Maybe thought it was going begging, too. Turns out she was mostly right.

"It's okay to not want to be in there," I say. Sitting on this bench, you might not be able to see the house, but you can still feel it. Big, wide, high, and freezing bright—redbrick sandstone and Georgian bar windows. And small, narrow, low, clammy dark. It makes the hairs on my skin stand up straight and stay that way. "It's okay to be scared of what you—"

"D'you ken in America, there's such a thing as a breastaurant?"

"Gramps. Come on."

He's not really my grandfather. He's the bachelor brother of Mum's dad, so a great uncle, although he's been Gramps to me just as long as I've been Pinky to him. The radio maintainer on a boat, he told me, is one of the most important jobs of them all. Before we moved in permanently—Mum, Brian, and me—I'd spend hours at the big table in the kitchen, helping Gramps fix up old wirelesses and CBs, while he taught me how to Jackspeak. I was the bait that they dangled; the grandchild he'd never imagined he could have. I think I probably knew that even then. I think Gramps probably did too.

He sets down his mug, leans forward, hangs his fists between his legs. "Crows make everything sound sinister, you ever notice that, hen? Bad creepy, like something's about to take a big old hold ae you, and you cannae see whit."

The crow is in our only tree: a big gnarly thing that grows big gnarly apples we never eat. The bird blinks at us, gives another scornful *caw* before taking off for next door in loud, vicious flaps. And I shiver, try not to care that Gramps is pretty much right, because he only said it—same as the breastaurant thing—to shut me up, to shove me left instead of right.

"On a boat, every fucking thing sounds like that," he says, proving me wrong yet again. "Whales, skimmers. Pretty much anything upstairs. Sunshine pills." He snorts at that. Takes one hand out of its fist to draw it loud against his stubble.

"Bombs," I say, even though I know full well what they are. "Depth charges."

He looks back at the empty tree. "Loud or quiet, that's all it ever is. Hot or cold. Dull as watching paint dry or so fucking scary you forget your own name."

Normally, it takes him a long time to get to this point. Normally, he tells me about being a fisherman in the fifties and sixties instead. Funny stories about being drunk on duty, or smuggling whisky and fags, or fishing illegal fish in illegal places. Sticking it to the Coast Guard and the Port Authority. But maybe he feels it too. All that clammy, rank dark creeping into the day, creeping into our skin. He isn't fit enough to go down to the mission on Leith Docks every day anymore, and I know that's made a difference, even though it's a shit hole. Even though nearly every submariner he's known is dead. Once a year at Christmas they'd present him with a bottle of Sailor Jerry rum, an old joke that stuck even though he only ever touches Old Navy, and his dad, a determined Irish Catholic, christened him Gerald. *Nicknames are like long memories, hen,* he told me once, *every jack has one.* He didn't like the rum and he didn't like the mission. He just didn't ever want to be here, that was all.

"And you're lying on your bunk—which isnae your bunk 'cause it smells ae the other dozen ratings whose bunk it is too when they're no' on tricks—boiling hot and stinking raw, listening to all them creaks, the whistle wind ae the wee vent next to your ear; praying it'll no' stop tormenting you 'cause that'll be something bad, something worse; hearing the oppo next to you or above you or below you screaming that the donkshop is flooding or a steel fish is chasing him. 'Cause lying in them bunks is like lying in the ground with worse than six feet ae dirt above you, even afore you're deep and diving, holding your breath on Silent Routine, while the pings ae fucking skimmers echo round and round, getting louder and closer, and you cannae speak, you cannae breathe, you cannae move, you cannae turn, so you put your hand against that cold whistle wind, and think ae the few metres of black, drowned space between it and the thin metal skin keeping everything else out, and you—"

"Gramps," I say, pressing my palm hard against the shake of his hands, squeezing his fingers. "Not like that. You know not like that. Not *you. I.*" Because he uses that *you* to water down what happened to him. He uses it to hide, to distance himself. To pretend maybe that nothing ever happened to *him* at all. And that isn't just a bad idea now, it's a dangerous one.

He squeezes briefly back. Closes his eyes. He goes on shaking, and it's like his whole body is vibrating. The bench too. He used to be so much more than this. Sometimes, I lie in bed, unable to sleep even on good nights, and wonder what it's like to get older, smaller, *less* in this horrible house. Sometimes I feel horribly certain I'll find out.

"Christ, I used to be able to spin a good dit," he says, trying to smile. "No' much else to do but play cards, listen to records, smell your own armpits, or spin a good story. The donkshop boys used to pay me in bum nuts and Nelson's blood, and I'd wax wild about anything wet. Heligoland Bight, Nautilus, New Atlantis." He smiles bigger. "Moby Dick if they'd a mind to listen to a story about topside swabbies."

I try to smile too. "Donkshop is the engine room," I say, making it sound like a question, even though he knows I know. "And you were an engine room artificer."

"I ken whit I was, hen," he says, but he says it gently. In amongst all of his old *Nat Geos* are books about the Mediterranean U-boat Campaign; smudged and brittle papers and logs and blueprints jammed between their pages and dust jackets. Trying to interpret them is like trying to read Latin: some of it you can guess, and the rest is an exotic lexicon that's really a brick wall. What I care about the most, what I've studied the most, are the pages of deck plans and cutaways, the frantic arrows and asterisks that Gramps has scrawled all around the dull, smudged margins. And one acronym that appears again and again, scribbled ugly and hard, sometimes all the way through the paper. *DFG.*

Gramps swallows. "HMS *Torque* was one ae the first T class diesel-electrics. Nearly three hundred feet and a thousand-long tons. Eight bow torpedo tubes, two amidships, forty-caliber deck gun. Maximum operational diving depth ae three hundred feet;

estimated crush depth ae six hundred and twenty-six. Fifty-seven crew. She was my first station, first posting. Third ae May, 1939."

He knows I've heard all of this before too, but this is just how he does it, how he gets around to doing it. Like he's getting ready to lance an infected boil that will only recur again in a few days. In the worst kind of way, he is.

"War hadnae started yet, didnae look to us like it was going to and no one told us any different." He shrugs. "She was a good boat, ken? Brand new. Course we were only in the Gare Loch then. Didnae quite appreciate whit sharing the same space with gear and food and mould and roaches and fifty-six other jacks who last had a shower or decent shit three months ago would be like. Or whit living under the sea and the worse on top does to you." He swallows again. "Fear, ken? It's like a virus. It's in the stinking air you breathe, and you cannae escape it 'cause it's the only fucking air you've got."

"Gramps—"

"Aye, I ken," he says, scowling, pissed off. Whether at himself or me I can't tell. "Not *you. Me. I.*" He takes back his hands, studies their palms. "I was a Back Afty. Back Afties always worked the most and shortest watches 'cause the heat in the fag end is like a bog. Thick and wet and it chokes you just about dead. We'd poke Charlie at the weapons guys, the Fore Endies, swaggering about like the fucking heroes ae the hour. Always having a weed on about something." He glances at me and tries to smile again; this time it nearly works. "Ask me, there's never been much skill in feeding steel fish into tubes. We were the ones kept us alive every single day. Bloody *front cun*—" He closes his mouth so fast, I hear the snap of his teeth.

"I'm twenty-two, Gramps," I say, and my smile works better

now too. The wind has picked up, bitter with the sea and the cold. It scours my lungs clean. "I've heard that word a few times before."

"Aye, well. No' from me you havnae." He stops, breathes deep too. Behind us, the house has shrunk smaller, quieter. "I had a few good mates on the *Torque.* Even afore the sea trials started. Donkshop oppos got to ken each other pretty damn quick, whether we wanted to or no'. Chief Sto was a good steady guy from Lerwick; went by Scurs, on account ae his beard. Every boat wants a good steady Sto and a good steady Jimmy, 'cause they're the ones calculate and set the trim afore diving. Get that wrong and it's so long and thanks for the fish.

"The *chief* chief was an arsehole called Dogs. He was pusser-built, ken? Every fucking thing by the book. And a face like a seaboot—just this blank, black stare, like all he lived for was to give you a scrubbing. He'd hand out double watches and take your mess share like he was giving a black dog for a white monkey, and that was bad news for me all right, 'cause back then I had about as much respect for authority as I did for lassies or wars."

He sounds breathless now, as if he thinks he's running out of time. Or air.

"Hibee was one ae the electrical mechs. I shared a hot bunk in the starboard corner ae the third compartment with him and another ERA called Tug. Top rack under the aft ventilation pipes. Shittiest bloody bunk going. We all came from the same part ae town. Turned out we even went to the same school. We'd spend hours just talking, bleating, chewing the fat." He finally stops, squeezes his hands back into fists, stares hard down the length of the garden. "Tug had a wife and two girls. Hibee was going to get married in the summer. Glasgow Fair. They were good mates to me. They were good. . . ."

When he lets go of his fists I see that the ends of his fingers have gone blue. I lean against him, bump his shoulder. "Come on, keep going. Talk to me."

"For Christ's sake, lassie. It doesnae help."

"It does. You know it does." I leave out the *sometimes.* Neither of us needs to hear that. "What is *DFG*?"

His intake of breath is sharp, loud. "Whit?"

"*DFG.* What does it mean?" I've never asked him this before. Don't know if it'll help or hurt. But needs must. I see the moment when he realises I must have seen his scribbles on those deck plans and cutaways, because his shoulders relax, his breath exhales in a frozen cloud.

"Deep, Fast, Green. It's a watch handover." He snorts. "Means 'All Is Well.'"

"And?"

"And whit?"

"Why is it important?"

"It isnae."

"Come on, you promised you'd try." Even though he didn't. "Why did you write it all over those plans? Why is it important?"

He shrugs again, but it turns into a shiver. "It's just something I do. Something I did."

It starts to rain. Not hard—soft slow smurry that's nearly sleet. We should go in, I know. But right now, I'm still not sure which is the more dangerous: out here or in there.

"Every rack had a locker. One cubic foot. Second day I was on the *Torque,* I got a penknife and scratched *DFG* inside its metal door. That's all. For good karma, good luck, whitever."

He gives me an unexpectedly wry smile. "Didnae work."

"It's really cold, Gramps. We should get you back inside."

This time when he looks at me, his tired grey eyes are fierce. "You shouldnae have to be here, doing this. Looking after an old man like me."

"Gramps."

"You should be at that fancy law school on South Bridge."

I avoid having to look at him by making a big production of our getting up off the bench, covering both of our heads with my cardigan as the rain turns heavier.

"I'm serious, hen," he says, louder, snappier. "You shouldnae have—"

"There's no money, you know that. That's all."

"I've got money," he says, because we've had this conversation many times before too. There already is money—enough that I don't qualify for either a bursary or crisis grant—but Mum and Brian are about as likely to take over the care of Gramps as loan any of it to me.

"I don't want your money. And I do want to look after you."

He's stiff after sitting so long in the cold. He winces and limps his way back to the door.

"This gives me time. To be sure it's what I want. And until I am—or not—I can save just about all the money I'm earning in the King's Arms, can't I?"

He stops, smiles. "Backing and filling—that's good, Pinky. You argue a convincing case." His voice goes quieter. "You should be in school."

"I'm fine, Gramps. I promise."

He limps up the steps, pushes open the back door with only the slightest of hesitations. "I'm sorry, lassie." He doesn't sound sorry.

He sounds mad. Maybe that's how he's able to keep on opening that back door. He's always been grumpy, impatient, cantankerous. He keeps three bags of M&S sausage rolls in the freezer for his future wake: calls them his *fancy horse doovers*, with DO NOT TOUCH printed big on three bigger labels—and he checks on them every day to be sure. On his ninetieth birthday, he got drunk on rum and pink gin and squared up enough to Brian that we didn't see him again for nearly a week. *Fucking Big OD*, Gramps calls him. Which I know is the very worst thing you can be christened on a submarine, even if he refuses to tell me what it means.

Inside the warmer scullery, he turns, takes hold of my hands and my gaze and keeps hold of them hard. "I'm sorry."

"I know." I smile and manage to mean it. Manage to hide my dread behind it. Squeeze just as hard back. Because even though everything is getting undeniably worse: him, the house, the frequency and power of those dark and twisting down nights, he's still as strong as an ox. We all know he's not going anywhere anytime soon. And of the four of us, I'm maybe the only one who's glad.

• • •

When it's worse, the house doesn't just clank and rattle and groan and breathe wet dark. It screams. It moves. And even in bed, I'm tossed and shaken like one of Mum's bad vodka cocktails. Like there's a fault line right beneath our house and it's getting bigger, wider, cracking open. Even when it slows, quietens, I have to cling onto the pillars of my headboard as we drop too fast and too long through endless nauseating fathoms.

What used to be claustrophobia is now suffocation. Asphyxiation. Everything dims except my panic, my need to breathe, to run, to escape, even though I know I can't. The house won't let me. I try to hold on to holding on, and I try to breathe, to calm down, to see, but everything squeezes down to the smallest of pinholes: a prick of light in the dark. And when it goes quiet, except for my heartbeat, which is thundering hard enough to hurt, someone sits down heavy on my chest and pours wet concrete into my lungs.

I shake, I sweat. I choke. Sometimes I puke. Sometimes I pass out. Sometimes I scream. And Gramps and Mum and Brian and the house scream back at me.

No one else hears it. No one else sees it. The noise alone is enough to make our heads and ears ring for days, but no one has ever come knocking, no one has ever reported us to anyone else. Because they're outside. And we're inside. Because fear is like a virus. Fear is in the stinking air you breathe, and you can't escape it because it's the only fucking air you've got.

• • •

When it's worse, the boat lists quick like the planesman's lost the bubble, and we're dropping, dropping, too sharp and too fast, the trim angle too big. A crash dive. We stagger to our stations; me to the After Ends and all its panels: the angles and dangles and gauges that tell me nothing I cannae already hear. The pressure hull stressing, creaking. Fixing to scream.

The lights go on and off. Stay off, come on. Go off again. The heat is wet enough to sting and blur. The angle is bad enough to have away anything no' screwed down. I grab hold ae the bulkhead frame as Dogs and Tug try to grab hold ae me. The floor grates are slick. No' a crash dive. We're going down too fast, too quick, too *wrong*.

I can hear the propeller, the rudder, and stabilisers even past the roar ae the turbines and the shouts and screams ae the amidships crew. I've time enough to feel uncommon bad for the front cunts in the quicker sinking bow, with only torpedoes and flooding tanks for company, and then I'm on my knees, ears popping, joints twisting, slamming into the starboard engine shaft, the heat exchangers, as we keep on going, keep on dropping, keep on angling down, the pressure gauges spinning wild just like a bad American war movie, just like my belly, those creaking screams slowing to louder, badder bangs, and I think, I'm going to die here. This is where I'm going to die.

And then we hit the bottom.

• • •

"The first rule ae Alzheimer's Club is dinnae talk about Chess Club."

It's not as cold today. There is no crow in the gnarly tree.

"You don't have Alzheimer's."

He snorts, sounds nearly sorry. "I ken."

We both have coffees, strong ones. Behind us, the house feels like a wall of water instead of red sandstone. A forty-foot high wave about to break over our aching heads. Cold. Black. Impatient.

He's bound to have heard this morning's fight—about the clanking, shaking, choking horror of last night. About money, about putting Gramps in a bloody home. But there's no way. Because *this* is his fucking home. And as much as I hate this house—as he hates this house—there's no fucking way we're pushing him out of it.

"Maybe they've got a point, hen," he says now, and his voice is hoarse, just like mine, just like Mum's and Brian's. Too much screaming.

He turns to look at me properly, and the horror, the guilt,

the shame in his face is too much on top of everything else. When he reaches out a hand to stroke my face, its tremor is much worse too. "My God, lassie. Look at you. I'm so sor—"

"Stop it." Because we all look like I do. We all have headaches and tremors and dark purple shadows under our eyes. We've all forgotten what a good nights' sleep feels like.

"It's me, Pinky. It's not this house."

But I think it's both. I think of Mum and Brian always telling me I have to earn my keep, while I don't know what the fuck they do to earn theirs. I think of Brian scowling at me this morning and saying *then he's your bloody responsibility*, as if he wasn't already. But that's fucking fine. I think without me, without someone giving a shit, trying to help, even if it's just to take the edge off whatever the fuck this is, we'd be suffering a lot more than just terrifying nights and near asphyxia. Yes, it's getting worse, I know it's getting worse. And I've thought about running away many, many times. But sometimes a fever has to get hotter and hotter before it breaks. And here's the thing. Despite all their talk and their threats, Mum and Brian aren't about to leave either.

"I just want you to be safe," Gramps says, and I know it's not just for me. Ever since I've known him his back has been bowed under the weight of so much guilt I'm always surprised he manages even to get out of bed in the morning. I've paid attention to it. That guilt is my only working theory.

"Then tell me."

"It doesnae—"

"Yes it does." I look at the high red walls of the house beyond the end of our garden, and I think, *it has to.*

"I had a girl once," he says. And I can't object, can't give into my impatience, because I know this is the only way he can do it.

I lean back, nurse my coffee. "You can't call us girls."

"Eh?" His frown makes me want to smile. It makes me remember the Belgian art student whom Gramps christened Axel Le Big Bad-Ass, and neat shots of Navy Rum when he dumped me on Christmas Eve. Gramps's grin when I told him it was the worst day of my life. The stroke of his hand against my cheek. *Hen. It's only the worst day ae your life so far.*

"Or ladies. Or lassies. Or *hens.*"

"Well whit the bloody hell is it I can call you then?"

"Women. We're women."

"They're just words mean the same thing," he says, but he's smiling too. "All right. I had a *woman.*"

"When did you meet her?"

"When I tried to sign up for the Royal Scots. She was one ae the nurses doing medicals up at the Royal Infirmary on Little France. Her hair was black like Hartwood coal, and her eyes were the blue horizon over the firth. Full ae sky and freedom." He shows me his teeth. "Told me I had a pigeon chest and flat feet, and would have to join the navy instead."

"What was her name?"

His smile changes, and I don't miss the small glance he gives behind us. "That's just for me, hen."

And I nod, nod, nod, because he's never told me any of this before.

"We spent just about the best weekend ae my life in a tin can van in North Berwick afore I got that first post up north. When I left, she gave me this little wooden box same colour as her eyes, full ae letters she'd written for me. So no' even the BFP could keep us apart."

Something stings behind my eyes, and for a moment it's far bigger, stronger, than the pain, the worry, the fear. Even than the cold, black, impatient wave. She is why he has never married, never had children. Why he's alone. Why he let us move into his big, empty house. She is why he loves me. "She died."

He nods, studies the palms of his hands. "Bad shit always has to happen, hen. It's life's one guarantee. But good shit, that's a lottery, and some folk just ain't born lucky. She died a year afore the end ae the war. Second influenza epidemic."

I give him a brief hard hug which he doesn't respond to beyond letting out a sigh and an ugly choked laugh. "Bloody hell, this hasnae helped at all, Pinky."

And I know he isn't only referring to that still growing shadow behind and above us. The hands in his lap have become fists and their tremor is back.

"It was just a test dive," he says, his eyes faraway, voice dull. "That was all. No' even that: just a tank water survey. The Fore Endies had to open the test cocks, check the internal torpedo tubes were flooded. One was blocked, some brass hat said later, and the Fore Endies didnae see it, didnae use prickers to clear it. Bow cap indicator panel was laid out like it had been designed by a kid hopped up on lemon sherbets." He stops, and when he forces open his fists, a few nails have broken through skin. "No idea whose fucking fault it was. Maybe the Fore Endies. Maybe the shipbuilders left something blocking the valve. Those upstanding brass hats invoked the old get out ae Crown Privilege, so guess we'll never ken." He shrugs. "Doesnae matter much, I guess, to the folk it killed."

I put down my coffee, press my hands over his. "Tell it like it was. What it felt like." He has never told me any of this either. I don't want to push him too hard, even though I'm certain that I have to. This flat monologue won't mollify that black waiting wave. And I'm trying not to act like this is any big thing: him telling me—finally telling me—what he hasn't, what he's refused to tell me for months. Because he *has* to tell me. And it *has* to help; it *has* to make a difference. I already know what happened to the HMS *Torque,* of course. It has its own wiki page. But knowing hasn't helped at all. If anything, it's only scared me shitless. The horror of it.

"The inner tube ae number five opened," Gramps says, and now his voice shakes. "And that's when the water came in. We sunk and sunk fast. First I kenned ae it, we were already going down. Steep. Bow first. The alarms were too late. Scurs's and Dogs's screaming orders were too late. It was too late to do anything but hold on and hope I didnae get smashed against anything could kill me afore we hit bottom.

"That happened fast enough too: Seabed was maybe only hundred and thirty, forty feet down. The bow hit first and hard. Fore Endies didnae stand much ae a chance. And then the ones ae us in the stern that hadnae already been shaken loose were left dangling, hanging on, and *fuck* it was hot, hen. Hot like Hell on a June day. The boat was shrieking blue murder, her head stuck right and deep in the bottom I could tell, and behind me I could hear the propeller and rudder, churning nothing but air.

"I was holding onto the handwheel for the outboard exhaust and hydraulics—and I'm telling you, you've no idea how heavy you are till you're dangling from a wee fucking metal wheel over a drop that could kill you in about a dozen different ways. A mech called Happy—dinnae remember much more about him than that—was hanging off the metal frame of the elbows, maybe only a couple feet lower down, and he looked right up at me when the boat settled back some and he lost his grip, bounced off just about everything nailed down and no', till I heard his back go in this one big crack.

"We moved quick, 'cause you cannae give yourself too much time to think about your situation. You do that, you start asking yourself how the fuck anyone could ever get out ae something like this, and that's when you panic, that's when you willnae. I started climbing down to the donkshop hatch. Maybe half a dozen jacks were already there, standing on the compartment bulkhead, looking up at the rest ae us, ducking or moving out ae the way every time one ae us let go and bounced. Scurs was yelling, pulled me down the last few feet, but I could see he was banged up pretty bad, a snapped bone was pushing up through his forearm and his nose was busted near flat; the rest ae him was a bad white-grey. Hibee came down right after me. By the time we got the hatch open, there were nine ae us climbing through it, and that's how we kept on doing it: dogging down the hatches, scrambling down every passageway, using every handhold, collecting off-watch jacks like Tug as we went, trying no' to look too long at jacks like Happy.

"We got to the escape chamber afore anyone else. Didnae ken how till a fifth hand said the captain and sig were trapped between brokedick auxiliary panels and the busted-up overhead to the conning tower. So we waited. The angle was maybe fifty-five degrees by then. Already the heat was getting worse and the air was getting bad. Everyone was coughing, shouting. It's never no oxygen you need to worry about in a boat. Unless it's full ae fucking water. Most times, it's whit you breathe out that'll kill you.

"Most everyone survived up to that point. Even a few ae the Fore Endies turned up after a while. The captain was pretty out ae it—his head was bashed up enough that he couldnae speak right—so the CO, some fancy boy from the BRNC, took over command, made us sit tight, wait till we were discovered. No' many ae us were up for that—Dogs 'specially: He got right up in that CO's face and told him plain that the only folk would rescue us was us, but that kind ae cagg never goes down well with fancy boys. Never has, didnae then.

"Ten hours it was in the end we waited, and by then there wasnae one ae us no' feeling like we were going to die just like that: wedged up against bulkhead hatches or each other; burning, choking, drowning in air. When the CO pipes up he thinks he can hear a skimmer upstairs, Dogs finally snaps and gets up, screams *'Shit in it!'* just about loud enough for some ae us to stop being deaf, and he knocks that fancy boy clean out, eyes all the other officers like he wants them to have an opinion too.

"*'We're going now,'* he says. *'My guys first.'*

"And even though that's never how it's supposed to go, pound to a penny it wasn't the first time it did. He got us all up, but in the sudden-quick rammy, only him, me, Tug, Hibee, and a wrecker—might have been called Banjo or Pony—made it to the chamber's inner hatch ahead ae anyone else. I never saw Scurs at all; remembered after about that ugly bone sticking up out ae his arm, and the big hard turns ae the escape chamber's outer door. There was plenty more bobbery—even some more punches—afore something like an evacuation line was made. Everyone was sweating neaters again by then. Always the way it is on a boat, remember? Feast or fucking famine. Soon as you stop thinking you're a dead man, you turn into Roadrunner on speed.

"There was only ever room for one person at a time in escape chambers back then. I went up third, after Tug and Banjo-or-Pony. Hibee wouldnae go afore me; we argued back and forth long enough for Dogs to start yelling *'Shit in it!'* again. His eyes were wild mad and blinking sweat, but they couldnae find us. Most ae us had started going blind by then, but he was already there, I'm about as sure ae that as anything else.

"And I was fucking scared. Of everything between me and freedom: the crew, the air, the pressure hull, ballast tanks, outer hull, hatches, the sea. The fear. So I went next. I left Hibee without even a good-bye—Hibee, who used to sing 'Mist Covered Mountains of Home' in his sleep and was getting married to Jenny Ann Cunningham during the Glasgow Fair—and I climbed into the escape chamber, shut the inner hatch on him and all those other white-grey faces, secured it. Looked across at the hatch to all that outside, looked down at my fingers, twitching, itching to open it, and prayed like a brown job waiting to go over the fucking top.

"And that wait was the longest wait ae all. The water started coming in and I couldnae stay still, couldnae catch my breath, even though I kenned the compartment was supposed to flood, had to flood. And my fingers kept on jumping, twitching, itching towards that outer hatch even though I kenned I couldnae open it till all the air was gone. Even though I kenned I had to get ready to blow and go, had to fill up my chest with just about as much ae that bad air as I could stand. But all I could see was outside, all I could see was escape, even if it meant I had to die to get it. Doesnae make no sense to anyone except the you at the time, but that's whit the fear inside a boat does to you. It's just about the worse possible thing you cannae stand.

"When the water closed over my face, my head, I had to fist my hands under my armpits to keep them from opening that outer hatch; had to turn my nearly blind eyes straight onto the go light and nothing else. And when the light finally went out, I pushed open the hatch, pushed right out through, and secured it behind me again so quick it felt like I couldnae have—that I had to still be trapped inside that chamber, waiting with my fists. The cold and space ae all that outside shocked me enough that I wanted to let go ae all my air straightaway, but when I looked up I could see the sun, I could see freedom, and I swam for it fast and exhaled slow till my lungs flattened out and the dark shadows in my eyes became big black spots. And then I broke up above the surface like a fucking humpback, smacking back down again, choking on waves and wind, squinting up at the spindrift and sky."

He's been staring fixedly at the gnarly tree and the back fence beyond it, but now he turns slow towards me and blinks. His eyes are red and dry. "I was the last jack to escape HMS *Torque.* No one else ever came up after me."

My heart sinks, even though I was expecting it. When I read the wiki entry and the three survivor names, I hoped he wasn't the last, and knew he probably was.

"That couldn't have been your fault," I say. "You secured the outer hatch."

"It is my fault Hibee never got to marry Jenny Ann Cunningham, and no one can tell me different, no' even you." He waves my objection away before I can even get it out. "Whichever jack got into the chamber after me was the one fucked it for everyone else. Maybe it was Hibee, maybe the fancy boy, maybe Dogs—he was fixing to go postal all right—but whoever it was, they had a bigger dose ae the fear than me, Tug, or that wrecker called Banjo or Pony, 'cause they never managed to stand it, to stop their fingers. They never managed to wait. They opened that outer hatch afore they should have, and it did for everyone else in that boat, 'cause the escape chamber would've been fucked after that. They'd have drowned quick, but every other jack would have had hours to think about dying from carbon dioxide poisoning afore they did. Deafness, blindness, headache, dizziness, confusion, palpitations, shortness ae breath, tremors, sweating." When he looks at me again, his eyes are sad sorry again. "Guess I dinnae have to tell you whit all that feels like, lassie. And at the end, convulsions and pain so bad it makes you go mad. Fifty-four men." He closes his eyes, pinches the skin between them. "They salvaged her a few months later, and brought the bodies out, full naval honours." He snorts, and it turns into an ugly cough. "Ran her aground at Uig the day war was declared."

"Gramps—"

"I dinnae blame that fourth jack," he says suddenly, as if it's the most important thing of all. "The guys inside, they wouldnae have blamed him either."

"Why not?"

He shrugs, looks back at the tree, the fence, the sky, and his voice drops to a whisper as if he's afraid the house will hear him. His eyes are even more afraid than before. "Because everyone deserves to escape." He swallows. "And most times they cannae do it on their own."

A sudden cold wind rustles the tree's leaves, fans the hairs already standing up straight against my skin. And I realise something. Something terrible that drowns dead all of my relief at Gramps finally telling me about the *Torque.* This hasn't made a difference. This confession, this *lancing,* hasn't mollified either the house or its cold, black, impatient shadow. We're still trapped helpless inside, both. We're still suffocating inside terrible clammy dark weight. We're still just waiting for all that fear and fury to break over our heads. Because there's still something else. Something so bad Gramps can't bear to even think about it, never mind talk about it. Something so bad that he's had to give me—he's had to give this house—what happened to HMS *Torque* instead. I know it.

Because something is better than nothing.

Because worse is not worst.

• • •

When it's the worst, I can't see, can't breathe, can't even scream. The world explodes around me, throws me against metal and plastic and rubber. I bleed. I fall. I crawl. I scramble to stand, battered against corners and sharp edges, borne away by violent walls of water. I bleed. I fall. I choke. I drown. My skin is icy cold. Incandescent with heat. I choke. I burn. I suffocate.

I find my scream as the boat dives down, down. Too hard, too fast. Alarms screech. My stomach drops. My heart stops. My ears pop. Dread is panic is terror is horror. Is fear.

I crawl. Clouds of wet mist close up my throat. I choke. I burn. I drown. I suffocate. I hallucinate.

A big cavernous house with red sandstone walls and Georgian bar windows.

The overheads and bulkheads crumple, rush in towards me. I put out my hands to stop them. I fall and choke and burn and drown and scream—

—*Make it stop. Gramps. Make it stop.*

And right before I know it won't, it does.

• • •

—and I think, I should have died here. That's whit I ken. This is where I should have died.

• • •

He won't get out of bed. Maybe he'd feel better if he did, if I somehow managed to get him up and across the landing, down the stairs, and back outside, but I'm pretty sure that he's past all that now. That we're past it. I feel just about the worst I've ever felt. My throat hurts and my ribs ache, my breath is shallow. It rattles even when I'm not coughing. I have cuts and bruises everywhere, enough that I've had to cover all of me under clothes and make up. Normally, Gramps would notice, but not today. Today, he looks even worse than I do.

Still, he props himself up against his pillows, grins with all of his teeth when I come in with two mugs of coffee.

"How do you think the unthinkable, hen?"

I pass the mug across to his trembling hands, watch the coffee spill out over his bruised and bloodied fingers. I sit down next to the bed with a lump inside my throat so big I don't even try to swallow it. "Dunno, Gramps."

"With an itheberg."

I start to cry, and he spills more coffee in trying to reach for my hands.

"It's okay, Pinky. It's okay."

I stand up, push away from the bed. "It's not fucking okay! In what way is any of this okay?"

He sets down his coffee. "Come here. Come here."

And I go, of course, because I could never not. And I let him hold me close, rub my back, stroke my hair. Whisper in my ear, "I cannae escape this. I cannae. And you cannae save me. But I can save you."

I draw back then, make him let me go, sit down next to him on the bed. And when he sees me shaking my head, he shakes his own in anger.

"There has to be an ending, lassie. Everything deserves an ending. And that's whit this is." He glances at the ceiling, the walls, the pea-green cupboard opposite the bed. "It wants an end."

"Then tell me what that end is," I say. *"Tell me."*

His frown is impatient, nearly belligerent. "It'll no' help. It'll no'—"

"I don't care. Tell me anyway." I look at him and I don't look away. "Tell me, and maybe then I'll do what you want me to do."

He sighs, looks up at the ceiling. The house is smaller now. Its ceilings low and too smooth. Its wide panelled doors shrunken, their corners and architraves curved like lozenges. The walls are closer, their silk print wallpaper mute silver grey.

Gramps leans back against the pillows, looks down at his bruised and battered hands like he's only just noticed them. "About a month into the war, less than six after the *Torque* went down, I was posted to another T class boat called the *Trigon.* After a spell ae patrolling for U-boats in the Atlantic, they sent us to the Med to blow up Italian boats and freighters instead. Captain was a guy called Holloway, anchor-faced through and through. A real Navy man. Some jacks thought that was always a bad thing, but no' me.

"I was a proper boat rat by then. As used to the noise, the crush, the heat, the dark, the stink, the feast and the famine as any rat can ever get." He smiles thin. "It was much worse than the *Torque.* There were boxes ae gear and provisions stashed everywhere: passageways and bunks, the showers, the After Ends. We stunk. Washed once a fortnight if we were lucky. Stayed submerged during the day and surfaced at night. Never saw the sun at all. The only thing more crowded up than us inside that steel can were the fucking cockroaches: big, black ugly fuckers that wouldnae die even if you smashed off their heads.

"I shared a donkshop bunk with two EAs: a fifer called Shiner, who got rechristened Admiral ae the Narrow Seas on account ae him spending most part ae every day honking his guts up. The other guy, Ginger, was whit we called a leg iron, a check valve. A useless arsehole. He spent most part ae every day sewn up or high. Kept a stash ae methamphetamine in our rack locker, industrial strength stuff like the Luftwaffe Stuka tablets—built to keep you awake for days and send you around the bend while doing it. I didnae make any mates on the *Trigon*, didnae want them, didnae get them. I was already a Jonah. Every jack on that boat kenned I'd been on the *Torque* when she went down. Kenned I'd been the last one out. That kind ae thing matters, 'specially in wartime, same thing as never wanting a woman or a left-handed jack or a sky-pilot and his bible onboard either. I didnae give a shit. Just went on doing my time, working it down, waiting for the fucking war to end and my life to start over on the surface.

"I had some fear still. Some dread. No point in pretending I didnae. The Med was a much more dangerous place for a boat to be than the Atlantic. More traffic and clearer water. Harder to hide. But the war was the war by then. And a posting was a posting. You can get used to just about anything if you do it long enough.

"And then, one day. One fucking day. There was something else. Something I wouldnae—couldnae—ever get used to. Didnae even try.

"I got off watch around noon. Found the admiral had yodelled all over our bunk and the one below it, and I was tired and fucked off enough to kick up a bigger stink than he had. The chief found me another, and I was already half asleep in it afore I realised. Starboard corner ae the third compartment. Top bunk under the aft ventilation pipes.

"It's strange whit bad familiar does—it gives you the kind ae déjà vu that yanks you back and shoves you front, till you're no' sure if it's rage or dread you've got; if it's a memory or a promise. Happened so often on war boats, we came up with a name for it. Bad juvu. I lay in that bunk, wide awake and trying no' to remember for maybe four hours straight, boiling hot and stinking raw, my ear pressed up against that cold whistle vent, listening to the creaks and moans ae the drowned space on the other side, till I couldnae stand it anymore. I got up. The rack lockers were never locked—anyone wanted to bone something away it wasnae like you couldnae take it back again you looked long enough—and I was fixed to eat something, read something. Anything so I could shake that bad juvu. But I never did see whit was inside that locker. Never got past opening its door."

"DFG," I whisper, and my fingers are cold against my mouth.

Gramps smile shakes. "All Is Well." His eyes look black. They fix ahead, on the pea-green cupboard door.

"The *Trigon* was the *Torque*?"

He nods and swallows, and I know it's because he can't speak.

"Oh, Gramps."

He clears his throat and ends up coughing hard. Something rattles down inside his chest, trying to come up. "Wasnae all that unusual for a grounded boat to be recommissioned during the war." His smile is the worst one yet; it makes me want to hide, close my eyes, run away. "But you were never supposed to ken it. You were never supposed to ken exactly how many men had died a slow bad death in it. Or whit they looked like, whit they smelled like, whit they screamed out in their sleep."

"Did you tell anyone?"

"Did I tell anyone?"

"No," I say, looking away from those black and bloodshot eyes. "You couldn't tell anyone. You couldn't tell them that—"

"I couldnae tell them." He takes another deep and creaky breath. "But there was no getting rid ae the bad juvu for me. Every day for weeks, months, I went on working watches in that donkshop, walking those passageways and compartments, laying in my bunk, and all I could see or feel or hear was the *Torque.* Whit it had felt like to hold on, to fall, to sink, to crash, to choke. Scurs screaming at me to climb the fuck down, his arm bone sticking up through his elbow. Happy letting go ae the elbow frame, that one big crack as he bounced from the starboard engine to the port-side bulkhead, his blood pooling watery pink inside the engine hatch. Dogs screaming wild mad and blind, *Shit in it! Shit in it!* Whit it had felt like to blow up through a hundred and forty feet ae freezing sea, and then tread waves on top ae it, waiting for someone—anyone—to come up after. And so all that dread went from memory to promise quick smart. It followed me around like the worst kind ae boat stink. Oh, I had the fear all right, and I couldnae leave it behind, couldnae wash it off, couldnae get used to it enough that I stopped being able to smell it.

"I was convinced we were going to die. I was as certain as Hogmanay comes after Christmas. And bad enough that I couldnae function for thinking about the how. The when. Bad enough that just about the only thing I could think about was throwing a wire rope over the pipes in the head and tying a noose afore I could find out.

"And then my body got sick too. Fever, sweats, chills, insomnia, disorientation. Doc diagnosed viral pneumonia. They couldnae get me off the boat quick enough. Transferred me onto a hospital ship in one ae the allied convoys off Malta first opportunity they got."

He looks across at me again, and his eyes are wet, shining. And I don't need a wiki page to know what happened, what he's going to say next.

"I never went aboard the *Trigon* again. Two weeks later, she was sunk by an Italian corvette off the west coast ae Sicily. All hands lost. Fifty-six men."

When he turns his face towards the window and the back garden, he doesn't hide his tears quick enough. They splash against his pyjama top, his long thin arms.

"Dinnae ken for sure how they died, but there are only so many ways you can die on a boat like that."

"Gramps—"

"Sunshine pills could have blown a hole in both hulls, ruptured her enough that the Med came in and everyone drowned. Would have been the best way to go, I guess, if you had to pick, but usually those pills were like firecrackers—a lot ae fucking noise and that was about it. When she saw the corvette, she would've dived. Couldnae not. You only surface under attack when there's nothing else to do. Maybe they got hit deep. And any rupture floods the boat ten times faster when you're deep. Only thing to do then would be close all the hull valves, open the air flasks into the ballast tanks, aim the boat up, open the throttles all the way, and pray Poseidon's been getting it regular.

"But they must have had Saltash luck with that 'cause they never came back up again. Closing the hull valves would've stopped the flooding, but the pressure ae all that water already inside would heat up the air enough to burn and smoke. Enough to choke you with thick hot mist. Meantime, the nitrogen would be binding to your blood, putting your head in a tight-winding vice, showing you Hell or Wee Willie Winkie on a headless horse. And all the time, you're sinking deeper, deeper, 'cause you're big down in negative buoyancy now and your engines are toast. The lights go out and the boat starts screaming soprano. The welds along bulkheads and overheads start to crack. Oil lines and pipework split and burst open. Operational max diving depth ae a T class was three hundred feet, remember? Crush depth, six hundred and twenty-six. The Med round Sicily's nearly four and a half thousand. That's how it would've been, I reckon. Blast wave, drowning, burning, choking, sinking, soprano. Seeing Wee fucking Willie Winkie on a headless horse, and then being crushed flatter than a Scotch pancake."

I look at his angry profile, at the gnarly tree and its waving branches outside the window. I think of last night. I think of the night to come.

"She's still down there. They're all still down there. Never happened afore or since. One for the record books. A boat going down twice, most every hand lost." His smile is twisted. "Maybe if they'd known about me that would've been a different kind ae record. After all, I'm the bloody one—"

"None of it was your fault! You weren't supposed to die on

the *Trigon* any more than the *Torque*! How can you think just because you survived that—"

He turns back to me, reaches again for my hands. "'Cause I escaped the *Torque* fair and square, hen. But I deserted the *Trigon*."

I snatch my hands back. "No, you didn't. You were sick! How—"

"I wasnae sick. I had a virus, sure, but it wasnae the kind got you shipped off boats." He takes in too big a breath and straight-away starts coughing, enough that I can hear that liquid rattle is louder, bigger, deeper. He gives me that wry smile again, and I want to cry again. "I couldnae take it anymore. Not any ae it. The waiting. The wondering how and when. All that fucking fear. So I boned some ae Ginger's stash. Enough that I passed for sick—contagious sick—and got myself off that boat afore it killed me. Afore *I* killed me. And I have to take the can back for that. I do, hen."

He looks at me, nearly triumphant, and I know he's expecting anger, disappointment, condemnation, something. And looks worse than disappointed when he doesn't get it.

"It wasn't your fault. For fuck's sake, if they'd known—if anyone had gone through what you had, they'd have done the same." I take hold of his hands so tight, I feel his bones creak. "Please. You have to let go of it. The guilt and the shame and the—"

"I cannae, Pinky. I've tried. It's no' me anymore." He looks up at the low ceiling, across at the silver grey walls. "Some viruses, they never go away. If you're lucky, you can get years, decades maybe, ae remission, but that doesnae mean you're no still sick. That doesnae mean it's no still there, right inside ae you, waiting with fists. And I'm just too old, too tired, that's all. For the waiting. The wondering how and when." His grip is loosening and his eyes are heavy, his irises rolling backwards with each slow blink.

"Go to sleep, Gramps," I whisper. Even though I want him to do anything but.

"Leave this place to your mum and the Fucking Big OD downstairs," he says, his words slurring, his fingers slipping out of my grip. And I don't have the heart to tell him that they've already pissed off, dragging their suitcases and ingratitude with them. "Leave this place to the ghosts, hen."

I light his ugly candles. Watch him sleep. Watch his fingers twitch against the sheets. Watch the shallow rise and drop of his chest. Listen to the low rattle inside his lungs.

I ignore the house. I don't look at its dimming windows and shrinking doors, nearing walls, dropping ceilings. I don't smell steel and smoke and mould and shit and sweat. I don't feel the icy cold and incandescent hot, the unstable floor beneath my feet, the lurches of my belly, the rumbling pressure inside my ears. I don't hear creaks and bangs and rattles and rushes and klaxon alarms. I don't see Wee Willie Winkie on a headless horse.

But when Gramps sits bolt upright with a screamed intake of breath, I only manage to breathe and scream back once the house has retreated again. I'm shaking so much my teeth are chattering.

"Lassie!" Gramps cries, and for a moment his eyes can't find me, as if he's gone blind.

We cling together until the end of the worst of it passes, but when I draw back, I'm the only one still crying. There's a steely determination in his face now. Maybe even a smile. One I'm afraid of.

"It wasn't your fault," I say, because it's become a mantra, an incantation. There's nothing else I *can* say.

He looks beyond my shoulder, points to the dresser with a shaky finger. "There's a big jiffy bag addressed to you in the top left drawer," he says. "Afterwards, I want you to come back and get it."

"Gramps. Please. It wasn't—"

He closes his fingers over my fist, rubs my wrist with his thumb. "It's okay, lassie. I think I ken now. I think maybe all ae these years all I've been doing is treading water." His smile grows bigger. "Waiting for my boat to come in."

"No. *No.*" I can't bear to let go of him, even though I'm seized with the need to move, to get up, to do, to fight. "You don't have to stay. You don't have to do this."

"I think I do." He looks nearly serene. But his eyes are still black. Black and afraid. More black and afraid than they've ever been. And they are what keep me here, anchored to this bed, to this boat, to him. He doesn't want to stay here any more now than he did then. It's just fear. The weight of it. The longevity of it. His want—his need—to open that outer hatch before the chamber has flooded full of water.

He digs his nails into my knuckles. Hard enough that I can't keep holding on. "I want you to go outside now, Pinky."

"No, no, no. It's not your fault. It's not your fault."

"Hey. Hey!" He pinches my chin to turn me towards him. The pads of his fingers slip in my tears. "Listen to me." He moves nearer until we're close enough that I can see the gold and hazel of his eyes deep down past the black. He strokes my wet cheek. "You cannae save me. Remember? But I can save you, lassie." He exhales. "I need to."

When he lets me go, he gives me a little push. I stand up. I look down at him and he looks up at me.

"I love you, Gramps."

He smiles, wipes his cheeks with those shaking fingers. "I love you too, Sarah."

As soon as I step across the bedroom's threshold, I smell the smoke of candles going out, and the door slams shut with a metallic clang. The house gives a long, thin scream of rage, and I run across the landing, cling to the bannister as I half fall down the stairs, as the house starts to list forward and port. In the kitchen, the lights go out and the angle steepens. The house screeches and rattles and drops like a stone. The walls of the scullery buckle and scream and crack. On my hands and knees, I crawl through the back door. Into sunlight and cold wind.

I sit on the stone bench. I cry with closed eyes. I listen to the crows. I listen to the house.

When I go back inside, everything is silent. And his bedroom is full of oakwood and autumn light and sweet new air.

• • •

There was money in that big jiffy bag. Enough money for law school ten times over.

I book the mission for the wake. Take all his unopened bottles of Sailor Jerry and his *fancy horse doovers* inside their DO NOT TOUCH bags down to the docks before the service in St. Michael's. Maybe a dozen people come. I don't know any of them, and I'm pretty sure none of them knew Gramps.

Mum and Brian come back less than a week later. The second morning, I walk in on them sitting at the kitchen table, talking about redecorating Gramps' bedroom purple and green before moving themselves and their Ikea king-size in. And I'm not as mad about that as maybe I should be, because the house is already growing dark again. Its walls smell of mould, its windows mildew. The lights flicker on and off, even in the day. The ceilings are too low and the floors too untrustworthy, as if we spend our days walking through a boggy wet field under heavy wet skies. And I know they feel it, I know they know it. But Gramps left them this house, and that's a different kind of bog for them—the kind they don't even want to escape.

He is the only thing that still keeps me here. Because he *is* still here. I feel him—in those walls and windows and ceilings and floors—his snorts and jokes and wry smiles. His guilt, his sadness, his shame, his fear.

On a freezing December day, nearly six weeks after the funeral, I lie on Gramps's single bed and look out over the back garden, up into a white-grey sky empty of clouds. The Heart Foundation people are coming tomorrow to take away everything that was his—everything, at least, that Mum and Brian don't want—so I suppose this is another good-bye of sorts. When the sky gets greyer, darker, I get back up and wander between the dust sheets and cloths, stop in front of the pea-green cupboard.

The inside smells so potently of him, I almost close it again straightaway. But I don't. I run my fingers through his trousers and jackets, two wire racks of brown ties, and that's when I see the sleeping bag. Not rolled up, but spread out along the bottom of the cupboard, unzipped and open. I crouch down, push in past his clothes, and get in, pull its soft inside back over my knees. There's the whistling whisper of a draft against my ear:

maybe from the flanking chimney breast or a gap in the plasterboard. In the brightest corner lie a lighter, a pouch of tobacco shag, and half a dozen half-burned pig fat candles. Something catches my eye on the lowest inside panel of the door, and I lean back towards it, pull it closer, run the pads of my fingers across its wood. *DFG.* Scratched deep and careful with a penknife.

I didn't think my heart could hurt any more, but it can, it does. This is where Gramps went. On bad nights—the worse and worst nights—this is where he hid. This is where he waited.

This is where he is now.

I don't know how long I stay there. Too long. Not long enough. It's dark by the time I stretch out my stiff legs to leave and my foot hits against something with sharp edges. When I push the door wide open to let what little light there is back in, I see the blue wooden box.

I can't not open it, and feel a lot better about that when sitting on top of all the old letters addressed to him, there's one addressed to me.

His writing is big. Untidy. It makes me want to smile even before I've read it.

*Make the good shit happen, Pinky.*

*Don't wait. Don't give it a fucking choice.*

I cry. And then I laugh.

Because we're haunted by a house that is haunted by a man, who spent his life haunted by a submarine that was haunted by the ghosts of a hundred and ten men. Because when you think about it, it's nearly funny. One for the record books. How do you think the unthinkable?

With an itheberg.

• • •

I've packed a bag. I've written a letter of my own. And when I lie on my bed tonight and look up at the ceiling, I won't feel dread or shame or misery. Or fear. Because tomorrow will be different. Tomorrow, I will leave this house and never ever come back.

And I'll take Sailor Jerry with me. Inside a wooden box full of sky and freedom, the same shade of blue as his girl's eyes.

Because everything deserves an ending.

Because everyone deserves to escape, and most times they cannae do it on their own.

Because All Is Well.

And I'm making the good shit happen.

# Natalya, Queen of the Hungry Dogs

*John Langan*

*In Memoriam Lucius Shepard*

## I

When it came, Hunter's e-mail was brief, blunt. "Well," it read, "that's wife number three packed her bags and gone. Said she cared too much to watch this thing have its way with me. Pity. If she'd stuck it out a little longer, she'd have done quite well for herself. She may still. I haven't told the lawyers. Anyway. The doc says it's a matter of weeks, at most. Why don't you come up for a couple of days? Bring a bottle of something good. Maybe two. You know the way."

"What should I do?" Carl asked his wife after she had read the message over his shoulder.

"You mean you aren't going?" Melanie said.

"No, I am going."

"Then what . . . Ah. You don't know how long you'll be there."

"He shouldn't be on his own. Not now."

"Doesn't he have a daughter?"

"They haven't spoken for fifteen years. She stopped talking to Hunter when he married the second time. I suppose it's never too late, except it almost is."

"What about his brothers and sisters? Isn't he one of four?"

"They don't talk much. There's one brother he's on good terms with, but he lives in Austria."

"Well, it isn't as if he's alone."

"Nurses aren't the same as family."

"You aren't family."

"I'm close enough."

Melanie sighed. "You have coverage at the dojo?"

He nodded. "Indrani can do the four-thirty classes, and I'm pretty sure Tara and Jeff can teach the five-thirties. The only day I'm not certain about is Saturday. I'll have to call Carmen, see if she's available."

"You should take the Subaru. I'm pretty sure I read something about there being snow on the ground in Vermont already."

"Will do. And babe?"

"Yeah?"

"I love you."

"Of course you do."

## II

Of the many stories Hunter Kang had shared with him over three decades of friendship, the one Carl Kimani returned to as he packed for the trip to South Burlington, was that of Hunter's first death. "Not near death," Hunter had said. "Death. I was gone for at least five minutes before I was revived." They had been sitting at a booth in Pete's Corner Pub in Huguenot, drinking Heinekens, after a particularly grueling workout at their karate school. They had known each other six months.

"What happened?" Carl said.

"Riptide," Hunter said. "My dad decided to take the family to the Jersey Shore. This was after my little sister died—I told you about Natalie, right?"

Carl nodded.

"That's right, I did. We had been in mourning for, it must have been a year by then. Dad packed us into the van, including Mom, who insisted she didn't want to go, and drove to Point Pleasant. Sprang for three rooms at the Neptune Motel, one for him and Mom, one for my older sisters, and one for me and my little brother. It was . . ." Hunter shook his head, smiling. "Man, it was fantastic. One of the best things my old man ever did. Maybe the best. We spent our days at the beach, with a break at lunchtime for subs at a deli a couple of blocks away. At dinner, we had pizza or hamburgers, and were allowed to watch TV in our rooms until eleven o'clock, which was unheard of. You remember *Simon & Simon*?"

"Sure."

"That was the first time I ever saw that show. I loved it. Anyway, our second to last day at the beach, I swam into a riptide. The next thing I knew, I was being carried away from everybody, out to sea. I didn't know what to do. I tried swimming toward shore, but I wasn't strong enough to keep myself in place, let alone fight my way to the beach. I started to panic. It wasn't long before I was screaming for help, waving at the rest of my family. At first, they thought I was showing off. By the time they realized what was happening, I was going under.

"If you were forced to pick a way to die, drowning isn't the worst. Don't get me wrong, it's pretty bad at the start. You thrash and cry, struggling to keep the water out of your mouth and nose. In what seems like a matter of seconds, though, you're overcome by a feeling of tremendous peace, and you let the process that's started, continue. After I went under for the final time, I looked at the water around me, which was this luminous blue, and thought this was the color of death, and it was beautiful. Even at this age—we're talking eleven years old—I was aware that what I was experiencing was a kind of gift, not like what Natalie had been through, the year before.

"My sister Vicky was the one who reached me first, and not my other sister Heather, which was strange, because Heather was on the swim team at her high school, and Vicky was captain of the chess club. Vicky also knew that the way out of a riptide is not to swim against it, but sideways to it, parallel to the shore, until you're free. This was what she did. As she was turning toward the beach, Heather joined her, and together, my sisters brought me in. When they delivered me to my dad, though, I was dead. No heartbeat, no breathing. If you could have hooked me up to an EEG, I'm sure it would have showed no brain activity.

"For what might have been the first time in his life, Dad froze. Here was a man who had immigrated to the US from Busan with a degree in graphic design and a bank account with just enough in it to let him live outside LA for three months. At the end of six weeks, he had a job with a small advertising company; within six years, he was chosen to head up their office in West New York. During that time, he met my mom, which meant dealing with her parents. Let me tell you, however progressive their voting record, when it came to whoever was dating their Lily, Grandpa and Grandma McMaster were not terribly thrilled with their daughter dating and then becoming engaged to an Asian. Apparently, Grandma said to her, 'Marriage is hard enough as it is. Why do you want to complicate it?' Nice, huh? But the two of them stuck to their guns, and when Dad moved east, he took his wife and young daughters with them. Together, they built a life for themselves in Jersey. The family expanded, two boys and another girl. At five, his youngest daughter was diagnosed with a rare form of bone cancer, which took two agonizing years to kill her. Throughout all of it, he had remained steadfast. Mom called him her rock, and I think the rest of us viewed him that way, too. Now here I was lying lifeless in his arms, a second child lost within the span of twelve months. It was too much.

"Fortunately for everyone, my mom hauled me away from him and dropped me onto the sand. She pumped my chest, turned me on my side to help the water pour out, rolled me on my back, pinched my nose, blew two breaths into my lungs, and started a set of chest compressions. My sisters, my brother, my father gathered around us, along with some other people who had witnessed Vicky and Heather dragging me out of the surf. One of the bystanders ran for a lifeguard (all of whom, needless to say, were fucking *useless*). Dad started to speak to Mom, words to the effect of, 'Honey, he's gone,' but she stopped him with a look that killed the sentence in his mouth. She labored over me. She pressed down on my sternum one, two, three, four, five times, switched to my head to fill my lungs, went back to working on my heart. The seconds advanced, each one carrying me that much further from her, but my mother's pace did not slacken. She was a dentist—did I ever tell you that? Met my dad when he came in with an abscess. Romantic, eh? She was six years older than he was. Packed up her practice in San Marino and opened a new one in Jersey City, while managing a steadily expanding family. When Natalie was given her diagnosis, Mom brought in a second and third dentist so she could spend the maximum time possible with her. She took my sister's death hard—not that the rest of us didn't, but with Mom, it seemed almost personal, as if death had targeted her child, in particular.

"Well. Mom put all of her effort—her concentration, her strength, her will—into her fight with the Grim Reaper. It was as if she was prying his grip from me one bony finger at a time. Right as the ambulance pulled up in the parking lot, I opened my eyes and sucked in a gigantic breath. Heather shrieked. Dad burst into tears. The EMT's insisted on taking me to the hospital, which my parents agreed to. Mom rode in the ambulance with me. Dad followed with everyone else in the van. On the way there, as the EMT was fussing over me, Mom leaned in close and whispered, 'You know what happened to you.'

"I nodded. The fact of my death felt too enormous to fit into words; it crowded the back of the ambulance with us.

"She glanced at the EMT, and when he looked away to check something, she said, 'Did you see anything?'

"I knew what she was asking. I nodded again. 'Natalie,' I said.

"Mom inhaled sharply. 'Really?'

"'Really,' I said. 'She was glowing—she was surrounded by yellow light. She was wearing the Hello Kitty T-shirt she liked, the purple one, and her favorite jeans. She held out her hand to me, said where she was was beautiful and peaceful. That's all I remember. The next thing I knew, I was sitting up on the beach.'

"'Oh, baby,' Mom said. She sat back, one hand over her mouth, her eyes full of tears. 'Oh.' If the EMT noticed, which I'm sure he did, then I'm also sure he thought she was overcome by what had almost happened to me. He was half right. She didn't ask me anything else, not there, not during the day I spent in the hospital, not during the trip home. In fact, she never mentioned what I'd described to her again. But after that, I had the sense she wore her grief for my sister more lightly, as if it were no longer a heavy coat, but a light scarf."

Hunter raised his hand. "Before you ask, because how could you not, no, I did not see my little sister in a full-body halo. She did not speak to me. You want to know what I experienced while I was dead? Nothing. One moment, I was floating underwater, my vision closing off, and the next I was on the beach, coughing up the water still in my lungs. In between was a blank. It wasn't like being asleep. I had no sense of the passage of time, no sense of anything. I simply . . . wasn't.

"Of course, I couldn't tell my mom any of that. I knew what she wanted to hear—what she needed to hear. So, I told her. I lied, but . . . when she was dying, she was at peace with it. On her deathbed, she told my sisters Natalie was coming for her."

After a sip of his beer, Carl said, "Not to play Devil's Advocate . . ."

"What?"

"The kid who went to twelve years of Catholic school would argue you didn't see the next life because you weren't heading there. It wasn't your time."

"I was dead. That sounds like it was my time."

"Not if God didn't want it to be."

"Yeah, well, tell your inner Catholic child to come talk to me after he's been dead for five minutes. Then we can compare notes, talk about what God wants."

• • •

## III

On a clear, cold Wednesday morning in early November, Carl took I-87 from the Beacon-Newburgh exit north to Route 7, on the other side of Albany, which he followed east out of New York into Vermont. Once over the border, he turned north again with 7, driving along the western edge of the state, toward South Burlington, a place Hunter had declared among the most civilized small cities he had spent time in, with the perfect proportion of bookstores and good restaurants, and within easy distance of Canada, his second favorite country. "Although," he had added recently, "the way things are going here, it's edging closer to the top spot." Set on a hill a couple of miles southwest of the city, his large house was surrounded by evergreens, which did not diminish the view of Lake Champlain with the Adirondacks beyond from its windows. The fruit of Hunter's years as a photojournalist, as well as of a handful of prudent investments, the house was a source of mild envy for Carl, whose modest Cape was, now that the girls were at college, plenty big enough for him and Melanie, especially with the garage converted into a study. But a spacious residence had been Carl's fantasy since a childhood spent sharing fifteen hundred square feet of raised ranch with his parents, older brother, and younger sisters.

When he expressed his jealousy to Melanie, his wife reminded him that Hunter's abode had been paid for by bullets zipping past him, once pinging off the helmet he almost never wore, not to mention, by threats from local warlords and field commanders, a few of which had drawn perilously close to coming true. His Pulitzer, his books, his house had been earned risking his life to show the world sights it didn't want to see, but needed to. All of which was true, nor had success curdled Hunter's personality. He was essentially the same guy Carl had met when they started karate classes together in their early twenties, at the Double Dragon Dojo in Poughkeepsie. These days, the principal difference in Hunter, as he himself liked to say, was that he could afford the top-shelf single malt he preferred. (In fact, he was part owner of a small distillery somewhere in Scotland; Carl couldn't remember its name.) Yet this did little to dilute Carl's envy for his friend's dwelling. As far as he was concerned, if you had to select a location in which to live out your last days, Hunter's was about as good as any.

Or so he thought. He wondered if Hunter shared his opinion, if he spent his time conscious of the understated beauty surrounding him, or if the prospect of his impending end, the one he'd already tasted, chased other concerns from his mind.

The road passed between the gnarled ranks of an apple orchard, and without warning Carl found himself remembering his first and only HIV test, taken at twenty-three, when he was not long out of a relationship which had given him a case of the crabs cured in one long night, and trust issues which would require longer to treat. Over a pitcher of cheap beer, he had relayed the tale of his ex-girlfriend and her infidelities to a coworker at the Office Max he was then assistant-managing. Instead of the chuckle and expression of commiseration he was expecting, Porter had stared at him with concern. "Dude," he said, "please tell me you were using protection."

"At first, sure," Carl said, "but then she was on the pill."

"Have you been tested?"

"For what?"

"What do you think? AIDS."

"Oh," Carl said, "I don't think I—"

Porter cut him off. "You were having unprotected sex with a girl who was cheating on you with someone who passed on crabs to her. Who knows what else he might have given her?"

"But . . ."

"You really want to chance it?"

He didn't, and so Carl had gone to the Department of Health to have his blood drawn; although, self-conscious about meeting someone he knew there, he drove twenty miles up the Hudson, to the office in Wiltwyck. After sitting on a molded plastic chair in the waiting room, Carl was directed to a closet-sized office, where he sat on another uncomfortable chair while a nurse dressed in a brown pantsuit and cream blouse asked him questions about his sexual and drug-use history before instructing him to roll up his sleeve. She filled a vial with his blood, taped a cotton ball over the spot on his arm, and gave him a slip of paper with his ID number on it and told him his results would be ready in two weeks.

Carl had spent that time trying not to think about the test's outcome. In unguarded moments, though, he would recall his older brother's best friend, Wayne Ahuja, who had suffered with and then died from AIDS-related complications over the course of a year and a half. Ever skinny, Wayne had become positively skeletal as his health worsened, his skin yellowing from the cancer consuming his liver. Toward the end, he had lost vision in his left eye, and for reasons of which Carl was unsure, had taken to walking with a cane. Throughout his decline, Wayne had retained an exasperated sense of humor, complaining of dying from a fling with a paralegal, and not a debauched weekend with Freddy Mercury. While he refused to be despondent—at least, publicly—about a month before he entered hospice care, Wayne said to Carl, "You know, I'm going to miss not seeing Paris."

They were sitting on the back porch of Wayne's mother's condo in Beacon. Manny, Carl's older brother, was helping Mrs. Ahuja in the kitchen. It was a warm spring day, but Wayne was wearing a cardigan and a blanket draped over his shoulders. Carl said, "Paris?"

"I'm treading perilously close to stereotype, I know," Wayne said. "I can't help it. I've always loved France. When my father was alive, he used to fly to France for business. He always brought me a souvenir, a little Eiffel Tower, French comics. The way he described Paris made it sound like the most amazing, wonderful city. In high school, I took French 1, 2, 3, and 4, all with Madame McCarthy, who was a flake. My junior year, there was a class trip to Paris, but we couldn't swing it, financially. My first real crush was on an exchange student from Besançon my senior year; he was beautiful and totally clueless, just thought I was very friendly. I'll say. In college, I majored in French. One of my teachers, Claude, was from outside Paris, and I used to ask her about the city in my terrible French. I watched every French movie Blockbuster had on the shelves. I read *The Stranger*, first in English and then (slowly) in French. A lot of poets, too, Rimbaud and Verlaine, Baudelaire, Valéry. I liked Baudelaire the best; Rimbaud always seemed like he was trying too hard to play the bad boy.

"Anyway, my plan was, once I finished college, I would work for a couple of years, stay with Mom to save money, and then spend a summer in Paris. I intended to hit all the tourist spots, the Eiffel Tower, Notre Dame, the Louvre, Shakespeare & Co.

I fantasized about finding a job while I was there, but hadn't figured out how to make that happen. I wasn't concerned. I assumed I had time. You know what they say happens when you assume?"

"You make an ass of you and me," Carl said.

"There you have it."

That was their last conversation; the next he saw Wayne, he was lying in his coffin in a funeral home in Fishkill. The final expression on his face suggested disappointment, as if, after his lengthy suffering, whatever Wayne saw approaching was anticlimactic. Carl had not forgotten the look, made uneasy by what it suggested.

The apple trees gave way to open fields dotted with rocks. As the date of his test result had approached, he remembered, he had noticed a sensation at the limit of his perception, not unlike the feeling of pressure his ears registered during a change in altitude. No amount of swallowing or yawning affected this pressure; indeed, it strengthened each day. He noticed, too, the people and objects around him outlined ever-so-slightly in black, as if they were comic book illustrations and he aware of the inker's hand. He recognized the link between the sensation and the black haloes and understood both as by-products of his escalating anxiety. Yet he could not shake the suspicion that this was more than an elaborate hallucination, that he was perceiving these things more than inventing them. Perhaps they had always been present, waiting for a situation of sufficient duress to disclose them.

By the time Carl was driving Route 9 to the Rhinecliff-Wiltwyck Bridge, he had decided that what he had grown aware of was death, was the void, the nonexistence atop which everyone and everything sat like soap bubbles quivering on the surface of dark water. At any moment, an individual bubble might burst, or dwindle to nothing, and the remaining bubbles would shift to close the gap, and it would be as if the particular bubble had never existed. Crossing the bridge high over the Hudson, he felt himself as hollow as any mix of soap and water blown into a sphere, his life a momentary structure fated to collapse.

Threaded through this apprehension, however, was another, of the sheer loveliness surrounding him. From the mid-afternoon sunlight bright on the corrugated surface of the Hudson below, to the chrome shine of the bumper in front of him, from the fine hairs on the knuckles of his right hand resting on the steering wheel, to the long blades of green grass nodding on the other side of the road as he drove off the bridge, beauty met his eyes wherever he turned them. A long line of passengers waiting to board a Trailways bus for Manhattan might have been figures in a painting by Brueghel. The buildings on either side of Broadway glowed with Technicolor vibrancy. A group of children running home from school could have stepped fresh from Renaissance marble. The impression swelled like a great piece of music rising to a crescendo, in its own way as pitiless as the sense of death with which it was entwined. Lightheaded, he parked up the street from the Department of Health. He was in the grip of an experience more profound than any he had undergone since the death of his father two years before, a moment in some ways adjunct to the earlier one. It continued as he once again entered the small office, where a different nurse, wearing a green dress and a necklace of large green beads, passed him a piece of paper on which he read the word NEGATIVE. Nor did it cease upon his return to his car, where he sat with the engine off and let relief spill through him. Perhaps the imminent dread of death lessened somewhat, but his recognition of the glory of the world did not. It held steady, even climbed a few rungs higher. By the next day, it would diminish considerably; while the morning following returned him to normal.

After that, the closest Carl drew to perceiving the raw, unfiltered beauty around him were the births of his daughters. Random moments in the intervening decades offered glimpses of loveliness, but nothing to compare with what he had known during his swing into death's orbit. He wondered if Wayne Ahuja had known the same beauty as he was dying, if perceiving the world's grace was compensation for losing it, if the disappointed expression on Wayne's face post-mortem was because whatever came next could not approach the beauty he was leaving.

On his left, the ground dropped to Lake Champlain, across whose shining breadth the Adirondacks stood in a line like the wall to some unimaginable kingdom, their jagged heights draped in snow.

## IV

Despite previous assurances that he would do so, Hunter had not paved the long driveway to his house. It was a nod to privacy, a complement to the NO TRESPASSING signs nailed to the trees at the end of the drive; albeit, one easily overcome by anyone willing to take the quarter mile rutted dirt slowly enough to avoid scraping their vehicle's undercarriage. For most of its course, the driveway ran between dense rows of tall red pine. Amidst the trunks to the right, Carl glimpsed a figure in jeans and a red jacket, a woman walking beside a golden retriever, who ran and gamboled about her. *That didn't take long,* he thought; although the woman could as easily be Hunter's doctor, checking her patient's status, or his lawyer, here to review details of his will. She could have offered to take out the dog as a kindness. *Or maybe she's the reason his third wife left him.* Hunter had always been charming, to put it mildly. In fact, it was a particularly credible threat from one woman's angry boyfriend that had brought him to train at the Double Dragon. His flirtations and an extended affair had strained his first marriage far past what Carl had been certain was its breaking point; the end of the same affair had undone marriage number two. With Hunter's third trip to the altar, Carl had wondered if his friend might be ready to settle, but it would hardly be surprising to learn that, even in the face of a terminal diagnosis, Hunter remained restless.

*And what business is that of yours?* Melanie might have been sitting in the car with him. *That isn't why you're here, is it?*

"No," he said.

The trees thinned and fell away, revealing the short hill atop which Hunter's house sat. The architect had been after something in the spirit of Frank Lloyd Wright, and had constructed a long wooden box with a flat roof and a western wall composed of two stories of windows, which Hunter said made the place a bitch to heat during the Vermont winters, but offered stunning views of the lake and the mountains. The driveway climbed through tall grass to a pair of garage doors set in the hillside below the southern end of the house. An olive, late-model Range Rover was parked in front of one of the doors, an older blue Volvo before the other. Carl tagged the Range Rover as Hunter's, the Volvo as belonging to his dog-walking guest. He stopped far enough behind the vehicles to allow either's departure. He retrieved the plastic shopping bag with the bottles of Auchentoshan and Talisker in it, and stepped out of the car for the walk up the stone steps to the front door. The air was cold and damp, brimming with the promise of snow.

Hunter opened the door as Carl was leaning to press the bell. "Hey!" he said, "You made it!" He looked terrible. The weight he had accumulated with his semi-retirement was gone, devoured by his sickness. He was as thin as he had been when he and Carl had met, thinner. A belt cinched on its last hole secured his jeans to his hips, while his blue and white flannel shirt enveloped him like a small tent. A faded blue baseball cap shielded a face drawn to the bone. Carl embraced him, and his friend felt insubstantial, more fabric than flesh. *It's as if he's already gone.* They released one another, and Hunter gestured at the shopping bag. "Is that what I think it is?"

"Water of life," Carl said.

"Bit late for me," Hunter said, "although I swear, it's what's brought me this far. You know how long the docs gave me? Three months. 'Put your affairs in order,' they said. 'This is gonna be quick.' That was nine months ago, almost ten, at this point. Who could have guessed? But come in, come in," he said, retreating inside the house.

Carl followed, passing along the front hall to the living room, a vast open space across which were scattered couches, love seats, and easy chairs, all upholstered in the same black padding, each oriented more or less toward the large flat-screen TV hung on the wall to the left. A doorway in the same wall led down another hallway, past a number of closed doors on the right, a wall of windows on the left, which showed the tops of the red pines and, beyond them, a shining stretch of

Lake Champlain, a cluster of the Adirondacks. They emerged into the kitchen, which was centered around a sizable island whose gray and white marble top glowed with the afternoon light. Hunter continued to another doorway, which admitted to a smaller room, its walls lined with tall bookcases stuffed with volumes shelved without apparent regard to size, subject, or author. Facing the windows and their view, a pair of easy chairs in the same black padding as the living room furniture flanked a small table, atop which rested a pair of glass tumblers and a jug of water. Seating himself on the far side of the table, Hunter nodded at the glasses and said, "There you go. I'll trust you to decide which bottle we finish first."

"You don't think it's a little early?" Carl said. "Don't you want to have lunch?"

"Early was a long time ago," Hunter said. "I'll have Annie order us a pizza when she gets back. You like mushrooms? Don't worry about it. We'll order two pies. You can get what you want."

"Fair enough," Carl said. He removed the bottles from the bag, set them beside the glasses. "As I recall, you favor the Auchentoshan."

"You recall correctly, sir."

He poured three fingers' worth into one tumbler, reached for the water. Hunter raised his left hand. "Don't bother."

"Do I have to give the speech about how the drop of water unlocks the Scotch's flavors?"

"At this point, I prefer my experiences undiluted."

"If you insist." Carl placed the bottle on the table and settled into his chair.

"Ahhh," Hunter said, smacking his lips after his first taste. "This is the stuff."

"It's even better with the water," Carl said.

"You don't let up, do you?"

"Nope."

"Dying's looking better and better."

Carl supped from his glass. "What's the latest on that?"

Hunter shrugged. "We're in the bottom of the ninth, two outs, two strikes. Not much longer to go. Maybe a week or two. Maybe less."

"You seem in pretty decent shape, all things considered."

"You mean, for a guy who's already a skeleton?"

"Is that what's different about you? I thought it was your hair."

"You're not wrong about that." Hunter removed his baseball cap, revealing a head rough with stubble.

"Chemo?"

"Yeah." Hunter returned the cap to his head. "I stopped a month ago, once the docs told me there wasn't any point. Had you seen me while I was on that stuff, you would've had no trouble believing the end was nigh. Since I discontinued it, I feel pretty good. You know, for a guy who's on his way out. It's strange: This is what got my mom. I'm five years older than she was, but in the end, heredity won." Hunter raised his drink, frowned. "Goddammit, why is this empty?"

"Hang on," Carl said, and poured him another generous portion of Scotch.

"Good man," Hunter said.

"Still a no on the water?"

"Why do you insist on asking questions you know the answer to?"

"Hope springs eternal, or something." Carl's glass was almost finished. He refilled it with less than he'd served Hunter, added a drop of water. Outside, on the lake, a boat was heading south. Exactly what type of vessel it was, he couldn't say, only that it was neither sailboat or speedboat. A yacht? Maybe. It appeared to be making good time; long waves rolled away from it in a V.

"What about you?" Hunter said. "How's Melanie? How're the girls? Everything okay at the dojo?"

"Good, good, and yes," Carl said. "Melanie's not long back from a trip out west to a couple of shows. She did pretty well at one of them, may have found a new outlet for her jewelry. Deb has one more semester to go at Binghamton, then she's looking at NYU for her master's. Art history. Karen's at community college, leaning toward nursing. We're up to a hundred and fifty students at the studio, give or take."

"That is good."

"I can't complain." Carl tipped his glass at Hunter. "Any word from—it was Jill, right?"

"Gillian, yes," Hunter said. "And no, nothing. You never met her, did you?"

"Once," Carl said. "At the party you had for your book, the one about New Orleans after Katrina."

"*American Atlantis.*"

"That one. Melanie came with me. She met Jill, too. She didn't like her."

"Your wife is a very perceptive woman. Which is why I've never asked you what she says about me."

"It's not all bad. She thinks you have a good eye."

"Coming from Mel, that's high praise."

"I take it Francesca hasn't been in touch."

"Believe it or not, she has. Nothing like your old man's

imminent demise to bring you to his doorstep. She was here last week for a few days. I wouldn't call it a good visit, but I didn't expect it to be. She had a chance to say what she wanted to. Where I could, I explained and apologized. Not everything that's happened to her has been my fault. We left things about as good as we could."

"I'm sorry, man."

"At least I saw her."

"How about the woman I saw on my way in? Walking a golden retriever? Is she—did you say her name was? Annie?"

Hunter nodded. "Her name is Antoinette, Antoinette Mazarine; although she prefers to be called Madame Sosostris. It's . . . her professional name, I guess."

"Exactly which profession is she in?"

"She's a psychic, fortune-teller, that kind of thing. She's here to help me with some stuff."

"Such as?"

"Drink up," Hunter said, emptying his tumbler and holding it out for more. Sunlight turned the lake into a sheet of bronze, made the mountaintops burn white.

## V

At some point thereafter, Carl looked at the Auchentoshan and saw that the bottle was empty. Simultaneously, he realized that he was drunker than he had been in years, since his last visit with Hunter, when the two of them had stayed up after his book release party drinking their way down a bottle of high-quality rum, which Hunter took straight, and Carl mixed with various leftover sodas. The next morning, much to Melanie's mingled amusement and irritation, he had suffered a hangover so blinding he crawled into the back seat of the car and lay there while she drove them home. "Melanie isn't here," he mumbled, the statement filling him with crushing sadness.

"What?" Hunter said.

"Nothing." With great care, he leaned over and lifted the Talisker from the table. He attempted to remove the seal from the cap, which proved a far more laborious task than he thought it should be. Finally, he peeled the last bit of plastic from the bottle's neck and twisted the stopper free.

"At last," Hunter said. "I thought I was gonna die of thirst."

"You live next to a lake," Carl said, amazed at his ability to pour the contents of the bottle into his friend's held-out glass.

"So?"

"So, there's plenty of water there." He gestured at the windows, outside of which, the water was dark blue, the mountains heaps of shadow crowned by clouds lit red and orange.

"Yeah," Carl said, "but . . ."

"But what?"

"We're almost—we—we only have one bottle left." He nodded at the Talisker, whose contents were already noticeably diminished.

"Don't worry," Hunter said, "we can get more. There's a liquor store in town."

"Sure," Carl said, "but neither of us can drive. Not like this, in this state, this state of drunkenness." He was finding it difficult to express himself; he wasn't sure the words he was using meant what he wanted them to.

"Not us," Hunter said. "*Her.* Annie. Sosostris. Madame. When she goes for the pizza, she can pick up another bottle. Or two."

"Oh. That's okay, then."

"See? Problem solved."

"Wait. Did we order the pizzas?"

"Of course, we did. Remember? Mushroom for me, cheese for you."

"I never said I wanted cheese."

"Well, why didn't you? It's too late to change now."

"No—I mean, I don't think we called anyone."

"We didn't. Madame Annie did."

Had she? Carl couldn't recall anyone entering the study after the two of them, but neither could he bring the last couple of hours into focus. "Are you sure?"

"Sure I'm . . ." Hunter's voice trailed off. "Dammit. Didn't we?" He placed his glass on the table. "Tell you what. One more, and if the pizza isn't here, we'll go order it. Mushroom for me, cheese for you."

"Hawaiian," Carl said.

"What?"

"Hawaiian," Carl said. "Or maybe you call it Canadian. I know I had it in Canada. At a knockdown tournament in Toronto. Ham and pineapple."

"On a pizza?"

"It's delicious."

"Ugh."

"That's what I want. It's delicious."

"Whatever you say."

"Hawaiian is what I say."

"I thought it was Canadian."

"Either way."

There was more conversation after that, but Carl couldn't

keep track of it. Some of it involved Hunter lecturing. He was a great one for holding forth when in his cups, was Carl's friend. "The French call them . . . What do they call them? *Les fantômes de* . . . something." Hunter's one last drink turned into another two, or three, and Carl tipped a couple more servings into his tumbler, and the Talisker was done, which seemed an unbelievable, a ridiculous amount for the two of them to have consumed in a couple of hours. Except the view out the windows had gone dark, and the room's track lighting was glowing—had Hunter switched it on? Or did the study have some kind of light sensor? Or maybe that woman, Annie, had looked in on them and turned on the lights. Did it matter? No, what mattered was that their pizzas hadn't appeared. Which meant that someone hadn't delivered them. Or ordered them. No pineapple and mushrooms for them. From the windows, a pair of middle-aged men regarded them from the comforts of their padded easy chairs. *Jesus, when did we become so old?* Still holding his glass, Hunter heaved himself from his chair with such force he staggered forward a half dozen steps, almost losing his balance before recovering. Waving for Carl to follow him, he staggered from the room; although Carl wasn't certain of his friend's destination, the kitchen or some other spot deeper within the house. Either way, his eyelids had grown incredibly heavy, as had the rest of him. Full of Scotch, he supposed. Who knew alcohol weighed so much? He set his tumbler on the table, closed his eyes, and unconsciousness rose over him in a flood

## VI

He woke needing to pee, urgently. On legs not fully awake, he lurched from the chair, swaying with the effort not to tip over.

The room spun like a carnival ride winding down. *Still drunk,* he thought, though not quite as much as he had been. The utterly disconnected feeling had subsided, replaced by the sense of being on a one to two second delay, requiring the slightest bit more time to respond to his surroundings. There was a bathroom somewhere nearby. At different moments throughout the afternoon and evening, he and Hunter had risen to seek it out. *On the other side of the kitchen, on the way to the living room. Third door on the left.*

Though the kitchen seemed to have expanded dramatically since he had crossed it last, he succeeded in navigating to the hallway where the toilet was. His bladder relieved, he exited the room and continued along the hall to the living room, whose assorted seating was dimly visible in the moonlight falling through the windows. Whether Hunter had shown him his room, he couldn't remember, nor was he sure enough of his recall of the house's layout, especially drunk and in the dark, to want to search for it. He would crash on one of the couches. First, he would have to venture out to the car for his bag.

As he exited the front door, a pair of lights clicked on to either side of it. The temperature had plunged; his breath vented from his mouth in a cloud. Mist floated near the ground. The steps to the driveway sparkled with frost; he descended them with care. At the foot of the steps, another set of lights, these positioned over the garage doors, snapped to life. Down here, the mist rose higher, denser, catching the light and holding it, submerging the cars in a lake of pale radiance. It was colder here, too. Gooseflesh raised up and down his arms. Carl hurried to the Subaru and lifted his bag from the back seat. He shut the door, and caught something out of the corner of his right eye.

Standing near the edge of the woods, a child regarded him. The mist reduced it to an Impressionist blur, but its size suggested eight or nine. It appeared underdressed for the cold in a red T-shirt and jean shorts. A sleepwalker? From where? Did Hunter allow campers on his property? Who would want to spend the night outside in this weather? Carl took a step forward, halted. There was something else out there. Closer to the tree line, a pair of shapes paced back and forth, weaving in and out of the pines. Lean, low to the ground, they could have been mountain lions, except their trunks were too long, their legs spread to either side in a way that suggested a spider's limbs more than a big cat's. Their heads, too, something was off about the heads, a disfigurement the mist would not allow him to see clearly. They were too long. Fear icier than the air sliced through his intoxication. Could these be dogs? They didn't seem to be menacing the child, at least, not yet. He dropped his bag and felt in the front pocket of his jeans for the knife tucked there (ironically, a gift from Hunter). He considered calling the house on his cell, but his friend was likely to be deeply unconscious; nor was Carl certain of Annie's location. Knife retrieved, its blade unfolded, he advanced toward the child, his eye on the twin creatures behind it.

The closer he drew to all three, however, the harder they were to see. The mist thickened until only the glow of the lights at his back indicated direction. Left hand up in a guard, right ready to stab, he moved in small steps, sliding the soles of his sneakers over the ground to minimize an attacker's ability to knock him off his feet. "Hello," he said. "My name is Carl. I don't know if you can see me, but I'm walking to you. I don't want you to be frightened, but there are a couple of animals out here with us. They're probably just dogs, but I don't know them, so I think it's a good idea to be careful. Can you tell me what your name is?"

In reply, the air erupted in high pitched laughter, like the lunatic cries of a pack of hyenas. Carl started, his heart hammering at the base of his throat. He stopped where he was. The hysterical yelps subsided, replaced by a new sound, the scrape of skin over dirt. Something was treading a wide circle around him; he was reasonably certain it was not the child. The hairs on the back of his neck lifted. He turned with the noise, doing his best to keep the knife aimed at whatever was producing it. *Of course,* a voice in the back of his brain said, *this would be a good way to distract you from an attack to the rear.* "One thing at a time," he murmured. *Should have held on to the bag, could have used it as a shield.* "Too late, now."

Without warning, the lights over the garage went out. Momentarily blind, Carl tensed, listening for the paws he was certain were about to run at him. None did. As his eyes adjusted to the dark, he saw that the mist had thinned to a fine vapor, and that he was at the edge of the woods. Of the featureless child, the strange predators, there was no sign. He stared into the trees, but if anyone was standing amidst their dim ranks, he could see neither them nor any animals.

For a second time, manic laughter filled the air. Glancing over his shoulder as he went, Carl retreated to his car, bending at the knees to retrieve his bag. Finally, the garage lights popped on. He was half expecting to find the child standing at his elbow, one of the big predators ready to pounce, but there was nothing there.

• • •

## VII

Certain he would not be falling asleep any time soon, if ever, Carl dumped his bag next to the biggest couch in the living room before heading to the kitchen. Although his nerves were humming with adrenaline, he could feel the drag of the alcohol his system had not processed. He found a glass in one of the cupboards and poured and drank four and a half cups of water. Given how much Scotch he had imbibed, there was no way he was escaping a hangover, but he figured he would do what he could to minimize it. Depositing the glass in the sink, he returned to the living room, where he settled onto the couch. He had no idea what time it was, only that it was late, far later than he was accustomed to being awake these days. *Old,* he thought, *you're so old.*

The next he knew, he was climbing out of sleep, prompted once more by the urge to urinate. No time seemed to have passed, but a look out the windows showed the sky washed with faint light, herald to the dawn. He found the bathroom more easily this time, and foregoing modesty, left the door open while he peed. The chamber music echoed through the hall. While he was washing his hands, he heard mixed with the water's hiss another sound, what might have been the squeak of sneakers on the floor outside the bathroom. He shut off the tap and waited, listening.

Nothing. He dried his hands and walked to the kitchen. Another couple of glasses of water, then back to the living room, where the couch was waiting to receive him.

## VIII

Breakfast smells (coffee, sausages, toast) and sounds (the stuttering burp of the coffee maker, the sizzle of oil in the pan, the ticking of the toaster) roused him to late morning sunlight. Head complaining at the effort, Carl sat up. It wasn't as if he hadn't seen this coming. At least he'd remembered to hydrate; otherwise, the hangover would have been mortal.

Hunter was waiting in the kitchen, standing at the stove cooking sausages in one pan and scrambled eggs in the another. A gray tracksuit floated around him. Aside from his sunglasses, he showed scant evidence of the previous day's excess. "Hey, Sleeping Beauty," he said. "How're you feeling?"

"About two steps from death," Carl said. "How is it you're even moving around?"

"Please," Hunter said. "You think that's the most I've ever had to drink? I tell you about the time I was in Chechnya, following a squad of Russian *spetsnaz*? Those guys spend all night working their way through a case of vodka, then are on the move at dawn, fighting by breakfast. If you want to run with them, you have to be able to keep up with them."

"I'm amazed your liver survived."

"Yeah, well, I did lay off alcohol for about a month after I came back from that assignment. What do you want to eat? Eggs? Sausage? Both?"

"For the moment, this'll do," Carl said, lifting the mug of coffee he'd poured. "I don't suppose you have any oatmeal."

"Yeah, there's a box of the instant stuff in the cabinet to my left. Apple and cinnamon, I think."

"That'll be fine, thanks."

They sat on high stools at the kitchen island, Carl with his coffee, Hunter with a plate of sausage and eggs. Through the windows, Carl watched a hawk skim the tops of the evergreens.

"Actually," Hunter said through a mouthful of food, "that was among the drunkest I've been."

"No 'among' for me."

"Yeah?"

"I've never been what you'd call a heavyweight, but I've put away my fair share of booze. Not like that, though."

A smile broke over Hunter's face. "Good. I like the idea of our final visit being marked by a memorable event. You'll always be able to say, 'The last time I saw Hunter, we drank more Scotch than I ever had before or since.'"

"Couldn't we have gone out for a nice dinner, instead? Or a game of miniature golf, maybe?"

"Nah. Think of it as being like Vikings on the eve of a big battle, working themselves up for it."

"We're fighting a battle today?"

"What would you say if I said yes?"

"I'd say I wish I stayed home, sent you a nice card, instead: 'So long, nice knowing you.'"

"A card? Really?"

"A nice card. You'd love it. They'd show it off at your funeral."

"After I was killed in the battle you bailed on."

"It would be some card," Carl said. "Speaking of which, are you planning a memorial service?"

"Yeah." Hunter nodded. "Immediately after I go, there'll be a small gathering in Burlington, at one of the galleries. Then, in the spring, there'll be a bigger event down in Brooklyn, a retrospective of my work with remarks by a few of my friends and colleagues. If you're available . . ."

Carl's throat tightened. "Sure."

"Good. Thank you. I'm just about done writing your speech. I figured we could rehearse it later."

"What? You don't trust me to tell the truth?"

"That's exactly what I'm afraid of."

"So, what's the plan for today?"

"Finish your coffee," Hunter said. "You should probably have your oatmeal, too."

## IX

After breakfast, Hunter led Carl to the guest room, which was on the other side of the study, up a flight of stairs, and along a short hallway. "I'll see you for lunch," Hunter said. "I have some dying stuff to attend to."

"Right," Carl said.

The room was on the east side of the house, what Carl thought of as its back side. Instead of a wall composed of glass, a pair of regular-sized windows gave a view across an overgrown field behind the house to the tree line. Low hills rolled in the distance. Resisting the temptation of the queen-sized bed, Carl showered in the attached bathroom, dressed, and called home.

"How hungover are you?" Melanie asked.

"It could be worse," Carl said.

"That bad."

"Yeah."

"Did you leave any Scotch for today?"

"Technically, it was today when we finished the second bottle. I think it was, anyway."

"Wonderful. Well, I'm sure Hunter has more liquor, just in case there's anything left of your liver. How is he?"

"Honestly, he's in better shape than I was expecting. Don't get me wrong: He's skin and bones, with an emphasis on the bones. But I imagined he'd be confined to bed, too spent to say much; instead, he's up making scrambled eggs and sausages this morning. As far as I can tell, he's as sharp as he ever was."

"He's led a pretty active life. He must have a lot to draw on."

"I think you're right."

"Has he said anything about his ex? Jill, was it?"

"Gillian, yeah. Not really—only that he hasn't heard from her. There's another woman staying here, Annie something. I saw her yesterday on the way in, walking the dog. I haven't met her, yet."

"Really."

"Apparently, she's a psychic. Hunter says she's here to help him. I don't know with what."

"I'll avoid the obvious remarks," Melanie said.

"I thought the same thing, but I'm not sure it's the case."

"Either way, Hunter's a big boy. Anything else going on?"

Carl hesitated, weighing a description of his early morning driveway encounter with the child and the weird animals. Already, though, the event seemed distant, dreamlike, if not a product of the Scotch, then colored by it. He settled for, "Not much. I ran into a couple of coyotes when I went out to the car for my bag." The instant the words left his mouth, he realized how false they sounded. Even through liquor-clouded lenses, the things he'd seen had not moved like coyotes. He remembered their strange, spread-eagled crawl, their elongated skulls. No, not coyotes, and not cougars, and not anything with which he was familiar.

"Holy crap," Melanie said. "What did they do?"

"Oh, they prowled back and forth in front of the woods for a minute or two, and ran away."

"Be careful. It's more wild up there."

"Yeah," Carl said, but he had an obscure feeling it was too late for caution.

## X

There wasn't space for him to practice his morning (now afternoon) *kata* in the guest room, so once he and Melanie had said their good-byes, Carl made his way downstairs. He was considering finding a spot outside, but during the time he had spent in the guest room, clouds had thickened the sky, obscuring the Adirondacks and releasing torrents of snow. In the kitchen, he stopped to watch the crowns of the red pine swaying this way and that, as if engaged in a vast conversation about the snow accumulating on their branches. Behind him, a voice said, "It's supposed to last all day."

He turned, and saw a woman standing on the opposite side of the kitchen island. Late twenties, he guessed, dressed in a white cable-knit sweater and jeans, her chestnut hair pulled back into a ponytail. On the marble in front of her, a number of oversized cards had been arranged in a circle—Tarot cards. The woman was holding the rest of her deck in her left hand. "Sorry," she said, "I didn't mean to startle you. I'm Annie."

"No need to apologize," Carl said. "I'm Carl. Hunter maybe said I was coming?"

"He did. I saw you on the driveway yesterday."

"You were walking a dog."

"Rufus, yes."

"Where is he? I haven't seen him at all since I've been here."

"Hunter's rehoming him with some friends. I took him over there yesterday afternoon."

"That's . . . oddly responsible of him."

"You aren't the first person to say that to me." Annie picked up the card at the top of the circle and returned it to the deck.

"Am I interrupting you? Because if I am, I can get out of your way."

"It's all right," Annie said. "I was done, anyway."

"I take it from the cards you're Madame Sosostris."

"Guilty as charged."

"What were you doing the reading for? Or can I ask you that?"

"I was—you might say I was checking on Hunter."

"And?"

"Your friend is very sick."

Carl nodded. "Yeah. A week or two, he said."

Annie lifted the last card from the island. Without looking at Carl, she said, "It's a little less. Days, really. If he passed this afternoon, I wouldn't be surprised. You shouldn't be, either." She placed the deck on the island.

"That's . . ." The words were a roundhouse kick to his unprotected head. "I mean, I knew he didn't have long. It's why I'm here. But I assumed we'd have a little time together. He's—he seems fine."

"Hunter possesses more willpower than anyone I've ever encountered. I'm fairly certain that's what's keeping him going at this point."

"He's always been stubborn."

"Yes, I can believe it."

"We met in karate class," Carl said, crossing to the island.

He slid out a stool and seated himself on it. "I don't know if he's mentioned this. There were some things he was good at right from the start. Free sparring, in particular: he was fast, and he was ferocious. He would hit you four times before you knew what was happening. The forms, though, the *kata*, were a challenge. He had a hard time remembering the sequences of moves, and then performing them at the proper pace. For some students, this would not have been a big deal. They would do whatever *kata* they were responsible for well enough to earn their next promotion, and that was that. Not Hunter. He wanted his forms to be perfect. Every time he made a mistake, it was back to the beginning, running through the form until he had it right, no matter how long that took. I used to practice with him after class was over. We would stay an extra hour, longer. While we were training, his focus was absolute. Those sessions made me a better martial artist. Without them, I doubt I'd have ended up with my own studio."

"He told me a version of that story," Annie said. "In it, he wants to go home, but you insist he keeps working until he does the form properly."

"Well, there may have been a little of that," Carl said. "What about you? How did you meet Hunter?"

"On a message board. He had some questions he was looking to have answered, and he reached out to me. We corresponded for about a month, then he invited me up here."

"Oh."

"I'm not sleeping with him, if that's what you're wondering."

"No," Carl said, glancing away. "I mean, it's none of my business if you are."

"You're right," Annie said, "it isn't. But I don't want anything distracting you from what we have to do."

"Which is?"

"Help him as he leaves this life."

"That's why I'm here."

"I'm not talking about another marathon drinking session."

"Thank God," Carl said, and smiled. "It's been years since Hunter and I discussed these things, but time was, he didn't have much use for notions of the afterlife. I'm guessing that's changed."

"Yes and no," Hunter said, entering the kitchen. He had changed from his gray tracksuit to a white long sleeved T-shirt and jeans. His faded blue baseball cap perched on his head.

"Hey," Carl said.

"You're ready?" Annie said.

"Getting there," Hunter said. "First, my friend and I need to discuss a few things."

"We do?"

"Why don't you make yourself some lunch? There's plenty of stuff in the fridge." Hunter pulled a stool toward him and climbed onto it, adding, "I'm not hungry."

"All right," Carl said. "How about you, Annie? You want anything?"

"Thanks, I'm fasting."

While he was retrieving bread, cold cuts, and mustard from the refrigerator, Carl heard Hunter say, "Well?" and Annie reply, "It's as good a time as any. You see what's happening outside." Hunter said, "I take it you checked the cards." Annie said, "I did. Let's put it this way: You're lucky your friend is here." Hunter grunted. Annie said, "Do you want me to give you time with your friend?" "It's all right," Hunter said, "I don't imagine this'll take too long."

His smoked turkey and Swiss assembled, a glass of milk poured, Carl resumed his place at the island. "So," he said to Hunter. "What is it you want to talk about?"

"It's my sister," Hunter said.

"Which one, Vicky or Heather?"

"Neither," Hunter said. "Natalie. The dead one."

## XI

"Come again?" Carl said.

"I lied to you," Hunter said. "All those years ago, when I told you about me dying."

"Your first death."

"Yeah. Don't get me wrong, the drowning part was true. My heart stopped. I was gone. My mother had to resuscitate me. The lie was me saying there was nothing after I died."

"Okay."

"I'm just gonna describe what happened," Hunter said. He swallowed, licked his lips. "Start with me underwater. My vision closing off, contracting to a single point. It was like the reverse of the stories about moving through a bright tunnel. I seemed to be traveling backward along a dark passage, away from the light. Or, could be the light was moving, leaving me behind. It was a little frightening, but mostly, I was sad watching it go. I'm pretty sure the sensation of floating was the last thing I felt.

"And then I was on my hands and knees, gasping. I was no longer in the water. I was back on land. Not the beach, though. My fingers and knees were pressing into thick, gray mud. I was still wearing my swim trunks. I looked up, and saw the mud rising to a line of scrub grass. Overhead, dense gray clouds blocked off the sky. I stood, and glanced behind me. An enormous brown river, so wide its other shore was a distant line, flowed from left to right. Patches of mist hung above its surface, which swirled and eddied with competing currents. Despite that, I had the oddest impression I was watching a gigantic snake, something fit to wrestle Godzilla, sliding to a destination I didn't want to know. I turned and headed for the grass. The mud made it slow going; I kept tripping and almost tripping. I wasn't upset or scared—well, maybe some, at the prospect of a monster snake. What I mean is, I wasn't especially freaked out at slipping under the waves and opening my eyes next to a river. Could be I was stunned, overwhelmed, but I mostly remember being curious about this place, which didn't resemble the afterlife I'd learned about in Catholic school. I knew enough Greek mythology to think of the River Styx, except there was no sign of Charon the ferryman, and the rest of the shore was empty.

"As I approached the grass, I saw stands of trees, birches. In their midst was a structure—when you were a kid, did you make forts out of old cardboard boxes? You know, big ones, like the kind an appliance comes in?"

"Sure," Carl said.

"What was in front of me was the biggest box fort I had ever seen. It was the kind of thing my siblings and I would have fantasized about building. There were boxes of all sizes, some large enough to hold a refrigerator. A low wall of cereal boxes separated a cluster of the biggest boxes from individual boxes scattered around its perimeter. Some of the boxes had pictures on them, the kind of crude figures small children draw, done in mud. Seeing the fort filled me with happiness. This was the kind of afterlife I wanted. Plus, I assumed the fort meant there were other kids here. I didn't know who, but if they built something like this, I was sure we would get along. I hurried forward.

"As I passed one of the boxes outside the low wall, I saw the word JAIL written on it. From inside, someone whimpered. I stopped beside it. The box was washer- or dryer-sized. I circled it to see if there was an opening in one of its sides, a door to the jail. None. I leaned in close to it and said, 'Hello?'

"Right away, a pair of voices burst out crying, 'We're sorry! We'll be good! Please let us out!' One of them started sobbing, the other went on pleading to be released. They both sounded young, four or five.

"'Hold on,' I said, 'I'll get you out of here.'

"Upset as the kids were, I thought they'd be happy to be released. But the one who was crying cried harder, and the other one shouted, 'No!'

"'Why not?' I said. 'You guys don't sound like you're having much fun.' I ran my hands over the top of the box, searching for a loose corner to pull on, but the flaps were sealed tight.

"'No,' the kid said again. 'If she finds out, we'll be in trouble.'

"I said, 'Aren't you already in trouble?'

"'Please,' the kid said. 'We have to stay here.'

"'How come?' I said. 'What did you do? Who put you in here?'

"'The queen,' the kid said. 'We made her mad, so we had to go to jail.'

"'Who's the queen?'

"The other kid's sobs had diminished; my question revved

them up. 'She's *awful*,' the first kid said. 'You should probably run away before she sees you.'

"The second kid stopped crying long enough to wail, 'I don't wanna be a dog!'

"I didn't know who this queen was, but if she was ruling over a box fort, I guessed I could handle her. I said, 'This isn't fair. You guys shouldn't be in here.' Which only provoked more protests and sobs. I crouched, sliding my hands along the base of the box in search of a hole or tear an opening I could work to enlarge. Nothing. When I stood, I saw my sister, Natalie, standing on my left, between the jail and cereal box wall.

"She looked the same as she did in the photographs hanging around the house. In the year since we'd buried her, I had stared at those pictures a lot, afraid that, if I didn't, I would forget her. Her hair had grown in to what it was before the chemo took it, down well past her shoulders. She was wearing a cardboard crown, a red T-shirt, and jean shorts. She was barefoot. She cocked her head and said, 'Hunter? What are you doing here?'

"'Nat!' I said. Strange as it sounds, I think this was the moment I realized I was dead; I mean, when it really hit me. I ran over and threw my arms around her, the way I never had while she was alive.

"She stiffened. 'This is my place,' she said.

"I released her. I said, 'You're the one who put those kids in that box?'

"She nodded. 'I'm the queen,' she said.

"'They're little kids,' I said. 'One of them's crying.'

"Natalie walked to the box and bent over to it. She said, 'I'm the queen. Isn't that right?'

"'Yes!' the kids shouted. 'Yes, you're the queen! Yes!' The

first kid added, 'Please let us out, Your Majesty. Please. We'll be good. We'll do everything you say.'

"'Come on, Nat,' I said. 'Listen to them. They're really scared.'

"'They're fine,' she said. Leaning on the box with her left hand, she trailed the fingers of her right over the cardboard. She said, 'They're going to be my dogs. Aren't you? You're going to be my dogs. Aren't you? Aren't you?' She turned the question into a song: *'Aren't you, aren't you, aren't you?'*

"In response, both kids cried. I mean, they cut loose, with the kind of full-throated abandon kids can tap into. I said, 'Nat, come on.'

"'Shhh,' she said, holding her index finger to her lips.

"The crying continued, until it wasn't crying anymore, it was laughing, then screaming, the hysterical laughter of someone who's been overwhelmed by the joke. It sounded too big for the box. The kids started to pound on the walls, shaking it.

"'Nat!' I said. 'Please! Will you let them out?'

"'Here,' she said. She straightened, put her hands on top of the box, and pulled the flaps apart. The pounding ceased, but the laughing continued. With a mocking bow that was pure Nat, my sister stepped away. 'Happy?'

"I ran to the jail, ready to lift one or both of the kids out. The cardboard prison was empty. The laughter seemed to surround me. For a moment, I thought my sister had played an elaborate joke on me, allowing the kids to exit the box while I was distracted by her theatrics. I circled it, but aside from the laughing, there was no sign of them. 'What's going on?' I said. 'Where are they?'

"Natalie didn't answer. She gave me this look—her face went

blank, except for her eyes, which burned like blowtorches. She said, 'Shut up,' and the laughter died away. 'You don't belong here,' she said to me. 'This is my place. I'm the queen here.'

"I said, 'Nat—'

"'Stop calling me that!' she screamed. 'That was my old name. Now I have a new one. I'm Natalya, Queen of the Hungry Dogs.'

"I started to laugh, but her expression stopped me. I decided to shift to big-brother mode, because even in the afterlife, I still had that over her, right? I returned her stare with a frown of my own and said, 'Listen—'

"Apparently, my sister hadn't gotten the memo about me still outranking her. She said, 'No, you listen. You don't belong here. I don't want you here. This is my place. I made it. You need to leave.'

"'I can't leave,' I said. 'I drowned. I can't go back.'

"'I don't care,' she said. 'Leave.'

"'Nat,' I said.

"'Queen Natalya.'

"I had forgotten how stubborn—how ornery my little sister could be. I was annoyed, and under that, scared at the prospect of spending the rest of eternity with someone so unreasonably hostile to me. I mean, I was her brother, for God's sake. Shouldn't we be sticking together?

"From the way Natalie was acting, the answer to my question was no. I felt my irritation bubbling into anger. 'Well, Queen Natalya,' I said, 'what if I don't want to leave?'

"'Then I'll make you,' she said.

"'You and what army?' I said, a favorite taunt from our childhood.

"'This one.' She raised her right hand to her mouth, put her index and ring fingers between her lips, and blew. Her whistle was sharp and clear. Immediately, the laughing returned, but louder, as if it was coming from dozens of throats. I saw movement in a stand of trees to my left, and watched as a pack of animals raised themselves from where they'd been lying on their bellies and sides. I glanced at the other groups of birches, and the same thing was happening in each of them, these animals standing."

"Animals?" Carl said.

"Man, I don't know," Hunter said. "They were on all fours, which made me think they were the Hungry Dogs Nat had referred to. But they didn't look much like dogs. They were hairless, and tailless, and their heads—there was something wrong with their heads. They were misshapen, no two in the same way. Some were long and knifelike, others squashed flat. This one's jaw was too big for its mouth, that one's ears flared like fans. You might have thought they were a child's drawings, brought to life. Or death, I guess. They were the source of the laughter, each one a voice in the mad chorus. They started in our direction, and they didn't move like any dogs I'd ever known. They crept along the ground, the way you would if you were sneaking up on someone. Of course I could see them, but I had the sense this didn't matter. They wanted me to watch them coming closer. I was suddenly conscious of myself in my bathing suit, with no means of defense but my hands and feet, which seemed woefully inadequate for the job. The laughter seemed to draw a line under that fact, to emphasize how defenseless, how vulnerable, I was. I didn't know if I could die a second time, but I guessed I could be hurt. I turned to Natalie and said,

'All right, I'm sorry. Maybe there's someplace else I can go.'

"'Too late,' she said, with all the smugness of a gambler holding a winning suit.

"'Nat,' I said.

"'Queen Natalya,' she said, 'Sovereign of the Hungry Dogs. Who are going to tear you to shreds.'

"I bolted. There was no point in running any direction but the river, so that was what I did. At my back, I heard Natalie whistle, and the thunder of the dogs' feet as they leaped into pursuit. My hope was to reach the river, splash in and let its current carry me to safety. Or at least, away from my sister and her animals.

"In the time I'd spent talking to Natalie, however, the distance between her box fort and the muddy shore had expanded to the length of a couple of soccer fields—not so far apart as to place the shore beyond reach, but enough to give the dogs a decent chance of bringing me down. I'd always been a fast runner, faster than anyone else in my grade at school, or two grades ahead of me, for the matter. A glance over my shoulder at the assembled dogs chasing me spurred my feet to move even quicker across the grass. But the dogs were running on four feet, which had to give them the advantage. By the time I was halfway to the river, the leader was right on my heels, its laughter dropped to a low chuckle. I veered right, left, faked right, trying to do what I could to increase the distance between us. The dog's teeth snapped at me, missed me. My heart was pounding so hard it felt like it was about to burst out of my chest; my lungs were filled with fire. Funny, a small part of me picked up on this and thought, *Wait a minute. You're dead. How can you be getting tired?*

"It didn't matter. I had reached the shore. At the edge of the grass, I threw myself forward in what I intended to be a long jump, but was more my arms pinwheeling, my legs flailing, as if I could swim through the air. I landed off balance, in a half skid, and my feet went out from under me, dumping me on my back, hard. Before I could do anything, the dog was on me. Its snout tapered to a jagged blade. It raised up on its hind legs, and drove the blade into me, right here." Hunter's hand pressed the middle of his shirt.

"Holy shit, did that hurt. I had never experienced that kind of pain before; in comparison, drowning had been almost pleasant. It stunned me, as if I'd been plunged into freezing water, this full-body shock. The dog jerked its head loose from my midsection. Blood splashed my face. I wanted to raise my hands, protect myself from its next strike, but the most I could force my arms to do was tremble madly. The dog prepared to skewer me again. This time, its target was my throat. I shut my eyes.

"And nothing happened. No stabbing pain pierced my neck. I opened my eyes to darkness—no dog, no shore, no river—and then the world rushed at me. I was still on my back, but my mother was above me, her knotted hands pressing my sternum, my older sisters and younger brother leaning in to watch Mom's efforts, my father standing just beyond them, as if afraid he'd jinx Mom if he was too close, too hopeful. After that, it was pretty hectic: the paramedics, the ambulance ride to the hospital, the exams to check my status. I didn't forget what happened to me while I was dead, but I . . . put it to the side, you could say. There was no doubt in my mind as to its reality. I still hurt where the dog had impaled me. But since this reality didn't align with anything I'd been taught to believe about the life to come, I needed time to process it. I can't remember: Did I ever tell you about my mom asking me if I'd seen Natalie?"

"You did," Carl said. "You told her she was happy, surrounded by glowing light."

"Yeah," Hunter said, "because how could I say her daughter was ruler of her own little hell?"

"Is that what you think it was?"

"Not exactly," Hunter said, "but not too far off."

"So, wait," Carl said. "What about the whole 'I died and there was nothing' bit? Not to put too fine a point on it, but for as long as I've known you, you've been pretty insistent about that."

"Like I said, I lied. Or, not exactly. By the time you heard the story of my first death, I pretty much believed what I was saying. Or I believed I believed it. I don't know. In my late teens, I went through a phase where I became obsessed with near-death experiences. You know, rising out of your body, moving along a tunnel of light, being greeted by all your loved ones. I read every account I could lay my hands on, searching for a narrative that matched up with what I'd been through. I couldn't find one. I moved on to scientific studies of near-death phenomena, and learned that there were biochemical explanations for all of it. The tunnel of light was caused by the firing of certain neurons as your eyes shut down. The vision of your loved ones was a last-minute effort by your brain to fool itself about what it was undergoing, a final delusion. It made a sense I couldn't argue with. I had always been a creative kid; my brain had just come up with a more elaborate fantasy. Yes, it had felt real at the time, but a lot of things had seemed real to me when I was a kid. I used to be very religious; I'm sure I must have told you."

Carl shook his head. "You didn't."

"Oh yeah. Altar boy, morning and evening prayers, Bible study, the works. My parents had this series of books, *The Catholic Encyclopedia,* big, oversized volumes with gold covers, and I would slide one out from the bookcase and sit leafing through it. I didn't just believe in Catholicism intellectually, I felt it viscerally. Jesus, Mary, the saints were these living presences I swore I could sense, as was the Devil. By the time I was a teenager, though, my faith had started to waver, mainly because I discovered girls, or maybe I should say, they discovered me. Either way, I knew all of the Church's prohibitions against anything other than the most chaste kissing, but when Marcie Roy unhooked her bra, all of that went out the window. I was smart enough to be able to rationalize what we were doing, but I also recognized my mental gymnastics for what they were, a type of bad faith, believing my own bullshit, and this revelation was the first crack in the wall. Considering how devout I had been, my belief crumbled remarkably fast, undermined by good old sex.

"The point is, if I had been wrong about religion, which had been at the center of my life, then the chances seemed petty good I had been mistaken about my post-death encounter with Natalie. If there was a difference between the two, it was that what I'd been through with my sister and her dogs retained the vividness of actual experience. I told myself it was due to the extremity of the situation which had produced it. Let's face it, you're probably thinking something along those lines right now, aren't you?"

"You were young," Carl said, "and it was a horrendous event. It wouldn't be a surprise if your mind tried to protect you from it. Although . . ."

"What?"

"If it were purely a matter of distracting you from your end, you would think the fantasy would have been more pleasant, less threatening. You go into the light, you meet your sister, and that's all, folks. This is way outside my area of expertise, though, so there could very well be another explanation I'm not aware of."

"Like residual guilt over the death of my sister."

"I suppose. If what we're talking about is some kind of defense mechanism, I'm not sure that works."

"You're right," Hunter said, "it doesn't. I want to say it took me a long time to reach the same conclusion, but I knew, on some level, I knew all along. I couldn't admit it, was all."

"What changed? The cancer?"

"Before that," Hunter said. "About six years ago, I saw Natalie again. I was back in Afghanistan, Kabul, to shoot a piece on the rise of heroin addiction there. I was working with a journalist from the *Guardian*, Janet Singh, and she had been told about a spot under one of the local bridges where the addicts gathered. We took a taxi to the place, and sure enough, there were all these men sheltering under a structure that might have gone back to the Soviets. This was in the middle of winter, January, and it was freezing. Janet found someone to talk to, a young guy who had the worn-out look long-term users get. He had a frankness I associate with certain kind of addict; it's like their drug use has reduced everything in their lives to the essentials, which is maybe not so strange.

"Anyway, we asked the guy the usual questions. How did you start using? How did it affect your relationship with your family? Is the drug hard to come by? Are you afraid of the police? My

Pashto isn't very good, but it didn't need to be. The guy gave the same answers you get from addicts the world over. Until it came to his dealings with the cops, when he said something that caught my attention. 'There are good cops and bad cops,' he said, 'but the men are more worried about the little girl.'

"'The little girl?' Janet said.

"'Yeah,' the guy said. For about the last week, a girl had been showing up among them. It wasn't unusual for there to be kids under the bridge, but this girl dressed like a westerner, in a red T-shirt and shorts. Taking her for the child of an aid worker or a journalist, one of the older men tried to shoo her away. In return, she did something to him.

"'Did something?' Janet said. 'What? What did she do?'

"The guy became embarrassed, looked at his shoes. 'She put her finger to his forehead,' he said, 'and the old man fell down in a fit. His eyes rolled back in his head; foam came out of his mouth. At the end of it, he was dead. Since then, everyone avoided her.'

"Janet took the story for a variety of collective hallucination, which is the rational interpretation. I hadn't thought about what happened after I drowned for I can't tell you how long—not consciously, anyway—but right away, I was back beside the box fort. It was as if I'd been punched in the solar plexus. All the air rushed out of me. I bent over, hands on my knees. Janet noticed, asked if I was okay. I shook my head. Hard as it was to speak, I asked the guy if the girl was wearing anything on her hair. I didn't know the word for crown, so I swirled one hand around my head. His eyes grew large, and he nodded, said she had on a *taaj* like a child would make. 'Who is she?' he wanted to know.

"I couldn't think how to answer him. Janet wanted to know what was going on. I started to say, 'Nothing,' but it was obvious that wasn't true. Did I mention I'd been in the country for a week? I didn't, did I? You could guess, though. I looked up at the guy, and standing ten feet behind him, there she was: Queen Natalya, Ruler of the Hungry Dogs, my dead sister. She hadn't changed much since I'd seen her last, four decades earlier. She glared at me with hatred pure and freezing as an Arctic gale. I panicked, told Janet we had to leave, apologized to the guy we were interviewing, dug in my pocket for some cash to press into his hand. I was terrified Janet was going to notice the girl in the red T-shirt and jean shorts, wearing the cardboard crown, which of course she did while I was attempting to hustle her from under the bridge. The addict had already turned and seen Natalie, and he leaped back the way he might have if he'd seen a cobra raised to strike. 'Who is she?' he asked. 'You know that little girl?' Janet said. I told the guy to steer clear of her. I didn't know the word for ghost, so I settled for calling her bad. Janet said, 'How is this child bad?' She was trying to step around me, to get to Natalie, who was radiating malice, who was radioactive with it. 'Please,' I was saying, 'we need to go. We can't stay here.' But Janet was having none of it. 'We have to find out what this girl is doing here,' she said. 'No, we don't,' I said. While we were arguing, Natalie turned and ran the other way, out from beneath the bridge. Everyone gave her plenty of room. Janet pushed me aside and set out after her."

"What did you do?" Carl said.

"I walked to where the cab was waiting, got in, and returned to the hotel, where I sat at the bar consuming more alcohol than I had in years. This wasn't convivial excess; this was shot after shot of overpriced vodka to numb the memory of what I'd seen. Eventually, Janet showed up. She'd chased Natalie into a maze of alleys where she'd lost her. She was tired, and pissed, and wanted answers I was too drunk to give her. Let's face it, though: had I been sober, I doubt I would have told her the truth, either. I was deeply afraid, in a way I'd never been. Scratch that. The fear—the absolute *dread* hollowing me was what I'd experienced as a kid, when I worried about Hell. The joys of religion. Once you know about something like that, you start to wonder if you might wind up there. It leaves you with the sensation of being horribly exposed, as if your skin is made out of glass and everything you are is on display. It did for me, anyway. Part of an overdeveloped superego, I thought when I left the Church. Sitting at the bar, I felt all the old fear, vulnerable in a way I hadn't standing across a tent from a Sunni chief pointing his .44 magnum at me. I finally told my friend I'd freaked out because the girl we'd seen looked exactly like my long-dead sister, which had triggered all kinds of emotions I wasn't prepared for. If you're going to lie, keep it as close to the truth as you can, right? Janet wasn't satisfied. We'd been in enough high stress situations for her to know I didn't lose my shit, not like that. But she let the matter drop, for which I was grateful. It was the last time we worked together, though. Two days later, I left Kabul on the first flight I could snag. I spent the intervening time firmly ensconced at the bar.

"So that was weird," Hunter said, "but maybe it was an isolated incident, right?" He shook his head. "Nope. On and off since then, Natalie has appeared to me. While I was shooting wildfires in the hills above LA, she was visible between a pair of flaming trees. In eastern Ukraine, she was in the middle of a group of rebels creeping through high grass. I saw her on the roof of a burned-out car on a side street in Aleppo. Always, she wore the same, hate-filled expression.

"My most recent encounter came the week following my cancer diagnosis. I decided I wanted to drive down to the Jersey Shore, revisit the site of my first death. Morbid, perhaps, but there you have it. Do you know, in the years since, I hadn't been back to that beach once? Not so surprising, I guess.

"With traffic, it was a ten-hour drive. I went alone, didn't want to bring Jill with me. I suppose that was a sign the marriage was on its way out. I left at breakfast, arrived in the early evening. The town had taken a beating during Sandy: There were still gaps where beach houses had stood. I had an idea I would find a motel room, spend a couple of days on the shore. I stopped at a deli, bought an Italian combo hero and a Coke. Being there might have been all kinds of traumatic, but parking on a side street, walking toward the beach, I was kind of exhilarated. The sky was hung with low puffy clouds the sun was filling with red and gold light on its way to the horizon. I strolled onto the beach, which was mostly empty, sat down halfway to the ocean, and ate my dinner while the waves rolled in. If there was one place I was certain of encountering Natalie, this was it, ground zero for our first meeting. Or, not first, but you know what I mean. Our first posthumous run-in. I wouldn't go so far as to say I wasn't concerned about it, but I was less worried than you would have anticipated. Maybe what I needed to do, I thought, was to confront my sister here, where everything had started. Call it a version of taking the fight to the enemy.

"All my bravado went straight out the window when I saw her running toward me. She burst from the waves, already moving full-tilt, her arms out low to either side, her fingers curved into claws. Her mouth was open in a scream that made me nearly piss myself. Where the ocean foamed behind her—I don't know how to describe this—it was full of the Hungry Dogs, I couldn't say how many of them, rising from the water and falling back into it, as if they were trying and failing to gain form. Natalie's bare feet pounded the sand. Her clothes were dry, as was the cardboard crown. I'm not sure I can convey how frightening it was. It—she had lost none of the intensity, the single-mindedness kids have, and that we spend our adult lives attempting to recover. She didn't hate: She was hate. She was no bigger than she'd ever been, but her screaming surrounded her, made her part of something enormous and terrifying. I swore I could hear the dogs laughing in the waves.

"I didn't waste any time. I left my sandwich wrapper and bottle where they were and fled for the car, which sounds easier than it was. My feet kept threatening to slip from underneath me and dump me on my ass. At my back, Natalie's scream expanded. Legs burning, I reached the pavement. Natalie's scream was deafening; it vibrated right through the center of me. I glanced over my shoulder, saw her a dozen steps away. Whether I was going to reach the car before she reached me was looking like a close thing. Thank God for keyless entry; I jammed my hand in my pocket, found the remote, and pressed the unlock button. My shirt jumped as Natalie swiped at it, missed. As we drew even with the car, I sped up, running past the driver's side door and then dodging left, around the trunk, to the passenger's side. It was the kind of trick I used to play on her when we were growing up, and it worked now, as it had worked then. I flung open the passenger's door, threw myself into the car, and hauled the door shut, locking it.

"Natalie was furious. She circled the car three times, and I swear, her scream was as loud inside the car as it had been outside. My heart was pounding, my head swimming. How ironic would it be for me to die from a heart attack here and now? I forced myself to move. If Natalie gained entry to the car, I had no plan. I sidled into the driver's seat, started the engine. My sister came to a halt directly in front of me and stood there, screaming. I'll admit, I considered shifting into drive and stepping on the gas."

"Why didn't you?" Carl said.

"Because whatever she had become, she still looked like my little sister. I reversed away from her, and burned rubber out of there. Natalie didn't pursue me, but her screams rang in my ears the entire way home."

**XII**

"I assume this is when Hunter called you," Carl said to Annie.

"Eventually," Hunter said. "For the first twenty-four hours after I pulled into the driveway, I was certain Natalie was on her way. Any minute now, I was going to look out the window and see her springing up the front steps. I didn't, but I didn't sleep all that much, either. I started chemo a couple of days later. My oncologist had recommended aggressive treatment as my only hope. As I believe I may have said, it kicked my ass. I was terribly afraid Natalie would appear while I was sitting on one of the hospital's comfy chairs, IV'd to the stuff that was nuking my body in hopes of frying the cancer first. I was tense, irritable. Jill was gone from the house a lot, which I can't say I blame her for.

"Finally, I decided I had to start talking to people about Natalie. I don't mean psychologists. I already had a decent idea of the interpretation they would offer me. My original experience was a fantasy constructed ad-hoc by my mind to fool itself into believing it wasn't facing extinction. Its ambiguous nature owed itself to unresolved guilt over my sister's death. My recent visions of her were the result of decades of poorly treated PTSD brought about by the accumulated stress of the places I'd covered. What had happened was a full-blown psychotic incident, precipitated by my recent diagnosis and its poor prognosis. That sound on target?"

"I'm not a shrink, but yeah, I guess so."

"The people I was interested in were the ones who would take my story at face value. I started with the local Catholic priest. Faith of our fathers and all that. He was followed by Episcopalian, Lutheran, Greek Orthodox, Methodist, Presbyterian, Baptist, and Unitarian clergy, after which, I moved to conservative and reformed Judaism, then Zen Buddhism and Tibetan Buddhism. I didn't have much luck with any of them. Assuming they didn't think I was playing some kind of weird joke on them, most of the men and women I spoke to opted for the psychological view. The Episcopalian and Unitarian were more flexible; each of them suggested I might have encountered a Hell that was adapted to me, specifically. The Tibetan Buddhist raised the possibility that what I took for my sister was a kind of wrathful god, a figure who appears to you once you're dead to frighten you toward the right path. There was no doubt Natalie had scared me, but none of our meetings had driven me to enlightenment. And I couldn't understand why my younger self would have merited a trip to Hell, and why my little sister would have been waiting for me there. No, none of it was especially helpful at explaining the story I told. I went online, hung out on all sorts of out-of-the-way message boards. This was how I found Annie." Hunter nodded at her. "There was this woman on one of them. She was being—I guess you would call it harassed by what she thought was her brother, until she found out he was out of the country, on a month-long trip to New Zealand. This . . . figure was making all kinds of weird shit happen to her. Annie wrote a long response to the woman's post which made me think she might be the person for me to talk to. I messaged her, sketched out the parameters of my situation, and asked if she had any insight into it. She replied straight away, said she'd do some research and let me know in a day or two. Which she did.

"And to cut to the chase, here we are."

"Here we are," Carl said. He stood from the kitchen island, carried his dish and glass to the sink. "If one of you could tell me exactly where here is, that would be helpful. Specifically, what is it you're planning, and why do you want me to be part of it? I mean, I assume that's the point of all this, to persuade me to assist in your—are you going to perform an exorcism? some kind of casting out of the evil spirit?"

"No," Hunter said. "All I need is for you to walk with me for a little while."

"This is one of those it's-more-complicated-than-it-sounds deals, isn't it?"

"No," Hunter said. "Or yes. Somewhat. Annie, feel free to jump in."

"Hunter's telling you the truth," Annie said. While Hunter had been telling his stories, she had quietly removed six Tarot cards from the deck, and placed them at what appeared to be the points of a hexagon. "He has to cross dangerous terrain. Having a friend with him, especially one he's known for so long, will help."

"Dangerous?"

"She means Natalie's turf."

"The box fort place?"

"Her kingdom, yeah. With the Hungry Dogs."

"I don't think I understand."

"Hunter's become entangled with his sister's domain," Annie said, "to an extent that will make it difficult for him not to be caught there. I've worked out a map to guide him through; however, once he sets foot in it, Natalie is going to do what she can to keep him with her."

"You want me to fight your sister for you?" Carl said.

"I'll deal with Natalie," Hunter said. "It's the dogs I'm worried about."

"I'm protecting you from them? I'm still not sure what they are."

"They're souls," Annie said. "Of children, as far as I can tell. Drawn into Natalie's sphere and warped by her."

"Jesus," Carl said. "What are we talking about? I thought she was a ghost."

"Imagine," Annie said, "that when you die, you have to cross from the land of the living"—she placed her index finger on the card at the top of the hexagon and slid the digit to the card at the bottom—"to the land of the dead. Let's not worry about that place. What concerns us"—she moved her finger to the center of the space—"is what lies between."

"Isn't that supposed to be a tunnel of light?"

"Or the river Styx, or a Valkyrie leaning to grab you from her winged horse, or—you understand. It's reactive. You're likely to encounter whatever you expect to. The majority of those who enter it succeed in reaching the other side. A few turn back, try to return to this life, which generally doesn't go well."

"Ghosts."

Annie nodded. "Among other things. A few souls become lost in this middle ground. They see somewhere they want to remain, so they do. Call it Limbo, albeit, of a highly personalized kind. There, the dead change, go feral."

"Hunter's sister is a feral ghost?"

"Yes, and from everything he's described, she's a powerful one. She's learned how to employ the landscape's reflective quality to alter other souls."

"But she's a kid—was a kid."

"You have children?"

"Two, daughters."

"Then you have direct knowledge of a child's creativity and will power. What do you suppose would happen if you placed a particularly bright and strong-willed child in a place where those qualities would have an immediate effect on her surroundings?"

"Okay," Carl said, "you have a point. But what are the other kids doing there to begin with? I'm guessing there's some kind of connection among family members, which would explain why Hunter was drawn to the place. Those kids, though, the ones Natalie's transformed, what brought them to her? Shouldn't they have been traveling their own paths?"

"Most do. As I said, it's possible to lose your way, and once that happens, to wander into someplace like Natalie's domain. There, you're liable to her influence."

"To what end? Why would she do all this, change other kids into monsters, chase after Hunter?"

"Boredom," Annie said. She began to collect the Tarot cards

in front of her. "Eternity is long. She wants Hunter because he escaped from her, because he escaped back to life. Think of a frustrated child. I would guess she's been searching for a way to extend her pursuit of him ever since that afternoon. How she accomplished it, I'm not sure. Single-minded persistence, obviously, but combined with some quality of the places Hunter went which allowed her to push through into them. Possibly the connection to trauma, to pain, suffering. Those kinds of extreme states weaken the barrier between our world and Limbo."

"If she's this strong, why not grab him, drag him off to her kingdom?"

"I don't know," Annie said. "To do something like that requires tremendous power and knowledge. Natalie has the one, but may not have the other. Or she may know he's dying, and have decided it's easier to wait."

"So you kick off," Carl said to Hunter, "and Natalie's waiting to turn you over to her dogs for a rawhide bone. I understand you have Annie's map through Limbo, but I don't see how you ever get to use it."

"Because we're cheating," Hunter said. He doffed his baseball cap and set it on the kitchen island, grabbed the bottom of his T-shirt and pulled it over his head. In the wintry light, his chest and arms were pale, the skin tight against the bone, painful to look at. His flesh was covered in designs executed in pale red ink, what might have been a child's approximation of letters, except the longer Carl studied them, the more they grew to resemble not so much letters as animals, fantastic creatures whose outlines stirred the hairs on his arms. He said, "What . . . ?"

"Camouflage," Hunter said. "It won't hide me from Natalie,

but it should make it harder for the dogs to track me." He folded the T-shirt, placed it beside the baseball cap.

"Should," Carl said.

"Hey, none of this is the kind of thing there are manuals for. We're doing the best we can."

"What about me? Where's my camouflage?"

"You don't need any." Hunter unbuttoned and unzipped his jeans, and lowered them. Underneath, he was naked, his emaciated skin a canvas for more of the strange characters.

"Dude," Carl said.

"Our theory," Annie said, "is that Natalie and the dogs will be focused on Hunter. The sigils will throw the dogs off Hunter, while your presence will confuse them further."

"A living guy in Limbo is not something they've seen," Hunter said. He folded his jeans, set them on top of the T-shirt.

"Are you saying they can't hurt me?"

"No," Annie said.

"You're the living weapon, remember?"

"Seriously? I run a small dojo in small city in the Hudson Valley. Most of my students are under ten. Half my classes I spend in fun activities so the kids won't get bored."

"Don't sell yourself short."

"You want to know the last time I was in a fight? Not a sparring match, but an actual fight? I was thirteen, and the other kid cleaned my clock. And this was a human being, not some kind of monster."

"All right," Hunter said, "how about, you're all I've got?"

"That's hardly a ringing endorsement. What happened to your *spetsnaz* buddies?"

"Dead," Hunter said, "except for the one who's in Syria."

"Son of a bitch," Carl said. "How am I even supposed to accompany you?"

"At the moment," Annie said, "the next world is very close. When you're talking about this kind of geography, the places move in relation to you. Just over the border, Natalie and her dogs are waiting. She's so concentrated on Hunter, she won't notice if I slide our place and hers into conjunction."

"You can do that?"

"Under normal circumstances, no. You need knowledge and power, remember? I have plenty of the former, but nowhere near enough of the latter. Natalie has power to spare, however, and I've worked out how to siphon off a sufficient amount to put my knowledge to use."

"Annie's gonna drop us behind enemy lines," Hunter said, "so to speak. We'll have a head start on our pursuers; plus, we'll be that much closer to our destination."

"Your destination," Carl said. "I still have to return from this excursion. Which I'm going to do how?"

"Once Hunter has reached the other side of Natalie's domain, I should know. I'll release the spell holding the worlds together, and you should be carried back here."

"There's a hell of a lot of maybe to this plan."

"Yeah," Hunter said, "there is."

Carl sighed. "It amazes me that I'm having this conversation."

"You've always been pretty gullible."

"Very nice," Carl said. "Okay. When is all of this supposed to happen? Do you know how much longer you have?"

"Until about two hours ago," Hunter said.

Snow filled the kitchen, swirling around the three of them.

• • •

## XIII

"What do you mean?" Carl said. "You're . . . ?" Unsaid, the word lay leaden on his tongue. Heavy, wet snowflakes pattered his face. The temperature was plunging.

"Don't worry about it," Hunter said. He crossed to Carl, grabbed his left shoulder with a hand that felt as solid as it ever had. Snow stuck to his bare skin; his breath misted the air. A mix of emotions, grief, incredulity, anger, surged in Carl's chest, making him sway as if still drunk. His eyes moistened, dissolving the snow clinging to his lashes.

"We're on the clock," Annie said. She had fanned the Tarot deck on the marble in front of her and was using both hands to push certain cards out of it. Snowflakes eddied about her, condensing into clouds that rushed away from her.

Hunter relaxed his grip on Carl. "Madame Sosostris," he said, "thank you. I couldn't have done this alone."

Without looking up from the cards, Annie said, "You're right."

"Come on," Hunter said, moving toward the hallway to the living room.

"One moment," Carl said. He wiped his eyes. A magnetic strip on the wall to the left of the sink held a series of rubber-handled knives hung points down in ascending order of size. He selected the second largest, just shy of the butcher knife at the end, and tugged it loose.

From the doorway, Hunter said, "Ready?"

"No," Carl said, testing the knife's weight, its balance.

"Excellent."

In the hall, the snow thickened, the flakes becoming smaller and denser, almost ice pellets. They rattled against the windows, clattered on the wall, stung Carl's face and hands. Raising his left hand to shield his eyes, his right ready with the knife, he said to Hunter's back, "This already sucks."

"Yeah, well, try doing it naked."

"About that: Couldn't you have found a way to do this clothed?"

"Sorry. I didn't realize you'd be so intimidated."

"Intimidating is not the word I'd use for your scrawny ass."

Carl glanced at the windows, but the storm outside had reduced the view to driving snow. At his feet, mist carpeted the floor, rising to his knees as he moved forward. "I feel like we should be having some kind of heartfelt conversation," he said. Icy snow clung to his hair, his ears, the back of his neck.

"What is it you want to talk about?"

"I don't know. Did it hurt? Dying?"

"I took some pills," Hunter said. "I went to sleep. At the end, I panicked a little, thought, 'Oh my God, what am I doing? What if all of this is bullshit, and I'm killing myself because of it?' But it was already too late; the only thing I could do was trust the plan Annie and I had come up with."

"How about now?"

"How do I feel? Weird. Half of me is elated. It's like, it worked! Here I am! The other half of me is scared shitless. I've deliberately made myself vulnerable to my sister and the Hungry Dogs. Those things, man . . ."

"I know."

"What do you mean?" Hunter slowed, cast a glance over his shoulder.

"I saw them," Carl said. "Last night. Or technically, I guess it was this morning. When I went out to the car for my bag. There were a couple of animals at the edge of the woods. I couldn't see them very well. Even with the garage lights, it was pretty foggy. I thought they might be coyotes, except they didn't move like any coyote I've ever seen."

"Sounds like them."

"I think I saw your sister, too. There was a kid dressed in a red T-shirt and shorts."

"She probably wanted to check you out."

"That's reassuring."

At the end of the hall, a framed eight-by-ten photograph hung. Hunter paused to study it, giving Carl time to join him. One of his better-known efforts, Hunter had taken it in the aftermath of Katrina's inundation of New Orleans. It showed a man and woman waist deep in water, straining to hold on to a rowboat crowded by four frightened children, a pair of dogs, and an assortment of worldly goods, including a cooler, a microwave, and a television weighing down one corner of the boat. Water foamed around the hull, the man appeared to be on the verge of losing his grip, the woman's face was contorted with effort, two children were crying, one of the dogs was attempting to scramble over the side. The photo was one of those iconic images of the disaster, part of the visual library news directors and documentary filmmakers went to for their pieces on the storm. Now, every last one of the figures in it had been replaced by Natalie, including the dogs. She looked on with concern at her struggling attempt to fight the current threatening to carry her away. Tongue lolling, she leaned against herself, who wrapped her arms around her tightly, eyes closed.

"Well," Carl said.

"Yeah," Hunter said.

As they emerged into the living room, the snow lost its ferocity. Carl lowered his hand. The space was full of trees, red pine mixing with birch, rooted in the hardwood floor. Couches and chairs scattered among them. The mist reached above his and Hunter's heads. He said, "I love what you've done with the place."

"I wasn't sure," Hunter said.

"No, it totally works," Carl said. "Gives a real, 'You're going to suffer a horrifying death here' vibe."

"Exactly what I was aiming for."

They advanced quickly, Hunter aiming for a group of three pines beside a recliner. About four feet up, the trunk of the middle tree had been scored with a series of short, shallow cuts, forming a symbol somewhere between a diamond and an eye. Hunter gestured at the mark. "All right. That's one of the runes Annie's using to stitch everything together. We can use them to guide us. More importantly, you can follow them out of here."

"I thought I was supposed to be whooshed to safety."

"That's the plan, but I figure we should have a backup."

"Can't argue with that."

In the middle distance, a larger pine was faintly visible. Skirting an end table, Hunter set off toward it. The snow had returned to large, damp flakes, which dropped around them in slow, lazy motions. To the left, a shape appeared: a brown box, big enough to hold a washing machine. On the side facing them was written HUNTER in childish letters. "Jesus," Carl said. Hunter did not comment.

The same blend of diamond and eye stared at them from the second tree's bark. Hunter brushed it with his fingertips. "Okay," he said. "The next part is tricky. We have to walk in a more or less straight line until we come to a tree that's forked at the base. It shouldn't be too far, but distances can be tricky, here. The important thing is to maintain our direction."

Carl nodded. He switched the knife to his left hand, flexed the fingers of his right. "After you."

Two steps from the tree, the mist congealed, rendering Hunter dim, insubstantial. In the dim light, the red figures written on his skin appeared clearer, as if the mist were a lens bringing them into sharper focus. Carl had the momentary impression the symbols were carrying Hunter, a mix of strange creatures and unfamiliar characters taking him through the mist. "You with me?" he said. The mist muffled his voice, making him sound farther away.

"Yes, sadly."

First on the left, and then the right, Carl heard the click of claws on hardwood. They were being paced, by several animals, from the sound of it. Glances to either side showed only mist. He returned the knife to his right hand. "Hey," he said.

"I know," Hunter said. "Nothing to do but keep going."

Now the claws were behind them, as well. The skin between Carl's shoulders tingled. He said, "I thought you were supposed to be camouflaged."

"Who says it's me they're tracking?"

"Great."

Another box, this one tall and narrow, loomed directly in front of them. "Shit," Hunter said. HUNTER'S FRIEND was scrawled on it. Carl's mouth went dry. He approached the box, reached out his hand to touch the words. The mud in which they were written was still damp. He wiped his fingers on his jeans. He felt his distance from Melanie, the girls, from everything he knew, a gap vast and profound. The claws herding them slowed but did not stop. Cold filled him, his interior weather mirroring the exterior conditions. "Oh," he said, "I am fucked."

"Not yet, you're not," Hunter said. He stepped closer to Carl, caught his elbow. "Come on." Carl nodded, allowed Hunter to tug him around the obstacle.

On the other side of the box, the dogs struck. To the right, claws scrabbled on the floor. Raising his left hand to guard, dropping his right to stab, Carl pivoted at the sound. As he did, another set of claws raced at him from the rear. He half turned in that direction, and the first dog smashed into his left knee. The pain was instant, overwhelming, taking him from his feet. Although he landed on his elbows, adding injury to injury, he held on to the knife. With the shock broadcasting from his leg, it was the most he could do. His assailant continued into the mist, as did the decoy, passing close enough for him to feel the drum of its paws through the wood. In this position, he was horribly defenseless, his back open to the teeth of the next attacker, but he could not move, could not draw sufficient breath to voice the curses streaming through his head: *Fucking fuck oh motherfucker fuck me you fucker fuck.*

Laughter burst around him, a shrieking choir whose volume suggested it issued from a hundred throats. Had it not been for the hurt, his nerves would have glowed with fear. As it was, he registered the approximate number voicing their delirium and added one more curse to his mental litany: *Shit.*

Hunter crouched beside him. "What happened?"

"My knee," Carl said, nodding at it.

He felt Hunter's hands on his leg. "No sign of a bite or cut."

"No. Hit it with their head."

"Right," Hunter said. He caught Carl under the armpits, started to lift. "Let's go. You don't want to stay here."

Of course he was right. With Hunter's help, Carl pushed himself to standing. His knee protested, but took his weight.

"You need to lean on me?" Hunter said.

"I think I can manage."

Accompanied by the laughter, and under it, the snicker of claws on wood, the two of them resumed their trek. The snow had tapered to scattered flakes, which circled them like moths. Cold numbed Carl's fingers, ears, face, made his nose run. He passed the knife back and forth between his hands, tucking whichever hand was free under the opposite armpit to warm it. At least the movement helped the pain radiating from his knee, allowing him to breathe more freely. But as the hurt ebbed, a tide of dread pushed in to take its place. A solid shot from one of those things and he was left helpless. How was he supposed to handle the laughing horde trailing them?

A red pine materialized in the mist, split at the foot into a pair of thick trunks whose lower branches were barkless, dead. On the trunk to their left, Carl recognized the diamond/eye symbol. The right fork was inscribed with the figure, too, but this one was surrounded by a tall rectangle, above and below which were cut short horizontal lines. Hunter stood beside the left trunk and pointed into the mist at about a forty-five degree angle from where they were standing. "This way," he said, and set off in the new direction.

At first, Carl thought it was his imagination, or an acoustic trick played by the moisture around them, but as they left the latest signpost behind, so did the laughter diminish in intensity. He wouldn't have sworn to it, but it seemed to be moving away from them. For a brief time, individual yips and screams continued to sound perilously close, and then the only noise was his and Hunter's feet on the floor. He said, "Is this the part where I say it's too quiet?"

"Another one of Annie's tricks," Hunter said. "Won't last forever, but it'll allow us to put some room between us and the dogs."

The mist was thinning, trees coalescing to either side. Hunter veered slightly to the right, to a young pine whose slender length bore the familiar mark. At the tree, he turned ninety degrees to the left and continued walking. "You know," Carl said, "I'm not sure I'm going to be able to remember this route."

"Relax," Hunter said. "You won't have to, remember?"

"And if something goes wrong? What happened to the contingency plan?"

"Nothing's going to go wrong," Hunter said. "We made it this far, didn't we? Jesus, when did you become such a worrywart?"

"Two kids and one business ago."

"It's fine. Everything's fine. Why do you have to be like this?"

"Because I'm the one looking at a future as the chew toy of the damned."

On their left, a collection of geometric silhouettes, smaller rectangles and larger squares, appeared through the mist. Another couple of steps, and the shapes resolved into a series of shoeboxes stood on end, forming a half circle before a pair of square boxes. Beyond this arrangement, further boxes were visible, clusters of low boxes interspersed in front of a line of bigger boxes, which were joined in what might have been a tunnel whose ends continued into the mist. Behind the tunnel, assorted boxes stacked three, four, and even five high formed precarious towers. Here and there, a birch rose in the midst of the constructions. Clearly, this was the box fort of Hunter's story, but it had grown from fort to metropolis, its full dimensions obscured by the mist. There appeared to be writing on some of the boxes, but between the distance and the mist, Carl could not read any of it. He said, "Wow."

"Natalie was never one for half measures."

"I can't help thinking how cool this looks. Is that crazy?"

"You have to respect her dedication."

They proceeded within sight of the cardboard city for ten minutes, more, past long, narrow boxes balanced to form a succession of archways, past a massive collection of coffee-mug-sized boxes meticulously layered into a ziggurat whose flat top stood as high as Carl's head, past tiny jewelry boxes arranged upon the floor in great spirals and stars. Mixed with his admiration and dread, Carl was aware of a new emotion, pity, for a child whiling away the endless days of her afterlife in yet another game. "Do you suppose," he said, "your sister has anyone else with her? Not the dogs, I mean another person."

Hunter shrugged. "My previous trip, she was the only one I saw. It's hard for me to imagine her tolerating another kid for very long. If an adult wandered into this place, I expect she'd consider them a threat to her authority."

"She must be lonely, though."

"Yeah, well, she's kept herself busy, hasn't she?" Anxiety strained Hunter's words.

"Is it much further?"

As if in answer, Carl saw a trio of red pines ahead. The trees on the right and in the center bore Madame Sosotris's symbol. Hunter strode between them. Carl followed. "We're most of the way there," Hunter said.

"That's good. Right?"

Instead of replying, Hunter stopped. Carl was on the verge of asking him what was wrong, when he saw the girl standing directly in front of them, a large animal behind her.

Natalie Kang might have been any nine- or ten-year-old entering an early growth spurt, all long skinny arms and legs. Her thick black hair reached past her waist and was in need of a brush. She was barefoot, wearing denim shorts and a red long-sleeved T-shirt. A cardboard crown circled her hair. Looking at her there in front of them, Carl was reminded of his daughters at that age, brimming with energy, possessed of surprising depths of melancholy and reflection, as well as titanic mirth. She was much smaller than he remembered, which was a ridiculous observation, because he had glimpsed her just the night before, but Hunter's stories had caused her to grow in Carl's memory to a raging monster, twelve feet tall.

When she shifted her large brown eyes from her brother to Carl, however, any reassurance her appearance might have caused withered. The gaze she directed at him was of pure, distilled malice, of hatred concentrated into its coldest form. He thought of Deb and Karen unhappy, of the rages they could fly into, the expressions of raw anger that would lower their brows, straighten their mouths. What was scalding him now like a jet of liquid nitrogen was the same emotion focused over decades, refined to a degree far in excess of what was humanly possible, tolerable. Briefly, he had wondered if Hunter might have misjudged his sister, misinterpreted her actions; now, he saw, his friend had not. Her eyes swung to Hunter, and it was as if Carl's skin warmed.

"You're naked," Natalie said. Her eyes narrowed, as if she

was attempting to decipher the characters on Hunter's skin. Something was off about her voice; it had a worn quality, as if it had been too long at the same pitch. Carl found it simultaneously frightening and sad.

"Yeah," Hunter said. "Hi, Nat."

"Don't call me that," she said. She raised her chin. "I am Natalya, Queen of the Hungry Dogs, and you are trespassing in my kingdom. Who is this?" She pointed at Carl.

"He's a friend. He agreed to come with me on my way through here."

"Why does he have a knife?"

"To protect himself. There are some pretty scary things in these parts."

"You mean my dogs."

"Yes, I do."

"You're right," Natalie said, "he should be afraid of them." She glanced behind her, and the creature at her back crept into view.

At the sight of it, Carl's stomach dropped, and despite himself, he said, "Jesus Christ."

The size of a big dog, a Great Dane or an Irish wolfhound, it slunk close to the floor, slender limbs out to either side like an enormous insect. Its hide was the damp white of flesh left days under a Band-Aid. Its head was awful, a pair of jaws distended by a cage of fangs the length of Carl's hand. Eyeless, it tasted the air with a fluttering white tongue whose edges were ragged from its teeth. A low chuckle rolled from its throat. The Hungry Dog positioned itself in front of Natalie, sitting as best the awkward arrangement of its limbs would allow, and turning its monstrous head in search of the palm she laid on it. She said, "This is Sam."

"Hi, Sam," Hunter said.

"Don't talk to him," Natalie said, her words laced with contempt. "He's mine."

"Okay," Hunter said, hands held out in apology, "I'm sorry."

"They're all mine," Natalie said. "Now you are too."

"Can we talk about that?"

"No."

Left hand low, palm forward, right hand holding the knife close to his body, Carl slid next to Hunter, who said, "Are you sure? I'm going to the summer country; maybe you could come with me."

"Why would I want to do that?"

"To see Mom and Dad."

"Them? They let me die."

"I don't think that's—"

"Shut up," Natalie said. "When I got sick, I asked them if I was going to die. 'Oh no,' they said, 'we would never let that happen.' I did everything they told me to. I took their stupid medicine, which made me feel terrible. All my hair fell out. And it didn't work. I died anyway. Before I did, Mom and Dad promised me I was going to heaven. 'You'll be lifted up by angels,' they said, 'and brought straight to Jesus. You'll see Grandpa Hugh again.' But there weren't any angels. I didn't see Jesus, or Grandpa Hugh. I wound up here. I saw a box fort and stopped at it. I didn't know where I was. I thought I was in Hell. I didn't know why; I didn't know what I had done. For a long time, I was so scared. Then I got tired of being afraid and got mad." Natalie lifted her hand from the dog (Sam) and he lurched to his feet. She said, "I knew when Mom and Dad died. I was ready for them. I was going to show them this place. I was going to ask them why they'd lied to me. I was going to make them apologize. Only, I missed them. Both of them. I went to find them, and I couldn't. It was like they didn't want to see me. Don't you think they would have? Don't you think they would have come looking for me?"

"I'm sure they did," Hunter said. "After I returned from here—after I was resuscitated—you were the first thing Mom asked me about. 'Did you see Natalie?' she said while we were in the ambulance."

"She did?"

"Yes, really."

"What did you tell her?" Eagerness blended with Natalie's anger, softened the stern cast of her features.

"I said I'd seen you."

"Did you tell her about my kingdom?"

"No, I did not."

"Why not?"

"To be honest, I was pretty freaked out by it. I thought Mom would be too."

Natalie's face hardened. "So even if she had wanted to find me after she died, she couldn't have, because you didn't tell her the right place to look."

"Whoa," Hunter said. "Hang on a minute."

Carl didn't pick up on the exact cue Natalie employed, but he caught the dog rocking back, gathering himself to leap, and pushed in front of Hunter as the creature sprang. For an instant, the Hungry Dog hung in the air, his abundance of fangs spread wide. Ice water flooded Carl's chest. Sam drew nearer in fits and starts, as if in a series of slides caught in a stuttering projector. Somewhere inside Carl's head, a voice was saying, *Move move move move move.* When the dog was an arm's length away, he did. Aiming for Sam's throat, he snapped the knife straight out, exhaling sharply as he twisted his right hip into the strike. The dog came in lower than he anticipated, however, and the knife drove into Sam's open mouth, piercing his tongue and lower jaw. Fangs tore Carl's hand as the dog jerked his head left in an attempt to avoid the weapon that had already wounded him. His momentum carried him into Carl, who released the knife and stumbled backward, thudding against Hunter and knocking the two of them to the floor. Sam landed next to them, thumping on his side, and immediately started wailing, a frantic cry half-way to a laugh. On his ass, Carl scooted clear of the thrashing dog, colliding with Hunter and forcing him back too.

"Dude," Hunter said when they were a safe distance, "your hand."

Carl raised it. It was bright red with blood streaming from the furrows Sam's fangs had dug in it. "Jesus." His head swam. He was aware of pain, incredible pain, astonishing pain, the moment his ravaged hand came into view, but he was more concerned that neither his thumb nor his middle finger seemed capable of movement. Nausea fought with panic in his throat.

"Holy shit," Hunter said.

At first, Carl thought his friend was commenting on his hand, until he saw what was happening to Sam. All over him, the dog's pale flesh was quivering, losing its solidity, becoming gelid, sliding partway from his limbs and torso onto the floor, then regaining its integrity and retracting up his frame. In some places, what reformed was not the shape of the Hungry Dog, but of a child, a seven- or eight-year-old, Carl would have guessed. An arm, a leg, a hand, a foot, a shock of curly red hair, a green eye wide with agony and fright, all blended with the dog's monstrous features, while he continued his laughing wail, pawing at but unable to dislodge the blade buried in his lower jaw.

"Hush," Natalie said, and Sam's cry diminished to a whimper. Mingled with his whining were sounds that might have been words; Carl thought he could pick out, "Hurts." Natalie crouched in front of the dog, her left hand on his head, her right reaching amidst his fangs to grab the handle of the knife. She murmured something to Sam, too low for Carl to hear, and tore the knife from his mouth with a downward stroke that split his lower jaw to the throat. Carl and Hunter shouted. The halves of his jaw flapping, pinkish blood venting from his open neck, Sam reared on his mismatched hind legs and fell over. His eye rolled frantically, then fixed. He sighed, shuddered, and was still. His body began to slide apart.

"What the fuck, Nat?" Hunter said.

"You broke him," Natalie said. She dropped the knife, stood, wiped her hand on her shorts. "He'll go back to his doghouse until I can fix him."

Hunter raised himself to his feet. He held out his right hand to Carl, who took it in his left and used it to help him up from the floor. The pain from his injuries was excruciating. "How're you doing?" Hunter said.

"Have I mentioned how much this sucks?" Trying to keep the hand elevated, Carl pressed his right arm across his chest.

"You might have."

"I don't think I'm gonna be much good for anything else," Carl said. Natalie had kicked the knife away.

"That's okay. It isn't too far from here. I'm pretty sure I can make it on my own."

"You are going nowhere," Natalie said.

"Are you sure?" Carl said. "Do you know which direction you're supposed to be heading? Because I have no idea."

"I said, You are going nowhere." Natalie advanced toward them.

"Yeah, I think so," Hunter said. "Hang tight; it shouldn't be too long."

"That's assuming you succeed."

"Ever the voice of encouragement."

"I SAID, YOU ARE GOING NOWHERE." Natalie was standing beside them. This close, hatred poured from her in freezing waves. "You are mine," she continued, addressing Hunter, "and so is your friend. I rule here. What I want to happen, happens. I want both of you to suffer, so you will. There's a box waiting for you, big brother. I've been preparing it for a very long time. Maybe I'll sic what comes out of it on your friend. Maybe I'll let the dogs have him, for what he did to their brother."

"Nat—"

"Queen Natalya."

"Yeah." Hunter shook his head, and leaped at his sister, catching her in a tackle that brought them crashing to the floor. Almost too fast to see, Natalie twisted, planting her feet against Hunter's chest and kicking with enough force to shove him away from her, mist rolling about him. She sprang up, ready for Carl, but he was hurrying to Hunter, who grimaced, his left arm wrapping his ribs. "Well, that worked," Carl said, extending his left hand.

Behind him, Natalie's voice thundered, "GIVE IT BACK!"

In his other hand, Hunter held his sister's crown. Waving away Carl's help, he staggered to his feet.

"GIVE IT BACK!" Trembling with fury, Natalie glared at the two of them. Loosed from the cardboard circle, strands of her hair lifted as if in a breeze. "GIVE ME MY CROWN, HUNTER!"

Hunter shook his head. "No can do, Nat."

In response, Natalie screamed, an ear-splitting shriek which lasted longer than Carl would have thought humanly possible. Somewhere deep in the mist, a distant pack of laughs answered. "Now you'll see," she said. "I won't bother putting you in your box. I'll let the dogs get you. You're going to be so sorry, Hunter. They're going to hurt you so bad."

"Thank you," Hunter said to Carl, "for coming with me. I don't know if I could have made it this far without you. I'm sorry about your hand."

"That makes two of us."

"I love you, man."

"I love you, too. I hope you make it."

"That makes two of us." Crown in hand, Hunter turned left and ran.

"HEY!" Natalie shouted after him. "HEY! COME BACK HERE, HUNTER! HUNTER!"

Already, the mist was closing around him, rendering him ghostly, dulling the slap of his feet on the floor. For an instant, the strange red symbols written on him appeared to float in the air, then they faded from sight, as well.

Natalie didn't waste any more time. Without another glance at Carl, she sprinted after her brother, her long black hair streaming behind her like a banner.

## XIV

Laughter roared around Carl, raged, together with another sound, the rumble of many feet, of hundreds of feet, running at him. The floor shuddered with their approach. How many

Hungry Dogs were there? Carl's hand throbbed. If one of them left the chase, he was in trouble; two, and he was finished. *Hang tight*, Hunter had said. Easy for him to say. The laughter swelled. The floor jumped under him. *Hang tight.*

As fast as his legs would carry him, Carl ran, aiming ninety degrees from the direction in which Hunter and Natalie had vanished. Laughter pursued him, enveloped him. The floor bounced like a trampoline, throwing him into a stumble that almost sent him sprawling. To his right, a stand of birches waved like reeds in a wind. He considered sheltering in them, rejected the idea. An arm's length in front of him, a dog loped from right to left, its head an assortment of blades. Closer still, another crossed behind him. This direction, the mist was heavier, which he supposed was equal parts to his advantage and disadvantage.

Snow rushed against him. He slowed, shielded his face with his left hand. "HUNTER!" Natalie's voice boomed on his left, made him flinch. He quickened his pace. The Hungry Dogs' laughter ebbed, swelled, ebbed. The shaking of the floor subsided. Ahead, someone panted with exertion. "Hunter?" Carl said. Faintly, he heard Natalie shouting, but could not decipher her words. Snow stuck to his skin, clung to his hair. At least it numbed his injuries.

His feet were starting to drag. There was something to the right, a squat form about which snow swirled. Its outline was too regular for a tree. Carl jogged over to it. Made of gray brick, it stood waist high, a foot and a half on each side. Set in its flat top was a shallow bowl of dull metal. Snow silted the bowl, spackled the column's sides. Carl walked around it, but could see no markings on it, no hint of its purpose. One of Natalie's creations? He couldn't be absolutely sure, but didn't believe so.

He squatted to study it more closely, using his left hand to balance himself. As he did, he realized his fingertips were touching not wood, but soil. Pulse leaping, he brushed his hand over the ground, confirming his discovery:

He had left Natalie's domain, and Madame Sosostris's path through it. He was lost.

## XV

For a long time, Carl stood beside the brick pillar, as snow drifted against it and the blood flowing from his wounds began to freeze. He could attempt to find his way back to Natalie's kingdom, but there seemed little point in doing so. If Hunter had succeeded in escaping her, then Madame Sosostris would have performed whatever action was necessary to unlink Limbo from the world of the living, and Carl would be entering a hostile environment from which there was no escape. He did not imagine Annie would or could keep the worlds locked indefinitely—she had mentioned the tremendous power required to do so, hadn't she?—so if Hunter did not reach his goal, if Natalie caught him or if he ran off course, there would come a moment when she would have to effect the separation, anyway. Which would yield the same result of him returning to Natalie's domain, except he and Hunter would be suffering together. He could continue into this new precinct of Limbo. The brick column was evidence at least one other person inhabited or had inhabited the area. But what if that individual was as hostile as Natalie, another feral ghost? What if they were worse, at the head of their own army of monsters? He could not risk wandering further into this territory.

The snow continued.

• • •

## XVI

At some point, he crouched against the brick pillar, thinking it would offer him a modicum of shelter from the elements. He supposed it did; although it sharply curtailed his view of his surroundings. He was too cold to let that sway him. How long had it been since Hunter and he had set out on their journey? A couple of hours? Was that possible? It felt as if he'd followed Hunter along the hallway out of the kitchen days ago. Attempting to conserve body heat, he huddled tight. Could he die, here? Given that he could be hurt, it seemed likely. What would it mean, to die in the afterlife? Would he notice? Or was there some deeper level of existence waiting under this one?

His family would not know what had happened to him. Presumably, Annie would call 911 to report Hunter's lifeless body. One look at the empty pill bottle beside it would tell the cops how he had exited his life, while a conversation with Hunter's doctor would explain why. No doubt, the investigating officers would have plenty of questions for Annie, but Carl didn't think she'd have any trouble answering them. He was less certain how she'd respond when they asked about the owner of the other car parked in the driveway. Her best option would be to hew as close to events as she could, to admit she didn't know. In short order, what started as a call about the death of a famous photojournalist, apparently at his own hand, would have developed into a missing person case involving his long-term friend, the owner of a shotokan karate studio in Beacon.

What would the cops assume had happened to him? More importantly, what would Melanie think? She would have leaped in the car the instant the call to her ended. An accident would seem the most reasonable explanation. In this version of events, he went for a walk in the woods surrounding his friend's house and suffered some kind of mishap, tripped, fell, knocked himself unconscious, then froze to death in the storm. A heart attack would work as well, despite a clean bill of health at his last checkup. The lack of any trace of his body on Hunter's grounds would lead to the search being expanded to neighboring properties, possibly down to Lake Champlain, whose cold waters would offer a compelling explanation for the absence of his remains. The cops might posit he had slipped and fallen into the lake. How long would it be until the search was called off, suspended? What would the official verdict be? Missing, presumed dead? Yet the coincidence of him vanishing at the same time his friend ended his life would lend his disappearance an aspect of mystery which would birth conspiracy theories as quickly as the internet could midwife them. The prospect was almost enough to bend his mouth into a smile, except that the same open-endedness would haunt Melanie and the girls.

From Carl, from Dad, names which over a lifetime had become synonyms for stolid, calm (if unexciting), dependable (if forgetful), the man who had been one quarter of the family would assume a new identity, or rather, lack of identity. He would become a cipher, a blank onto which Melanie, Deb, and Karen would write whatever anxieties and doubts they'd had about their relationships with him. Melanie would fear he had left her for a new life with another woman, one of the younger black belts whose fawning she teased him about. Deb and Karen would worry they'd been abandoned by a father who had only ever feigned interest in them and their lives. With time, perhaps the girls would accept that he had died in an accident which had hidden his body, but he doubted Melanie would.

She would know something was not right about his vanishing; the low-level marital telepathy they had developed over their decades together would tell her the situation was off. Would she seek out Madame Sosostris, demand more of an answer than the woman had provided the police? And suppose Annie acquiesced to her request, told her everything? What then? Assuming Melanie didn't take Annie as either lying or insane, what could she do? What options could Annie offer her? Without the power she had drawn from Natalie, she could not access this place. The best Melanie could expect was to know her husband was forever lost to her. Grief for her, for what she had not learned she already had lost, shot through him like a steel pin fixing an insect to a board.

Nearby, footsteps crunched in his direction. Wondering if Hunter had failed in his efforts and had managed to track him here, he raised his head. But no, he did not recognize the young man advancing toward him. For one thing, he was clothed, wearing a peach dress shirt, charcoal slacks, and black loafers. For another, everything about him, the colors of his clothes, the tone of his skin, even the shine of his eyes, glowed with a rich light, as if the midday sun were shining full on him. The man's expression, however, indicated he knew Carl. Squinting at the snow pelting his face, the man approached Carl until he was standing over him. In a pleasant voice, he said, "Your ride's here, kiddo. Time to go."

## XVII

"Who are you?" Carl said through chattering teeth.

"The gift horse you're looking in the mouth."

"I'm sorry," he said, bracing himself against the pillar as he struggled to stand, his legs complaining as they unbent. "It's just—"

"Your friend's sister, yes."

"You know about her?"

"Some."

"Can you tell me if Hunter got away from her?"

The young man shook his handsome head. "I can't. What I can offer you is a way out of here."

"Is this a trick?"

"This is not a trick."

"Then why are you doing this?" Sudden suspicion widened his eyes. "Are you an angel? A god? God?"

The young man burst into hearty laughter. "That's terrific," he said. "What a difference a change of clothes makes, I swear." Noting the blend of consternation and embarrassment on Carl's face, he added, "I'm sorry. I shouldn't have expected you to know me. The last time you saw me, I was in considerably worse shape. Actually, the last time you saw me, I was lying in the coffin in the Miskowski Funeral Home in Fishkill."

Here, Carl realized, was Wayne Ahuja, his older brother's friend, dead these many years, one of the multitude consumed by AIDS and its attendant infections. The delay in his recognition was understandable. Even before his sickness, Wayne had been skinny, the type of kid, it was joked, who had to stand in the same place twice to cast a shadow, who had to run around in the shower to get wet. In contrast, the man in front of him had the robust dimensions of an Olympic swimmer. He wore vitality with the same ease as his immaculately tailored shirt. Nor did the difference end there. When Carl had known him, Wayne had been reserved, guarded, a consequence of being out at a time and in a place whose attitudes were struggling to advance. This Wayne was suffused with self-confidence. It was as if he was seeing Wayne not as he would have been had he lived, but as the best possible self he could have been. Wonder and bewilderment competed to find their way into speech; what emerged from Carl's mouth was a compromise: "Why?"

"Are you saying you want to stay here?"

"No," Carl said, "no, no, of course not. It's—I don't understand. I thought I was trapped in this place."

"I supposed it does seem a little *deus-ex-machina-y*, doesn't it? Just when all hope seems lost, the handsome ghost from your past swoops in to rescue you. Well, more like, trudges across a snowy waste, but you get the picture. It's because of that," Wayne said, pointing at Carl's torn right hand. "Blood was spilled. Whenever that happens in this neck of the woods, it creates all kinds of opportunities."

"Like what?"

"Don't ask. Be glad your friend's sister didn't know about it, or she wouldn't have spent two seconds on him." Wayne turned to the pillar, on top of which a couple of inches of snow had accumulated. With the flat of his hand, he swept it clear, then scooped out the snow remaining in the metal bowl. He waved to Carl. "Give me your hand. No, the injured one."

Carl removed his hand from its position against his shoulder and held it out. Wayne took it in his warm grasp and guided it over the bowl. Rotating the wrist this way and that, he inspected Carl's mostly frozen wounds. "I'm sorry about this," he said, and squeezed Carl's hand tightly.

Pain burned his fingers and palm. He yelped, went to jerk

away, but Wayne's grip did not lessen. From numb, Carl's hand was aflame, flesh and bones luminescent. Fresh blood streamed from the grooves in his skin and pattered onto the bowl, striking it with a tinny music. "That should do," Wayne said, and released him.

"Fuck!" Carl said, cradling his reinjured hand.

"Again, I apologize." Wayne peered at the bowl, watching Carl's blood slide down its sides into a crimson bubble. The blood quivered, elongated, shooting up the bowl's curve in a straight line. Wayne pointed in the direction it indicated, about twenty degrees to their left. "This way," he said.

Snow whirled around them. "There's a hell of a lot more walking in the afterlife than I expected," Carl said.

Wayne chuckled. "It isn't far."

"Can I ask you something?"

"You want to know what it's like."

"Heaven, yeah. Hunter called it the summer country."

"What makes you think that's where I come from?"

"You didn't?" Carl glanced at him.

"No, I'm teasing you," Wayne said. "If your friend reaches it, he'll be happy."

"I would hope so, after all this."

They proceeded in silence for a minute or two, until Carl said, "That's it?"

"That's it."

In front of them, a low wall made of flat black stones layered thigh high barred the way. "Here we are," Wayne said. "Do you think you can get over this on your own, or do you need a hand?"

The stones were a single layer deep. Carl stepped across with a minimum of effort.

"And there's my answer," Wayne said. "All right. Continue straight on and you should see your destination in about five minutes."

"Thank you," Carl said. "I wish I could come up with something better to say."

"You're welcome."

"I still don't understand why you were the one who came for me. Not that I'm complaining; I just wondered."

"Do you remember the last conversation we had?"

"Yes. You told me about wanting to go to Paris."

"That was a bad day. A horrible day. I was in a lot of pain, and I was starting to understand I didn't have much longer. All the stuff about France had been such a central part of who I was, how I saw myself, and it was going to be lost, to go down to the grave with me. I was depressed and I was afraid. You allowed me to talk about something I loved one more time—for the final time, as it turned out. It was comforting, at a time when comfort was in short supply. For my remaining days, I appreciated that.

"Plus, you did a good thing for your friend. I admire that. I could help you, so I did. You get a Get-Out-of-Jail-Free card. Why not, right?"

"No argument here," Carl said. "One last thing?"

"Yes?"

"If you happen to see my friend—Hunter—tell him I'm glad he made it."

"Should I see him, I will."

"Thanks."

"Go home," Wayne said.

Carl did.

• • •

**XVIII**

More like ten minutes after he departed Wayne, Carl noticed the mist thinning, disclosing the trunks of trees around him. The snow had not let up; indeed, it had gained in intensity, accompanied by a wind that sliced through him to the bone. Carl advanced to one of the trees, saw that it was a red pine, and his heart lifted in his chest. Moving from evergreen to evergreen, he continued forward. The wind whipped away the last of the mist. He was walking through the woods lining the driveway to Hunter's house; through the blowing snow and the trees, he could see his Subaru, and beyond it, the steps climbing the slope to the house's front door.

A tremendous wave of emotion rose in Carl, sent tears flooding his cheeks. The snow, the trees, the car, glowed in his sight, suffused with beauty. The wave broke, became joy and relief and a fierce love for the world and everyone in it. The snowflakes were a miracle, the trees astonishing, the car a work of art. He could not contain himself: He broke into a run toward the house, where his old friend's body lay on the bed in the master bedroom, an unreadable expression on its cooling face.

**Epilogue**

The surgery to repair Carl's hand took place at the UVM Medical Center. He had blamed his injuries on an attack by a stray dog he'd encountered when he went outside to practice his *kata*. The explanation was simple enough to repeat to the police convincingly; although it necessitated a series of rabies shots he couldn't refuse and maintain the illusion. The doctor who treated him at the ER strongly recommended operating as soon as possible, which opinion the surgeon on call endorsed. Already on her way up, Melanie met him at the hospital, where a slot had opened early the following morning. “Holy crap,” she said when she saw the bandages wrapping his hand. “A dog did this?”

Although he hated lying to her, Carl said, “Yeah. It was the craziest thing.” Which was perhaps not as much a lie as he had thought.

After the surgery, while he was in the recovery area, surrounded by tall green curtains through which various nurses came to check his vitals, Hunter appeared to him. Melanie had ducked out to run to the cafeteria for a cup of coffee and a snack. Carl was lying with his eyes shut, riding in and out of consciousness. He heard the curtain rings jingle, felt someone sit on the end of the bed. He assumed it was Melanie, but when he opened his eyes, saw Hunter. Still unclothed, his skin still a canvas for the red figures, Hunter was wearing Natalie’s cardboard crown, perched unsteadily atop his larger head. On the floor beside him, a Hungry Dog sat awkwardly, its head an elongated wedge.

Carl was aware that he should be terrified, but whatever drugs were coursing through his system dulled the emotion to a mild concern. He said, “You’re still naked.”

“Yeah,” Hunter said.

“I take it this means the plan failed.”

“No,” Hunter said, “it didn’t.”

“Then why are you here?”

“I couldn’t do it.” Hunter looked down. “I made it. We made it; Natalie chased me all the way there. We must’ve made some sight, me running bare-assed down the middle of this cobbled street, her hot on my heels, screaming her head off. She finally brought me down, started punching and kicking me. I wouldn't let go of this, though." He pointed to the crown.

"Wait," Carl said. "Heaven has cobbled streets?"

"This part does. You know what it reminded me of? Have you ever been to St. Andrew's, in Scotland?"

"Heaven is like Scotland?"

"I'm sure the Scots would agree with that. It's not important. Anyway, there we are, me on the cobblestones, Natalie beating the shit out of me, and the next thing, there are people in the street. I want to say they were there all along, it just took us a minute to see them. I don't know what the hell that means, either. Their clothes were these incredible colors . . . I can't say exactly how, but they separate the two of us, form a circle around Natalie. She's furious; she's shouting at the crowd, running up to and pushing them, punching a couple. They don't react. Or, they don't react the way you would expect. They talk to her, reassure her, tell her it's okay, everything's all right. As they do, they're doing this thing with their hands." Hunter mimed moving his back and forth, as if he were playing tug of war and drawing the rope to him. "I'm thinking I should run, escape my sister while I have the opportunity, but I can't stop watching. I swear, I can almost see these people drawing something out of Natalie, like long, silvery webs. Eventually, she goes from running around inside the circle, to standing still, to sitting, then she lies down and falls asleep right there in the middle of the street. Some members of the group leave, others keep on with the hand stuff.

"I was so relieved; I can't tell you. A woman approached me, said we should see about getting me settled. 'What about my sister?' I said. 'Oh, her, too,' she said. Just like that. As if Nat hadn't been this raging monster.

"And it hits me, what about the Hungry Dogs? I'm thinking about Sam, about what we saw happen to him. I'm thinking about I don't know how many of these creatures, these kids, there without their queen. I'm thinking about what I've witnessed with Natalie. If there's a way to, I don't know, get her back from whatever she had transformed into, then shouldn't there be a way to reclaim them, too? But who's gonna do that? I can't bring Natalie out there, and I can't ask any of these people I don't know. I can't say it isn't my problem, because . . . well, I can't. How could I enjoy this place knowing this pack of kids was wandering around the box fort, wondering what happened? I asked the woman I was talking to if she could help my sister, could connect her with our parents. She said she would, so I put the crown on my head and set off the way we'd come.

"It wasn't hard to find the path back to Natalie's kingdom. Once I arrived, most of the dogs avoided me. I could see they recognized the crown, but had no idea what it meant for me to be wearing it. A few approached me, but this guy," Hunter nodded at the dog at his feet, "was the only one to stay. So far. I can't say why, but I think his name is Rudy."

"Hi, Rudy," Carl said.

The dog stared at him blankly.

"Although I could be wrong," Hunter said.

"How are you planning to retrieve them?" Carl said. "Who they were?"

"I have no idea," Hunter said. "If Natalie could transform them into these things, then I figure there's a way to return them to who they used to be. I just have to find it."

"Sounds like it could take some time."

"It's not as if I'm doing anything else." The bed creaked as

Hunter stood. So did the Hungry Dog (Rudy?). "Okay, I just wanted to drop by, check on you. I don't foresee myself having a lot of adult conversations in the immediate future." He moved toward the green curtain.

"Be careful," Carl said.

"I'm already dead."

"And for God's sake, get some pants, Your Majesty."

"Kiss my ass, peasant."

The curtain rings sang, the dog's claws clicked on the floor, and Carl was alone. When Melanie returned, she saw her husband wiping his eyes with the back of his unbandaged hand, but she did not ask him about it, not then.

"And if he were wrong, well, what would be the harm in that? Better to be wrong forever than to live without hope."—Lucius Shepard, "Limbo"

*For Fiona*

## ABOUT THE CONTRIBUTORS

A winner of both the Shirley Jackson Award and the International Horror Guild Award, **Dale Bailey** is the author of *In the Night Wood,* as well as *The End of the End of Everything, The Subterranean Season,* and five other books. His work has twice been a finalist for the Nebula Award and once for the Bram Stoker Award, and has been adapted for Showtime Television. He lives in North Carolina with his family.

**Nathan Ballingrud** is the author of *North American Lake Monsters: Stories, The Visible Filth,* and the forthcoming collection *Wounds.* His novella, *The Visible Filth,* is currently being made into a film, due in early 2019. He has twice won the Shirley Jackson Award. He lives in Asheville, NC, with his daughter.

**Aliette de Bodard** lives and works in Paris. She is the author of the critically acclaimed Obsidian and Blood trilogy of Aztec noir fantasies, as well as numerous short stories that have garnered her two Nebula Awards, a Locus Award, and two British Science Fiction Association Awards. Her space operas include *The Citadel of Weeping Pearls,* set in the same universe as her Vietnamese science fiction novella *On a Red Station, Drifting.* Recent works include the Dominion of the Fallen series (set in a turn-of-the-century Paris devastated by a magical war), which is comprised of *The House of Shattered Wings,* its standalone sequel *The House of Binding Thorns,* and the novella *The Tea-Master and the Detective.*

**Richard Bowes** has published six novels, four story collections, and eighty short stories. He has won two World Fantasy Awards and a Lambda Award, among other things. His classic 9/11 story "There's a Hole in the City" got a fine review in *The New Yorker* and is online at *Nightmare* magazine.

He's recently had stories in *Black Feathers,* the Wonderland-themed *Mad Hatters and March Hares,* and *Welcome to Dystopia.* His F&SF story "Dirty Old Town" will be a chapter of a book he's writing about a gay kid with magic in 1950s Boston.

Next year Bowes will have, among other things, stories in *Welcome to Dystopia* and *The Salon of Dorian Gray.*

**Pat Cadigan** sold her first professional science fiction story in 1980 and became a full-time writer in 1987. She is the author of fifteen books, including two nonfiction books on the making of *Lost in Space* and *The Mummy,* one young adult novel, and the two Arthur C. Clarke Award–winning novels *Synners* and *Fools.* She has also won the Locus Award three times, and the Hugo Award for her novelette "The Girl-Thing Who Went Out for Sushi," which also won the Seiun Award in Japan.

She can be found on Facebook and Pinterest, Tweets as @Cadigan, and lives in North London with her husband, the original Chris Fowler, where she is stomping the hell out of terminal cancer. Most of her books are available electronically via SF Gateway, the ambitious electronic publishing program from Gollancz.

**Siobhan Carroll** is an Associate Professor of English at the University of Delaware, where she studies the relationship between the history of exploration and science fiction. A writer as well as a critic of speculative fiction, she contributes genre-blurring stories to magazines like *Beneath Ceaseless Skies* and *Lightspeed* and to anthologies like *Children of Lovecraft* and *Fearful Symmetries.* She has lived in the United States since 2002, during which time she's been acquainted with the hard work performed by immigration lawyers, officials, and activists. For more of Siobhan Carroll's fiction, go to http://voncarr-siobhan-carroll.blogspot.com.

In writing "The Air, the Ocean, the Earth, the Deep," she benefitted enormously from her conversations with Amelia Wilson at the U.S. Department of Justice and from the public-facing work of volunteer organizations like the Sojourners Immigration Detention Center Visitor Program and First Friends. What errors the story contains are all her own. For more on detention centers, or to volunteer as a visitor, go to http://sojournersvisitorprogram.blogspot.com and https://firstfriendsnjny.org/volunteer-2.

**F(rancis) Marion Crawford** (1854–1909) was an American writer who lived most of his life as an expatriate in Italy and who was best known in his lifetime for his historical novels. His posthumously published short-fiction collection, *Wandering Ghosts,* features most of the tales that constitute his weird fiction legacy.

"The Upper Berth," now considered a classic, was first published in *The Broken Shaft: Unwin's Annual for 1886.*

**Indrapramit Das** (aka Indra Das) is an Indian author from Kolkata, West Bengal. His debut novel, *The Devourers* (Del Rey / Penguin India) was the winner of the 2016 Lambda Literary Award for Best LGBTQ SF/F/Horror, and shortlisted for the 2016 Crawford Award. His short fiction has been nominated for the Shirley Jackson Award and has appeared in several publications and anthologies, including *Clarkesworld*, Tor.com, and *The Year's Best Science Fiction.* He is an Octavia E. Butler scholar and a grateful graduate of the Clarion West Writers Workshop, and received his MFA from the University of British Columbia in Vancouver. He has worn many hats, including editor, dog hotel night shift attendant, TV background performer, minor film critic, occasional illustrator, environmental news writer, pretend patient for med school students, and video game tester.

**Terry Dowling** is one of Australia's most respected and internationally acclaimed writers of science fiction, dark fantasy, and horror, and the author of the multi-award-winning Tom Rynosseros saga. He has been called "Australia's finest writer of horror" by *Locus* magazine. *The Year's Best Fantasy and Horror* series featured more horror stories by Dowling in its twenty-one-year run than by any other writer.

Dowling's horror collections are *Basic Black: Tales of Appropriate Fear* (2007 International Horror Guild Award winner for Best Collection), *An Intimate Knowledge of the Night* (Aurealis Award winner), and *Blackwater Days* (nominated for the World Fantasy Award). His recent publications include *Amberjack: Tales of Fear & Wonder* and his debut novel, *Clowns at Midnight,* which London's *Guardian* called "an exceptional work that bears comparison to John Fowles's *The Magus.*" His latest collection, *The Night Shop: Tales for the Lonely Hours,* was published in 2017. His homepage can be found at terrydowling.com.

**Brian Evenson** is the author of a dozen books of fiction, most recently the story collection *A Collapse of Horses,* which was a finalist for the Wonderland Book Award, and the novella *The Warren*, which was a finalist for the Shirley Jackson Award. He has also recently published *Windeye* and *Immobility*, both finalists for the Shirley Jackson Award. His novel *Last Days* won the American Library Association's award for Best Horror Novel of 2009. His novel *The Open Curtain* was a finalist for an Edgar Award and an International Horror Guild Award. Other books include *The Wavering Knife* (which won the IHG Award for best story collection), *Dark Property*, and *Altmann's Tongue*. A new collection of his stories will be appearing from Coffee House Press in 2019. He is the recipient of three O. Henry Prizes as well as an NEA fellowship. He lives in Los Angeles and teaches in the Critical Studies Program at CalArts.

**Gemma Files** has been a film critic, journalist, screenwriter, and teacher, and has been an award-winning horror author since 1999. She has published two collections of short work (*Kissing Carrion* and *The Worm in Every Heart*), two chapbooks of speculative poetry, a Weird Western trilogy (the Hexslinger series: *A Book of Tongues, A Rope of Thorns,* and *A Tree of Bones*), a story cycle (*We Will All Go Down Together: Stories of the Five-Family Coven*), and a stand-alone novel (*Experimental Film,* which won the 2015 Shirley Jackson Award for Best Novel and the 2016 Sunburst Award for Adult Fiction). She has two upcoming story collections from Trepidatio Publishing (*Spectral Evidence* and *Drawn Up From Deep Places*), and one from Cemetery Dance (*Dark Is Better*).

**Ford Madox Ford** (1873–1939) was a British writer who based his *Parade's End* tetralogy of novels, written between 1924 and 1928, on his service as a propagandist and soldier during World

War I. Although he wrote short stories in addition to novels, criticism, travel essays, and poetry, it is his critically acclaimed novel *The Good Soldier*, regarded as one of the greatest novels of the twentieth century, for which he is remembered.

"The Medium's End" is one of his few pieces of supernatural fiction.

**Jeffrey Ford** is the author of the novels *The Physiognomy, Memoranda, The Beyond, The Portrait of Mrs. Charbuque, The Girl in the Glass, The Cosmology of the Wider World, The Shadow Year, The Twilight Pariah*, and *Ahab's Return*.

Ford's short fiction has appeared in a wide variety of magazines and anthologies, and has been collected in *The Fantasy Writer's Assistant, The Empire of Ice Cream, The Drowned Life, Crackpot Palace*, and *A Natural History of Hell*.

He lives in Ohio in a 100-plus-year-old farmhouse surrounded by corn and soybean fields and teaches part time at Ohio Wesleyan University.

**Alice Hoffman** is the *New York Times* bestselling author of *Faithful*; *The Marriage of Opposites*; *The Dovekeepers*; and *The Rules of Magic*, the prequel to her cult classic *Practical Magic*, selected as a LibraryReads, Indie Next, and Reese Witherspoon Book Club pick. Hoffman's most recent novel is *The World We Knew*, published by Simon & Schuster, September 2019.

British Fantasy Award–winning **Carole Johnstone** is a Scottish writer, currently enjoying splendid isolation on the Atlantic coast of the Isle of Lewis in the Outer Hebrides. Her short fiction has been published widely, and has been reprinted in Ellen

Datlow's *Best Horror of the Year* and Salt Publishing's *Best British Fantasy* collections. Her debut short story collection, *The Bright Day Is Done,* and her novella *Cold Turkey* were both shortlisted for a 2015 British Fantasy Award.

The story of HMS *Torque/Trigon* is based on the true fate of HMS *Thetis,* a T-class sub that sank during sea trials in Liverpool Bay on June 1, 1939, with the loss of ninety-nine men. There were only four survivors. After being salvaged and repaired, it was recommissioned as HMS *Thunderbolt* in 1940. It was sunk by an Italian warship off the coast of Sicily on March 14, 1943. All hands were lost, and HMS *Thunderbolt* was never recovered.

For more information on the author, go to carole johnstone.com.

**Stephen Graham Jones** is the author of sixteen novels and six story collections. Most recent are the novella *Mapping the Interior,* from Tor.com, and the comic book *My Hero,* from Hex Publishers. *Mapping the Interior* won the This Is Horror! Award for best novella. Stephen lives and teaches in Boulder, Colorado.

**Richard Kadrey** is the *New York Times* bestselling author of the Sandman Slim supernatural noir books. *Sandman Slim* was included in Amazon's "100 Science Fiction & Fantasy Books to Read in a Lifetime," and is in development as a feature film. Some of his other books include *The Grand Dark, The Wrong Dead Guy, Metrophage,* and *Butcher Bird.* He also writes comics, including *Lucifer* and *Hellblazer.*

**John Langan** is the author of two novels, *The Fisherman* and *House of Windows,* and two collections, *The Wide, Carnivorous Sky* *and Other Monstrous Geographies* and *Mr. Gaunt and Other Uneasy Encounters.*

With Paul Tremblay, he coedited *Creatures: Thirty Years of Monsters.* One of the founders of the Shirley Jackson Awards, he serves on its board of directors. Currently, he reviews horror and dark fantasy for *Locus* magazine. Forthcoming is a new collection, *Sefira and Other Betrayals.* He lives in New York's Hudson Valley with his wife and younger son.

**Alison Littlewood**'s latest novel is *The Crow Garden,* a tale of obsession set amidst Victorian asylums and séance rooms. It follows *The Hidden People,* a Victorian tale about the murder of a young girl suspected of being a fairy changeling. Alison's other novels include *A Cold Silence, Path of Needles, The Unquiet House,* and *Zombie Apocalypse! Acapulcalypse Now.* Her first book, *A Cold Season,* was selected for the Richard and Judy Book Club and described as "perfect reading for a dark winter's night."

Alison's short stories have been picked for many "year's best" anthologies, and have been gathered together in her collections *Quieter Paths* and *Five Feathered Tales* (a collaboration with award-winning illustrator Daniele Serra). She won the 2014 Shirley Jackson Award for Short Fiction.

Alison lives with her partner, Fergus, in Yorkshire, England, in a house of creaking doors and crooked walls. She loves exploring the hills and dales with her two hugely enthusiastic Dalmatians and has a penchant for books on folklore and weird history, Earl Grey tea, and semicolons. You can talk to her on Twitter: at @Ali_L, see her on Facebook, or visit her at alisonlittlewood.co.uk.

**Bracken MacLeod** has survived car crashes, a near drowning, being shot at, a parachute malfunction, and the bar exam. So far, the only incident that has resulted in persistent nightmares is the bar exam. He is the author of the novels *Mountain Home, Come to Dust,* and *Stranded,* which was a finalist for the Bram Stoker Award, and two collections of short fiction, *13 Views of the Suicide Woods* and *White Knight and Other Pawns.* He lives with his wife and son outside of Boston, where he is at work on his next novel.

**Nick Mamatas** is the author of several novels, including *I Am Providence* and *Hexen Sabbath.* His short fiction has appeared in *The Best American Mystery Stories, The Year's Best Science Fiction & Fantasy,* Tor.com, and many other venues. Nick is also an anthologist: his books include *Haunted Legends* (co-edited with Ellen Datlow), *The Future Is Japanese* and *Hanzai Japan* (co-edited with Masumi Washington), and *Mixed Up* (co-edited with Molly Tanzer).

**Vincent J. Masterson** was raised in Chesapeake, Ohio, and earned his MFA from the University of Alabama. He has taught a variety of English and creative writing courses to adult learners, international students, and undergraduates. He is currently an adjunct professor of English at Palm Beach State College in Boca Raton, Florida.

**Seanan McGuire** lives, works, and occasionally falls into swamps in the Pacific Northwest, where she is coming to an understanding with the local frogs. She has written a ridiculous number of novels and even more short stories. Keep up with her at seananmcguire.com. On moonlit nights, when the stars are right, you just might find her falling into a swamp near you.

**Garth Nix** has been a full-time writer since 2001, but has also worked as a literary agent, marketing consultant, book editor, book publicist, book sales representative, bookseller, and a part-time soldier in the Australian Army Reserve.

Garth's books include the YA fantasy Old Kingdom series—*Sabriel*, *Lirael*, *Abhorsen*, *Clariel*, and *Goldenhand*; YA SF novels *Shade's Children* and *A Confusion of Princes*; and a Regency romance with magic, *Newt's Emerald*. His fantasy novels for children include *The Ragwitch*; the six books of the Seventh Tower sequence; the Keys to the Kingdom series; and others. He has cowritten several books with Sean Williams, including the Troubletwisters series, Spirit Animals Book Three: *Blood Ties*, and *Have Sword, Will Travel*.

His most recent book is *Frogkisser!*, now being developed as a film by Twentieth Century Fox/Blue Sky Studios.

**Joyce Carol Oates** is the author most recently of the novel *A Book of American Martyrs* and the story collection *Night-Gaunts*. Her work has appeared in previous anthologies of Ellen Datlow's, including *The Doll Collection* and *Black Feathers: Dark Avian Tales*. She is a recipient of the Bram Stoker Award, the National Book Award, the PEN America Lifetime Achievement Award, the National Humanities Medal, and the A.J. Liebling Award for Outstanding Boxing Writing, and the 2019 Jerusalem Prize.

**M(ary) Rickert** has published three short story collections: *Map of Dreams*, *Holiday*, and *You Have Never Been Here*. Her stories have been in numerous anthologies, including Library of America's *American Fantastic Tales, The Big Book of Ghost Stories, Nightmares: A New Decade of Modern Horror,* and *Shadows and Tall Trees 7.* She is the winner of the Crawford Award, the World Fantasy Award, and the Shirley Jackson Award. Her first novel, *The Memory Garden,* won the Locus Award.

Before earning her MFA from Vermont College of Fine Arts, she worked as a kindergarten teacher, a coffee shop barista, a Disneyland balloon vendor, and a personnel assistant in Sequoia National Park. Visit her at mrickert.net.

**M. L. Siemienowicz** lives in Melbourne, Australia. She has had short fiction published in speculative and literary venues such as *Nightmare, Aurealis,* and *Overland.* Her work has been reprinted in "year's best" anthologies, including *The Best Horror of the Year* and *Australian Dark Fantasy and Horror,* and her novel manuscript, *Pretty Roadkill,* was shortlisted for the 2018 KYD Unpublished Manuscript Award. Find her on Twitter at @clockworkquill.

**Lee Thomas** is the Bram Stoker Award– and two-time Lambda Literary Award–winning author of the books *Stained, The Dust of Wonderland, The German, Torn, Like Light for Flies, Down on Your Knees,* and *Distortion,* among others. His work has been translated into multiple languages and has been optioned for film. Lee lives in Austin, Texas, with his husband, John.

**Paul Tremblay** is the award-winning author of seven novels, including *The Cabin at the End of the World, A Head Full of Ghosts, Disappearance at Devil's Rock,* and *The Little Sleep.* He is currently a member of the board of directors of the Shirley Jackson Awards, and his essays and short fiction have appeared in the *Los Angeles Times*, EntertainmentWeekly.com, and numerous "year's best" anthologies. He has a master's degree in mathematics and lives outside Boston with his wife and two children.

**A. C. Wise** was born and raised in the Montreal area, and currently lives in the Philadelphia area. In addition to short fiction appearing in publications such as *Clarkesworld*, Tor.com, and *The Year's Best Dark Fantasy and Horror 2017*, she has two collections published with Lethe Press, and a novella, *Catfish Lullaby*, published by Broken Eye Books. Her work has been a finalist for the Lambda Literary Award, and won the Sunburst Award for Excellence in Canadian Literature of the Fantastic. She contributes a monthly short fiction review column to *Apex Magazine*, and contributes to the Women to Read and Non-Binary Authors to Read review columns to the Book Smugglers. Visit her at acwise.net.

## ABOUT THE EDITOR

**Ellen Datlow** has been editing science fiction, fantasy, and horror short fiction for almost forty years. She currently acquires short fiction for Tor.com. In addition, she has edited about ninety science fiction, fantasy, and horror anthologies, including the annual *Best Horror of the Year, Fearful Symmetries, The Doll Collection, The Monstrous, Children of Lovecraft, Black Feathers, Mad Hatters and March Hares,* and *The Devil and the Deep.*

She's won multiple World Fantasy Awards, Locus Awards, Hugo Awards, Bram Stoker Awards, International Horror Guild Awards, Shirley Jackson Awards, and the 2012 Il Posto Nero Black Spot Award for Excellence as Best Foreign Editor. Datlow was named recipient of the 2007 Karl Edward Wagner Award, given by the British Fantasy Society for "outstanding contribution to the genre"; she was honored with a Life Achievement Award by the Horror Writers Association, in acknowledgment of superior achievement over an entire career; and she was given the World Fantasy Life Achievement Award at the 2014 World Fantasy Convention.

She lives in New York and cohosts the monthly Fantastic Fiction Reading Series at KGB Bar. More information can be found at ellendatlow.com, on Facebook, and on Twitter at @EllenDatlow.